THE STONEHENGE SAGA: COMPLETE

by J.P. Reedman

First published in two volumes as 'STONE LORD' AND 'MOON LORD' by Mirador Publishing 2012, 2013

Complete revised edition, c J.P. Reedman, 2017

THE LEGEND OF KING ARTHUR—
THE ERA OF STONEHENGE

BOOK ONE-STONE LORD

DEDICATED TO RICHARD 'KIP' CARPENTER

PART ONE—MERLIN: MOONRISE

CHAPTER ONE

The Stones demanded blood.

Blood to bathe their stony feet, to bind their cumbrous bodies to the earth.

So it had always been. The Chosen would die, the marked One touched by the spirits since birth.

In the settlement of Faraon, the child who was Chosen dwelt with his mother in a filthy lean-to that bordered the pigsty and the midden. His boy-name was Lailoq 'the Friend'—but his name was a lie. He had no friends among the people ruled by the chieftain Vhortiern.

Lailoq was an outcast, a scapegoat, along with his mother, Keine of the White Streak. Children spat as he walked by, and elders made signs against evil when he went around on his daily chores, a clay pot balanced on his head and a sack of kindling bound to his scrawny back.

His mother, Keine, was to blame for his misfortune. She had been beautiful once, desirable, perhaps even a potential bedmate for Vhortiern himself. But she had a white streak in her dark hair—an ominous sign, a flaw that beckoned to interested spirits—and one night, twelve Sun-turnings before, those spirits came to claim her. She had drifted away from the Midwinter fire-feast to enter the woods, the taboo area of the Old Hunters. Three days she went missing, and the people beat ancestors' thighbones on the ground and mourned for her as one dead.

However, on the new Moon's rise, she returned, dazed and raving, telling tales of bears with the voices of men and crows that stood tall as young saplings. They had danced with her in the forest and begged her to join them. Their leader was called Min'kammus; stag's horns crowned his head and his cloak the pelt of the spotted deer. He had led her through the dance, and wetted her lips with fire-mead, and eventually he took her away from the ring of dancing beasts and danced with her in the way of men with women. She fled at night's end, fearful of what she had done, of the dread being she had lain with in the shuddering forest, but it was too late. The horned chief, whatever he was, man or beast, god or spirit, had left her with a gift—or curse—from that solitary coupling. The seed of his unnatural loins blossomed like a dark flower in her belly, and Keine soon grew great in size to match the pregnant full Moon.

Lailoq had come squalling into the world on an eve when Tarahn the Thunderer smote the hills with his thunder-axe and sent the deer of doe-eyed Fleesh running in fright. Small and dark, with a long, black-furred head and deep, bird-like eyes, he resembled a wizened little old man rather than an innocent newborn babe. Six fingers grew on his right hand, a sure mark of the malevolent spirit-world.

So it was no surprise, some twelve years later, that he was Chosen be given to the Stones. It was not a common thing, not any more, though such sacrifices had been frequent enough in the times of the early kings of Albu—the bloody but glorious days of the tin-kings Samothos, Sarron and Longho, and before them Raven-lord Brahn and his sons Brito and Amaethan, who brought agriculture to the land.

But when Vhortiern and his men were unsuccessful in raising the final two stones of their holy circle at Din-Amnon, and the pillars tumbled down, crushing heads and smashing bones, fearful and frenzied whispers went through the tribe: "The Ancestors are angry! The Ancestors want blood and bone! Something must be done, a gift must be given!"

Chief Vhortiern had no doubt what the gift must be, and who. Axe in hand to assert his might, he went to Keine of the White Streak in her hovel, and asked for the boy. Keine shrieked, wailed, and tore her hair, but he would not be moved by her torment. The boy Lailoq, sitting by the pitiful, half-dead fire, said nothing, but went quietly with the chieftain to be prepared for the act of making the stones sacred.

The time of the sacrifice was set for twilight, when the veil between the worlds of the living and dead grew thin, and barrows on the hills opened their stony wombs and released the ghosts of the Ancestors, for good or for ill. Wearing masks and painted with ash and ochre, the village folk began their procession from Faraon toward the high ground where the unfinished stone circle lay under a blood-streaked evening sky.

Even incomplete, the ring was a marvellous sight. Two massive portal stones of white quartz, twice a tall man's height, lay stretched out on the grass before empty stone-holes that yawned like waiting mouths. Behind them stood a neat oval of stunted blue-green stones, open to the East and aligned on a gap in the sunset-bloodied peaks of the Holy Mountain known as God-of-Bronze.

Vhortiern entered the circle first, as was his right as chief, followed closely by the village Shaman, the Old Woman of No Name, who had lived longer than any other in the tribe, and had blood-ties to almost all. An infant's skull hung on a loop round her neck, and a mask with a wooden nose curved like the sickle-Moon covered her shrunken face. The mask's eyes were ochred scallop shells brought from distant seashore, and masses of dung-stiffened grass hair fanned out from the rim, giving the mask a crazed, grotesque appearance.

It was the face of Death. Of She-Who-Guards.

Behind the chief and the shaman walked the important men of the tribe, harsh vertical stripes and rib-bone patterns daubed onto their torsos, their thick manes of hair plaited into fantastical knots and tails. Their wives trailed after, painted moss green from head to toe, the colour of death and Otherness. Both sexes danced as they processed into the circle, beating on skin drums and making hideous keening sounds with pipes made of perforated bone.

They surrounded the sacrifice, the fatherless boy, circling, swooping, spitting, calling on the Ancestors to take him and his evil luck away and let their stone circle stand. Lailoq walked amid them as if he feared nothing and merely looked on this as an adventure. Some folk sneered and nudged each other. "Look, he is simple," they whispered. "He does not cry, he does not know he is to die…"

Overhearing, the boy fixed them with an unnerving smile, and something about his dark, sharp face made them quail and reach inside their cowhide tunics to touch the talismans that hung there.

Lailoq had been dressed and adorned for the role of sacrifice—the only time he had ever worn anything other than scraps of skins. A pale linen robe tumbled to his calves, and his long black hair had been greased back with pig-fat and twined with the feathers of hawks. His face was painted a livid blue, the colour of a corpse, to show that he was already dead to the tribe, already half in the Otherworld.

Vhortiern gazed at him uneasily. He wanted this night to be over. He was not squeamish about breaking the boy's head and letting out his spirit, for he thought the brat should have been exposed at birth—but there was a depth, a darkness, in those glittering and somehow ancient black eyes that almost unmanned him.

Unconsciously, he stroked the worn, gold-pinned head of his war-axe, the Good Striker, a thousand years old and made of jadeite from a half-forgotten motherland beyond the shores of Albu the White. Tonight Striker would drink, and the stones would drink too, and the angry Ancestors, always demanding their due, refusing to be forgotten, would allow the Man-stone and Mother-stone to rise and stand together, framing Sun and Moon and Holy Mountain.

A sound from Lailoq made him jump, and he eyed the brat with renewed suspicion. Would this be the beginning of tears, of fighting and begging? He felt suddenly old and tired, all too aware of his own vulnerable young sons, asleep back in his hut in Faraon. He just wanted the sacrifice to be over and the stones to rise, a lasting tribute to the spirits that would make them whisper his name with pleasure and confer fruitful harvests on his folk.

He let his hard, jaded eyes travel to the scrawny, linen-clad boy, who had wandered up to the diamond-shaped Mother-stone and was staring at it if willing it to leap up from the ground and fly. Suddenly the child squatted down, staring intently into the empty stone-hole beside the menhir, making the Chief fear the brat was going to jump in and start some futile fight for existence there in the gathering gloom.

Instead, the boy kneaded the earth with his horrible six-fingered hand—like some beast's paw, Vhortiern thought with a shudder—and suddenly his eyes gleamed, glowed even, green sparks breaking their deep darkness. Vhortiern scowled, making a sign against evil behind his back. He thought of Stag-man and Bear-man and Crow-man in the woods, tumbling white-streaked Keine whom he had once desired, and getting this fey, half-animal child, and he knew it was right that Lailoq should die…

The brat was making a low, guttural noise, a self-satisfied kind of growl. He snapped his long brown fingers at the chieftain, his stance one of an equal, not of one whose life was forfeit for the good of the people. "Chief Vhortiern, you must not use Good Striker tonight!" the boy cried, his voice harsh as the shrieks of the bird of prey he resembled. Not a child's shrill voice, but that of a fell spirit, surely. "If you slay me, it will not make the stones stand. You will raise them but they will fall again, like dead men. You will bring other children to them, one by one, till the village's child-wealth is all spent and only crones and greybeards dwell in Faraon, weeping for their lost future. Never will your stones stand, and the village will become a cursed place of dust and bone."

Vhortiern's face grew white; his heavy brows bristled. "What do you know, you who are the Son of Nothing?"

Lailoq smiled slyly, his strange, fevered eyes sucking up the last of the lingering light. "I know much, much more than you think, Chieftain. In the village pigsty I listened to the grunts of the Great White Sow, dead-eater and prophecy-maker. I understood her tongue. From her, I learned how to commune with the dead in their cairns and with the hunting spirits who wander the forest. I have heard the voices of the trees and conversed with salmon in the rivers. And I hear voices calling me now, from deep beneath the earth."

"What voices are they?" Vhortiern grunted, unable to control the shivers that ran up his spine. Why did this unseelie creature disturb him so? He was just a boy. A tainted boy.

"The shrieks of Wyrms, two great serpents that battle and slash each other with their fangs!" Lailoq licked his lips almost eagerly. His tongue looked too red, too bright, to the uneasy Chief, and it was pointed like a snake's. "One is Moon-pale with eyes of flame, the other fire-red with breath of smoke. They battle for supremacy under this hill, and their shudders are what make the stones fall!"

Vhortiern felt sick. He should have guessed some evil slumbered on this hill. An old burial mound had been cleared away in order to build the circle; its bony occupants had come from another tribe and he had smashed the skulls and cast them into the offerings shafts near the village. It had been a foolish move.

The Old Woman with No Name limped forward now, removing the mask from her dried-up, toothless sack of a face. Ugly as she was, her eyes still shone a brilliant sea-blue, and they were keen and intelligent. "So, boy, if what you say about these Wyrms is true, what must be done?"

"Old Grandmother," said Lailoq, "let the men come and re-make the pits to hold the stones. They must be wider and deeper, and the women must help too by packing their bases firmly, with no gaps. The packing stones must be magic stones, red ones for the red serpent and white quartz for the pale one. Once the stones are properly laid down, they will seal the angry serpents below us, and the stones will not fall."

Vhortiern glanced at the Old Woman; he feared her, disliked her, even, but she was versed in lore and magic, and he had no choice but to ask her advice. "What is your counsel, old one?"

The Old Woman with No Name put a painted claw on Lailoq's greasy dark head; she looked almost fondly at him, and for a moment Vhortiern noticed a similarity in the thin but determined jaw, the jutting bird-beak nose. He had not noticed such a look before; the boy had seemed to him completely foreign, a changeling creature. Could the Old One have lost her edge and decided to protect this cursed boy because of some real or imagined kinship?

"Let us try the way he describes," she said. "He is half of the Otherworld; maybe he speaks truth. But if he fails to quiet these Serpents-Under-Earth, I myself will break his skull and add his knucklebones to my necklace."

And so, shortly before the next full Moon, the stone holes were dug anew, using the shoulder blades of oxen as shovels, and the two menhirs were tipped into them and packed firmly at their bases with skull-sized chunks of quartz and red sandstone. The Old Woman sprinkled lamb's blood on the stones, and kissed them and bowed to them, while men and women wove a spiral dance around the ring, and singing and feasting went on in the village for seven nights and days, until the full Moon crested the utmost peak of God-of-Bronze and sailed West into the Deadlands.

At last the stones stood, proud and tall—without the blood of a fatherless boy to hold them fast to the ground.

As for the Child, the Chosen One, he was no longer an object of scorn and hatred in the village. Men still feared him, but he was also revered for his wisdom in the matter of the stones. His rags were burned and offered at the circle, and the Old Woman gave him a deerskin tunic painted with magic signs. She wove bronze rings in his hair and hung a blue bead shaped like a star around his neck on a thong.

And on the Feast of the Summer-lord, when the dawn Sun made a path of gold between the massive portals of Din-Amnon, the youth stepped forward with all the tribesfolk watching, to be made a man of the people. Vhortiern gave him a bow and quiver of arrows and cut the marks of manhood on his cheeks, then rubbed them with woad that the women had ground that morning. A lock of his hair was cut and burned as an offering to the Ancestors, and the ashes scattered in the grass. So too, were his fingernails pared and then burned.

"Swear that you will serve me," said the Chief sternly, "as my magic man, from this day forward. Swear this oath, and use your wiles and wisdom to protect me and mine from the Otherworld, and you will be held higher in esteem than my best warriors!"

"I swear." Lailoq smiled his unnerving crooked smile. "I will serve you till the day you go to live among the Ancestors, great Chief Vhortiern."

Vhortiern extended his hand, thick as a club and massed with scars as pale as the white serpent now pinioned below the Man-stone at the entrance to the sacred circle. "Then let you take your place by my right hand side! Cast off your childhood name of Lailoq, and choose you the name by which a man shall be known!"

Lailoq lifted his arms toward heaven, as if embracing the Sun, which hung like a fiery eye in the Eastern sky. He took a deep breath as he stared into the heavens, searching, seeking, summoning. A shriek sounded high above, and a winged shape suddenly darkened the face of the sun, before plunging down like a deadly dart, straight towards Lailoq.

Vhortiern shied away, grimacing, while the women watching outside the circle began to wail in terror.

They fell silent when they realised the creature did not attack. It glided gracefully onto Lailoq's upraised arm, talons carefully seizing his forearm without puncturing flesh. It flapped lustrous wings and uttered a sharp cry from its hooked beak.

It was a Merlin, a hawk, a shrewd predator who flew among the lonely hills, seeking prey.

"From now on, you will call me by the name of this beast that is my brother," said Lailoq, who was no longer Lailoq—and the hawk that was his totem-animal screamed defiance into the growing light. "From this day forth I shall be called the Merlin."

The Merlin of Din Faraon thrived in his new honoured position. Wise and canny, he advised Vhortiern in matters of commerce and war, and soon traders from far and wide traversed the green hills to reach Faraon, making white tracks across the countryside with the passage of so many feet. They traded skins and beads and weapons, all under Merlin's shrewd gaze, and soon the daggers of the men of Faraon grew longer, and they replaced their old stone axes with fine new ones of bronze.

Merlin himself continued to learn the lore of all within heaven and earth under the tutelage of the Old Woman of No Name…who, to her young pupil, was not nameless. She had whispered her secret, true name, Buan-ann, into his ear at his initiatory rites, as a sign of her trust and approval.

"I won't lie and say I wouldn't have killed you, if it had been asked of me," she cackled, when she took him into the nearby forests to gather mushrooms that would open the spirit-world, and willow-bark to soothe the villagers who had bone-bend and tooth-rot, "but I always hoped it wouldn't come to that. Man with no father…pah…" She spat on the forest floor. "I can see the Old People, the Hunters, in you, boy. Their blood's in me too, probably in most of us, if truth be known. And undoubtedly something of a hunter was in your mother, too, that fateful night she vanished! Ahhheee." She laughed at her own ribald joke, slapping her thighs with gnarly hands.

The Merlin laughed too, like any young lad fascinated by talk of the secret rite between man and woman of which he had no real knowledge as yet. But he was more curious about other things Buan-ann had told him. "Who are these hunters; what is their tribe?"

"We do not know, for their tongue is like gravel falling from the hillsides! They were here before us, long before, and our fathers have been here long enough. They do not farm or build homes; they travel like the wind, eating only woodland berries and flesh of wild beasts. They are now almost gone; their life was a harsh one. Some eventually became farmers like us and hence our blood is mixed."

Merlin nodded, glad to know that his father was perhaps not a forest-demon and but a man. He would not tell any but Buan-ann that, though—a suspected otherworldly origin could aid him in his role as magic man.

Buan-ann smiled at him, all gums save for one grizzled tooth. "Your secret is safe with me," she laughed "Now come, I will teach you the song that pleases old River-woman, so that she will not suck you down to her reedy bed when you go swimming!"

A year passed, and one night shortly after the Feast of Lambing, Buan-ann did not rise from her bed. The women attended her, but no potion could bring her back, and by dawn her spirit had begun the journey across the Great Plain to the Summerlands of the West.

She was carried from her hut on a plank of stout oak, held by the strongest youths of the tribe. She had been wrapped in deer hide and her hair combed and braided. Flowers wreathed her grey head and her neck was draped with amber, like golden tears on her silent breast. Beside her lay a rattle to show the gods in the Otherworld that she was a magic-woman and by her head was placed the ball of worn quartz in which she had divined the future. She was carried to a high hill with a flat top; a spirit-stone gazed out from here, pointing toward the dark slopes and rilled fangs of God-of-Bronze, which men whispered was an entrance to Ahn-un, Land-of-the-Dead.

Here she was laid out on a pyre of hazel-wood. The villagers milled round, women first, men following, singing and dancing as they circled her bier. Then, when they had whipped themselves into a frenzy of grief, they lit many torches and hurled them onto the pyre with much wailing and keening. The dry wood crackled and went up in great orange flames. Flesh hissed, and Buan-ann's skull shrivelled and blackened, bowing down toward her ball of quartz, as if summoning its power to guide her upon her final journey.

Merlin sang and howled, leaping like a young deer beneath the smoke-filled sky and pretending it was rain on his cheeks and not tears. She had been a good friend—the first ever for friendless Lailoq, and he was grieved to lose her wisdom and companionship.

When the pyre had burnt to ashes, Merlin picked through the wreckage, muttering the chant that calmed dead souls. One by one, he placed the charred and fragmented shards that had once been his mentor in a wide-brimmed urn.

He halted for a moment, breath ragged, as he spotted something shining in the heap of ash and calcined bones.

The crystal ball, bright and pure as if the fire had not touched it.

He knew then: he was meant to have it. A final gift from Buan-ann as she departed to the Undying Land. A sign for him, that he was indeed the one to take her place and commune with both man and spirit. He placed the still-hot ball to his forehead and prayed, while the sky shone with all the fires of the gods and the women carried Buan-ann's urn away to the river, to mingle her ashes with the waters that streamed out towards the flowing sea.

As the year grew warmer and the feast of the Longest Day and Shortest Night came and went, Merlin sought audience with Vhortiern and announced that he would be going West, to continue learning the wise-man's craft with the great high wizards who dwelt on Mhon. Grumpily, the chief granted his permission, but made Merlin swear not to stay past the autumn Equinox, the Day of Balance, when neither Light nor Dark had power over the other. "The traders come at that time," he said, "and your slick tongue soothes them better than my rough one. You owe me that tongue, boy...I mean, Merlin; it is I who saw your... greatness... and spared your life. Remember that."

So the Merlin set out for the North, carrying only his copper dagger, a bow and a shaman's hazel staff, to visit the Oak-Seers who lived in the groves of Mhon, the Mother Isle, which jutted like a spear-head into the stormy seas between Prydn and its sister isle, Ibherna. He stayed with them awhile, and they taught him of the movements of Sun and stars, and how the great spirits had made them so, and what would please those heavenly beings and keep them upon a steady and favourable path. Then, with the Oak-Seer's aid and blessing, he travelled onwards in a coracle of bark and skins, and, borne by a skirling tide, reached the shores of Ibherna itself, deep green under a red Sunset.

Trudging inward from the coast, over many days he sought out the sanctuary of the native goddess, Brygyndo, Fiery Arrow. Brygyndo was worshipped in a wooden temple in the heart of a great earthen ring; nearby were the tallest standing stones found in Ibherna, near equal in size to the great monoliths of Khor Ghor, that most famous of Temples that lay upon the Great Plain in the south of Albu.

Inside the temple precinct, an eternal flame burned before Brygyndo's Three-faced effigy, and a priestess known as Brig-ahn who was healer, birthing-woman and deadly archer, tended the hearth and minded the statue.

This Brig-ahn, a tall woman with crimson-stained hair and ear and lip plugs of jet readily invited the Merlin into the sanctuary, as was the wont of her cult; no one seeking succour or solace was ever turned away from the Shrine of Fiery Arrow. Merlin made his offering to the Lady of that place—a gleaming lucite arrowhead with long barbs, so thin and painstakingly crafted it could only be used by the spirit-world—and then sat in meditation, breathing in the herb-scented smoke that coiled round the chamber. He had chosen to come here because he wished to follow the footsteps of another Merlin, who had visited Brygyndo's shrine countless lifetimes ago, studying the God-stones that guarded the sanctuary. An ancient forebear Merlin who had brought his followers to the peaks of God-of-Bronze, where they quarried pillars of bluestone, a type of doleritic stone speckled with white flecks that made them resemble a starry night sky. These stones were dragged to the coast and sent on a perilous journey to the south, where they were used to build the inner circles of Khor Ghor, the Dance-of-Great-Spirits, on the barren expanse of the Great Plain.

The priestess Brig-ahn gazed at the youth, cross-legged amid the smoke, and her eyes were hooded, thoughtful. "Times of change come to our sister isles," she said. "The world is changing, as the world must. Rumours have come that many great cities in the hot seas of the south have fallen into fiery ruin, that corsairs harry their shores and survivors have taken to the hills. We are more fortunate here, in our isolation, but even so there has been an increase in Sea-Raiders in the last year—black-bearded men from far in the East, the likes of which we have not seen before. Some call them demons, but they are only men. Greedy men. They seek gold, they seek tin, but they wish to take all for themselves and not to engage in legitimate trade. Several villages on our coasts have been burned by these raiders when they were denied access to our mines."

Merlin nodded. "The rumours of these Sea-Pirates have come to my ears too, brought by the traders on the Golden Path that runs through God-of-Bronze, whose peaks gaze out towards Ibherna. But in the valleys, my people have not encountered them; we have kept safe. The mountain regions have always repelled unwelcome visitors."

"They will come, nonetheless," said Brig-ahn, sighing deeply. "Their greed and fury will eventually make them leave their boats and fare far ashore. Even mountains will not hold them back, if they think there is plunder to be won, and foolish, timid people who will offer them no challenge."

Merlin rubbed his chin, with its haze of youthful stubble. "If you can, Great Lady, give me counsel in this matter, as your predecessor of ancient days gave wisdom to the Merlin of old, the Merlin who raised the temple of Khor Ghor with arts learned from Ibherna's own Stones."

The priestess sighed. "Our peoples are fractious and have ever been so. Prydn needs a chief who will be strong enough to gather the tribes together, to lead them against these incomers, using new ways of warfare that the invaders will not expect."

"You are not thinking of my chief, Vhortiern, are you?" Merlin laughed mockingly. "He dreams of his days as a warrior, but his belly grows fat and his arm trembles."

Brig-ahn shook her head. "In the south of Albu, men still gather every year at Khor Ghor. Back many lifetimes ago, five chiefs—Samothos, Sarron, Longho, Harbron and Gorbonian—came to that place, marked by five settings of stones that stretch to heaven, and they forged the laws that men of the Isle of Prydn lived by. Samothos held supreme sway above the rest, as king of the Great Trilithon, the place where the Sun dies at Midwinter, and under him the isle grew strong and prosperous. But then, plague laid the kings low and their line was extinguished. No high-king has ruled Albu the White for many generations. The time without a strong leader must come to an end, and a king return to Prydn. A king…and another Merlin like the Merlin of old."

The young shaman was silent, but his heart suddenly leaped, beating like a wild, trapped thing against his ribs. Khor Ghor, the temple of the Ancestors, receptacle of Sun-Face and Moon's eye! Khor Ghor, a mighty marvel begun by his own namesake, the Merlin of ancient times, one of a long line of Merlins. Perhaps he would be next in that illustrious line, the next to reap undying fame amidst the frowning pillars of that great structure, unique among the monuments of the tribes of Prydn. A place some called, in dread, the Tomb of all Hope, with its five inner trilithons forming portals that led into the Otherworld.

Brig-ahn smiled at him, almost slyly, cobweb creases fanning out from her pale blue eyes and too-rich mouth. She had seemed quite youthful at first, with her flame hair and painted cheeks, but now she had suddenly grown old, an ancient crone, both wise and deadly, hiding behind the veneer of youth. She might be twenty summers old, or two thousand. "Your eyes are on fire at the mention of that dread place! It is in your heart, is it not? And so it might well be. For are you not known as the Merlin, like he who raised the first stones? Are you not Chosen, the child of no mortal man? Yes, even here, the rumours have come of a fatherless boy who found two Wyrms that fought beneath the earth and tamed them."

Merlin scowled, looking like a petulant lad rather than a powerful, albeit youthful, shaman. "My chief, Vhortiern, has bound me to him, by my blood. I may not leave Faraon while he lives. So I have sworn"

"Blood." The Priestess stoked up the sacred fire. Shadows leaped around the thatched temple, stretching long from the triadic carving of Fiery-Arrow on its plinth before the hearth. "Blood bond may be broken in many ways. Think on this. You know it to be true, and you will know, when the time comes, what you must do… But do not think too long; for if action is delayed, the sea-men will come and destroy all you hold dear."

Pondering the Priestess's words, the Merlin left the sanctuary of Fiery Arrow the next morn and began his arduous journey back to Prydn. Journeying to the seastrand, where men fished along the shore, he gained passage across the waters by offering a fisherman a weather-spell to protect his coracle from the tumultuous tides of Mahn-an the Sea-lord. Reaching the coast of Prydn after a long but uneventful crossing, the shaman bade the old sailor farewell, then shouldered bow and staff and began a forced march toward the stark silhouette of God-of-Bronze. He reached the boundaries of Vhortiern's territory close to the Time of Balance, just as he had promised.

As he arrived in the village, coming on weary feet down the long track over the moor, he felt a creeping unease. All looked the same, the clustered huts with their belching smoke-holes, the pigsties and the heaped midden, the little stream where the women beat clothes on rocks. But he felt a change, subtle and indescribable, as if, in the time he was absent, all he knew best had been wiped away, making it a very different place to that which he had left.

His unease heightened when one of the village children, recognising him, rushed forward with a loud squeal. "Merlin, Merlin, you've come back to us! Look what I've got, Merlin!"

The child, a little lad named Starn, held up his arm. On his wrist was a beaded bracelet. Merlin had not seen its like before, tiny seed-like beads in rainbow colours sewn on to a strip of cloth. He knew, though, that it was cheap and ill made, and there was a smoky, unknown fragrance that clung to it, an alien perfume that reeked of faraway places.

"Starn, where did you get this thing?" he asked sternly.

The child looked afraid; he hid his arm with the cloth bracelet behind his back as if fearing Merlin would snatch his prize from him. "Just some traders, Merlin. They have been in Faraon since the day after you left. They are funny men, Merlin. Their hair curls like sheep's wool, and they pour oil on it—how it stinks! They paint their eyes too, like women. But they are rich; they have many good things that we have never seen before. They tell such wonderful stories of faraway lands where the Sun is always shining."

"They have been here a long time for traders," Merlin muttered, half to himself.

"Yes. But that is because chief Vhortiern plans to wed one of the stranger's women."

Merlin's eyes widened in shock and anger, but he fought to hide his rage from the child. "You have done well to tell me, Starn. Now, run along, I must see Vhortiern at once."

Grasping the hilt of his dagger, he slowly entered the village and approached Vhortiern's large hut with its carved doorposts all bloodied from offerings to household spirits. The skin flap across the door was pinned aside, and he could hear raucous laughter and the clink of drinking beakers within.

He pushed his way into the hut and stood blinking, forcing his eyes to adjust to the gloom. Vhortiern sat cross-legged on a fur, decked out in his chieftain's finery, three golden buttons on his tunic, his dagger and axe on one knee and Good Striker upon the other. His wives, Kymidei and Tyndri squatted beside him, dripping with necklaces of blue and honey-coloured beads. They were entertaining several well-fed men with wiry black hair and prominent features, whose long curled beards gleamed under coatings of scented oil. They wore tunics in colours Merlin had only even seen in rainbows, and the swords at their belts were long and grooved.

"Merlin, my friend, you've returned!" shouted Vhortiern, his face flushed from the honey-drink he had imbibed. "Meet Kaash and Ven, traders from afar. They have come seeking tin. Our tin. The have offered us great things in exchange, barrels of the magic drink of their land, fine jewels that will make us the envy of Albu…Even a fair daughter of the tribe, the Rho-han." He pointed to a sullen dark girl crouched by one of the woolly-bearded strangers, her brown eyes mutinous, her lower lip in a sullen pout.

Merlin did not like the look or stance of these men, or the girl, and wouldn't have even had not Brig-ahn warned him of the Sea-Raiders. "I would not rape the wealth of our mountains for a mere tub of foreign drink," he said harshly. "Or the unwilling flesh of a woman scarce better than a slave."

One of the foreigners, Ven, spread his be-ringed hands and flashed a wide grin. His face was long and his teeth were large, like a horse's teeth. "Do not fear, my friend." He spoke the language of Prydn in a thickly accented voice. "I forgive you your distrust and harsh words. But your folk have so much tin and gold, what little we take will not harm your supply at all. As your chieftain," he stressed the word, "has realised, your tribe will most fortunate if you cooperate with us. Just think of the treasures that we could bring you from our homelands! No enmity need be between our peoples; once Rho-han and Vhortiern wed, we will be almost as kin."

Merlin's face darkened with fury. He was young but no fool. Unlike Vhortiern, he could see the cold insincerity in Ven's eyes, the disdain for northern savages who would gladly trade their tribe's freedom for a few baubles. "Our tin lies in the heart of the mountain known as God-of-Bronze," he said between clenched teeth. "It is a sacred mountain. It is said to be one of the entrances to the Deadlands of Ahn-un. If you strangers go there uninvited, I will call the wrath of the mountain down upon you!"

The dark-bearded men cast each other angry, darting looks. Vhortiern's face purpled. "Merlin! They are to give us swords and spears, arms such as we have never owned! We could rule the entire West—or more! None surely would have the strength to stand against us, with the sea-strangers at our backs."

"At our backs, ready to stab us with their sharp daggers!" cried Merlin, and he whirled around and grabbed the tunic of one of the foreign men, dragging him from the mat where he squatted and hauling him to his feet.

"Where are the rest of your men? What have you planned? That we show you our mines, then you slaughter us all?"

The man flailed clumsily, his teeth bared like a mad dog's against his raven beard. Merlin slung him towards Vhortiern and the girl Rho-han. He fell with a crash at Rho-han's feet, crushing pottery beneath him. The girl leapt up with an angry shriek and fled from the hut into the twilight while Ven shouted furiously after her.

Vhortiern bellowed and drew his dagger from its horn sheath; it glowed like a tongue of flame in the gloomy hut. Merlin's eyes sparked in his thin, dark face, already weather-beaten despite his youth. "Do you dare, chief? Do you raise hand to one who speaks with the spirits? Think deeply before you strike, what that deed could bring you!"

At that moment, the hanging in the door of the hut was torn aside and two village youths tumbled in, panting and wild-eyed. "What do you want?" roared Vhortiern, striding towards the pair with dagger in hand, ready to strike anything, anyone, in his anger.

"There are men in the wood, armed men!" cried one of the boys, waving his arms frantically. "We've seen them! They attacked Yde when she was washing clothes by the ford, but she got away..."

"I warned you, chief!" cried Merlin, rounding on Vhortiern with flashing eyes. "This is the price of your greed!"

Immediately Vhortiern's attendant warriors sprang into action, grabbing Ven and Kaash and binding them. Vhortiern himself staggered out into the smoky twilight, axe in one hand, dagger in the other, shouting 'To me, warriors, to me!" One of his older sons blew on a great cow's horn and the rest of the warriors of Faraon poured out of their huts, raising knives and axes of both ancient stone and new-wrought bronze. Shouting in fear and excitement, eager for action, they streamed down the hillside toward the wooded valley below, cloaked with a cap of mist that concealed both friend and foe.

Merlin did not follow them. His heart felt heavy, his mind troubled. All his learning, his natural-born arts, yet he was oath-bound to a fool who would sell his own people for a girl and a few trinkets. A vision entered his mind of the other Merlin, the one who had used his Arts to build the circle of Khor Ghor. He longed to be such a one, whose power would be remembered forever, whose memories were whispered from the stones to the grass to the everlasting sky.

In that instant he knew what course he must take. Oath or not, he had to leave the oppressive atmosphere of Faraon. Maybe he would become a priest of Khor Ghor, as he desired...or maybe he would be slain as an interloper by unfriendly priests, shot full of arrows and dumped in the ditch...His fate, his future, was in the hands of the spirits. What he would not do is waste more time in a backwater where he would grow old and die with his potential unrealised.

Snatching up his staff, he stalked from the village and hurried to join the Golden Road that wound past Din-Amnon and curled like a Wyrm's tail across the ridged brow of God-of-Bronze. Women and children called after him—he could hear Keine weeping, but he did not glance back at them lest his resolve was lessened.

As he reached the soul-stones on their lonely moor, the first stars were coming out, dancing over their dark tips. He paused and bowed in respect to the Ancestors, remembering how close he had come to joining them, aware they still might be angry because they did not receive the gift of his blood. He noticed that a piglet's carcass had been placed at the foot of the mother-stone, its eyes plucked by the ravens.

A pig when it should have been a child...

Suddenly out of the wispy night fog a figure rose, lurching and lumbering, malevolent. Despite himself, Merlin jumped in alarm, his breathing ragged... and then he recognised Vhortiern.

Vhortiern bloodied to the shoulder, the Good-striker a gory mess in his hand.

"Why are you here?" asked Merlin. "Should you not be in the valley, seeking to undo the evil you have wrought?"

"The battle is over. I have killed the foreigners—all of them," panted Vhortiern. "Ven's head." He reached under his woollen cape and flung a gaping severed head to the ground. It bounced along by Merlin's feet, and he stepped away in disgust. "I brought it here to appease the Old Ones, who will be angry at me, for it was I who let these wolves in amongst our people."

His eyes suddenly narrowed. "But why are you skulking around by the stones? Where were you during the battle?"

Merlin's face turned hard as flint. He raised his arm, and his Merlin-hawk flew down with a cry and flutter of wings. "I leave Faraon again, Chief. This time for good. I will not stay in this place. You have sullied it with the blood of those sea-devils that wanted our tin…and our freedom as a people. I go to Khor Ghor, to see if they will have me, and maybe the wise there can raise a force against these ill-starred men who will seek our shores as long as there are men like you to let them get a foothold!"

Vhortiern made a strangled sound, half-enraged and half-surprised. "You are my magic-man. I forbid this! You have brought luck to Faraon, and if you go, all I value may fail…" He grasped Merlin's shoulders, shaking him, spittle flecking his lips in fury as he shouted, "You swore to stay with me…"

"Until the day you go to the Ancestors…"

Merlin's copper dagger leapt out of the dark like one of the stars above the mountains. It pierced Vhortiern's chest, drove deep. "You are old, Vhortiern; old kings must die before their dotage causes crops and the wombs of beasts and women to fail," he said coldly. "Go now to the Ancestors; your sons are young and hale and will be better rulers than you."

Vhortiern sank to his knees, face white with shock. He grasped at his chest; blood welled between his fingers and splattered the ground like red rain. He staggered against the long Man-stone, then thudded to his knees. Good-Striker rolled in the grass beside him.

Merlin picked up the chief's axe, beautiful, polished, its head jade-green beneath a slime of blood and brain. It was a fine thing, ancient and full of power. He raised it to his lips and whispered, "Make it swift, great Ancestors. Take the life of this one as final payment for sparing mine, and may my blood-debt to you be finished forever."

He swung the axe and it crashed into Vhortiern's temple. The big man crumpled silently, his skull a shattered ruin, and Merlin watched his death-throes in solemn contemplation, divining the future from his last twitching contortions. He noticed, with a sense of elation, that the already stiffening fingers on Vhortiern's out flung arm pointed to the south—toward the gentler lands of Albu and the pathways that led to the fabled temple of Khor Ghor.

CHAPTER TWO

Merlin wound his way up to the spires of God-of-Bronze, the Golden Road a pale ribbon beneath his feet. He passed the outcrops where the first Merlin had quarried the bluestones of Khor Ghor, and bathed his feet in the healing springs that sprang around the sacred dolerite. Then, to pay the stone-spirits for his safe passage, he sheared off a single lock of hair to leave as an offering on the capstone of the tiny ancestral tomb on the summit of the mountain. The shorn strands blew away like smoke, towards the South.

Towards Khor Ghor.

Descending from the mountains into tamer lands, he abandoned the Golden Road, fearful of encountering traders heading West, who might give information of his whereabouts, willingly or not, to Vhortiern's vengeful kinsmen. He set out across open country instead, climbing banks and fording streams, sending his hawk ahead and following its shadow on the grass.

He passed through the Valley of Wolves, where he walked with drawn bow and watched every rock, and crested the Bald Hills and the Black Hills, where no trees grew and the earth was dark and ashen as if it has been burned in ancient fire. Then he began a slow journey South into lower, flatter lands covered in deep vegetation, until, at last, he reached the banks of the mighty, green-brown river sacred to the spirit Ha-bren, who every year caused a great tidal bore to roar inland, sweeping all before it. Ha-bren could be dangerous and capricious, but not to all men—she allowed many to sail and fish her waters unharmed. Still, in order to ensure her favour, Merlin tossed her a quartz pebble from the magic-bag at his waist before continuing his journey along her banks.

Ha-bren must have been pleased by the gift. Not long after he deposited the pebble, Merlin saw smoke rising from a gaggle of huts near the riverbank. He had been guided to food and lodging. As he drew near, he noted the pungent smell of fish, and wrinkled his face in disgust—fish was taboo to his people, who ate only meat and grain—but he forced his revulsion down and approached the village's wattle fence. His hawk gave a disgusted cry and soared away, as if he, too, found the reek of the place foul.

Immediately scavenging dogs and fishy-smelling children poured from huts and surrounded Merlin, the children wide-eyed and bouncing with excitement, the dogs barking and snuffling at the hem of his robe. They were followed by a pack of curious women, all rather unappealing and smelly, and then several warriors, who left off drinking, snoring, and boasting round the evening fire to see what the commotion was about.

They gazed at Merlin suspiciously, fingering their axes, till he cast back his cloak to reveal the robe beneath – a knee-length sheath of tanned hide painted with mystic symbols, the edges sewn with ancient teeth of dog and wolf and boar. Buan-ann had aided him to paint it and sew the points on in the prescribed order, and it was obvious even to these strangers that the robe was the attire of a magic-man.

The people drew back then, gasping, slightly afraid, especially when Merlin's totem-hawk suddenly appeared, dropping onto his wrist and uttering a challenging scream to the throng.

The chief of the tribe, an old man with stringy grey hair bound in a knot high on his head, ambled forward, hands outstretched. His face was leathery, his mouth toothless. He walked with a limp, but despite this defect, his clothes were carefully crafted, with expensive conical buttons of jet fastening the front.

"Welcome, holy man!" he cried. "You may dine with us this evening, and stay the night if you so desire. My son had gone hunting and will be away till the new Moon—his hut is empty."

Merlin smiled. The tribes of Prydn had a custom that favoured a lone wanderer on the road. They were generous to a fault to those with special gifts: magic-craft, tale-telling, metallurgy, healing or dagger-play. A chief who was stingy, whose hearth was unwelcoming to guests, would soon be a laughing stock for miles around. No one would willingly besmirch their honour by being niggardly, and especially they would not do so before one who spoke with the spirits, lest he call a blight to wither the crops or spirit their babes off to Ahn-un.

Surrounded by the curious children, Merlin entered the communal feasting hut, his hawk still flapping on his arm. He was handed a beaker of honey-mead and a haunch of pig. It tasted good, and he realised how weak and hungry he had become on his long journey. Across the room he spied the tribe's shaman, an ugly man with a sly, canny face shaped like a crescent Moon, with a jabbing chin and bulbous brow that strove to meet. Moon-face must also have had a dedication to the Lady Moon, for he had a crescent tattooed between his brows, and his deerskin cloak was patterned with the lunar phases picked out in tiny beads.

The Shaman was kneeling by a hearth, cooking something that sputtered and sizzled on a spit. "Come, young stranger and man-of-magic," he wheedled. "Come, hawk-man, and see what we do here in Ha-bren's village."

Merlin had little interest in what Moon-face was doing. Nevertheless, he did not wish to offend his hosts, so he sent his hawk flying back out into the night, causing the gathered women to scream as its wings brushed their heads. He then squatted by the shaman, and saw that Moon-face was cooking a fish over the fire. Its juices foamed and spat; its mouth gaped and its big luminous eyes seemed to bulge at the young watcher. Again, Merlin fought his instinct to gag at the sight and smell.

Moon-face smirked, obviously aware of his discomfiture. "Is it 'gesh' for you, do you have a taboo on sea-flesh?" he cackled. "'Tis a pity, for this fish is the Salmon of Knowledge. Eat its flesh and you will have greater knowledge than any mortal man." With that, he grabbed the fish himself and bit into its shining scales. Juices spurted out and ran down his skin, but he had evidently miscalculated how hot it would be, for he let out an agonised howl and flung the fish from him.

The flopping, sizzling thing landed straight into Merlin's lap, as the villagers nudged each other and sniggered with mirth. He slapped it away, but his thumb sank into the roasted flesh, and he bit back a pained cry as the hot juices burnt him. Instinctively he placed his scalded thumb in his mouth, and the essence of the taboo creature passed into him.

He sprang up at once, glaring angrily at those gathered in the hut. "You think me some poor man of the mountains to jeer at," he snarled. "Beware, I say, lest you be cursed for your inhospitable ways!"

The people parted as he stormed from the tent, burnt thumb in his mouth like a petulant child. He heard snorts of laughter behind him, which both riled and concerned him. Safe passage in these unknown lands depended on his ability to convince the tribesmen that he was untouchable, worthy of honour and hospitality. He had not convinced these folk.

In the hut the chief had loaned him, Merlin lay down with his staff and dagger close by his side. The strange taste of the fish lingered in his mouth; he spat onto the ground once or twice but could not rid himself of it. At least it had not killed him or turned him into some foul beast!

When he finally found sleep, after many hours, he began to dream... He was a fish, like the one he had tasted; the Father of all fish, the Salmon of Wisdom with the Fire in his Head. As he swam, he felt the presence of pursuers, dark men along the water line who prodded the water with barbed spears, seeking to hook him, kill him.

Using the Salmon Leap, the champion's leap, he flew up through the water in a spray, soaring high above the heads of his foes. And as he leaped, ringed in the light of the rising Sun, he began to change. From fish that leaped high, to a bird of the air.

A hawk. His hawk.

A Merlin that soared over the forests of Albu toward a conical green hill that filled him with strange excitement and longing…

"I must go!" He sat up in the fuggy dark, eyes shining like those of a wild beast. It was silent in the riverside village, with only the occasional wail of a babe or the bark of a dog breaking the stillness. Yet something was stirring, coming his way. Merlin could feel it with a new, inborn sense.

He gazed at his blistered thumb. "The Salmon of Wisdom…Knowledge given me by my enemy's own mocking."

Quietly he crept between the dark huts, making his way towards the river. He halted, slinking into the shadows of one round hut, as two warriors swaggered past in a haze of alcoholic fumes. "He's not one of us," he heard one say. "He's ill-starred. Did you see the magic crystal he carried at his belt? It would go well in my hut, a gift for my new wife. Why should such as he have it? We should throw him to the fishes he despises so much."

The other man's teeth glinted in his coppery beard. "Let us do it. You can have the bright ball. Just let me search his pouch for other wealth…"

The two warriors picked up pace and Merlin swirled by them, silent as a breath of wind, a trick he had learned from Buan-ann. His fears had been proven; these men had no honour and were out to rob and kill. His lip curled in a snarl of outrage; in these lands even a magic-man was not safe…surely an affront to the spirits themselves!

Reaching the river, he spotted the tribesmen's canoes, tethered like animals to pegs in the thin, Moon-bathed mud. Cutting one free with his dagger, he paddled it into the centre of the flow, the sound of the oar no louder than that of fish leaping in the dark

A few moments later, there were angry shouts from the village. Torches flared. He grinned and spat in the direction of the huts, murmuring a powerful curse on the faithless and the false. As if it already had taken effect, a stray spark from the watch fire landed on a thatched roof and it burst into sudden, unexpected flame. Screams of fear and anger filled the night. Merlin watched for a moment more, coldly satisfied, then paddled on into the shadows, with the flip-flop of fish all around him and the soft laughter of the spirits soughing through the bushes to speed him on his way.

Merlin abandoned the canoe many miles upstream. His arms ached, and he knew, if he pursued, he could not keep up the pace against experienced boatmen. So he decided to proceed inland on foot.

Using his staff for support, he walked for what seemed an eternity, until the soles of his skin footgear hung in tatters. But still onwards he walked…

And walked…and walked…

Villages came and went; he made cautious stops to gather supplies and ask directions, but he never lingered. Like a man caught in a dream, he shouldered his pack and wandered on…

And on… And on…

His shoes soon disintegrated utterly; he caught a hare with help of his Merlin-hawk and made its pelt into a pair of new boots, which he padded with grass woven into a matt. He fed the hare's giblets to his eager bird, then walked on, uncomfortable because the hide had not been properly dried, but grateful he was not barefoot.

And still the path wound on, seemingly endless, deep into the strange southern lands far from the mountains of his birth.

Eventually, he felt the ground changing beneath his feet, becoming soft as a maiden's pliant flesh. It was Woman's land here, void of the harsh masculinity of his homeland of gods and giants. In his nostrils he could smell water and earth intermingled—women's elements, unlike fire and air, which were male.

Cresting a low rise, he suddenly spotted a conical hill on the horizon. It dominated the surrounding landscape, looking somehow unnatural, as if man, or maybe a god, had sculpted its form. It was the hill of his dream—deep green, with a spiral-path winding up to its crown and water pooling at its feet. The evening Sun was passing over its shoulder, and the lake below gleamed dark as jet, sucking in the lingering light.

Entranced, he hunkered down and watched as the Sun fell from heaven and the water at the base of the hill turned scarlet—a lake of blood, the birthing-pool of the holy hill. Slowly, the gory welter of sunset faded from the West. Jewel-like stars now glimmered on the surface of the lake, reminding Merlin of the white speckles in the stones on God-of-Bronze.

"What is this place?" he whispered. "Surely it must be one of the Hallows of Prydn."

Rising, he continued with renewed vigour toward the holy hill, skirting the edges of the now-sullen lake. He trod carefully, for the ground became even wetter, saturated with rank marsh-water. Glancing down, he could see that he walked on a mesh of ancient withies, laid down in some bygone time to aid passage across the fen. A little god-doll carved from a slab of bog-oak squatted in the marsh near the head of the track, its quartz-pebble eyes glinting in the dusk. Fireflies ringed the figure's head, making a crown of dancing light. Merlin bowed to the effigy in respect, but could not sense if it welcomed or warned him.

Further along, he spied the pointed roof of a hut set on an islet in the heart of the marsh. It was so quiet he guessed at once that it was the house of some idol or spirit rather than the dwelling place of mortal men. Respecting its sanctity, he avoided its lintelled doorway and continued to skirt the boggy lake.

Just as he was beginning to despair of ever walking on solid land again, he spied a trail that led from the water's edge. Mist was rising around him now, as the cool of the night strove against the warmth of the day, and some of the stars went out, blotted by the opaque cloud. Merlin scanned what he could still see of the sky and realised it was very late; the Moon had westered. It was time for him to sleep like the sunken Moon, lest weariness made his steps clumsy and he ended up sinking in the bog amid the slimy marsh-eels.

He peered around, eyes straining in the murk. Off to one side, he could see a tree on a rise, guarding an entranceway or passage formed by several natural boulders. He stepped towards the gap and nearly bumped into a wooden post covered in carvings that he could not decipher. He ignored it, although he realised it might be perilous to do so, and entered an enclosure surrounded by close-set, stunted trees. They were laden with small ripe apples, and the grass below their boughs was full of fallen fruit that gave out the sickly-sweet smell of decay.

He could hear water running and stumbled through the gloom towards the sound. His feet splashed into the stream before he saw it. Ice-cold water swirled around his calloused soles, soothing them. He sighed in utter pleasure.

He followed the small stream further into the enclosure. A sharp tang hung in the air, stronger even than the fug of the rancid apples. Recognising the sharp coppery scent, Merlin felt the hair on the back of his neck prickle.

Fumbling in his belt-pouch, he drew out his flint strike-a-light and a piece of tinder. Swiftly he kindled a small torch and held it aloft.

Shadows swirled about the garth, retreating from the flame. Merlin stood on the edge of a pond fed by the tiny stream. Offerings lay on its shores: wheat sheaves bound with twine, a broken pot with spiral designs, the upended top of a skull that rocked mournfully, ominously, in the wind. The sharp tang rose even more strongly here and Merlin knelt and cupped the water, bringing it to his lips. It was pale, pure and clear, seemingly untainted, and yet…the waters tasted of blood.

There was no mistaking taste and scent. It was as if he were drinking the blood of the Earth itself, of Great Ahn-ann whose breasts were hills, whose body spawned all living things. This spring and the coiled hill beyond were very holy places indeed. Holy, but fearsome and filled with dark mysteries, women's mysteries of which he knew little.

Awed, he knelt to pray to the patron of the blood-water spring…but he heard a harsh breath in the dark, a swish of long robes.

Before he had chance to react, the cold blade of a bronze dagger pressed against his throat. Warm breath tickled his ear, and a woman's voice said, "Who are you stranger, who have come unbidden to the Garden of Afallan? To enter here without the permission of the Lady of the Lake makes your life forfeit!"

He froze, scarcely daring to breathe. "I am friend, I mean no harm. I am a wanderer who comes in search of wisdom. The Ancestors have guided me here."

"Have they now?" the woman said mockingly. "The Ancestors are capricious, or did you not know? Perhaps they guided you here to be sacrificed to them."

The dagger poked his neck; he felt a drop of blood slide over his collarbone. He was filled with real fear. He had not envisioned his life-force going to feed this bitter, metallic-tasting pool. "The land may want my blood," he croaked, "and if that is what the high ones decree, that is my fate. But I would not gladly die before seeing Khor Ghor."

The woman's breath railed between her teeth. "Khor Ghor? What business do you have with that mighty place? If it is merely to gawk, there are screens to shield the holy of all holies from unworthy eyes. You would not be welcome there—you are, by your tongue, a rude mountain man."

Anger kindled within Merlin, overcoming his fear of the woman's dagger. "I seek the priesthood. Barbarian I may be to you, woman, but I tamed the Wyrms of Faraon, I have studied in the groves on Mhon, and I've held counsel with the priestess of Brygyndo in Ibherna."

The knife suddenly dropped away. "Interesting." A hint of mirth deepened the woman's voice. "Maybe you are more than just a hapless wanderer after all. Maybe you were guided here for a reason. Turn around, slowly mind…If you disobey, my dagger will strike your heart quicker than lightning."

Slowly Merlin turned around. A girl stood on the green grass, a deadly copper rapier in her hand. Autumn-brown hair wound with strips of blue felt tumbled to her waist, and a white-gold lunula circled her neck. Spirals were painted on cheeks and chin. Fringed by dark lashes, her eyes were as green as the conical hill of his dreams. A thin robe blew floated around her, ephemeral as the mist, hiding little of the slim, wiry body beneath.

"Who are you?" he breathed. She seemed so beautiful, standing in the starlight; she put all the women of his tribe to shame. But there was a deadly, dangerous quality to her beauty. It reminded him of a snake, mysterious and exotic with its piercing eyes and dappled skin, but with fangs ready to bite the foolish hand that reached to touch. He would not dare touch this lady. He half wondered if she was human at all, or one of the Everliving ones, who could take on human form at will.

The girl was looking him up and down with her unsettling, grass-green eyes. "You are younger than I thought at first, and less ugsome. Though you could use a meal…and a bath. But not in the sacred lake…unless you wish never to come out again." She giggled quietly, her laughter unsettling. "My sisters and I alone can swim there and live. I am Nin-Aeifa, priestess of Afallan, the Apple-garden, and guardian of the Tor where Hwynn the White Fire, lord of the mortuary and son of Nud Cloudmaker, rides every Sovahn to collect the shades of the dead. With my sisters we form the ring of Nine Maidens who tend the Sacred Cauldron of Inspiration, boiled by fires that never wane."

"I am known as the Merlin," Merlin said simply, and at that moment, his hawk descended from the clouds to flutter round his shoulders. Merlin was oddly pleased to see Nin-Aeifa jump at the sight of the bird before regaining her regal composure.

"You continue to surprise," said Nin-Aeifa. She sheathed her rapier. "Follow me."

The young priestess led Merlin to a round hut outside the enclosure, within sight of the great cult house that stood on the artificial island in the lake, but not too near it. She gestured Merlin onto a pallet of furs, then reached for a drum made of gut stretched taut over a wooden frame. She tapped out a sharp tattoo, bringing a flurry of younger girls, who carried in trenchers heaped with pork, and beakers brimming with a drink made from fermented apples, the likes of which Merlin had never tasted before.

"Eat, Western stranger," commanded Nin-Aeifa, "and slake your thirst to your heart's content," and Merlin did as he was bade, uncaring in his hunger that juices smeared his face and dripped onto his clothes. As the apple-ale hit his belly, his tongue loosened in a way that was unusual for him, and he began to tell Priestess Nin-Aeifa about his old life, of the serpents that caused the godstones to fall, of Old Woman Buan-ann and the warnings of the priestess of Fiery Arrow. He even told her how he had slain Vhortiern and given him to the stones.

Nin-Aeifa sat cross-legged, stroking her chin thoughtfully. Merlin was amazed; she was so young yet appeared so wise, as if the knowledge of centuries was locked within the body of a girl. "Rumours have come to Afallan," she said, "that Eckhy, one of the elder priests of Khor Ghor, is ill with a disease than thins his blood. It is thought he will not last more than one more Winter, two at most. When he passes to the West, magic-men from all over Prydn will gather to compete for his position in the Great Temple. Maybe his death will be new life to you, outlander; perhaps it is true, that the Ancestors sent you from your mountain realm to take his place. This may be a good thing. Many of the priests there are old in both body and mind, and seem not to see the perils of these troubled times. Maybe Khor Ghor needs new blood." She laughed again, the not-quite-pleasant laugh of the garden. "And if not, the Stones may well have your blood anyway. They do not like pretenders there."

"I am no pretender," growled Merlin, flushing with annoyance.

"Well, good." She smiled impishly, tossing her blue-streaked hair over her shoulder. "You will have nothing to fear then."

"I will press on to Khor Ghor at first light," said Merlin. "I will make myself known to the priests before this Eckhy passes."

"No, you will not." Nin-Aeifa sidled up to him; suddenly he noticed how sweet she smelt, but it was the cloying scent of the rotted apples in the enclosure, a scent dark and earthy and unsettling, an overwhelming brew both fair and foul. "You have eaten my food—the food of Otherness—and drank my ale, brewed with the waters of Life and the apples of Afallan. You are mine for a year and a day. But no, do not cast me those angry looks; yours will be a fine captivity. I will teach you many things that you must know before you reach Khor Ghor. Right now you are but a boy of some talent…you must go there a man of Many Talents."

He dared not defy her; knew he could not, that her bright blade would snake out to seek his veins if he resisted. And he was not entirely sure he wanted to resist. The offer of learning appealed; his inquisitive mind was fast as flame and, like flame, craved more fuel to burn. He felt strange other yearnings and longings too, in his chest, and in his loins. He had not had much truck with women of his own clan, who had seemed like dull, dumb oxen, worn down with care. But this creature, fire and water and cloying apple-scent, she was a match for him, one of the Touched Ones, an equal of his own kind.

"I will stay," he whispered hoarsely. "I want you to teach me…everything."

"Oh, I shall…" In her hand, she held a small round cup laced with perforations; she lit its powdered contents with a bit of kindling from her hearth and the room was suddenly wreathed with curling, pungent smoke. Enchanted smoke that went to the head and gave men visions of the Otherworld.

The clouds wreathed her and he saw her face, haloed by the smoke, a face serene and young, yet cunning and dangerous. A goddess's face. Her crescent collar gleamed like the Moon as she took it off and raised it, kissing it before setting it aside. Then her flimsy robes slithered away, pooling on the floor, and she flung herself down upon the furs, her supple legs and floating autumn-leaf hair tangling with his limbs, and her lips, apple-laced, burning hotter than the fire against his yearning mouth.

***

The days marched on into months, and the trees in the nearby groves turned red as blood, then became thin as skeletons in a barrow. The Year Turned, the Sun falling into the sacred lake on the shortest day, and the dance of the seasons began again, with new buds sprouting on the trees followed by flowers and leaves, and gradually, the gold and reds of yet another Autumn.

Merlin and Nin-Aeifa lived as lovers in her hut below the Tor, and as she had promised, she taught him all she knew of magic and the spirits of the water and the dead, and he taught her of his mountain ways, and the gods of sky and stone. He gave to her his secret name, Lailoq, and she whispered that she had been born Hwyndolona, child of a priestess of Afallan, and she was consecrated to Hwynn, god of the Mortuary, by both name and upbringing.

"When I leave this place, will you come with me, be my wife?" Merlin asked one day, when they lay beneath her sheepskins, with a wind that bore the first bitter hint of winter whistling about the roundhouse.

She glanced at him, eyes fathomless. "Never. I am a Maiden of the Cauldron. If I were to go with you, my honour would go too. I would have to kill you."

"Maiden!" His hands slid over the rises and valleys of her lithe body. "I hardly think so."

She gave him a glare that immediately stopped his ministrations. "Maiden merely means that the servants of the Cauldron never wed. It does not mean we must remain virgin, though some choose that path. Every year at Midsummer we bathe in the lake on the first full Moon after solstice, and it is said the Lady of the Spiral Crown purifies us anew."

Merlin settled down into the warmth of the furs, pressing against the swell of her hip. "Forgive my rash words. I am but a man and do not know the women's mysteries. Women...the doom of the Merlin!"

"It may be so," she whispered, and turned away into the dark.

***

The next morning Merlin went to gather healing plants in the nearby woods. He was alone, for Nin-Aeifa had gone to the cult house in the lake, attending to matters of the Cauldron. Distantly he could hear his lover and her fellows singing and chanting, as they began the preparations for Savhan, the night when the dead came from their barrows and walked the dark beyond the firelight. It was when Hwynn himself rode forth, head burning with White Fire, and collected new spirits to take into the Deadlands.

Merlin had gathered half a basketful of fungus when he became aware of a faint rhythmic vibration in the earth beneath his feet. He lay down and pressed his ear against the ground. Yes, something was coming. Something large...far larger and heavier than a man or even several men. Winds arose, and the fallen leaves eddied as if dancing in anticipation. Shoving his woven basket beneath a bush, he hastened to the ancient trackway that wound through the marshy woodland where he collected his mushrooms, mosses and herbs.

At the end of the track a figure appeared, mounted on a great black horse. This sight frightened Merlin at once, for men seldom rode those great wild beasts; they were sacred to the spirits, and had hooves and teeth to fight off the advances of men. Some tribes captured them and kept them as totem animals, and it was said the kings of Ibherna ate their flesh after boiling them at their inauguration feasts, but his people just avoided them...they were the children of the Lady-of-Horses whose head was a woman's but who ran on four legs.

The galloping animal drew closer; he could now see its wild eyes and the froth on its muzzle, and a shaggy, raven mane plaited with what looked to be human finger-bones. Astride its back was a man, or something man-like, with silver-white, bleached hair that billowed like a cloud of fog. Its face was narrow, lean, painted in black and white, its contours those of a skull...or was it paint indeed, for there seemed to be no human eyes in the darkness of its sockets, just pinpoints of bright blue light?

Merlin shuddered and dropped to his knees, heart pounding with both terror and elation. Surely this was Hwynn the White himself, riding to the Holy Tor to bear the souls of the newly dead back to Ahn-un, where Hwynn and his sire Nud would judge them, before sending them on to the Plain of Honey, or casting them back into the world as vengeful ghosts. Fearfully he peered up, and saw with terrified excitement, that there were now three great dogs bounding alongside the unearthly rider, their coats white as untrodden snow and their flapping ears the hue of old blood. They bayed, howled, and snapped at the air, frenzied by the mad flight of the skull-faced rider.

Fighting down his fear at being in the presence of such a holy one, Merlin struggled back to his feet. "Oh Great Lord!" he cried. "What tidings do you bring to Afallan this day?"

The skull face turned, white hair foaming around it. "I come from the lands where Abona makes the waters swell." A gravelly voice rang out, reminiscent of the clatter of winter icicles, of long bones in rifled cists upon the hills. "I come bearing the spirit of one who has passed, one who will now live forever with his mighty forefathers from the Times-before-Time. Eckhy the old, the wise, priest of Khor Ghor, has now lain upon the mortuary platform for the prescribed turning of the Moon, and will now come to rest for a while under the Hill." He parted his cloak of shredded black pigskins, and revealed a drum-shaped chalk box upon his knee, decorated with surprised, watching, faceless eyes. "His heart, his spirit, lies within."

The vision of the sinister reliquary box was gone in a flash and the unearthly rider with it, pounding on his sweat-stained steed along the track toward the Tor, domain of Hwynn, son of Snatcher, Son of Snarer.

Merlin stepped onto the path and stared after the fearsome figure as it dwindled into the distance, the attendant hounds yammering around the horse's hooves. "So...Eckhy is dead," he whispered. "And as the Moon accounts it, it nigh on a year and a day since Nin-Aeifa bound me to her. I am free of her constraints, and I must go."

There was a shriek from above and his totem-hawk descended from the trees and dug its talons into his uplifted forearm. He was surprised, for the bird had not come to him for a while, though he had oftimes spotted it circling in the sky, wary of the settlement of the Ladies of the Lake yet still tied to its mortal brother.

"You have returned, my friend," he said, stroking the feathered head. "You will be my one companion on the road to the Temple of the Ancestors."

A stab of pain needled his heart as he spoke to the bird, but he forced it away. Nin-Aeifa had made her choice, and he had made his. Quickly, without a backward glance, he hurried away into the wintry woods, his hawk flying up above his head, spiralling and screaming as if goading him on.

And in the cult house in the lake, the Nine Maidens paused while stoking the fire round their sacred Cauldron, and they heard the hounds and hoof beats of Hwynn the White upon the beaten path, and suddenly Nin-Aeifa cried out with knowledge and loss, "He is gone!"

Her Sisters, thinking she spoke of the spirit of the old one that Hwynn carried, began to keen for the dead, and to tear their hair and faces. Nin-Aeifa joined in their mourning, her hands clawed and a shroud across her face.

But it was not for any ancient temple priest she wailed.

It was for the death of love, and the end of youth, and the twisting of destinies in the unassailable hands of fate.

CHAPTER THREE

Darkness shrouded the Great River known simply as Abona—the River. It was the prime waterway of Albu and the most holy, hence the simple, defining name; the recipient of ancient soulstones on a long journey from the West, and a source of life and death and cleansing.

Merlin sat in a canoe while a lean, wiry, river-man poled the craft through weirs, past tall stands of reeds and round islets where strange birds, disturbed by splash of the paddle, rushed up shrieking into the shadows.

Overhead the stars wheeled in the vault of sky, their white points scattered amid the tangle of trees on the riverbank. Fish flopped in the water, their passage leaving rings on the swell, and Merlin, listening carefully, fancied he could hear the song of the river-mother who lay, green and weedy, on the beds below:
"Lay di lay, for a thousand lives' span
The river will run where the river ran
I was here ere great stones stood
I saw them borne on rafts of wood
But I shall flow while stones may fall
Old Mother shall outlive them all!"

"Where am I now?" he asked his guide, whose services he had hired at a village downriver in exchange for a handful of bluestone chippings.

The man grunted, continuing to pole the craft. "Not far from the Temple. On the right…" he paused, waving one arm into the blackness, "are the Resting Places of great Kings, and the Giant's Dance beyond them, where their shades may look upon it. Continue to follow the river and you will come to the Old Circle, where the Spirit-Avenue begins, leading over the hill and across Mai Mor, the Great Plain, up to the Stone of Summer itself. If you turn your back to the Avenue and following the river South, you will soon see the Place-of-Light upon a plateau, marked by posts and lit by torchlight. This is where the folk who are not priests dwell."

Merlin craned his head around, smelling the air, eyes seeking in the deep darkness. "Pull into the bank," he ordered, nodding towards a spot where the reeds were thin.

The man bared his teeth. "I would rather take you to the settlement. There will be ghosts walking in the fog. Not all are happy to be dead, not all have joined their Ancestors on the Plains of Honey!"

Merlin grinned, his eyes twinkling. "I fear no Wight. Indeed, I would gladly talk to the dead tonight!"

"You are mad," said his companion morosely, but he pushed the coracle in against the bank as Merlin had asked. "I do not suppose I will ever hear of you again. My wife will thank you in her prayers for the lucky bluestones."

Merlin climbed out onto the bank, his skin shoes slopping in the mud. "You will hear of me again. Remember the name of the Merlin! Remember it, and pass it to your sons and to your sons' sons' sons! My name will live forever!"

"Mad!" the boatman repeated, as Merlin vanished into the scrub growing on the riverbank. Then, as shivers that were not brought by the chill of the wind rippled down his spine, he began to paddle madly toward the wholesome, welcoming fires of the Place-of-Light.

Merlin wandered a while, before finding a track. Cut into the chalk, it wound up from the verdant banks of Abona and snaked north, glowing faintly in the starshine. Hoisting up his heavy, tooth-fringed robe so that his legs were bare and free, he began to follow it. The night was cold, and rags of mist fluttered past him like the souls of the dead that the boatman had warned him about.

Suddenly, one of the dead men's barrows came into view, huge and round, blocking out the starlight, circled by a white chalk ditch that kept the spirit of the corpse—if he still lingered on the mortal plain—within its sacred boundaries. A decaying memorial pole loomed on the mound's summit, facing North-East, where the Sun rose at Midsummer.

Merlin felt power flow from the tumulus, cold lines that twisted like serpents beneath his ill-shod feet. Approaching, he crossed the ditch and knelt by the pole, examining carvings of axes and chevrons and spirals. Around him, the air sighed, and he suspected old barrow-man was stirring; that he, loving life as a warrior of Khor Ghor, had not yet crossed the Great Plain to the Deadlands of the ultimate West where the chosen played eternally on the Plain of Honey.

Hastily, Merlin fumbled with the pouch at his belt and drew out some dried herbs wrapped in a large dark leaf. He crumbled them between his fingers, thrust them into his mouth and forced himself to swallow, despite the bitterness that caused him to grimace and gag.

For a while, he sat cross-legged, the wind hissing in the grass and in his sleek black hair. Gradually, a dull cramping sickness gripped his belly and he forced back the urge to heave. Zigzag flashes obscured the edges of his vision, while the centre of his gaze became an undulating black tunnel. His heartbeat grew loud, echoing in his ears, while a fine sweat covered brow and torso, to be licked away by the rising breeze.

A splitting pain gripped one side of his head, almost as if some primeval monster was squeezing it with vicious claws, trying to rend his skull and steal his brain as a man might suck a wild bird's egg. He closed his eyes against the throbbing agony, and when he opened them again…He was there.

The warrior. The grave-wight. He was one of the old ones, one of the first men of tin. He carried a bow and golden baskets glittered in his hair. His face was green and glowing, alternating between a skull and livid flesh, and in his hand he brandished a dagger of ancient style, phosphorus flowing from its blade in a stream like a comet's tail.

Merlin felt a surge of both fear and elation. "I welcome you, mighty Ancestor!" he cried, kneeling with his head almost upon the bony feet.

"Why do you wake me from my sleep of a million nights, from my dreaming with my beakers and my arrows and beloved gold?" asked the Wight, his voice the eerie sough of wind in bare branches. It was the inhuman rasp of one who has no throat, no tongue of mortal flesh with which to speak.

Merlin gazed up, suddenly fierce. "Because I can!"

The dead face looked almost surprised. But then the jaw dropped and a grating screech came from the desiccated throat, a terrible sound that Merlin only just recognised as laughter. "You are not as other men if you, in truth, wish to gaze upon such a creature as I!"

"I am not as other men," replied Merlin. "Indeed, some say I am not a real mortal man at all, for my sire was of the spirit world. Hence, I do not fear you. It is learning I seek."

"To what purpose?" The creature leaned over him, smelling of cold earth and long-dead flesh. "You have hawk's eyes. I do not trust you. Hawks rent my flesh when I was dead."

"Tell me the secrets of Khor Ghor. It is there that I go this night, to become a priest—the greatest priest ever—of that temple. I must have knowledge in order that they will accept me, a youth and a foreigner."

The Wight's teeth grinned through rags of flesh. "Secrets should stay secrets, but as you have compelled me here, know this-- I lived when the lintel-ring was raised. The great stones came from the north, from near the temple of the Eye. Many hands pounded these stones into shape--the work of men, not gods, brought with blood and hard labour. Wooden platforms were built skyward to put the capstones in place, a work never seen among the stone buildings of men, truly a fitting tribute to the Ancestors and to Bhel Sunface and Mother Moon. And when it was done, we carved upon some of the stones, putting marks upon them from our respective beliefs—the image of She-Who-Guards, the Axe that bears the power of the Sun, the Blade of Power. And the priestesses, the dancing women, came and honoured the Great Stones, weaving in and out until their cries of ecstasy greeted the dawn…"

"You honour me with your knowledge." Merlin bowed, awed by this being who had witnessed the raising of the greatest temple in Prydn, who had walked in an era when stone fell before metal and Midsummer became secondary to the great feast of resurrection in Winter's heart.

The cold wind blew more fiercely; goose bumps sprouted on Merlin's bare legs beneath his robe. The mist went sailing in great ragged loops down the valley, while stray leaves tumbled and fell like dead men on the valley sides. He swayed and fell, and went tumbling with the leaves, rolling over and over, unable to gain footing, while behind him the ghostly, ghastly laughter of the barrow-man split the night until, suddenly, his gaunt, surreal figure flickered out as a flame is extinguished in the wind. Only the night and the wind trod upon the lowering bulk of his great barrow.

Merlin staggered dazedly to his feet heavy-headed and unsteady, and trudged on, his vision still distorted from the effects of the potion he had consumed. Up ahead, he noticed a lofty rise crowned by an unassuming earthwork and lit by the hard crescent of the Westering Moon. The place looked deserted, but its height would enable him to survey the lands below and plan his route.

Breath a cloud of white before his mouth, he clambered up the rise. As he climbed, he could smell a sickly tang, the same sweet but hideous scent he had recognised beside the Holy well in Afallan. The scent of decay, of dissolution.

The scent of death.

Cresting the bank of the earthwork, he immediately knew why. The hill was covered by excarnation platforms, some with hunched figures lying upon them, others bearing completely skeletal bodies, their rib cages stark beneath the cold, thin, bone-light of the Moon.

As he stumbled forward, his feet shifted millennia of teeth and small bones fallen from their owner's corpses into the grass. They tumbled like shimmering pearls in the muted starshine.

Merlin noticed one platform that loomed higher than the rest, and seemed to be of recent construction. The body lying on it was furled in the shredded remains of a blue robe that fluttered like a sail in the breeze. The face had been picked clean by birds and other scavengers, but the hands, still retaining some flesh and tendon, grasped a boar's tusk and a shard of magic quartz.

Suddenly he realised who this sky-burial must be. "Eckhy the priest," Merlin murmured.

There was a rushing sound, another skirl of wind, and suddenly the spirit of the old man appeared, thinner and less substantial than the Tin-man in his ancient mound, and less threatening. He was like a dim reflection of life, ready to break apart like an image seen in a raindrop or on a puddle. "You have come, I know you would," he said. "It was foretold a Merlin would return to the Temple."

"Do I have your blessing, old one?"

"Aye, but your desire will not come easy. Many covet a place in Khor Ghor. But you alone will have spoken to the dead of the Stones, as well as the living priests. You belong to our world as well as the world of men. Look, Merlin…look over and see the Dance-of-Spirits in its majesty."

Merlin peered out from the height, gaze sweeping over rises and ridges dotted with barrows, some overgrown with spiky thorns, others glowing white, their chalk faces still bare and their ditches newly dug. Beyond them, pallid in the starlight, on a plain long denuded of forest, stood the Temple; the Year's Turn, the Circle of Eternity. Its lintels rose into the night, beacon bright, while its barrier-ditch glowed with an eerie earth-light. The worked, smoothed stones of the outer ring grinned like a row of even teeth, with utter darkness gathered in the spaces between them.

"It is not a place for the faint hearted," said Eckhy. "Some have come with foolish posies and gifts of pebbles, but this is not a place of simple charms and cures. Khor Ghor is a place of power, a place of Kings that were and Kings that will be."

Merlin stared at the gigantic structure, hot and cold chills rippling down body. He felt as if his very spirit was being sucked from his chest into the unearthly blackness between those massive stones. He was afraid…yet he wanted to plunder that blackness too. He too was part of the darkness, the mystery that lay beyond safe firelight, and if any could tread those paths unscathed—it was the Son of No Man.

"Do you fear what you see, boy?" asked the shade of the old priest, pointing to the Stones, while the substance of his thin arm unravelled like mist. He was being drawn back into the darkness, back across the Plain to the Holy Hill where Hwynn had taken him to enter the Otherworld, to begin his long journey from Ahn-un to the Plain of Honey.

"I do," replied Merlin. "But not a fear that would put me to flight. It is a fear that has also set a fire alight within me—I want to know more."

"Then you, like your namesake, will surely become one of the great priests of that hallowed Place," said the spirit, and he abruptly vanished with a hiss like escaping marsh-gas, leaving only a bird-ravaged body high on a wooden dais.

Merlin stared at the bundle of bones that had been a man, and climbing onto the platform placed pebble offerings in the dead man's empty eyeholes as a token of thanks and respect. Finishing, he swiftly left the hill and hurried across the chalkland on a well-worn trail. It led between the upturned bowls of warriors' barrows and the disc-shaped tumuli of forgotten queens, before petering out a respectful distance from Khor Ghor's bank, which formed a stark boundary between the profane world and the world of the Ancestors.

Heart drumming against his ribs, he cautiously approached the earthwork, watchful for any guards. Mere feet away, the outer sarsens were like pale, malformed giants dancing in a ring, joined together for all time by their lintels. Beyond them, the mighty five trilithons that were symbols of both death and power roared up into the night, the largest man-made structures Merlin had ever laid eyes on. He knew their names from age-old lore: Throne of Kings, decorated with dagger and axe; the Arch of the Eastern Sky; the House of the North Wind; the Western Guardian, and tallest and most imposing of all, the Great Trilithon, Door of the Setting Sun, with its massive lintel towering high above the rest. More ominously, this trilithon was also known as the Door into Winter and Portal-of-Ghosts.

Not yet daring to approach the heart of the sanctuary, Merlin wandered Sunwise along the edge of the bank. His eyes scanned the shadows; he saw ghosts, watching shyly, but no living men, or any guards. He had heard that though Warrior-Priests traversed the Plain all night, they did not tarry long in the Stones themselves—it was too fearsome a place to linger after Sunset.

Indeed, at that moment Merlin's own heart quailed and he wished momentarily to be very far away, where there was fire and the comforts of men. But, then, unexpectedly, there was a rush in the dark, a brush of wings against his cheek. He nearly screamed, but took control of himself at once, watching as a huge white owl, its eyes the colour of amber beads, beat shadows back with its wings before vanishing amid the Stones.

The Owl was the totem of the Guardian, the Lady of the Watching Eyes, whose rectangular symbol was graven high on the Western trilithon.

Merlin had his omen, his welcoming.

Taking a deep breath, he crossed the divide and passed beneath the lintels of the outer sarsen ring.

A hedge of bluestones greeted him, crowding around him like old friends. Stones from his own lands, the jagged mountain that was God-of-Bronze, with its views across the waves to Ibherna. Damp with dew, the stones gleamed bluish-green, the Western ones tall and elegant, the others more roughly formed, though two, one pointed and the other broad, were exceptions. They were the Old Father, with his peaked head, and flat, broad-faced Grey Woman; progenitors of the tribes of Albu embodied in stone.

Leaving the bluestones, Merlin crossed the circle and came before the Altar, the Stone of Adoration, the godstone that held the very essence of the Circle's power. Green and faintly glittering, it was backed by the enormous Door into Winter, which opened the way for the spirits of the departed to fly across the Great Plain, following the path of the setting Sun.

This was the centre of all things, caught in a circle that had no beginning and no end. Awed, Merlin knelt on the chalk floor and bent his head to the ground in homage to the Stone of Adoration. He could feel energy rushing through the earth, the beat of life itself. It soothed him, comforted him as if he was a child. Sighing, he stretched out beneath the dark skies, watched over by the guardian Stones.

Heaviness crept over his limbs; his body went limp as a babe's. He feared nothing here, not spirits, not angry guards. His eyelids dragged down, and the darkness of sleep overcame him.

"Should we kill him?"

The prod of an arrow's tip between his shoulder blades brought Merlin to wakefulness. Biting back a cry, he struggled to wake from his potion-addled sleep. The world tilted. He could see he was still in the centre of Khor Ghor, lying slumped against one of the sarsens, but the sky was blood red with approaching dawn.

Turning his head, he saw two men glaring at him. He guessed they were warrior-priests of the temple, both young, clad in woven tunics and with bronze bands holding back their hair. The one prodding him had some kind of northern ancestry for his long locks were corn-coloured, braided in front and hooped by gold rings. The other had wild, curling russet hair, and dark tattoos ringing his eyes, giving him the semblance of Owl's eyes. Both carried bows, and daggers with hilts of horn.

"So, the sleepy one wakes!" The tattooed man nudged him with a toe. "How dare you, ragged one, come in here and lie like a dog at the fire in the holy of holies."

"You are lucky you are not dead," said the blonde man, lip curling in a sneer. "What have you to say for yourself, stranger?"

"I say... who is leader here? Neither of you I would wager."

The men glanced at each other with mingled expressions of anger and perplexity. "You must be Moon-touched, boy!" choked the tattooed man. "To speak so to the guardians of Khor Ghor, when the very arrows that mete death are pointed at your heart!"

Merlin stared into the man's eyes. "If you had really sought to kill me, you would have done the deed by now. You do not know what to make of me, do you? You don't know how I got here, passing your careful guardianship..." He smirked mockingly. "You wonder if I am a spirit, or a sorcerer…after all, you could not tell your superiors a mere mountain boy slipped into Khor Ghor and slept the night among the holy Stones, while you huddled outside like frightened women!"

The tattooed man gritted his teeth. "Stop playing with us, boy. Who are you, who comes here with such audacity, mocking us?"

Merlin flashed a vulpine smile. Suddenly he looked older than his captors, as old as the Stones themselves, and somehow sinister, with his beak-nosed and strangely archaic face, its high planes streaked with sweat and dirt, the deep-set eyes bloodshot from his magic spirit-brew. "I'm son of no Man. They say my father was a spirit from the forest. I have studied the mysteries within earth and within the sky. I have made stones stand that have fallen. I have killed a chief and have tasted the apples of Afallan. The Salmon of Knowledge has blessed my tongue, and the Lady of the Lake my body. And so I come here to join the priests of Khor Ghor and replace Eckhy the old."

The warrior-priests glanced at each other, anger replaced by surprise and even a touch of fear. "If what you speak is truth," said the tattooed one, "you must come with us right away, to meet the leader of our Order."

Dragging him from the centre circle, they skirted the Summer Stone that marked the year's longest day, before hurrying down the parallel arms of the processional Avenue, which led over the fields before curving sharply toward the River Abona. However, the priests did not take Merlin this way. Instead, they left the safety of the Avenue and herded him along the top of a ridge studded with huge, swollen tumuli, some of the largest burial mounds Merlin had ever seen. Cow carcasses rotted in their ditches; offering to placate restive spirits.

"Seven kings sleep here," said the yellow-haired priest. "Lords who wrought Khor Ghor of old. This is not a Land of the Living, stranger-boy; it belongs to the Dead, and there may be horrors in the morning mist that freeze your heart."

"Not mine," retorted Merlin. "The Dead have been as much friend to me as the living, priest."

The party journeyed onward in an Easterly direction. The rising Sun was a burning red eye through the dwindling night-fog. In the distance, Merlin could see a range of sloping hills, curved like a woman's body, the chalk scars on their slopes gleaming in the growing light. And not far away, facing the hills, was a settlement on an escarpment that overlooked a shallow dell and the river beyond.

The sight of this holding awed him, but he kept his expression impassive, not wishing to appear a gawping and unsophisticated country fool. He had never seen a settlement so large, never really knew that one existed. Standing on the highest point of the plateau was a great round temple, lintelled and open to the sky in similar fashion to Khor Ghor, but wrought from stout oak timbers instead of stones. A scatter of barrows hugged the temple's sides, as if the dead sought to press in upon this place where the living worshipped.

A short distance away, a circular earthwork shone white as bone in the half-light. Hundreds of rectangular houses clustered around its edges, and at the centre stood a mighty cult house, once again circular and open to the sky. A pair of soaring totem poles fronted this house of the spirits, and a wide pathway, smoothed by the passage of countless feet, curved from its doorway toward the river lying in the dip below the settlement.

The blonde warrior-priest gestured with his bow, pride and the rosy light of dawn bringing a flush to his face. "Look and wonder, newcomer. You gaze on Deroweth, place of oaks, place of the wise seers—the greatest dwelling in all of Albu, maybe all of Prydn."

"It is a mighty place," Merlin agreed, his gaze sweeping over Deroweth. "Though quiet, considering it has many dwellings."

"You have not seen it in Midwinter, when chiefs come from all over the Five Cantrevs, bringing their women, children and herding beasts. The priests pass laws, disputes are settled, marriages made…but best of all is the Great Feast on the day Bhel Sunface dies and is reborn! Even the dogs of Deroweth are glutted with meat on that night, and beacons burn on every hill to greet the rebirth of Bhel from Ahn-ann's womb."

The warrior-priests and their captive soon reached a house standing near the entrance to the great henge. It was of highest quality, long and rectangular, with stout oak walls—the dwelling of a man of status. Smaller huts straddled its sides, with middens at the back and strong scents of cooking wafting from them—but there was no midden near the big house or signs of domestic life. All was clean, perfect, and holy.

The fair priest rapped on the door, before entering the house without further ado. "You had best be respectful," his companion hissed into Merlin's ear as he shoved him forward, jabbing him in the back with the tip of a barbed arrow. "You don't know how lucky you are that we've let you live to come before our High-Priest!"

The interior of the house was dark, wreathed with smoke from a large fire-pit at the centre. A sleepy-looking old woman, bunched-up hair straggling from a bone pin, was stoking the flames. She did not even glance up at the newcomers. Merlin's eyes darted about, taking in everything: the painted symbols on the walls, pots sealed with clay plugs lined up on wooden shelves, rich furs and weavings that enshrouded the boxed-off sleeping cells. The opulence confirmed his first impression that whoever dwelt here was indeed held in high esteem.

"What have we here?" A hoarse voice sounded from the back of the hut, bodiless, its owner shrouded by the roiling smoke. "Why this intrusion so early in the morning? Bhel has hardly risen."

"We have a captive, great one." The blond guard shoved Merlin forward. "He was caught in the Stones. The disrespectful dog had spent the night there, curled up at their feet! We would have punished him in the usual way, but he claims he is a magic man come seeking admittance to our Order."

"I am eager to see this brave or foolhardy one!"

The smoke eddied, and a tall man stepped from behind a skin curtain. He was one of the oldest people Merlin had ever seen, well beyond his fiftieth summer. His hair was so white and fine, it was almost a shade of pale blue, the colour of snowfall at twilight. His long beard was equally pale, tumbling in tendrils over his floor-length robe. Serpent tattoos slithered round his frail arms and coiled in knotwork designs above his eyes, which were shrewd, sharp, grey flints beneath a ridge of frosty brows.

"I am Ambris, Speaker-to-Immortals," he said. "High priest of Khor Ghor. Is it true what my priests tell me? That you broke the sanctity of the Stones and lay amongst them while you slept?"

"It is true, Great Lord." Merlin bowed to the stately elder. "I was in the Stones. But not to desecrate or bring dishonour. They called to me, and all the mighty Ancestors of old called to me too. I come from the mountains far away, but that is my home no longer. My home, my heart tells me, is here, serving the temple of Khor Ghor. I know the number of your priests is less by one, and I would fill that empty place."

Ambris stepped forward and caught Merlin's face in his withered hands, staring into the youth's eyes and searching the depths of his heart, his soul, with a glance that cut like a dagger-blade. After a few minutes, he let his hands fall. "I can see no falsehood in you. Fervour, aye…and maybe, just maybe, some kind of power. Who are you?"

"I am called the Merlin. The hawk that also bears that name is my totem; one travels with me, he comes and goes with the wind, as I do."

Ambris's brows lifted slightly. "There have been other Merlins here, before our father's, father's, father's time. One came to Khor Ghor when the land was forest; he danced the Horn-dance with the Moon, and raised great poles as beacons to the spirits above. He gave his name to these isles—the Merlin's Precinct. Later, there was the Merlin who brought the skystones from the West; floating them down rivers while wolves howled on the bank and strange men flung spears. Three is a magic number, Merlin. Maybe, as the third Merlin, you will be the greatest and most famed Merlin of all."

The priests who had escorted Merlin to Deroweth were gawking. They had obviously expected anger from the High Priest, maybe even an ordered execution. "High One," owl-eyes muttered, "You speak like he's one of us already! Surely he will have to pass the test!"

Ambris glanced at the man with irritation. "Do not fear; he will have to pass the test like every other priest." He turned back towards Merlin. "There is a bed and food here, within my hut. You may make yourself at home. When the next full Moon comes, it will be time to choose a new priest to replace Eckhy, who is lost to us. A competition of wisdom will take place. No man shall have an advantage above the other; no priority is given for status or age. You have as much chance as any other competitor, young stranger. But if you fail, you must leave in the dawn and never return on pain of death. The Stones will have chosen and if they reject you, you must never set foot in their presence again."

The night of the full Moon rolled round after what seemed an interminable time, during which Merlin had stalked around the settlement like a beast trammelled in a cage. He explored the entire settlement, guided by one of Ambris's many attendants, committing to mind and heart the places of power: Woodenheart, with its gateway facing Magic Hill at Midsummer, and the Hallows in the centre of the great chalk ring, which was focussed on Midwinter Sunrise in reverse to Khor Gor, where the dying Sun was framed by the arch of the Door into Winter.

He knew he must not fail in his testing, lest he be cast into the wilds, a tribeless man—there was no going back to God-of-Bronze and those far off Western lands, not with Vhortiern's blood on his hands. Sighing, he reached to his belt-pouch, brought out Buan-ann's crystal ball and wiped it on his fringed cape. He held it up and stared at the sky through its heart, but today the magic stone was misty and vague, showing him nothing.

"Master Merlin, it is time to make ready." One of Ambris' acolytes appeared from a hut and gestured to Merlin to follow him. "You must be prepared and purified for tonight's testing."

"Are the other men who seek a position here also?" Merlin asked, following the acolyte as he was bidden.

"Aye, Lord Tyllion arrived yester eve from Peak-land, and Uinious from the East this morning, just before the Sun was up. That is why there is so much activity here today. Most of the year, except at the times of festivals, only the priests dwell in Deroweth. The common folk live in the Place of Light, on the Hill of Golden Graves where the tin-men set up their tent-camps long ago, but some have been employed by Lord Ambris to come down to tend to the newcomers."

Merlin glanced over near to Woodenheart, where a gaggle of children, women, robed priests and priestesses, dogs, pigs and even a roving ox milled about in disarray. A cacophony of noise filled the air: geese honking, dogs yapping, babies wailing, women laughing and shrieking, and suddenly he saw a man the size of a black bear sweeping around the circle of onlookers, touching the foreheads of children, laying hands on the bellies of women in blessing. "Is that one of the would-be priests?"

"Aye, Tyllion from Peak-land, which is a land of high hills many miles north, bounded by the Great Dark Forest and guarded by the Mother Mountain and Shining Tor. His folk have blood-ties with Khor Ghor going back many generations to the days of Samothos. Jet is much traded through Tyllion and his people, who purchase it from the Brighi along the northern coastal cliffs."

"And the other man? Uinious?"

"He prays in Woodenheart. He is less boastful than Tyllion of the Peak, but no less determined! Come now, O Merlin, we must make you ready so that you can stand proudly with the other two."

Merlin followed the solemn youth to one of several smaller wooden buildings that stood between Woodenheart and the Hallows. These round huts were for the priests and priestesses, where they washed themselves, performed purification rites, and meditated before commencing with their daily lives. Like the larger wooden temples, these cult-houses were aligned on events in the sky: one on the Moon, which was for female initiates only, one on the rising of the Seven Sister Stars, and another with opposing entrances that faced Sunrise on the Equal-days when light and dark were balanced.

He was taken into the Circle of the Seven Sisters, where several priests awaited him. "Kneel," ordered a hard-faced man in a peaked red hood, and he roughly pushed Merlin to his knees beside a lit fire. Other priests came forth and stripped him of his robes, beating his body with willow-switches, to purify the flesh and drive out any evil humours that might linger in him. Lips taut, he bore the pain without complaint, while sweat mixed with blood upon his bare back.

Once the ritual beating was done, the priests raised him up and painted him from head to toe with symbols, the marks of his tribe and the mark of an initiate. Then they brought back his robes and draped them around him, and gave him his crystal to hold, and they bound his raven hair with a long pin made of bone.

"You are ready," said the red-hooded one. "You may go to Woodenheart to join the others."

Merlin walked across the frosty ground. Dusk had begun to fall, and tendrils of mist curled up like the reaching hands of the untold generations of dead that lay in the barrow cemeteries just beyond Deroweth. Across the field, the bulky Khu Stone, or Hound's stone, sank down into an eerie white cloud, with only its grizzled tip sticking out, sharp as a spear.

On the far side of the plateau the Moon was rising, fat and cold and pale as a skull, casting chill light over Holy Hill and the lands below. "Oh Eye-Goddess of Moon and Dead Men," whispered Merlin, "look kindly on me this night! They say you were here even before Bhel Bright-face, and that you see into the hearts of all men. Then see I am the one who best shall serve Khor Ghor and the Isle of the Mighty!"

Prayer finished, he tore his eyes from the Moon and entered the lintelled gateway of Woodenheart. Inside, a forest of posts and standing stones confronted him. Priests glided between posts and menhirs, ghostly in their rustling robes and fantastical masks. They beckoned Merlin forward, toward three stones that leaned in toward each other like conspirators whispering secrets.

A cove. A sacred space that resembled the mouth of a tomb.

Ambris stood within the cove, his flowing hair a nimbus of red in the light of fires that burned in hearths on either side, the flames fanned by attendants who cast strange powders and oils upon them. On the floor, before a cairn of flints, squatted barrel-chested Tyllion, looking more like a strongman than a shaman, but wearing mystical symbols on his face, and with a holy man's rattle in his hand. Uinious, contender from the east, was kneeling beside him. He was more suave and smooth than Tyllion, with a sandy, bifurcated beard sewn with blue beads, and a strangely cut tunic fastened by toggles and a fancy bronze pin that must have come from beyond the Northern Sea. He was younger than Tyllion, and his shrewd hazel-green eyes darted everywhere, measuring the mood in the temple.

So these were the challengers…Merlin's lip curled contemptuously. He knew he was the right choice, that these others cared mostly for their own prestige, but how was he to convince the assembly that he would be a greater asset to the Temple than they would? Beads of nervous sweat popped out on his forehead, and he clutched his seeing stone, damp fingers streaking the quartz as he begged the spirits for a sign.

Ambris clapped his hands, and the temple priestesses brought round the Beaker of Peace, brimming with the fermented honey-mead that only men were allowed to drink. Each one of the priestly candidates took a draught, savouring the rich golden taste and the rush of fire in the belly that followed soon after.

Uinious was first to speak. "I come from the East to the West, and will bring new ways and ideas to Khor Ghor and its peoples. The gods have always been with me; I killed a wild cat at nine and my first man a year later."

"I shall bring new ideas too!" roared Tyllion. "Northern ideas!" He took another swig from the Beaker and wiped his red, dripping lips. "The gods have always smiled on me, as much, if not more, than you, Easterner. I have wrestled a bear in a darkling forest, and overseen the bringing of the black jet from the sea cliffs. I have seen the Antlered Man ride from Dark Dale and up the shivering slopes of Mother Mountain, and welcomed the Moon home in the cove of Ar-bar. I know the lore of all living things; I know the names of kings and chiefs who ruled on Albu's shores since time immemorial!"

He stood up, cleared his throat and began to half-sing, half-chant reams of names of people long barrowed away, dust in the wind. The list was obviously pleasing to a few onlookers who doubtless fancied themselves the direct descendants of these ancient worthies, but Merlin grew bored and restive. Any decent storyteller could recite the annals of the Ancestors as well as fat Tyllion.

Uinious grinned savagely as the cumbrous man finished his litany with yet another slurp of honey-mead from the ceremonial Beaker. He tossed back his long, thin head, making the beads in his oiled beard clack like bones. "I have skills that can help us grow closer to the gods and gain their favour. I am skilled with herbs and plants; my knowledge of these is beyond compare. I know of plants that can make a man fly high enough to kiss the icy lips of Mother Moon—and others that, with a mere drop, could fell every living creature in this settlement. I will tell you their names: hemlock, henbane, deathcap…"

Merlin leaned forward, supporting his chin with his hand, eyes glazing over at the prospect of another lengthy bout of posturing. Uinious's plant-lore was hardly new; he had learned the same years ago, when Buan-ann first took him to the woods to train him in the shamanic art. He was so bored, listening to the old ones' flapping tongues, he half-wished the Sea-Raiders would attack that very moment, so that he could test his wits and powers against them.

As Uinious droned on, prattling about his amazing studies of Sun and stars in the wooden temples of the East, Merlin reached for the Beaker of Peace. In its depths he could see the Moon's reflected eye, watching him. Careful to remain unseen, he dropped several mistletoe berries into the brew before draining it to the dregs. The Moon had called to him, with her white horns; he would commune with the spirits, not with these two fools, eaten up by a quest for their own glory.

A few minutes later, his head began to throb, one-sided, in the usual manner. His central vision became a spinning tunnel that guided him toward the spirit realm. The walls of the world fell away; Woodenheart's posts grew huge, spiralling up into the starry sky. The heat of the fire vanished abruptly, the flames turning ice-blue, and the big sarsens that stood in the cove seemed to be rocking in their beds. Across from him, Tyllion had butted in over Uinious and was droning out some stale, ancient folk-tale, much to the annoyance of his rival, whose eyes had narrowed dangerously. Tyllion's rumbling baritone seemed to have become unnaturally slow and deep, wobbling in and out of Merlin's hearing.

"I have something to say…" Merlin's voice rose above the drone, distant and unearthly in his own ears. It was like the voice of someone else, someone older, stronger and more powerful. An ancient, long-gone Merlin, speaking from beyond the veil…"It is my turn, and I have words of greater importance than these pretty tales!"

"You are an insolent brat!" Tyllion roared petulantly, heaving his huge bulk up and clawing for the haft of his axe, but Ambris laid a firm hand on his shoulder and pushed him back to the ground.

"Remember where you are, Tyllion. Under our Law, the boy has the right to speak. He has said nothing so far, while you and Uinious have spoken enough for ten!"

Merlin glanced around him, in strange ghost-world born of his potion. At his feet, by the little cairn of stones on the Midsummer alignment of the temple, a ghostly child was playing with a pebble. She was a small thing, bird-frail, with eyes of mismatched colours. She was touched by the gods, like Merlin himself, but her fate was not his—though he nearly had shared hers, at Vhortiern's circle.

"Help us, Merlin of Albu," she said in her whispery ghost-voice. "Or my sacrifice will mean nothing, and my grave will lie forgotten beneath burnt timbers." She knelt on the cairn of flints before the cove, stroking the stones with thin white fingers.

Merlin reached out to touch her cheek, but his hand went through her and touched the flint that topped her grave instead. "A child lies here," he murmured, quietly but loud enough that the surrounding priests could hear, "her head was split so that her spirit could guard this place with her ardent innocence. She will weep for an eternity if either of these blusterers becomes a temple priest; they are old and the world they knew is passing. It is time for youth to triumph, for youth to build this land anew!"

The onlookers gasped at the young man's presumption. Ambris smiled behind the rim of the Beaker of Peace. Merlin rose, gesturing for the gathered assembly to follow him. Arms held aloft, he walked between the posts of Woodenheart and out into the night, where the rising gale went screaming around the settlement and over the plain, dispelling the last scraps of ground-fog on its boreal breath.

In the distance the hump of the Great Spirit-Path, a linear earthwork far older than Khor Ghor itself, stretched out across the fields like the white leg-bone of a fallen giant. A thousand stars crowned its bank, twinkling like watchful eyes. Some said stars were the most ancient of the dead, set in the firmament to watch over their descendants. If so, they were all out to witness the events of this momentous night.

"Why have you brought us here?" Merlin heard Uinious's dismissive snarl. "There's nothing to see! It is cold, and dark…A waste of our precious time!"

"Silence!" ordered Merlin. "And behold!"

In the Northwestern sky, beyond the end of the Spirit-Path, a flash of light tore the blackness asunder. Merlin went cold, then hot, then cold again, as if spirits were touching him, passing through his body. He gave a shuddering cry of ecstasy and, ignoring those around him, began to run towards the light in the heavens. Behind him, he could hear shouts and cries, but he paid them no heed.

Out in the field beyond Woodenheart he paused by the Khu Stone, the Stone of Hounds. He could now see the guardian spirit-dogs, snarling around the menhir, red-eared and red-eyed, their bodies white as the chalk of the plain. They ceased their growling and yipped in delight as he raced towards them and sprang upon the stone, teetering on its tip with his arms outstretched toward heaven.

"Sacrilege!" he heard someone bellow and he knew that many arrows were aimed at his back. He did not care. They would not slay him. The signs were in the sky, and he could read them.

He, alone.

"Look you!" he cried. "In the North-West there sails a comet, an omen from the gods! It is a portent."

Behind him he heard puffing and mumbling, and he was vaguely aware of a growing crowd, furled by the shadows.

"And what do you think this comet betokens, Merlin?" He heard Ambris's muffled voice. "Speak now, or speak never again in this company."

Merlin took a deep breath, the cold night air searing his lungs. His head reeled and his tongue felt swollen, hanging heavy in his dry mouth. Letting the trance-state of the mistletoe engulf him, he rocked drunkenly on the Khu-stone, and gestured to the sky.

To the comet with a great bright tail that sailed through the Western heavens, emerging from the Deadlands to betoken new Life.

"The Armed King-Dragon rises in his chariot of stars..." Words tumbled from his lips, flowing like water from somewhere deep inside him, without thought or rehearsal. "But ascending his realm, he shall fall, crown shattered, while Firetail, the Dragon of the Flaming Star beats the drum of War with his bright tail. Strife is coming to the shores of Prydn, but so too the Bear in the Wain, the Dragon's heir with his shield of the sky; and he will be known unto you as Bronze-Wielder, Hammer-Hand, Stone Lord. But the child who will become the man is not yet born upon earth, and those who will give him blood and sinew know not yet their part in destiny's play. I, the Merlin, shall be the one who moves them in this game, and when the Stone Lord is grown to man, he and I shall weave a tale betwixt us that will last ten thousand years!"

Face flushed with ecstasy, Merlin turned from the streaking comet and stared down at the gathered sea of faces, some approving, some shocked, a few openly hostile. But none disbelieved his words, his prophecy; he could see fear and elation, hope and worry within their watchful eyes.

The stars spun above, and suddenly he felt the world lurch, and then he was falling...falling...tumbling from the top of the standing stone, while the phantom hounds bounded in excitement. His brow caught an edge of the sarsen and blood sprang out, which the hounds lapped with their ghostly tongues.

"Blood," he murmured, as black spots spun before his eyes, "is this what you still want from me? Well, I swear if you will give me what I desire, you will have me in the end—not in one death but Three."

The stone seemed to shudder under his touch, and then Merlin fell down into merciful blackness.

Merlin woke around the middle of the next day, head pounding like a solstice drum and his hair clogged with dried blood. He was lying on a bier of woven withies inside Ambris's house, with a warm and woolly sheepskin over him. The high priest was sitting cross-legged on a fur by the fire-pit, arms folded and eyes closed as he meditated on events beyond the world. Slowly he opened one keen eye, and fixed his young guest with a stare. "So you are awake."

Merlin sat up, clutching his cramping stomach. The headache and nausea always came after close contact with the spirit-world. He could barely recall all that happened the night before, only that he had spoken words of prophecy to the gathered priests. Tidings of a king, yet to be born. A Great King that was to come. "It is dawn...that means the choosing is over. Where are Uinious and Tyllion? Did they..."

Ambris shook his head. "They are gone."

"Gone? Gone where?" Merlin had an unsettling vision of both men striding arrogantly up the Avenue to be initiated as priests of the Temple, congratulating each other that even though neither had been deemed supreme, they had both trumped the mad boy from the West.

"Gone home," said Ambris quietly. "Where else?"

Merlin sprang to his feet, despite his heaving guts and reeling head. "You...you mean..."

"Aye, Merlin," said the high priest. "It is you who passed the test. After that show you gave us last night, few supported those two tedious bores from afar!" He laughed quietly, his face breaking into a thousand merry lines.

Merlin staggered out of the hut into the hazy morning mist that hung over the settlement. A thin trickle of black smoke rose between the oak pillars of Woodenheart, while away in the culthouse a drum was beating, its rhythm matching the beat of his blood. Overhead the Sun's eye was a bleary orange ball, looking down upon him with favour.

Merlin fell face forward onto the packed chalk, kissing the blessed earth, taking the crumbs into his mouth. He belonged here, he had always known this was so, and now he had proved it. "Ancestors, Lord Bhel and Lady Moon, I thank you for this honour. I will not shame you. I will honour you in life and in death."

Ambris came up beside him, and raised him from the ground, brushing the chalk from his clothes. Merlin leaned over and grabbed the hem of Ambris's robe, raising it to his lips. "I will serve you and the temple well; I swear it, my Master. I am young but I beg you—do not doubt me."

"I do not doubt you," said Ambris. "The truth is clear for those who have eyes to see."

"I am here for the sake of Albu, high one. I am here to usher in a time when the people will have no fear of raiders from afar.... Though it will not be through feats of arms on my part. I am many things, but no warrior."

"No, and neither am I, nor many who have followed the path of communion with the spirits," said Ambris. "Like you, I have been looking for many years among the tribes, seeking one who can take the role of High Chief of Albu. Five hundred years has it been since there was one ruler over the Five Cantrevs of the West; the Great Trilithon has stood empty, home only to the spirits and the dying Sun. I have searched and have seen many chiefs with strength and heart, but none has been the One who can lead all men, rallying their hearts and strengthening their hands, no matter their differences of birth or custom. Our people have one great fault, Merlin, and it is that they spend too much time fighting amongst themselves to see the danger all Prydn faces if the Sea-Raiders are not halted."

Merlin clenched his fists. "The omens in last night's sky foretell the ascendance of the King we seek. He will come, even if the Wise must meddle with the hearts and minds and flesh of ordinary men."

Ambris leaned heavily on his oak staff. "I am old now, Merlin. The quest, I fear, is no longer for me to pursue. But I shall tell you of one that might be of interest—my sister's son, who dwells in the land of Dwr. I read the stars at the hour of his birth, and saw portents there, although there was...weakness too, a shadow in him that I do not understand."

Merlin glanced up with interest. "Tell me more of this kinsman of yours, Lord Ambris"

Ambris's eyes glinted beneath his snowy brows. "He is fourteen summers, tall as a spear and good enough to look upon. His hand is steady on the bow and he fights with the courage of the bear. His name? It is U'thyr. U'thyr Pendraec of the Dragon Path of Dwr."

35

PART TWO—U'THYR: MOONSET

CHAPTER FOUR

U'thyr marched along the long white back of the Sacred Dragon mound, the winter wind clawing his dark braids back from his face. On one side of him the fields of the Dwr, the People-of-the-Water, undulated and rolled away into an icy fog. Near the sides of the Dragon mound, a spirit-road that ran nearly a mile across Dwr territory and dwarfed the similar monument near Khor Ghor, burial mounds clustered like children round a great mother, their summits yellow with old dry grass that had withered after the summer.

Reaching to his belt, U'thyr lifted up a severed head, gaunt and stinking. He dangled it on high by its thick bush of tangled black hair. Its tongue protruded as if poking out disrespectfully at the ancient dead in their clustered mounds. "Ancestors!" shouted U'thyr. "I bring you the head of the leader of those scavengers who dared set foot on Dwr soil, bringing violence and grief to its rightful peoples. Let it be known that while there is breath in my body, none of this creature's kind shall ever settle on Dwr lands, or even have the right to walk here as free men!"

He tossed the head from him; it bounced on the mound's bank, and rolled into the half-silted ditch. Immediately a flock of rooks descended, eager to taste its flesh.

U'thyr, the Pendraec, the Terrible Head, stood upon the top of the bank, feeling the current run beneath his feet, in the soil. He spread out his arms, buffeted by the wind, and, he was sure, by the fleeting spirits of those who had passed before, generation upon generation, their bones mingling with the earth, making it rich and fertile for their descendants through the ages.

He felt good. There was nothing he liked better than to slay a few of the hateful invaders. Smiling, he took his dagger from its calfskin sheath and examined it. Bright bronze, the colour of the dying Sun, reddened and strengthened by the blood of enemies of Prydn. Carefully, he took the flint knife he always carried at his belt as a back-up weapon, and used it to make a notch in the polished antler hilt of his dagger. Eleven Sea-Pirates under his belt. And he was still only ten and seven years old.

He longed to tell Merlin, high priest of Khor Ghor, of his latest victory. Merlin had mentored him since U'thyr was a boy, taking over from his Uncle Ambris, when Ambris sickened with fever one winter and went to the heavenly Ancestors. Merlin, in fact, took a bit too much interest in him, always questioning him about when he would take a wife, wanting to know what girls he bedded, or wanted to bed…and then chiding him if he thought they were 'unsuitable.' Embarrassing stuff, for, as young chief of the Dwr, he was enjoying having his choice of the willing village girls, and heard no complaints from amongst them.

Still, he would be glad to see Merlin again and share meat and tales of battle with him at the Great Midwinter Feast of Deroweth, when the Sun died and was reborn at Khor Ghor, and men could celebrate that winter and shadow would not endure. The feasting would go on for over a week; there would be dancing and drinking and song, and babies and marriages would be made and alliances between clans forged…and sometimes broken.

Slipping his dagger back into its sheath he headed for his village, tucked into a hollow in the side of The Pen or Head hill, which overlooked the great twisting dragon-path as it snaked across the downs. He could smell the hearth-fires burning, and hear the village women singing as they packed for the long trek to Deroweth.

Passing the first hut, he saw his mother, Indeg, directing her serving girls to load the best woollen blankets and sheepskins on to a large wooden cart. All around was hustle and bustle:

other carts being loaded, women chasing over-excited children, sheep and cattle driven hither and thither by flushed-faced shepherds with their yapping dogs. Only the very old and the sickly would remain at The Pen, guarded by a few unlucky men chosen to miss the festival.

U'thyr slipped up behind Indeg, made a playful grab for her. "I am back, mother, just in time for the Winter Celebration. The beaches are safe, probably till spring. The stories and tales of the strength of the men of Albu should keep the intruders away."

Indeg hugged him, her face flushed. "I heard of your victory. The entire West knows that Indeg's son is master not only of the Dwr, but of all Albu! Did you bring anything for me from your travels, my dearest son?"

"You will have an amulet made from the skull of the black-bearded leader of the Sea-Raiders," promised U'thyr. "I will carve it myself and get my friend the Merlin to place charms upon it to benefit you. But first our friends the ravens and the rooks must feast upon the ugly creature's flesh to clean it away…And now…" U'thyr nodded toward the weighted-down carts, groaning beneath excited celebrants and their goods, "we should put our thoughts to happier things, to meetings of friends and kin at Deroweth."

"Maybe you will find a nice wife of noble status this year," said Indeg hopefully.

U'thyr snorted. "You're nigh as bad as Merlin, marrying me off to every girl who has half-decent lineage and a face slightly more comely than an aurochs' arse! When the time comes, it will come. Now let us get a move on! I've been travelling several days and look forward to feasting with my men and the other tribes of the West."

Nightfall three days hence found the people of the Dwr arriving at Deroweth. They were not the only arrivals; chieftains major and minor from all over the West and South of Albu had begun to descend on the site. A few had even journeyed from beyond Peak-land, tall men sweltering in furs too heavy for the temperate southwestern climes. Tents and yurts were set up on the downs, while families of high status crowded into the empty wooden longhouses that thronged the bank of the Great Circle; their homes this time of the year alone. The whole site, usually reserved for the priests, was a buzzing hive of activity: traders setting up stalls, women and children thronging outside the temples, dogs running about half-mad with excitement, herdsmen driving wild-eyed cattle and shaggy brown sheep into pens where they would be either sold or slaughtered. In one corner, a huge wattle enclosure held dozens of half-grown pigs that squalled and dashed around crazily as children lobbed chunks of mud at them, eliciting the wrath of the pig-boy, who chased the giggling youngsters away with a big stick.

All the longhouses were decorated with holly and ivy, while the great cult houses gloried in renewed splendour, their timbers painted red and their internal hearths alight and puffing out great clouds of dark smoke into the faded winter sky. Skulls of beasts were affixed to their broad lintels, amid bunches of white-berried mistletoe, the plant none but the priests dared touch, sacred to both Sun and Moon, the symbol of peace and fertility. Drums were beating within the great circles, shaking the earth and summoning the tribesfolk to celebrate and chase the darkness of winter away.

Down by the banks of Abona torches glowed in the icy fog as womenfolk poured the ashes of their Ancestors, saved especially for this occasion, into the cleansing swell of the holy river. Their keening and lamenting rose to mingle with the primal thud-thud-thud of the great drums inside Woodenheart and the other cult houses.

U'thyr squatted on the chalk bank of the Great Circle, surveying the activity below him. People in all manner of array strode past. Beakers were raised and honey-mead and beer consumed until men went rolling down the banks into the ditch. There was much laughter and a lot of shouting, as a pair of young hotheads started pummelling each other over a rosy-faced girl with yellow hair, who was simpering and feigning horror, when one look at her round, flushed face told how much she was enjoying the whole sad spectacle.

U'thyr snorted in bemusement. To think his mother and Merlin wanted him tied to some wench and acting just like those besotted fools! He'd trust no woman. A man's trust should lie only in his dagger and axe.

His attention was drawn from the fighting youths by the sound of a horn, blown repeatedly, that cut through the dwindling twilight. Peering through the smoke toward the Khu-stone, he spotted a party of newcomers, a good-sized troupe with many sheep and cattle, fronted by warriors in stout leather jerkins and red woollen cloaks, one of whom was blowing on a huge ox-horn bound with copper. "All hail to Gorlas of Belerion!" the warrior shouted between discordant blasts of the horn. "Lord of the farthest West, master of tin, tamer of bronze, trader of axes…"

"King of braggarts, by the sound of it," murmured U'thyr, who had arrived at Deroweth with little ceremony. Still, his interest was piqued, for he had never met this Western chief, and he leaned forward straining his eyes into the growing gloom.

The red-caped warriors marched past, followed by Gorlas's shepherds with their flocks for trade and slaughter. Pushed by two youths, an enormous wooden keg trundled by, sloshing some kind of alcoholic drink, followed by a gaggle of sweaty, red-faced women rolling a gigantic Moon-like disc of cheese—both gifts to the Temple to declare Chief Gorlas's wealth and power.

A whip cracked and the horn blasted with even more furious intensity, and two chunky carts rolled into view, shuddering and juddering across the uneven ground. On the first lay a man, big as a bear, reclining on a bed of rich furs. His hair was blue-black, almost like that of a Sea-Pirate, falling in coils almost to his waist. A golden Moon-collar circled his throat, and his bare chest was tattooed with fantastical animals. His beard was cut short but it was thick and bushy and covered much of his broad, thick-jawed face. Rings and ornaments jangled in his tresses, proclaiming his wealth and rank.

"So that's the man who thinks so highly of himself!" laughed U'thyr, not very impressed. The man was so fat, he looked as though the only way he could kill an enemy would be to crush him with his bulk!

U'thyr let his gaze wander from the corpulent tin-lord to the cart behind. Sitting on a pile of soft sheepskins was a woman clad in expensive blue-dyed linen. She was young and very small, almost child-like in appearance, but there was toughness in the set of her shoulders and the arrogant tilt of her jaw. She had long, loose, wavy dark hair that held a hint of copper fire, and a diadem of a pale, Moon-coloured metal that U'thyr had never seen before bound her brow.

"She is a comely woman, is she not?" U'thyr glanced over to see Merlin walking toward him, dressed in his robes of priesthood, a long tunic of tanned hide fringed with the claws and teeth of foxes, badgers, boars, dogs and even the canine of a great wolf that the local villagers had brought down one Winter. A staff topped by a human jawbone was in his right hand, for when he wished to speak to the Dead. Around his neck hung the skull of his long-dead totem-hawk, bound in bronze, with chips of faience for eyes. "But do not stare too much…I've heard Gorlas protects her as a bear protects its young! And can you blame him?"

U'thyr looked over in surprise at his friend, his mentor. He usually thought of Merlin, with his grey-flecked hair and craggy visage, as an old man, unlikely to talk of the charms of women, but he remembered that in truth that the priest was only a handful of years older than U'thyr himself. "Is she his daughter?"

"No, his wife! Gorlas is lord of a tin mine in Belerion and very rich; in fact, he sometimes trades with our enemies to swell his riches, which is why you have not seen him here before; he is not popular amongst the other chiefs. And the girl...the girl is daughter of an ancient family of Belerion; they say her Ancestors' Ancestors came from the Drowned Lands where the Little Sea now flows. He saw her dancing within their holy Circle on Bhel's Eve, and was so overcome by lust that he ran into the stones and snatched her away, kicking and screaming, right in front of the shaman. Her father was so vexed he came here to Khor Ghor to ask the priests to intervene. We decided to let Gorlas keep the girl if he would wed her honourably and pay reparations in gold and cattle to her sire and to the dishonoured temple. He did as asked and within nine Moons the girl bore him a daughter. This secured her position with him, for all his other three wives proved barren—a sure sign the spirits were angry."

"Why has Gorlas come here now, when he is unpopular through his dealing with the sea-folk?"

The corner of Merlin's mouth quirked upwards. "Can you not guess? He has a daughter but that is not enough. Now that the spirits smile on him, he has come to ask them for a son."

U'thyr nodded toward Gorlas's wife, who had climbed down from the cart and gone to the fat man, stretching a hand to help him ponderously descend from his fur bed. "And what is the name of this Western woman, with her silver brow and fierce eyes?"

"Y'gerna," said Merlin. "That is her name. The Queen."

Gorlas and Y'gerna began walking slowly toward the great portal pillars of Woodenheart, surrounded by their followers and the curious crowds of Deroweth. A sudden sire to see more possessed U'thyr, and he scrambled to his feet, almost tumbling down the bank in his haste.

Merlin frowned at him. "Where are you going, U'thyr? We have only just met and off you run like a deer in the wood! I need to know of your doings in the land of the Dwr, of the raiders and the outcome of your battles."

"Merlin, forgive me!" U'thyr bowled humbly, hoping he appeared suitably apologetic. "But I…I must also ask a favour of the spirits in Woodenheart. Very urgent. I must not delay. I will be back as soon as I may."

"A favour, eh?" Merlin tapped the jawbone on his staff with a fingernail, making an annoyed click-click-click. "Just make sure this 'favour' is asked of the gods…and not that girl! Or about that girl!"

"Girl!" U'thyr felt colour flood his face. "I am not…I swear it…"

Merlin waved his hand dismissively. "Go, U'thyr. But be careful. I need your arm against our foes; I don't want it hacked off by bull-headed Gorlas of Belerion!"

U'thyr slid down the bank and pushed his way through the milling crowds. He could feel a tension rising in the tribesfolk, charging the air like lightning. They were almost hysterical with mingled joy and fear: knowing that if the gods so willed the warmer days would soon return, yet terrified that their prayers and sacrifices would not suffice, and Bhel would die upon the Altar at Khor Ghor and never rise again.

Thrusting the wild-eyed revellers, the endless yapping dogs, the trundling sheep, he stepped over the threshold of Woodenheart. Its posts soared around him, as imposing as living trees and red from the heat of the great hearth at its centre, where the little child's grave-cairn lay crossing the Midsummer alignment.

A priest and priestess stood on either side of the cairn, listening to the supplications of a line of men and women. Unlike Khor Ghor, which was the gathering place of spirits on their way to eternity, this temple was a place of life as well as death, its pillars like fossilised trees, permanent and undecayed. People came to Woodenheart to pray for the easy passing of dying elders and sickly babes, and for the birth of strong infants and the continued fecundity of both the womb and the field.

Ahead, half-shrouded in the smoke that billowed from the hearth, U'thyr spotted Y'gerna's arrow-straight back, draped in her long dark hair. Gorlas was clutching her arm as if he feared she would run away, but U'thyr scarcely noticed him. Just a fat old man, puffed up with pride, not worth noticing.

The tiny woman approached the priest and priestess. They turned her around three times, chanting, before leading her deeper into the temple, to the three-sided cove of standing stones that were both tomb and womb. She knelt on the floor, hair spilling like midnight water around her. "Grant me a son, O ancient ones, spirits of earth, spirits of grave!" she cried. "My lord desires a son to rule after him, strong and healthy."

The temple priestess, whitened by chalk from head to toe, stepped forward carrying a set of old, bleached antlers, symbol of the feminine. The priest, painted such a shade of dark blue he looked almost black, moved alongside her, bearing a huge stone phallus decorated with mistletoe. The priestess laid the antlers before Y'gerna and began to chant, holding up her bone-white arms to the sky. The priest's deep voice sang out in answering incantation, and he began to whirl and dance around Y'gerna, waving the phallic sceptre and thrusting it at the heavens and at the supplicant and her husband, who stood staring at the spectacle, his face red and sweating like a piece of cooking meat.

When the priest was done, the priestess took Y'gerna's hand and raised her to her feet. Her eyes rolled and she leaned on the girl's shoulder. A tendril of drool trickled from the corner of her lips. "Yes…yes…" she croaked in a voice coarsened by the smoke of the pyre. "A child shall come to you…. A male child…a special child…" Her fingers caught in Y'gerna's blue robes, clutching at the girl's stomach. "Within the month he will be conceived; he will be a great hero beyond compare. His name will be sung for eternity!"

The priestess stumbled away, shaking, worn out by her prophecy. She dropped, panting, to all fours beside the fire. The priest lay down the sacred phallus. "It will be so," he said. "The spirits have spoken. Go now!"

Y'gerna turned on her heel, her long locks swinging. Gorlas followed her like an eager dog, his podgy face florid and smug. "Well, that is good news. Come, wife, let us go to our tent and make sure the prophecy comes true!"

Y'gerna scowled and lashed out at him with a small, clenched fist. "Don't bother me, you uncouth oaf! I am tired; we have been travelling for days. Let me have at least one night in peace where I may forget my 'duties!'"

Gorlas sprang away from her as though he had been burnt, his face so suffused by blood it looked as though his bloated cheeks might burst. Y'gerna seemed not to care that he was angry. Without a single glance at her furious, shamed husband, she swept from Woodenheart and out into the frosty winter night.

Intrigued, U'thyr followed, skulking in the distance among the festive solstice crowds. He did not want Gorlas to spot him. Or Y'gerna, for that matter. He just wanted to watch her, light and lithe as a river spirit, brave and fierce as a she-bear. A woman so pleasing to look upon, with her narrow waist and arrogant but lovely face….

Stop it, he chided himself, feeling foolish. He was nearly as bad as the two lads fighting over the yellow-headed trull…There were plenty of good women available who were not bound to other men.

He paused, hiding behind a greybeard who was dragging a stubborn goat along and cursing as the animal butted him with stubby horns. Over the man's bony shoulder, he could see Y'gerna walking down the wide path that led to the banks of Abona—the Path of the Sun, which would light up on the morn of the shortest day. But it was not the Sun she went to greet, hours away in His bed in Darkness, but Mother Moon, sailing across the distant tree tops. She raised her arms and began to dance, tossing back her hair, moving her slim hips. She sang in a low voice, in a language U'thyr did not know but recognised; the tongue of the Firstborn, who came to Prydn after the Great Ice melted from the land, and hunted great elk and wolves and bear in forests that had now vanished. Later, others speaking new tongues

40

came to Albu, bringing a settled way of living that supplanted the old hunting life. With the end of the hunter, the old language died too, and languages of trade became paramount. Still, a few words of the First Tongue were heard occasionally on the lips of certain sturdy, dark men who still lived a semi-nomadic existence, and some rivers and hills bore names that had no meaning in the common Western tongue.

He paused, watching, and felt a fire burn in his loins unlike any such longing he had ever experienced before. The other women he had lain with seemed dull and trivial, creatures of lowly clay. Y'gerna was a being of the Moon and the night, flitting to and fro like the fireflies that buzzed over the walls of Deroweth.

Like a man possessed, he stumbled forward onto the metalled Path of the Sun.

Y'gerna must have sensed his presence; she ceased her frenzied Moon-dance and turned. Her eyes were midnight hollows; the shadowy webs of her lashes dark on her cheeks. "Why do you stare, stranger? Do you always go about gawking at women you do not know?"

He suppressed a grin. "Not always. Never in fact, before this night."

"It is not seemly."

"Then you should find a place to dance alone, lady. Only a man made of stone would not be entranced by your grace and beauty."

She laughed sharply, and then snorted, "You have a honeyed tongue! What are you...a singer of songs?"

He approached her, shaking his head. He could see stars reflected in the dark pools of her eyes and caught in her damp-frizzed hair. His heart thumped madly. "No, lady. I am head chief of the mighty Dwr. My lands stretch from the sea to the Great Fort of the Plain, Mai Dhun, to the spirit-path that is known as the Dragon's Back."

"You are young to hold such a vast realm." She looked impressed; he could feel her sharp gaze scanning his features, running approvingly over his torso and down his slim, leather-clad legs. He flushed furiously; he was used to appraising women, not the reverse.

"My father recently passed to Otherness," he said, attempting to hide his embarrassment in words. "He fell to the arrow of a Sea-Pirate. And so his lands are now mine to rule."

Y'gerna chewed her lips. "I am sorry for your loss. I do not like the Sea-people. My husband curries their favour, but I can read deceit and hatred in their eyes."

U'thyr stepped up to her, touching her blue-clad arm. "Why are you with that treacherous fool? He is old and foul, with one foot in the barrow! He does not deserve you."

Her lips pursed, a small hard bud. "He is wealthy and he is powerful, lord of tin and master of many cattle. He is the father of my daughter, Morigau. He claimed me by conqueror's rights and gave my family much-needed wealth. Is that not enough for any woman? Or can you offer me more?"

She tossed back her hair and stared intently into his eyes, her stance fierce, with her legs braced apart and her arms folded. He was all too aware of the Moonlight shining through the fabric of her gown, and the beckoning play of shadows between her breasts.

"If you leave him," U'thyr said gruffly, "I will make sure you and yours will never go short. I will bring you gold from Ibherna, amber and jet from the North and blue star-beads from the South. You will want for nothing, nor will your kin, and you shall not have to endure the lusts of an old, fat, failing man."

She leaned toward him, her hair brushing his cheek, her breath a whisper against his ear. "You will have to kill him, you know."

A fierce, hard look came into U'thyr's gaze. "If I must." He reached for her, breath heavy, wanting in that instant nothing more than to pull her down into the grass, Gorlas and Merlin be damned

She danced away from him, light as a linden leaf in the starshine. "You are a bold fellow, aren't you? I like that. But you need to prove yourself to me by brave deeds, not by brave words. I will leave you now to think on this, U'thyr Pendraec. And on this, lest you forget me when the mead wears off." She sidled up to him and let her fingertips drift seductively down his skin-clad thigh, and then, laughing, she sprinted off into the crowd of late-night revellers, leaving U'thyr staring helplessly after her.

Merlin found him a short while later, sitting on the bank staring moodily into the night. "Where have you been?" chided the High Priest "You said you were coming back to discuss important matters with me. But no, I find you moping here with a face sour as an unripe apple! What is wrong, U'thyr? Has the drink curdled in your belly?"

U'thyr leaped up, a sudden spark of green fury in his eyes. Merlin almost stepped back, but did not; he would not show such weakness to his young protégé. "Merlin," snarled U'thyr, his voice harsh, "I must have her! No other will do!"

"Who? What?" the shaman frowned, and then, as realisation hit him: "By Bhel's blood, I knew this was going to happen from the moment Gorlas and his party arrived, and you were there with your eyes where they shouldn't be! This is folly, U'thyr, folly and madness! She is his wife, you fool! We need to be making alliances, not breaking them! Start fighting amongst ourselves, and we are doomed; the Sea-pirates will overwhelm us!"

"I do not care!" U'thyr's tone was hard, dangerous. "It is as if the gods planned the hour of our meeting, and gave me a quest to take her for my own. If I can steal her from Gorlas, maybe the words the priestess spoke in Woodenheart will be relevant to me, not that slobbering half-man!"

Merlin's face grew very solemn and still. "Words? What words were spoken? Tell me, boy!"

"The priestess said Y'gerna would bear a son…a child who would grow so great he would be remembered when we are all dust in our barrows!"

Merlin's eyes grew distant, black; he thumped his staff against the packed chalk. "So…it is her…it must be her. How the Ancestors toy with us! Well, if it must be, then it must be, broken alliances or not. U'thyr Pendraec, I will do what I can to get you this woman. But you must make me a promise…."

"What promise is that?"

"That the firstborn son, this special child, will be given to me at birth, that I might raise him in my own way."

"Yes, yes, whatever you wish." U'thyr waved his hand as if swatting at flies. He was not interested in some putative child, god-touched or no, other than the honour it would bring his line. All he wanted right then was to quell the flames of his passion between Y'gerna's promising thighs, and of that alone could he think.

"Give me two days…the Solstice is upon us," said Merlin, "It will do not good for any of us if the Sun does not return in spring!" He flitted off into the shadows, leaving the younger man burning with his unfulfilled desire on the banks of Deroweth henge.

U'thyr eventually sought the Merlin's hut, where he was invited to sleep as a token of friendship. Under sheepskin rugs he slept fitfully, until, shortly before dawn, he was woken by the sound of mournful horns blowing. Groaning, he clambered to his feet, tugged on his boots and trews, and took from a small wooden box the symbols of his chieftaincy, passed on through many generations; gold tresses to clasp his hair, arm-bands that twisted round the biceps like copper-coloured snakes, a bronze diadem decorated with serpentine spirals—the crown of the Head Dragon. He donned them swiftly; fastening the gold buttons on the tunic with chilled fingers, then wrapped his warm fox-fur cloak around him, and went out into the dark-before-day.

Outside the sky was lightening, the night-fog turning violet. Frost glittered on the ground. A solemn drum was banging inside the cult-house in the centre of the earth circle, while Woodenheart and the other smaller timber temples were silent and dark. All around the people of the plain and visitors from the Five Cantrevs flitted like grey ghosts, some with faces painted into skulls, others ash-smeared, dark and sombre. Quietly, with none of the laughter of the night before, they hastened toward the Hallows to wait for the imminent dawn.

U'thyr followed the crowd, alert for any sightings of Y'gerna, but he saw neither her nor Gorlas. He castigated himself inwardly, unsettled by his own weakness where she was concerned; he must strive not to think of her till after the ceremonies were done, least the spirits be angered and play cruel tricks on them all…

Silently he entered the cult-house, stepping over a crescent of skulls that had been chosen from the many sacred bones carried to Deroweth from afar, and took his place among the great of the Five Cantrevs, who stood ranked between the oak posts that stood open to the sky. The common folk crowded outside the circle, silent, and expectant.

Down by the river, the sound of chanting started, and the drummer at the back of the cult-house began to tap out a faster rhythm. The sky above Magic Hill in the South-East flushed crimson, and suddenly a solitary flame flared beside the waters of Abona, slashing through the mist, chasing back the night and any malevolent wights that might reside in it. The chanting grew louder, and the tongue of flame became a glowing circle of fire, round as the Sun himself, casting out sparks and fiery tendrils into the gloom. Slowly, as the flames intensified, it began to bob up the slope from the great river toward the dawn-aligned temple.

At the embanked entrance of the Great Circle, U'thyr could now see the source of the flames. Surrounded by a score of priests, Merlin was bearing aloft a huge, spoked wooden disc that had been set alight. Symbolic of the Sun, it blazed into the darkness, imitative of the solar events that would soon occur.

"Today Bhel Brighteye dies and is reborn!" the Merlin cried, holding the solar-wheel aloft. "His Mother is angry, for she is now the Old Woman of Gloominess, The Watcher of the Dead. As a Great Sow who eats her own farrow, she has chased him and bitten him till he is weary and wounded, for he is growing old and weak. He will bleed upon the stones of Khor Ghor this Winter's eve…and then he will be reborn, the Young Son, growing fairer and stronger. If ever it was not so, then the world we know would perish!"

An awed moan rose from the waiting crowd. Women began to wail and tear their hair. Men stomped and cried out to the heavens, raising bronze axes to the still-twilit sky.

Merlin stepped into the cult-house and cast down the firebrand, which was extinguished by the other priests, who flung crumbled chalk upon it, burying the ashes under a mound that resembled a miniature barrow. Then he turned back toward the undulating bulk of Magic Hill and opened his arms wide, his voice rising in a wordless cry of both joy and despair.

At that very moment, the rim of the Sun peeped out from a small gap in those distant snow-crusted hills, a red burning eye, sullen and without warmth. It ascended swiftly, a ball of blood, livid colours staining the sky around it. Sullen beams struck the metalled path that led to the river, and a shaft of wavering, uncertain light streaked into the heart of Deroweth, cutting a path across the grass and entering the lintelled archway of the great cult-house, piercing the shadows beyond.

Another moan came from the crowd, and the drummer inside the temple beat on his drums in a frenzy. People fell on their faces, bowing toward the South-East, while warriors blew on horns and waved bullroarers that made a terrific, thunderous sound.

Merlin made a jerking gesture with his arms and the noise ceased abruptly. The drums started again slow, steady, but with an added beat, a touch of menace. One of the priestesses ventured forward, her face and naked body blackened with ash, carrying a black-feathered chicken below one arm. She was Night, her hair a snarled tangle of darkness, her teeth in her ebony face as sharp as the fangs of the creatures that prowled the midnight hours. Another woman joined her, body striped with yellow and crimson ochre, bearing a squawking red-feathered bird in her hands. She was the Day, the dying day when Night held mastery over the weary Sun.

Together they entered the cult-house and promptly sacrificed the two chickens, cutting their bellies with flint knives and mingling their blood as day mingled with night at that auspicious time of the year. The women then painted each other with the blood, the essence of life, and daubed it on the carved faces on the stout posts of the unnatural forest that surrounded them, while Merlin read omens and portents in the birds' entrails that lay coiled across the chalk floor.

Heading back outside, the priestesses began to dance a circular, halting dance, and the women of the tribes joined them. The men clapped and shouted. Suddenly one priestess stopped and pointed to the entrance of the Circle: 'Look, he comes, he comes—the cursed one!'

Through the gap came a black billy-goat followed by a man wearing a hideous bull-horned mask. He bore a club, which he used to swat the goat, forcing the frightened beast forward. The animal was dressed outlandishly; a garland of holly on its brow a mock crown that slipped over one rolling, terrified eye.

"Evil!" shouted a priestess, gesturing to the bewildered goat. "Cursed. Drive him from this place, so that he will take away your sins, your pains, your wickedness. Let him take away famine, plague and death…Let all the ills men suffer fall on his cursed head!"

The tribesfolk began to hurl lumps of chalk, handfuls of grass, a finally stones at the frightened animal. They screamed with rage, cursing the goat and cursing every ill that afflicted them—aching bones and abscessed teeth, children who died in infancy, wives lost in childbirth, husbands slain in strife. Their eyes became fierce and wild and they would have run forward and torn the animal to bits had not the priests held them at bay.

This unfortunate beast was not for their pleasure. He would go to Khor Ghor, to please the Old Woman and her Son and take the troubles of Albu's people into the West. At one time, in days long gone, it was a Man who made this sacrifice when the land was invaded, when crops withered and babes went hungry…but for now, a fine, healthy animal crowned with holly would do to appease the forces of heaven and earth.

Merlin looped a rope round the beast's neck and led it toward the river, where waiting rafts and coracles bobbed along the banks. The masked Teaser shuffled behind, swinging his club, forcing the goat onto a raft, where men trussed it with hemp ropes. Next, the temple priests processed to Abona, singing and chanting. A group of elite supplicants followed them, warriors, chiefs and high status women who were permitted to enter the stones of Khor Ghor on that night only. Many bore funerary urns packed with cremations; others carried bones scraped clean ro be interred around the ditch. They clambered into the boats, and the party set out into the purple morning, the goat's bleating becoming fainter and fainter as the current carried it farther downstream, to the Old Circle and the start of the Avenue.

The rest of the celebrants spilled out along the verdant banks of the great river, tossing in cremations, wailing and praying, splashing themselves with the cleansing waters of old River-Woman. U'thyr walked along proudly with members of his warband, long-shanked Kol, swift-handed Rivan, Govna the smith of the Dwri, who wrought doughty blades. He tried to keep his mind on spiritual matters but his thoughts kept slipping back to Y'gerna dancing under the Moon. He glanced around surreptitiously, hoping to spot her, but could not see her in the heaving throng milling about on the banks of the river.

After a long walk, the tribesfolk reached the start of the Sacred Avenue. They hurried along it, crying out to the heavens, beating the path with the thighbones of Ancestors. Mothers with babies strapped to their backs held up yellowed, age-worn skulls, clacking the jawbones and making a sinister, rhythmic noise amid the ululations of the mourners and the reedy skirl of bone pipes.

Reaching the bend of the Avenue below the ridge of the Seven Kings, where mighty white barrows stood glittering with frost, the celebrants paused, gaping and awe-struck. The great sanctuary of Khor Ghor rose up on the Plain before them, shining like a beacon, its stones warm in the crisp winter light, the shadows of trilithons and freestanding menhirs running like black fingers across the grass. Two fire-pits glowed before the entrance, and priests were driving long-horned cattle through in rites of purification. Drumbeats came from within the circle, slow and steady, bouncing from stone to stone, while deep, otherworldly horns blew in the heart of the sanctuary, almost sounding like chthonic voices as the great megaliths reverberated to the sound.

The celebrants halted outside the henge bank, for this was as far as was permitted for most. Excitement hung in the air, and men drank heartily from beakers before ritually breaking them, killing them as the Sun was killed on this day, and soon the people of the five Cantrevs became very noisy with the shouts of boasting, cheering, intoxicated men. The women did not drink the honey mead—a man's drink—but they had a thinner brew of their own that made them just as merry as their menfolk.

Like the others, U'thyr hastily imbibed as much of the mead as he could. The more a man could drink without vomiting or unconsciousness, the higher in in esteem the others held him. It was also thought that the effect of the mead could put one into close proximity with the spirit-world, while giving a warrior courage and unnatural strength.

He had just downed his fourth beakerful when he saw Y'gerna caught within the ring of revellers, her hateful bloated husband flapping about her like some sinister, flesh-gorged raven. Clad in a tight dress of tanned deerskin, her hair was braided many times, the braids set off by blue beads. A great chunk of honey-hued amber from the north rested on a thong between her breasts.

He could not keep his eyes off her, and he felt both the fire of the mead and the fire of his lust well up in him. Heat suffused his face, although the air around him was cold.

As if sensing his stare, Gorlas turned his head towards him, his piggy black eyes full of anger. It was almost as though he sensed that here was a rival who could bring his whole world crashing down. He scowled evilly, his face twisted like that of some hideous demon from the Otherworld.

The sight of Gorlas's contorted visage turned U'thyr's lust to white-hot rage. He wanted the man dead, and his hand stole to the antler hilt of his dagger. His companions milled about him, seeing the murderous look in his gaze, and tried to calm him. Violence among rivals was forbidden at the temple, with harsh penalties exacted, especially on this sacred day.

Knowing of this prohibition, Gorlas swaggered over, his beard split by a white gap-toothed grin. "You stare at me…at my wife," he said. "Maybe, one day, when you are grown, you will get yourself a woman as fair as Lady Y'gerna. That is, if some angry husband does not cleave your skull first. I would smite you myself, but it is Solstice. And Gorlas of Belerion is magnanimous."

U'thyr made a lunge at him, but Kol and Govna grabbed his arms and dragged him back.

"You will be sorry you spoke those words," U'thyr snarled. "When I split your skull and let your spirit out, and lie that very night between Y'gerna's thighs!"

Gorlas laughed. "Idle threats, from a boy who is a chief but has gained it only through lucky descent from his betters! Prove yourself a great warrior and then maybe I will battle you. I could use some sport! But now, I would not even raise my dagger to you, it would be an insult to the might of my arm. I do not fight children!"

U'thyr flushed; he knew he was the youngest of all the chieftains in the Five Cantrevs. "Prove myself I shall!" he spat. "Tonight, back in Deroweth, I will claim the Champion's Portion, in the way done of old, and be lord of the feast with nothing denied me! Then you will be sorry, old man!"

Gorlas's face went pale but he promptly regained his composure. He laughed harshly, dismissively. "I hardly think so. If you follow such a course of madness, my young friend, you will be dead before the night is over!"

CHAPTER FIVE

U'thyr made another lunge at Gorlas but his warband pulled him back, keeping him from committing an act deemed sacrilegious, especially outside the very portal stones of Khor Ghor. Kol yanked U'thyr's arms behind his back, keeping his fingers well away from his dagger, while Govna poured a brimming beaker of mead over his head, making him roar with rage but having the desired effect of distracting him from his enemy.

"Hush, my chief," said Govna, as U'thyr bellowed and kicked at him, his sodden hair straggling in his drink-maddened eyes. "You must cease this fight with Gorlas—for now. It is almost time! The Sun is almost dead!"

A sudden blast of noise came from the shielded heart of Khor Ghor: a cacophony of chanting, wailing and blowing horns, flat and sinister.

Merlin appeared in the central arch, seemingly in a trance, holding up a bloodied dagger of harsh black stone—an ancient artefact from a thousand years past. Standing between the Watchers, he wiped the gore in streaks upon his face and licked the blade. Behind him, the Sun was going down in a welter of blood, setting puffy-ridged clouds on fire. Slowly, slowly the orb tumbled through the firmament, until it was framed, the bloody eye of the dying Winter-god, between the immense arches of the Great Trilithon, Door intoWinter. It hovered briefly above the shimmering head of the Stone of Adoration, and then sank into the West, utterly vanquished.

"He is dead…but he will rise again!" Merlin held his sinewy arms up to the sky in ecstasy. "And so too will a great Chief, greater than the men of today, a man like unto our blessed forebears, those mighty ones who braved the seas to come to Albu the White! I have read this in the entrails, in the death throes of the Chosen Beast and I have read it in the patterns of the sky! It will be, and Albu shall be great once more! As Bhel Sunface will rise on the morrow, strong and renewed, so too shall the fortunes of Prydn rise!"

The crowd cheered. Some men began to leap and stamp their feet before the pit-fires and the gross bulk of the Stone of Summer. Women joined hands and danced a circular dance around the outside of the bank, singing to the Sun that was gone into the Land of the Dead, and to the Moon, the woman's planet, that was rising in ghostly majesty over Magic Hill in the East.

The priests and supplicants inside the stone circle began to process out of the ring, two acolytes dousing the fires at the entrance, as the Sun itself was extinguished. The crowd began heading back down the Sacred Avenue, mood lighter now that the Merlin had foreseen the rebirth of the Sun and a new dawn for Albu. The drummers came along behind, still playing, while masked flautists leaped amongst the crowds blowing on their bone pipes.

Back in Deroweth, the warbands of U'thyr and Gorlas sought desperately to keep the two chieftains apart. Now that U'thyr had, in Gorlas's opinion, doomed himself by boasting of the deeds he would do, the older man took the opportunity to make U'thyr's boasts known to all the peoples of the Five Cantrevs. Waving a beaker about, as mead slopped down his arms and torso, he pointed to his young adversary. "Look over there!" he slurred. "A young pup who thinks he's a hero! Who thinks he has right to my wife. MY wife! Ah, I cannot wait to see him humbled. He said he would claim the Champion's portion! "

Red-faced and furious, U'thyr tore himself away from his men and stormed towards the leering Gorlas, only to find his path blocked by a herd of squealing young pigs being driven by two acolytes of the temple. The animals were fat and rosy, fed with honey to make their meat taste sweet. They would be slaughtered today, chased by the young men of the tribes, who would shoot them with arrows, making sport rather than mere slaughter, with the man who slew the most being awarded 'the Champion's portion'—the right to eat the first of the cooked flesh, from the largest, juiciest pig in the herd.

Raising his arms to the sky, U'thyr cried out in a great voice, "Let no man speak me ill this day, for I will claim the Champion's portion! I will be Lord of the Feast, the Winter King! But..." he paused as the sea of faces around him grew thicker, deeper, interest piqued by his show of bravado, "I will not be testing the strength of my bow arm tonight! I will become one with my quarry, I will become the Sun himself, chased by the Hag of Winter, his dam and his bane! I will run with the pigs!"

A gasp rose from the crowd. In their father's father's day, it was customary to have a man run through the heaving, squealing herd of pigs, while the youths let fly with their barbed arrows. If the man lived—and frequently he did not—he was feted as King-for-a-day, and had his every wish granted and the Champion's portion on his platter. If he died, pierced by many arrows, his remains would be thrown under the pig bones in the great middens around the settlement.

"Do not do this, my son!" U'thyr's mother Indeg staggered up to him, face twisted in anguish. "What madness has possessed you? You are a chieftain, not some callow boy out to prove his manhood! You must not risk yourself this way!"

"Begone from me, woman!" snapped U'thyr. He was beyond reason now, the mead, the celebration, and his unslaked passion bringing him almost to the point of what some called the warrior's madness, where a man might foam in rage like a beast gone mad.

The crowd stirred restlessly, their faces flushed and a strange primal eagerness in eyes that sudden grew bright and small and dangerous, desirous of excitement and blood. They jostled each other, elbowing and pushing to get a better view.

The acolytes rounded the pigs to one side of the white chalk walls, while helpers set up temporary fences, forming a long straight avenue similar in appearance to a spirit-path. The village youths fetched their bows and their most lethal arrows with translucent quartz tips and goose feather fletchings. They hollered and yelled, strutting like peacocks before the village women in bright headdresses and paint, setting arrows on fire and shooting them high above the waters of Abona in brilliant barbarous display.

U'thyr stepped forward, handing his beaker to Kol. Slowly he stripped off his tunic with its rich gold plate, and handed it over, too, followed by his armbands and diadem. Govna ran up with a pot of ground ochre and drew protective designs on his torso, zigzags and whorls, the surprised eyes of the Guardian. When this ritual was completed, U'thyr bound up his long leaf-brown hair with a pin of bone, and unsheathed his dagger.

"I am ready!" he shouted. "I will run with the pigs and be the Winter-King!"

The crowd roared its approval; beakers clashed and clattered. Vaguely U'thyr could hear Gorlas yelling, "Die, die, DIE!"

Face set, U'thyr swung over the fencing and dropped in amongst the pigs. They squealed frantically and dashed in all directions, bashing into walls and each other. U'thyr launched himself forward, his calves slamming into the slower pigs' bottoms, almost making him fall. Mud and faeces oozed under his feet, as he swayed, struggling to keep his footing as the frightened beasts swarmed around him.

Suddenly he heard a sinister hiss, like the sound of a dozen snakes. Out of the corner of his eye, he saw the young men draw and release their arrows.

The race was on.

The first arrow took out a pig just in front of him. The animal fell, stricken, a clean kill. The people watching on the sidelines and the henge bank loosed a roar of unanimous delight. U'thyr leaped over the twitching carcass as the rest of the arrows whistled around him, some hitting the ground, others finding their marks among the terrified pigs, who were now almost screaming in fear, their voice high-pitched and surreal, almost like the shrieks of tortured human beings.

U'thyr darted forward again, zigzagging from side to side of the run as more arrows whistled overhead. One nicked the tip of his shoulder, drawing blood, but he hardly noticed. He just ran faster, weaving in and out of the mass of frightened beasts. Faster came the arrows and more thick, their fletchings momentarily dimming the Moon, but U'thyr eluded their barbs and only the pigs lay dead and dying in the run.

The people began to chant his name, "Pendraec, Pendraec, PENDRAEC!" over and over, and to stamp their feet in rhythm with the chanting of his name. It spurred him on even more. He leaped high into the air now, while arrows whizzed below him, then went into a roll as flint tips thudded into the earth around him...

Leaping back up, he bounded toward the far end of the run. Up on the banks he could see the stout frame of the hated Gorlas silhouetted against the stars, with Y'gerna a smaller silhouette at his side. Merlin was hovering several feet in front of them, his face inscrutable in the flickering torchlight.

Another arrow hissed by, the wind created by its passage caressing his cheek like the cold finger of death. He dropped to all fours, crawling amidst the blood and entrails and shrieking animals, whilst another volley sailed overhead and thudded into pigs near the end of the run. They dropped, twitching in their death-throes.

U'thyr tossed the bodies aside. He was near to completion of his task now, unscathed except for the small wound to his shoulder. Blood streaked his chest but he paid it no heed; it was like protective war paint. He was so close to the finish he could see his men; his mother's anguished face; the impassive visage of the Merlin. Hands reached over the rails, trying to touch him, the day-king, the Champion of the Winter feast, and to lift him out of the blood and filth to safety and to glory.

But no, he had one more act of courage to perform as Champion of the Feast. He must choose the animal from which the sacred portion would be carved. Glancing around, he saw one particularly large black pig rushing back and forth, grunting and foaming in fear. Its eyes were red, almost mad in its terror. For a moment, man and beast looked each other in the eye, and then they came together in brutal conflict, rolling amidst carcasses and steaming dung.

U'thyr reached to his belt and snatched out his dagger. "Brother, you have fought the good fight tonight!" he whispered into the pig's bristly ear, as he put his knee across the fleshy neck and yanked back the head. "Be pleased that your spirit will be honoured, and that your flesh will go to nourish the people of the Five Cantrevs!"

With that, he slit the pig's throat and released its life force into the night. Standing up, he grabbed the carcass and raised it over his head like a trophy. Blood showered over him, mingling with the red stream from his own wound.

The crowd cheered again and hurled down boughs of holly and mistletoe, for he was without question the Winter-King, king for a day.

U'thyr heaved the pig's carcass up, flinging it over the fence toward Gorlas and Y'gerna where they watched on the bank. It fell with a thud before them, split throat showering blood. U'thyr then vaulted over the rail and stalked over to his kill, dragging it up by the head. "I claim the Champion's portion!" he cried, his voice guttural, almost animalistic. "Does any here gainsay me?"

There was no answer. Gorlas's face was a twisted mask of rage—and fear. In silence, Merlin strode over and began to paint designs on U'thyr face and shoulders with the warm blood of the pig. Then he flung out his arms and shouted, "Hail the champion, lord of the feast, Midwinter's King! Let nothing he asks for this eve be denied him!"

A wolfish grin split U'thyr's bloodied visage. "I ask but one simple thing…" He stepped toward Gorlas and Y'gerna, noticing that the girl was staring at him with dark, admiring eyes.

He stretched out his hand, filthy and red. "A kiss from the lips of this queen who has driven the cold of winter from my flesh with her presence."

The crowd muttered; Gorlas's face was thunderous, but he knew he could say nothing to the winner of the Champion's portion. Y'gerna reached out and placed her slim fingers on U'thyr's bare shoulder. "For the Champion," she said, and she tilted her face to his, her dark hair raining back like a waterfall, past her slim hips, almost to the backs of her knees.

U'thyr devoured her red mouth like a wolf, tasting his own blood, salt, the mead they had both drunk that night.

The moment was broken by an enraged scream from Gorlas. "This is outrageous! Champion of the feast or no, I will not be made a fool by some young hothead! I shall leave at once, and never come here again! Khor Ghor is corrupt and the spirits will soon speak their anger. And you…you harlot…" He snatched Y'gerna's arm and yanked her away from U'thyr, "You've had too much to drink! Go find your attendants, and make ready for the journey back to Belerion!"

He pushed Y'gerna out into the darkness and followed her, cursing and shoving her to make her go faster.

U'thyr turned to Merlin, eyes wild. "I must kill him now! I cannot let her go…"

"Silence!" The Merlin laid a warning finger to his lips. "You will have what you want, I will see to it, but we will do this my way, so that there will be as little blood spilt as possible, and none here in this holy place of priests. As I said before, we do not want war with the men of Belerion, who have long been allies of Khor Ghor and also of Ar-morah across the Short Sea. Meet me at Moonset, by the Khu stone...and put your trust in me."

The rest of the night dragged for U'thyr, despite his position as Champion. He feasted, tearing off huge chunks of meat then throwing the half-eaten remains to the hungry dogs, which ran from reveller to reveller, tongues lolling and tails wagging frantically. He drank deep heady brews that made his head spin. He dandled women on his knee, some dark, some fair, some red as fire…but they could not drive out his lust for Y'gerna. It was as if she had bewitched him with some ancient woman's magic.

At last, the fires started to die away and the people disappeared in twos and threes to seek their huts and tents. U'thyr called his warband to him, and, with their weapons concealed under their cloaks, they wandered through the smoke and mist to seek Merlin at the Khu-stone.

The shaman was waiting by the hump-backed menhir, wrapped in a skin cloak with a hood pulled up to hide his face. "Follow me," he said, and he led the small party out across the night-cloaked expanse of the Great Plain.

"How far has Gorlas got, think you?" U'thyr strode next to the older man, dagger unsheathed and jaw tense.

"His rage carried him swiftly for a few miles," Merlin smirked, pushing back his hood. He had repainted his face; it looked frightening beneath the Moonglow—skull-like, a symbol of death to come. "But he's not so young, and his bones ache…and I slipped a sleeping drought into his drink at the feast, and he took three draughts of it!"

U'thyr laughed sharply. "His gluttony may have served me well!"

Merlin's eyes glimmered. "I then sent a tracker to follow his trail. Gorlas has camped for the night at the old fort of Sarlog, which lies betwixt the plain and the lands of the Willow."

"Sarlog…never did I think the site of its broken ramparts would be so sweet to me," murmured U'thyr and he lengthened his strides, knowing that Y'gerna was waiting for him there. Waiting for him to free her from her husband, to take her to his bed, to claim her as his own woman

Soon the crown of Kar Sarlog appeared on the horizon, a whitish blot against an obsidian sky. Vast earthen ramparts, partly ruinous, spiralled upward to form a vast black cone. The sides were chalky and strewn with bushes, attesting to the fort's desolation, but on top tents rustled in the breeze and fires flickered. U'thyr would have rushed for the main gate immediately, but Merlin held him back. "No. That would be folly. Gorlas will be half-expecting you to follow him, and his men will be on guard."

"We should have brought more warriors!" snarled U'thyr. "Stormed the place, and killed them all…"

Merlin's eyes flickered. "I told you—no more blood than is necessary! You will get what you desire…I promised I would help you, did I not?"

"Then work your magic, wizard!" snapped U'thyr.

Merlin knelt on the ground, hands splayed on the earth. He closed his eyes and began to chant. He rocked back and forth, teeth grinding, calling on unearthly forces to help him, to help U'thyr. Reaching into his belt-pouch he brought out a switch of rowan and beat himself with him until blood beaded on his flesh—his own sacrifice, himself to himself, on this night of power and destiny.

For a long while, nothing happened. U'thyr began to stalk back and forth, his eyes wild as a caged beast's, the cold wind licking droplets of sweat from his agitated brow. His men looked helplessly one to the other; they did not ken the ways of sorcerers or even of their lust-maddened chief.

Suddenly Merlin leaned back on his heels, panting, drooling, his face-paint smeared. His eyes were black as coal, inhuman, the pupils distended and the whites full of red veins. "It is done!" he rasped. "Look into the valley!"

U'thyr and his men gazed into the vale that swept down from the Western side of the hill-fort. A white mist was curling, rising, rolling toward them. Higher and higher its tendrils reached, blotting out the stars, sucking in bushes and trees and rocks. The men huddled close together, warriors or no; for they half fancied they could see faces in that mist—cold dead faces, eyeless skulls, yawing mouths of beings that detested the living that walked beneath the Sun.

"The mist is the Faeth, the fog of Oakseers," said Merlin. "It will last but a few hours. Go now, U'thyr and call Gorlas to combat. When he is vanquished, take his battle-helm and place it upon your own head. You will seem as Gorlas to his people, and you can go to the Lady Y'gerna without detection."

U'thyr looked at his mentor, suddenly grateful. "Merlin, my friend, my helpmeet, I have been acid-tongued towards you this eve. What can I give you, to repay all that you have risked for me?"

Merlin inched up to the younger man, his dark gaze locked with U'thyr's. "I told you before. One thing only will suffice. A child. The child. The first male child that you get on Y'gerna. That is all I ask."

"Yes, yes, whatever you want, it is yours…"

"Then go…and may the Ancestors smile on you!"

U'thyr scrambled up the hill, tripping on rabbit holes and roots hidden by the sorcerous Faeth. Ahead, he could see the gateway, undefended, open like a mouth inhaling the unholy mist of Merlin. Fires flickered beyond, hissing in the sudden damp.

"Gorlas of Dindagol!" he shouted, drawing his dagger. "I, U'thyr son of Kustenhin call you out for single combat! You have insulted me, who became Winter's King through my prowess, and you have shown disrespect to the Temple of Khor Ghor. You are not a man in my eyes, but a beast—a foul, rutting boar that needs to be culled!"

A roar of rage sounded from within the encampment, and moments later U'thyr saw the helmeted figure of Gorlas silhouetted against the guttering fires, a huge stone battle-axe in one hand and a bronze rapier in the other. His warriors milled around him, bleary eyed, not sure what or who was attacking

"Where are you, U'thyr Pendraec?" Gorlas shouted. "Show yourself!"

"No, you come to me—alone!" cried U'thyr. "Or are you so fearful that you must surround yourself with younger, doughtier men!"

Gorlas roared again and launched himself through the gateway. His warriors blundered after him, uttering war cries that fell dead in the mist. They crashed down the slopes of the fort, tripping on stunted shrubs, sliding on winter-rotten leaves as cold and slimy as dead flesh…and then at the bottom, the enchanted fog curled up to engulf them, all arms and legs and twisted faces full or sorrow and hate. There came a soft whirring noise, like the fluttering of a bird's wings wildly beating—or the wind through the fletchings of an arrow in the dark—followed by a series of muffled shrieks and then deathly silence.

U'thyr and Gorlas found themselves alone on the hillside, the mist forming a circle, an unearthly arena, around them. Purposefully, U'thyr stepped toward his adversary, his dagger held in ready, every muscle tensed. Gorlas dropped into a crouch, growling like a beast, and indeed he looked much like an animal in his rude fur cloak and grotesque helmet fashioned from a boar's head.

For a few minutes, they circled, each getting the measure of the other, and then, uttering an unearthly yell, Gorlas barrelled forward, head lowered, the boar's tusks on his helm thrust forward like a pair of additional weapons. U'thyr sprang back in surprise; he had expected an axe swing or a slash from the rapier. He stumbled against a tree, and Gorlas rushed past him, the impetus of his attack carrying him beyond his intended quarry. Slipping on leaves, he managed to halt himself and turn around ponderously…in time to see U'thyr bearing down on him, dagger upraised.

Panting, he flung up his axe and U'thyr's blow smashed against the wooden haft, cutting a great gouge. There was a crack, the wood parted, and the black polished axe head thudded to the ground.

Gorlas yelped in fury, but his anger turned to mirth as he saw that his opponent's weapon had suffered a similar fate. U'thyr's bronze-bladed knife had bent with the power of his blow, and was in danger of snapping in two.

"I have you now, young fool!" Gorlas grunted, raising his rapier. "You should have stayed in Deroweth with the womanish priests. You would have reigned as chief for another year, but now the Dwr shall have no ruler and I shall make a drinking cup of your skull. I shall make that faithless whore Y'gerna drink from it every night."

"I am not done, Gorlas," said U'thyr, falling into a crouch. "I still have one weapon—the strength of my arms!"

Gorlas laughed. "You! Thin as a reed! Know you that I once wrestled a wild boar unarmed and won—hence the head upon my helm!"

"Looking at that mangy token, the battle was many long years ago," U'thyr retorted. "Once your limbs were doubtless strong. Now they are merely fat!"

Gorlas snarled and leaped at his adversary, his blade making slashing sounds through the chill air. U'thyr ducked and swung a balled fist into his stomach, making the older man double over and gasp for breath. Purple-faced, Gorlas stumbled in his direction, dagger stabbing aimlessly, free hand groping for a handful of cloak, tunic, hair…

U'thyr darted behind him, trying to kick through the banks of sodden leaves on the ramparts of the fort. He slipped and fell heavily amid the slimy mulch, and Gorlas made a wild lunge with his knife, thinking his luck was in, but U'thyr grabbed a handful of the mouldering leaves and rammed them into his face.

"You fight unfairly!" screamed Gorlas. "You fight like a maid afraid of being tupped!"

"You are the one who fights like a coward—a man with a weapon against one with none!" U'thyr shouted back.

"I have had enough of your tongue!" Gorlas yelled, and he lunged at U'thyr once more, adrenaline giving him a speed unnatural in one so fat and indolent. Like a maddened ox, he charged at U'thyr, arms flailing madly, pointlessly, his mouth open in a frothing, mad shout.

And U'thyr, with the litheness of youth, once again sprang up into the misty darkness, swinging on the bough of a shrivelled hawthorn tree above the reach of Gorlas's sword. The fat man, as before, blundered forward, carried along by his mad, headlong rush and the weight of his own corpulent frame.

He began to slip on leaves, as U'thyr had done, his legs bowing and his cloak billowing and tangling with bushes. The hillside beneath him was tilting, while around him rose the Faeth; its coiling tendrils full of sneering, jeering faces and hooded, accusing figures. "What evil magic is this?" he screamed, and he slashed wildly at the phantoms with his rapier.

Still he was propelled forward, unable to stop his forward rush, toadstools crushing to pulp beneath his boots, branches whipping his cheeks, cobwebs breaking over his eyes and obscuring his vision. He was gathering speed, sliding, slipping, knee-deep in mud and mulch...

And then, suddenly, his feet were free and kicking....

In cold air, with no solid earth below him.

He hung in mid-air for a moment, as if dangled by some giant's child, and then suddenly he began to fall, to plummet like a stone toward whatever lay below, shrouded in the eerie fog. He shrieked once and the faces in the mist twisted with mirth and anticipation.

Through tearing eyes, he saw the mist opening below him, parting to accept his heavy frame. There was grass, and mud, the bottom of a ditch...and the fallen trunk of a hoary oak, with bare branches radiating out from it like sharpened spears.

"No!" he shrieked, clawing at the mist, the sky, and then he hit the fallen tree and lay like a sacrifice upon an altar, head back, eyes wide, the spoke of a huge tree branch jutting up through his belly. Blood pattered on the floor of the ditch.

U'thyr slid down the embankment to the side of his fallen foe. Gorlas was clearly dead, his eyes already glazing. Carefully U'thyr removed his helm with its ugly mask and placed it on his own head. Unfastening the dead man's cape, he wiped it free of blood spray as best he could and wrapped himself in it.

"May Merlin's magic make me seem enough like Gorlas!" he muttered, and he began to climb back up to the entrance of Sarlog fort.

He passed through the gates unchallenged. He saw some men looking at him quizzically, and snarled in a gruff voice, the sound distorted by the swirling fog: "He is dead; the fool who mocked me is dead. Go back to your rest."

"But lord, what of the warriors who went out with you tonight?" asked one old man, his face creased with worry. "Where are they? Why are you alone?"

U'thyr kicked a water bucket over, spraying the man. "I've fought a battle for my life and you pester me with questions? They are chasing my enemy's men, hunting them down. They will not be back for hours yet for I have ordered that they slay every last man."

Gorlas's people murmured, nodding, glad at his words, and comforted to think that their enemies were put to flight. U'thyr turned from them and blundered through the sea of hastily thrown up tents, looking for one that seemed as if it might belong to a chieftain. Sweat poured down his face under the reeking helmet of Gorlas.

Up ahead he spied one tent that was larger than the rest, its sides painted with chevrons and zigzags. Two small braziers glowed before the doorway and he could smell the scent of burning herbs, sweet on the night air.

She was in there, waiting for him—he knew it.

Breathing heavily, he approached the door and flicked back the entrance flap. Inside a stout woman was poking a fire with a stick, and he felt his stomach knot with anger and disappointment. But then, behind the woman, he spotted Y'gerna lying on a bed of sheepskins. Slowly, languorously, she was combing her dark locks out with her fingers. Coy, she looked over at him and a small smile touched her lips.

The woman by the fire had stopped stoking the flames and was peering nervously at her mistress. Y'gerna flicked a hand at her. "What are you gawking at, drab? Get out, you know my lord is always filled with ardour after his conquests."

The woman bowed and scurried away. Y'gerna rose, letting the sheepskin round her shoulders drop to the floor. She was lean and lithe; her wiry body scarcely showing any signs that she had born a child nigh on a year ago. "Let me undress you, my lord," she said hoarsely, reaching out to unfasten his cloak, and as it dropped to the floor: "My lord…U'thyr!"

U'thyr said nothing, he had no flattering words, no pretty lover's speeches, but that did not anger Y'gerna—she did not want them, this fierce Western princess of the old blood. He jerked her towards him, and she kissed him as fiercely as he had kissed her on the ramparts of Deroweth, drinking of his mouth as if she meant to draw out his very soul.

Maybe she had done exactly that. He had never felt like this before, possessed by a kind of madness.

Gasping, he fell forward, bearing her down into the mounded piles of furs and skins. Her hair streamed out, dark as night-time water, tangling around his arms, flowing over the hard peaks of her high, round breasts. She was like some primeval deity lying there, a goddess of earth and love and war, with her dark eyes glowing and her lips red and wet. She could be his life…or his death.

Outside he could hear Gorlas's folk beginning a dance round their fires, a victory dance that would soon turn to tears. Drums started slowly and rhythmic, and so too did he move with Y'gerna, twined in the oldest dance of man since time began.

Out in the valley beyond Merlin heard the drums and glanced up at the darkened hilltop. Making his way across the ramparts, he spied the body of Gorlas of Dindagol lying as it had fallen, his blood feeding the hungry earth below him.

"So U'thyr has succeeded!" The shaman glanced up toward the shadowed gateway of the ancient camp. "He must be lying with the woman even as I stand here."

He clapped his hands and slowly, slowly, the mists receded. A great joy overcame him, as in his mind's eye he beheld a vision of the future, of the great man that he would mould to his will from childhood. He began to dance and whirl, stamping in time with the drums from the hillfort, calling on the Ancestors to bless this night, to bless U'thyr and Y'gerna's loins, to bless the child that would be born to give his strength to Albu the White.

CHAPTER SIX

The Sun came up in a cold, watery haze above Sarlog. In the encampment, the folk of Belerion lay sleeping, worn out by their long trek and the dancing of the night before. Even the dogs slumbered, twitching by the remains of the fires.

Only one woman stirred, bleary eyed, her heart filled by an unknown sense of dread. The warriors had not returned. On silent feet, she crossed the centre of the fort to the unmanned gateway and stared down the hill. The fog of the previous night had burned away and the naked branches of trees stuck up like the denuded bones of skeletons.

She cocked her head, trying to focus. There seemed to be something lying in the bottom of one of the mighty defensive ditches, a crumpled bundle of rags slung over a tree. More bundles lay scattered through the woods beyond, empty sacks of clothes. A sick fear suddenly rose in her gut and she strained her eyes into the morning Sun.... and began to scream.

Her shrieks brought instant wakefulness to the rest of the tribesfolk. Leaping up, they ran to the gate and peered down. More women started to wail, and the men rushed down the slope, drawing daggers from their belts. In horror they found their best warriors dead, slain by arrows in the night, and their lord, Gorlas, lying impaled upon the great tree, the birds of carrion already gathering about him, squabbling over morsels of eyes and nose.

They dragged his corpse free and, howling and keening, hauled it back up toward the encampment, his dead weight resting upon their shoulders.

"This is madness!" wept the woman who had first spotted the corpses. "I saw Lord Gorlas enter my lady Y'gerna's tent last night...saw him with my own eyes! Or maybe it was not a living man I saw; maybe it was an evil wraith out to bring death to us all!"

"No, it was no spirit!"

The folk of Belerion halted in their tracks. The Merlin, high priest of Khor Ghor, was standing in the centre of the camp, leaning heavily upon his shaman's staff. He looked hard and hawkish, his face tired but triumphant. The hawk's head in bronze upon his breast glimmered in the strengthening light. "It was no spirit that wrought this doom upon you—It was the hand of man. But it happened because the Ancestors frowned upon you, for blindly following Gorlas, who consorted with our enemies, and slighted the priests of Khor Ghor just yester eve. Now, because of his folly, you will have a new lord over you, and you will work your tin mines and pay a tithe to Khor Ghor and the spirits to atone for Gorlas's errors."

The people murmured, looking at each other with not a little relief. When they found the warriors slain, they had been certain the killers had slated them for a similar end. Gorlas's death they could come to terms with; though feared and honoured, he had never been loved by his people.

"Who is this great warrior who has killed our chief and will rule us from this day forth?" asked one old woman, her voice high and tremulous.

"I am that man."

U'thyr stepped from Y'gerna's tent and stood before the tribesmen. He still wore the helm of his fallen foe, with its curved tusks and harsh bristles, and in his hand he held both dagger and axe as a symbol of his authority. "I am U'thyr Pendraec, the Terrible Head, chief of the Dwri and the great Dragon Path. I have killed treacherous Sea-folk and I have killed your black-hearted chief and taken his woman for my own. You need not fear me, unless you try to raise hand against me, or do me disrespect."

At that moment, Y'gerna herself stepped forward, hair in disarray, wearing only a skin she had hastily wrapped around her. "Listen to him!" she cried. "This man may seem fearsome, but I swear he will treat you all with fairness. He has no wish to harm you, that I know."

The serving woman whose husband lay dead at the foot of the hill spat at her. "A curse on you...you who are tearless though your husband lies dead! You let him in, didn't you? You contrived this between you, you bitch-in-heat!"

She stumbled forward, trying to lunge at Y'gerna, but Merlin stepped into the way. "No, it is not the girl's fault. I spun a glamour that gave U'thyr the semblance of Gorlas. And so he entered Y'gerna's bed. If she is tearless, it is because she knows what her duty must be. She has no choice but to cleave to U'thyr."

Y'gerna bowed her head, hiding her smile beneath the curtain of her hair. The old man made her flesh crawl, but she was grateful that he had spared her the tribesfolk's wrath.

"Now..." Merlin turned to U'thyr. "We should return to Deroweth. You can make preparations to send these poor wretches back to Belerion with one of your men, who can oversee them and get the wealth sent to you in Dwranon."

U'thyr stepped uncomfortably from foot to foot, his jaw tightening. "No, Merlin, I have thought long into the night, and have other plans. I will go to Belerion and live with Y'gerna in the fort of Dindagol. Think of it...the Sea-folk come most often to those regions; I can make sure they get no more footholds in our land!"

"What of your own lands?" Merlin shot him a dark look. "Who will defend them? The chief of Duvnon's kingdom lies between Dwranon and Belerion; it will not be so easy to cross between the two without conflict. To say nothing of taking many days."

U'thyr shook his head. "My mind is made up, Merlin. I will go to Dindagol, and leave the management of Dwranon with men like Kol and my young cousins."

Merlin poked a bony finger into U'thyr's chest. "You...you disappoint me! I had such hopes once, but you were always hardheaded and rash. But, be that as it may, I hope you are not trying to escape because of the promise you made me!"

"Promise?" He looked genuinely puzzled.

"The promise about the boy. Your son. Born of your night with Y'gerna."

U'thyr tried to laugh; it came out a hoarse croak. "What makes you so certain there will be a child? If it were so quick and easy, any young fellow might get half a dozen each new Moon!"

Merlin stared into his face, his eyes black with anger. "There will be a child. And you will give him to me. Just remember that, U'thyr Pendraec. You will give him to me."

The months rolled by. Winter bloomed into the fairest spring men could remember, then a blazing summer with blue skies and red sunsets. By Autumn, the folk of Belerion were bringing in a bumper harvest, and Y'gerna gave birth to a boy-child just after the feast of the Corn-Lord, where men and women bundled together in the furrows as the last sheaf was cut down. There was rejoicing among the folk of Belerion, who had grown loyal to U'thyr Pendraec and his woman, after their initial reservations after the bloody death of Gorlas.

But U'thyr was not happy, though all about him celebrated. He turned his head away from the flower-topped cliffs and the blue sea and looked inland. Waiting...Dreading...

The thing he feared most happened one night when the Moon was full and men could feel the hint of old magic in the air, touching the standing stones, awakening the spirits, drawing back the barrier between the world of men and Otherness. U'thyr woke in the chieftain's hut on the hill at Dindagol, with its rampart ring of lichened boulders. He felt strangely uneasy. Outside, at the foot of the cliffs, he could hear the waves crashing, smiting the land as the hammer smote the anvil --a sound that still unnerved him even after all these months. It was an alien realm here, surrounded by the magics of the sea-god Mahn-an, who rode the wave-caps on a seal's back, and blew fog and storms in on his bitter breath.

Rolling over, he saw that Y'gerna was still fast asleep, her head pillowed on her arm. Whatever it was wakened him had not bothered her in the least.

Quietly he rose and walked over to the cradle of woven birch boughs in the corner, where their infant son slept wrapped in a sheepskin. The baby was silent, also in deep sleep. He had no true name as yet, but his parents called him Art'igen, the bear-that-is-to-be, the Cub, in order to fool passing evil spirits into thinking he was not a human child and hence of no consequence. Call your babe 'brave' or 'fair-face' at birth, and the old dead ones in their barrow-tombs might become jealous and spirit them away, leaving gnarly, unseelie things in their cradles instead.

"Sleep on, my dark one," U'thyr said, ruffling the infant's hair with a finger, and then he left the hut and stepped out into the shadows.

It was a pleasant night, with the warm orange Moon burning over the sea, its light making an enchanted road across the waves. The wind was a warm caress against his face, and the air tasted of salt.

Silently, U'thyr left the confines of the dun and walked along the rugged coastal path atop the cliffs. Sea-grasses whipped his ankles, and his hair was a banner in the breeze. He stopped by the little waterfall that tumbled over the black bastions of the cliff and knelt down, surveying the land and the endless waters before him. For all its beauty, it made him shudder—the cliffs seemed stark, frightening, the sea too deep, too fierce, frothing up like a dog gone mad. Strongly, he felt that something dwelt beyond, waiting for him, something that he did not want to face.

He almost hoped it would be another attack by Sea-People, in their long fast ships that darted like fish down the Western coast of the mainland, skimming past the lands of ancient kindred tribes—the Iverri, the Vasca and the Albianis who looked out toward the Isles of Prydn from across the Little Sea.

He could deal with Sea-Pirates. It was a promise made in the heat of lust he could not deal with.

His heart skipped a beat. Down on the beach he caught a glimpse of movement, a greyish shape contrasted against white shingle. The figure was standing in the mouth of a sea-cavern men called Mahn-an's Maw. An ill-starred place that sucked in dead bodies lost at sea, and where exploring children often drowned in the fast-incoming tides. It was whispered Fhann, wife of Mahn-an, would sing the children into enchanted sleep, then hungry Mahn-an would flood the cave and carry their drowned bodies into the deep.

But it was not the Sea-god he feared tonight.

It was a man. But a man unlike other men.

His fears were realised as the figure below left the cave-mouth and started in his direction, climbing a well-worn path up the cliff-face He could see a flutter of stained robes, flowing silver-streaked hair, and a staff topped with a jawbone.

Like a craven, U'thyr hid in a wind-stunted bush, praying to all the spirits that the old man would stumble and fall down the cliff side.

The gods did not listen,

The Merlin reached the top of the cliff and gazed straight at the bush where U'thyr hid, with his hard, black, bird-like eyes. "Come out, U'thyr," he said mockingly. "It is not fitting that the lord of Belerion and Dwranon hides away like a fearful girl."

Shamefaced, U'thyr stepped from the shrub to face his old mentor. "So you have come."

"As I said I would. I speak no lies, U'thyr Pendraec. Are you able to say the same? Are you an honourable man who keeps his bargains?"

U'thyr flushed. "Do not doubt me. You will have what you want...but are you sure you must do this thing? The child...there will be others later, he is my heir...."

"And so he will remain," said Merlin dryly. "But I will foster him. Many tribes practise fosterage. Now give him to me. I am not here to pass the time, my duties lie elsewhere. Reports have come that both raiders from Ibherna and Sea-People have been harrying the coasts in Duvnon, and I have been trying to rally local chiefs to band together and fight them, although the battles may not be in their own lands. This was a job I had hoped for you, U'thyr, to be the high war-leader of the tribes. But you have lost the fire, between your dark queen's thighs!"

U'thyr hung his head, angered by Merlin's words but unable to find any words of his own to answer him. In silence, he walked back to his hut, the Merlin walking briskly at his side. Entering the door, he saw Y'gerna sitting by the glowing embers of the fire, feeding the baby Art'igen, the bear-cub. "Merlin!" she said with surprise and some trepidation as the shaman swept into the hut. "What brings you to Belerion unannounced?"

Merlin paused, his brows raised. "Has he not told you? Has U'thyr, the brave and terrible Head, been too fearful to tell his own wife about the will of Merlin?"

Y'gerna whipped around to face U'thyr, her eyes darkening with alarm. "No, he had told me nothing! U'thyr, what is the meaning of all this?"

U'thyr's face reddened and his lips moved soundlessly.

"I shall tell you if U'thyr cannot," said Merlin. "When U'thyr first became enamoured of you, he asked for my help. He would have done anything for an hour in your arms. And so he promised me the fruits of your night together, Lady Y'gerna....he promised me your son."

"No!" Y'gerna put Art'igen down and sprang to her feet. For a moment it looked as if she would attack Merlin, but instead, she turned on her silent, shame-faced husband. "You bastard!" she screamed, launching herself at him, tearing at his tunic and hair, biting at his neck like a crazed animal. "How could you do this to me? How could you keep this terrible secret from me? I despise you..."

"Shut up, woman!" U'thyr grabbed her wrists, holding her away from him as she spat and struggled, kicking out at him. "What's done is done. The boy will come to no harm; you know the Merlin will treat him well. Many lads are fostered out to great men's families."

"But you didn't tell me..." she sobbed, the fight suddenly gone from her. She sagged at the knees, looking faint. "How could you? He is so small, not ready to be taken away..."

U'thyr grabbed her as she started to fall, gathering her close. Tears were streaming down her face, hot, helpless, angry tears. "I promise you I will make amends. Gold, amber, garments and circlets imported from over the sea. I'll put another six strong sons in your belly! But we must let the Merlin take the Cub—I cannot break the promise I made."

His strained gaze flicked over to Merlin and he nodded, mouthing the word, "Go, now!"

The older man picked up the baby from the rush-mat on the floor, wrapping it in a fur, then tying it in a sling across his chest. Without a further word to U'thyr or the sobbing Y'gerna, he left the round house and walked back through the courtyard of the fort toward the sea.

As he reached the last hut of Dindagol, nestled against the ramparts, he suddenly sensed eyes upon him. Turning, he beheld a small girl child, no more than three years old, watching him from the entrance of the hut. Black-haired and dark-eyed, her face was a tiny, petulant heart. She was observing him intently, her thumb in her mouth. Merlin noticed copper bangles rattled on her wrists; he guessed she must have some status among her people.

"Where you going?" she asked, letting her thumb drop.

"Far away, to lands near the great temple of Khor Ghor," he replied.

"You take baby?" She toddled over and grabbed at the furs that wrapped the Cub.

"Yes. I am to foster him."

A strange expression crossed the elfin face; a look too old for such a young child. A look of resentment…even malice. "Good…no like him! My da not come back, and new man is with mam…and baby. I sent to nurse."

"Ah…" Merlin let out a long exhalation. He knew the truth now; this strange dark child was Morigau, Gorlas's daughter by Y'gerna, replaced in her mother's favours by U'thyr and the new baby.

"Would you not take Morigau too?" the child asked, hopefully.

Merlin knelt down, staring into her eyes. "No, you must stay and look after your mother. She will need you now that Art'igen is gone."

Again, that troubling expression of malice crossed Morigau's face, making her look almost like some small demon. "Me should go to temple…not brat!" Her eyes glowed, green-brown in the wan Moonlight, and Merlin felt his heartbeat quicken.

It was as if she had a bad spirit within her. Perhaps her father's ghost was still angry about his death and had possessed her. Young as she was, she already exuded a kind of darkness, and he knew, instinctively, if she were left unchecked, she would attempt to bring all his plans crashing down in ruin…

He glanced at the seawall, the bright stars beyond. The sea was rumbling over pebbles on the beach. It would be easy to snatch her up, muffling any cries, and hurl her down into the waters. Mahn-an would take her, and her malignant spirit would no longer be there to threaten her brother and Merlin's dreams.

But…he could not do it. He would kill when the spirits demanded their due, but she was no sacrifice, no Chosen One—the spilling of her blood would be cursed, not made sacred. Such an act would cause dissension, even war, in Albu, and he had no doubt U'thyr and the men of Belerion would hunt him down without mercy.

No, he had to leave her be… but he would remember the darkness in her, and try to make sure she was kept well away from the swelling rises of the Great Plain and her younger brother.

Turning from the child, he hurried out through the gate of the fort and down the hillside, slipping on the long sea-grasses with their crusts of glittering salt. In his arms the baby began to grizzle, its voice high and thin on the night breeze, the cry of a gull, the wail of a spirit out of the cold cairn.

"You'll wish you took meeee, old one!" Merlin heard Morigau's voice rise up like some malevolent death-spirit in the night. "Not him! Meeee!"

Unsettled by the vehemence of the fey dark child, the high priest of Khor Ghor hurried on toward the boat moored in the shadows of Mahn-an's Maw and the safety of the lands he knew.

PART THREE: ARDHU—SUNRISE

CHAPTER SEVEN

The horse galloped across the green field, flanks rippling, nostrils flaring in the chill wind. Art'igen watched, taut as a bowstring, transfixed by the grace and power of the animal before him. He wished he had the same kind of fluidity, the strength of rippling muscles and powerful flanks, but he was still just a boy in training, in his own eyes ungainly and clumsy.

Just wait, his foster-father had said, and you will surprise yourself.

Wait! It seemed Art's life was all about waiting, and he was growing impatient.

Art'igen was fifteen and had not yet been made a Man of the Tribe. He lived with his foster-brother, big, ugly but amusing Ka'hai, and his foster-father, Ech-tor, who was a smith. At one time, as a metalworker, the tribe would have regarded Ech-tor as a magic man, just like the great Merlin of Khor Ghor (who often came to visit Art'igen, teaching him the magic patterns of the skies and many other things). Smiths knew how to make the sword come from stone, and how to turn dull base metals into the axes and daggers of kings.

Now, though, in Art'igen's day, a smith was still a highly honoured trade, if not thought to be of otherworldly mode. Ech-tor, however, was spirit-marked by another art unrelated to the forge—his love of horses, those fearsome animals who ran free in the wilds, some hunted for meat by tribes who wanted to ingest their strength, the rest being shunned by those who deemed them creatures that only the gods dared sit upon.

On Ech-tor's little steading, a few miles from the important settlement of Marthodunu, lying between Khor Ghor and the stones of Suilven, the Crossroads-of-the-World, the Smith kept six horses which he had captured and tamed. Hence, his old name of Tor had been changed to Ech-tor, Tor the Horse-Man. And men came not only to watch him make the daggers of bronze and serpentine armbands, but to watch him and Ka'hai slip twine bridles onto their horses' heads and ride them up and down amid the frightened sheep and pigs in the yard.

Art'igen was considered too young and callow to partake of this sport, but Ka'hai told him that soon this would change. Indeed, it was almost time for his initiation into the tribe, and the time of choosing of a new name, his adult name. This was a fraught time for Art'igen, not knowing what would be expected of him when the priests gathered the boys of the tribe together in the Sweat Lodge of Marthodunu. What name would they give him, to identify him forever more? It could be Tall Spear or Stag-fleet, which would be honourable names to bear, but likewise it could be Scowling-Face or even something as grotesque as Pig-eyes. Art'igen knew a lad called Pig-Eyes, a fat, red-haired boy who puffed and grunted when he ran, hence the unflattering name.

"Art!" He heard a familiar voice, and looking around saw Ka'hai riding toward him on his horse, Hen-gron. He had rounded up the golden-maned mare that Art'igen had watched in her wild race across the sunlit meadow, and slipped a twine bridle over her ears. "Art, come here, I have something for you."

Art'igen ran over to his brother, a big bluff lad with sandy, rough-cut hair and light, light eyes that spoke of some strange northern ancestry. Despite his size, he was quite a shy, gentle youth, who preferred horses and dogs to strutting around with boastful lads of similar age. "Here." He grinned at Art'igen, "I have a present for you, since you are now fifteen summers old and about to become a man. My gift for your naming day is this mare, Lamrai is her name."

"Mine?" Art'igen gasped, astounded.

"All yours, little brother," replied Ka'hai, handing him Lamrai's reins. "Now, let us see if you can ride her! Father and I have already taught you the crafts of wood and metal, and the use of dagger and bow. Now, we will teach you how to ride—a feat seldom seen in Prydn. It may be of great help to you one day—or so said the Merlin."

Carefully, Art'igen grasped Lamrai's Sun-honeyed mane, and with the litheness of youth, vaulted onto her back. He yelped and slid about for a bit, while she snorted and danced at his unfamiliar clumsiness, and Ka'hai covered his mouth with a hand and suppressed a laugh.

But Ka'hai's eyes were kind when his mirth was quelled. "Go on," he said. "Touch her sides with your heels. Ride her up to the Hill of the Old People on yonder rise…" He nodded towards a distant round barrow that stood on the crest of a nearby slope, marking the territory for the past few hundred years. "You must become one with her, as you would with a beautiful woman…"

Ka'hai's big, plain face broke into a grin as he saw Art'igen squirm in embarrassment. Youths of Art's age were not permitted to dally with village girls, even if the girl was already marked as a woman of the tribe. That could come only after Art had a name and status; then he could take a wife or wives if he could afford more than one. But Ka'hai had seen him looking at the girls of the nearby settlements, and knew soon it would be time for him to do more than just look.

Art'igen querulously tapped his heels onto Lamrai's flanks. With a toss of her head, the mare trotted forward. Another tap, slightly harder than the first. Lamrai broke into a canter.

"That's it, brother!" Ka'hai yelled. "Ride like the wind!"

Face flushed with excitement, Art'igen slammed his heels into the mare's sides. She leaped in fright at the sudden punishment, and Art'igen let out a strangled yelp as she suddenly bolted from the yard, heading toward the desired rise but at a breakneck gallop. He clung desperately to her mane, the coarse golden hair whipping his cheeks and stinging his eyes, while behind him Ka'hai stood, hands on hips, roaring with laughter.

After the initial panic, Art'igen became used to the hard beat of the gallop. He steadied his position, moving with the movements of his steed, raising himself up to see above her head. Trees flew by, a green blur, while up ahead the hump of the marker-barrow rose, a black blot against the cloud-strewn sky. It was a moment of magic—Art felt as if he were indeed one with the horse, a mythical six-legged man-beast that could fly over ground that would take an hour's walk on foot. He almost fancied that Lamrai's heart was beating in time with his own, symbolic of their joining on that day. Any chief who could learn this art, this communion with a beast of four legs and broad back, would surely become great beyond words, especially if he ordered his men to take mounts as well. They could ride hither and thither to protect their lands, fighting with bow and long spears from horseback…. Dreamily he thought of it—an army of men with himself at the fore, travelling the Four Corners of Albu.

His reverie was brought to an abrupt end as Lamrai mounted the slopes of the barrow. A rustling noise came from the bushes sprouting in its ditch, and the mare suddenly threw back her head and shied to the right, eyes rolling in fear. Art'igen went flying over her head, arms and legs flailing at air, and landed in a hunched ball on the grass, bruised but unharmed. Lamrai, now seemingly calm, trotted off down the side of the barrow, cropping grass that grew rich and green from the nourishing bones below.

"Stupid beast!" Art'igen muttered petulantly, his pride wounded more than his flesh. In the distance, he could hear Ka'hai bellowing with laughter. "What could have made her behave in such a way?"

He rolled over, groaning…and then he saw what had frightened the mare. A man was standing atop the barrow; lean and wiry, with grey-dark hair in long braids round a lean, sharp face. A hawk's skull plated with copper hung round his neck, and a staff topped by a worn human jaw rested in his right hand.

"Merlin!" Art'igen shouted joyously, leaping to his feet. He was always glad to see the old shaman, proud that such a one, chief of the holy men of Khor Ghor, would take an interest in him. Despite the distance from Marthudunu to his abode at Deroweth, Merlin came at least once a year to see Art'igen, to teach him various lessons and to instruct Ech-tor as to what he wanted for the lad. Art was not sure why Merlin was so interested in his education, but a boy his age did not ask questions of the great ones. He simply assumed that his closest kin had died when he was a babe and hence he was given to the temple, and that Merlin had placed him with Ech-tor to ensure he would grow up useful to the tribe.

Merlin nodded toward the youth. "I did not expect to see you rolling in the grass like a babe," he said dryly.

Art blushed. "I was riding, Merlin. Riding a horse! I fell off...but that won't happen again! Ka'hai is teaching me! Just think, would it not be a great war-tool, to ride horses..."

"Indeed," said Merlin, with a taut smile, "but not if you dream away so much you fall off and are trampled by them!"

Art's blush deepened and he stared at his feet. "I will learn; I will not fall again!"

Merlin grinned again. "You will fall. We all do along the long, hard paths of our lives... but you will rise again as all strong men of Albu must!" He stretched out a veiny brown hand to Art'igen. "Come, rise, young Art, I have news for you. Exciting news!"

"And what news is that?" asked Art'igen, excitedly. Few diversions came to Ech-tor's holding, with the exception of the occasional traders or warriors seeking new weaponry. Art had only been to the great henge of Marthodunu once or twice, despite it being only a few miles hence. As a boy, he was not entitled to join the rites and had only viewed it between festivals, when it was empty, its huge banks covered in mist from the nearby river.

"It is the time for your manhood rite," said Merlin. "I have put your name forward and the priests there have said to bring you."

Art'igen's eyes gleamed; he tried to control his excitement, and not look childish and over-eager. "This is great news, Merlin! I had not expected the call till the autumn, after harvest fest, at earliest. "

"The priests listen to me—I am the Merlin," said Merlin. "I want to see you made a man-of-the-tribe as soon as possible...because much is afoot in Albu, and it is men the tribes need, not sheltered boys. After some years of peace, the Sea-Raiders have been harrying the coasts of Belerion and Duvnon again. Some have even sailed down the rivers, making paths inland. The chieftains are uneasy, and in their fear, they may grow some common sense at last and stop fighting petty quarrels amongst themselves! They have agreed choose a high chief, the supreme Head, as we had of old; he who will be Stone Lord, Master of the Great Trilithon and Son of the Sun. This event is something I want you to witness."

Art was nearly jumping with excitement. He had heard the tales of chiefs and warriors around the fires, of men who painted themselves blue and men who spoke different tongues, of some who pierced their noses with bone, and some who were tall as giants, their great arms a-clatter with bangles of polished shale. He had only seen the few travellers, cloaked and dusty, who sought smith Ech-tor's wares, and as a boy, he had not been allowed to speak to them. He had watched them from afar, men with Sun-bronzed faces and scars, all the while burning with impertinent youthful questions that went unanswered.

"Ah, Merlin, my friend, I thank you for this gift! It is a great honour," he cried. "When do we go?"

"As soon as possible." Merlin glanced at the Sun's position in the sky. "The chiefs of the Cantrevs and their wains are on the move even as we speak. Go collect Ka'hai—he will also want to witness this great day—and gather whatever possessions you need. And bring the horse; it will make you look good!"

"If I don't fall off," said Art'igen sheepishly, with a small grin.

"I will pin you on there with my magic if need be," said the Merlin fiercely. "Just that one time!"

The Merlin, the two youths and their mounts departed the Ech-tor's holding and headed across the downland of the Valley-between-Hills. It was arable land and they saw farms dotted about and lone shepherds driving their flocks of woolly brown sheep. As night fell, they came into a thin grove of silver birches, their branches whistling and whipping in the wind like the hair of a dancing maiden. Merlin stopped and sat down in a little rounded bowl formed by the roots of several ancient trees that had lashed themselves together, strangling each other as they fought for purchase in the rich, deep earth. He scraped together some dry twigs and lit them with his flint strike-a-light, murmuring a short prayer to the flame to keep it bright and warm.

Ka'hai tethered the horses to a tree, and then slumped against its trunk, wrapped in his piebald cowhide cloak. Almost immediately, his head drooped and he started to snore; the day was warm and he was not used to walking so far from the smithy. Ignoring the big lad, Merlin handed Art'igen some strips of dried meat from the bag at his waist, then stretched out his thin legs until they were almost in the fire. He chewed a mouthful of jerky in thoughtful silence, his sharp eyes locked on the dark-haired youth across from him.

Art felt mildly uncomfortable. Merlin had never subjected him to that kind of silent scrutiny before. It was embarrassing…especially as he did not know why the priest stared with such intensity. Measuring him up. Judging.

Eventually Merlin spoke. Night was drawing in now; the thin fingernail of the Moon hung suspended above in a swaying web of ghostly branches. "Art'igen, what do you know of the making of Khor Ghor?"

"Only what the storytellers sing. That the first Merlin, blessed be his spirit…" He glanced anxiously at the older man, who was possibly—who knew?—reborn with the spirit of that much Esteemed Ancestor. "The first Merlin brought the stones from the West by magic, after winning them from Ibherna in a terrible battle! It is said that he floated them through the air all the way to the Great Plain!"

Merlin's eyes were hooded. "A pretty tale, but just a tale. Wiser lore-masters will tell you how he dismantled the stones with cunning devices, and raised them again in the same way—with the wisdom of his thought, not any magical art. Ardhu, come follow me. We will not be long. Ka-hai will be quite safe."

Merlin got up and entered another section of the darkling grove. Art'igen followed, carefully picking his way between snarled roots and animal burrows. Up ahead he spotted a stone, furred with moss: the capstone of a mighty burial cist, a chamber to contain the bones of some great warrior, his knees drawn up in foetal position as he awaited rebirth, his long-fleshless face turned toward the rising Sun in the East. It was not a particularly pleasant place to visit in the dead of night, with the wind rushing and dancing about, keening through the moving branches of the trees. What if the old barrow-man was lonely, hungry, seeking to draw the unwary living into the Lands of the Dead?

"Art'igen," said Merlin, "do you think you can move that stone?" He gestured to the capstone with its cupmarks that held the tremulous Moonlight.

Art stared at him as if he had gone mad. "Of course not! Many men would be needed to drag such a heavy slab!"

"So it may appear…but watch me, Art'igen." Merlin approached the stone and set his hand upon it. He shut his eyes; the wind lifted his hair, Moonbeams turning it to a mist of silver and shadow. His lips moved soundlessly, invoking who knew what beings. He gave the capstone a small but sharp shove… and the stone moved. It swivelled round, grinding on pebbles beneath its underside before settling again with a dull thud.

Art was silent, but his mouth was hanging open. He forced his jaw to shut, afraid that he looked like the village fool, gawping and incredulous. "Great is the magic of Merlin!" he gasped.

"Magic? Some would see it as such," said the priest. And then, leaning close to the youth, his eyes hollow as those of a skull: "Others would call it an art. Remember this, Art'igen, and if I ever ask you to move stones for me, do not hesitate and have faith. Remember this night, and cast all doubts away."

Merlin was so ardent, so impassioned, that Art felt a thrill of fear run from head to toe. But he bowed his head gravely, and said, "Whatever is the will of the Great Merlin, my mentor."

They returned to the encampment, where Ka-hai still snored beneath the tree, and the horses contentedly cropped grass beneath the Moon. Merlin eased himself onto the mossy ground with a groan—already he suffered the chronic bone-ache that afflicted almost all older folk in Prydn—and soon he was snoring as loudly as Ka'hai, his cloak thrown over his head.

But Art'igen could not sleep, not after seeing that huge stone moved by one man's hand. In silence, he sat staring at the changing sky, thinking on what he had witnessed, while growing excitement knotted the pit of his belly. It was only after Moonset, when the wind sank to a sigh and the little grove was black with unbroken shadow, that he finally allowed himself to sleep.

And as he lay curled on the grass, Merlin got up and sat over him, singing and humming, casting his spells, treating with the spirits and elements that they would protect and assist this dark young bear, son of the Head Dragon.

The three travellers reached the henge of Marthodunu early the next day. The sky was fair and the huge banks towered high and bright beneath the Sun. Unlike Deroweth, there were timber building actually built upon the earthworks, their roofs shining in the early light. On one side of the settlement, the coiled snake of Abona made a natural watery boundary before winding its way across the flatlands: following its course, a traveller would eventually reach Deroweth and the Place-of-Light. It was the umbilical cord that bound the holy places of the land together.

Merlin entered Marthodunu first, through the great Northeastern gap. Art'igen and Ka'hai followed, all eyes, trying not to gawk at the unfamiliar sights around them. To one side, a priestess sat moaning and incanting, her face blue-grey with clay, mimicking a corpse's pallid visage. She squatted above the unmarked tomb of the guardian of the gate, a young girl whose stunted bones had marked her as chosen many centuries ago. Merlin tossed a chip of bluestone at the priestess and she smiled a toothless grin and bowed, swaying on her bony painted legs before placing the chip on a gathered pile of offerings given by incoming travellers—shells, pebbles, bones, flints.

Further on, at the heart of the huge complex, was a mighty mound, raised by the hand of man, but nearly as big as a natural hill. A ditch surrounded it, and water glistened palely at its foot, a sheet of blue mirroring the morning sky. Beyond the mound stood more timber buildings and an earthen enclosure that resembled a small arena or amphitheatre. It was here that most of the people were heading.

It seemed that many of the chiefs of the Five Cantrevs and their wives and warriors had arrived during the night or around dawn. They clustered by the amphitheatre surrounded by crude wagons heaped with furs and grain to offer to the priests of the henge and to use for barter with each other.

Ka'hai and Art were now staring openly, unable to feign adolescent disinterest any longer. These people, men and women alike, were as magnificent as the tellers-of-tales had painted them. One highborn woman had fire-red hair, caught up in golden wires, and a crescent necklace of imported jet from the north. Another was almost impossibly old, her wrinkled face dominated by tribal scars and a lip-stud that distended her mouth, but she appeared to have much power and prestige—thick cones of pure, decorated gold fastened her dress, and amber droplets swung from the ends of her grey braids. One lord was tall as a spear, with tattoos of beasts on his body, and he shaved his face and the sides of his head, which left a huge tufted plain of grain-golden hair on top, waving like a flag in the breeze. Yet another was muscled and dark of aspect, with a plate of fine gold stretched out upon a linen tunic and jet plugs in ears and the bottom of his nose. They all jostled and shouted, trying to establish dominance, along with their equally bright contingents of warriors, all boasting, bragging, and strutting in their finery, while their less lordly companions, wrapped in undyed sheepskins, unloaded the carts and started bargaining with the crowds of onlookers who had come in from the nearby farmlands. Some had even brought girls to marry off—the maidens giggled and tittered, making eyes at the handsomest, most gold-rich warriors.

A lanky priest in a brown robe approached Merlin and spoke to him earnestly. A moment later, he came over and beckoned to Art'igen. "Come," he said in a sharp voice. "You must prepare yourself."

Art was led away by the priest, but not before Ka'hai has whispered, 'Good luck to you, little brother!" in his ear. He was taken across the great enclosure, up to the earth-turfed house that squatted like a crouched beast on its lofty banks. The house had a low door, its gable painted with chevrons. The priest thrust aside a screen barring the doorway and pushed the lad inside.

The interior of the hut was boiling-hot; Art had never felt anything like it, even on the hottest summer's day. A huge fire roared in a pit sunken into the ground, and around it clustered half a dozen lads, stripped and shining with sweat, all looking decidedly uneasy. Behind them clustered some priests, greasy-haired in the heat, faces florid above their long beards. They chanted and sang; one drummed. Behind them, where the flames from the pit cast little illumination, were a row of bowed heads, bald heads, heads devoid not only of hair but flesh: Ancestors brought out of old tombs to witness their children's children ten times over become men of the tribe. Some were merely bones, on others drying had caused bone and skin to fuse; some of the latter were dressed in clothes, as if they were living men, with ochre rubbed on their bony cheeks to give the semblance of renewed life.

"You—take off your tunic," ordered the head priest, turning to Art'igen. Art quickly obeyed, and the priests clustered round inspecting him for any flaws. A boy with a shrivelled arm, a clubbed foot or a sway back would never be a proper man...though he could sometimes find a haven amongst the priests and shamans.

"He will pass," said another priest, nodding. "He is sound and hale."

"Kneel," the chief priest ordered, gesturing to the other lads to likewise get down on their knees.

Art knelt down, sweat starting to trickle along his spine. The priests were chanting loudly now, lifting up great switches made of bound willow withies. Crying out, they struck the bare backs of the kneeling youths repeatedly, beating any evil spirits from their flesh, making them pure before the watching Ancestors and the ever-present spirits that resided in the earth, the air, the water and the holy fire.

When they were finished, they cast the bloodied branches into the fire and danced around it as they were consumed. Then they took the hot ashes, rubbed them over the boys' wheals, and painted symbols on their brows with them. Through all of this, the young men remained silent, not a sound passing between them—one groan of pain, one tear in a smoke-filled eye, and that lad would be judged a failure, a child to be returned to his mother's hearth for another year.

Once this face painting was completed, the head priest led the boys from the hut and herded them across the grass to the circular arena, the ring within a greater ring, which Art had noted when he arrived. It was still thronged with the visiting chiefs, who sat on sheepskin rugs in the fore; behind them clustered the humble people of the surrounding lands, craning to see the display. For boys from the outlying farmsteads and small settlements, this parade was a good thing—often, if they showed themselves worthy, they would be invited to join a chief's warband. This was Art's great hope; as much as he honoured his foster-father, he wanted to go beyond the forge, to see the great temples spoken of in song, to fire the bow and wield the axe in defence of the green hills of his home.

Inside the earthen amphitheatre, small and cramped in the shadow of the Great Barrowhill, the boys began to march in a circle. Pipes wailed, drums thumped, and the youths danced with wild abandon—the fire-warrior's first dance in honour of the Risen Sun. High they leapt, nimble as the deer, supple as the salmon, reaching toward the Bright Lord of the Everlasting-Sky. The men and women on the banks shouted and catcalled, choosing favourites, jeering at those who were not light of foot or pleasing to look at. Art was glad he did not hear any insults thrown his way.

The drums and pipes died suddenly and a cudgel thrust into his hand. One older lad, already an adult, was coming toward him from amid the gaggle of priests and their followers. His face was painted in red and black stripes and his oversized mouth was stretched in a nasty grin. In his hand, he held a spiky blackthorn club, which he swung menacingly.

On the banks, the tribesfolk and foreign visitors began to chant and stamp their feet. The dull thudding made the ground reverberate beneath Art'igen's bare soles, almost as if the earth itself had gained an audible heartbeat. Art's own heart speeded up, as both fear and excitement blazed through him, and then he made a rush for the older youth.

The lad sneered and hopped easily out of the way and Art stumbled past him, almost falling with the impetus of his rush. The crowd booed. Face burning, he whirled on his heels and lashed out again at his smirking opponent. He was obviously quicker than the other lad expected, and this time Art's cudgel met with his wrist. He jerked back in surprise and then red rage filled his eyes. He was very tall and long-legged, and he sprang high into the air, a warrior's leap, and aimed a vicious blow at Art's head with his foot. Art'igen anticipated his move; he had seen a horse kick out under an unwelcome rider many times on Ech-tor's holding. Dropping his weapon, he grabbed the other youth's leg and tipped him over backwards. He fell with a crash on the sandy soil, breathless and gasping in shock and dismay. Art'igen hurled himself onto his chest, pinning him down, and tore the blackthorn club from his fingers, holding it menacingly above him as if to strike a deathblow.

Behind him, he could hear the chiefs and warriors from the Five Cantrevs shouting and clamouring: "Finish him, boy! It is an honour to be blooded on your first day as a man! Kill the weakling!"

Art looked down at his adversary, his face paint smeared, his chalk-whitened hair filled with dirt. He was only perhaps a year older than Art himself. His eyes were still defiant but fear had crept into them. Art raised the club, to an accompanying roar from the audience. It would be an honour; he could bestow the youth's spirit upon the ever-eager Ancestors who always welcomed new faces in the realm of the Not-living.

But no. He could not do it. It seemed too great a waste… He looked down at his vanquished adversary and prodded him with his foot. "What is your name?"

The young raised his head. "Betu'or. Of the people of Marthodunu."

"Betu'or—a name of two meanings, am I right? King of Battle and Knower-of-Graves. Well, Betu'or, you will live this day and the knowing of graves may not be for many years yet. Be glad this day, for I give you back your life, which was mine to take. Some would not show mercy but I say it is better to keep a valorous man of the tribe to fight our truefoes. Rise now, and go. "

Betu'or scrambled up and sped from the enclosure. Some of the men in the crowd booed in disappointment, but the women were laughing and clapping, and eventually their menfolk put their bloodlust aside and followed suit.

The chief priest of Marthodunu swept towards Art'igen and took hold of his arm, raising it on high. "This one today shall be proclaimed a Man-of-the-Tribe, free to wed, to wield arms, to participate in rites to please the Old Ones and the spirits. He is born anew, his life as a man just begun, and a new name he must have. What shall it be?"

"He fought like a bear out there!" someone yelled from the crowd. "Like a bear!"

The priest inclined his snowy head. "He was Art'igen…the bear-that-is-to-be. A true Bear he is now, and true is the spirit if the Bear within him.. From this moment forward let him be known as Ardhu—the Dark Bear."

"Ardhu, Ardhu!" chanted the crowd, and the sound of Art's new adult name echoed round the steep walls of Marthodunu and reached up to touch the very vault of heaven and the realm of Sun and Moon.

CHAPTER EIGHT

Ardhu and Ka'hai spent the rest of the night getting very, very drunk on beer and fermented honey-mead. It was the first time Art had been permitted to drink alcohol, which was deemed fit only for adult males, and he was going to make the most of it. The Merlin kept an eye on them both from a perch high on the henge bank, and pretended to give them disapproving glances (although he was secretly amused.)

Finally, when Ardhu fell over, clutching his belly, and started to retch, the shaman wandered over and poked him with the tip of his staff. "Enough for now," he said. "You need some rest. When the chiefs meet tomorrow to choose a High Chief, I want you to witness the event with a clear head and undimmed eye! Do you understand?"

"Yes, Merlin," said Ardhu meekly. "But I really haven't drunk that much…"

He rose to prove his steadiness to the older man, and promptly fell over with a yelp. Ka'hai bellowed with laughter, his big bluff face red and shiny.

"Come on, Ka'hai, help me lift him," Merlin ordered curtly, and together they carried the protesting Ardhu to Merlin's tent, which was pitched by the river. The tents and yurts of the lords of the West were all around, brightly decorated, some billowing pungent smoke from their smoke-holes. Torches and rush lights flared, while warriors paraded by with huge hounds trundling at their heels and beautiful sloe-eyed women on their arms. It seemed a magic world of nobility and splendour to a youth who had spent nearly all his days at Echtor's smithy, away from even the normal daily life of the local villages. "Merlin…" he said suddenly. "Now that I am accounted a man…I want to be a warrior. Like them!" He flapped his arm wildly in the direction of the men with their dogs and daggers and haughty amber-draped women.

A chunky man with a nose flattened by many a fight and a face as coarse and lumpen as a slab of weathered sarsen, scowled in Art's direction. "You looking for a good thumping? What are you staring at, boy?"

"Not your ugly face I'm sure, Bohrs!" Merlin retorted, peering over Art's shoulder at the squat warrior. "Actually, my ward was…admiring you! Now come and help an old man, and cease your bluster."

The scowling warrior, not daring to cross a priest, especially one from Khor Ghor, scowled ever deeper but obeyed without question. Joining Ka'hai and Merlin, he grabbed one of Ardhu's arms and dragged his dead weight over to Merlin's tent. "My thanks, noble Bohrs!" gasped Ardhu, clutching feebly at Bohrs' cloak, while the older man curled his lip contemptuously and tried to rip the cloth free. "If I ever become a great warrior, I would have the likes of you in my band!"

"That's about as likely as a flying sow!" snorted Bohrs, and he stumped off with great aplomb, his dignity hurt by the familiarity of this silly, young drunk.

Merlin dragged his ward inside the tent and pushed him down on a pallet of dry grass; his eyes shut almost as his head hit the floor. Ka'hai, exhausted by lugging his little brother about the henge, fell forward in a drunken stupor, half over Ardhu's bed, like some giant, shaggy guardian dog. His jaw dropped and the usual ear-splitting snores came out.

"Sleep now," Merlin ordered, making a sign of protection over both young men. "Tomorrow you must be bright and alert. It will be a great day for Albu, the day the high one returns to the Temple and the Men of the Cantrevs!"

Ardhu awoke with an aching head that beat like a drum. Outside the tent, he could hear real drums, and the low, mournful bleating of horns. Scrambling up, his stomach lurched and he thought for a moment that he would be sick.

Instantly the Merlin was beside him, thrusting a beaker full of a foul-smelling liquid into his hands. "Drink swiftly—it will ease the griping of your belly," he ordered. "Then you must get ready, we must hurry so that we can get a good position at the meeting."

Art hastily downed the brew and almost immediately felt less ill. Colour returned to his cheeks. He stood up and let the Merlin fuss around him like an old woman, greasing his dark hair with bear-fat and binding it back from his brow with a copper diadem wreathed in snake-like designs. Then the priest took a tunic of soft leather from a container of sweet-smelling bark, and pulled it over Ardhu's head, fastening buttons of amber with golden crosses on them that were symbols of the Eternal Sun. It was a regal outfit and Ardhu's eyes were round with amazement. Surely, he would stand out a mile, and look too ostentatious amongst his elders and betters. But he dared not question Merlin's motives. He kept his silence as the older man reached into his belt-pouch and drew out a tiny clay box, which held two very ancient hair-tresses made of beaten sheet gold. They were battered from wear; ancestral goods handed down from generation to generation, gathering power as they gathered years. Deftly he clipped them on to two small braids he had made in the front of Art's hair.

"I...I cannot accept this gift!" Art was stunned, since gold was only for great chiefs and their kin, and men of magic and art. Not for poor boys of unknown parentage. "This gold is an heirloom, belonging by rights only to the children of the last man who owned it."

Merlin looked at him solemnly. "And so it does, Ardhu. All I have given you—the tunic, the armbands and the hair tresses are your legacy. They have lain in wait for you many a year. There were your father's possessions."

"My father!"

"Did you not think you had one?" Merlin's bushy eyebrows rose quizzically. "Did you think a spirit begat you, as is rumoured about the Merlin?"

Ardhu flushed. "I never much thought on my blood-parents; Ech-tor and Ka'hai were father and brother to me. And you, Merlin, acted as the kindly grandfather."

"Not so kindly perhaps," said Merlin, lips narrowing. "I had my reasons."

"So who am I?" Art turned and stared into Merlin's eyes as if hoping to read the truth of his lineage there. "Who wore this tunic and ancient gold in his hair? And where is he now? Is he here? Is that why you brought me, so that he could witness my initiation as a Man-of-the-Tribe?"

Merlin shook his head. "He is dead and in his barrow these ten years. He was a fine youth, but his head was hot, and the lure of the flesh led him astray. I had hopes he would be a great chief once, possibly the highest of all chiefs. But he locked himself away in his own little world with his woman and turned his face from the greater matters of Albu—in the end, it proved his undoing. He trusted where no trust should have been given, and during a feast in which he hoped to make pacts of peace, the men of the Sea pulled their curved knives and stabbed him to death."

Ardhu's face was taut, full of mixed emotions. This news scarcely seemed real; it was as wild as a tale told round the fires. "His name...you have not told me his name!"

"Ardhu, your sire was U'thyr. U'thyr Pendraec, the Terrible Head. You are Ardhu Pendraec, true scion of Uthyr's line and of the ancient house of Belerion through your mother, Y'gerna. You will be a leader like your father. And who knows what else you will be, Dark Bear."

Filled with shock, Art followed Merlin out into the enclosure of Marthodunu. He was the son of U'thyr Pendraec! Who had not heard the tales of the young chief who had fought many battles and stolen the dark-eyed wife of Gorlas of Belerion? The chief who had been Prydn's great hope...until he vanished into the West, sequestering himself with his bride Y'gerna until his untimely death by treachery. They said that after his death, the tribe had feasted for ten weeks upon his burial mound, slaughtering cattle every night and tossing their remains into the ditch. Seven captive Sea-Raiders had been dispatched to the Otherworld with him, their cremations lying over his face in rough, squat urns, their spirits bound to serve him for eternity.

"Art, stop dreaming; we are coming to the meeting place," said Merlin, and glancing up, Ardhu saw that they were entering the amphitheatre where he had completed the manhood rites the night before.

The same crowd of chiefs and warriors were there, but the mood had changed. Darkened. Some men were openly arguing, and Ardhu was alarmed to see that many openly carried axes or daggers. No one laughed in this grey morn, the ribaldry and merriment of the night past was forgotten.

"Here is the Merlin, wise priest of Khor Ghor!" someone called, and Ardhu felt a hundred pairs of eyes swivel in his direction. He raised his chin, trying to look stern and unconcerned, despite feeling distinctly uncomfortable. "Ask his counsel in this matter!"

The chief with the horsetail of yellow hair who Art had noticed the previous day stepped forward. "I am Per-Adur. I believe I should be battle-lord of Albu; no, all of Prydn! I have never been bested in battle, and show my enemies no mercy. None will set foot on our shores without meeting my blade and my arrows."

"No, you are too young and green for such an honour. I have taken more heads that you!" Ardhu saw Bohrs strutting about, a whole row of gleaming daggers thrust into his belt. "Merlin! Tell this fool that he is unsuitable!"

Merlin frowned. "Same old arguments! Same old noise! I swear these fools would argue over each other's prowess even as our shores burned!"

The two rival chiefs were staring at Merlin, their faces grim and angry. "We have been talking and debating all night, magic man," said Per-Adur. "Do not accuse us of taking this matter too lightly! Where were you when men spoke of the fate of Albu the White and Prydn last night?"

"In my bed," said Merlin dryly. "But I am sure many lands were rescued and foes slain in the bottom of your beaker!"

"You mock me!"

"I do! I mock all those who think the loudness of their shouts will put a claim on the lordship of Albu! No, there will be another way; I am high priest of Khor Ghor and I have talked for many Moons...no, Sun-Turnings, even...with my fellow priests from the Great Temple, and from Marthodunu and Suilven and Arb-ar in the Land of the Mother Mountain. We have communed with the spirits, and they have told us a test must be performed... Man must do what is seemingly impossible to do!"

"What is this test?" shouted Bohrs. "I will do it! I am not afraid."

Merlin crooked his hand. "Come, all those who would be master of the Isle of the Mighty. Follow me...if you dare."

Merlin, surrounded by a bevy of priests and seers from the various temples of the Five Cantrevs, left the entrance gap of Marthodunu, a crowd of warriors surging behind him. Ardhu and Ka'hai tagged along in the rear, intrigued, though Ardhu was less interested than he might have been yesterday. His mind was churning, filled with the wonder of his revealed parentage. He wondered if Ka'hai knew.

Before long, the party reached the grove of birches where Merlin, Ardhu and Ka'hai had spent the night on their journey to Marthodunu. Merlin and the priests went in first, chanting and hailing the spirits, then, when they were satisfied that no malign forces denied entry to the wood, they beckoned the rest of the party into the trees.

The chieftains poured into the grove, trampling the foliage, slipping on leaves and rotten mushrooms. Ardhu looked through the sea of foliage and moving bodies and saw the Merlin standing beside the huge burial cist with the cup-marked lid—the stone he had moved with his magic.

"Below this capstone rests the bones of a great warrior," Merlin said solemnly. "One who lived in the elder days, when men were as giants. Tall as a sapling he stood, so big that when he died the very flames of the pyre could not consume him totally, and his kindred had to pack his ashes into the straight bone of his back! But that was not all that was remarkable about him. He was a great man who knew the secret of bronze and the way of the warrior, and to mark his prowess, he bore at his belt a knife from distant Ar-morah, land of our kin. Carnwennan it was named, and if his enemies saw it unsheathed, shining like the Sun itself, they trembled and quailed in fright. That blade lies in the tomb, waiting for a new great ruler to take it up. The man that moves this great stone and takes up Carnwennan shall be the rightful master of the Five Cantrevs. He will be war-chief of Albu, and lord of the Great Trilithon, Door into Winter."

The chieftains murmured darkly, looking one to the other as if Merlin had gone mad. He was, after all rumoured to have run wild once, during his quests for wisdom as a youth.

Then, slowly, they approached the capstone, long lines of men, grim faced and determined. Their usual bravado had vanished and been replaced by a steely determination. Their task was at hand—shouting and display would do no good. It would not move the impassive ancestral stone.

Bohrs was the first. He whipped off his shaggy cloak and flexed arm muscles bulging under a lattice of tattooing. "I am known for my strength. I'll wager that I am strongest amongst you. If any shall move this stone, it is likely to be me!"

So saying, he leaned down and set his shoulder against the mighty capstone. He pushed. Nothing. Grunted and strained. Nothing. Red-faced he grabbed the stone in both arms, clasping it as he would a lover, and pushed, grappled, struggled. Curses fell from his lips, sweat channelled down his face. Still nothing happened.

"Out of my way!" Another lordling pushed him aside. "You've failed. I will try my hand!"

And so on it went, with both the mighty and the lesser all trying to move the stone. It would not budge, not even an inch. Men sweated and swore and called on the gods and spirits and the priests to bless them, but nothing seemed to work

Ardhu, standing with Ka'hai at the back of all the activity, could only marvel at the vain display of strength. It seemed impossible that he had seen this very stone move under the hand of the ageing Merlin. He was beginning to wonder if he had dreamt the whole thing.

"That is enough for the day!" Merlin's sharp voice suddenly echoed through the grove. He stood forward, arm upraised to signal a halt. "The Ancestors have favoured no one who has tried to gain the dagger in the stone. You must retire for the night and begin again tomorrow when we are fresh and rested. I will stay here awhile to seek guidance"

Grumbling, the chiefs and warriors left the grove and set up a temporary encampment around its periphery. Ka'hai and Ardhu had no tent, unlike the highest-born chiefs, whose followers had brought supplies from Marthodunu, but that did not bother them. They merely wrapped themselves in their cloaks and nestled down on the grass near a fire, where they lay staring up at the night sky, unable to sleep, still fired up by the excitement of the day.

"What do you think will happen?" Ka'hai whispered to Ardhu sometime after midnight, when the fire at last fell to embers. Above the sky was a dark vault filled by pinpricks of light, a thousand watchful eyes, a thousand souls who had passed over the Great Plain to the Deadlands. "Do you suppose anyone will be able move that stone?"

Ardhu took a deep breath; a strange excitement was knotting his belly. "Ka'hai...Don't go to sleep just yet. Now that its dark and the fire's out, I want to show you something. Quick, while no one's looking..."

Silently the two youths rose. Around them, the camp slumbered, save for a few tottering drunks and a couple of bored guards who leaned on their bows, staring morosely into the night and dreaming of warm skins and sleep.

Quickly and silently, they turned and entered the grove with its precious, hidden treasure. They glanced about furtively, in case they bumped into Merlin, who had still not returned to camp after the unsuccessful testing. "I don't like it here!" whispered Ka'hai, his face white. "The old one in his tomb might not be happy with all that's been going on. Merlin might not be happy either, to have us poking about..."

Ardhu put a finger to his lips. "Hush, Ka'hai. Be brave. Can you see Merlin? Wherever he is, it isn't here."

Side by side, they approached the cist where Carnwennan lay amid the ashes of its long-dead master. Moonlight, slanting through the tree branches, danced on its capstone, the immovable stone that had been the cause of so much pain and frustration during the day. Fireflies wheeled in the air, filling the glade with an eerie, iridescent light.

"What are you planning to do?" asked Ka'hai uneasily. "We've looked at this thing all day!"

"Ka'hai, the night we bedded down here, Merlin brought me to this burial-stone. He showed me something I thought I would never see."

"What was that?"

"How a man, an ordinary mortal man, might move a stone many times his weight."

"But Merlin...is half of the spirit world, you know that! The rest of us are of common flesh. You have seen how the mightiest warriors failed to shift the block."

"But Ka'hai, he told me, from his own lips, that it could be done. Told me, and showed me! He told me I could do it myself, if I had faith!"

Ka'hai laughed. "You must be dreaming, little brother!"

"Then if I am dreaming...let me wake!"

Ardhu sprang forward, placing his hands upon the capstone. It was cold to touch, ice-cold, the lichens and moss slimy with night-dew. "Spirits, be with me this hour!" he whispered, and then he pushed with all his might, using the sideways movement he had seen Merlin use.

At first, nothing happened. Ka'hai shook his head. "Come away before we're in trouble!"

Ardhu ignored him and pushed again, shoving the cist-lid in a Sunwise direction as if he sought to spin it in a circle. And suddenly there was a noise, as before, a deep, ominous groan as if the stone itself cried out, then the sound of pebbles crushing and stone grinding fitfully on stone.

"By the Everlasting Sky, it's moving!" Ka'hai yelped, his eyes bulging in terror and amazement.

Ardhu kept pushing. The stone was turning swiftly now, shifting to one side, arching out and away from the granite cist below. Air full of the scent of cold earth and ancient decay blasted up into his face.

"I...I've done it!" He dropped to his knees beside the stone, gasping, breathless with exertion and excitement.

Ka'hai ran over, throwing himself down beside the younger boy. He peered into the cist. "Look, there, I can see it, I can see it!"

He pointed downwards with a tremulous hand. Ardhu, still gasping for air, peered into the cist. Deep below, he could see carvings on the stone, a pattern of human feet that symbolised the walk of the dead from life. A broken urn, lying on its side, spilled out ash and bone…and a short, broad dagger of archaic design. Its bronze blade was green from the long passage of years, but the hilt, wrought of antler and affixed with rare, white-gold rivets, still gleamed like the rising Moon, as fair and unmarred as the day it was made.

"I can't believe it!" Ka'hai sprawled over the edge of the burial-chest, reaching down. Carefully he brought up the dagger Carnwennan, frail but beautiful in the Moon's misted glow. "Art, you've done it! This must mean…you…"

At that moment, a torch flared in the glade. Then another. And another. The Merlin strode out of the shadows, his eyes like obsidian flakes, and his mouth drawn into a severe line. Behind him were other holy men from Marthodunu and elsewhere, and, hard on their heels, packs of craning chieftains and warriors.

"What is going on here?" demanded Merlin, striking the tip of his staff into the earth with a noise like muffled thunder. "Why have you come to this holy place, unbidden, when all others are abed? This is not a place for childish games!"

The two youths sat motionless, dazzled by the torchlight and by Merlin's anger, too ashamed and fearful to speak.

One of the warriors spoke instead: "Lord Merlin, what is in the big lad's hand?"

Merlin rounded on the youth. "Show me, Ka'hai!"

Ka'hai lifted up Carnwennan, proffering it to the priest. "Merlin, please don't be angry. Ardhu was just showing me…."

An expression of genuine shock rushed over Merlin's face. His visage became skull-white, drawn. "The dagger! The sign of lordship! Ka'hai, was it you who moved the stone to get it?"

Ka'hai licked his lips. A look of longing filled his eyes. "Yes…Yes, it was me. I moved the stone and claimed Carnwennan! Does that make me lord?"

He turned and suddenly met Ardhu's shocked, reproachful gaze. Instantly, he hung his head in shame, tears burning his eyes. "No, I lie. Forgive me. I did not touch the stone. Ardhu was the one who moved it…Ardhu is the one who rightfully has won the sword."

So saying, he turned to Ardhu and bowed low, handing the fragile blade to its rightful owner.

"The sword has been taken from the stone!" cried Merlin, striding over to Ardhu and holding out his torch so that the flickering light fell over the youth's face, revealing him fully to the throng. "The spirits have spoken. Prydn has a new leader, come to raise our isle to the greatness of old and to repel our sworn enemies!"

There was an angry murmur from the gathered tribesmen; a hum like a hive of infuriated bees. "But he is only a boy!" someone shouted. "A beardless lad!"

"Yesterday you saw this boy made a man," said Merlin sternly. "Now you see the man become your King. Praise him! Ardhu, lord of the West, the chosen one." Turning, he knelt in the leaf-mulch by Ardhu's feet, his head bowed. "I, the Merlin of Khor Ghor, do swear to serve you until the breath is gone from my body or the sky falls, whichever comes first."

"This is madness," another chief roared from the shadows. "Even if this callow youth was acceptable, who, by the holy Sun, is he? We do not know his father's house or mother-line. He may not even be a true son of Prydn, for all we know!"

Merlin sprang to his feet; smiling now, fierce and wolfish. His voice was the crack of a whip. "Ardhu's blood could not be truer. For he is the son of U'thyr Pendraec, the Terrible Head, who once ranked high among you. His mother-line is Y'gerna of Belerion, the Land of Tin. It was I who worked the magic that brought that pair together, I who took their child

73

from his cradle so that he might be raised to become a great leader! I, the Merlin, tell you this—is there any man who would gainsay me?"

There was a stunned silence. The warriors still looked surly, but there was doubt in their expressions too. And in many of the more youthful men, there was building excitement. They had been chained too long, hanging on the cloak-tails of elder chiefs who wanted to drink and recount the old days rather than defend their territories from the peril from the sea.

"He looked on me with favour!" The harsh, deep voice of Bohrs suddenly rang out. Bohrs, who had scowled at Ardhu on his first night as a Man-of-the-Tribe. "Yestereven, after the festivities, the new King of Albu looked on me with favour! He asked me to assist him to his tent! I am truly blessed! I will pledge my dagger-arm to him!"

"And I too!" A lighter voice rang out; tall Per-Adur with his horse-mane yellow hair. "I would have moved the stone myself but had not the strength. The boy-king did. The spirits have spoken!"

Merlin smiled, sly and secret in the shadows of the grove. A victory. It was only one battle, and the very first, but he and his young ward had won.

At the next full Moon Ardhu, the Dark Bear, son of the Terrible Head, mother-born of the Tin-lords, was brought to the temple of Khor Ghor to receive the blessing of the Ancestors, and to accept the Sacred Signs of Kingship from Merlin.

The young man was dressed in his father's tunic and hair-tresses, and Carnwennan was bound at his side in a deerskin sheath, its rusty blade replaced anew by the arts of Ech-tor. Silent and stern, his body painted with protective symbols, he was guided by priests along the Sacred Avenue, past the great Sun-Stone and the Guardians, and into the sanctity of the Khor Ghor itself.

Merlin stood in the shadow of the Great Trilithon, beside the Stone of Adoration. He was dressed in his full priest's regalia: a painted skin cloak and long robe fringed with the teeth and claws of many beasts. A bull's horn headdress sat on his brow and his face was wreathed in chalk spirals that circled his dark eyes, making them look huge and surreal. By his feet rested a woven basket, its contents shrouded by a skin.

"Come forward," he beckoned, "and kneel before the spirits of this place, who rule the movements of the heaven and confer fertility upon the earth. Be humble in their presence and those of the Ancestors who made you, their long dead flesh into yours."

Ardhu sank to his knees. He glanced upwards, trying to take in the sights few mortal eyes were permitted to see. The stones—how high they were, how massive! The shimmering, micaceous sandstone block of the Altar-stone loomed above him and beyond it the tallest of the blue-tinged Ancestor-stones, which had come from the Western lands, the birthplace of the Merlin. On his right, one cumbrous trilithon faced due West, and on its face he could see the rectangular carving of She-Who-Watches-the-Dead. She had no eyes, no face, just a carved crook springing from her head, but he could feel her presence watching him, deciding the plan of his life and the hour of his death. He shivered slightly.

"Look at me, Ardhu son of U'thyr." Merlin spoke, his voice deep with emotion. Today is a day of great portent, of great change. A new era is dawning in Albu, in all of Prydn, and you and I will be as Sun and Moon, rising in splendour and power before the people. Do you swear to follow my guidance is this venture?"

"I do swear it."

"And will you honour the Stones and those who have gone before?"

"I will honour them."

"And will you give your life for the land, if it is asked of you?"

Ardhu hesitated; a cloud streaked over the face of the Sun, and shadows suddenly galloped around the stones, turning their stark faces sinister, frowning. "I…I…will..."

"Then you shall be granted the symbols of high chiefdom, which no man has borne for hundreds of years, since before our father's father's time."

Merlin drew forth from his basket a round shield embossed with bronze. The rectangular image of the Guardian was graven on its gleaming surface, which was the colour of the dying Sun at Midwinter. "This is Wyngurthachar, Face of Evening. Let it shield you as you shield the folk of Prydn."

Reverently he fastened the shield on Ardhu's left shoulder; it was heavy, and Ardhu staggered a moment at the unexpected weight before recovering his balance. "My shield," he said. "Shield of Albu against her foes."

Merlin reached into the basket again, drawing out an item wrapped in dried moss. The covering crumbled away beneath his fingers to reveal a golden lozenge, incised by mystical, geometric designs. He held it aloft, catching the Sunlight; it flashed as though in answer to the burning orb in the heavens. "The breastplate of the Sky. Some say it was once used as a tool to assist the architects of Khor Ghor, others that it plots the motions of the Sun, and the dance of the rising stars."

He fastened the plate to Ardhu's tunic with thin leather thongs, before lifting up the last item from the woven container. It was a ceremonial mace, its polished head wrought from a fossil. Five lightning-like decorations of bone encircled the wooden handle, their number signifying the five trilithons of Khor Ghor. "This is Rhon-gom, the lightning-Mace of kingship," said Merlin. "With it, you may smite down your enemies as lightning smites the earth."

Ardhu took the mace, running his fingers over its smooth dome, feeling its energy flow into him. It was as if all his forefathers, from their long houses under the hill, were passing their strength and courage to him. "If I can be even half as worthy a ruler as my Ancestors, I will not have lifted this mace in vain," he whispered to the all-seeing sky, the all-knowing stones.

Merlin gestured the young chieftain toward a screen raised before the left-hand stone of the southern trilithon known as the Gate of Kings. This trilithon had the finest tooling and crafting of the hard sarsen, giving the structure a very sharp and precise appearance above all the others. Art frowned; what could be behind the screen of stretched deerskin, shielded from all eyes except those of holy men and ghosts?

"One of the Hallows of Prydn lies behind that covering," said Merlin. "Only a true leader, a true king, can touch it and live."

Reaching out, the Shaman thrustthe screen away.Ardhu gasped. There, fitted within the stone itself, was a dagger of gold, longer and thinner than those used in the West—a thing of great beauty, sgining brightly as the afternoon sunlight slanted into the great circle. Beside it, were several large, glame-coloured bronze axes, also beaten into the hard sarsen, and around them dozens of smaller axe carvings.

"Symbols of kingship," said Merlin. "The sword of the Sun and the axe of the Sky. Come, forward, Ardhu of Prydn and set your hand upon this stone, your legacy, your destiny."

Ardhu reached out a trembling hand. What if the Merlin was wrong? What if he proved unacceptable in some way? Would fire gush from heaven and smite him?

But no…his palm came to rest upon the shiny, smooth gold, hot from the Sun, and no angry rebuttal came from heavens or earth.

"It is done!" Merlin shouted, and now his voice was great, bouncing around the circles, carrying to the priests and chiefs and warriors gathered outside the banks of the temple. "The rightful ruler has set his hand upon the Sword-in-the-Stone! The kings of old have return at last to the green fields of Albu the White, and a new Age of Men has begun!"

CHAPTER NINE

"A king must have a suitable dwelling place, a pre-eminent camp where he may gather his warriors and confer with them." Merlin shuffled around his hut in Deroweth, his silvered hair incandescent in the watery early morning light streaming through the door. An acolyte in a grubby robe was attending his fire-pit, baking bannocks for the priest and the young king who still lay abed under a pile of furs.

"But why, Merlin?" Art rolled over, stifling a yawn with his fist, looking both sleepy and impossibly young. "I like being here with you, my friend and advisor. And Deroweth is well known to all as a place of great learning and might—and so it has been for many generations."

Merlin shook his head. "Your position is still precarious, because of your youth and the circumstances of your birth. If you stay here for too long, wicked tongues will wag and men will say you are my pawn, a puppet-king under the control of the priests."

"And do you not control me?" Ardhu said carelessly, flopping onto his back as he yanked on his tunic, trousers and boots. "Since you are telling me to get out, and I must obey whether I wish it or not?"

Merlin shot him a sour look. "If I did not know you were jesting, well, you are not so old or so mighty that I might not tan your hide!"

"Hah!" Art smoothed down his sleek dark hair and twined a bronze circlet around it. "Like to see you try."

"Do not tempt me beyond endurance, whelp! Now come, I will show you the place I think may be suitable for building."

The priest and the young chief left the hut and strolled down the metalled road to the river, joining the well-worn track that led toward Place-of-Light. It was a fine day, with Sunlight rippling on the swell, and dragonflies whirring and darting above the reeds on the water's edge. Halfway along, not far from the barrow-ridge of the Seven Kings, Merlin turned aside and lead Ardhu into a boggy field. The twin banks of the Avenue cut across it, running down towards the curving silver snake of the river and the robbed stone-pits of the Old Circle. Above, shadowing the sacred pathway, rose a mighty hill with a tip like the prow of a ship jutting toward the eastern Sunrise.

Merlin gestured to it. "Your domain, Ardhu. Can you not see it? A huge fort of stout oak, gazing out toward not only Khor Ghor and Deroweth, but to Harrow and Magic Hill. A place of warriors …a place of legends!"

Arthur gazed up at the hill, its banks green with oak and elm, and silver birch with graceful boughs that fluttered like pennants against the rain-washed sky. His mind whirled, and suddenly he could envision all that his mentor had said—earthen ramparts and wooden palisades, and a mighty hall the likes of which had never before been crafted in Albu. "What is this place called?" he asked.

Merlin stared at the tree-clad heights, shadows stretching down from its prow-like tip. "Kham-El-Ard. The crooked High Place."

"I am surprised no one has built here before."

"It has been thought of as a haunt. A pool gathers at the foot of the hill that retreats and then grows, like the tides, like the Moon…a place of women's magic. This magic has kept men away. That, and spirits from the hunters' time. In the time before Dreams they came to the pool and gave thanks for their kills with gifts of flints and weapons."

"I fear no ghosts." Ardhu stepped forward. "I am glad you have showed me this place, Merlin. I think much can be accomplished here."

Merlin nodded. "I have already sent for great woodworkers in both East and West to come here. They are following the Tin-routes across land even as we speak. Many men want to catch a glimpse of you, even beyond the Five Cantrevs. Word of a King returned to Khor Ghor has spread like a summer fire!"

"Merlin, let us explore this hill, and not return to Deroweth till late. If this hill is to be the place of my high seat, I want to know every inch of it."

The shaman nodded and the young king and the older man walked into the shadow of the great hill of Kham-El-Ard. Skirting its broad base, they reached an area where water rose from the ground and weeds and fronds waved in the wind. Trees and brush grew thickest here, twining and twisting, branches forming an impenetrable backdrop to a round pool formed between the bank and a wide curve of Abona. Tendrils of fog hovered over the seed-speckled surface, showing that the spring feeding the pool was warm, heated by some great furnace within the heart of the earth.

Art knelt on the shore of the pool, breathing heavily, eyes scanning the waters and the dark foliage beyond. Merlin stood motionless, his feet crushing the flint tools of bygone men where they lay on the bank, suddenly reminded of Afallan, where he had loved a bright-eyed priestess called Nin-Aeifa. The dark lake, filled with mystery, the waters of Life and Death…

"Ardhu…someone is here!" he suddenly rasped, and he reached for Art's shoulder with one hand and pulled his dagger from his belt with the other.

Ardhu rose, his gaze intent on the waters. The mist was rising more strongly from the surface; coiling up into vast ghost shapes that streamed out upon the wind. Merlin could smell the magic in it, the glamour of Otherness. Time did not advance; it was as if the movement of the Sun himself had stilled, and all the woodland was silent, as if even the birds and beasts held their breath.

There was an eerie tinkling sound, and the mists began to part. Out onto the lake glided a raft, poled by a stately woman. At first glance, she seemed almost a creature of the Un-world, maybe even the spirit of the wild places. Braids stiffened with lime tumbled to her hips; blue faience beads danced along their length. She wore a long, green skirt of twisted thongs interspersed with what seemed to be dried aquatic weeds and all down the front of her deerskin bodice were sewn hundreds of tiny shells and quartzes, swinging and clashing and making merry noise as she moved. Her head was bowed so that her face was hidden, but her exposed hands and throat was daubed with paint made from a paste of fish scale and chalk, which gave her a faintly surreal glitter as the thin Sunlight wandered over her.

"Ardhu the Dark Bear…" Her voice rang out over the pool, a voice of wind and rushing water. "You come to claim your kingdom, and I, the Lady of the lake, come to greet you."

Merlin jumped and his face flushed then paled. That voice…he knew it, dreamt of it when he grew weak and the wants of mortal flesh came upon him, making him bitter and morose. Nights when he turned and groaned in his furs, the arthritis nagging in his back, his brain afire with dreams of long, water-scented hair and white limbs that coiled around him, taking his will, his powers, even as he took his pleasure.

He peered across the water, trying to control the tremble in his hands. Yes, yes, he could see her face more clearly now, and it was she, Nin-Aeifa, one of the Nine Maids of Afallan. But in the intervening years, she had changed. Changed greatly.

Gone was the sprightly, quick-tongued girl who had pressed her dagger to his throat in one instant, then led him to her bed in the next. She was still beautiful, but it was a ruined and surreal beauty: her left eye was blind, milky, an orb that gazed only upon the Otherworld. The other eye was as he remembered, but full of care and sorrow. She was thinner and somehow more regal, the planes of her face sharp as flint beneath the bleached and plaited mass of her hair.

"Nin-Aeifa," he breathed.

"Merlin." She smiled and it was like the Sun lancing through clouds. "I thought we might be bound in some way to each other, even if not in the way I once desired."

Ardhu glanced at his mentor. "You know this...this woman?"

"Indeed," murmured Merlin. "I know her well."

"More than any other living man," said Nin-Aeifa.

"Why have you come here, from the far-off dreaming isle?"

She shook her head and smiled again. "Wise Merlin has been so busy with his young king; he has not noticed what has taken place around the Great Plain. The High Priestess of Afallan heard of the coming of the King, and sent forth a band of priestesses to minister to him, to bring him great gifts of great power. We have built a dwelling in the vale beyond, where the lakes mirror the stars and the Sun. I am chief of those holy women; I am the Lady of the Lake, second only to High Priestess Vy'ahn of Afallan."

She then turned from Merlin and stretched out a hand toward Ardhu. "Dark Bear, come and let me gaze closely upon you. I wish to see the chosen one!"

Ardhu hesitantly waded out into the water. Leaves and weeds curled about his calves. The water was warmer than he expected and strangely soothing.

"Nin-Aeifa, you be careful with him!" barked Merlin. "Remember—he is mine."

Nin-Aeifa smiled again, and this time her expression was cruel. "Yours? You take another man's son, when you will not beget your own? But fear not, the Lady of the Lake shall not interfere with the wiles of the Merlin. Not yet. But the Nine Maidens may claim him at the end, as all go back to Mother Ahn-ann."

Ardhu had now reached the edge of Nin-Aiefa's raft. She knelt down, catching his face in her glittering, glimmering fingers, with nails long and pearled as talons. Her blind, smoky eye, weird and unblinking, was almost pressed up against his own eye. "Yes, you are the one," she said. "I can see into your heart, I see your past and your future. King you will be beyond compare, if you fall not into folly. Merlin has taught you well and no doubt armed you well against your enemies. But I have a weapon beyond peer that waits for the touch of your hand. One of the Lords of eld bore it, its blade forged by magic smiths who came from distant lands of Ice Mountains, and at his death it was consigned to the waters of this sacred pool, an offering to the spirits of this most ancient place."

"And what is this talisman of which you speak?" Ardhu asked through chattering teeth.

"It is called Caladvolc, the Hard Cleft," Nin-Aeifa replied. "Look below you, Ardhu the Dark. It is there. Waiting"

Art stared down into the waters swirling around him. The Lady moved her hand and it seemed to the young chief that the mists lingering over the sacred pool parted, darting away like errant spirits. Below, the water was clear...and something burned orange beneath its surface, down among the waving weeds.

Maybe that is why the water feels warm! Ardhu thought dully. That...that glowing thing, whatever it is, is heating the pool...

As if of its own volition, his hand reached down below the surface of the water. Ripples ran out across the holy spring. He could hear Merlin shouting from the bank, but he could not make out the words; they were remote, unclear, like echoes in a cavern. In the trees above, a bird screamed and he saw the limed hair of the Lady fanning out above him, turned to white ash by the backlight of the Sun. She was smiling, but the smile was not necessarily one of friendship....

He slipped under the water, into the land-under-wave, a kind of otherworld or underworld. All was green-tinged, the Sun above a sickly blob distorted by the swell within the spring. Weeds caressed him, drawing him down...down...into the dark...past broken beakers and lost flint tools, old bones and a half-mouldered wheel with fishes streaming between its spokes.

And there, amidst the detritus, an accumulation of offerings from the time before time, lay a rapier—the longest bladed weapon he had ever laid eyes on, longer even than the famed daggers of the princes of Ar-morah. It was wrought of fine bronze, and on its blade were the chevrons and magic insignias of the long-ago chiefs of Khor Ghor. The light filtering through the spring water bounced off its blade, causing the fiery glow Art had seen from above.

Reaching out, Ardhu grasped the pommel, laced with hundreds of gold pins, and pulled it from its nest of slimy fronds. With a cry, he kicked upwards, leaving that watery underworld and cleaving the surface of the pool like an arrow, the sword held above his head in victory.

"Merlin, I have it!" he cried. "I have the sword Caladvolc!"

"And so you do." The Lady of the Lake spoke behind him. "Soon you must needs use it. The Lake Maidens have received messages that the Sea Folk are raiding anew, coming in ships across the Little Sea and even into Habren's swell; the lands of Duvnon burn even as we speak."

Ardhu grasped the sword, glowing like a firebrand in the Sunlight. "Then I must go to meet them. And prove myself beyond a doubt to the chieftains of this isle."

"It is too soon!" Merlin snarled as he stomped along the trail back to Deroweth with Ardhu following, barely able to keep up with the older man's long, angry strides. "Your camp not even built, the men still doubtful, training only just begun, both theirs and yours. I had hoped inclement tides would have kept the raiders away a bit longer…"

Art increased his pace until he matched that of the priest. His face had suddenly lost its youthful candour and become a granite mask, hard as one of the standing stones of Khor Ghor. "We must manage with what we have. Ka'hai and Ech-tor have brought ponies and horses from the Western moors and they are reasonably trained, if not perfect. Anyone who can sit a horse will ride, even if he must be tied in the saddle! I will ride at their head, as is my place."

Merlin glanced over at the young man. He looked less a boy now, the lines hardening on the sharp planes of his face, showing the man he would soon be—if f he lived that long. Gone were all traces of youthful indecisiveness, of deference to the man who had mentored him—there was a shadow of his father U'thyr in him, but more besides. Something sterner and far greater than U'thyr. "So be it, then, my lord," the shaman said with a wry smile. "You will go, and the gods go with you."

By the next full Moon, the men of Ardhu's warband were ready to journey to the coast. Dressed in leather jerkins studded with copper and cloaks sewn with insignias of their respective families, they gathered at Khor Ghor to receive rallying words from their leader. Each one, armed with a bronze war-axe, a dagger, and a bow, stood proudly in an archway of the circle, every man an equal within the curve of that never-ending ring, no man higher or lower than the next.

Only Ardhu was pre-eminent, the Stone Lord, master of the Great Trilithon. He stood with Merlin upon the height of the huge lintel, with the Face of Evening on his shoulder and Caladvolc in his hand. His green-dark eyes were ringed by spirals of blue war paint, while his hair was plaited ornately and fastened in a knot with a long bone pin. The Sun flashed off the Breastplate of Heaven, making him look indeed like a son of the gods, of the Sun himself.

"Today we ride for Duvnon!" he shouted, his voice echoing in the sanctuary. "Today is the day you set out for immortality! Today is the beginning of a great adventure for all of us, when brave ideals and brave words are turned into brave deeds. Together we will crush our enemies, and all of Prydn will praise us, for as long as the Stones shall stand!"

The warriors began to cheer, raising their daggers to their young lord atop the height of the trilithon. He in turn raised the Lightning-Mace Rhon-gom, and they marvelled to see it, shining pale against the broad blue sky.

Art scrambled down from his high perch, using the secret hemp ladder that hung on the reverse side of the trilithon, and beckoned the men from the sacred enclosure. He led them across the fields to where Ka'hai, Ech-tor and a load of boys in their service were gathered with the horses and ponies. "We ride," declared Ardhu. "Our enemies will not be expecting men on horseback; I have heard they believe we fear horses. Remember, if they speak, do not listen to their words, and do not gaze into their snake-like eyes lest they entrance you. Strike them down as you would strike down a maddened boar! Strike hard and fast for Albu the White…for all Prydn!"

The men cheered again, but some were looking a bit warily at the horses, who stirred uneasily, sensing excitement in the air. Ka'hai and Ech-tor had set to teaching the warband to ride, but it was early days yet, and many a proud would-be warrior had bruised his arse and his pride during a riding lesson. Merlin looked at the men thoughtfully, his brow knitting in a frown. "They are still not sure, they could break faith with you at any time…Ardhu, do you want me to ride with you, hold them in check?"

"No!" Ardhu's reply was vehement, his face stern. "You said yourself they will not heed me if they think I am merely a tool of the priests of Khor Ghor. I must prove myself to them in this battle—or perish."

He whirled away from the older man and reached for the reins of his mare, Lamrai. Swinging up onto her back, he held up Rhon-gom and Carnwennan, the two signs of his kingship. "We ride!" he shouted. "To glory, to a free Prydn…or to death!"

The other men and boys mounted, clumsy but eager, and soon the Great Plain was filled with the dust of thundering hooves and the cries of excited warriors, rising above the wails of the women and children who had come to see them leave. Those left behind huddled in the swaying grass, keening and sobbing, not knowing if any of their loved ones would return from those far distant war-torn coasts.

Merlin stared after the warband, his own heart filled with unrest and foreboding, no different to the weeping women. This was the test above all other tests, and he, great magic-man though he was, did not know if he would see Ardhu Pendraec again in that world, or only in the next.

The journey to the coast seemed to takean eternity. The company stopped in various villages along the way, some friendly, some less so. Occasionally one or two men would slide from their horses and slip silently into the darkness, their nerves broken as the coast approached, but usually some bright-eyed village youth would leave his mother's hearth to ask if he could ride with the young King Ardhu. And so defectors were replaced; indeed, the numbers in the band swelled considerably. And, most importantly, Art's main circle of men remained stalwart and loyal: Bohrs with his blustering voice and brawny arms; Betu'or, whose life Ardhu had spared; Ka'hai, who was as good as a brother to his lord; the twins Bal-in and Bal-ahn, kin of Betu'or; tall Per-Adur with his golden mane and aristocratic manner.

One evening, as they rode through the foggy dusk, Ka'hai sniffed the air. His big, lunkish brow wrinkled. "Art, I can smell burning, somewhere out ahead."

Ardhu took in a deep breath and nodded. "Burning thatch. And worse, I fear. I can also smell the salt; it must be the sea."

"Aye, indeed it is, Lord Ardhu." Bohrs rode up, nodding. "I know it well. We are at the junction of two rivers the Glain and Duv'las, where they meet to flow into the sea. I'll wager the pirates have taken over the arm of the Glein; there were a few rich villages there, where they used to bring in gold from Ibherna and beyond, and export shale and axes."

"Well, there is but one way to find out." Ardhu urged Lamrai forward through the fog.

The band soon reached a cliff top covered with many scrubby trees stunted by continuous blasts of wind from the sea. The mists began to part, and down below they could see a river shining dully in the failing light. On its banks stood the smoking ruins of roundhouses, and the fields that ran up to the base of the cliff were smouldering. Dark shapes lay sprawled in the furrows; it was too far to say for sure that they were men, but Ardhu's band knew they could be nothing else.

Along the riverbank were moored three large foreign ships, their red and black sails furled. The sound of singing and raucous laughter lifted on the night air.

"Let us kill them!" cried Per-Adur, from behind Ardhu and Ka'hai. "Look what they've done, the murdering scum!"

"Silence!" Ardhu raised his hand. "We must not behave as fools. We must approach with stealth, not shouting and rushing in like mad men, with anger taking away our wits! Bal-ahn, you and your brother Ba-lin, go down to the right, and circle the village where it meets the water. You are both strong swimmers, just like a pair of otters; I want you to go out to the raiders' ships. And burn them."

The two brothers—twins born at one birthing and hence thought to share one soul—grinned at each other and nodded. Pulling up the hoods of their deerskin cloaks, they dismounted their horses and slipped away into the shadows.

Ardhu likewise dismounted and passed Lamrai's reigns to Ka'hai. "I will go down first," he said, looking from his foster-brother to the other young men of the warband. "I want to speak to the pirate leader, to let him know that Albu is not his to do what he wills. To let him know there is a high king at Khor Ghor once again."

Ka'hai tried to protest but Art silenced him with a stern look. "Keep your bows ready but do not come seeking me until…" He gazed into the East where the Moon was hovering, a thin white sliver between fleeting clouds. Expertly he deduced its course across the sky, using arts taught to him by Merlin, at night amid the Stones. "Do not come to me until the Moon appears fully over the water. When you do ride down from the cliff, I want the enemy to see you on your horses. They will not be expecting such a sight."

"Take care, Ardhu," Ka'hai's voice was a cracked whisper; he licked his lips nervously." Don't do anything too stupid!"

Art grinned and clasped his foster-brother's shoulder. "You know you can trust me on that score!" Hefting Wyngurthachar onto his shoulder, he vanished into the shadows.

On foot, he wound his way down the hill to the river. The stink of fire and death hung in his nostrils; he felt a cold rage rising up to clench the pit of his belly. Ahead of him reared a sentinel stone, the Ancestor marking the territory of that riverside tribe…but its face was smeared with blackened blood and it leaned at an angle, where the invaders had tried to topple it from its pit, desecrating the site and driving off the spirit of the place. That made the young king even more angry; it was as if all the generations of people of Albu had been violated, the land itself raped by these foreign invaders who cared for nothing but tin and gold.

Passing the teetering stone, he caught sight of a man by the river. He had a woolly black beard to his waist and an aquiline profile. Robes of a lurid purple hue Ardhu had never seen before frothed round his ankles; the hem was fringed with gold wires. He held an ornate cup from which he sipped daintily, almost effeminately. Indeed, Ardhu thought he looked rather womanish in his flowing, brightly coloured garb; the rims of his eyes were also painted with dark smoky lines. He was talking to another man, his head shaved like a slave, who sat scribbling on a tablet, an activity alien and rather abhorrent to Ardhu. He had heard rumours that men in far off lands wrote down tales of gods and wars, but it was not the custom in Prydn. It was considered taboo, even if one had the art—surely it was better to learn the lore of one's people and pass it down around the fires, than to write it on clay or bark, where any enemy might make use of it, stealing the sacred names of living things and sapping their power?

Shaking his head, he took another step forward. Blood begin to pulse in his veins and a light sweat broke out on his face. His resolve wavered momentarily as, for the first time since he left Deroweth, he felt fear tighten his belly. Merlin was not there to guide him…and he was just a fifteen-year-old lad who had not yet been blooded. He bore the arms and regalia of a king, but how would that help him against these strangers from across the sea?

In that second, the black-bearded man turned as if sensing his presence. His robes swirled and Art could see daggers at his belt, long and deadly. "Who goes there?" the man barked, first in his own tongue, which sounded like the cawing of crows, and then in a rough version of the tongue of Albu. "Show yourself, I know you are out there."

Ardhu stepped forward, moving into the ring of fire. The bearded one's hot little eyes raked over him, as black and oily as his long tumbled beard. They lit up slightly as they touched on his golden breastplate and belt buckle, and the helmet he wore

. "Welcome, my young friend!" The man extended a hand jangling with rings. "I can see you are a man of worth and standing in your community. Please, let me get you a goblet of wine. Who is it who does us the honour of this visit?"

"Kind words indeed," said Ardhu, his own voice coming out harsh and flat. "From a man who has slain the people of this village without reason and left their bodies for the ravens in their own fields."

"Ahhh…" The bearded man gave a huge, theatrical sigh. "That. It was a pity. We tried to make ourselves known to them, to let them know we were peaceful traders. However, they did not or would not understand us. They attacked us. We had no choice but to retaliate."

"Women and children attacked you too, did they?"

The man shrugged. "Casualties of battle, alas. It was nothing personal. We did not make them suffer. Why does it concern you, stranger? Those lowly river-folk were obviously not of your status." He gestured to Ardhu's shield and gold adornments.

Ardhu's eyes narrowed. "You asked my name and you shall have it. I am Ardhu Pendraec, son of the Terrible Head, war leader of Albu and high king of the West. Those 'lowly river people' you slew were my people, and if I am too late to defend them, at least I will avenge them!"

The man's fixed smile transformed into a vicious snarl. With a lightning-like motion, he yanked a dagger from his belt and hurled himself at Ardhu. Art stepped back, yanking out his flanged axe and flinging up Wyngurthachar at the same time. The knife-tip slammed into the shield, cutting a brief channel, and then snapped off with a loud crack. The pirate grunted in dismay, but immediately snatched another dagger from his belt, this one with a wicked serrated blade.

Ardhu stepped back and spun in a tight circle so that his enemy could find no obvious place to strike. Then, unexpectedly, he dropped to one knee on the muddy ground.

His opponent's eyes glistened evilly. He assumed that Ardhu had slipped in the mud. With a ululating battle-cry, he launched himself at his adversary with his knife high in the air, raised for a killing stroke

Ardhu waited until the man was directly above him, the cruel blade beginning to descend. Then, uttering a war cry of his own, he struck out with his axe, shattering the bigger man's left kneecap in one blow, and bringing him down screaming in pain.

Ardhu rolled out of the way of his flailing body and sprang to his feet. Out of the corner of his eye, he saw the open-mouthed scribe drop his parchment and run. No time to stop him…he had to finish what he had begun.

Bending down, he grasped his enemy's thick hair and yanked his head back. "Ask your gods for their forgiveness and mercy—you will get none from Ardhu of Albu," he said harshly, and he drew Carnwennan across the raider's throat and released his life force out upon the ground.

Ardhu stood for a moment in shock, as blood spewed from the severed jugular, soaking his leggings and felt boots, and the feral light in the pirate's eyes faded into nothingness, leaving him a lifeless husk, food for crows. Art began to shiver; his first kill, but he took no joy in it, despite knowing what the raider had done.

He had no time, however, to dwell on the less glorious side of death and battle. He became aware of other sea-pirates arriving on the strand, exiting their tents and coming in from the ships, addled with drink and bleary-eyed, angry as disturbed bees for being awakened from their drunken slumber by the noises in the village.

There were too many for him to take on, he knew that at once. Staring up into the vault of the night sky, he saw the Moon, a bent sickle, over the troubled waters of the Glein. The Moon had risen where he had predicted it would, using Merlin's skills…

A shriek ripped through the darkness, a blood-curdling war cry. Out of the night-mist galloped Ka'hai, Per-Adur, Bohrs, Betu'or and the other warriors of the warband, waving axes of stone and bronze, their faces painted with patterns and their hair full of feathers. Their mounts champed and rolled their eyes, unnerved by their riders' unearthly cries. Nonetheless, they drove them on with heels and hands, crashing them through the foreigners' watch fires and barging straight into the line of confused pirates—who only just seemed to have noticed that their leader lay dead upon the shore, his blood seeping into the earth of the land he had violated.

The raiders quickly recovered from their initial shock, and tried to form a ragged line of defence against Ardhu's men. Most, however, had left their best weapons on the boats, and soon many fell beneath pounding hooves or the downward strike of an axe or stone hammer. Realising they were outnumbered and at a gross disadvantage on foot, they began to retreat toward the moored ships.

"Stop them, they're getting away!" Bohrs roared in rage, slamming his heels into the flanks of his pony and spitting with fury as the frightened animal refused to budge.

"Wait! Look!" Art pointed across the water. "Ba-lin and Bal-ahn! They have reached the boats!"

Out in the dark a solitary tongue of flame appeared on the deck of each ship. It grew bigger and brighter, then whooshed upwards, following the line of riggings and folded sails. Fire! Sparks shot up into the air; smoke billowed in pale clouds over the river.

The sea-pirates knew their game was up. Some threw themselves from their ships into the Gleyn and tried to swim ashore, but the men of Ardhu's warband rode them down in the shallows, trampling them with their mounts or felling them with their huge, ancient axes. Bodies bobbed along the shoreline; the currents of the Gleyn turned a sickly crimson.

And so was the first battle of Ardhu Pendraec, the Stone Lord, the Terrible Head, won in the West. His first battle as king and the first time he had spilled blood.

It would not be his last.

CHAPTER TEN

Ardhu sat within a hut in the riverside village, recovering from the events of the night. He drank from a beaker, slowly, reflectively, while Ka'hai fussed about him like an old woman, combing blood clots from his hair, and rubbing ointments and unguents onto his bruises and scrapes. This killing of men; it was a nasty business. Ardhu wondered if he ever would grow used to it—the stink, the screams, the sensation of the dagger slicing through flesh, and then that strange, fearful emptiness as the adversary's spirit slipped into eternity. He glanced at Ka'hai, himself newly blooded that day, and wondered if he felt as disturbed and shaken as he—his foster brother who was so gentle with animals, but who had just killed five men. Ka'hai's visage showed no emotion; he just worked on, finishing his ministrations of Art's grazes, before wrapping a fine cloak around his shoulders and fastening it with a huge disc-brooch surmounted by a golden cross, the symbol of the Sun himself.

Outside there were yells and cries as the rest of the war band danced around the fire, drunk with victory, drunk from the contents of their beakers. They had raided the stores of the sea-pirates and had found new drinks to imbibe, among other delicacies, and they were enjoying themselves tremendously.

"Are you going to join the men?" asked Ka'hai. "They expect to go amongst them, praising the might of their arms."

Ardhu smiled wanly and got to his feet. He was bone-weary, his eyes gritty as if they were full of sand, but he dared not let go of his fragile hold on his warriors. "If they want me there, then it is my duty to go," he said, and he walked stiffly from the hut.

Rapturous applause and joyous shouts from the men greeted him, as they danced around a giant pyre made from the pirates' possessions. Trophies of war surrounded them: kegs of drink and dried meats, strange foreign armour and weapons, and a dozen severed heads mounted on stakes of driftwood.

The dead eyes of the heads seemed to glare balefully, reproachfully, at Ardhu as he approached through the smoky darkness. He avoided their blank gaze; he could not forget that although they were his enemies and deserved to die, they were also men who once breathed even as he did.

"My men, I greet you!" he said to his warband. "And I praise you, the greatest warriors ever known. Such courage will be remembered forever."

Deep in his cups, Bohrs staggered up to his chief. "Will you reward one of us with the Champion's portion?" he bellowed "One who was better than the rest!"

Art took his arm and guided him back to his place by the fire. "No, Bohrs, there will be no one champion. You are all champions. As there is no beginning and end to the Great Circle of Stone, so there is no one higher or lower in my band of men. We are equals, fighting toward one goal—the freedom of Prydn."

Another cheer went up, and Bohrs plopped down drunkenly, splashing the heady liquor in his beaker across his ruddy face. He laughed and shook himself like a wet dog, to howls of mirth from his companions.

Suddenly two warriors came through the smoke and river-fog dragging something between them. "My lord," shouted one—Ba-lin, one of the twins who had fired the pirates' ships. "We've found another man, hiding. He was unarmed and begged for mercy, we did not think it right to kill him. At least until we had your permission." He grinned wolfishly.

"Let me see this man," Ardhu ordered.

Ba-lin's twin Bal-ahn kicked the prisoner forward; he fell on his knees before the young warlord. Art recognised him at once as the shaven-headed scribe he had first spotted in the village. He looked thoroughly miserable, covered in mud, his teeth chattering with fear. Close, he saw that the scribe's features did not quite match to that of the raiders, and deduced he came from some other tribe.

"What do you have to say for yourself, foreigner?" he asked.

The man spoke slowly, in a broken version of the tongue of Prydn, "I beg for your mercy, young lord. I am but a slave; I had nothing to do with the injustices done to your people. My own suffered likewise many years ago, and I was spared only because of my skill with words—I can both read and write."

"A slave. I thought so by your cropped head. Well, you are a slave no longer. Your masters are all dead."

The man looked confused. "Do you take me for your own slave now, lord?"

Ardhu shook his head. "In my kingdom I prefer my men to serve me of their own free will. I have no use for men with your skills, either—only those who can wield a bow or dagger."

"Then what are you going to do with me," the man said flatly.

"What do you think? I am not a monster, like the wretches you served. You are free."

The man looked up, amazed, his mouth hanging. "Young lord, you are too merciful. How ever can I thank you!"

"In one way. I will give you safe passage across the Narrow Sea, and when you arrive on the mainland, I want you to spread the word far and wide that Ardhu Pendraec holds Prydn, and that he will tolerate no incursions from men who seek not lawful trade but thievery and murder. Take this message to the ends of the known world! But tell them too that Prydn is open to trade with all those who come with honest hearts, and that the King of Albu is stern but also just and fair!"

"I will tell them," said the slave, and suddenly there was a new light in his eyes. "My name…the sea-folk called me Pal. But I am Palomides. I was the youngest son of a lord who lived on an island called Delos. Years ago, there were friendships between your Isle and ours and much trade; two holy women of your race even settled in our land and their tomb is decorated and revered by local maidens even today. This was many centuries past, when these Pretanic isles were ruled by Brytto, who gave his name to them; and by his son, Blessed Brahn, big as a house, with a raven as his totem."

Ardhu clapped his hands and roared with laughter. "I like this, friend. A, man from far across the sea who knows more of our history than most native-born sons!"

Pal gave a little bow. "As a younger son I was not desired as either warrior or statesman. So I grew learned about the ways of men in the world around me. It was a good thing, lord. My learning probably kept me alive."

"And long may it be so," said Ardhu, placing a hand on his shoulder. "Now go, my men will see that you have safe passage."

"Wait." Palomides' eyes darkened. "I must tell you. There are two more Sherdan ships further along the arm of this inlet. The pirates on them have treated the locals as harshly as here."

Ardhu frowned and his men muttered and felt the edges of their axes; but there was a note of despair in their voices too. They were weary from long travelling and hard fighting; they had more than their fill of blood and slaughter for one day.

"And," Palomides stared at his feet. "There is even worse afoot, I fear, my lord. One of the leaders, Husrubal, was in meeting with some of your own kind—men from the northern islands off the tip of the land called Kaladhon."

Fury ignited in Ardhu's eyes. "Who? What are their names?"

"Forgive me if my memory slips…I heard but whispers in the night…One was... Loth… Loth of Ynys Yrch, the other Orion…no, Urienz."

"The pig from the Isle of Pigs and his kinsman,"grunted Bohrs, making a rude gesture. "Do you know what they wanted, foreigner? They were far from their homes."

Palomides swallowed. "They asked the Sherdan for help. Help to remove a boy-king of the West, who had become too powerful for his own good." He looked at Ardhu. "I wager they spoke of you, lord. And it was with no love."

"Traitorous wretches," growled Bohrs through gritted teeth. "I knew they would turn way back at Marthodunu, even though they grudgingly swore to support you!"

Ardhu wiped his arm across his face. He looked tired and drained, purple circles underscoring his eyes "This is ill news but not unexpected. Our thanks, Palomides of Delos. You may have been more valuable than you realise. Go now, and farewell — maybe, we shall meet again. And if you do ever come to these shores again, I will make you a man of my warband—the different one, the outsider, with different skills and much knowledge."

Palomides bowed again. "If the Gods will it, it will be so."

Then Art beckoned to two of his men and they led Palomides away, toward the coastal settlements where sea-trade had been the lifeblood of the locals for over six hundred years and boats travelling afar with tin and copper were plentiful. Once he had crossed the channel safely, he could make his way across the continent using ancient trade routes that led through the forests of the Middle-Lands to the mighty Rivers Rhinn and Rhon. With luck, and no attacks from hostile tribes or evil weather-spirits, he could then follow the rivers Eastward and be home with his long-lost family within two Moons.

Art quietly thanked the spirits for the Delian man as he mulled the information the slave had imparted. He had to move quickly, before the other pirate raiders became aware of the destruction of their fellows…and before Urienz and Loth's men arrived from the northern isles.

Turning to his warband, he said in a voice that grated like stones on the shore: "No time for celebrating! No time for sleep! We must go on and cleanse Albu of these invaders and traitors. When that is done then may we rest-whether it is in our furs or in our barrows!"

He raised the Lightning Mace to the sky, its white bone mounts shining in the dark; and above the sky suddenly answered, lightning flaring sullenly under the belly of the livid clouds that had been gathering in the North. The horses whinnied and skittered, frightened of the storm, and the men felt the energy in the air, the electricity crackling in their hair.

"We ride on!" cried Ardhu, and he ran to Lamrai, vaulting easily onto her back. Just as the storm broke, and rain slashed down like tears of a tormented god, the warband galloped from the riverside, and toward the haunts of their enemies.

The next two battles of Ardhu the Bear were harder won than the first. The Sea-Raiders had seen smoke curling in the air, and sailed into coves and sheltered areas where they set up watchful camps. This time there were no words spoken between the two opposing forces; the air instead was full of the sound of war cries and then with the screams of the injured and dying. Art's men were, for the most part, young and unskilled, but their youth and strength gave them an added edge—that and their sturdy mounts, which they drove over their foes as they fell. As Ardhu had hoped, the Sea-Raiders were not expecting horsemen, and had no time to devise a way to stave them off.

Eventually the fighting was over. Again, Ardhu sat in the dark, hair and skin bathed scarlet, his garb purple with dark, clotted gore and the stink of death all around him. On the river ahead, he could see fires leaping as a ship aflame slowly sank beneath the waves to the jeers and shouts of his victorious band. He wiped his face, his burning eyes, wishing for nothing more than sleep and clean clothes.

Ka'hai came to join him; he too was smeared with red blood, his hair-knot crimson and his blue eyes startling and somehow almost monstrous against the scarlet-streaked mask of his face. "Art…you are hale?" he asked, hunkering down beside his foster-brother. "We have done it—no pirate is left alive; the warriors have taken their heads and hands and feet and placed them under boulders so they will never walk as spirits either here in Prydn or in the Otherworld."

"And our men?" Art looked at him grimly, leaning on the hilt of Caladvolc the Hardcleft. "What of our losses? This time, I know we were not so lucky."

Ka'hai sighed. "Lucky enough, considering that we are all green in the arts of war, save for Bohrs and Per-Adur. The main body of warriors from Marthodunu and Place-of-Light is unharmed save for scrapes and gashes. But some of the youths and new recruits picked up along the route to the Gleyn will not be going home to their green fields and forests. But such is the way of war, and they knew that. They are now riding over the Great Plain, young forever."

Art rose, gesturing to his torn, stained clothes with sudden anger. "This disgusts me…I reek of death! We have leather-workers amongst us; hunt down a deer and kill it, and have them make me a new tunic to wear. I am not such a savage I would rejoice in wearing my enemies' blood!"

Ka'hai glanced at him solemnly. "Wear your soiled robe with pride, Ardhu. From this day forward, garments of such hue will be the colour of royalty, of battle and sacrifice for the Land."

Ardhu shook his head bitterly. "Noble speech, but hiding the ugliness that is truth. I tell you, brother, although it may not be so honourable, the tilling of soil is preferable to the killing of men."

"Oh, I agree, Art—I'd rather be with my horses that here, stinking of gore, but that is not our lot, I fear. Wear the royal purple blood-robe, my friend, and remember its colour comes not just from the wounds of your enemies but from your own blood."

The two youths walked down to the water's edge. The fallen of the warband lay in rows, curled into foetal position by their fellows, their sightless eyes turned, as was tradition, toward the rising Sun in the East.. There would be no barrow-burial for them, nor cremation with urn-burial, for the women were the ones who moulded containers for the ashes of the dead, and they were far away. No, the fallen would be burned, and their ashes given to the waters, the air and the earth.

"Gather the wood," Ardhu commanded, and Ba-lin, Bal-ahn, Betu'or and others went out into the darkness and came back bearing as much dried kindling as they could find. They stacked it around their fallen comrades and packed the crevices with chunks of dried moss and lichen. When the pile was heaped high, Ardhu used his flint-strike-a-light to kindle a torch. He thrust the brand into the driest part of the pyre and the flames leapt up, twisting and turning, illuminating the faces of the living and giving the false glow of life to the faces of the dead.

"There is no time to linger and mourn," Ardhu said as the flames spiralled. "The kings of the North are coming…We have no time for grief!"

Leaving the pyre burning brightly in the night, the warband of Ardhu the Stone Lord rode on toward the gathering forces of Urienz and Loth.

The warriors made camp in a little valley of pleasant aspect, with a winding stream and rocky ground scattered with rowan trees. The valley lips were high and ridged, making it an ideal place to pitch camp in safety, for it would be easy to spot any unwelcome visitor silhouetted against the backdrop of the vast, open sky.

"We'll rest here for a few days," said Ardhu. "Get some decent food into us, if the hunt is good, and tend our wounds. Ba-lin, Bal-ahn, you scout ahead and see what you can find out about the movements of Loth and Urienz and their followers."

The band set about making camp, some throwing up temporary shelters while others took their bows and headed into the deeply wooded valley-side to hunt for game. Ba-lin and Bal-ahn, like two eager pups, grabbed their bows, and went bounding up and over the lip of the vale and away, their war-whoops echoing through empty spaces broken only by the cries of hawks and other passing birds until that hour.

Ardhu pulled off his ragged, bloody tunic, freeing himself at last of the sight and smell of bloodshed. He yanked on a long, baggy, yellow-brown kirtle his men had looted from one of the sea-raider's troves; it hung on him almost like a woman's dress, and he snorted in derision, and pulled his belt tightly around his waist, cinching the garment up an inch or two. Hah…in his eyes it looked fair fit for a girl, but at least it was clean! Thrusting Carnwennan into the top of his felt-lined leggings, he walked away from the camp and followed the stream, seeking a place where he might bathe and sit away from the noise and clamour of the others for a while.

Gradually he noticed the stream widening, fanning out toward a line of gnarled trees that ran up to a wall of grey, slate cliffs. The cliff tops were stark, ridged with fangs of wind-battered stone round which the wind made eerie moans. Above this piteous keening, he could hear the rush of swift-flowing currents, and a churning roar, like a giant's grinding teeth, as that water poured into an unseen basin.

"A waterfall," murmured Art, picking up speed as his curiosity deepened. He had never seen water falling from height before; Abona ran smooth and deep, save for a few eddies round the weir when the river was full after winter storms. But Merlin, whose ancestral lands had held such wonders, had told him of the white foaming hair of the water-spirits that fell over the bones of the land, and the deep green tears they shed into the fathomless pools below them.

Ideal places for mortal men to wash away the cares of the world…

Hastily he entered the trees, splashing in the stream's shallows, savouring the coolness on his bruised and blistered feet. Sunlight dappled a carpet of deep, drenched moss and flickered on the little crests of water that played round his ankles and slapped the slime-streaked boulders in the swell.

The trees suddenly parted and there before him reared the falls: a frothing spout of water that jetted over a tongue of dark green stone before falling, ringed by rainbows, into a pool where bubbles broke over pebbles worn into fantastic shapes by the ceaseless pounding of the torrent.

And spoiling Ardhu's view of this earthly paradise was a stranger.

Ardhu felt a fearful knot arise in his belly as he stared at the unwelcome one. Was this truly a mortal before him…or was it one of the Everliving Ones, the spirits who lived in the hills, the stones, and wild places of earth? For surely no human could have the face and form of the man who stood before him, balanced high above the falls on the jut of stone where the waters began their rapid descent, practising warrior's-arts with a long and deadly spear that he thrust towards the belly of the sky.

He was a Man of Bronze.

Red bronze was the head of his spear, and pale bronze the skin on his bare shoulders and lean, tightly muscled torso. His hair, a rippling mane of waves that hung down his back, was also golden-bronze, and there were rings of copper threaded through its length. The planes of his face were high and fair, without flaw or defect: the nose sculpted, the jaw, which he wore clean-shaven—firm without viciousness, the lips curved but not womanish. Under a noble brow, his eyes gleamed rich, tawny amber. It was as if the Sun himself had stepped down onto that high perch and taken on the semblance of a human being in order to enjoin with human affairs.

But then the perfect stranger stumbled, his foot slipping on sodden waterweeds and nearly spilling him into the flume, and his perfect mouth loosed a florid and very human oath, and Art, watching from below, knew at once that it was no god preening and parading on that lofty perch. It was just a man. A man who had the temerity to look like a god to Ardhu's eyes.

Fear and awe changed abruptly to annoyance…an embarrassing stab of jealousy. He was King of Prydn, who, at fifteen summers had won three battles in as many days—how dare this man wander around as if he owned this wood and water!

Harsh words burst out almost as if from a stranger's mouth: "You! Over there! I wish to use this place. Finish your practice and be on your way!"

The Man of Bronze halted and swung round to peer over the edge of the waterfall, his sun-bright face calm but mildly curious. He caught sight of Ardhu and his tawny eyes narrowed, although his lips rose in a mocking smile. "Who is this boy who speaks to me in such a haughty manner?" he asked in Ardhu's own tongue, though he spoke with a strange, outlandish accent. "I thought by the tone that surely it must be some great warrior, some mighty chief. Instead I see a child in a silly robe that he must have stolen from his sisters!"

"How dare you!" spat Ardhu, face reddening with rage. "You know not know who I am?"

"No, I don't…and you certainly do not know who I am!" retorted the shining stranger, leaping down the stony outcrops of the side of the falls with the fluidity of a sure-footed wildcat. "I am An'kelet, He-of-the-Striking-Spear, Prince of Ar-morah, son of the high priestess Ailin of the Lake of Maidens and King Bhan. And I may well be the greatest warrior in the West of the world."

"The greatest braggart, more like!" shouted Ardhu, and in a sudden frenzy born of exhaustion and frustration, he hurled himself at the taller man.

The bronze stranger seemed unconcerned and even slightly amused. "You want to fight …so be it, young fool. I will douse your hotness in the waters of the falls by the end of the day!" With a deft movement he cast his great spear into a nearby tree where it stuck, quivering, its embedded point releasing a stream of sap as red as blood. "Let it be hands on then, no weapons. I would not raise a weapon against a child; it would bring no honour."

His words, as intended, inflamed Ardhu even more. The young chief rushed at An'kelet and tried to seize him, to topple him over into the pool and stop his prideful boasts. He was no great wrestler, but he had competed in fun round the fires, and what he lacked in bulk he made up for in swiftness of movement and wiry strength. Surely, one good headlong rush and he could wipe the mocking smile off that too-handsome visage…

A moment later Art was on his arse on the hard rock, gasping. He stared up, unbelieving and bewildered, at the tall fair man looming above him, who had shot round him with lightning speed and tripped him up, kicking his legs out from under him with a swift blow from a lean, hard foot.

"What evil magic is this?" he mumbled, wishing he had his own magic-man, the Merlin, with him to do battle against this unnatural warrior from Ar-morah. "Fight me properly…you…you water-creature!"

An'kelet sighed. "What more do you ask from me? I have already laid down my spear! Would you have me tie my hand behind my back too? I told you, boy—I am the best warrior in the Western world. Be it with weapons or hands, I will win!"

Ardhu's eyes blackened; burgeoning jealousy and self-doubt grew large in him again. Surely, the gods loved him; they had given him the sword from beneath the stone—not this foreign stranger with his lazy smile and conceited boasts. Uttering an enraged cry, he struggled up into a half-crouch and slammed his head into his opponent's stomach.

The blow hit home…but did not have the effect Art desired. The bronze man staggered back for a brief second, but immediately fell upon him again, pinioning his arms behind his back. "A nasty, angry little boy, aren't you?" he mocked. "I told you, you need to cool off by having a ducking!" And without further ado, he hurled Ardhu into the emerald pool.

Art sank into the green depths, the water churning like a primordial cauldron around him. Immediately he kicked out and began to swim, striking out for the foam-laden surface. He burst through the spume and bubbles to see his adversary hunkered down on the bank, grinning and laughing.

Laughing at him! At Ardhu, king of Prydn!

A cloud of rage descended on the young warlord. Irrational thoughts of revenge filled his head. Although he vaguely knew it was ignoble in a fight where weapons had been downed, he reached under the water and drew Carnwennan from its hidden place in the band of his leggings.

"You will laugh at me no more!" he shouted and he sprang from the pool and slashed wildly at his opponent's startled, perfect face.

The next moment he was on his knees, gasping for breath. An'kelet's hands were around his throat, fingers pressing hard on his windpipe. No longer was the bronze man playing, teasing—now he was full of deadly intent. His eyes were narrowed, his face serious and deadly.

"Who are you? Who sent you, assassin? Was it Loth of Ynys Yrch? You are not just some local peasant lad, are you? Not with that fine dagger! Speak now, or you will never speak again!"

Ardhu struggled to answer; black spots streamed across his vision. "I…if Loth and Urienz are your enemies, then in truth you must be a friend of mine, for they are my enemies also."

An'kelet did not release his grip; he dragged Ardhu up, his eyes boring into the younger man's. "Is that so? Who are you, if that is true? And how did you come by that noble dagger…How could it be yours, unless you are a man of worth…or a cutpurse and thief, a looter of barrows!"

"I am Ardhu…" Art croaked. His head felt fuzzy, the world was spinning. He had never felt the Otherworld so near. "Pendraec. The Terrible head. The blade is mine by right. It was won from its barrow-guardian by moving the great stone. I am the King of the West!"

Through dimming vision, he saw An'kelet suddenly blanch. "My lord, forgive me, I could not know!" he cried, and at once he released Ardhu's throat from his death-grip.

Ardhu sank to the ground, eyes streaming and puke dripping from his chin, as, before him, the mighty Man of Bronze went down on one knee and bowed his head to him.

Ardhu and An'kelet walked across the field toward Art's war-camp. The tall foreigner had donned tunic and cloak, and although he looked less godly in his woven garb, his high birth was obvious by both his mien and his possessions. A fillet of thin gold held back his hair, and a small, ancestral axe-talisman fashioned from polished jadeite hung round his neck. His felt boots were of many colours, his belt-ring of shale, and at his belt hung two great, long Armoran daggers with golden pontille hilts—Arondyt and Fragarak the Answerer. On his shoulder rested the great barbed spear Balugaisa, which, he told Ardhu, was wrought from the spiky hide of the sea-monster Kon-khenn.

"Here…" he was rummaging through a fox-skin bag, "I have mosses that will heal your throat where my fingers bit into you. It will aid the bruising."

Art smiled wryly. "You heal too? Are you the world's best healer just as you are the world's best warrior?"

An'kelet grinned. "My mother, the high priestess Ailin, said the ability to heal is one of the greatest of all arts. She showed me much healer's magic, once even cutting a roundel from a man's skull so that evil spirits can fly from his mind!" He pulled a tuft of moss from the bag and handed it to Ardhu. "Here. Try it."

Ardhu did as An'kelet told him, still wondering at this odd shining man from over the sea, who was unlike anyone he had ever met before. Despite the hostility of their initial encounter, he found himself beginning to warm to the stranger. Although An'kelet brimmed with confidence, and was better to look at than a human man had a right to be, there was something appealing about his open manner, and his eyes, when not burning with the light of battle, were kind.

"So, Prince An'kelet, what brought you to Albu from our cousin-land of Ar-morah?"

An'kelet gave him a sideways look. "My father Bhan died before my birth, hence none of his lands became mine. My mother, as I told you, is a priestess; she lives with twelve maidens on an isle in the heart of a silver lake, in the middle of the mighty forest of Brokhelian. These women were rumoured to be the most beautiful on earth; they tended a holy cairn surrounded by eighteen cup-marked stones that represented the Moon's Great Year. When the time arrived that the Moon came down from the sky to dance over the temple, the priestesses would seek lovers from amongst human men, for that one night only. My father came to the isle, drawn by the rumoured beauty of the women—and by his own lusts! He coupled with my mother on the lakeshore and sought to carry her off to be his wife…but he did not know all of what took place upon that island. The Maidens of the Moon, driven into frenzy by their dance, tore him apart with their bare hands and scattered his bones into the lake. Nine Moons later I was born on the same silvered shore where I was conceived, and from it took one of my many names An'kelet-of-the-Lake. I was happy there for many years, but when my manhood rites were completed, I was forced to leave, for it is forbidden for a grown male to dwell on that isle, and so I went to stay with my mother's kinsman, King Hoehl. I grew restive there too, though, as a landless man, and decided to seek my fortune in Albu. We in Ar-morah had heard rumours of a mighty young war-lord and I was curious to see for myself if he was worthy of the strength of my arm."

Ardhu grimaced. "And there I was acting the fool…"

"It is forgotten, lord," said An'kelet, wide-eyed. "There is no shame in it. My presence merely startled you when you were weary and sore-hearted, and you were not yourself. I am to blame."

Ardhu waved his hand, urging him to continue. "So, you had heard of me over the Sundering Seas. But here you are, far in the mountains of the West, near Sylur lands. And you speak of my enemies, Loth and Urienz, as your enemies too. How has this come about?"

"I set sail in the winter when the waves were high; I am no sailor and forgot how the winds of Prydn are fierce and its weather-spirits capricious! No wonder the men of the East call your people 'Dwellers Beyond the North Wind'! My ship was blown beyond its desired port in Belerion, and was beached on the coast near Mhon. I went ashore and continued my travels on foot, and came at the Feast of Lambing to the village of a chief called Ludegran. He was well glad to see me, foreveil neighbours had plagued him, and he looked to the sharpness of my spear, Balugaisa, Spear-of-Mortal-Pain. He is old but kindly, and I pitied him; his only son is dead, and his men, like himself, grow old; many of the tribe's youths have perished in raids from the sea. He spoke of you with great hope, lord, and said he had seen you lift the great capstone to reveal the magic blade."

Ardhu nodded. "Yes, I recall Ludegran from the gathering at Marthodunu. Old but keen-eyed and quick of wit. He never spoke against me, as some of the others did."

"I was just about ready to leave Ludegran and search for you," continued An'kelet, "but then further evil befell. A messenger came from the North—from the chiefs Loth and Urienz. Ludegran was asked to join them in rebellion against you, and to support Loth in a bid for High Kingship of all Prydn. He refused, Loth threatened dire revenge, and now scouts have brought word that fighting men are issuing from the North, by sea and by land, to burn the villages of those who refuse to support them, and join forces with those miscreants who do. And when their numbers are swelled, they will march to the Great Stone temple of great fame, and cast you down."

"So, they are well on their way," said Ardhu bitterly. "I had word of their treachery, and it is because of their threats that I have brought my warband to this place. However, it is evil news that they are so near at hand, for my men are weary…having three times fought the Sea-Pirates and won."

An'kelet clapped a firm hand on Art's shoulder. "Well, you need not fear so much now, lord. I am here, the master of the shining spear. Together, all the evils of the world will fall before us!"

When Ardhu and the Ar-moran noble arrived at the camp, Ardhu's warband were just as intrigued by the newcomer as Art had been. They gathered close, curious, eyeing his weapons, especially the great, pronged spear, which was not a weapon used much by the men of Prydn, who preferred bows, daggers, and axes of stone and bronze.

Ka'hai looked a bit wary, however, and rubbed his big, broad chin with a grubby fist. "I don't know, Art," he murmured to his foster-brother. "I wish Merlin were here. Oh yes, he is likeable…amazing, even, but what if the men take to him and desert you? Do not be offended! But men are fickle and he is like a light to which lesser moths will cluster."

"Yes, I know the foreign prince is a special one," said Ardhu heavily. "Knew it so much that I acted in a shameful manner when first I met him. Look…" He pointed to the finger marks on his neck. "He put these on me and brought me back to my senses. He has marked me now and humbled me; no matter if the men are loyal or not, I will know in my heart he is the better warrior and more worthy."

"Then why did you bring him here?" snapped Ka'hai, brow furrowed with anxiety. "Surely that is madness!"

"Because it was his aim to join our cause…and because we need men like him, men beyond compare. Men who will inspire. We need him on our side, gathering warriors to us, to our cause, rather than drawing them to whatever quest is dear to him. Do you understand?"

"I…I think so… I pray you're right, brother." Ka'hai chewed his lip.

At that moment, An'kelet cast his spear in a demonstration of its power, and the warband cheered as it split a rotted tree stump nigh in two. "A fine cast!" yelled Bohrs. "Ardhu, is this one to join us this day? We could use a long throw like that, to split a few raiders' black hearts!"

Ardhu inclined his head gravely and approached An'kelet, hands out. His voice was steady. "That is solely up to Prince An'kelet; let the decision be his."

An'kelet drew himself up to his full height and smiled. He then drew his long dagger Arondyt with its gold-pinned pommel and presented it hilt-first to Ardhu. "I will fight with you, against the enemies of Prydn that are also enemies of Ar-morah. And please, do not call me 'prince.' There is only one lord-chief here and can ever be—Ardhu Pendraec, King of the West."

He sank to one knee, still holding up his dagger. Ardhu took it and touched it to An'kelet's brow and to his shoulder as a token that he accepted this bronze stranger as one of his own men, and then he gave the blade back to its owner, who rose with a smile that blazed like the Sun at Midsummer.

"My lord," An'kelet said. "Now that I am your sworn man, can we set off to halt these bastards, Loth and Urienz? My spear is thirsty and my spirit crying for battle!"

"I'm just thirsty!" grunted Bohrs. "Ach, man, we've been battling for days!"

"There will be respite, before the big battle," said An'kelet. "Come, I will show you the way to the dun of chief Ludegran, where you will receive meat and drink to cheer you."

They upped camp before the Sun had reached the noon position, mounting their weary steeds and heading northwards, while around them the countryside grew more rugged, the mountains taller and the air more clear. Above their heads, the sky was alive with wheeling seabirds, sunlight flashing off their outstretched wings, their cries shrill and lonely like the calling of lost spirits. "I can smell salt in the air," said Ardhu, lifting his head and scenting the wind like an animal, in a way Merlin had taught him.

Riding alongside him on a pony that had belonged to one of the warriors who fell on the seastrand, An'kelet nodded. "Yes, we are not far from the sea—the sea that divides Albu from its sister isle Ibherna. The sea that brought men to Prydn years ago, and still does, but now they are men filled with plans of hate and conquest. Ludegran's holding is just over yonder hill; he has moved his people from the valleys to a high place that overlooks the sea—a shrewd move, for the sea is where the danger lies, and he can now easily keep watch. This fort is an extraordinary structure, I have not seen its like…I am sure, in the future, its merits will catch on."

"Alas, this is how it shall be in many places, I fear; men will hide behind stout doors in high places and leave their farms behind," said Ardhu. "I myself have built a hilltop fort, Kham-El-Ard—you will see it when we head back south. But back to this Ludegran: will he welcome so many of us, eating his supplies, drinking his mead? Although he supported me at Marthodunu, it is hard for men in these perilous times to feed unexpected guests."

"He will regard your presence as a great honour," replied An'kelet. "And your bows and daggers a great relief. You see, he has a reason greater than most lords to want his walls unbreached, his house defended. Behind the stout posts that surround his holdings he hides a great treasure!"

"A great treasure?" Art's dark eyebrows rose. "What kind of treasure is this?"

An'kelet grinned and tossed back his golden-bronze hair, setting his hair-rings jangling. "A most unique treasure, and the old man guards it with his life. In his walls he holds the White Phantom, fair beyond compare!"

"White phantom? You mean like a barrow-spirit? What a strange thing to trammel within the walls of a dwelling; such should stay behind the walls of henge and ditch!"

An'kelet laughed, his white teeth flashing. "No, my lord-friend. A goddess! A queen! His foster-daughter Fynavir of Ibherna, who was set to marry his son as Harvest-tide, had the lad not died. Ludegran worships her and fears for her safety, should he fall in battle. As well he might; I saw the northern emissaries' lustful eyes when they saw her!"

"A girl!" said Ardhu, with some disappointment. "Is that all?"

An'kelet laughed. "You are young yet, lord, I imagine women are not as interesting to you as hounds, horses and swords. Not yet."

"And I suppose you are the world's greatest lover, as well as the greatest warrior," said Ardhu teasingly.

"If I chose to be," said An'kelet, face suddenly serious and his eyes vaguely shadowed "Both woman and men have offered themselves to me. But, in truth, I take a more restrained approach to…pleasures… than most. I grew up on the Lake of Maidens where most of the priestesses knew men only once in their lives, and killed the men who took them, in atonement for their virginity."

An'kelet pulled his short cloak tight around his shoulders; the wind was rising, cooling. "Death was the fruit of the lust of men; I saw this. My own father succumbed to it. I believe yours did too, my lord, if the tales are true. I swore as a youth I would not be swayed by such lusts; that I would only worship and love what was pure and holy. I will not, I pray, be taken by passions that bring only doom and pain for all concerned."

"But surely you want to continue your line. That's what the Ancestors desire of us!"

"Maybe. But I do not think they frown on me." He grinned. "Do I look as though I am in disfavour?"

"You are a strange one, An'kelet," said Ardhu, laughing.

"I would not deny it, young lord. You will never meet my like again!" An'kelet tossed his head again, and his clear laughter mixed with the jangle of the rings in his hair rang out across the grey, empty land.

The path ahead narrowed and the trees melted away to become clusters of thorny bushes. Over the steep ridges ahead, the sea was now visible, slate grey and shining dully. Far to the West, the green curves and swells of Ibherna rested under a pall of cloud.

"Look," said An'kelet. "Ahead is the fort of Ludegran, ready for war."

Art peered into the Sun. High on a plateau before him rose a fort with earthen ramparts newly dug. Stakes sharp as spears bristled at the bottom of the ditches, waiting to impale the unwelcome. A wooden palisade circled it, made of stout oak. He felt a small thrill as he looked upon it; for surely this was what Kham-El-Ard would look like one day. Only his citadel would be twice as big, twice as grand, blessed by the rising Sun on its eastern flank, and on the other side facing the Temple and the Great Plain.

An'kelet set his heels to the flanks of his pony and joyfully thundered toward the gates. A multitude of heads immediately popped up over the ramparts; Art could see a line of drawn bows. "Peace! It is only I, An'kelet-of-the-Lake!" called An'kelet, waving his spear above his head. "I've returned to help you, my friends, and I have brought with me Ardhu Pendraec, King of the West, my ally and my friend. Unbar the way and make us welcome!"

There was scuffling in the entrance to the fort. Barricades of wood and sharpened poles were hastily pushed aside.

An'kelet rode through the gap, his bright hair streaming like a banner, and Ardhu and his band followed after to cheers and the blowing of ox-horns.

CHAPTER ELEVEN

"Welcome, Lord Ardhu, Terrible head, chief of Khor Ghor and the West."

An old man, beard white frizz, rheumy eyes the colour of rain-wet slate, walked up to Art and bowed deeply. He wore a checked tunic with a sash tied over one shoulder; the dagger at his belt was of an ancient type with a handle of horn, and he wore an ancestral wristguard as a bracelet, its red stone pierced by three great studs of gold. "You may remember me from Marthodunu. I supported your cause."

Ardhu nodded. "I remember. I wish we could have met here in happier circumstances. Your stronghold intrigues me; it should hold out many foes."

"I pray you are right, young lord." A shadow passed over Ludegran's gaunt face. "Foemen are on the march. I see Prince An'kelet has met with you already; I trust he has told you of Loth's treachery, and of the threats he has made against my people. And against you too, of course. He resents that he could not lift the stone and take the kingly blade."

"Yes, I know about Loth, and his twisted brother," said Ardhu. "We will deal with them, and if the spirits will it, few if any of their men will return to their unfriendly, wind-blasted homeland! Do you have any news on their movements?"

"Nothing as yet. I have scouts in the villages along the coast, ready to send warnings when they arrive. But come, you look weary; news has come from the West that you have already been victorious in many battles. You will eat and drink with me and mine, and we will make a fitting reception for your brave heroes."

Chief Ludegran led Ardhu towards a massive roundhouse that stood in the shadow of the fort's retaining wall. Torches lit a path to its door, and the Westering Sun turned the thatching of its sloped roof to flame. Carved household deities with eyes of flint capered at the threshold, and a bull's skull loomed above the door-lintel, horns poking the sky.

Following Ludegran, Ardhu entered the smoky darkness of the house. For a rural chieftain away from main trade routes, Ludegran lived in moderate opulence. Furs of bear, wildcats and beavers hung on the walls, making the room warm and cosy. Woven pennants bearing blue and red designs—the symbols of kingly clans—hung between the furs. Skulls of boar and horse lined the roof beams, and several human skulls, either enemies or Ancestors, hung suspended over the deep fire-pit, which was tended by ash-smeared women who continuously poked and prodded, and fed the flames with logs of ash and oak. At the back of the house, several screened off areas marked the sleeping compartments of the highborn, their floors strewn with rushes and mounds of goatskins.

An'kelet, who had followed Ludegran and Ardhu into the roundhouse, was peering around. "My lord Ludegran, where is your fair treasure, who brings joy to us all?"

Ludegran smiled. "When strangers are at the gate, I hide her away—as any man would do with such a lady of value. She is here, watching even as we speak! War-chief Ardhu, let me present to you the White Phantom, noblest and most blessed woman in Prydn: Fynavir, daughter of red Mevva."

A screen shifted aside, skin hangings stirred and a slender figure emerged into the sultry glow of the fire-pit.

Knowing that Ludegran's 'treasure' was but a maiden beloved by a doting foster-father, Ardhu fixed a polite smile to his face, fully intending to murmur a few pretty words and then get on with men's discussions of war.

Abruptly his smile faded.

The girl was indeed magic, a goddess, as An'kelet had said. Like her name, White Phantom, she was truly white—almost unnaturally white, the palest girl he had ever seen. Moon-silk hair drifted in a sea of cobweb strands to her waist, and her skin was pearlescent, rose-tinted on her high cheekbones. A red robe with a fringe of bronze was wound about her, while a great Moon-collar wreathed in magic symbols clasped her neck.

Ludegran noticed Ardhu's appreciative stare. "My fosterling Fynavir is a Princess of Ibherna, Lord Ardhu—her mother the great Queen Mevva, the Intoxicator, who men say is a goddess-on-earth. She was to marry my lad, Brokfel, and make an alliance between our people and those of the sister-isle, but…he died. We have not yet heard what Mevva and her husband, the Ailello, wish for Fynavir now. No doubt they will seek another match before long."

An'kelet standing beside Ardhu stepped forward and kissed Fynavir's on each of her pale cheeks, a brotherly kiss of friendship but one that made Ardhu feel strangely uncomfortable nonetheless. Strangely jealous. "The Sun goes down and we live another day—and the great King Ardhu is amongst us!" he said. "Will you aid in our merrymaking tonight, my fair friend, as we wait for the approach of our enemies?"

Fynavir smiled and nodded, then left the roundhouse with other girls of the village crowded around her. They soon returned with beakers that brimmed with honey-mead, roundels of aged cheese, and wooden trenchers of beef and pork for the men. Musicians followed close behind them, blowing on bone flutes and horns of cattle and tapping out a steady beat on small skin drums painted with chevron designs.

"Come, Fynavir," An'kelet teased, catching at the hem of Fynavir's rust-red gown, "will you dance for us tonight—a victory dance to inspire the men of the tribe? Your feet are as light as falling leaves and pleasing to the spirits."

"It is not up to me, friend An'kelet," said the pale girl, pulling the fabric of her dress from An'kelet's fingers but smiling at him nonetheless. "It must be as my foster-father wishes—and our revered guest, the mighty warlord Ardhu Pendraec. He is a man of dagger and axe, who may not be given to watching the dances of maidens."

Regally she swept up to Ardhu, who sat cross-legged on a skin beside Ludegran. "My lord?" she questioned. Her teeth were like pearls, her eyes, beneath curving silver brows were chips of green ice. "Would you have me dance?"

"Ah…uh...yes…" he stammered, flushing to the roots of his hair.

"Foster-father?" She looked at Ludegran, who was beaming, full of pride as if he was her true father.

"Of course! If my esteemed guest wishes it, it shall be done."

Ludegran snapped his fingers and the pipes and flutes and drums came together to form a loud and frantic tune, wild and sensual and unearthly. The onlookers of the household stamped their feet and chanted in time to the beat as the foreign princess let her red robe fall, revealing a strange ritual dress beneath—a short woven top that left her belly bare, a belt with a round bronze plate, and a short skirt of individual woven strands that barely hid her modesty and revealed long, milky legs and smooth thighs. Gracefully she began to twirl on the rushes, arching backwards and leaping into the air, using arms and hands to gesture and pose, whipping and tossing back the silken hair which coiled and frothed round her almost-exposed hips. She seemed almost in a trance as she danced, her eyes closed, her lips slightly apart, beads of sweat breaking out on her flesh and slipping down her neck, between her full, hard breasts…

Art stared, transfixed, the contents of his beaker slopping onto his deerskin leggings as his fingers suddenly turned to jelly. His men laughed; he ignored them. A strange heat went through him, rising up to his face, making his ears burn. He had little experience with females; once he had become king Merlin had warned him against being too free with willing girls—"You are a great chief now, and many will try to be your friend or lover in order to share your power and fame. This will not do for one of your stature. Take low-rank women if you must ease your flesh, but a proper match with a female of similar standing to yourself must be made. I will find you a wife who will bring you riches and no shame!"

Ardhu wished Merlin were here with him now to advise him. Surely, surely, the shaman would agree that this girl, a princess from over the West Sea, would be a fitting match for the Stone Lord, the Terrible Head.... Oh spirits, but what madness possessed him to even think of a match so soon! He'd only just met her, and had grunted at her like some savage, and ogled her like some lust-addled oaf. She probably thought he was coarse, clumsy and thick, but it was as if a mad fire was burning in his brain, and even worse, in his loins....

"Chief Ludegran, I must...get some air!" He dropped his beaker, spilling mead all over the floor, and pushed his way out of the roundhouse. Pausing by the door, he took a quick look back. Seemingly unconcerned by his sudden departure, Fynavir was now dancing for An'kelet. Anger and jealousy leapt up in him like a wild fire, and, ashamed, he hurried away, almost knocking over a startled serving-woman carrying a platter of mutton.

Face grim, he stormed over to the palisade behind the hut and kicked the wall with all the force he could muster. It hurt, but the pain brought him back to his senses. Slightly. He knew better than to go into the roundhouse right now lest he behave in a way that was less than kingly. Sighing, he climbed up onto the palisade and stared moodily into the descending night, uncaring of the curious stares of the men positioned as guards on the wall.

"Lord Ardhu..." A voice soft as the Moonlight drifted through the shadows. He froze. It could not be...

Turning around slowly, he gazed into the glacier-green eyes of Princess Fynavir. She had donned her red robe and a cloak of sewn beaver-pelts, and had tied her hair into a long braid, but still she looked heartbreakingly lovely, there in the muted starlight.

"My lord, I pray I did not offend you with my dancing." She placed a gentle hand on his arm. He nearly jumped with the unexpectedness of her touch.

"Offended?" he laughed coarsely, trying to sound unflustered. "Of course not. It was just...different...to the dances of my people. As were your garments. They were...short."

She nodded. "My father was the third Ailello of my mother, Queen Mevva, and he was a man from over the Northern Sea, and it was to his homeland I was sent in fosterage as a young girl. I was to marry a northern chief who would bring amber from the Sea of Beltis to Ibherna in return for our gold. I grew up in the Women's House there and learned the dances of spring, to invoke the Sun and the spirits who make crops and women's bellies grow. It is their style of garments I wear, carried home in a cedar box when my intended husband died of tooth-rot. My mother ordered me to bring the dress; she said prospective husbands would like it."

"Well, I certainly liked it," Art mumbled, even as he reddened, hating his bumbling, foolish tongue. She must surely think him a stupid, callow youth, not only an unworthy ruler but useless as a man.

Fynavir smiled. "My mother is seldom wrong about the wants of men. She has had more lovers than I can count and men clamour to bed her for both her beauty and her reputation."

"Does your father not complain?" Ardhu looked shocked.

A shadow passed over her face. "He is dead. Every seven years the old Ailello is given to Krom the Bloody Crescent, that some call Stonehead, at his temple of thirteen stones, and my mother takes a new young strong Ailello as husband. All are pawns to my mother, who men say is goddess-of-the-tuath or tribe. Even I, her only living daughter, am but a useful tool. However, I am unlucky with husbands, it would seem, much to Mevva's dismay!"

"And what now for you?" His heart started to pound dully in his ears. He wanted nothing more than to reach out, to touch that soft pale face, the long, swan-like neck, and feel those white, half-revealed thighs against his...

"I do not know," she said softly. "It all depends on if we survive the attacks of these chieftains from the North. If we do, I am sure my mother will find some other who wants a goddess' daughter for a bride, or a golden bride price. Or both."

Ardhu reached up, suddenly catching hold of her arms. She gasped ever so slightly, eyes widening, unsure as to his intention. "You won't be bartered like that if it's not your wish," he said forcefully. "Do you understand? You are in Albu now, and if I say you are free to do as you will, then so it will be."

She shook her head violently. "No! You would not dare risk ten thousand spears sailing to your shores!"

His eyes darkened; suddenly he was his father's son indeed, scion of impetuous hot header U'thyr. "I would risk it! I am Ardhu, king of Prydn! I am the land and this land is mine! Do you understand me, foreign girl? Your redheaded mother with her paramours and scheming ways holds no terror for me! Understand?"

"My lord, forgive me!" She drew back and dropped into a position of obeisance.

His face softened; he caught her arms and drew her up to him. The Moonlight was shivering on her brow and in her eyes, bleaching them of colour; she was like a mist-wraith ready to vanish on the wind. But she was of earth too—all too well he remembered her pale, round thighs, their promise barely hidden by the swinging strands of her skirt. "You are forgiven," he said, "but do not doubt what I say to you again. I would never lie…not to you, Fynavir White Phantom."

She glanced up, wondering, and before she could protest, he took her in his arms and covered her mouth with his, while the guards on the ramparts nudged each other and muttered behind their hands.

"Ardhu…" Fynavir pulled away first, but her hands were still resting on his shoulders. "Lord, you honour me, but I fear I will bring no luck to you. As I told you, both my betrothed husbands now lie in their barrows."

"Three is a blessed number and I will break that fatal charm," said Ardhu dismissively. And when Fynavir opened her mouth to protest: "I warned you not to doubt me!"

He was about to say more, but suddenly a wolf howled in the valley beyond the fort. It was a lonely cry, long and drawn out, borne aloft on the bitter night-wind. A score of other howls soon joined it, rising and falling, peaking in intensity as the Moon shone out from behind a patch of flying stratus.

"Wolves," breathed Fynavir. "I'd heard they sometimes came into these hills but not in recent years; they fear the halls of men."

Ardhu leaned over the wooden parapet, eyes straining into the dark cup of the valley below. "The wolves are indeed running tonight, with sharp teeth and fierce bite," he said grimly. "But they are not the kind who runs on four legs! Those voices do not belong to beasts. They belong to men. Loth and Urienz and their lot of mad Northerners have arrived."

"To the gate!"

The cry went out into the night. Ardhu's warband and Ludegran's men assembled in the yard of the fort, while the women, including Fynavir, were hustled into the roundhouses and placed under guard. Art stood with An'kelet on one side and Ka'hai on the other, Caladvolc in hand, waiting. All around him his men and their allies began igniting torches, filling the dun with a flickering light that spilled over into the shrouded fields beyond. Archers climbed onto the top of the walls, positioning themselves, their painted faces almost inhuman in the sputtering torchlight. War-chants went up, and horns were blown, their mournful tone matching the eerie cries of the false man-wolves skulking in the shadows beyond.

Ludegran climbed up on the barricades in the gateway of the fort and gazed out. Shadows were swirling and leaping in the fields and forests. "Where are you, Loth?" he spat. "I know you're out there. Show yourself, if you are not craven!"

The shadows parted and two men strode forward. Ardhu, peering over the barricade, recognised Loth of Ynys Yrch and his kinsman Urienz. Loth had been a handsome man once and still had a roguish appeal, despite a scar that ran from the edge of his eye to his chin and a tendency to run to fat. He was tall, broad-shouldered, with a short, neat beard, and glossy dark brown hair cut bluntly at the shoulder. Blue eyes cold as the seas around his island stronghold gazed out from under heavy brows. Golden sun-whorls were stitched to his studded tunic, while a necklace made of the serrated teeth of some sea-beast clacked around his neck. Over his shoulder was draped a wolf-pelt, the head used as a hood –a trophy he must have acquired far from his homeland—for no wolf-haunted forests grew on the barren, wind-blasted isles of the Northern seas. Ynys Yrch was known as the Isle of Pigs, for those hardy beasts, sacred for their oracular powers, were the only beasts that thrived in Loth's domain.

Beside Loth stood his brother Urienz, who held territories on the shores across from Ynys Yrch. He had been less favoured in his appearance, a big, barrel-chested man whose hair had receded from his brow and ran down his back in a thin, mud-brown plait. One eye had been lost in some long-ago skirmish; many of his teeth were missing too. He wore a bearskin cape, complete with claws and head, adding to his fearsome appearance.

"I am here, Ludegran!" shouted Loth. "You're still resisting me, I see, though now from behind walls and wood! What a fool! If you had joined with me and marched on that snot-nosed priest's puppet who has usurped the kingdom of the Great Stones, you could have shared in the glory, and your people would have lived as free men honoured for their part in our victory! Now you force my hand-I must slay you all down to the last woman and child. Except for the white maid you treat as daughter…" He grinned lasciviously. "If she is as fair as my messengers report, I have other plans for her!"

"Shut your foul mouth, traitor!" Ludegran called back, enraged. Red spots burned on his wrinkled cheeks. "Speaking with an evil tongue is all you are good at, you lord of a petty realm where neither trees nor beasts thrive, where the Summer Sun hides His face, and the cold makes a man's heart wintry and cruel! You speak ill of the Lord Ardhu, but he brings us peace and freedom from foes from beyond…while you and your like bring death to our own people!"

"Your loyalty to the boy-king is touching," Loth sneered, his eyes narrowing. "But what good will it do you? Is Pendraec here? Can he help you? No doubt he is tucked up in his warm house being coddled by that conniving old fool, the priest called the Merlin."

"No, he is here with you now, listening to the words that bring you shame!" Ardhu suddenly leapt high onto the barricade, with the firelight glowing red on his golden breastplate and patterning the face of Wyngurthachar. "I am here, false chief, man of serpent's tongue, creature of no honour. I will always be ready to defend those who are in need, and who are loyal and true, not just to my rule, but also to Prydn. You are not one, and you will pay the price."

Loth looked startled for a moment but almost instantly regained his composure. "It is you who will pay," he snapped. "Come down and speak your brave words to my face…boy!"

There was a rush of wind in the dark next to Ardhu. A war cry split the air and a brazen figure sprang over the barricade and hurtled headlong toward the two rebel chiefs. It was An'kelet, his spear raised on high, his face contorted with the warrior madness known as the 'warp-spasm.' Some men got this rage from drinking specially concocted potions wrought in the Moon's dark, but to others it came naturally, making them as strong as beasts, nigh as powerful as gods, terrible and implacable in their madness.

Whooping, he descended on Loth, thrusting at him with his great barbed spear. Loth shouted an oath and stumbled back, smashing at the spear haft with his big dolerite battle-axe. It was no good; An'kelet was twirling like a mad thing, muscle and fire and the flame of fury. Loth could touch neither him, nor his spear. As the bronze man of Ar-morah drew close, drawing his long bronze blade Fragarak from the sheath at his belt, Loth turned tail and ran into the midst of his milling warriors, vanishing in the sea of skin-draped figures.

On the walls, the men of Ludegran hooted and laughed derisively. Warriors began to pour over the top of the barricade and rush toward the war party of the traitor chiefs.

Seeing that An'kelet was fixated on finding Loth, Ardhu went after the cousin, Urienz, who was still standing his ground near the entrance to the fort. They locked together in hand-to-hand battle, slashing at each other with their grooved blades. The edge of Caladvolc sliced Urienz's knuckles and blood flowed, black in the sickly Moonlight. The older man roared in rage and charged like a maddened bull at his young opponent, throwing both of them onto a patch of trampled, muddy earth. Caladvolc and Wyngurthachar tore free of Art's hands with the impact, the sword flying across the ground to land several feet away, just out of reach.

Urienz began to laugh, his huge belly wobbling. Mud was daubed on his florid cheeks like war paint. "I will crush you, worm! I am a wrestling champion…and you are nothing. I will smash your spine, then take your head and make your skull into a drinking-cup!"

Violently, he grabbed Ardhu's shoulders and slammed him against the earth. Art's head struck the ground and stars showered across his vision. Urienz's great knee slammed into his gut, knocking the air from his lungs, and then the warrior's arm pressed down across his windpipe as he sought to pinion him for a final killing blow.

But Urienz was slow and unwieldy, long past first youth and fat from supping on too many tender young pigs for too many years. He had also not looked to see if his young opponent had any other weapons.

He had missed Carnwennan—the White Hilt. The Sword from within the Stone.

In a lightning motion, Ardhu drew the small but deadly blade from its hidden spot against his leg, and thrust it into his enemy's back, just above the kidneys. Urienz screamed, and the blood poured in an awful waterfall from his yawing mouth to spill all over the face and chest of the youth pinned beneath him.

Ardhu heaved Urienz's bulk to one side and leapt up, gasping, as Urienz flopped and flailed like a fish on a hook. "You saw me take this blade from under the Stone!" he said, holding up the dripping blade. "You knew what it meant, and you swore to honour it. You and your vile brother have angered the Ancestors by your actions, and so you have paid the price. The sword you falsely swore to serve has now taken your life."

Urienz stared up at him. "Not…a boy…" he mumbled, bloody foam making a strange and horrid red beard on his trembling chin. "Was wrong. You are…a monster!"

"I am my father's son," said Ardhu darkly, and suddenly he did not seem a boy at all but some dark god of death, powerful and ruthless. "The Terrible Head. I am also the Dark Bear…and you wear my emblem, the skin of the bear, and that offends me. It also rightly makes you my prey."

With that, he retrieved the fallen Caladvolc, and in a brutal motion drew it across Urienz's throat and sent his enemy's spirit to the otherworld. Then with another downward slash, he took Urienz's head. Lifting it in a shower of gore, he carried it to the cliff edge and hurled it toward the night-clad sea from whence the traitor had come, dooming his spirit to wander aimlessly forever.

Returning to the sprawled body, he took Urienz's bearskin cloak as a trophy and wrapped it about his own shoulders, a final insult against the spirit of his vanquished enemy. The great bear's head, preserved by careful drying, loomed over his own head, while the massive paws hung down with huge nails still intact. He was the bear, not Urienz—the Great Bear of Albu, where even the constellations spoke of his might.

He suddenly felt as one with his namesake animal, almost as if its spirit had entered him. Casting back his head, he roared like a bear into the night, "I am the King! I am the Terrible Head and no foe of Prydn will withstand me!"

Shaking with surges of adrenaline, he hurried back through the trees and up the slope to see how his warriors fared against Loth's men. Reaching the lower rampart of Ludegran's dun, he found the battle nearing its end. It had been a short, sharp skirmish, and Loth's forces had not fared well. Most of the men of the North lay dead, shot with arrows or ridden down by the horsemen of Ardhu's warband. The air reeked of blood; the rooks and crows and ravens would soon feast.

An'kelet was standing in the centre of the carnage, like the golden effigy of some solar deity, a smile on his face and his right foot firmly planted on the neck of Loth of Ynys Yrch, who lay sprawled on the ground, weaponless and utterly helpless.

Seeing Ardhu, An'kelet beckoned him over. "Lord," he called, "I have saved him for you…It is you he betrayed so foully, so you must be the one to have the honour of taking his head."

Ardhu strode up to Loth, staring down into the blood-smirched face of his enemy. "Your brother Urienz is dead," he stated harshly. "I wear his garb as my own. I have hurled his head into the sea, so his spirit will now wander the misty strands incomplete and lost. What will you say to me that will make me spare you the same fate?"

"You are not what I thought you were!" panted Loth. "Neither the wizard's pawn nor a jumped-up boy of no skill! I was wrong about you, and I was wrong to doubt the choosing of the old one beneath the stone, whose dagger White-hilt you wear. I have been prideful and foolish…and it has brought me to a sorry pass. Ardhu Pendraec, if you are as merciful as you are powerful…show me clemency this day and let me return to my islands. I will not bother you again; the mainland holds no more attraction for me."

"Don't trust him, Art!" cried Ka'hai, staring with hatred at the Northern chief. "He is as slimy as an eel. Kill him and put an end to it."

Ardhu beckoned to An'kelet. "Get him on his feet. Whatever he has done and whatever I chose to do with him, he will not grovel in the dirt like an earthworm."

The bronze warrior grabbed Loth by his tunic and dragged him up, forcing him to stand before the young king. Ardhu stepped forward, his face only inches from his opponent's, the tip of Caladvolc touching his throat. He stared into Loth's cold eyes for a moment, then lifted his hand and struck him across the face with all the force he could muster.

"Get out of here," he said as Loth tumbled onto the ground with a thud. "Go, before I change my mind. And if you ever set foot in these lands again, I will not only have your head, but I will march North and set your bleak islands ablaze from end to end, and wipe every one of your clan from the earth and cast down your Ancestor-stones and break your barrows and grind the bones to dust, so that no one ever shall know that your treacherous breed ever existed in the world of men! Spirits, so hear me, and know that I will hold true to this if Loth of the Yrch islands should defy me again!"

Wordlessly, Loth scrambled to his feet and ran blindly for the trees on the hillside, his arms flailing and his teeth bared like a frightened animal. The warriors of Ardhu and Ludegran hooted derisively and called insults after him.

"You should have killed him, I reckon," said Ka'hai heavily, shaking his head. "He'll never change. He may never set foot on the mainland again, but I'll wager he'll still find a way to cause mischief!"

"We'll just have to watch his movements." Ardhu stared into the blackness where his adversary had vanished. "I would not kill him and risk more dissension among the tribes. We spend too much time fighting each other as it is. I do not wish to give some Northern lordling cause to create rebellion in his name. We need some kind of alliance between the Chiefs, even if an uneasy one, if we are ever to defend this island from invaders."

Now Ludegran came up to Ardhu and clasped his shoulder, his fingers trembling. "Mighty is the sword-arm of the Terrible Head! You have surely saved us from what would have been certain doom, even with our stalwart walls and brave bowmen! Chief Ardhu, ask anything of me and I will grant it if I can, in token of my gratitude and endless friendship!"

Art paused, blood rising suddenly to his face. Only one thing interested him in Ludegran's dun. A girl white as snow, with a goddess for a dam. The Merlin might be angry, but it would be a good alliance, surely the old man could see the wisdom in it. The seas between Albu and Ibherna would be made safe, and a link forged to the goldmines of the fabled green isle.

"I ask for one thing only." Ardhu folded his arms. "I ask that I might take as wife the Princess Fynavir, daughter of Mevva the Intoxicator."

Ludegran looked surprised but pleased. "Her mother must be consulted, of course, but I am sure she will agree to this match. Who could be a better husband for her daughter?" Turning around, he motioned to one of the women who had ventured out to view the aftermath of the battle.

"Go, Edel, fetch Fynavir from her chambers!"

The woman ran back into the dun and appeared a few moments later with Fynavir, wrapped in thick furs against the night chill. She glanced around anxiously, not certain why she had been summoned. Seeing her distress, An'kelet smiled at her, and the worried lines on her brow immediately softened at his concern.

"Fynavir." Ludegran placed his hands upon her shoulders. "In the time you have dwelt with my people, you have become as a daughter to me. I had hoped you would enter my family, but alas, due to the death of Brokvel, it was not to be. I have worried what your fate would be, knowing that you did not wish to return to your mother's hearth, but now I can assure you that this will never happen, barring any objections from Mevva. The great Chief Ardhu, Bear-chief and Terrible Head of Prydn has brought great honour upon us both—he wishes to take you as his wife."

Fynavir's lips parted; no sound came out. Her eyes travelled to An'kelet, who had stopped smiling. "Foster-father, I know not what to say…" she finally managed. Her voice trembled.

"He pleases you, does he not? Girl, I am lord here, and know what went on upon the walls last night! Is there some reason why you should not marry King Ardhu?"

"No, he is a great warrior and a comely chief. But I…I…" Her voice faltered and again her gaze slid towards An'kelet, as if hoping he would speak, finding a reason why this match should not occur. Instead, he stared at the ground, leaning heavily on his spear.

"Then it is settled!" Ludegran clapped his hands. "You will marry King Ardhu. I will send messengers to Queen Mevva and the Ailello on the morrow. Fear not, Ardhu, Fynavir will not bring just her beauty to your marriage bed. She will also bring forty head of cattle and golden treasure from her mother's hoard."

Ardhu grinned like a mad thing. "So much the better. Ludegran, if Mevva agrees to the match, have Fynavir sent to me for the Feast of the Rage of Trogran at the Crossroads-of-the-World. That is an auspicious time for fruitful marriages."

"It will be done," said Ludegran, clasping hands with the younger man to signify a deal had been struck.

The warband then set about celebrating both their victory and the forthcoming marriage of the king. No one even noticed that Fynavir had retired, alone, to her sleeping cubicle, or that the usually ebullient An'kelet had grown suddenly solemn and pensive, drinking from his beaker as if the only solace in the world was within its depths.

CHAPTER TWELVE

The Merlin was angry. Ardhu guessed it as soon as he rode into Deroweth, and could see no sign of his mentor, only pale-robed priests flitting to and fro between the houses with countenances sour as unripe apples. "Where is he then?" he said curtly to one priest, as he slid down from Lamrai's back and flung the reins to Ka'hai.

The man frowned from under the peak of his white linen hood. "He awaits your arrival in his hut, lord Ardhu. He is aware that you are home."

"Is he? Well, not much of a greeting for his king!" Angrily, Art stormed towards the Merlin's hut, with its grandly decorated doorway facing away from the sharp winds that raked the ridge overlooking Holy Hill.

Flinging aside the deerskin hide that hung in the entrance of the house, he thrust his way inside, blinking in the gloom. "Merlin…why do you shun me? Have I not driven off the invaders? Conquered Loth and killed the treacherous Urienz? What is wrong with you, man? I come home expecting glory and celebration, yet see nothing but grim faces and bowed heads."

Merlin's face loomed out of the darkness. He looked wild and fierce, eyes scored by dark rings, lips twisted in a sneer. "Yes, you have done all the deeds I trained you to do. But that is not all you did, is it, Ardhu Pendraec? You did much more. Yes, much, much more. News came of your victories, but also of you taking a foreign prince into your warrior's fold. Even worse, it seems that you have arranged a match with the daughter of Mevva of Ibherna! Fool!"

Ardhu's eyes ignited, his anger matching the Merlin's. "I am not your pawn, Merlin. You said yourself it would be good for the tribes to see that I am my own man and not some minion of the Temple. And so I am. An'kelet is the greatest warrior in the world—and he is my friend, with whom I would entrust my life. And, as for the girl," he faltered here, his cheeks growing red. "You…you have not seen her, Merlin…"

Merlin spat on the ground in derision. "You are no better than your foolish father, swayed by the lure of a woman's tits and thighs! I was working on a match for you, and now those plans lie in ruins."

"Good!" Art shouted. "Why should I lie with some trollop with a face like a pig's arse just because you have chosen her for me?"

"Because I know what is right for you! For Prydn!" Merlin practically shrieked. Spittle flew from his lips, striking Ardhu's cheek and making him wince in disgust. "I have cast the bones, cast them many times. Each time it comes out the same…Look!"

He grabbed Ardhu's arm and yanked him down beside the fire-pit. On the packed earth lay a jumble of knucklebones, some new, glowing white in the gloom of the hut, some dark yellow, worn smooth from centuries of use. Merlin passed his long, brown hand over them. His eyes were hot, hooded.

"There it is, written in the bones of our Ancestors. Signs. Dire signs. See the centre? That is the serpent, with you, Ardhu Pendraec, at its head. The Terrible Head. Above your right shoulder is the Sun, brightly shining but burning with fierce power too—that is your stranger from Ar-morah. Above your left shoulder rises a crescent Moon, pale and deathly—the white phantom woman you have chosen in defiance of me. These two shall come together as the Sun and Moon come together at rare and terrible times when the earth plunges into darkness for a time. The shadows cast by their brief union may undo all we have worked to achieve."

A chill of fear rippled up Art's spine but he forced himself to face his mentor. "Pah! Quivering with fear because of some chance configuration of the bones! Why, the old women cast such bones for the price of a bead or two on feast-days; it is little more than an entertaining game to them!"

Merlin's hand shot out, grabbing Ardhu's tunic and dragging him towards him with a strength belied by his lean frame. "The destiny of this land is no game," he snarled "Or if it is, it is a game we must win. Do you understand?"

"I understand," said Ardhu frostily. "But I want you to understand too. I will have my own friends and companions. I will have the wife of my choice. If I have done wrong and misjudged their worth, I will pay the price and seek to make amends. Do you understand, Merlin?"

Merlin leaned back, his breath hissing through clenched teeth, rocking on his callused heels. He seemed suddenly old and tired. "Yes, I understand," he said, voice heavy with sudden weariness. "For all my hard work, you are still your father's son. I should not have expected otherwise. Go, and leave me in peace; in your absence I have been overseeing the workers who build the great fort of Kham-El-Ard, and I am weary from doing for you, you ungrateful whelp."

Ardhu left the shaman's house and returned to his men, who sat waiting on their mounts, a little dismayed that there had not been feasting and celebrations to herald their arrival.

"Trouble, Art?" Ka'hai raised one eyebrow quizzically.

"Yes," replied his foster-brother. "Merlin trouble! But he will get over it. He'll have to. In the meantime, let us move up river and look at the walls of Kham-El-Ard, then fare to the Place-of-Light. I suspect the reception there might be more welcoming."

Ardhu and the warband rode down river, stopping to marvel at Kham-El-Ard, where oak posts sprouted like trees on the heights, soaring up almost to touch the Sun Himself. It made Ludegran's promontory fort look humble and mean in comparison. Workers streamed in and out of what would eventually be a great gate with turrets for archers, while others dug banks with antler picks and shovels made of cows' shoulder bones.

Riding beside Ardhu, An'kelet looked impressed. "One day this place will go down in legend. I am glad that I shall play a part. Our peoples were always close through deepest time; may it always remain so, Ardhu."

The warriors passed on, following the banks of Abona, which narrowed and began to curve and coil like a serpent. Fording her waters at a weir where water boiled like a cauldron, they then rode East toward the settlement known as Place-of-Light. Standing on a slight plateau, this village was an ancient place of great renown, for here the first great smiths from Faraway changed Prydn forever with their knowledge of the riddle of metal. And more besides—for in their retinues they not only brought the knowledge of copper and gold, but the brewing of mead and ale, the manufacture of drinking-beakers worthy of great warriors, and a burial rite of individual graves, where a man's spirit could go into the West with his dogs and treasures, even his servants and children if that was his desire. The Galloen had not fought with the people of Albu and Khaledon, but they changed their lives irrevocably; the communal stone tombs of the Ancestors had been sealed, and circles such as Khor Ghor had been reused and remodelled, its vast structures of stone rearranged and made even more magnificent.

The warband spotted the settlement almost at once, rising on top of an escarpment that gave an unobstructed view across open lands from Holy Hill to Deroweth. A line of vast totem poles glowered on the lip of the scarp; behind them loomed the remains of ancient grave mounds and other holy places, some marked by posts, others by pits and deep shafts. Further behind, stood roundhouses and huts, where children and dogs played in the Sun. Cattle lowed in pens, fat with sweet grass, while woolly brown sheep trundled lazily between the wattle walls of the huts. Women sat weaving and making pottery, while men tanned deer and cowhides and dragged in sheaves of wheat to be ground for bread.

As soon as the band became visible, a joyous cry went up. A drum started to beat, and every hut seemed to disgorge a stream of children and women, all clamouring to see the returning warriors.

"I told you the reception would be better here," grinned Art, nudging his foster brother Ka-hai in the ribs. "Look, there is father!"

Ech-tor the smith was striding across the settlement, shoving aside infants and yipping, excited dogs. A huge grin split his face. He had abandoned his smithy near Marthodunu and come to live permanently in Place-of-Light, in order to be near Ka'hai and Ardhu. As the village's own smith had been barrowed the winter before, his skill was sorely needed—and much appreciated. In fact, he was considered special, having raised the young Chief himself, and he had even taken a new wife, Kerek, from amongst the villagers.

"My boys!" he cried, arms outstretched, as Ardhu and Ka'hai dismounted. They fell about in bear-hug embrace, while the other warriors laughed. "You have returned to us as blooded warriors of the People! You are true men now—ha, I swear, you even look taller! And Art, what is this we hear…that you have contracted a bride?"

"It is so," murmured Ardhu, aware that he was blushing. "It is said her mother is a goddess-on-earth. She is white as the Moon, and her name means 'White Phantom.' She will bring gold and cattle as her dowry."

Ech-tor glanced sideways at Ka'hai. "You next boy!" he teased. "You mustn't let your brother outdo you! Now come, we must all celebrate your safe return from battle and hear tales of mighty feats of arms!"

The feasting that accompanied the warriors' homecoming lasted for three days. Venison and boar was consumed and roast goose sizzled and spat over the fire-pits. Hazelnuts were cracked and consumed, and mushrooms boiled in broth flavoured by dried seaweed imported from the coast. Rare sweet treats were offered afterwards—wheat grains drenched in milk and left till they burst, then flavoured with honey, and possets of tansy leaves mixed with berries from the local woods. There was much merriment, and many a man back from his first battle looked with new respect at domestic life unmarred by war's violence, and set his gaze upon one of the unwed womenfolk. The girls themselves wove flowers in their hair and stained their lips with berry-juice, and acted shy and coy until they got their chosen warrior alone, when they then showed the female-starved men who really held the real power in matters of the heart. That was, of course, the practical older girls, eager to escape their mothers' hearths—the younger ones sat sighing over Ardhu or An'kelet, who treated them all like sisters and tolerated their constant Mooning and moping better than most of the other young men.

At the end of the third day, as the burnt orange eye of the Moon soared West toward the Stones and the Deadlands, Ardhu gazed down from the height and saw a familiar figure, staff in one hand, climbing slowly to the top of the plateau.

The young king ran forward eagerly. "Merlin! You have come! Have you forgiven me yet?"

Merlin pushed back his hood and spat onto the feet-impacted chalk, shining blue in the Moonglow. "No. But there is naught to be gained in dwelling on your rash actions. I must try to make the best of this situation. Maybe I can shield you from what I have seen in the pattern of the bones."

Ardhu lead Merlin into the headman's hut, and the feasting continued, though slightly more subdued now that Merlin's stern eyes were upon the crowd. The shaman was particularly interested in An'kelet and spent hours grilling him about his life back in Ar-morah. After he was done, he looked more relaxed; the faint hint of a smile even touched his thin lips.

"He is an honourable man," he said to Ardhu. "A great warrior, but child-like in a strange way. He is ruled by his beliefs, and when he has set his course upon something, he will follow his heart till the end, right or wrong. This is his failing…a failing you must deal with if he is to stay amongst your men."

Art sipped from his beaker, savouring the rich, fermented honey taste. "And what would you advise?"

"He must go to Khor Ghor and swear absolute obedience to you. This oath will bind him. If he strays from your path, the guilt will break his mind. That is the kind of man this stranger of bronze is—strong as a stone on the outside, but with a fatal flaw inside that might cause him to crumble as an ill-made pot crumbles. Pray you do not lean on him too much lest he falls and takes you down with him."

Ardhu looked at Merlin through drink-misted eyes. He hated it when the old man went on so. "He already swore to me, when we first met. He even renounced his princely title. Surely, that is good enough for you!"

Merlin thumped the head of his staff against the ground. "No, it is not. I want him to swear before the Ancestors, before the spirits that are all around us. A man may make noises of obedience in moments of triumph or gladness—then change his course when next the wind blows. I want to take no chances; as the son of a priestess An'kelet will be well aware of what his fate might be if he shatters the vows he makes."

"So be it," said Art, eager to keep the old man happy. "He will be sworn in at the Stones on the next auspicious day, under your guidance, Merlin." He counted on his fingers. "And then…it will be nigh on the time of the Harvest Feast, the Rage of Trogran, and we must set off for the Crossroads-of-the-World to meet my bride!"

"Aye. lurching from one folly to the next," Merlin mumbled into his beard, but Ardhu, eyeing him sharply, fancied that his lips bore the trace of a weary smile.

An'kelet's oath taking at Khor Ghor took place after the death of the Old Moon, when there was no Moon to be seen in the sky at all. This was a time when the elder powers and shades were strongest, crossing from their barrows into the world of men, rewarding their most faithful descendants and bringing mischief and even death to those who did not venerate them in the proper manner.

The Merlin and other priests of the Temple led the prince of Ar-morah from the Place-of-Light to the banks of Abona. The day was fair, the sky blue as woad, and a warm, surreal light clung to the leaves of the wind-tossed trees and set the waters of the great river sparkling like a breastplate of gold. Swans sailed on the surface, birds of Otherness, which, legend said, often turned into beautiful women who entranced men but stayed with them for but a year and a day.

On the bank, An'kelet was divested of his garb, and had the rings taken from his long hair. He was guided into the clear green waters, amidst streaming weeds of green that felt like surreal hands against his skin. The priests and acolytes surrounded him in the river, invoking Abona, the great Cleanser, to take away evil or malice from his heart, to make him born anew that day in the service of his chief.

T hen Merlin came up and grasped his head by the hair, forcing his head below the swell. Three times he did this, with three great cries, as An'kelet gasped and thrashed blindly around in the water.

"Now you are purified in the blessed way, and you may continue with your great journey," Merlin said solemnly, after the third dunking. "Rise now, and take the Sacred Avenue to the Dance of Spirits where your fate awaits you!"

An'kelet clambered out of the water on the far side of the river, and the acolytes brought him plain robes of undyed wool, a token of humility before his lord and the spirits. Then the party of priests gestured him forward, and he was taken into a small, banked monument, black with the ash of burning. Empty stone holes still showed as pits in the earth. An'kelet sensed this was a very old place, perhaps even older than the famous temple he had yet to behold, and it was a dark place too, scented with the funeral pyre. He shivered, wet and cold, as the wind blew.

Merlin bent and picked up a lump of charcoal. Approaching An'kelet, he drew symbols with it on his face, his exposed arms. "We can never escape what we are—that is, food for the pyre, for the worms in the barrow mound," he intoned. "Each day might be our last. So remember this, and wear with pride and knowledge the marks of those who have gone before, written in the ash that was their flesh."

Once he was done, the holy men and women surrounded An'kelet once more, guiding him towards a pair of parallel banks that streaked away across the fields like white, exposed bones of the earth—the Sacred Avenue of Khor Ghor that protected pious men from the malign ghosts that lurked in this haunted landscape of gods and Ancestors.

Halfway up the Avenue, the party halted and a priest came forward holding a blindfold, which he tied around An'kelet's eyes. Once it was on, the holy men turned him in a circle until he was dizzy. He knew it was a deliberate attempt to disorientate, to add to the strangeness and mysticism of his committal to the Young Lord—and it worked. He did not know if he walked into the Sun or with it at his shoulder, did not know who walked behind him or at his side, or even if they were still with him, or had allowed him to wander through some gap in the Avenue bank into sacrosanct lands where men feared to tread without powerful talismans.

At last, after stumbling up and down the rolls of the Great Plain, the Merlin called for An'kelet to stop. Time had passed; he felt the air cooling against his cheek, the first vapours of the evening. Hands reached up to his head, carefully removing his blindfold.

The Merlin was standing beside him, dark and saturnine in headdress and long robe with its clatter of animal teeth and claws. "You look toward the East, where the Sun rises," he said, and true enough, An'kelet found himself gazing out past the swelling mounds of the Seven Kings to the misted blue hump of Magic Hill. "That is where all life begins, with the rising of the Sun. But now you must turn from that toward the West, towards eternity and death. To your fate as a warrior of the king, sworn to die in his service. Do you still wish to procede, Prince of Ar-morah?"

"I do, Merlin of Prydn, the choice was made long ere now."

"Then turn and face the Tomb of Every Hope, the gates of the Sky, the circle of Sun and Moon. Face the spirits who guide us all, and face your sovereign King."

An'kelet turned, and a gasp was wrest from his lips. He came from a land where many stone monuments stood, of antiquity beyond all others: great marching rows of menhirs like jagged teeth, huge humped tombs with carven chambers, a single standing stone so large it had toppled the very day it was raised, its ninety-foot length smashing into fragments—but he had never before seen a structure like Khor Ghor, the Dance-of-Spirits. For it was solitary, unique, and would remain so unto the end of days.

Viewed from his low position in the bottom of the valley, the temple soared up toward the sky in towering layers. Each stone in the vast outer ring was joined to its fellow by mortise and tenon joints, a technique used in the construction of wooden buildings. An'kelet had never seen such an art put to stone before, and he marvelled at the smooth grey faces of the stones, beaten into shape by long labouring with stone mauls. Inside this outer ring were even larger structures—five massive trilithons built of sarsens weighing many tons. They soared several feet above the outer circle, with the trilithon at the far end being the tallest and most imposing. The Sun was setting and the red light angling down on the great megaliths turned them a magical shade of crimson-gold.

Filled with awe, An'kelet walked up the rest of the Avenue. A gigantic wind-beaten stone confronted him—the Stone of Summer with its wrinkled, natural inward face frowning in the direction of coming Winter. Striding past it, he stopped to reflect on the stone gate of the Three Watchers, also known as the Shadow-stones; sure enough, as the Sun tumbled in the sky, their shadows stretched long over him, black and cold as death.

Then he was beyond them and entering the sacred space of the circle. A ring and oval of small dark stones, some vaguely human in appearance, faced him like a stony army, while the trilithons and outer sarsens rose up and up, seemingly the very pedestals on which the heavens rested.

At the far end, beside a dimly glittering green monolith, stood Ardhu Pendraec, Stone Lord and king of the West, bearing the insignias of his Kingship—the sword, the mace, the shield, the dagger. The bearskin he had taken from Urienz was on his shoulders, too, snarling mouth open in silent roar.

Around him, framed in each archway of the great circle, were the men of his warband. An'kelet knew them all, but they seemed different now, no longer the battle-worn, weary lads he had met on campaign, but mystic warriors in cloaks of fur and feathers, with axes tied to their belts by bright peace bonds, and totemic talismans jangling around their necks.

His eyes slid from the men back to Ardhu, his lord, his friend, and a sudden chill went through him. He had honoured Ardhu before, as a man, and a valorous leader, but here in Khor Ghor he was more than that. Here he was a god, a sacred king, bound to the land, his destiny entwined with the very fate of Prydn. His destiny was in his face, suddenly both old and young; it was in his eyes, the green of the wildwood and the darkness of the tomb.

Awed, An'kelet sank to his knees on the bone-white chalk, his head bowed and his hands pressed to his face in supplication.

Ardhu approached him, his deerskin shoes making no sound on the packed chalk floor of the inner sanctum. "An'kelet of Ar-morah, you come here this day before the Ancestors and powers that move the world of men. Do you swear to renounce all others and follow my path, and join the Comrades of Albu from this day forth and ever after?"

"Lord, I do," An'kelet said hoarsely.

"And do you swear to be loyal to me, to protect me with the strength of your arm, to honour my wife and any heirs as if they were your own kin, forsaking your own rank or any desire for status of your own?"

"I…I swear it, lord."

An'kelet hesitated a moment as Ardhu mentioned his 'wife.' Fynavir. Briefly her image filled his mind, snow hair and glacier-green eyes, the hint of sadness that always lingered in the girl who had been bartered so many times by her ambitious mother. The maiden said to be a goddess's child, herself a manifestation of the sacred Land. The White Phantom of birth and death. The Full Moon.

But he must not think of her as anything but Queen. She was Ardhu's, and he had sworn his oaths to his mother long ago. Shutting his eyes, he sighed then murmured, "You will be as my god, Lord Ardhu, and your lady I will love above all other women—my goddess to worship and protect."

Ardhu lifted Caladvolc, its long incised blade incarnadine in the failing light. "Then I confer upon you the title of champion of the Circle of Khor Ghor, hero of Prydn. Arise, Lord An'kelet."

The sword descended, touching briefly the kneeling warrior's broad shoulders, and then it was drawn away and swiftly sheathed.

An'kelet rose, and Art embraced him, suddenly a youth again and not the stern-faced being, lord of life and death, that stood beside the Stone of Adoration, and the men came in and clapped him on the back, and were merry and encouraging indeed.

But Merlin, standing between the tallest two bluestones, looked bleak and wan. He had pushed for this oath taking, hoping it would deflect the disaster he had read in the bones, but he had heard something in An'kelet's voice that made him quail anew. Your lady I will love above all women…

"I will not let it happen," he muttered, hands clawing the dark rough side of the stones. "Ancestors, give me strength to stick a dagger through both their hearts should they betray us as I have foreseen!"

CHAPTER THIRTEEN

Ardhu and his men reached the outskirts of the great and ancient place known as the Crossroads of the World a few days after the three-week-long feast of Bron Trogran had begun. They had travelled overland from Khor Ghor to Marthodunu, where they rested for several days before journeying onwards, their numbers swelled by locals eager to celebrate the harvesting of the crops. Leaving the huge protective walls beside the gurgling Abona, they continued North, following a line of green ridges where ancient long barrows and abandoned camps kept watch over the changing landscape and the ancient paths that led to Suilven, Crossroads-of-the-World.

Riding along a worn trade-track that had brought men to this area for a thousand years or more, the company first spotted a circular wooden building perched high on the edge of a steep escarpment. It had a vast thatched roof and a ring of weathered grey stones circled it. Next to the site, a line of barrows stretched out along the horizon, ominous against the bright sky. The afternoon was warm and golden, the air thick as honey and shimmering eerily around stones and posts. A fire was burning by one of the stones, casting up a greasy smoke, and people in masks were spiralling in and out, in and out.

One of the lead dancers was a young man who, to Ardhu's surprise, wore women's garb: a crescentric jet necklace and big, hooped earrings of gold, each bearing a dangling blue star-bead. Tumbling to his bare feet was a long gown painted with odd symbols—rutting stags, phallic signs, the terrible Mouth of Mother-Watcher as Devourer who all men desire yet fear. His lips were ochred and so too his cheeks, while ashes made his deep eyes smoky and emphasised his brows. People were bowing to him, and touching his robes as if for luck.

Ardhu glanced at Merlin, who rode beside him, rather uneasily, on a small fat pony chosen for its placid nature. "What is this place we can see?" he questioned. "And what are those people doing with that strange half-man? We do not celebrate in this way at Khor Ghor."

"The temple is the Sanctuary," replied Merlin. "It is said it was a bone-house in the old times, where the Ancestors would be laid out while the flesh fell from their bodies. It has changed its function many times. Now the priests and priestesses of Suilven use it as a gateway to that hallowed place the Golden-Men called the Crossroads of the World. As for the beautiful boy, he is the Fhir-Vhan, the man-woman. He is both outcast, set apart from the tribe, and holy—he brings both good and bad luck. He embodies the dual nature of all things: day and night, Sun and Moon, male and female."

The warband approached the Sanctuary and dismounted their horses, bowing before the mighty stones and laying down offerings of meat and drink for the spirits and the priests and priestesses of the temple.

The Fhir-Vhan danced up to the party, waving a rattle made of an infant's skullcap. He held out his free hand, its fingernails of unseemly length, and gestured to himself. "A cowry shell or amber bead for blessing of the Fhir-Vhan on the Rage of Trogran," he wheedled.

Ill at ease with this unsettling figure, Ardhu pulled on Lamrai's reigns, drawing her away. "I don't want your blessing!" he snapped.

The man/woman's beautiful face turned ugly, malign. "Then you shall not have it. Nor shall you have children of your loins that will live to come after you, just as I, the Fhir-Vhan, have no living progeny!"

Merlin flung up his hand, making a symbol to avert evil and curses. An'kelet, Bohrs and Per-Adur drew their daggers. The Fhir-Vhan stared scornfully down his long, straight nose at them. "I fear no knife. No Fhir-Vhan lives to see more than one lunar year—death means nothing to me. I already belong to the gods."

Merlin was the first to make peace. "I crave your forgiveness, Fhir-Vhan. The King…" he stressed the word, "is not worldly in some matters, for he is very young."

The Fhir-Vhan gave a haughty sniff and turned his back on the party before resuming his mad dance around a cairn of flints that marked, deep below, the ashes of a hundred Fir-Vhans spread over the skeleton of the very first—a young male with the pelvis of a girl placed over his hips.

"No damage was done," Merlin said to Art, who gestured for his men to sheathe their weapons. "My avert sign shielded you. But by the Sun, Ardhu, keep your mouth in check when you are far from home or you will not live long enough to bed that fair woman who has bewitched you! Discretion is a lesson you still must learn!"

The warband left the Sanctuary and continued toward the heart of the Crossroads-of-the-World, following a sacred avenue that snaked, serpent-like, across the countryside. It was vastly different from the earthen avenue at Khor Ghor, being lined with rough-hewn sarsen stones, some long and phallic, others broad and shaped like diamonds. Celebrants flitted up and down the line of stones, bowing and praising them, pouring libations at their bases.

At last, the Avenue ended. A bank and ditch became visible, immense and glowing white. Cresting its height, Ardhu gazed into a chalk ditch that fell away to such a depth it was as if he gazed down into the very underworld. Beyond was a raised earth platform, and on it three immense circles of unhewn stones similar to those in the adjacent Avenue. In the heart of the far ring stood a setting of three enormous menhirs that represented the mouth of a chambered barrow, its function much like the trilithon arches of Khor Ghor—a place where the spirits could enter or leave the world of the living under proper intercession from the priests and shamans. In the centre of the nearest circle loomed a single mighty obelisk with a tapered point, taller than the Great Trilithon by a man's height, and garlanded by flowers and fronds. Girls were dancing around it, arms raised to the Sun, and wheat sheaves bound in their hair. Some were naked or partly clad; many seemed to have worked themselves up into a trance as they whirled and writhed to the steady beat of a drum.

The comrades rode back down the bank at Ardhu's command and began pitching tents amid the other temporary dwellings that sprawled for a mile across the field beyond the sacred space. Once the encampment was made, and the horses and ponies safely tethered in a makeshift corral, Ardhu, accompanied by Merlin, returned to the activities in the great circle. The rest of the men, freed from warriors' obligations at this happy festival, mingled with the crowds both within and without, some seeking the solace of drink and some of women.

Merlin drew Ardhu toward the entrance of the south circle, fronted by two cyclopean stones, one with a large cleft in it, forming a natural seat. On it sat the most grotesque woman Art had ever set eyes on. She was short, nearly a dwarf, and old, almost impossibly so, maybe sixty summers. Her face bore ritual scars that deformed mouth and nose, and her wide mouth, distended by a clay plug, was void of teeth. She wore only a loincloth and a swathe of perforated shells that dangled between pendulous breasts heavy as great stones themselves. She was bloated, edemous, her skin painted a livid shade of grey-blue. In one hand she held a sheaf of wheat and in the other a serpent that circled her wrist like a living bracelet.

"Who…or what… is this?" Ardhu hissed to Merlin. He had heard that the Crossroads-of-the-World, especially under its older name of Suilven, Stones of the Eye, was highly attuned to women's magic, dark and primal. Most men feared this magic, for they could never understand—how women bled but did not die, and how the Moon drank this sacred blood, and how the women let spirits come into them with a man's seed to be reborn as new babies for the tribes.

"She is Odharna the high priestess," replied Merlin. "The Old Woman of Suilven, the greatest Old Woman of them all. In her flesh is the spirit of the one we call Ahn'ann, whose paps are the hills, whose Womb is also the Barrow-hill. Mother of Life, bestower of Death."

The priestess Odharna, spotting Merlin, gave a crowing cry of greeting. "Merlin, Merlin of Khor Ghor, long has it been! Come closer; let me see how many new grey hairs I can count upon your head."

"Too many I fear, Lady Odharna." Merlin walked towards her and bowed. "I have had my hands full these many years guiding my young friend here toward his life's destiny. Among other duties of course."

"Aye, aye, the boy-king!" Odharna rocked back and forth with mirth. "News has come here of his deeds, the Eye of Suilven is ever watchful across Prydn! Here, bring him closer, let me see him!"

Merlin shoved Ardhu forward; the young man hesitated, disconcerted by this strange figure, who seemed half of the very stone she sat on. "Ah, don't be afraid." She grinned toothlessly, gums stained green-black from some leafy substance she had been chewing. "I shan't eat you; it's not the season to eat pretty young men, I am not the blade-toothed Hag till winter!"

Ardhu forced himself to bow to her, using the depth of his bow to avoid looking at her lumpen, clay-coloured body, which reminded him of a bloated corpse. "I like the look of you," the priestess was saying, while stroking the head of her snake as it coiled about her arm. "Like U'thyr, your father, but without his petulance. Still green though; still a boy in many ways, that much I can see by your demeanour—the fact you cannot bear to gaze into my face. But you will learn in time, you are bright enough." Her small, fat-enfolded eyes raked over him. "You come here to marry at the feast, do you not?"

"Yes!" he burst out, surprised. "How did you know?"

"There is little I do not know," she grinned. "I have heard of the party from Ibherna that comes with cattle and gold—but, more precious than that, a woman white as snow. 'White Phantom' is her name, and her mother rumoured to be a goddess, and men now say that the daughter is a goddess too, embodiment of the very soul of the land. You'll have to keep a good eye on her when you get her, lad…for many men would kill to lay with the Sovereignty of Prydn, and gain mastery of this isle."

Ardhu's face darkened with sudden apprehension. What a fool he'd been! He should have sent the warband to greet Fynavir and her attendants…

Odharna laughed. "Don't look so stricken. I have sent out my bowmen to guide the marriage-party safely to the Crossroads-of-the-World. They are still a few days away, but fear not, my men shall see your white lady arrives unmolested."

Art bowed again, truly grateful. "I am in your debt, High One."

"I dare say by the end of all things we at Suilven shall be in yours," the priestess retorted. "So let us say we are even, Terrible Head. Go now, and join the festivities—the games of Trogran have begun this day and there are races and archery, wrestling and the hurling of stones. The fields will come to life, and the corn-woman will walk in her golden dress beneath the dancing Stars …and all will be blessed for another year."

"But…" She leaned forward, lank hair coiling like black serpents around her enormous mottled bosom, "a warning—most come here for blessing but some for less noble purposes. Darkness walks among us. I can feel its presence. One comes whose heart is black with hate. Milk will sour and the corn fail and women grow barren where this cursed one walks. And it is you she seeks, and hates, above all."

With that, her great flat head fell forward onto her chest and she drooped against the stone, her mind winging into some great Otherness.

Ardhu and the Merlin walked away toward the city of tents that had sprung up beyond the banks of Suilven. "Merlin, do you think I am in danger?" asked Art.

"You are always in danger," replied Merlin dryly. "It is a requirement of your position. But yes, there may be added peril here at Suilven. I know the danger that Odharna saw, and

112

hence it is time to tell you… that your family is here at the Crossroads-of-the-World. I saw the colours of Belerion on their tents."

"Family?" Ardhu's eyes widened. He had never asked Merlin about any living relatives. He had assumed that, like U'thyr, they were dead.

"Yes, boy, you surely didn't think you had no kindred at all? I will take you to meet them, and I can assess the situation."

"I don't understand. You want me to meet them, yet imply they might be dangerous. Why would they seek to harm me?"

Merlin sighed. "Not all of them wish you ill. Just one. One who is jealous of you and all you have attained. I gazed into her eyes long ago and saw something I feared. She is touched by the spirits, boy; a powerful woman of magic—to be feared more than any man. She is your half-sister, Morigau."

"My half-sister! I wish you had told me earlier, Merlin. I could have tried to make amends!"

Merlin shook his head. "You cannot make amends. You cannot bring her father back from the dead or restore her position in her mother's heart."

Merlin stopped before a tent painted with flanged axes, and gestured to a servant wandering about with a water-jug in her hands. "Fetch your masters and mistresses," he ordered. "Ardhu Pendraec would meet with his family."

The woman scuttled away, and Art could hear voices behind the skin flaps of the tent. A few minutes later the hangings were swept aside, and several figures emerged into the summer afternoon. Foremost was a girl who Ardhu immediately guessed must be close kin to him. Her eyes were the same brown-green shade as his, and the planes of her heart-shaped face had a familiar cast. A golden band topped her long near-black hair and she wore woollen robes dyed a rich green—colour of death, of the Ancestors in their mounds. Several men and youths of varying heights and sizes emerged from the tent behind her, along with a second young woman holding a crying baby in her arms. She alone of the group had blue eyes, and her hair held the warm hue of an autumn leaf.

"Hail, Ardhu Terrible Head, lord of Stones and hammer of our foes," said the first woman formally, bowing to Ardhu with utmost grace. "I am Mhor-gan, daughter of U'thyr Pendraec and Y'gerna of Belerion—and your sister. Behind me are your uncles and cousins on our mother's side, Emys, Baradir, Yltid, and your other sister, Gwyar, who is married to Gorangon of Brig-ahn."

Ardhu clasped her hands and looked into Mhor-gan's greenish eyes, filled with sudden joy at this acknowledgement of their kinship. "The Sun's Face shines on this day of our meeting, sister!" he cried. "Has our mother come with you to the feast?"

Mhor-gan laughed and shook her head. "No, she seldom travels. She has a third husband in Belerion, and prefers to keep away from the intrigues and feuds of her children! Ardhu, lord, come into the tent and all the questions you have shall be answered in time!"

Art let Mhor-gan lead him into her tent. It was cosy and warm, with sheepskins on the floor and bed-spaces laden with furs. An incense-cup burned in a corner, releasing a heady perfume. Mhor-gan offered her brother a beaker of ale and he drank it gratefully in token of their new friendship.

"So, tell me, sister," he said, when he had placed the mug back on the floor. "How have you fared these long years of our separation? Are you wed? Betrothed? And why do you wear the colour of the grave-mound? "

Mhor-gan smiled, long lashes veiling her eyes. "Can you not guess, Ardhu? I am like your friend Merlin, I see beyond the veil into the spirit world. I can speak with the Ancestors, and I know the movements of Moon and Stars and Sun. I can make potions to heal or to kill. I have danced on the hill with the Korrig, the shining ones; hence, the folk call me Mhor-gan of the Korrig-han, the faerie, and it is their colour I wear. It is my desire to join the Ladies of Afallan, sisters in my art, and learn more of my craft. This men I must marry no man. We may well end up as neighbours, brother, for I believe I shall be put under the tutelage of the revered Nin-Aeifa, who dwells in the lake-lands near Khor-Ghor."

"That would be a happy day; great is the wisdom of my sister Mhor-gan! But tell me more…" He gazed into her eyes, probing. "You introduced me to uncles and cousins, and to my younger sister, Gwyar. But there is one more, isn't there? One who is not as the rest? What of our older half-sister, Morigau?"

Mhor-gan toyed uncomfortably with a clay amulet around her neck. "Our half-sister…I suppose you had best know, for knowledge can give protection. Morigau hates us both, Ardhu.You for 'stealing;' her father and her mother; me, for being gifted with the shaman's art. She has powers too, perhaps even greater than mine, but Morigau is blighted, Ardhu, cursed. All she touches goes awry, bringing grief to her and those around her."

"I feel pity for her," said Art. "I would not see her sundered from us if a friendship can be forged."

Mhor-gan shook her head vigorously. "Hatred is what she lives on, Ardhu; it is her life's blood. She will never be your friend. She is about to be married, even as you are...to your enemy, Loth of Ynys Yrch."

Art spluttered in range. "Loth! How did this come about?"

"The moment Morigau heard that he disputed your claim to kingship, she travelled the length and breadth of the land, risking her life in hostile territories to reach his lonely isle. Obviously Loth was impressed by her tenacity…and other things." She laughed bitterly. "Like our mother, Morigau has many charms that certain men find irresistible!"

Ardhu shook his head. "Bitterness between kin is an evil thing. If she is so twisted that no hand of friendship can be offered, then I am glad she will be in the cold north with that bastard, Loth. I have sworn to kill him if he should ever cross into Albu, and I make no idle threats."

"But dare you ban Morigau from the south, too? How the tribes would laugh—the great king Ardhu fearful of a woman, and his sister, no less! Morigau is clever; she is well aware of how things stand, and will use it to her advantage."

Ardhu frowned and stroked his chin. "You speak troubling words, sister."

"Forgive me," Mhor-gan said. "But you need to know the truth. But come, smile again, is it not true your bride is on the way to Suilven? Soon you shall be together. Surely that thought will help dispel the gloom brought by Morigau's hate!"

Ardhu reached forward and kissed her on both cheeks. "You are a wise woman indeed. I will turn my thought to what will be, rather than what may be. For all we know, once Morigau weds Loth, she may never again set foot beyond the frigid north!"

"We can hope," said Mhor-gan, lady of the Khorrig-han. "Hope is the best we have."

Later that night, Ardhu emerged from the tent and went alone into the great circles that made up the Crossroads-of-the-World. Fires roared between jagged sarsens, and the figures of frenzied dancers cast strange shadows over the trampled grass. In the far circle, wailing women were carrying skulls and jawbones in and out of the three-stoned cove. A priestess hunkered down, naked, head lolling and eyes rolling as she invoked spirits she alone could see. Around her, other revellers danced, reaching their hands up to the great Cross-of-Stars that was rising over distant Hakh-pen hill.

Ardhu glanced around, hoping to spot some of his men, or the Merlin, but he had not seen any of them since he had gone to speak with Mhor-gan. No matter—they had served him well these past months, and it was their right to join the great feast of the Harvest as much as any other.

Ardhu noticed a flurry of people leaving the main circles and processing down a secondary avenue of stones that branched out toward the night-shrouded West. The revellers chanted and waved torches, and a hot, smoky lust burned in the eyes of both men and women, repelling and yet intriguing the young chieftain. He let himself drift along with the flow of people, the river of humanity streaming out along the row of sarsens.

At the end of the avenue, the surging crowd slowed, pooled. Art threaded his way through the heaving mass to see what was happening. Dimly lit by the torches, he spotted another mighty stone cove, and beyond it the dark hump of a large, ponderous long barrow.

In the heart of the cove, a rite of the harvest was taking place. A figure wrapped round with wheat-sheaves danced wildly in the flickering torchlight, weaving and winding between the sarsens, casting handfuls of grain over the onlookers. Naked except for a bull's head mask, a man pursued the fleeting figure. He was painted with stripes, and he brandished a flint sickle, honed and deadly, an ancient relic handed down from generations past. He chased the Dancer-of-the-Wheat-Sheaves in a rough, clumsy dance of his own, hewing at the air with his sickle and stamping and bellowing like a real bull.

Art sat down cross-legged in the grass alongside other onlookers. A huge drinking vessel was being passed around. Ardhu drank deeply, mimicking those around him. The mead in the brimming pot rushed to his head almost instantly, and in a flash he realised it was drugged.

His stomach contracted. He was a king, not a priest…he did not seek to get closer to the gods by the taking of potions. He went to rise, to make his way back to the encampment, but hands reach out to pull him down.

Two young men about his own age were tugging on his cloak. "You…you're Ardhu of Khor Ghor, are you not?" one asked. "The Young King? Surely you won't leave before the dance is over? Your blessing would surely make the crops grow stronger next year."

Art flopped clumsily back into the grass. "Who are you?"

"Friends. Admirers. We have heard much about you. I am Ack-olon." A youth of middling height with a broad, confident face stepped forward and gave a short bow. "And this is my friend, La'morak." He gestured to the other youth, smaller and less stocky, his tawny curls braided with feathers. "Would you care to share our drink and food? It would be an honour."

Ardhu did not know how he should respond. His head was light from the draught of tainted mead, and the thought of not being quite himself made him uneasy, but if he refused the lads' hospitality, it might be bandied about that he was high-handed and thought himself too good for people outside of his band. He wished now that he had consulted Merlin before blundering off and joining in the celebrations. Or maybe taken An'kelet with him.

La'morak was pushing a brimming beaker into his hands. "Drink, my King! First taste to you, the wielder of the sword from the stone, who has so bravely fought our enemies."

Ardhu drank, the thick, cloying mead running down his chin.

"And more!" Ack-olon shoved another beaker his way, this one full of frothy ale.

Again, he downed it, all too aware of the hot eyes of the youths on him. Surely, this was some sort of a test by these two young warriors—seeing if he, younger than they, could compete with them in the man's world of the feast.

A sudden shout from the cove drew his attention away from his companions. The Dancer-of-the-Wheat-Sheaves was twirling within reach of the vicious flint sickle, and the bull-headed man was hewing frenziedly at the golden coat. Suddenly he nicked a strand of twine binding the sheaf and the whole casing tumbled away, showering onto the onlookers, who grasped at the tendrils and took them for luck.

Where the Wheat-Dancer had been was a young girl, naked save for her streaming red hair. Her eyes were huge, the pupils swollen with mushroom-potion, looking inwards to otherness and emptiness. Her lips moved faintly in invocations as she reached towards the bull-masked man.

A priest in a conical bronze headdress emerged from the crowd and tied plaited strands of wheat around the two, binding them together. The masked man cast away his sickle and grabbed the girl to him, all lust and fury, with no gentleness. She met him in like passion, clawing his bare back with her nails, crying out wordlessly toward the hag-face of old Mother Moon as She soared overhead, a bent crescent heading West to the land of the Dead.

Together they fell onto the trampled ground, coupling like beasts before the assembled celebrants. The priest with the tall bronze hat and seven acolytes danced wild rings around them, offering up the jawbones of those whose spirits they hoped would be reborn and casting down carved chalk balls that symbolised the fertility of man and beast. The onlookers cried out, moaning and shrieking along with the pair on the ground; men and women started to pair off and run out into the darkness, tearing at their clothes, their eyes full of Moon-madness and unbridled desire.

Hot blood rushed to Ardhu's face. He had never seen rites like this before. He knew of course how it was between the sexes; he was not ignorant. But he had grown up in a small homestead of a widower, and if Ech-tor had women, he had met with them on his trading journeys when Ka'hai and Ardhu were left at home to mind the forge and tend the animals. Then, since his coming of age he had been in the Merlin's care, and until he met Fynavir had hardly so much as spoken to a girl…

The youth called Ack-olon nudged him in the ribs. "Surely that should be you there with the Corn-Maiden, since you are King," he said, his voice an insidious whisper. "That's how it was in the old days. The King mates with the Lady who is the Land."

"I have a woman…I am to be married during the feast," said Ardhu. He cursed himself inwardly even as he spoke. He had been foolish, naive. His companions' behaviour had gone beyond harmless testing; their eyes were glittered with amused malice, and their whole demeanour reeked of arrogance and impudence. They had some grudge with him. He knew the sensible thing to do would be to retreat into the milling crowds before any more trouble found him.

But La'morak had hold of his arm, his fingers like a vice. "Surely you should have her here, this night. It is only right that you, as King, should make the great marriage with your Queen."

Ardhu groped at his left boot, seeking Carnwennan in its hidden sheath, and then remembered, with a sinking feeling, that he had left it at the encampment along with Caladvolc, obeying the rule that forbade weapons in the circles of Suilven. He began to struggle, but the drugs in his first bowl of mead and the alcohol in the second and third made his head whirl and his knees and arms jelly-like and weak. He struck out at La'morak and missed, plummeting forward onto his belly on the ground.

He could hear the two young men laughing, and he tensed, half expecting to feel fists rain down on him, or even weapons…but then a figure came drifting out of the darkness, as if from some shadowy dream, a figure that swayed towards him, hands beckoning, dancing on delicate feet, bringing welcome memories and a shiver of both fear and desire.

The dancer was wearing a heavy wooden mask carved into the semblance of a raven with a long bone beak and eyes of glittering jet. A vast cloak made of hundreds of shining black feathers floated around the figure, rustling in the rising breeze.

Leaning over Ardhu, the dancer tapped him sharply on the shoulder with the beak of the bird-mask. The feather cloak briefly parted and he caught a tantalising glimpse of white flesh beneath.

Art started to grin, a silly, lecherous, drunken grin. Surely, surely no girl would know to dance for him in such a way…except Fynavir. Fynavir the White Phantom, who had danced in her foster-father's halls for him and awoken the fires in his loins. She must have arrived sooner than expected and devised this strange meeting, though he had no idea why she would play such games with him. He knew so little of women! Maybe this teasing game of courtship was part of her people's tradition; in foreign parts tribes did things differently—in Fynavir's homeland of Ibherna, he'd heard it was even usual for a king to mate with a white mare, which was then sacrificed and boiled into a broth. He was glad such an act would not be required of him; he fancied girls not horses!

La'morak smirked and pulled Ardhu roughly to his feet, pushing him in the direction of the masked woman. "Your Queen awaits, King Ardhu," he said, his voice husky, harsh, tense with excitement. "The one bound to you in life, in death. Go to her, the Great Queen, and know your destiny."

Ardhu stumbled toward the raven-woman. He tried to lift off her heavy mask, but she caught his hand, and instead drew it under her cloak, pressing it against hot, bare flesh, a conical breast that, oddly, made him think of the shape of a grave-mound.

He almost cried out with surprise at the jolt of fire that ran from head to crotch, but she laid a calming finger against his lips. "Come, come with me," she whispered, and she drew him away from the firelight illuminating the cove, and out into the shadows of the darkened fields, away from La'morak and Ack-olon, away from the celebrating people of Suilven.

Beyond the firelight, there was total darkness save for the stars. To the left Ardhu could see the vague silhouette of a mighty stepped hill, an earthen pyramid shaped like a barrow but much larger than the tomb of any man. It was the Hill of Suil, the Wise Eye, one of the wonders of Prydn, and a Tomb of Tombs that held no mortal bones. Some said it was the sepulchre of the Sun in Winter, others that it was mighty Ahn' ann's own body, from which she birthed the holy springs that rose nearby to join the Head River Khen. Some gave the Winter Sun a name; they called him Zhel, and said he was Ahn'ann's son, and that when he died on the shortest day he was buried in a golden coffin in his Mother's earth-womb to await rebirth as young, virile Bhel, the Sun of Summer.

But to Ardhu, wandering through that dead land with the raven-cloaked woman, he could think only that it resembled one thing—the great white breast of a goddess, caressed by the four winds and the wavering starlight. A giant replica of the warm, living flesh his questing hand had touched. Cold chills ran down his spine, but fire leapt up in him too, a primal heat that matched that of the man who played the corn-king at the Cove.

"Where are we going?" he asked his companion, trying once again to get a look under her concealing mask.

"You'll see, my king," came the muffled voice. "Not far now and then…" She swirled her feather cloak, revealing for one second the pointed hills and dark valleys of the tempting flesh beneath. "Your desire and your destiny will become one!"

They walked further and the night deepened. The noise from the great henge was a mere buzzing on the wind. Rounding the flanks of the Hill of the Eye, the raven-woman set off across country, crossing the sacred stream of Suil and hastening for the hilltop above. Ardhu followed silently, wanting to rip away that cloak, to fall with her into the furrows of the fields, and to give up the last vestiges of his childhood in her arms. To become one with her as the Sun became one with the Earth, quickening the crops and all nature to life.

Nearing the top of the rise, he spotted a finger of stone, a dark hummock with the fading Moon hanging over its end.

A long barrow.

It was the mightiest structure of its kind that Art had ever seen. On the Great Plain most of these early burial mounds, some already two thousand years old, were mere earthen piles, their wooden mortuary houses, once draped with the hides of oxen, long collapsed and decayed. But here, the barrow had chambers and forecourt of stone, and at the front of all was a great, wide, sealing stone, its threatening bulk seeming to shout 'I forbid!" into the darkness.

The lust in him almost died away in the presence of that stern, frowning Ancestor-stone. This was a place of haunts and shadows, not a bed for lovers to lie in.

The woman at his side noted his hesitation and slid her arms around his waist, rubbing herself against him. "Don't be afraid!" she whispered in his ear, nipping the lobe with sharp little teeth. "Here the spirits can bless our union. Here a great Ancestor might come into me even as you will, and breathe soul into a child in making."

Ardhu flushed. He had not even thought of that possibility. But how good would that seem to the people, not only leader and conqueror, but also founder of a new dynasty of kings…!

He let himself be led around the stony fangs of the forecourt to the blocking stone. There was a gap between it and the arched roof of the cairn, and Raven-woman wriggled into it effortlessly, again giving him a tantalising glimpse of white legs and smooth buttocks.

He followed all too eagerly.

The night wind shrieked over the hill as if laughing at the folly of a lust-blinded young man.

Ardhu awoke early the next morning in a tangle of bones…and living arms and legs. Daylight was filtering dully through gaps around the blocking stone. He stared. On either side in niches were stacks of bones, skulls in one place, long bones in another. Empty eyeholes regarded him. Their owners were long dead, but the air smelt damp, foul, retaining the resifue of death and decay.

Tearing his gaze away, he stared at the woman sprawled next to him. She lay curled on her side, naked on the feather cloak, but still wearing the bird-mask. She had refused to take it off during their lovemaking, and he supposed, as before, that this was some strange custom of her people, so he dared not press her too far.

But now, the union was done; morning had come and she need not hide any longer. He crawled closer to her, taking in the curve of her hips, the small but perfect breasts which had been painted with ritual signs, now smudged by hands and lips. She was thinner than he had imagined she would be, and darker-skinned, though it was hard to tell through the paint and dirt from the floor of the cairn.

Lovingly he reached out to remove the clumsy mask, to free the Moon-white hair and kiss the pale full lips of Fynavir…

A lock of midnight-black hair tumbled over his hand.

His heart began to thud against his ribs. What madness was this?

Less gently, he pulled the mask away.

And looked into a dark, fine-featured face that was a feminine copy of his own visage. Greenish eyes, wide-set and knowing, regarded him with amusement. A small but sensual mouth, red and languid, smiled.

"Who …who are you?" he cried, hurling the mask away. It shattered against a stone and feathers flurried.

The girl rose onto her haunches, tossing back her ebony mane. "Haven't you guessed? I am sure the Merlin and Mhor-gan warned you of me! I am Morigau…your half-sister."

Bile rose up in Ardhu' throat, burning like fire. Shame reddened his face. This…this creature had tricked him…tricked him into breaking a terrible taboo. One of the greatest of all taboos. If any of the tribes were to find out, he would lose his kingship, and probably his life; it might even start a civil war in Prydn, as other men strove for supremacy.

Morigau seemed to read his thoughts. "Don't worry," she said haughtily. "I am not going to go about telling the world. My fate would be worse that yours, which would be a clean death at least. Me—they'd pin me in a bog."

"Why have you done this?" Ardhu cried. "Hate I could fathom, but not this terrible act! You…you are surely a shape-shifter, a witch! I could have sworn you were Fynavir!'"

Morigau's lips tightened to thin lines; her eyes glowed, cat-like. "You saw what you wanted to see! Like most men you were led by your man-thing…and not this…" She tapped her forehead. "Do you want to know why I deceived you? Well, hear my words, brother: I had a father, whom I loved—he was taken from me by your father. I had a mother too; she forgot me when you were born, and even when Merlin claimed you, she never loved me again. I am going to show you what it is to lose, Ardhu. To lose everything, as I have: my father, my mother's heart, Belerion, which would have been my birthright, had Y'gerna not wed U'thyr. All that is left for me is to marry a pig like Loth of Ynys Yrch, so that I may live with a queen's status. I blame you for that too, Ardhu Terrible-Head, bastard of U'thyr, whose barrow I spit on!"

"If I had my sword I would kill you!" Ardhu shouted, smashing his clenched fist against one of the great megaliths of the chamber. "You are sick, twisted."

"I'm not afraid of you," she said scornfully. "Rage, little boy! I have powers, just like your friend the Merlin. You would not dare touch me…especially as the Eye-Goddess, lady of the tomb, has breathed a spirit into my belly to mingle with your seed. Nine Moons from today a child will be born…"

He stared at her, horrified. "You cannot know such a thing for sure!"

She smirked evilly. "I am a witch—you said it yourself! I saw it in the bones cast three times three. Once I was certain the signs were right, I arranged the time of our coupling to follow the phases of the Moon that guides all women. I will not be wrong. My Woman magic is strong."

She wrapped her arms round her knees and her eyes were filled with burning fire. "Traders visiting Belerion have spoken of great kings in sun-burned lands far away, who marry their sisters to keep the bloodline pure. That is what our son will be, Ardhu—a pure son of Albu. Through him, I will claim back all the lands I lost, and he will love me as no other ever has. Never will there have been a child of such beauty and power. Be warned, Ardhu—brother—he will be the Dark Moon that eclipses your Sun!"

She leaped to her feet, her face warped with hatred but also ecstatic at the thought of the future she foresaw. "Today I will continue my journey north to the realm of my husband-to-be. I am sure he will be pleased to find out he has got an heir on me so soon. He will never know another's seed grows in his field. Farewell, Ardhu. Thank you for your gift." She leaned over as if to kiss him, but viciously bit his lip instead, drawing blood.

He cried out and sprang back, repulsed.

Morigau laughed, standing with her lips reddened with his blood like some malign war-goddess. One droplet rolled down her skin, pooling in the hollow of her throat. She flicked it away with a finger and, casting Ardhu a mocking and contemptuous glance, snatched up her feather cloak and climbed hurriedly from the tomb.

Ardhu staggered after her, his stomach heaving with the enormity of what he had done. He did not know what steps to take; killing Morigau was all he could think of, but he was weaponless, and she was blood-kin, and a woman.

And a magic-worker, set to marry his enemy, Loth.

Standing on the barren hillside, with the cold morning wind blasting into his face, he watched as Morigau traipsed blithely down from the burial cairn and was greeted by La'morak and Ack-olon at the bottom of the rise. They hugged and embraced in a congratulatory way, and he realised that not only had the youths been sent to entrap him with drink, that the familiarity between Morigau and her henchmen was more akin to that between lovers than mistress and servants.

With a cry of grief and despair, he sank down onto the dew-drenched soil and pounded the earth with his fists.

CHAPTER FOURTEEN

Later that morning, Ardhu sought out the palisaded enclosure beside the waters of the Khen, a sorry, grim-faced figure with a cut and bloodied lip and shadows in his eyes. He had sat for hours in the cold wind beside the Old Ones' barrow, cursing himself, Morigau, the very gods who could allow such deceit. Eaten by shame, he would have stayed even longer, but suddenly he heard the blare of horns, and standing on the ancient mound saw a stream of unfamiliar banners heading toward the palisade, followed by the flags and pennants of his kin and his own warband.

Unnerved by this flurry of activity, he cursed and ran from the hilltop toward the palisade enclosures.

An'kelet met him at the great gateway of stout oak. "Praise the spirits that you are here! The Merlin has been searching for you. The men were growing uneasy."

Art glanced at his friend, his insides clenching with revulsion at the memory of the taboo that he had broken. He could tell no one the truth...not An'kelet, not Ka'hai, certainly not Merlin. "I was drunk..." he said gruffly. "I fell. I've been in the fields sleeping it off."

An'kelet gazed at his troubled face, and frowned, but kept his peace—who was he to pry if Ardhu wished to keep his secrets? "There is news, Lord, news that should gladden your heart. The Lady Fynavir has arrived, bringing cattle and other riches in her train."

The last vestiges of colour drained from Ardhu's already pale face. How could he face Fynavir, so soon after...? If it had just been a tumble with some willing local girl, even a temple priestess, no harm done, none would think of it ever again or hold it against him. But to break such a powerful taboo as that which bars the mating of close kin, with such a powerful magic-woman, in such a holy and dreadful place....

He ran his hands through his lank and dirt-clotted hair, over his pounding forehead. "I must make myself presentable for her, An'kelet. Come; help me dress in my ceremonial clothes so that neither she nor I will be shamed."

Ardhu went to his tent and An'kelet followed. As his lord's right-hand man, he washed Ardhu's face and painted it. He braided his long dark hair and placed his copper helm upon his brow. Carefully he buttoned him into the leather tunic with the golden breastplate of King Samothos fastened to the front, and girt Caladvolc about his waist. Lastly, he handed him the Lightning-Mace with its gleaming mounts and fossil head.

Hiding his inner turmoil as best he could, Ardhu stepped out of the tent into the milling crowds inside the palisade enclosure.

The first thing he saw was Merlin descending on him like an angry hawk. The Shaman grasped his arm, fingernails biting flesh. "Where have you been? Why do you play the fool? You spoke to Mhor-gan; she warned you, as I did, of possible danger here at Suilven, and yet you ignored us, and vanished without telling a soul. You are lucky you are not lying in some ditch with your throat slit from ear to ear!"

"Merlin, enough!" Ardhu flashed back. "You will not chide me like some wayward child in front of my people! Take me to Fynavir and hold your tongue at least till we are alone!"

The older man fell silent, sparks of fury leaping from his eyes, but he obviously thought better of making a scene. Face dark as a storm cloud, he ushered Ardhu toward a large group of people hovering around a newly-raised cattle pen at the back of the enclosure. Cows lowed and stomped as men leaned on the rails, remarking on their size and heartiness.

"Before you, Chief Ardhu, is Princess Fynavir's bride-price, sent from Mevva of Ibherna," said Merlin. "There are also three hounds, a goblet carved from amber, and a gold clothing fastener for your cloak. Ka'hai is looking after everything."

"It is good to have received such wealth, but only Fynavir and her well-being matters to me. Where is she?"

"She comes…dressed in her bridal gown and ready to greet her husband-who-will-be." Merlin nodded toward a tent guarded by several foreign warriors in outlandish clothes, and ringed by girls and women straining to catch a glimpse of the mysterious white woman who had come to wed the young king of the West.

Suddenly the tent flap was pushed aside and Fynavir emerged, attended by two young women from her homeland. The sight of her took Ardhu's breath away, deepening his guilt over his tryst with Morigau the night before. She was truly a vision, an earthly goddess like her mother, but where Mevva was red, the colour of blood and sensuality, Fynavir was snow-white and pure, unstained, a creature born of cloud or mist. He almost expected white trefoils to blossom and dance at her feet.

She was wearing the badges of nobility, of a queenly bride—a bronze circlet that glowed against the snow of her hair and a shining pectoral cape wrought from a single sheet of beaten gold, fashioned by great art to resemble pleated cloth. Linen marriage-robes fell from eyelets along the cape's edges, sweeping the ground with a fringe made of thin gold wires. As stunning as the cape looked, Fynavir was clearly uncomfortable wearing it, for the shoulders were so narrow and inflexible she could scarcely bend her arms. She moved at a shuffle, looking nervous and disconcerted, while women and men alike touched her for luck.

"Fynavir." Ardhu held out his cold and dirty hands, green with barrow-mould, and made to clasp her soft white hands.

Then he stopped. He was filthy. Contaminated. Unfit to touch her.

He dropped his hands abruptly, and stared at his feet, leaving Fynavir stunned and hurt with the murmuring crowds all around her.

A priestess of the Sanctuary came up, tall and thin in her hooded robe. "Shall I send for the Old Woman of Blessed Fame, and prepare the circle for your marriage-binding, lord?"

"N…no!" Ardhu objected more harshly that he had intended. "I have decided that the best place to wed is my own territory, at the Temple of Khor Ghor. I would leave for there as soon as possible."

A gasp went through the crowd, and the people suddenly shied away from Fynavir as if she was now accursed. The priestess's weather-beaten face was thunderous. "If that is your wish, you must go—you are the Young King," she said. "But some may see this decision as an affront both to Suilven and the spirits."

Ardhu made no reply but signalled for his men prepare for departure. Merlin's visage was livid, but he kept his peace and stalked along behind Ardhu, clutching his staff until his knuckles were bleached as bone.

Art nodded at An'kelet, who stood in white-faced silence, as shocked by Ardhu's rejection of the blessings of Suilven as the rest of the company but loyalty staying his tongue "Ank, escort the Lady Fynavir back to the Place of Light, will you? Make sure her men need for nothing, and that the animals are well tended and don't escape along the journey. I will ride ahead with the Merlin. We have much to discuss. Things I cannot even speak of to you, my friend."

The warband moved across country, passing the harvest-hill that was a miniature twin to Zhel's Barrow before following the wild borders of Savarna's wood toward the South. Merlin and Ardhu were far ahead of the rest, out of earshot and almost out of sight.

Fynavir rode on a fat pony that had been requisitioned from one of the warriors; she had never sat astride a horse before, and so An'kelet led her steed on a sturdy twine rein. She glanced over at him, noticing how the hazy summer light shimmered on cheekbone and smooth forehead, and made a halo of his waving amber hair. She had missed him, her friend from Lodegran's dun, who, as a foreigner himself, had understood her sense of never truly belonging. He had made her laugh, had taught her to fire a bow and tame a hawk, and she had danced for him once, as she had for Ardhu, but he, bound by the oaths set on him by his priestess mother, had merely kissed her hand afterwards and walked away.

"I am not sure about riding," she said dubiously, trying to strike up conversation. "It seems unnatural…"

"You will grow accustomed," An'kelet replied with a smile. His teeth were white and even, not worn down by grit like so many others'. "It is a swift way to travel—and for warriors, riding gives advantage in most kinds of battle. Ardhu wants us all to learn to ride."

Fynavir tensed, and she stared at the ground. "I displease him."

"Don't be foolish!" An'kelet shook his head.

"Then why did he not take my hand? Why has he postponed our marriage, and enraged the priestesses of Suilven?"

An'kelet sighed and flicked his horse's rein, guiding it closer to Fynavir's pony. "Art is young, Fynavir. Sometimes he acts with no thought. He is…moody."

She laughed a little. "I thought only women were prey to their moods! But I will take into account what you say. I hope I can trust your word, and that you are not just trying to pacify me."

He gazed at her with seriousness. "I would never lie to you…my queen. Ardhu is as my brother, and I will serve and love the both of you until there is no breath left in my body. If I should break this vow, many the sky fall upon me, my bones remain unbarrowed and my spirit be bound to earth forever."

He spoke with such passion that she blushed and glanced away, embarrassed. Heat crept up into her face. She was all too aware, suddenly, of An'kelet's near presence ; his muscled arms, bare in the heat, his golden male beauty making him shine like a spirit born of the Sun Himself….

You should not think of him thus! she told herself sternly…

At that moment, a hare bounded out of a mossy bank and dashed, legs pumping, in front of her pony. The stocky little animal reared on its hinds, while Fynavir grappled hopelessly with the reins then, in desperation, flung her arms around its neck. The pony rolled its eyes and bolted, thundering over the rocky terrain toward a winding brook lined with ash-trees.

"Fynavir!" She heard An'kelet's voice call frantically after her. Sunlight shattered on the rocks about her, rippling like golden fire on the free-flowing stream. Wind raked her hair and the world tilted, earth becoming sky, sky becoming earth …and then a hefty branch hung with lichens smashed into her shoulder and sent her crashing to the ground amid the pointed rocks.

An'kelet was at her side with such speed it was as if he had flown to her on the wings of a magical swan. Face pallid with concern, he flung himself on the ground next to her and lifted her carefully in his arms. She could feel the beat of his heart against her cheek, the beat of her own heart madly, wildly, against her bruised ribs…and suddenly the world seem to lurch again, but not in an unpleasant way. It was as if time itself had stopped, and all the world had become unreal, a place where only she and An'kelet existed, locked in a golden circle of light, far from the fights and troubles of kings and warriors.

And An'kelet…he gazed down at her in silence, her hair spilling over his lap like a cloud, and Fynavir knew he felt what she felt, and that he feared it, and yet desired it more than anything else on earth.

"My Lady…Fynavir…" he whispered hoarsely, and he gently turned her around in his arms so that she faced him. The golden light was all around them, the brook beside them roaring, its spirit rising to protect them, embrace them. She closed her eyes, felt his breath mingle with her breath, the faintest touch of his mouth on hers, rich with the taste of honey and meadowsweet....

Suddenly a shadow fell over them, and the magic circle was diminished, its light smothered. They both glanced up as a raven soared overhead, its voice harsh and mocking, doom-laden.

"An omen!" Fynavir whispered, covering her face in fear.

An'kelet's hands dropped from her shoulders; his visage was white and drained. "An evil spirit possessed me.... I should not have acted so. Forgive me."

Tears sprang in Fynavir's eyes; coldness clutched her heart. She had nearly betrayed her husband-to-be, her king, and put both her own life and An'kelet's in jeopardy with her wantonness.

At that moment, Ka'hai and Bohrs rode up. "Lady, are you hurt?" Ka'hai swung down from his horse.

"Only my pride." She wiped her eyes with the back of her hand. "But don't fear for me, lords of the West—I will not break from such a tiny bump, I am made of sterner stuff than that! I have a wedding-alliance to make between your peoples and mine. I will not fail in my duty."

She got up, ignoring their proffered hands, and managed to clamber with minimal fuss back onto her pony, which was now cropping grass calmly beside the stream. She gestured to Ka'hai to ride beside her, and set heels to her mount, driving it back up to the main entourage waiting on the trackway.

An'kelet was left behind, seemingly forgotten by his fellows, kneeling on the cold stones under the branches of the gnarly ash, watching Fynavir's white tresses stream away into the distance like a trail of wind-blown smoke.

She did not look back.

The sky was dark with promised rain, the clouds bunched into fantastical shapes of giants and gods. Shafts of sunlight spiked through tiered cumulus, lighting up the rolling barrow-downs around the temple of Khor Ghor, illuminating first one mound and then another, making chalk ditches and half-grassed summits gleam with otherworldly luminescence.

Inside the great Stone Circle, the warriors of Ardhu Pendraec stood in their ceremonial robes, one in each archway, facing in towards the Altar-stone. Ardhu stood upon the height of the Great Trilithon with Merlin at his side, invoking the spirits of Everlasting Sky—Nhod the healer, Cloudmaker, lord of the milky way; Moon-Mother with her bone-white eye; and Bhel Sunface with his radiant head that gave life to all the world.

Below them, beside the Stone of Adoration, Fynavir stood in her bridal gown with its unparalleled cape of gold. She looked small and alone amidst the towering megaliths. She felt uneasy, for though these Stones were strange to her, in her own land she knew of Stonehead, the Black Crooked One, surrounded by thirteen pillars, who demanded a tithe of milk, corn and children every seven years. And so it was everywhere—the spirits always demanded a sacrifice; there was always a price to be paid...

What did the Ancestors who ruled Khor Ghor want as payment? And who would pay it?

She shivered, and it was not from the biting wind that seemed to blow, day and night across the plain, bringing inclement weather from the West and battering the stones on that side of the circle.

Glancing to one side, she spied An'kelet among the warriors. His head was bowed, the wind casting his copper-gold hair in wild disarray. A sudden shaft of light touched him, and he was instantly all gold, a scion of the Sun himself.

She looked away hurriedly, fearful that he would notice her furtive glance, afraid her eyes would reveal the fearful secret of her heart.

Merlin and Ardhu were descending from the Door into Winter using a rope ladder that priest-acolytes then removed and rolled up. The shaman was stern-visaged, and unwelcoming; Fynavir had sensed that he did not approve of her. She knew he could be a danger if his opinion did not change, and determined she would put no foot wrong and win him to her cause.

The Merlin stalked up to her and grasped her hand, thrusting it into Ardhu's with little gentleness. Art grinned at her shyly, looking like the boy he truly was beneath the warrior's veneer, and squeezed her chilled fingers. Merlin then drew a cord made of gold wires from his belt-pouch. He wrapped it about their twined hands, knotting it again and again, until it dug into their flesh, binding them together.

"By these bonds, you are joined, King and Queen of Khor Ghor and the West, high lord and lady of the lands of the Dwri, the Duvnoni, and other client kingdoms. The spirits have entrusted you with these positions and you are their representatives on earth—son of sky, the Great heavenly Bear who rules the Northern heavens, and daughter of Earth, the White Lady who lies within the chalk below us, the very bones of Albu, our fair land. Together it is your duty to rule the tribes well and to give them a strong line of kings from the joining of your flesh…"

Merlin gave Ardhu a sudden piercing look from under his brows, and both Fynavir and Art blushed profusely, neither gazing at the other.

"So it is done," said the Merlin, and he waved his staff over them, lightly touching them on brow, on breast, on Fynavir's belly and Ardhu's thigh. "Hail to the Lord of the West and his Lady!"

The warband cheered and drums were beaten. A sweet smell went up as priests lit incense cups and walked around the stones, bowing and supplicating them, pouring offerings of animal blood and alcoholic drink at their bases so that the Ancestors might also join in with the wedding feast.

Once finished, they halted and turned toward the North-East. Their drum fell silent—but another in the distance was beating, slow and sensual. Up from the river came a party of women to attend to the bride and prepare her for the wedding night ahead. Three times three they were: a holy number, three maidens, three women of childbearing age, and three withered crones. Naked save for short skirts and paint, they capered and shrieked and wailed, occasionally lifting their skirts and exposing themselves—an age-old gesture said to ward off evil spirits and protect against lightning.

The men within the stone circle stared at the ground, or else covered their eyes—it was ill-luck for males to gaze upon these women as they danced for the fertility of human and beast, and even a furtive, stolen glance could make a man blind, or, worse, impotent.

The women surrounded Fynavir, touching her with their stained hands, leaving red, chalky, and ashen handprints all over her splendid robe. They guided her to a great flat bluestone at the front of the circle, standing beside a peaked 'male' stone, its mate through long eternity. They crowded around it, rubbing themselves against its rough surface, pressing Fynavir forward until she too was embracing it, this old Mother stone that had seen generations come and go. She could feel its rough surface through the thin linen of her bridal robe, and it seemed to grow warm as she touched it, making her body tingle, and her thighs grow warm.

For the first time since she had entered Khor Ghor she felt less afraid. Whatever spirit dwelt in this Ancestor-stone, it felt benign, even loving… unlike crook-backed Stonehead with his Moon-sickle that harvested human lives.

The women took her by the arms and drew her away from the female stone. Slowly they retreated from the great circle, holding hands and making a circle of their own, dancing Sunwise around Fynavir as they chanted and sang.

Down the Avenue they danced, and the Sunlight and shadows of that day enfolded them until they became mere dots on the horizon by the swelling mounds of the Seven Kings.

"Go now," said Merlin to the men of the warband. "Let there be feasting and merriment among the peoples until the break of dawn. King Ardhu of Prydn now has his Queen."

The men fared forth to high Kham-El-Ard, where Merlin's builders had finally completed the Great Hall, a structure unlike any other ever raised in the isles. Crafted to the specifications of the shaman, its design was influenced by past meetings with travellers from beyond the mighty river Rhyn and the Pillars of the Western World, who brought tales of the splendid palaces and strongholds of faraway lands.

The hall stood shining in the pallid Sunlight, a true place of heroes with its mighty gables and lintelled door that faced East to catch the rising Sun. Rectangular in shape, it resembled the small houses that clustered about Deroweth, but was many times their size and covered with carvings of gods and spirits that seemed ready to leap into life. Unusually, high portholes were cut into the sides to let out smoke and odours, and screens of stretched calfskin were attached to them on frames to keep out inclement weather.

The men set about drinking, and many ribald jokes were told, and boasts made that would never be carried out. Warriors wrestled, and a young aurochs, standing nearly six foot at the shoulder, was dragged up the hill and pole-axed before the doors of Ardhu's Great Hall, its blood being used to paint the threshold and bring good luck to the consummation of the marriage. The beast's head was then buried in a pit by the gate, a silent watcher that gazed toward the terminus of the Avenue.

Gradually day faded to early evening, and the light became warm. Red rays of Sun shot through the bunched clouds in the West, making the entire fort of Kham-El-Ard glow like fire. Down below, in the twisted trees near the Sacred Pool, a horn suddenly blared, its voice rising eerily up to the heights. Birds scattered from their perches at the sound, soaring into the sky like the souls of the dead taking flight.

"It is time," said the Merlin, "for the purified bride to come to her husband to fulfil the sacred marriage and bring great blessings on the people of the West. It is time for all to depart save Lord Ardhu."

The warriors began to gather their possessions—strewn cloaks and beakers, lolling-tongued dogs. They streamed toward the gates of the half-finished citadel, hurrying before the light failed to get onto the riverside path that led to their tents up near the Seven Kings. They did not dare glance back towards the woodland at the foot of the hill, the haunted area where it was whispered the shades of the old Hunting-men still wandered, firing ghostly arrows across the mist-exhaling lake. Here their new Queen was being ritually cleansed before coming to the bed of the King—the beautiful white Queen who was on that night a goddess, not a woman made of mere flesh. A thousand years before, any man who gazed upon the chief's bride in her purification rites would have been strangled and deposited in the holy waters of the lake, and although that tradition had lapsed, no man risked the displeasure of the gods by spying on her unveiled beauty.

"An'kelet, I would have you stay with me." Ardhu beckoned his friend to his side. "The fort seems too empty. I know it must be so till the warband's dwellings are built…but still. I would not be alone up here."

"Alone? You won't be alone." An'kelet smiled wryly. The smile did not reach his eyes.

"I meant unguarded. I could have chosen to celebrate the wedding night at Deroweth, but that is a place of priests and the half-world. I am a man, and this hill and the structures upon it are of the now-world—and they are mine, as Ardhu Pendraec, King of Prydn. Hence I want to bring my bride here, to the hall where she will be the first Queen of many over long generations to come."

An'kelet shifted uneasily, making circles in the dust with his felt boot. His confidence seemed to wane like the dying Moon. "Ardhu…my friend, I beg you, choose another…."

Ardhu frowned, perplexed. "I thought you would be honoured to be the king's Man on this night—the guardian of the Marriage Chamber."

"Yes, An'kelet of Ar-morah, surely you would not deny your sworn lord."

Merlin suddenly flapped in, saturnine and hawk-eyed, his cloak and hair and beard straggling on gusts of the ascending breeze. His piercing gaze darted from An'kelet's pale, guilty face to Ardhu's perturbed one. "What an honour, to protect the bridal bed of your beloved King and his comely Queen!"

"I…I cannot…" A glistening bead of sweat trickled down An'kelet's forehead, despite the coolness of the impending night.

Again, down in the trees below Kham-El-Ard, the horn sounded its mournful note—closer, this time. The chanting of the women could be heard as they began to ascend the hill.

"Maybe you should tell Ardhu why, Lord An'kelet." Merlin's voice was a growl. "Tell him the truth."

An'kelet turned to his friend, his chief, his eyes pleading. "I cannot stay here tonight… What you ask is geish—taboo for me."

"Taboo?" Ardhu shook his head. "Why? What do you mean?"

"He's making it up." Merlin pointed an accusing finger at An'kelet. "I warned you, Ardhu. The bones do not lie."

"Be silent!" Ardhu blazed back at him. "An'kelet, I order you to speak!"

An'kelet drew a shuddering breath. "I told you of my mother, the Priestess Ailin, and how I am sworn to purity, as she dictated, in order to keep the power of my arm. I must not, therefore, be party to the joining of the flesh, which could lead me to weakness."

"Nonsense!" Merlin stamped his foot. "He hides the truth, Ardhu!"

"Believe me or not, I must not stay!" cried An'kelet. "Punish me on the morrow, if it is your will!"

Face white with shame, he stumbled from the hall. Neither Ardhu nor Merlin called after him. As he ran, he spotted the women coming up the hill. Fynavir walked amongst them, proud and cold, a white, frosted flower. Her garments had been stripped from her, and she had been painted head to foot with symbols of luck and fertility, and blue flowers were twined in her unbound hair.

He paused for a moment, unable to tear his gaze away from her naked beauty. His breath came low and heavy; he felt stirrings he had kept long suppressed. And fear, a terrible fear… If Fynavir was goddess on earth, she could be death as well as life. His death, the death of all that An'kelet, greatest warrior in the West, had ever striven for…

He cast himself on the ground, covering his eyes. The marriage party passed, and the doors of Ardhu's Great Hall closed as the women brought Fynavir to the bridal bed with many women's charms upon her.

And An'kelet, scrambling back onto his feet, howled like a beast in pain, and ran like a madman out into the Deadlands of the Plain, where the barrows clustered and mortals did not walk. He had told his first ever lie, to his best friend and his lord; heart and mind and body had all betrayed him that night.

And in the sky the new-risen Moon watched his torment: a white and haunting ghost whose face was that of Fynavir.

CHAPTER FIFTEEN

A year passed at Kham-El-Ard. Carpenters and craftsmen finished work upon the halls and walls, and as Merlin had foreseen, the fort stood in unparalleled splendour—a mighty citadel with woven banners flapping above the gate and guards strutting along the ramparts. The prime warriors and their wives had relocated there from Place-of-Light, living in small houses around the periphery of the fort. Despite the loss, Place-of-Light continued to thrive as it had done for centuries, ever since the gold-men came from overseas; indeed, its population swelled as youths arrived from all over Prydn to join Ardhu's warband. Not every youth was suitable, of course. Many were hotheaded and ill-trained, so Ka'hai, Bohrs and Betu'or took to teaching them the arts of war—the strike with the slingshot, the death thrust of the dagger, the blow of the war-hammer.

The coasts were free of the snake-like ships of the Sea-Raiders and Ardhu and Fynavir rode out in splendour as far West as Belerion, and wherever they went, they were hailed as gods-come-to-earth. The weather remained unusually settled from the Winter Solstice on through spring and summer, and everywhere crops sprouted in abundance, promising a fulsome harvest. Few old ones passed into the Otherworld, and less bone-ache, tooth-loss and rickets plagued the tribes. Children were born, and lived in record numbers, along with their mothers.

It was as if the earth itself had become fertile with the union of the young King and his white Queen...but there was no sign that Fynavir herself would present the people of Prydn with Ardhu's heir. Each month the village crones looked to her and gossiped, but every turning of the Moon she stole away to the Women's House in the lake valley to spend five days away from her husband until the priestesses of the temple purified her and returned her to her husband's bed.

But Ardhu was none too worried by the absence of a child. They were both young, and not every coupling produced a babe—he knew that. When the Ancestors decided that a long-dead Great One should be reborn in flesh, then they would make it so, breathing spirit into the woman's womb. This could happen now or months hence; the Ancestors were capricious.

In some ways he was glad no child had come, as yet—he was just enjoying being married to Fynavir. After initial shyness, even slight reluctance, she had warmed to his embraces, and her long, strong dancer's legs wrapped round him in the lovers' dance helped him forget the dark, wild lustfulness of Morigau, his eternal shame, and his hidden secret.

But shortly after the first anniversary of their marriage union, Merlin came to Ardhu as he sat beside Fynavir in the Great Hall. Torches lit the high, carved roof-beams and incense burners let off sweet fragrance, while Art sat with his queen upon a nest of furs and pillows stuffed with dried grasses. A warm fire burned in a pit before them, and they passed back and forth a fine imported cup carved from a single lump of amber

"Your sister wants to see you, Pendraec," said the high priest curtly.

Ardhu turned bone-white; he thrust the amber mug at Fynavir. "My sister! Where is she?"

Merlin glanced at him suspiciously, noting his discomfiture. "What ails you? You look as if I told you the Great Sow herself was rooting for your blood! I am talking of your younger sister Mor-ghan...Ana, who lives in the Lake Valley with Lady Nin-Aeifa. She has asked for you at the secret cave below the fort."

Ardhu relaxed, colour flooding back into his face. "Ana! Yes, of course! She has joined the Lake Maidens. What does she want?"

Merlin shrugged. "Her tidings are not for me, Ardhu. You must meet with her yourself."

Ardhu rose from the floor, scattering furs.

Fynavir made to rise too. "Shall I come, Art?" She quite wanted to meet this mysterious sister; she had seen the Ladies of Lake worshipping at the Sacred Pool below Kham-El-Ard, but they wore concealing veils and painted their faces white like the dead, and she had never dared speak to them.

"No, it is a private matter between my kinswoman and myself," Ardhu said distractedly, dragging his bearskin cloak round his shoulders. "I shan't be long. An'kelet will entertain you while I'm away..." He nodded at his friend, who sat to the right of the fire, beaker in hand, half-hidden in shadow. "Sing her a song for me, will you, Ank? A ballad from your homeland. Something sad that will make her miss me, and then welcome me home again in the best way a woman can!"

An'kelet bowed his head, expression hidden by the amber locks of his hair. "I will do what I can to please her, lord."

"Good—that is as it should be! Keep my place warm for me!"

Ardhu slid down the path that led from the summit of the hill, and walked around the base of the mound with its dry defences rimmed by sharpened poles. Passing onto the eastern side, trees rose up in leafy abundance, and the smell of water and old things, growing things, reached into his nostrils. Wind rushed in the treetops, making an eerie hissing, and lonely birds cried out, their shrieks reminiscent of the cries of lost spirits.

Ardhu glanced gratefully toward Carnwennan in its secret sheath against his calf. He was reasonably certain he would meet no hostile humans so close to Kham-El-Ard, but denizens of the spirit-world were another matter. He did not know how well his earthly weapons would fare against spirit-beings, though he had heard they were fearful of metal, since many came from the Time Before, when weapons and tools were of bone or stone.

Ahead of him, he saw a gap in the ash, elm and holly, yawning like some prickly foliate mouth. Though it, the waters of the lake where he had gained Caladvolc gleamed silver-blue, a mirror reflecting the graceful, swaying branches and the scudding clouds in the sky above.

He walked to the edge of the water, feet sinking in the mud, feeling suddenly cold and alone. Perhaps he should have allowed Fynavir to accompany him...but maybe Ana had things to say that Fyn could never hear...

Ardhu took another step forward, into the long reeds that grew in the shallows. They clacked together, noisy as the teeth in a dried old skull. Where was Mhor-gan? He did not like these games; all his sisters played too much with such flummery and drama, while he liked things straightforward and plain.

He scowled, wishing he were back in the hall. Suddenly a whistling noise filled his ears, a high whine like that made by some particularly malevolent insect. He paused for a second, frowning, before recognising the sound for what it was...and with a cry he dived into the reeds, throwing his arm over his head for protection.

An arrow! It had just skimmed past the tip of his ear...he could feel the flesh stinging in its aftermath. Glancing over his shoulder, he saw the shaft sticking in a tree behind him, still vibrating from impact.

Drawing Carnwennan with a sullen flash, he began to creep slowly through the reeds. Mist suddenly rose up, curling from the water, obscuring trees, shrubs and landmarks. The waters rippled, and out of this mist came Mhor-gan in a narrow boat made of skins, poled by a tall man who seemed a creature of the wild, with a cloak made of hawk feathers fluttering around him, and a hawk-mask covering his face. Mhor-gan carried a bow, an arrow to the string.

"Mhor-gan!" Ardhu shouted in vexation, leaping from the rushes. "What kind of folly is this, shooting at me? You could have killed me!"

"I could have killed you, brother." She looked at him and her eyes were strange, feral, and he knew at that moment she was more than his sister—she was one of Nin-Aiefa's priestesses, possessed of the spirits. "But I would never have done so. Take it as this—a warning. My dart may not seek your heart, but the knife will forever be ready to strike you."

"So I am in danger, then? Is that why you have come?"

"Follow me to the cave and we will talk." The boat ground into the shallows and Mhor-gan stepped elegantly from it, her deerskin-clad feet scarcely seeming to touch water or mud. Her hair hung loose, dark as the shadows, but tinted red in the flame of the torch her companion kindled.

She led Art through the woods at the foot of a hill to a cave that stretched away into the hillside. It was not entirely a natural construction; great sarsens slabs lined the sides and had been hoisted up as capstones. The lichen-stained rocks were painted with faded signs.

She went in and knelt by a small hearth, throwing dried mosses and other fodder on it. Deftly using a strike-a-light, she kindled a flame and fire rushed up with a great whoosh, turning the cavern roof black almost instantly.

Ardhu stared around in amazement. The walls were painted with many pictures—scenes of setting Suns and rising Moons, and men at the hunt, and women at the dance, and men and women in the oldest dance at all... And at the very back of the cave, almost worn away, were vague outlines of tusked and toothed beasts Ardhu could not name, from the Time-Before-Time of the Hunting-Men.

Mhor-gan sat down cross-legged and Ardhu followed suit. The Hawk-headed Man stayed standing, perhaps guarding.

"Ardhu..." Morgan's voice was a whisper. "News comes from the north. Our sister Morigau..." She paused, eyes shadowed by her eyelashes, swaying slightly as if she might fall.

"Yes?" Ardhu's voice emerged a hoarse croak. What did he wish—that Morigau were dead? It happened often, even among the young—a sudden flux, an unexpected wound, and the barrow gaped ...

Morgan's head shook. "She has given birth to a son on the Isle of Pigs. She has called him Mordraed."

Ardhu went cold, then hot, then cold again. His heart thumped so loudly he was sure Mhor-gan and her man must hear it. "And Loth of Ynys Yrch, he is pleased to have a healthy son?"

Mhor-gan raised her head, a bitter little smile playing on her lips. "He is pleased, or so it is reported. Even though some malicious gossips count their fingers and say that the brat was born too soon to be his. But you will know more about that than I, Ardhu Pendraec."

Ardhu was silent, and then said slowly, "Perhaps you know more than you should. Who told you? Merlin?"

"How I know doesn't matter," said Mhor-gan. "All I know is that Morigau will use this child against us as a warrior uses his sword. It is said he was born with a caul over his head and is marked. It is rumoured she has fed him blood with her milk to whet his appetite for war. I have looked into the waters of the cauldron and seen running blood, and Mordraed's face and the walls of Kham-El-Ard burning."

Ardhu shuddered. "I will kill Morigau...I will kill her and the child."

"No, you cannot." Her fingers gripped his arm. "A kinslaying would bring all of Loth's forces down upon us, and many others would join his cause. Even if you proved victorious in battle, a taint would lie upon you, and Morigau's plot to topple your rule would be accomplished."

"What would you have me do, then, Ana? You are a holy woman—guide me!"

"Always take care. Trust not even those you love the most." Her eyes became shadowy again, her jaw tense. "Harden your heart and steel yourself. Think of war, and do not spend too much time in the pleasures of the hall. This is not the time of a gentle earth—it is an Age of Stone! And so your heart must be. Never let your guard down, Ardhu."

She glanced over at the Hawk-man, standing still as a monolith, gaze directed toward the cave's mouth. "Come, cousin," she said softly. "It is time to introduce you."

The feathered figure turned towards Ardhu and lifted the beaked mask from his head. Art saw a face not much older than his own, framed by dark hair, with the look of Mhor-gan and his other kin from Belerion. "Who is this?" he asked. "And why have you brought him to me?"

"This is our cousin, Hwalchmai, Hawk of the Plain, son of our mother's sister. Since the day you ascended the throne, he begged me to send him to you. But I would not till the famed Skatha the Shadowy, who dwells on the northern isle that bears her name, trained him in the warrior arts. Nor would I send him hence until taught by the priestesses in the ways of the spirit. For we have seen that there is a great quest ahead of Hwalchmai, one that will be sung for a thousand years and more. Right now, he is but a young sapling, with roots still seeking purchase, but he will fight and take the crown of old holly…or perish in doing so. But that is long away. For now, he will be one of your chief men in the warband, the most courteous of your warriors; and if An'kelet of Ar-morah stands on your right, Hwalchmai shall guard the left with an arm as strong as the oak-tree."

Ardhu frowned. "Ka'hai, Ech-tor and Bohrs train new men, and we choose the best amongst them. They would not be pleased to see a newcomer march into the hall and take a place without trial."

"Then a trial there will be, "said Mhor-gan. "Now, before your eyes, will Hwalchmai show his skills. The greater testing will come later, as was prophesied."

The slender woman nodded to Hwalchmai, and he bowed to her and to Ardhu. He then began the warrior's dance, the chant of the hunt. Taking his bow, he fired several shots in succession over the lake, and to Ardhu's surprise, he brought down game with every shot—a roe-deer springing through the foliage, a bird that soared between the trees, a fox slinking through the waving ferns. Running over to the fallen beasts, he slashed them across the throat with his honed dagger and caught their warm blood in a handled beaker, drinking in their power and essence with their life-juices. Finishing, he gutted and skinned them, preparing the meat for the hall of his king and taking the skins for his own use.

"As fleet as the deer, am I," he said, wrapping the skin around him, "and as wily as the fox." He tied the fox's red tail into his hair. "But I am also as loyal as the dog that lies by the fire and guards the homestead."

Ardhu smiled, and placed his hand on his shoulder. "I do not doubt it. And now, my hound, you will bark for me, and guard my fort and all who dwell in it."

Mhor-gan's lips curved faintly upward as the cousins began to talk in a less formal manner, discussing warcraft and horses and feasting. It was good to see the pleasure in Ardhu's face. She feared he would not look so if he knew that, at that very moment, Morigau, his one-time lover and his bane, was meeting with the Merlin somewhere out on the Great Plain.

Merlin huffed along the track in the twilight, the butt of his staff thudding against the firm earth. His bones ached; he noticed it now whenever he had to move with swiftness, a burning pain that gnarled his joints, especially in knees and back. He gazed down at his thin hand, clutching the staff; his knuckles were knotted and deformed, already an old man's hands, though, mercifully, not enfeebled yet.

He cursed, his breath a white fog before his lips. He had no wish to come out here on the summons of the she-hag, Morigau. But better he came, level-headed, than Ardhu, who was still callow enough to lose control in the demon-woman's presence, whether by killing her or falling for her dubious charms as he had at Suilven. He would like to ring her neck himself, no matter how pretty it seemed, but he dared not, for the same reasons he couldn't allow Art to kill her—she was Loth's woman, and he'd use her demise as the perfect excuse to come rampaging down from the north, bringing the wild tribes of the isles and forests with him. Even if Ardhu's warband rode out to meet him, taking in additional warriors from the Land of the Mother Mountain and the Brig-ahn who dwelt on the high moors, this would then leave the entire West and south open to attack or infiltration from the mainland coasts. Rumours had come that the pirates were sheltering in coves along the rocky shores of Armorah, just biding their time until they thought they could sail unchecked into Albu once again...

Up ahead, the slope of a bank rose up into the twilight, half-grassed, half- chalk—the Great Spirit path, built by the earliest Ancestors to separate the lands of the living from the places of the spirits. In the distance, he could see the sanctuary of the Stones, the massive sarsens violet-tinted in the dusk, slumberous giants that brooded over the Great Plain.

Watch over me, O Ancestors, he thought moodily, as he traversed the bank of the Spirit Path to the place he had arranged to meet Morigau, in this liminal area far from stones or settlement, the only fitting place to deal with this viper who had sprung from the same nest as Ardhu but sought to impale him with her poison fangs.

The rustle of a cloak made him glance around, and he spotted her, hovering like some malign imp atop the bank. Her hair was free like a young girl's, blowing in a black, tangled cloud about her. She had painted her lips and cheeks with berry- juice and her dark eyes, dominating her face, were smudged with ash that made them appear huge and dark, almost black. She looked at him and an expression of disappointment and then anger passed over her visage; she had obviously expected Ardhu to be there.

"No, he's not coming," said Merlin tartly. "He has no wish to see your face again after your foul deceit. It is me you will deal with, Morigau of Ynys Yrch."

She smiled sweetly. "So be it, Merlin. Maybe that is for the best. After all, we are cut from the same mould, you and me. We are ...equals."

Merlin's brows lifted until they vanished under his unkempt grey-streaked fringe. "Indeed? Interesting that you should think so!"

"Ah..." She descended from the crest of the bank, coming to stand beside him. She was short, like her mother, and similar in feature, with the same haughty arrogance and barely veiled sensuality that had attracted U'thyr to Y'gerna. "Don't you know? I too commune with the old ones. I too know the secrets of plants that harm and heal. I too study the movements of Sun and Moon. I have become priestess on the distant isles where I am also Queen. So we are indeed equals, cut from the same cloth. I do grant to you, though, as my elder, that there is much you could teach me."

Merlin said nothing. Morigau moved round in front of him, staring up into his face. "Merlin, Merlin, don't look at me that way! We don't have to be enemies..."

"No? After the evil you have wrought?"

Morigau pouted. "I blame you and your wiles for much of that, Merlin. But, be that as it may...I have changed since I lay with Ardhu at Suilven. My life is different now."

"Different? In what way?"

Her lips twisted into a mocking smile. "Can't you guess, Merlin? I am the mother of a fine, healthy son—heir of Ardhu Pendraec and recipient of all that I can teach him. Unclaimed he may be by his father, but one day he will wrest away all Ardhu has won."

"And you dare to speak to me of a peace between us!" snarled Merlin in anger.

"No, listen, listen!" She raised her hand. "I do not mean to anger you. I only speak truth, from one who has the Sight, even as you do. Ardhu is weak, plagued by the follies of his fathers; my son is strong, made of stern stuff in the north. Ardhu has married a woman they say is a goddess, but no news comes of a child of his loins; the goddess-of-earth does not favour them. I have looked into the fire and seen betrayal and death; even among his so-called friends…Can you tell me that you have not seen this too?"

"And what would your course be, Morigau?" Merlin's eyes were hard as sarsen.

"This…." In a practised movement, she tore open the toggles at the top of her robe, and let it fall in a heap to her ankles. Naked, she stood in the dying daylight, brazenly unashamed. She cupped her swollen breasts, holding them up like offerings. "For us to join, as man and woman. For us, two of a kind, to meld our power and knowledge and take on the leadership of Prydn until my son, under our tutelage, could become ruler. If you said yes to me, I swear you would not regret it."

She moved closer while the older man stood frozen like a statue. She wound herself around him, sinuous as a serpent and as deadly, writhing her slim hips against his, nipping at his neck with her sharp white teeth. "I have heard you live an austere life, Merlin," she panted in his ear. "Surely you do not want to live your entire life alone, without the pleasures of flesh. Surely you would prefer this…" she let her hand slide between his thighs, "to congress with naught but ghosts and spirits. Or perhaps you prefer to tup the dead," she finished cruelly.

Her last jibe goaded him to anger. For a moment, he had nearly succumbed to her, to the warmth of her willing body, to the sensations he had denied himself since he had left Nin-Aeifa at Afallan. But staring down into her carnal, cruel eyes, he realised that no pleasure would ever be found in her embrace—only devouring death. Strength and resolve returned to him, and that ember of traitorous desire that threatened to ruin him died like a flame under cold water.

With a cry, he grabbed her shoulders and flung her backward into the ditch. Drawing his knife, he fell upon her before she had the chance to rise, and pressed its blade to her throat. "I could take you and then kill you," he grunted, his free hand wandering roughly over her body, a motion meant to humiliate rather than excite, "and none would know your fate, for the animals and hungry spirits would chew your corpse to rags in the night. But, you faithless whore, you have nothing I want or need, nor ever shall. I can see now what evil magic you wrought on Ardhu, but it has no power over me!"

He rolled away from her and Morigau, spitting fury, sprang up and dragged on her gown. "You will pay for this outrage!" she spat. "Doubly. I offered you a chance…it will not be offered again. Enjoy your feasting and merry-making with my brother in your great hall of Kham-El-Ard; it will soon be at an end. The land will be in turmoil again, and by my hand."

"Loth would not dare to step on these shores again," said Merlin.

"I do not speak of the armies of my clumsy husband. That useless fool is too busy cursing Ardhu's name to gather men to him so that he can break the constraints my brother has laid on him. It is I who have reaped the whirlwind that is about to descend—I, alone. Though who will put blame on me, a priestess and a queen in the remotest part of Prydn?"

Merlin snarled between clenched teeth. "I knew I should have thrown you into the sea when you were but a puling brat! An evil spirit dwells within you, gnawing your innards!"

"You helped put it there!" she retorted. "But I have grown used to it now. And I have put the fire in my head to much use during my lonely hours on Ynys Yrch. When not rutting with Loth—he is like one of the pigs that roam those blasted isles, slobbering and gross, interested in only his beaker and bed—I have been raising a fine little boar bred from the most vicious sow I could find—a sow black as She-Who-Guards. I have whipped him and tormented him, and watched with joy as he became more vicious every day. I gave him potions to craze him, and fed him on the flesh of men—strangers who came unbidden to the isles, shipwrecked men from the north, unwanted brats…"

"You sicken me…" Merlin's voice was a groan.

Morigau went on animatedly, almost merrily. "He is eager to run loose now, my dear little boar. T'orc is his name, and along with his handler, Rhyttah, a man most loyal to my cause…" She smirked and Merlin guessed exactly what she meant by 'loyal.' "He will lay waste to the lands of Prydn. Ardhu will have never faced such a creature before, and Rhyttah himself is not like the effete men of the south with their perfumed hair and oiled flesh; his very cloak is woven of the beards of slain enemies. Soon Ardhu will join their numbers…not that the soft-faced whelp has much beard to add to Rhyttah's cloak!"

Merlin flung his dagger at Morigau, tormented beyond endurance by her mocking words. The throw was not accurate, but the point tore her dress and nicked her arm, drawing beads of bright blood. "You dare strike me!" she gasped, clutching the wound. "Just wait, Merlin, one day that blow will come back on you! I await that day with much longing! Now farewell!"

She sprang away into the darkness, running fleet-footed as a deer into a nearby stand of trees. Above the Moon was rising, crooked, the wane Moon, the death Moon.

Merlin stared after his adversary, Ardhu's bane, and felt sickness knot his belly.

CHAPTER SIXTEEN

"She was here on the plain!" Ardhu swept an agitated hand through his hair as he paced the Great Hall. "Why did you not tell me, Merlin? You devised this with Ana, didn't you? Sending me off with her to keep me out of the way while you treated with Morigau."

"Yes," said Merlin," and it was the right thing to do. Look at you, filled with fury. You would have fallen right into Morigau's trap, and done something you would later regret."

Ardhu slumped to his knees by the fire-pit. "I have already done things I regret. Merlin, Ana has told me that Morigau has...that there is..."

Merlin nodded gravely. "Yes. There is a child. She has passed him off as the get of Loth."

"If I could..." Ardhu's eyes blackened, and for a second Merlin recoiled, for the young man looked so like his half-sister it was disconcerting. "If I could, I would send my warriors throughout the land to kill any man-child born in the month of the Bhel-fires!"

"But that would make you as much a monster as Morigau."

"I know." Ardhu bowed his head. "And you know I would never in truth do such a thing."

Merlin raised his young lord up with a hand. "Now that you have shouted out your anger, we had best gather the warband and hold council. Morigau threatened not only you, but all the people of Prydn. We must be prepared for sudden attacks. It may be all angry bluster and wishful malice—but I fear not."

More than four months had passed before Ardhu had news of his kinswoman and her malign devices. The warband was gathered in the hall of Kham-El-Ard, drinking and carousing, most well into their cups. Some played foolish games with coloured pebbles, while others dandled their wives on their knees or pinched and pawed the serving women who brought them their beakers of mead and beer. The day was cold, the Winter Solstice gone by nearly a month, and the whole world outside seemed a bleak vista of grey and white—a haze of mist, a touch of frost, a sprinkle of trodden snow. Icicles clattered on the roofline of the hall, while in the valley below tree-boughs clashed together like skeleton bones, tossed on a bitter wind.

As daylight failed, the clouds gaped and it began to rain, an icy flow from the heavens that pattered on the thatching of the great chieftain's house and beat against the calfskin stretched over the window-slits.

Ardhu sat at the head of the hall, on a raised pile of furs, his legs stretched out before him close to the blazing fire-pit. An'kelet reclined on his right hand side, honing the barbs on the spear Balugaisa, while Merlin squatted on his left, impassive and ever vigilant, one eye fixed on the door, which shuddered in the rising wind, threatening to burst open and flood the hall with wintry chill. Fynavir knelt between Ardhu and An'kelet; eyes locked on the fire's flames. She wore her frost-pale hair loose like an unwed maiden, instead of in the customary hairnet favoured by married women—it was what Ardhu liked and expected.

And An'kelet too. She could feel his gaze travelling the graceful curves of her body, willing her to turn and face him. To let him know the truth of what she felt towards him...

Eventually she could bear no more, and she turned her head and met his ready smile. A small gasp left her lips and she hastily turned away again, clutching her handled mug with its watered-down beer.

"Fynavir, what ails you?" Ardhu leaned over, hand caressing her shoulder, running over the swell of her breast, past her hip to touch her stomach. "Are you...all right? Should I call a healing woman?"

She knew what he implied; his intimate touch said it all. Tears pricked her eyes. There was still no sign of any child. The only signs visible tonight were of her traitorous desires.

"I am fine, lord husband," she said. "A moment's giddiness...the heat...the drink...Perhaps I should go to our chamber."

Ardhu stared moodily at her. These turns were more and more frequent. She seemed, sometimes, to be drawing away from him, her embraces cold and less frequent, and her expression distant.

"Fynavir, do not shame me here," he hissed in her ear, suddenly cruel with too much beer and winter boredom. "Men will talk if you leave the hall. You are meant to be at my side. You are my Queen, and the spirit of the land is within you. If it is not right between us, the people will think that it is also not right with the Land itself!"

"And is it?" Tears stung her eyes.

"It would be if you would give the land an heir!" Ardhu snapped, and then, realising he had spoken too freely, wrapped his bearskin around him and glowered furiously into the smoke in the longhouse.

He had done it—spoken the unspeakable aloud before all. Merlin, tapping out a thin beat on a shamanic drum held between his bony knees, smiled a bitter, knowing smile. He did not hate the white foreign girl, but she was the worst choice his young king could have made. Maybe, with luck, Art would now see the unhappy truth and put her aside.

Feeling a stab of guilt for his outburst, Ardhu reached for Fynavir's arm. She was startlingly beautiful, her hair like the frost on the trees, her eyes green and stormy as the distant seas. Jet beads shone darkly around her neck and in her ears, startling against her unnatural whiteness. "Why don't you dance as you did before," he slurred. "Back in the hall of Ludegran. Dance for me, Fynavir, and show everyone that it is still good between us!"

"I...I can't..." she began, hand rising to her throat, but the spasm of anger that crossed her husband's face silenced her protests.

Reluctantly, she climbed to her feet, swaying as her head reeled. The men of the warband cheered; most secretly found her good to look upon, different in her whiteness to most of the native Prydn women who tended to brown hair or red. Musicians began to play on pipes, while Merlin's drum sent out a frenzied thumping.

Fynavir closed her eyes, imagining, as she always did when she performed her magic dances that she was other than she was. In her mind's eye, she was a swan, faltering on the wing, trying to fly away over a long, dark lake to join a long-lost mate in the shadows on the other side. She soared and swooped inside her head, and her body took over and mimicked the scene in her mind. On graceful toes she leaped around the fire, her head flung back revealing a long neck as graceful as that of the swan she envisioned.

Ardhu watched, enthralled, the blood running hot in his loins. He had been unkind, but by the gods, he would make it up to her. Blue faience beads, a golden- buttoned gown from over the sea...anything she asked.

Suddenly she ceased dancing. The image in her head lurched. The swan flew into the dark, and suddenly an arrow pierced its breast, and with a dying cry it plummeted down, falling, falling, and falling, toward the icy lake….

"No!" she cried, and toppled forward towards the burning fire.

A serving woman screamed.

Swift as the wind, An'kelet was at her side, catching her before she collapsed into the flames. He lifted her as if she were a child, carrying her away from the heat and the sparks that threatened to ignite her hair.

"An'kelet!" Ardhu leapt to his feet. His voice was harsh. He did not know why he felt angry toward An'kelet, who had done only what a loyal warrior would do. "Leave her be; I shall take care of her!"

An'kelet hesitated. Ardhu's eyes widened then blackened with fury. What was the fool up to, making him look like some boor who could not be trusted with the wellbeing of his own woman?

At that moment, there came a crash from outside. A huge gust of wind smashed opens the doors of the hall, and extinguished the torches at the entrance and the lamps full of burning fat. Even the fire dimmed down to a pile of sullen embers.

In the sudden blackness, someone shrieked in fear.

There was the sound of daggers being drawn. An'kelet placed Fynavir on a fur and drew Arondyt and Fragarak, while Ardhu unsheathed Caladvolc and snatched up the Face of Evening.

"Who goes?" he demanded.

Raiders he could deal with, but his spies had brought no news for weeks, and the great Ridgeways were empty. So close to Solstice, it was more likely that any unwelcome arrival at the feasting hall would come from the malevolent spirit-world.

The sound of hoofbeats answered his shout. The men and women in the hall shrank back, even Bohrs and Ka'hai, as a dark figure on horseback entered the hall and rode boldly across the rush-strewn floor toward the king's dais.

The stranger looked indeed as if he harkened from the Otherworld; surely, no mortal man had a countenance such as his. He was green from head to foot, in both skin colour and the colour of his tunic. Wild thorns and sprigs of holly jutted from curled hair and beard, and blood-red berries dangled from antlers sprouting from between his snarled locks. Against the green of his face, his eyes seemed large and reddish, monstrous. His teeth were filed sharp and white as the Moon, glowing as he laughed. Above his head, he brandished a great double-bladed bronze axe.

Ardhu leapt up, Caladvolc shining like a tongue of flame in the dimness. "Be you man or spirit, I will smite you if you do not leave my hall!"

The green rider ignored him and swung down from the saddle, swaggering arrogantly toward the young king and his men. "Fine words," he cried. "Fine brave words…but where is your hospitality, O jewel of kings! Ach, the warrior-circle of the famed Ardhu Pendraec is made of naught but mean men, holding their beakers and their dark plots close to their hearts!"

"You speak treasonously!" Hwalchmai, who had been sitting with Ba-lin and Bal-ahn, sprang from his seat and rushed towards the verdant apparition. "The Lord Ardhu is most generous of kings! He offers no hospitality to you, because your countenance is vile… as is your uncouth tongue! You deserve to die for your slurs!"

The Green Man peered down his aquiline nose at the young man before him, at the angry face and fierce grey-green eyes. He then laughed, the sound rising up to shake the rafters. "If you think I have committed such a grave crime, take my head, boy. Look…I will make the deed easy for you!"

He held out his huge, double-bladed axe, its long haft wrapped in oiled leather. Hwalchmai snatched it from him, stumbling as he realised it was heavier than he thought. His dismay at the brief loss of his footing elicited another peel of laughter from the Green Man.

"Surely my weapon is not too much for such a noble youth!" he bellowed. "But behold, I still bow to your great prowess! I will go down on my knees and bare my neck to the kiss of the blade!"

Grinning, he sank down before Hwalchmai and parted his mass of hair with big green hands. His neck shone in the dying embers of the fire—pale green like a corpse's skin.

Hwalchmai hefted the great axe. Sweat broke out on his brow. The axe's handle was slippery, sweaty; he fought to position it, to prepare for the lethal blow. With a cry he raised it over his head, and then brought it down with all his might, aiming for the tree-like neck, bulging with knots of veins....

And missed.

As if enchanted, the heavy-headed, foreign weapon dragged forward in his hand, tearing through clawed fingers as if trying to get back to its master's belt. The axe tumbled in the air, a flash of red, before thudding into the packed earth a few inches from the Green Man's ferocious head.

"A...ha!" he bellowed, springing to his feet and snatching up his fallen axe. "Brave words, but wavering hand! Can your honour ever be restored, young hothead? Not by ordinary means. Only if you come to my abode in Lud's hole, and play the axe-game with your head!"

Hwalchmai stared at him, furious yet fearful, eyeing the stranger's axe as if it were some living creature that might suddenly spring forward and strike him. He could hear the other men in the hall murmuring, some even sniggering—he was not liked in all quarters, for some believed he had risen in Ardhu's esteem too quickly, and only because he was blood-kin. Well, he would prove them wrong. He would pass the greatest test of them all, or die in the attempt.

"I will seek you out at this Lud's hole," he snarled between gritted teeth. "And I will play your axe-game."

"Good!" shouted the Green Man, with a rapacious grin, "I look to the hour of our meeting!" and he sprang astride his steed and galloped from the hall, out into the driving rain and wild weather beyond. In an eye's blink, he was gone, lost in the darkness of a storm-wracked winter night.

"Hwalchmai, what have you done?" Ardhu shook his cousin's shoulder." You have sworn your life away."

"I had no choice," said Hwalchmai, hotly. "To nay-say him would bring dishonour. Already I am looked on as an interloper who rides upon the fame of my kin. I will prove that is not the case and find eternal fame among the singers-of-song. Or else my head will decorate the Green Man's dwelling in Lud's Hole."

Hwalchmai did not go after the green stranger for another week; a terrible winter storm blew in from the frozen reaches of Kalydon, where the painted people dwelt amidst high mountains and uncharted forests, and turned all the land into a vista of white. Ice came with it, not just snow, borne on a screaming gale that gnashed men's flesh like wolves' teeth and left the trees and rooftops of Kham-El-Ard rimed with glittering icicles that fell and shattered with an eerie tinkling. Several head of cattle, terrified by the wild weather, broke free of their pens and perished while stampeding over a thinly frozen Abona and several shepherds on the eastern downlands did not return to their homes in the Place-of-Light.

"There is evil afoot in this storm." Merlin frowned as he leaned on his staff and stared out from the doors of Ardhu's Great Hall. "It comes from the North, where the devil-woman Morigau dwells. How she must laugh at us, soft in the South, trammelled here like beasts while she wreaks her mischief!"

Head bowed, he murmured invocations to the Sun, to the spirits in the snow-bound stone circle out on the Great Plain. The winds answered him, but they were cold, droning about him with icy malevolence.

As the storm finally died away, and the first hint of blue returned to the sky, Hwalchmai began to prepare for his journey to Lud's hole, packing a bag and wrapping himself in his thickest furs, stuffing straw inside his boots of felt and skin. Ardhu begged him to let the warband accompany him but he refused. "I must do this deed myself or no respect will be mine," he stated.

Bow and quiver of arrows strapped to his back, two sturdy daggers at his belt, he began to make his way down from the heights of Kham-El-Ard. It was not long after the Sunrise and the snowdrifts were red-tinted, as if stained from some gory battle. The eastern sky burned with crimson fire as the Sun's bleeding eye slowly ascended the dark hump of Magic Hill.

Ten steps he took, feet crunching on frozen snow, and then he cried out, "Ardhu! Someone comes to Kham-El-Ard this cold morn! Look!"

The gate-guards sprang into action, running halfway down the hill with bows nocked. Sleepy-eyed, Ardhu appeared on the ramparts, his bearskin wrapped loosely around his shoulders, his black hair storm-tossed. Sure enough a figure could be seen staggering across the fields towards the hillfort, a shambling shape amidst the ghostly fog-tendrils rising from the waters of Abona.

Fleet of foot, Hwalchmai was first to reach the stranger. He skidded to a halt as he realised the man was not alone—in his arms he carried the body of a young boy. A boy, blue-faced and stiff, who had been dead some days. Ash and blood smeared his livid face. He was no more than ten.

Hwalchmai stared in horror. The man stared back, face grimy, besmirched, and twisted with grief. His mouth moved but it seemed he had lost the ability for speech.

"What has happened? Where are you from?" Hwalchmai found his own voice. "Who has done this evil deed?"

The man spluttered, and wiped his eyes, before finally finding his tongue. His voice was ragged with sorrow: "I hail from Tarn Wethelen on the borders of the Dwri lands…and I come begging help from the Young King who men say protects the weak and helpless against tyrants and wicked men from afar. A week ago, our village and temple were burned to the ground by invaders. They spared no one, not even unarmed children…" He looked at the stiffened corpse in his arms and began a pitiful keening that cut eerily through the morning.

By now, Ardhu had reached the foot of the hill, with Merlin and An'kelet following closely behind him. Ardhu approached the man and placed his hand on his shoulder, while Merlin prised the rigid child's body from the man's grasp and laid it respectfully on the grass, head facing toward the rising Sun.

"If it is vengeance you seek, you have come to the right place," said Ardhu firmly. "The Warband will ride this very day, and your boy's death will be made good with foemen's blood. Who was it that attacked your settlement? The sea-folk? Or other Western chiefs?"

The man spat on the ground. "Neither. They spoke our tongue but with a strange twist. Northerners, I think. With them they had a totem-animal, a monster from the pits of shadow in An-un, the Underworld. A great boar it was, eyes like flame, tusks like knives. It was mad and ran amok, even as they did, goring and biting, and after the battle they fed it on dead men's livers…T'orc Is-gurth they called the beast, the Chief Boar, and its master who goaded it on was named Rhyttah Bad-adun, the Chief Giant. He was as fearsome as his creature, a hand taller than most men and one-eyed, and he wore a cloak woven from the beards of men he has slain."

Merlin clutched his staff, face twisting with anguish at the newcomer's words. "So she did not tell idle tales," he muttered. "Morigau did not lie, but worked her evil well. But she will not prevail…no, I shall see to it."

Turning to Ardhu, he caught his arm. "You must go and fight this new danger and crush it utterly. It is the doing of Morigau, your sister."

Ardhu spat an oath. "So soon! She must truly be a creature of Otherness; she flies around Prydn as no mortal could. What is your counsel, Merlin, to defeat this Boar and its Master?

Will axes and arrows be enough? The smell of magic is on this, wrought by the hands of Morigau."

Merlin's lips narrowed, tightened. "Ever since she was here, I have thought on this, conferring with my fellow priests and lore-masters at Deroweth. You are warriors, not magic men, and I would that you kept it so, and hunted down this fell beast with the tools of warriors made from sound stone and good, wholesome metal. But if all fails, and Chief Giant and Chief Boar elude you, there are others ways—but they are dark and perilous. If it comes to it, seek the Black Witch daughter of White Witch in her cave in the Uplands of Despair, and take from her the magic razor, tempered in blood, that lies upon her altar. It is will shear both the magic boar's bristles and the neck of cruel Rhyttah."

Ardhu turned back toward Kham-El-Ard, and ordered the men to go out into the fields and blow on aurochs horns, awakening all in the lands between the Place-of-Light and the circles of Deroweth. The fort on its height sprang to life, youths running here and there to get their masters' mounts ready and women packing bedrolls and provisions for the long journey. Warriors dashed amongst them, polishing weapons and making high boasts while attaching talismans to tunics or belts. Those to be left behind looked grim, but the warrior's faces were full of joy—the Solstice was over and they were half-mad with boredom and glad of this new challenge.

Fynavir emerged from her sleeping quarters, feet bare, a sheepskin wrapped around her. "Ardhu, what is happening… I heard the horns blowing!"

"It is time for battle again," said Ardhu briskly. "Not foreign raiders, this time, but our own kind. In fact…it is the doing of my own sister Morigau."

"The wife of the northern King? I heard from the jet traders that she recently bore a child….What harm could a woman fresh from child-bed wreak?"

Ardhu stared at his wife, scanning her face to see if she had any knowledge of the truth of Morigau's child, if any hint of scandal had reached her ears. Her green eyes were guileless. He breathed a sigh of relief. "She is not as a normal woman, Fynavir. A bad spirit resides within her. "

Fynavir pondered this for a minute, and her face clouded. She grasped his wrist. "Ardhu, why must you go? It is far away and you have already done more than any other chief in three hundred years. Wait till spring, when the weather is sweeter and if the trouble is still about, deal with it then."

Ardhu snatched his wrist away and reached for his mace, tucking it into his belt. "People—my people, are dying. I cannot leave them to their fate, or I would not be worthy of the title of High King."

"And An'kelet…he will ride with you too?" She hung her head.

"Of course. He is my battle-brother, and the best warrior in my company, though Hwalchmai soon shall be his equal."

Tears began to leak from Fynavir's eyes, as they did all too frequently. "I beg you…don't go! I have seen omens in dreams, and heard dead voices on the wind…I do not wish to be left here alone. Ardhu, let me come with you!"

Art burst into loud, frustrated laughter. "Now that would scare the enemy! Fynavir, the battlefield is no place for you. It is your duty as Queen to stay and attend to the running of Kham-El-Ard in my absence. There is a homeless man at the gate, and a dead child to be barrowed… these shall be among your tasks when I am away."

"Oh Ardhu, Ardhu…" she wept, pressing her hands to her face, and in embarrassment, he pushed past her to gather his shield and the rest of his things. He would never understand the woman; one moment seemingly indifferent, the next weeping if he stepped beyond the hill-fort's gates.

Leaving Fynavir, he proceeded to the entranceway of the fort, thronged by milling warriors and war-steeds, which champed and stamped and threatened to trample the dogs of the settlement as they rushed around in circles in the snow, half-mad with excitement. A few of the larger hounds were on leads, ready to be taken on the long road to hunt Chief Boar T'orc. Ba-lin and Bal-ahn were there, alongside Bohrs with his war-club and An'kelet leaning on his spear. Ka'hai was checking that all supplies for the long road were in place, aided by Betu'or and the brothers Brathac and Nerthac and lanky Cacamuri. Drust Thunderfist, who had a huge war-hammer made of black stone, was shouting a boast, while Glu Mightygrasp, wrestler of great renown, swore that he would tear T'orc into pieces. Hluk Windyhand, famed archer, was inspecting the fletchings on his arrows while sharing a swift joke with Anwas the Winged, fleet-footed scout and messenger. Wadu, Naw and Sberin, youths on their first foray with the warband, jostled each other with ill-concealed excitement, along with Is'govan and Isgowuin from the settlement of An-Dwra in the East. Ohsla Big-knife, Gillah Stagshank, and Ellidur the guide completed the band.

Ardhu gestured to Hwalchmai, whose own departure had been delayed in the drama of the morning. "Cousin, I know you have other journeys on your mind, but I would have you ride with us. I think you will play a part in this exploit before its ending."

"I have already sworn to go to Lud's Hole and meet the Green-faced Man."

"And so you shall. But you will come with us upon the road, at least to a point. Is that not acceptable to you? We may well need the might of your arm."

Hwalchmai grinned at his cousin. "It is acceptable, lord. I will be glad of the company, and who knows, maybe we can each help the other in our quests."

The company was ready to depart by the next dawn. The riverbanks were thronged with well-wishers who had come down from Place-of-Light. Mothers held up small children to watch the warriors pass, and old men cheered and shouted, reliving their youths in these bright new champions.

Fynavir stood silently in the great gateway of Kham-El-Ard, under the carved lintel with its grinning faces of gods and spirits. She looked a being of the underworld herself, wearing her gold pectoral cape with the long linen skirts billowing below like a shroud. Her hair was limed into a fantastic, white-coiled shape, and she had chalked her face as a token of her sorrow, turning her soft, lovely face into a surreal, emotionless, mask. Some superstitious folk even made signs against evil at the sight of her, behind their backs; she was their Queen, but she was foreign and different, and although they honoured her as Ardhu's wife and representative of the land, they did not love her.

Ardhu took her cold hands and kissed her on both cheeks, tasting the chalkiness of her face-paint. It was like kissing the earth of the plain itself, full of the bones of Ancestors… He shivered. He longed to kiss her lips, but she had frozen him out again, had spent the night curled under her furs, weeping. How tired he had grown of the sound, just as he had of the soughing, sighing winds that harassed the walls of Kham-El-Ard, making him long for his upcoming journey, no matter how dangerous.

"I leave my kingdom and all that is in it in your hands, Fynavir," he said solemnly. "Merlin will be at Deroweth should you need him, and Ech-tor will remain at Kham-El-Ard to assist with the running of the fort. Lads from Place-of-Light have also been recruited as guards."

"I will do my best to look after your realm, lord husband," she said softly, inclining her head. And then unexpectedly, she embraced him, anguish in her eyes. "You…and An'kelet, you must take care, do you hear? Don't take any unnecessary risks; you have both already proved your valour!"

Embarrassed in front of the men, Ardhu gently pushed her away. "Have trust in our skills, wife," he said, and then he turned to Ka'hai who was leading Lamrai toward him. She whinnied and danced on the half-frozen ground, eager to be away, to stretch legs cramped by the confinement of winter. Ardhu knew exactly how she felt.

Nimbly, he swung up on her back, and his men mounted alongside him, a gaudy crowd in feathers and furs, bronze and gold, with their mounts nearly as brightly decked out as the warriors themselves. Mounted on a mist-grey stallion, An'kelet rode on Ardhu's right, while Hwalchmai, seated on a beast as black as charcoal, protected his shield arm. As the warband drew ranks behind them, they unfurled the great woven banner of the Head Serpent, with its insignia of a golden lozenge between two spirals. A horn blew and then another and the company moved off toward the fords of Abona.

Fynavir watched them go, uncaring that those around her saw tears track down her dead-white cheeks. She felt their scorn, their eyes harsh as flails on her back. Some of the women were tittering, shaking their heads. "May the spirits bring you safely home," she murmured into the wind…but she did not know if it was her husband she asked the Old Ones to protect or the Prince from Ar-morah riding at his side.

CHAPTER SEVENTEEN

The warband moved rapidly across country. Day blended into night and the Moon faded and went dark, leaving only its attendant crown of stars. Dawn came again, slow and sullen, the Sun barely alive as yet, seeming not to have strengthened since Solstice eve.

At length they came to the settlement of Tarn Wethelen.

Or what remained of it.

All was charcoal and ash. A village turned from a place of light to a place of death and shadow. Not one hut remained, and scarce were the traces that they had ever existed, so thoroughly had the raiders burned them. Corpses of slain villagers lay amid the charred remains; they too had been caught in the conflagration and their cremated bones were scattered in the scant ruins of their homes. At least the wolves would not feast on their flesh.

Turning away from the grisly scene, still emanating the roast-pig scent of the funeral pyre, the company journeyed on toward Tarn Wethelan's temple, a mile away on a bald broad hilltop visible for leagues around. As they had been warned, it too lay in smouldering ruins, a trail of sullen black smoke spiralling up from its shattered remains to mingle with the sleet-heavy clouds. Dazed, the warriors rode up the hill and stopped before what had been the temple entrance. Some started to moan and keen; a few had visited here in happier times and remembered the magnificence now obliterated, never to rise again.

Once, an enormous wooden palisade had run inside a mighty encircling ditch, protecting the sacred area; two entrances had faced East and West, the eastern one with an imposing lintelled gateway that framed the rising Sun. Four circular arrangements of free-standing posts had made an unnatural forest in the centre, guarding a cove of three tall stones where the priests would treat with the spirits and perform rites to ensure the risings and settings of Sun and Moon.

Now that splendour had perished, leaving charred lumps overlaid by a crust of ash-smeared snow. The fire had been so voracious many posts had burnt right down into the their chalk-dug pits.The standing stones of the cove had been toppled into the ditch, and fires deliberately set under them so that they cracked into many pieces.

An'kelet gazed bleakly at the devastation. "How did they dare wreak such evil in a holy place? Surely they feared that the spirits would strike them down for their sacrilege!"

Ardhu's visage was grey as the surroundings; the smeared snow, the solemn sky, the lifeless winter-bitten hills in the distance. "My evil sister and those under her spell seem to fear nothing, my friend, be it in the sky, or in a barrow, or walking the green earth. I pray you never meet her face to face; she has the Aspect of the Old Gloomy Woman of Winter on her...."

An'kelet shuddered and made a sign against evil behind his back; the Gloomy Woman was a euphemism for the Death Crone, the Guardian, who sucked life from her own Son, the Sun, in Winter

"Where next from here, Art?" Ka-hai rode up, struggling with his horse, which was reacting in fear to the stench and smoke all around it.

Ardhu nodded towards Bohrs and a small knot of men who held the great hounds of the tribe on their tethers. The animals were restive, snapping at each other and tugging on the lead, sniffling and snuffling at the scored and blasted ground, their tails swinging like whips. "The scent of the raiders must be here, somewhere. Loose the hounds."

Bohrs let go of his dog, with a shout of encouragement. The tan hound bounded away, barking, and the rest of the pack raced after him, crashing through the ash piles, leaping up onto the broken embankments, their noses thrust into the wreckage. Bohrs and other dog-handlers went after them, scanning the ground for traces of footprints or animal spoor from the Chief Boar T'orc

At first Bohrs found nothing, and his wide face became as dark as a thunderhead in frustration. But suddenly his dog, Drudlwyn, gave a sharp bark and sprang on a brownish lump in the grass, clasping it in her jaws and worrying it. "Give that to me!" Bohrs leaned over and wrestled the scrap from his dog's jaws with much growling and snarling from the hound. "Hmm, Ardhu, what do you make of this?"

Art took the matted clump from Bohrs. It seemed to be a wad of coarse springy hair braided and sewn onto a scrap of cloth that appeared to have been torn from the hem of a garment. "I cannot say for sure, but maybe this hair is from the cloak of Rhyttah, which is said to be made from the beards of vanquished chiefs!"

"Just what we needed then," said Bohrs, and he snatched the clump back from Ardhu and thrust it under Drudlwyn's wildly working nose. "Find him, my girl!" he ordered the dog. "Bring us to this Rhyttah and his fat Boar...so we can all have boar meat for supper, then shave Rhyttah's chin as he has done to many others!"

The hound's ears lifted in excitement and the heavy tail thumped. Then, baying, she loped away, the rest of the dog-pack eagerly following. The men of Ardhu's warband pursued, riding single file through the steaming, dismal ruins of what had once been the temple of Tarn Wethelen.

The warriors journeyed West then North, then West again, wildly zigzagging across desolate, wintry lands, through hills furled with mist and over rivers frozen solid in their beds. Right up to the peaks of God-of-Bronze they galloped, below the very crags of Kharn Mennyn where the Spirits of Sky dwelt amidst sharp fingers of bluestone, then back across the harsh terrain toward gentler, lower lands that lay further North. They did not come across Chief Boar and Chief Giant, but they found their leavings—ransacked villages, desecrated holy sites, ravaged corpses left for scavengers to feast on. They tried to make decent the bones of those killed, then continued onwards, ever more determined to wreak justice on Rhyttah and T'orc. But slowly they began to feel an edge of despair, as they crossed endless gloomy expanses by day, and shivered round fires at night with the howls of wind and wolves in their ears. They might call Rhyttah a coward in boastful talk, but they were growing unnerved by both his refusal to meet them, and his continued path of destruction with T'orc. On several occasions, An'kelet brought up the name Merlin had mentioned—Ahnis the Black Witch, daughter of White Witch, who lived at the Valley of Grief in the Uplands of Despair.But Ardhu refused to seek her out, still putting his trust in keen blades and the smiting of axes against enemies' skulls rather than sorcery and dark dealings.

Riding with the company, Hwalchmai had almost forgotten his oath to find the Green Man and offer his neck to the axe. His quest seemed almost foolish, with the ruins of once-thriving settlements scattered across the land and widows and orphaned children wailing on the sides of the great Ridgeways that crossed Prydn. Fighting the enemies of his chief and land was surely a better cause than dying at a Moon-mad man's bidding. After all, what was the Green One, who had entered the king's hall unbidden that stormy eve? Maybe an evil spirit born from the cold and the darkness, maybe just an enemy seeking to cause mayhem and confusion... Honour in facing him? Maybe. But would the men of Ardhu's band think Hwalchmai an honourable hero, or just an honourable fool? Breaking his word was not a thing to be proud of, but neither was throwing life away on a whim.

Hwalchmai pulled his horse's reins and began the decent into a low-slung valley filled with tumbled stones and gnarled thorn trees. Ardhu and An'kelet were riding several paces behind him, discussing heatedly what the best course of action was with Rhyttah seemingly moving like the wind across Prydn. The rest of the warriors massed in the rear, three abreast on the narrow, stony trail that wound towards the valley floor. Hwalchmai could see the hounds in the basin of the vale, sniffing between boulders and skidding over the surface of a frozen brook. They seemed uneasy, almost afraid, their ears press flat against their narrow skulls and their tails down.

Suddenly he caught a glimpse of movement on the far side of the valley. Squinting into the gloom, he spied the figure of an old woman clad in black rags shuffling amid the boulders. As he stared at her, her hooded head swung round and she stared back at him with such malevolence he instinctively made a sign against evil with his hand. He could not see her visage clearly, due to the distance, but a brief glimpse had shown him a countenance mottled and twisted, abnormal. He now noticed too that the valley itself was abnormal, with no vegetation, save for thorny black scrub, and rocks that were white as bone, jagged as blades. An air of desolation rose from the barren and blasted earth, and by a stunted shrub, a flock of crows were pecking at the denuded carcass of some hapless beast.

The place felt foul, worse than anywhere he had ever ventured—could this be the fabled Valley of Despair? It certainly fitted the name!

Without waiting for the others, he drove his mare on into the valley. He heard Ardhu shout to him, his voice raised in annoyance, but a strange rash madness overcame him, and he paid his kinsman no heed. Going into the vale first and facing the hag in her den would surely prove his valour to the Men of the West for once and for all…

And then the mist came down. It came fast and it came suddenly, creeping out of cracks between rocks, from damp earth, from the ice of the frozen river. Cold tendrils swirled round him, rising into sinister shapes and yawing faces that melted in an instant. Chills rippled down his spine, and he drew his dagger and slashed wildly at the fog. He heard sounds deep in its heart; were they peels of laughter?

"Ardhu? My lord?" he shouted to his cousin, but his voice sounded abnormal in that grey amorphous mass, a muffled lifeless groan, a voice out of a barrow.

Pounding his heels against his steed's flanks, he stumbled on through the thickening greyness. He could see shapes, or so he thought, heard the faint trace of voices shouting his name. Then suddenly he was completely alone in a still grey world. Beneath him his mount was trembling.

Before long, the mist lifted slightly. He could see frozen water, a river course leading up to a small waterfall that had turned to ice. It shone blue, beautiful yet cold and perilous in the half-light, its motionless juts of water thrust out like spears in mid-flight. Below the icy prongs, sitting on a rock, was a woman—not the hag he had spied shuffling across the valley, but another. One much more pleasing to the eye…

She was older than Hwalchmai, but good to look upon, not toothless or sagging from bearing children year after year. Straight nut-brown hair hung to her waist and her wide eyes were earth-hued. Translucent skin made her eyes appear even darker, and freckles dotted her small nose like flecks of gold. She was dressed all in green, with a red sash tied about her waist.

Green. He shuddered suddenly, and his heart started to pound.

The woman rose and approached him. She held out a sprig of mistletoe, a symbol of peace. "You, young warrior, are the one my husband has been waiting for," she said. "The youth who serves Ardhu, High-King."

Hwalchmai nodded. "If your husband is the green warrior who comes and goes like a being from Otherness, then yes, I am the one who swore to come to him."

She smiled. "So formal. Please, be at peace. I have no quarrel with you. See! I have brought the sacred mistletoe, used in treaties between warring chiefs. Let us give each other the kiss of peace, and then, in trust, we will go back to my husband's domain at Lud's Hole."

Hwalchmai dismounted, and the lady approached him. "What is your name?" he asked. She was tall for a woman, close to his height, and she smelt of the greenwood, fresh and woody, underlaid by slightly acrid tang. He noticed why as he saw that her necklace, which he had first thought was made of coloured beads, was really a string of poisonous, inedible holly-berries. They oozed, white and yellow.

"You may call me Rhagnell," the woman said, and she kissed him soundly on both cheeks. He was all too aware of the proximity of her, the warmth that flowed from her supple frame.

She smiled and held out her hand to him. He marvelled at it, soft and white as if she had never worked in the field or skinned a beast for the pot. "Come, Hwalchmai of the court of Ardhu Pendraec. Come and face your fate, whatever it might be."

***

"Where, by the Sun, is Hwalchmai?" An'kelet whirled in circles in the mist, sure of nothing except that Ardhu was near him, a darker spot in the sombre sheet of greyness. "He was here one moment...."

"And gone the next." Ardhu's face loomed out of the fog, pallid but with eyes on fire. "There is magic here, An'kelet; I'd stake my life on it. Merlin can conjure such mists—he did once so that my father could carry off my mother—and I am sure he is not the only magic-user who has the skill."

"What shall we do, Art?" Ka'hai broke through the fog bank, brow furrowed with worry and nose red and dripping. "We can't see a thing! We could run right into a hedge of daggers for all we'd know."

"We must move forward," said An'kelet. "If there is someone beyond this mist who has no love of us, they will surely try and hem us in at the valley's exposed heart, attacking from all sides."

"But which way to get back out?" Ka'hai scraped his work-roughened hands through his damp hair, his face red with frustration. "Should we retreat? Going back up will be difficult, the shale is loose."

"Forward—and on foot." Ardhu swung off Lamrai's back. "If we ride about in the fog, the horses might slip and fall. We cannot afford to lose steeds or men in such a manner."

The warband slowly dismounted and Ardhu began to lead the party across the valley floor, over the weather-washed rocks and twisting roots. All conversation died away, sucked into the swirling fog; the atmosphere seemed oppressive, unnatural, and surreal. The hounds, sensing something was amiss, whimpered and hugged the heels of their masters' horses.

Suddenly they saw the cave, gaping like a monstrous mouth in the slate strewn valley side. A rust-hued stalactite hung down from the centre of its roof, the fang of some earth-giant ready to gnash the unwary, while evil humours drifted from its depths, reaching into their nostrils and making them gag.

"Pah!" spat Bohrs. "It reeks of death here. This must be a burial place!"

"Or a place of sacrifice," said An'kelet solemnly.

As they drew closer to the cavern, they could see that the place was indeed some kind of hideous shrine, though what spirit demanded such dark worship they did not know. Seven stumpy stones marched across the cave-mouth, forming a barrier against the profane world and on them rested a line of tiny skulls—the crania of children. More children's skulls could be seen in the gloomy cave interior, some stuck in natural fissures in the stone, others teetering on rotting poles. Lit tallow-cups illuminated the sad, bony faces.

"Truly this is a place of great darkness and despair," Ardhu muttered hoarsely. "Surely this must be the cursed valley mentioned by Merlin, and this cave the abode of the Black Witch daughter of White Witch."

An'kelet stared at the forbidding cave-mouth, face twisted with revulsion. "I think no other place is so accursed in all Prydn, my friend."

At that moment, a screech sounded within the cavern, a horrible, throaty sound that echoed on the dank, moss-furred stones. A torch flared, and a wretched, hideous figure shambled into view. It was a woman, old beyond any the warriors had ever seen, her back humped and her left leg dragging from some paralysing malady. Her face resembled a skull, gaunt and taut-skinned, the mouth open and yawing, foul with ulcerations that had eaten away one side of her lip and exposed the gnarled stumps of her teeth. Her eyes were red and rheumy, their unnatural colour made more striking by the blue face-paint she wore. A third eye was drawn in ochre on the centre of her forehead. Stinking rags fluttered around her like malodorous wings; they were dun-coloured and reeking…and looked suspiciously like strips of desiccated skin.

"I am Ahn-is, the Black Witch!" she cried, "servant of Kayagh, Old Woman of Gloominess, the Hag of Winter. Why have you come to my valley, you men of bow and blade? Have you brought an offering for my shrine?" She grabbed one of the skulls from its plinth and cradled it as she would a living child. "Long has it been since the little ones were fed to the Moon, under the wings of Owl-face, the Great Watcher with her wide open eyes! And so the land has diminished, the Old One grows angry, her winters grow wilder. Her Sun raises his head less freely; soon, he may remain in the dark underworld, defeated, and all the wailing of priests in Khor Ghor will not bring His Light to the world!"

"Blasphemer!" cried out Ka'hai from his position behind Ardhu and An'kelet. "You think the works of great priests like the Merlin of Prydn are less than the bloody sacrifices committed by a mad old hag!"

The Black Witch pointed a bony, crooked finger in his direction. "You mock me and recoil in horror, big ugly man, but do your deny your own Ancestors gave the best of their babes to the Moon, and that in those days the folk of our land were in the height of our strength and power?"

The warriors stirred uneasily. Many lives were given to the spirits in the Old Times, to encourage the Sun and make the crops grow, and please old Mother Moon with her bleak skull-eyes. The priests said that if the brightest and best were given to the Ancestors, the ancients would be pleased and ensure fine weather and fine harvests. These practices had dwindled over the years, with offerings of sheep and cattle substituted for human flesh. Only in rare occasions, when there was famine or plague or war, would the Great Sacrifice de deemed necessary.

The hag hobbled forward, leering horribly. "You will fail, all of you. The land cries for your blood. It may not be given on an altar, but that sacrifice will you make."

One of the lower ranks of warriors, Nerthac, gave a shout and swung his horn-filted dagger at the crone's midriff. A terrible shriek left her tumour-swollen lips and she leapt upon him like some grotesque, hopping spider, tearing at his face and throat with her twisted nails, snapping at his exposed flesh with rank green teeth.

Nerthac fell back, screaming, with the hag on top of him. Nerthac's friend, Cacamuri, rushed forward and tried to seize Ahn-is by her matted hair, but she turned on him with startling agility and grabbed his own long braids, bouncing his skull off the valley floor until the blood rushed from lips and nose.

"Do not underestimate me!" cried Ahn-is. "I am She who is in every Shadow, who guides the fatal arrow to its target, who judges the fatal blow. See me and fear me, men of the West! I will have what has long been due to me, blood and honour."

The men were beginning to waver. Other men they would have attacked and hewed at until either they or their opponents were slain. But this creature, frenzied and hideous…they did not know how to react. She was a woman, but not just any woman; a priestess certainly, and maybe more. It might bring the wrath of the Ancestors if she was killed—a punishment of blighted crops and empty cradles. The risk was too great.

Ardhu saw the paling faces, hands reaching to clasp talismans, lips moving in silent prayer. Adrenaline pumped through his body. He had to act quickly, or the lines would break and the warband would break asunder, to become lost in the sorcerous mist in the valley.

Drawing Carnwennan in a flash of light, he suddenly urged Lamrai forward and hurled the dagger at the Black Witch daughter of White Witch. The blade took the crone in the throat, burying itself deeply. She stumbled back, releasing Cacamuri, who crawled away, moaning and clutching his shattered nose. Hands fluttering, Ahn-is collapsed against the stone stumps at the mouth of the cave, knocking over skulls and tallow cups. The flames from the cups caught her skirts of dry skin and they began to smoulder, releasing an awful reek that turned the contents of one's stomach to bile.

Ardhu threw Lamrai's reins to An'kelet, and leaping from the saddle raced towards the thrashing figure of Ahn-is. He grabbed her hair and dragged her up, plucking his dagger from her flesh with his free hand. "Whatever you are, it is time for you to meet your gods," he said. "You have been too long living in your past. You will seal this place of dread with one final sacrifice—yours."

The witch grinned at him, light already dimming in her eyes. Blood bubbled on her lips as she grated, "So be it, it is as the Owl-faced one decrees. One cannot live till Eventide whom the Old One has touched at dawn! Remember this well, man. I can see Her behind your shoulder, looking with her wide-spiralled eyes. The land cries out for mighty sacrifice, and my old flesh will not suffice."

A shiver went up Ardhu's spine at all this talk of death and the ancient spirit-mother, whose plaque he knew so well on one of the five trilithons inside Khor Ghor. All men met her, eventually, for that is the fate of men, but it seemed that the hag was cursing him, bringing evil in where there was none before.

"Be still, you monster. If ever you served this land's good, it was long ago, and now you are nothing but a blight." He brought Carnwennan down again, glittering in the fog, and clove the witch's skull near in twain with the might of his blow.

The fear that had taken many of his men evaporated. They circled back round and crowded into the cave, casting down the pitiful skeletal remains in every nook and cranny, turning over the witch's big bronze cauldron and sending its rank, gelatinous contents spilling across the cave floor. The liquid mingled with Ahn-is's blood and a hissing went up like a thousand serpents.

At the back of the cave, Ardhu came across the Black Witch's sacrificial altar, a block of sandstone with a natural dip in the top. Livid stains marred its surface, and shrivelled offerings he did not want to begin to think about lay scattered at the base. On top, in the hollow, lay an ancient bronze razor, green with age, the surface decorated by ancient patterns. Old as it was, the blade was honed to sharpness; its edge winked wickedly in the dim light.

Carefully Ardhu picked it up and held it out to show his men. "The Razor of the Black Witch. Surely this will be the tool to shear the bristles of T'orc …though an evil thing it seems."

An'kelet gazed toward the entrance of the unwholesome cave. "It is—so let us fare forth and use it, then break it to make it dead. We must waste no more time; the mist is lifting."

Sure enough rags of fog were sailing by, shredded on a rising breeze. Feeble sunlight played off the pointed white stones that littered the bleak valley.

Ardhu grinned and ran out into the burgeoning sunlight, swinging lithely onto Lamrai's back. "Come, warriors of the West, raise your bows and keep your hands close to dagger-hilts!" he cried. "We go forward now to finish the task that has been laid upon us—to slay the boar from the North that plagues our land!"

CHAPTER EIGHTEEN

A hard ride of several days brought Hwalchmai to Lud's hole, the abode of the Green Rider and of Rhagnell, his wife. It stood in an area of ancient woodland, with a row of great natural rocks rising up behind it like a row of black fingers clutching at the skies. Clouds scudded over their tips, dappling their flanks with light and shadows, making the landscape truly look like the abode of gods and giants.

Lud's hole itself lay in a slight dip surrounded by dark trees. Serrated rocks stuck up, the bones of a fallen god, forming a natural barrier. At one end, the boulders gaped away revealing a dark cleft that plummeted straight down into the earth. Above the lightless entrance hung great wreaths of mistletoe and holly.

Rhagnell dismounted and beckoned for Hwalchmai to do the same. She led the horses to a ramshackle pen beside the cavern and hastily fed and watered them. Then she approached Hwalchmai, her brown eyes solemn, her long straight hair swinging in the breeze. "Do you still dare to set your head on my husband's block?" she asked.

"I am a man of my word," he said resolutely.

Rhagnell went to the cave mouth, beckoning for Hwalchmai to follow. The entrance was dark and gloomy, lit only by small flickering pots of tallow in crevices on the walls. Incense-cups were billowing, filling the air with the exotic scents...but they did not hide the underlying reek, sweet and sickly, of decay. Of rotten flesh.

"What is that smell?" Hwalchmai grimaced, raising a hand to his mouth.

Rhagnell's lips turned up at the corner. "Can you not guess? It comes from the others who have played—and lost—the beheading game." She took one of the tallow cups from its niche on the wall and held it aloft. On a little ledge near the roofline sat a dozen human heads, preserved by drying or by rubbing them with unguents and oils. Their eyes were gone but had been replaced by coloured stones; their skin was like tanned leather, brown and ropy.

Hwalchmai winced and glanced away, his hand instinctively going to his dagger.

A flight of stairs descended from this gallery of death, leading to another antechamber. Rhagnell went down them, solemn, stately, and Hwalchmai followed, cautious, unsure of what he would find.

When the young warrior reached the room below, he was amazed at how welcoming it seemed. A fire roared in a hearth, the smoke funnelling through a channel in the rock to reach the outside. The floor was strewn with sweet rushes, and herbs hung from above in woven nets, their fragrance, mingling with the scent of the incense cups, blotting out the reek of the preserved heads. A bench ran along one wall, and at the end of it sat the Green Man himself.

He was not in full ceremonial dress, although his shaggy robe was dyed green. He wore no verdant stain on his face and Hwalchmai could now see that he was old, over forty summers by the deep lines round his eyes and the grey streaks in his beard. So, he was not a man even in his prime...and yet he showed no sign of weakness, his legs sturdy as tree-trunks, his belly broad, and his shoulders wide and straining against the material of his tunic. He did not glance up as Rhagnell and Hwalchmai entered the chamber, but toyed with something that lay across his knees, hidden by the fall of his clothing and the shadows in the cave.

He looked up as Hwalchmai drew close, and he grinned. "So you have come, boy! Good, I need some sport to pass the winter. See...I have prepared for your coming!" He lifted the object on his lap, and Hwalchmai saw that it was his magic double-bladed axe. The Green Man had been honing it, sharpening the blade with a whetstone until its edge shone like cold fire.

Hwalchmai shuddered.

The Green Man hauled himself to his feet. He was a big man, taller than most in Albu, perhaps due to some ancestry from the Men of the Ice Seas, who were often tall as trees, or so it was said. "Don't look so stricken, lad," he rumbled, still grinning in his unsettling way. His teeth, for a man his age, were very white and even, with long canines that gave him a wolfish demeanour. "I'm not going to eat you. Indeed, I am going to give you a fair chance. I will not ask you to lay your head on the block tonight—it is not the auspicious time, the act must be done when the Moon is dark. That time will be in three days, and until then you will be fed, given a soft bed and well taken care of by Rhagnell. You can even leave if you wish; that's if you could bear the shame of such cowardice. What is your name, boy?"

Hwalchmai held his head high. "I am Hwalchmai, Hawk of the Plain, cousin to Ardhu, chieftain of Prydn, and of the High-clan of Belerion."

"A noble heritage. I would be glad to have your head decorate my hall. I am called Bresalak…the Contentious."

"A fitting name for you, for so you are," murmured Hwalchmai.

Bresalak ignored his comment. "Tell me, Hwalchmai of the high-clan of Belerion… what gift did my wife Rhagnell give you today?"

Hwalchmai stirred uneasily, ill at ease with this unexpected line of questioning. "Nothing that would bring you dishonour."

"Did I imply that I thought it would?" Bresalak roared with laughter and smote his knees with a hand. "By the gods, you are a strange fellow, Hwalchmai. But come, I ask a question. Show me what Rhagnell gave you."

"Do as he bids…" Rhagnell, standing near his shoulder, pushed him forward. "He will know if you lie; he can read men's truth."

Grimly, Hwalchmai leaned toward the green warrior and gave him the kiss of peace on his cheek. "This token of peace was the gift of the lady," he said. "I trust you will honour it…until the time when the beheading game must take place."

Bresalak laughed again, but there was a strange, strained note in his laughter. "Of course. Now I must go hunting in the woods and leave you here in my domain. Rhagnell will feed you and show you to your sleeping quarters. We will speak again tomorrow. Have a restful night, lord Hwalchmai."

With that, he gathered up his green robe, tossed a cloak about his shoulders, and strode from the cave.

"Sit." Rhagnell pointed Hwalchmai in the direction of the bench. He sat down and she brought him a handled beaker of heather-beer and a wooden platter of meat and cheese. When he had eaten his fill, she took his arm and guided him into an antechamber, where a bed of furs and sheepskins lay on the floor. Tallow lights hung suspended from the ceiling, casting flickering shadows around the walls.

"You shall stay here until the beheading game takes place," she said. "Sleep well, Hawk of the Plain."

She retreated, her long skirts and long hair rustling. Hwalchmai lay down, pulling a sheepskin over himself, watching water bead on the cavern roof. He swore to himself that not only he would not sleep well in this eldritch place, he would not sleep at all.

But despite his vows to keep wakeful, Hwalchmai dozed off sometime in the early hours of the morn. He was woken, suddenly, by the mournful hoot of an owl in the woods outside the cave. He sat up, heart hammering. An owl's cry was no good omen; the owl with its huge flower-like eyes was sacred to the Guardian.

Crawling out of the sheepskins, he pushed back the hanging that fronted the chamber and slipped out. The tallow cups had burnt down, and the only light came from the sullen glow of the hearth. Rhagnell was there, sitting cross-legged by the dying embers, crooning words he did not understand to something that lay in her lap. Her face was painted with strange signs and looked weirdly old, like that of a crone. She turned as he came into the room, and he hesitated, grimacing, as he noticed that on her lap she held a human head. She was oiling it, rubbing preservatives into the tanned leather skin.

"Are you repulsed?" she asked calmly, putting down the grisly artefact. "Do I frighten you?" She rose and walked towards him. He could smell the scent of the unguents she'd rubbed on the skull oozing from her skin, saw where sweat had tracked through her ceremonial face-paint.

He was too polite, in this strange house, to say ill words of her and maybe offend. Admitting fear was also not for a man and warrior of Ardhu's warband. "I am not afraid," he said. "Although I find this a strange house. But I would expect nothing more when its master is the green-faced rider."

Rhagnell laughed. "Do you find me fair, lord Hwalchmai?" She whirled on her bare feet, and suddenly he was all too aware of the thinness of her robe and how it clung to her flesh, damp with sweat and scented oil.

He stared at his feet. "I found you fairer without the paint," he said, trying to make light.

"Ah, but this," she pointed to her face, "is what I must wear, to speak with the spirits of the men my husband has killed. A face half of shadow, because I must speak with shades. It is something I have always done, for I have that gift. If you were my man, instead of Bresalak, would you forbid me to wear my dark face and walk only in the world of light?"

"Lady," he said, "if I were your man, I would give you free will to do as you would. It would not be my place to stop you from speaking to those beyond the Western Door."

She smiled, her teeth glowing white against her artificially blackened lips. "A good answer, my brave young Hwalchmai. "Now kiss me to prove your words are true, to prove that you are my friend."

He hesitated. "What of Bresalak?"

"He is far away on a midnight hunt, tracking down the wild one with his branching horns. Besides, there is no harm in it. Another kiss for peace and one for friendship." She reached up and plucked another sprig of mistletoe from a bunch that hung from a hook on the roof, and handed it to Hwalchmai. He took the green shoot, but to his embarrassment could think of naught but that the plant was also linked with fertility, its white juices resembling the seed of a man.

Rhagnell laughed. Hwalchmai almost fancied that she knew where his thoughts were leading, and he blushed red to the roots of his hair. The dark-eyed wife of the Green man reached out and touched his chin, drawing his face towards her with her finger. "Mistletoe is the key that opens all doors," she said softly, watching as he blushed even deeper at the double meaning in her words.

Struggling, he found his tongue. "I do not think its use is always well advised."

"Ardhu Pendraec teaches his warriors much in the way of courtesy and self-sacrifice," said Rhagnell, still caressing Hwalchmai's face. "He must be an extraordinary being…as he is barely more than a boy himself."

"He is extraordinary. And I am his kin."

"Go now, then, Hwalchmai." She leaned in and kissed him, first his cheek and then, grasping his shoulders, his mouth. "But remember, in two days the Moon will be in the correct phase. Bresalak will wish to commence the beheading game."

Hwalchmai returned to his chamber and fell into the sheepskins and furs. He tossed restlessly, sweat beading on his skin. He felt feverish; he hoped he was not becoming ill. The idea of offering his neck to the green-faced warrior seemed utter madness now; surely he must have been ensorcelled to follow such a doomed path. And then there was Rhagnell, loathly as she caressed the severed head of one of Bresalek's victims, but also filling him with a desire he dared not slake. He thought with both pleasure and despair of her dark, questioning eyes, and her wandering, oil-smeared fingers on his face. Fingers that had caressed a withered death's head…

Night passed into morning, and he heard the roar and bellow of Bresalek returning to Lud's hole. He wandered from his sleeping space, bleary-eyed, in time to see the massive man stride into the chamber, a deer slung over his shoulders. He hurled it to the ground and began to skin it, uncaring of the blood and innards that slopped across the floor.

Excited, Rhagnell knelt beside him, helping clean out the carcass. Her arms were red with gore to the shoulder; daubs of red marred her face. She was truly the loathly lady again, the tender of the dead, aiding her monstrous, surreal husband with the fruits of the hunt.

"There will be fine venison for your meal tonight, Hawk of the Plain!" boomed Bresalek, wiping his besmirched hands on his baggy trews. "Your last meal, maybe…if that is what the spirits will."

He got up from the floor, and approached the silent youth in the corner. "And what did you do when I was gone? Did my woman Rhagnell entertain you?"

"She entertained me as every woman should entertain a visitor in her household."

"Indeed. And did she give you anything? Anything at all… Come, show me, boy; I will know if you lie."

Hwalchmai stared into the inscrutable face, Sun-bronzed and leathery, with deep, green-flecked eyes under grizzled brows. "Two kisses, that was all, one for peace and one for friendship, and I give them in return to you." And he duly set the kisses of peace and of friendship on the Green Man's cheeks, though he felt inclined to neither.

The Green Man roared with laughter and stretched out his immense, muscle- bound arm, beckoning Rhagnell to bring him a beaker of mead. "Peace there will be until the Moon's phase is right," he said. "And aye, we can even be friends until that time. So for another day enjoy my home, and the company of my woman, and let us not think about the future."

Finishing with the deer, Bresalak went outside and did not return. Rhagnell continued tending to the meat her husband had left, and then turned her attention to the deer's skin, scraping it clean with an old stone scraper and stretching it out on a drying frame made from branches.

"Where has Bresalak gone?" asked Hwalchmai.

"He hunted deer, now he seeks boar," she replied. "Just like your lord, Ardhu."

Hwalchmai sighed. "Ardhu, who I should be with now! I am a man or honour and would not gladly break my word, but tell me, Rhagnell wife of Bresalak, why should I die just for some whim of your husband? We have no real cause for enmity."

She sighed. "Bresalak was touched by the spirits when he was young. He ran wild in the forest. He saw He-who-is-Oldest beneath his thunder-oak, antlers springing from his brow and leaves spilling from his mouth. It changed him. He devoted himself to his Lord of the wildwood, but there was one thing he could not accept—that he, like the foliage, would wither and die and a new young king supplant him. So, every year, he has chosen the best and brightest to play the beheading game…when he takes the head he feels the mightiness of the slain pass to him, renewing him for another year."

"He is mad," muttered Hwalchmai. "No mortal man may live forever."

"No, no man may," said Rhagnell, and she would say no more.

The day passed as if in a dream. Hwalchmai wandered outside, walking the woods of that wild place in a haze of anxious anticipation. Wind buffeted him, the trees roared and swept down with long branches. Everything around him seemed unusually bright, unusually vibrant—the rich greens of the mosses and leaves, the violet blue of the winter skies. And the smells! Water and damp earth, cold frost, and distant snow being gradually swept over the higher moorlands. All fresh and alive, taunting him with their beauty...for unless fate intervened, this would be the last such beauty his eyes would behold, for tomorrow he must face the Green Man's axe.

He wandered back to Lud's hole later that afternoon, after watching the Sun impale Himself upon the craggy fangs of rock that topped the long moor beyond the deep earth cave. Inside the fastness, Rhagnell had cooked some of the venison brought home by Bresalek; Hwalchmai ate in silence, and Rhagnell said nothing either, but merely stared into the fire with a strange lost look on her face.

As the tallow cups sputtered, and shadows danced around the main chamber, Hwalchmai departed for his room. He lay down but had been there only a short while when a shadow filled the stone doorway. He reached for his dagger instinctively...but let it drop with a clatter when he saw that his visitor was none other than Rhagnell.

Her hair fell unbound around her, autumn leaf hued, gold and brown and red combined. It was smooth and shone like metalwork, like Sun on a shield. A flowing robe, white as the Moon, and tied at the waist by a sash of green-dyed cloth, tumbled loosely to her ankles. She walked with purpose and her eyes swallowed the feeble, wavering light.

Hwalchmai propped himself up on his elbow. "Lady, what do you do here? I beg you let me rest and dream, for it may be the last night I can do so."

She knelt beside him on the sheepskins. "I have been here near enough three times three years, Hwalchmai, ever since Bresalak brought me here as a young and frightened girl. My father was a prince of the north; he traded me like a piece in a game in order to avoid Bresalek's axe. I have been loyal to my husband, and tended to all his needs. I have been a good wife to him. But I can sense a change in him, a weakening, and my own heart is changing too. For the first time I feel sullied, not like his wife, but his captive, his slave. He is no longer the great oak, stalwart against the wind—he is the vine withering on the ground, its sap spent. We have no children, Hwalchmai."

She spread her arms, the loose white linen floating around her so that she almost looked like a spirit. "Hwalchmai, untie my sash from my waist and keep it safe with you when you go to face Bresalek tomorrow. My token to you; maybe a help, and maybe not. It is in the hands of the gods and they can be cruel."

Hands slightly shaking, Hwalchmai reached up to untie the moss-green sash. It tumbled in verdant folds to the floor. His hands then drifted to the front of her robe, where the linen gaped with the unfastening of the sash, revealing a provocative slice of pale skin. Gently, he pulled back the robe from her shoulders and let it drop alongside the sash. She had a lean, athletic body, with narrow hips and round, firm breasts sprinkled with tattoos of spirals. He let his fingers trace the line of the tattoos, seeking, exploring. She wrapped her arms around his neck and drew his face up to hers and kissed him on the lips, three times, but no longer was it the kiss of friendship or of peace, but the kiss of a lover.

He pushed her down into the skins, admiring the play of the softly flickering tallow-lamps across her nakedness. He ran his hands through her glossy hair, spreading it out across the sheepskin, noticing for the first time that she still bore mistletoe, but it was artfully threaded through her locks, the berries cool and soft against his fingertips—much like Rhagnell's naked flesh.

She realised he had found the berries and smiled, coiling around him like a cat, drawing him down against her pliant warmth. "I am the key, Hwalchmai," she said.

Rhagnell left Hwalchmai's bed just before dawn. He heard her go, bare feet slapping on the stone floor of the cavern. He lay still for a few more minutes then rose himself, dressing quickly and binding on his belt with its daggers and axe. Last, he picked up Rhagnell's discarded sash and tied it tightly around his waist.

He went from the cave and out to the green grass before Lud's Hole. A sprinkle of snow had fallen in the night, and the rising Sun glittered on frozen fronds and boughs. A clean wind was blowing from the West, bringing the promise of kinder, warmer days.

He wanted to live to see those days…

Suddenly a shadow fell across him, wide as a broad-backed bull. Bresalek stood before him, grinning, his huge hands planted on his hips. He had been successful in his hunt again, but this time he had downed a wild boar. It lay over his muscled shoulders, its blood trickling down his tunic. With a grunt, he heaved it away and beckoned to Hwalchmai with a red-stained hand.

"Come closer, boy. Do not stand gawping like some sheep! This is the morning of the Beheading Game. The game I always win."

Hwalchmai approached the giant as bidden. A strange calm filled him. The Sun was brightening, sending long shafts of light between the spindly trees that surrounded Lud's hole. Surely, surely, he could not die this morning….

"So what did you do on your last evening, boy?" asked Bresalak. "Did you drink? Did you hope? Did my dear woman Rhagnell try to assuage your fears?"

"Indeed she did."

"And what did she give you this time? No more kisses of peace, I'll wager, for this morn no peace can be between us, only rivalry and death."

"No, no kisses of peace…" said Hwalchmai, unable to restrain an ironic grin. To think he had cuckolded this green monster, in his own den!

Bresalek's countenance whitened as he guessed the meaning of his victim's words. His gaze fell to Rhagnell's sash, bound tightly about the young warrior's waist. His eyes turned black as obsidian.

"To the place of Beheading –now!" he roared.

He stormed into the wood and Hwalchmai followed him. Soon they reached a raised mound with trees standing sentinel all around it. A single squat stone stood on the summit, a worn sandstone block streaked with ores that turned its surface red as blood. It was aligned on a gap in the crags beyond, where the Moon would rise and dance every nineteen turns of the Sun.

Bresalek gestured angrily to the worn block. "Kneel down and part your hair," he ordered, "as I did for you in the hall of Ardhu Pendraec. Otherwise, be known as craven, and un-man…and I swear I will kill you anyway, with honour or not—the choice is yours!"

"I keep my word," said Hwalchmai and he dutifully knelt before the stump and laid his head upon its surface. He wondered how many others had knelt in such a fashion, and how much blood had bathed that single worn-down monolith.

"Are you ready, boy?" Bresalak was swinging his great double-headed axe, the muscles rippling in his enormous arms. "Have you made your peace with your gods?"

Hwalchmai's eyes darted, as his mind frantically worked out ways to distract the giant. "Wait! Let me change the place where I kneel. I am ashamed that I die without great conflict of arms. Therefore, it is fitting I die gazing into the shadows and not at Bhel's bright and victorious face."

Bresalek snorted. "I care not which way you kneel, head to the East or to the West. All that interests me is taking that head and adding it to my collection. Be assured I will make that slut Rhagnell dress it and lie with it at her side, since she favoured you so much!"

Hwalchmai wriggled round the pillar until he felt the rays of the strengthening Sun warm his back. Bresalek stomped up in front of him, brandishing his axe. His movements were jerky, erratic, dictated by fury rather than by the rules of the Beheading Game. His hair and beard bristled and his cheeks were purple with simmering rage—uttering a strangled cry, he swung the axe upwards, preparing for the death-stroke. The axe-head caught the early Sunlight and turned to a ball of lambent flame…

The light was full on Bresalek's face, pure golden light from the East. He faltered, suddenly blinded, as the Sun rose even higher in the sky, its radiant beams smiting deep into his eyes like the spear of the Young Son who had been reborn at Solstice and now slowly grew towards the flame of his power at Midsummer. With an angry, thwarted yell, he lashed out wildly with his axe at the crouched figure of Hwalchmai.

And missed.

The deadly blade of the axe thudded against the earth, cutting into the icy ground and sticking there.

Before Bresalek had the chance to pluck it free, Hwalchmai leaped to his feet and charged at the giant man. "One blow you had….and yet I still stand and breathe upon the earth!" he cried triumphantly. "Now it is your turn to meet the fate you gave so readily to others!"

Bresalek cried out, a note of fear in his voice. He suddenly looked old, weak—as Rhagnell had said, a withering vine, ready to return to the earth, where he would moulder alongside a million fallen leaves, his flesh and bones feeding and nurturing all manner of living things.

He tried to flee, to make a mad dash into the trees, but Hwalchmai flung himself on Bresalek's back, kicking his legs from under him and bringing him to the ground. Tearing off Rhagnell's sash, Hwalchmai looped it around Bresalek's throat and twisting with all his strength. Breath cut off, the Green Man thrashed and flailed, his hands scrabbling uselessly at the ever-tightening garrotte. Hwalchmai continued to twist the sash with one free hand, while drawing his flanged axe with the other.

"Go now to the Ancestors, Green Man," he said. "On this winter's morn. I, Hawk of the Plain, have won the Beheading game."

With that, he struck Bresalek between the eyes with his axe, releasing the life-spirit from his skull. The huge body slumped into the grass, and Hwalchmai knelt by it and cut off the huge scowling head. He carried it to the pillar on the mound and set it on top, gazing sightlessly into the strengthening Sun that had brought ruin to its owner.

Then, arms and face and garments streaked with blood, Hwalchmai walked back to Lud's hole. Rhagnell stood outside the cavern, anxious and pale. When she saw his gore-drenched visage, she sobbed briefly, then wiped the tears away with her hand. "So it is done. Bresalek is dead."

Hwalchmai nodded. "Yes, and I must now hasten to join my kinsman, Ardhu, in his hunt for the boar T'orc."

"And what of me? What will become of me now that Bresalek is no more?"

"I leave that up to you," he said. "I would not compel you to come with me, for once already a man compelled you to do his bidding. But if you would ride with me, and share my bed, and dwell with me at the hall of Kham-El-Ard as my wife, it would bring me great pleasure."

"So be it," she said, and she ran round to fetch the horses and provisions for their journey.

Before bright Bhel Sun-face had reached his midday height, they were away toward the lands of the West, while behind them the black crows of the Death-goddess plucked the eyes from the severed head of Bresalek the Green Man and feathered their nests with his hair.

CHAPTER NINETEEN

At Kham-El-Ard, Fynavir felt full of unease. No word had come from Ardhu, not one message from the West. Traders from the Ridgeway spoke of the Chief Boar's rampages and how it seemed able to elude Ardhu's warband. "The beast is born of magic," they said, shaking their heads darkly. "A creature from the underworld. Maybe no man can ever harm it, and Ardhu will chase it till the day the Sun falls from the sky…"

Fynavir shivered, pulling her red fox-skin cloak tighter about her shoulders. She tried to set her mind to the stitching on a pair of shoes; her bone needle slipping in and out, in and out of the fine deer-hide, trailing a piece of dried gut thread. Outside, the wind was buffeting the Great Hall on its crooked hill, sighing in the eaves like a living thing. And perhaps it was a living thing of sorts, the breath of the world that could whisper the first hints of spring or scream like a foul and malevolent hag. It was screaming today, its sound an incessant torment.

"Ardhu, I pray you come back soon," Fynavir murmured to herself. The bone needle flashed in and out. In and out…"We need to set things right between us. A king should not be chasing across country on some fool's errand, even if a worthy one… He should be in his high seat, beside his queen. He wants an heir, I know he blames me that there is not one, but I will show him if only he will return to me. Prydn will have an heir!"

A sudden urgent rapping on the hall's broad door made Fynavir jump in fright. "Oh!" she exclaimed in alarm, as the bone needle pierced her finger. A drop of blood fell into her lap, soiling her tunic. "Who is there?"

The door creaked open. A dwarfish girl hopped in, dragging a clubfoot, and stood without fear or deference. Her forehead was abnormally broad and bulbous, and protruding eyes stared in different directions. Despite her unappealing visage, she had beautiful reddish-gold curls spiralling past her twisted hips. Fynavir recognised her as Brangyan, one of the Ladies of the Lake, her deformity marking her from birth as one touched by the world of spirits. And so it often was…children born with extra fingers, webbed toes, a squint, or a clubfoot were taken in by the priests and priestesses of various orders, for it was clear the spirits or gods had marked them.

"Greetings, Brangyan of the Lake." Fynavir inclined her head politely. A little knot of fear twisted in her belly—could this strange girl be bringing ill news? "What business have you in Kham-El-Ard this day?"

"I bear greetings from the Lady Mhor-gan, sister of Ardhu, sister of ravens, all-seeing lady of the funeral rite. She asks that you visit her in the lake valley where our Order dwells. She wishes to speak with you on a matter of import."

Fynavir's cheeks turned whiter than her hair. Ardhu. It had to be something to do with Ardhu. Maybe he was hurt…or worse. Or was it An'kelet? She wanted to grab Brangyan and shake her until she spewed the answer, but she knew that was not the way. "I will come at once," she said, scrambling for her thickest cloak against the biting wind. She could feel eyes of the women and men in the hall on her, inquisitive, concerned.

"Lady!" Her attendant, Khelynnen, a pretty maiden from the Place of Light, tugged on her sleeve, trying to draw her back. "You can't go tramping in the marsh-lands dressed like that! You need felt boots, an otter skin! And if you must go, shouldn't you take one of the lads as a guard? The days still draw in early, and both strange men and spirits may fare abroad in the night-mists!"

Fynavir tore the girl's fingers from her sleeve. "Peace…I am called, I must go." Quickly, she went with Brangyan into the outer ward of Kham-El-Ard, and down the slope past the defensive ditches with their rows of glistening wooden spikes.

"Your servant-woman need not have feared." Brangyan brought from beneath her cloak a small bow made just for one of her height. "I am the best archer in my order, and my arrows are treated with poisons that will stop a man's heart within a beat."

Together they walked down the well-worn track to the old Henge, before turning upstream and crossing the main fords of Abona, where River Mother's consort Borvoh the Boiling churned in the weir, restless from the heavy winter rains.

After a short journey through a land of withies ands soggy pools, they began a slow descent into long valley enclosed on either side by steep banks, though the northern side was higher and steeper, a barricade that cut the valley off from the sacred landscape of Khor Ghor.

However, the vale-side was a sacred place in itself and had been for many lifetimes, ever since the first Merlin had floated the skystones on rafts down the shining coils of Mother Abona, from the Western mountain known as God-of-Bronze. Tumuli littered the high northern slopes, facing toward the Great Temple on the Plain beyond, while on the far side of the river, beyond stands of deciduous trees, new farming systems had sprung up. A great livestock enclosure ringed the brow of the Hill of Ogg the Eloquent, where it was said the sky first whispered words to men and gave them the art of speech.

Brangyan led Fynavir away from the trackway that split the valley's heart and toward another fording place in the river, which surged into two channels before forming a small, mirror-bright lake. A wooden causeway jutted into the waters, its edges fringed by sentinel reeds, and at the end stood a roundhouse with a sloped roof that touched the water.

The House of the Nine Ladies of the Lake.

Brangyan gestured for Fynavir to mount the causeway and enter the hut. Nervously she walked along the creaking planks, glancing back hopefully at her companion, but Brangyan remained behind in the faded afternoon light.

Fynavir entered the roundhouse and glanced around. A fire burned in a hearth of stone slabs, its smoke spiralling up through the smoke-hole in the ceiling. Fresh herbs and medicinal plants hung from the rafters. Offerings lay on a many-shelved shrine at the back— crow feathers, a broken archer's wristguard, a shard of the spiralled pottery used before the Tin-Men came and found scattered all over most sites of veneration. Mhor-gan, Ardhu's sister, was kneeling by the fire, tending the flames that must never be allowed to die. "I am glad you have come." She spoke without glancing up at Fynavir. "We must talk."

Fynavir felt her heart begin to thud. "Is it…news of Ardhu? Tell me, sister, I cannot bear it! Is he dead?"

"No, No!" Mhor-gan rose and steadied her with a comforting hand. "Calm yourself. The Ladies of the Lake have many eyes, and we can assure you that Ardhu is hale and well— although he has not yet found his quarry, for the one that trained the beast made sure her minions served her well. However, T'orc's reign of terror is nearing an end—winter is almost over, the skies are growing bright. Chief Boar's men are weary of flight and want to return to their own hearths, while T'orc snaps at his own handlers…he wants naught more than to eat acorns and rut with wild sows in the forest! Soon, the warband will catch them, and Ardhu will mete out the justice of the King of Prydn."

"Why have you called me here, if not for news of my husband?"

"It is of you I wish to speak, not my brother. Have you forgotten what night is coming up soon?"

"All days have become as one since the warband went seeking the dread boar. Enlighten me, sister."

"It is Y'melc, the feast of Lambing. The beginning of spring. The day is ruled by Fiery Arrow, who breathes on the hearth-fire and wields both flame and lightning."

Fynavir nodded. "I know of Her. She has a sanctuary in the land of my birth, where the tallest stones in all Ibherna stand guard. I remember a little of her rites from my childhood, but I was sent to the northlands as a young maid and have dwelt in many foreign homes since then, and my memory does not serve me well. As a priestess, I beg you offer me guidance, that I may do the right thing on her Feast and give no offence to gods or men."

Mhor-gan smiled. "You must stand as Brygyndo that night, as queen of your people and the Fiery One's representative. You must pass from house to house and receive gifts, and in turn, confer luck and blessings on the people of Kham-El-Ard and Place-Of-Light. Then you will be put to bed with the bride-doll of the goddess lying beside you, and a magic wand hewn of an ash-limb; these shall be burned on a sacred bone-fire the next morning at Sunrise, and the ashes scattered over the fields to make them fruitful."

Fynavir's mouth worked; her eyes were bitter. "I am hardly a good choice if it is fruitfulness the people crave. So far, I am barren, and they all know my shame. The old women laugh behind their hands whenever I pass, or cluck with mock sorrow!"

Mhor-gan ran a practised hand over Fynavir's stomach, pressing, kneading, and eventually coming to rest near her hipbone. "When a new spirit is ready to go into the world, you will quicken. It is only a matter of time."

Fynavir hung her head; she could not look into the other woman's face beneath its loops of dark braids. "I am filled with doubt...I once heard a rumour among maidens that if ...if another is in your mind beside the one to whom you are vowed...that the spirits will send no child?"

Mhor-gan laughed aloud, teeth flashing. "Ah Fynavir...Ardhu has no other woman, he is enamoured of you! He defied the Merlin to wed you—no mean feat! What you heard was the chatter of silly virgins! Children are born from love, from hate, from long-time lovers and those who seek merely to ease their flesh on a lonely night! It is all in the hands of the spirits how and when the gift of babies arrive."

Fynavir still did not raise her eyes; scarlet stained her cheeks. For all her learning, Mhor-gan did not realise that she spoke of herself, not of Ardhu!

"Thank you for your words of comfort," she finally managed. "I will prepare for the feast of Y'melc, as you have directed, even though I am not worthy to emulate such an esteemed One as High Brygyndo."

"You are worthy in the eyes of the tribes. People everywhere have heard that you are the daughter of Mevva the Intoxicator. They hear tell of how your flesh is white like the chalk that is the bones of the earth, white like Mother Moon who draws the shades of the dead to her. To them, you are a symbol of white-cliffed Albu itself, and only the king of that land may possess you." She poked at the fire, her eyes suddenly shadowed. "And that is another reason why I have summoned you here today. It is not Ardhu's safety that worries me, but yours. Art has many enemies among the chieftains of Prydn—violent, fractious men who cannot see the good he does. The eyes of Afallan see far, Fynavir, and our ears hear what others miss. Many have spoken treasonously, seeking their own power; they cannot draw the sword from beneath the stone, but they can still abduct the white Queen, the sovereignty of Prydn, and claim king-right through you."

"That is madness!" cried Fynavir. "I am no goddess, I am not my mother! I want no man fighting over me, or treating me like some lucky talisman! I would stain my white hair blue if I thought it would keep these beasts of men away!"

"I fear it would not," Mhor-gan sighed, "not now that they have scent of what they desire—a white Queen, a whole kingdom. So, I beg you, although you must continue in your daily duties, be on your guard till Ardhu returns from the Boar Hunt. Lady Nin-Aeifa and I have gazed into the sacred lake and seen many things; some we fear, some we do not understand—the omens of the Otherworld are often not clear to decipher. But there is sorrow and fear, and love and triumph, a setting Sun and a wan Moon that is yet to rise. "

Fynavir returned to Kham-El-Ard, much troubled. But at least she knew that Ardhu and An'kelet were unharmed, which soothed the fears she found hardest to bear. In the days that followed, she tried to cast her worries aside and concentrate on preparing for Y'melc. With deft hands, she created the Bride, the god-doll, from dried sheaves of wheat and early flowers. With Khelynnen and other women, she went to the herdsmen to ascertain there would be enough roundels of cheese and pitchers of milk to satisfy all the celebrants, while leaving some to be offered to the Fiery One herself and to any wandering spirits that might chance upon the Feast. Houses were swept out and domestic rubbish tossed into the middens; it was a time when all life would be refreshed and renewed.

The eve of Y'melc soon came, a clear night with a hard frost and many stars. A full Moon, round and yellow as the cheeses that had been prepared for the occasion, hung over the heights of Kham-El-Ard and turned the sacred pool below into a silver mirror that reflected the faces of the nine Ladies of the Lake. The Ladies had gathered at Sundown and poured ewe's milk into the water before bathing in it, one by one. Now they all sat in a semi-circle, tallow cups burning in their hands, singing as they rocked rhythmically from side to side.

Fynavir let Khelynnen robe her in her finest kirtle, dyed red with the root of madder. The girl then combed down her wintry hair and circled her neck with seven rows of northern amber. Great crescent earrings from the mainland coast were placed upon her earlobes and ochre rubbed onto her cheeks. Ready to face her people, Fynavir lifted the Bride, the sacred image of Brygyndo, from its place beside the hearth and carried it into the courtyard, trailing grains of wheat and petals in its wake.

In the centre of the yard the priests of Khor Ghor had come to oversee the lighting of the Fire-Cross of Brygyndo. Although they celebrated the festival of the Ewe's milk, they played but a small part, for Brygyndo was not a spirit of stone or sky but of earth and childbed and hearth-fire. She was a patron of women, and women's lore and mysteries, though smiths revered her too, for her holy fire kept the forge hot and her breath hardened their metals.

Fynavir spotted the Merlin, hawk-faced beneath his hooded robe, and nodded politely in his direction. He frowned back at her, as always, distrust still evident in his black eyes, before turning away to kindle a torch with his strike-a-light. When the torch was ablaze, chasing shadows around the fort, he strode forth and touched the flame to the Cross-of-Brygyndo that the village folk had wrought from river-reeds. It burst into flame and the priests raised it on high and carried it Sun-wise around the enclosure, with its crooked, crazed arms shooting sparks into the darkness and threatening to ignite hair and thatch.

As the wood burned through and flaming fragments tumbled to the ground, the priests placed the Cross on a waiting, unlit pyre at the fortress gates. They blew upon it and chanted over it, and the eternal flame of Fiery-Arrow was kindled and roared up into the gloom, lighting the entranceway to Kham-El-Ard. The watchers roared in delight and ran forward with pieces of kindling, which they thrust into the hottest part of the conflagration. Within minutes, the night was alight with waving brands.

The procession moved down the great hill, following the course of Abona toward the Place-of-Light. Fynavir found herself scooped up with all gentleness by the mighty-armed smith, Ech-tor, the father of Ka'hai, and placed upon a wooden chair that two stout village youths hoisted onto their shoulders. "You are Blessed Brygyndo tonight," Ech-tor said. "Queen of them all. Therefore your feet must not touch the earth."

Laughing and singing, the party made its way through the marshy lands below the Place-of-Light, before winding its way up to the settlement on top of the escarpment. The whole village was ablaze with torches, and women singing and holding out bride-dolls and their own small children for blessing from the goddess.

Fynavir went amongst them in her chair, her own Bride effigy seated beside her, and bestowed on them gifts of grain and milk and cheese. In return, they gave her draughts of fermented milk, sweetened with honey, which made her head spin; mostly, she was used to drinking watered-down beer, for the more potent mead was deemed a drink of men. Unless you were Mevva, her mother, whose very name signified the golden drink of the gods.

She shivered. She did not want to think of Mevva, red and carnal, heaping scorn on the children who could never match her. Tonight she would only be Fynavir...and the Bride.

The festivities went on long into the night. Great stars set, and the Moon sailed West and grew small to the eye. Fires burned down, and were relit again, mead and beer flowed free, and mutton was served sizzling on wooden trenchers. Men and women started to dance, weaving round the fires, before leaping across the flames and vanishing into their huts or the nearby bushes.

Fynavir sat in a place of honour outside the headman's dwelling. She was nodding off, her lids heavy from the fermented drink, the battered Bride-doll leaning drunkenly against her shoulder. Khelynnen was completely intoxicated, and lay slumped against her mistress with her mouth open and little ragged snores coming out.

"Khelynnen…" Fynavir dragged herself upright and shook the girl's shoulder. "It is time for us to go. Long past time, I fear."

Heavy-headed, Fynavir stumbled across the settlement, clutching the Bride-doll to her as if it was a child. Khelynnen lurched after her, the bone pin tearing loose from her hair and spilling long dark coils over her befuddled face.

One of the lads who had carried Fynavir's chair from Kham-El-Ard approached them, a well-built fellow with a shock of auburn hair. "I am Drem son of Khas. If it is your will, Lady Fynavir, I will escort you back to Kham-El-Ard."

Fynavir hesitated a moment. There was little to fear for two women walking the short miles between Place-of-Light and Kham-El-Ard. Wild boars and wolves never came so close to human habitations, unless the winter was so hard that they were unnaturally hungry. As for men with bright blades and sharpened arrows, only those extremely brave or foolhardy would mount an attack right on the doorstep of Kham-El-Ard, even with the Bear away chasing the Boar.

And yet Mhor-gan had given her stern warning…

"Yes, we would appreciate your company, Drem, son of Khas," she said, a shiver running down her spine at the memory of the priestess's words. "I am sure you have a very stout arm to defend us from all manner of evil creatures—the hares and badgers, or perhaps old beaver-man in his dam on the river!"

"I will do my best, lady," Drem responded, his crooked teeth flashing in the dimness.

The three made their way down the escarpment, Drem leading, while Fynavir supported the stumbling and complaining Khelynnen with one arm while trying to carry the Bride-doll tucked under the other. She half-wished she had left the girl to sleep off the drink in some hut at Place-of-Light, but Khelynnen was a comely girl and might come to grief among all the high-spirited youths that dwelt there, training to become warriors for Ardhu's cause. Fynavir did not want to have a serving-girl whose belly would grow big as the full Moon over the next nine months.

Once the little group was on level ground, they headed swiftly across the boggy fields toward the river. The Moon was lost behind the trees, and a sharp breeze, heralding the approach of dawn, blew out of the East and made Fynavir tremble like a leaf in a gale.

Soon they reached the banks of Abona. Fish jumped in the dark, while a night-prowling owl hooted in the distance. Wind hissed in the grass, while trees creaked and groaned, their branches clacking. All natural nightly sounds, noises Fynavir had heard a thousand times before. Why then these feelings of unease, of rising panic, that burned away the warm cloud of drunkenness and made her suddenly, frighteningly sober?

Suddenly she saw it...a metallic glint between the boles of two large oaks. Darkness swirled, and immediately the minute gleam vanished like a glow worm snuffed out. But Fynavir sensed that something was out there, in the dark of the woods, and it was watching their progress with hot, intent eyes.

"Quickly, quickly!" She prodded Khelynnen, trying to force her to pick up her feet.

"Lady, I can't," the girl wailed. "So tired..."

Drem turned and glanced at Fynavir and saw the naked fear in her face, and his own big, raw visage whitened. "What is it, Lady Fynavir?" he whispered. "Why do you look so strange?"

She leaned over toward him and hissed in his ear: "There's a man in the bushes, maybe more than one. I can feel eyes watching us."

The youth began to sweat and his eyes widened with terror. He had not foreseen such a thing when he had offered to escort the Queen to Kham-El-Ard. The worst he had expected was to chase off a fox or a hare. Hand shaking, he reached towards the hilt of his dagger, given to him in his manhood rite just two weeks before.

Fynavir grabbed his wrist. "No," she said kindly, "you are too young. I will not have you give your life in a fight you cannot win."

"But Lady, I am sworn to protect you..." he began, but again she shook her head and pressed her finger to his lips.

"Drem, you are more use to me alive than dead. Do not be foolhardy. Do as I tell you, I beg you."

"Yes, Lady. What is your will?"

"We must keep walking, until I say otherwise. Maybe the stranger is just a passing traveller who is curious as to our doings. Maybe he will either come forth in friendship and all will be well, or maybe he will just journey on into the night."

At Fynavir's side, Khelynnen, sensing something was wrong, began to snivel. Fynavir tried vainly to hush her, while keeping attuned to the shadowed trees around her.

There...she heard it now...a heavy footfall to her right, followed by crackling of twigs and branches deeper in the woods. A frond swayed, and she caught a faint glimpse of figures moving, keeping pace with the two women and the lad as they hurried along the banks of the river.

Fynavir stared hard into the darkness that stretched ahead—miles ahead, it seemed. The hill-fort was not far away, but she knew these strangers would make their move long before she reached it. But perhaps...perhaps...

She tugged on Drem's sleeve, trying to seem commanding and reassuring at the same time. "They are all around us now. We must assume they are enemies. Drem, did I not hear that you ran straight and true, faster than the other village boys?"

"Anwas the Winged, who rides with noble Ardhu, is my brother. He is the fastest runner in the entire West but I am catching up."

"Then go...use those fast feet to fly to Kham-El-Ard. Tell them we have been attacked and that they must bear word to the Merlin and to the Lord Ardhu, wherever he may be."

"Lady, I can't leave you at their mercy..."

"Do as I say—this is my command as your Queen. As Ardhu's woman, I am the one most likely to be spared by them, the only one whose life may have value. Go. Go now and the gods give you speed!"

She gave him a hard shove in the back and he staggered out into the path. He cast her one pitying look and then bounded away into the darkness like a frightened deer.

As he broke for freedom, the woods sprang to life. Men jumped out of trees and from behind bushes. Arrows whirred and skittered on the path as they fired at Drem's retreating back. Khelynnen started to scream till a tall man with stone bracers on either wrist stepped up and struck her across the face, knocking her to the ground. She fell instantly silent.

"Stop it! She is just a girl!" Fynavir flung her god-dolly to the ground and raced toward the man looming threateningly over her serving-woman. She noticed that, beside his high status bracers, he also wore a leather jerkin with a plate of gold sewn to the breast, similar to Ardhu's Breastplate of Heaven. However, it was a rectangle rather than a lozenge, and was quite battered.

The man turned to Fynavir and smirked. He was of great height and no longer in the first flush of youth, although there was still a ruined comeliness to his face. Ruined, because a dagger had slashed one cheek in some bygone battle, leaving a gouge from the corner of his eye down to the edge of his mouth. Greying dark hair hung round his shoulders, and his eyes were pale grey flecked with amber. Wolfish eyes, without pity.

"So, you must be the fabled Fynavir, queen to the boy-king Ardhu," he said, eyes raking over her appraisingly. "Many chiefs speak of you beyond Khor Ghor, of your beauty and your otherworldly whiteness, and how you are born of a goddess. How you are Sovereignty, the Land itself, and how any man that possesses you will be the King! "

"Maybe men should talk less of women they haven't met and deal with hardships within their own folds," she shot back icily.

"Although you are white as snow, fire burns within you," he said, nodding. "I like that. I am Melwas, King of the Summer Country, and I claim you by warriors' right, and from this day forward you shall be as my wife and dwell with me in the Summerlands. Together we will rule Prydn, and the fledgling boy you wed will fall, toppled like a stone raised in a bed that is too shallow. "

"You are mad!" she cried. "Ardhu will hunt you down and kill you!"

Melwas sneered. "He is far away; do not think rumours of his exploits haven't reached the Summer Country! Indeed, he seems more interested in chasing his wild Boar than he does you, my little snow-white one. Maybe it is animals that hold his fancy, or the pretty man from Ar-morah whom they say always rides at his side. But fear not, I will attend to you every night, and soon we will have a whole hut full of sturdy, divine sons!"

She recoiled in disgust, though she knew it was useless to run. "You are Moon-mad if you think I'll willingly go with you!"

"You will come with me," he said, an edge of danger in his voice. "And without a fuss. Or...I kill this one, here and now." He grabbed Khelynnen's hair, dragging her to her knees and pressing the blade of his dagger against her throat. "And then I will take my men and burn down your fancy fort and the village on yonder downs. I'll kill the men and children but take the women as rewards for my men, and they will spit and curse you, for it will be your own selfish stubbornness that doomed their menfolk and made them slaves."

Fynavir stared at Khelynnen, who lay paralysed with fear, her eyes pleading. She could not be responsible for her death, nor the deaths of any of the people who lived nearby.

"Very well...you have won," she said to Melwas. "I will go to the Summer Country with you. Just leave the innocent folk of Kham-El-Ard in peace."

Melwas let Khelynnen's head fall. She crouched on the ground, weeping. "A wise decision. I would not gladly kill the lowborn; there is no honour in that. Come, woman, I must bind your arms and feet; I will not chance you trying to escape along the road."

Resigned, she meekly extended her hands. Grinning, Melwas tied her wrists and ankles with gut ropes. Lifting her to his shoulder, he carried her into the woods, where she saw the rest of his band waiting, a rag-tag group of hard-faced men armed with bows and staves. They had a cart with them, drawn by a dispirited-looking ox and filled with war-equipment and food supplies. Melwas dumped Fynavir in the cart amidst the bows and baskets; an object for future use, just like the cart's contents, spoils from a bloodless war.

"Don't any of you bastards touch her," he warned the leering men. "Or I'll feed your ballocks to my hounds. You mind she's not damaged in any way on the journey home …she's not some slut; she's going to be my wife."

The warriors prodded the ox with long sticks, and slowly the cart lurched away through the woods. The men roared and jeered, filled with crude mirth. Fynavir lay staring at the lightening sky, trying to hold back tears of rage and fear. Why had she been so foolish, so careless, when she Mor-ghan had warned her? She was a failure in all she did; it was as if the spirits conspired against her.

"Ardhu…An'kelet…you must find me!" she whispered desperately to the four winds.

Behind her, on the riverbank, the discarded Bride-doll broke apart in the breeze and its bright fragments dispersed upon the flowing water.

CHAPTER TWENTY

Hwalchmai and Rhagnell rode swiftly across country, seeking signs of Ardhu's men. Rhagnell had tracking skills, learned from years in the forest with Bresalek, and soon she picked up a trail, not of Ardhu, but of Rhyttah Chief Giant and his band of brigands.

"Pig-shite," she said, dismounting her steed and kneeling beside a pile of dung on the trampled earth. "With the marks of many footprints around it."

Hwalchmai grimaced in disgust. "Looks big enough to be horse-dung, but smells a hundred times fouler."

"That is because T'orc eats flesh, not grass," said Rhagnell solemnly.

They journeyed on, and began to find more evidence of the passage of T'orc and his guardians. A village lay burnt and devastated, and then another. Finally they found one settlement that still stood; it was large and had been hastily fortified by a ring of boulders and earth.

As they approached, a dozen archers leapt up onto the makeshift defensive wall and faced them with bows nocked. "What business do you have here?" called out an older man, who appeared to be a headman; he had bronze threads sewn in his cloak and carried a black basalt axe.

"We seek the warband of Ardhu Pendraec," replied Hwalchmai. "We seek to help him defeat Rhyttah Chief Giant and the great boar T'orc."

The chief spat on the ground. "He is about, for all the good he's done. He's chased the Boar for days, going round and around like a puppy chasing its tail! Yet he can never catch it, and every day more innocents are killed. The very rivers of our land turn red, and the clouds are full of the ashes of the pyre."

"It shall not be so much longer," said Hwalchmai. "The time of this evil is at an end. Which way did Ardhu's warriors go?"

The petty chief pointed with the butt of his axe. "West."

Hwalchmai and his lady galloped on, passing into wilder lands filled with wind-blasted trees and scrubby heathland. Suddenly Rhagnell yanked on her horse's reins, drawing it to an abrupt halt. "There is something in the wind…someone comes. We must hide."

Hastily, they hunkered down amid a jumble of huge, irregular boulders that lay as if tossed from some giant's apron. They held tight to their mounts' bridles of woven grass, willing them to be quiet and still.

Over the brow of the nearby hill marched a party of warriors, hard-faced men clad in the skins of wolf, bear and deer, with the heads left on to serve as headdresses. Their leader was a massive one-eyed man, with arm-muscles that rippled as he swung a flail toward the flank of a huge black boar that had a heavy bronze chain attached to its hind leg. It squealed and snorted, eyes glowing, and thrust honed tusks into the air. "Down you beast!" the big man growled at it, yanking brutally on the chain. "I know you'd love to gore me, but I am master here!"

"Chief Rhyttah, the animal grows wilder each day," said one of the warriors, gazing uneasily at the champing boar. "Blood-lust and the evil spirit inside it have made it mad. I fear even you will not be able to control it ere long."

"Nonsense," said the big man, Rhyttah Chief Giant. "I will control T'orc until the day he dines on the innards of Ardhu Pendraec. Then I will slay the boar and eat its heart, and ingest both their strengths into myself."

"Why do we not turn and meet Ardhu in battle?" asked the other man. "We traipse over the hills and dales like men Moonstruck!"

"You are no tactician, are you, Gronu?" Rhyttah grinned, his upper lip curling in derision. "I weaken him, tire him out. When at last I change course and meet him head on, with T'orc charging before, he will not be expecting the about face, and he will perish."

"May it be soon, Lord Rhyttah," grumbled the man Gronu.

"It will, Gronu, never fear."

In the clump of boulders, Hwalchmai drew his axe and would have sprung out in a rage, but Rhagnell wrapped her strong arms around his waist and pulled him back. "No, that is not the way! There are too many of them for us to take on, to say nothing of the beast. We must find Ardhu, and tell them what we have seen and heard."

"But they may well vanish into these harsh uplands again!" snarled Hwalchmai.

"No...this time there will be no escape." Rhagnell took her short woman's bow from her shoulder and raised it, putting an arrow to the string. Carefully she aimed through a crack between the lichenous boulders, seeking the flank or chest area of T'orc.

"No!" Hwalchmai grabbed her wrist; "you dare not shoot the beast. One arrow will not kill such a mighty one, but it could make him go mad. He might well kill Rhyttah and his men in his rage, but he would also turn on us, and we have no weapons to bring down such a powerful animal."

"I do not intend to kill him," said Rhagnell. "Just a little wound. A prick."

"Why?"

"You will see." Rhagnell shook free of her lover's restraining hand and aimed her bow again. "Trust me, Hwalchmai. I know what I must do."

This time, Hwalchmai allowed her to fire. The arrow skimmed through the grass, a low deadly shot. It grazed the hind leg of T'orc, tearing off a strip of flesh and bristle, then fell away into the moorland scrub. The giant boar squealed and danced about in anger, blood dripping from its wounded leg.

Unaware of the animal's wound, Rhyttah shouted an oath at the boar and hauled on its chain, waving his flail in a menacing way. "Move on, pig, or you'll have a taste of my wrath!"

"There," said Rhagnell smugly. "I have done what I intended. T'orc will lead Ardhu's warband to him by the trail of gore he leaves behind. A trail Rhyttah has not noticed. And I do not think he would dare touch the monster to bind the scrape, even if he did."

Hwalchmai hugged her. "You are as clever as you are good to look at. Now let us find my cousin and tell him our news!"

They came upon Ardhu's warband later in the day. The warriors were riding over a high ridge where bleak stone stretched to the sky and a cold wind was singing. Anwas the Winged, the tracker, knelt down on the damp earth, examining the ground, but his face was pinched and solemn; the soil was so deliberately churned by feet he could make no sense of what he examined.

Hwalchmai gave a joyous shout and spurred his steed ahead into the midst of the group. Laughing, he and Ardhu embraced. "So you still have your head, cousin!" said Ardhu, ruffling the other youth's hair.

"Aye, that I do. But Bresalek—the Green Rider—has lost his! And his life is not all I have taken ... with me is his wife, Rhagnell, a woman of noble lineage, who is now to be mine."

Ardhu glanced at Rhagnell and then back to Hwalchmai. "You amaze me, kinsman. Adept in the warrior's art, adept with fair women!"

Rhagnell urged her mount forward. "Ardhu, lord of the West, I greet you, but Hwalchmai and I have more to tell than of our doings. We have spotted your quarry on the other side of yonder ridge. They are growing weary…"

"Are not we all?" grumbled Bohrs, from behind Ardhu.

Rhagnell ignored him. "And T'orc is injured…"

"What?" interrupted Ardhu, his eyes widening. "I had no knowledge of that!"

"Nor could you," said Rhagnell, "for it was I who wounded him with an arrow. Just a scratch, but enough to leave a trail of blood that should prove easy work for your tracker!"

Ardhu turned again to Hwalchmai. "It seems you have chosen well in a wife—artfulness as well as beauty! Let us go now, and put an end to these long days of wandering in the wilds, chasing what has oft-times seemed like mist and smoke!"

As Rhagnell had predicted, it did not take long to pick up the trail of T'orc. Little clots of gore clung to grass and tufts of heather; carrion birds swooped down and pecked at them, cawing, eager for the feast. They flapped back up into the air, wings beating madly as Ardhu's men cantered past.

The trail went over a hillock and into a wooded coomb where stunted oaks clumped together like sentinels, forming a gnarly barricade. A black mountain rose to the sky above the coomb, its peak scalped bald by wind and the slate skittering down its sides. A cairn rose on the crest, jagged with stones like pointed swords.

"What is this mountain called?" Ardhu asked, feeling ill at ease. "Do any among you know?"

Drust Mightyfist made a sound. "I hail from this area. It is called Mineth Beddun—the mountain of graves."

The company could see no sign of Rhyttah or the boar on mountainside or in valley, but suddenly An'kelet nodded and pointed with his spear-butt to a thin trickle of smoke that wafted up between the trees tucked in the back of the vale.

"Someone has pitched camp in there…and they are being none too careful."

The warband entered the forest cautiously, picking their way over moss-furred roots. Anwas was foremost, searching for blood spots on the forest-floor, or other signs of animal or human passage.

Suddenly Ardhu's mount Lamrai began to tremble. Her nostrils flared and she danced fearfully on her hooves, tossing her head and fighting against Ardhu's control. She wheeled around, trying to head back out of the shadowy grove.

"What is it?" Ardhu stroked her neck in an attempt to calm her. "Do not fail me now, my noble one…"

At that moment, a terrible crackling noise filled the forest, an awful sound that resembled a thousand breaking bones. It grew louder, and the earth began to tremble. Slender birch trees swayed and danced, and then suddenly split asunder, fragments of bark flying hither and thither like spears.

A terrible, high-pitched squealing filled the grove, and suddenly Anwas the Winged was flung up into the air. He screamed in agony as he hurtled into the branches of a tree and hung from a fork by his cloak, with blood pouring from a gouge in his side.

T'orc the Chief Boar stood below him, pawing and snorting, his great jaws working and gnashing. Redness dripped from his tusks.

Ardhu stared at the ravening animal, his adversary. Surely the beast was more than just some maltreated creature, goaded to madness by his malign sister; Morigau must have summoned some evil spirit to enter its skull. It was grotesque—fat and bulbous, its skin the colour of an old corpse and massed with fly-bites and scabs, its head ugly and squat with a great wide snout dripping snot and froth. The eyes under leathery folds gleamed red and tufts of coarse, upstanding bristles as sharp as knives sprang out all over its spine and brow. Twisted tusks dripped with Anwas' blood.

As if sensing Ardhu's repulsed gaze, T'orc slowly turned away from Anwas to face the young king mounted on the trembling Lamrai. One foreleg pawed the ground, puffs of noxious mist surrounded flaring nostrils as the beast breathed heavily in the cold air.

"Look out!" An'kelet was the first to move. "He is going to charge!" The Ar-moran prince spurred his mare forward, aiming with his great long spear. He alone of the company had such a reaching weapon; for although the spear was popular upon the continent, the choice weapons for warriors of Prydn were still dagger, axe and bow.

With a cry, he launched the spear, seeking to smite a deathblow before T'orc could move. Unfortunately, the horses of the warband, terrified and fighting against their riders' control, bashed into the flanks of his frightened mount and caused his thrust to go wide. Balugaisa with its many tines scraped along T'orc's flank and stuck shallowly into his hindquarters.

An'kelet leaned forward over his horse's neck, one-handed and grim-faced, trying to drive home the spear, to get the deadly barbs locked within the stinking, cadaverous flesh of the beast.

The boar released a deafening bellow and whirled in a circle, biting at the shaft sticking from its flank. Not expecting such a sudden, powerful move, An'kelet was jerked violently forward, over his steed's withers and onto the ground. Immediately, the warband closed ranks to protect him from the crazed animal that squealed, shrieked, and stamped in pain.

Ardhu drew Caladvolc and pressed forward. At that moment, he spied shapes of men within the trees, their bows drawn. "Look out—they are firing on us!" he cried, and he flung up Wyngurthachar just as a score of arrows whirred between the trees. Several struck harmlessly against the Face of Evening and bounced aside; but out of the corner of his eye, he saw Per-Adur wince in pain and grab his shoulder. A black-feathered shaft stuck out of his flesh.

The attackers were surging forward, their voices raised in a horrible, ululating battle cry. They broke through the trees and flung themselves with abandon at Ardhu's warband, striking the horses' knees with great heavy stone war-hammers that crippled them instantly. Within minutes, many of Ardhu's men were on the ground, beside horses screaming and bucking in pain, while the great boar T'orc, crazed with its own injuries, stabbed at both beasts and men with its sword-sharp tusks.

Ardhu leaped from his saddle and slapped Lamrai's flank, sending her careering out of the wood, away from the battle scene. Here, in the green shadows, where roots reared like serpents and the air smelt of ancient death, was not a place where a mounted man could gain the advantage.

Caladvolc in one hand, shield upraised, he ploughed into the heaving mass of fighters, forcing his way through. A north-man screamed, pierced through the throat by Ardhu's blade, and fell away; T'orc's huge body crashed down on the flailing figure, and silenced his screams forever. Blood bubbled up in the churning mud, spattering Ardhu's shield and golden breastplate.

Art had now spotted Rhyttah, who was fighting hand to hand with Hwalchmai. He let his gaze fall over the huge figure, surely a giant's spawn by his great height, with a bald shining head tattooed with a black crescent Moon. Rhyttah grinned like a mad man, his teeth as uneven as flagstones, as he parried Hwalchmai's blows, and tried to get beneath his guard.

"Rhyttah Baddaden, Chief Giant!" shouted Ardhu. "You have claimed the beards of mighty kings to weave your cloak. Now at last I have hunted you down like the beast you are, and will have yours!"

Rhyttah brought his arm down with blinding force, shattering Hwalchmai's wrist in one violent motion and sending his dagger flying. Rhagnell grabbed her lover from behind and dragged him to safety, staggering in pain…but Rhyttah was no longer interested in him.

Instead, the huge man lurched toward Ardhu, his shoulders bunched, his war-axe swinging menacingly. "So, I meet the boy-king of the West," he sneered. "I have heard all about you from your sister Morigau. All about you. She had many interesting tales to tell as we rolled together in King Loth's own bed!"

"I'm sure she did," retorted Ardhu. "But nothing truthful ever came from my sister's lips; her words are the hisses of snakes, filled with venom. She has used you. And now you will die."

"It is not I who will die!" shouted Rhyttah and he lunged at Ardhu, his axe upraised.

Ardhu stepped back, and slashed at the big man's brawny arm. The tip of Caladvolc dug into his bicep, drawing bright red blood. Rhyttah's axe-blow went wide, and Ardhu closed in so that they were almost torso to torso, fighting hand to hand. Art kept Rhyttah's arm pushed up, over his head, with the blood running down, unable to use his axe. The big man, more than a head taller than the slight youth, was fumbling at his belt for another weapon, a long knife that he carried in a leather sheath, while Ardhu sought to block him and draw his own dagger.

"Look out! Ardhu, beware!" An'kelet's voice came from behind the fighting warriors, full of fear and urgency.

Alarmed, Ardhu half-turned...and saw T'orc bearing down on him. The animal was squealing in high-pitched tones that sounded almost like human screams; its eyes rolled in its fearsome skull and drool sprayed from champing mandibles. Its back bristled with at least a dozen arrows, none of which had come even close to killing it. An'kelet's great spear was still embedded in its hindquarter, its haft smacking into trees and men as the animal charged.

Ardhu whirled around, letting Rhyttah's arm drop, and tried to leap away to safety, but T'orc thudded against his legs, throwing him across the forest as if he were as insubstantial as a feather. He struck the bole of a tree and slid to the ground, the breath driven from his lungs. The impact tore Caladvolc from his grip and it went spinning through the air, landing with a clatter a few feet away.

T'orc was on him almost instantly. The ground shuddered beneath his hooves; foul breath blasted over Ardhu, hot and rank with carrion-scent. Death was in the creature's eyes, and pain and madness. With an enraged bellow, he thrust forward with his tusks, catching the inside of Ardhu's leg and tearing a long gash. Blood spurted out, soaking both Ardhu and the boar's bristling pelt.

"Ardhu, use the razor—the hag's razor!" Through a darkening mist he could hear An'kelet yelling, saw him leap over a fallen tree trunk and come running towards him with his long, foreign blade in hand.

Fighting waves of pain and nausea, Ardhu grasped T'orc's head in an arm-lock and jabbed violently at the piggy eyes, attempting to blind or distract his adversary. His free hand scrabbled wildly at his belt, seeking the sacrificial razor he had taken from Ahn-is's cave, but his fingers were slick with blood, and the honed weapon slid between his fingers onto the grass.

In the distance he could hear Rhyttah laughing, his voice booming out like thunderclaps: "Ha ha HA!"

A bolt of anger ripped through him at the sound of that mocking mirth; surely the gods would not allow him to die in such a way, mauled by some monster of his sister's making and jeered at by one of her twisted lovers. With a harsh cry, he punched T'orc straight on the nose with all the strength he had left. The boar squealed shrilly and backed up for an instant, before lunging forward again, slobbering and champing with renewed fury.

It was all the time Ardhu needed. Grabbing the hag's razor from the grass, he swung at the boar and slashed at its face. The razor's blade bit deep in the horny hide and blood spurted. T'orc bellowed again, but this time there was a note of fear in its cry. It began backing away from Ardhu, shaking its massive head in a spray of blood and mucus.

The hunter had become the hunted.

Adrenaline shot through Ardhu's body, blotting out the agony of his gashed leg. In a half crouch, he stalked T'orc as the boar retreated from him. He was like a beast himself at that moment, covered in both his own blood and the beast's, his face chalk-white and his lips drawn back in a feral snarl. "It is time for your spirit to pass, ugly one," he rasped. "Time to put an end to your terror."

The boar stopped abruptly, lungs pumping like bellows, its hindquarters trembling. It looked as though it might drop…but unexpectedly its eyes ignited, and uttering hideous grunts, it made one last assault on its enemy.

It did not get far. An'kelet rushed round to its right flank and grasped the still- swinging haft of his spear. With an effort, he managed to yank it free of the tough, leathery skin, and then plunged its barbed head in deeper, seeking the monster's vitals.

T'orc leapt in the air as Balugaisa dug deep. Ardhu was not its concern now; only the pain and the blood and the mindless terror as its tormented life neared its end. Ardhu staggered forward and threw himself on the beast's back, bringing the razor across T'orc's exposed throat and slashing wide the great vein of life. A huge jet of blood shot out, drenching the glade with stinking hot gore. The great beast slumped, with the young King still astride its twitching body.

"T'orc the Chief Boar is dead!" he cried, and he chopped the tuft of hard bristles from between the monster's ears and held it up as a trophy.

Across the clearing, Rhyttah cursed and turned to flee into the deeper parts of the forest. The men of Ardhu's warband immediately surrounded him with weapons drawn. They circled him like wolves, eager for vengeance for their own fallen, for their wounded king.

"Your followers are dead," said Ka'hai. "And now your demon-boar is dead too."

"I would shoot out his remaining eye!" cried Rhagnell fiercely, aiming at Rhyttah's face with her bow. "In returning for breaking Hwalchmai's wrist."

Hwalchmai cradled his wounded arm against his chest, face grim. "No, don't touch him, Rhagnell, Ka'hai, any of you. Ardhu is the slayer of the Boar…it is for him to decide the fate of this murderer, this slayer of innocent women and children!"

Ardhu clambered off the body of T'orc and limped towards his men. Blood was still running down his thigh; it was an evil wound, rough and jagged-edged, but at least it had missed the artery —he would not bleed to death. Face white, he approached Rhyttah and stood before him, the gore-smeared razor in his hand.

"You," he said in a voice deep and pitiless, "take off your cloak—the cloak wrought of the beards of slain chieftains. Now."

Rhyttah ripped out the pin at the neck of his cloak and let the mantle fall. Bohrs snatched it up, and examined it, frowning at such an unwholesome oddity.

"Burn it,"Ardhu ordered. "Let those dead chiefs' last remains go to join their spirits across the Great Plain."

Bohrs took out his strike-a-light and kindled a flame, and soon the woodland was full of the scent of burning hair.

"There…the cloak that symbolised your pride and your cruelty is no more," said Ardhu, still standing mere inches from his enemy. "Now…kneel. Kneel, I say!"

A mutinous gleam filled Rhyttah's single eye, but Bal-ahn and Ka'hai prodded him with their blades, forcing him to his knees before Ardhu.

Ardhu grabbed the long greasy black braid that grew at the nape of Rhyttah's neck and yanked his head backwards, exposing his throat. "I will shave you now, and shame you as you shamed and humiliated the unfortunate chieftains you slew." Raising the Hag Ahn-is's bronze razor, he roughly cut away the big man's beard and moustache, while the warriors of the warband laughed and jeered.

"Your braid must go too," he added, slashing through the coarse hair, then running the blade over the lice-caked scalp. "And the rest comes off too. A shaven head is the sign of a slave, and that is what you are, aren't you? A slave to Morigau!"

"She will ruin you yet…" Words burst from Rhyttah's bruised lips. "She has a weapon greater than any I could wield. She calls him…Mordraed!" He started to laugh harshly, almost maniacally. "Would your men like to know all about him, how he came to be?"

Ardhu went ashen. "Be silent, or your life will be forfeit this instant."

"Is it not already? Would you spare me, even after all the crimes of which you accuse me? I do not deny I did those things…and enjoyed doing them!"

"I might have a use for you. You know Morigau's…mind. I would not slay you purely for spite or for love of blood."

"Oh, the noble Lord Ardhu," sneered Rhyttah. "Spare me your mercy, boy. I will never help you or your precious, righteous cause. I spit on you and your mercy…" and he hawked at Ardhu, the spittle striking the centre of the young king's golden breastplate and running down in a yellow gobbet.

Ardhu's lips tightened. "So be it. No mercy shall be shown." Lashing out with the Black Witch's razor, he cut the Chief Giant's throat in one fluid motion. The huge man made a gurgling noise and crashed to the ground, his spirit leaving his body in a red tide.

An'kelet approached Ardhu, placing a hand on his shoulder. "It is done and over. Come, friend, we must attend to your wound. You are still bleeding."

Ardhu glanced down; he had almost forgotten his own pain, the ragged gouge marring his thigh. Looking at the oozing slash, a wave of light-headedness overcame him; his legs became as jelly and the world dipped and tilted alarmingly.

An'kelet's arms reached out to catch him as he fell. Ka'hai rushed over to grab his legs and help carry him away from the gore-soaked clearing to a sweeter-hued part of the forest. They laid him on the mossy greensward, using a cloak as a headrest, and Betu'or, who had some training as a healer, cut away the lacings on Ardhu's leather trews to examine the wound.

"It has missed the great life-river in his leg," Betu'or said, with some relief. "The bleeding looks bad, but properly packed, it will stop. The biggest fear I have is that the wound may get flesh-rot. None who get flesh-rot live to see another year."

Rhagnell stepped forward, reaching to a bag that hung at her waist. "I too had some training in healing, while I lived in the wilds. I have dried Midsummer's plant—that is good to clean wounds, and comfrey also. Fresh would be better, but we must do with what is available. After, we can gather oak-sap from the trees and use that to staunch the blood flow and make a seal. How well the young King heals is then in the hands of the Great Spirits."

Bohrs' face creased up, red and frustrated between bristling tufts of his bushy beard and equally wild hair. "Gods, why did this happen, when the great victory of Mineth Beddan is upon him? What if he is maimed? By law, a man cannot rule if he has a physical blemish!"

Rhagnell shot the burly warrior a harsh look. "The quicker you and the men go out and get me some oak-sap, the less likely it is that Lord Ardhu will be blemished. Now go!"

Bohrs and half a dozen of the men scattered, while the rest remained, gazing solemnly at their fallen chief and talking in low whispers.

After a while, Ardhu's eyelids flickered and he sat up, pale and shivering. "The boar…Rhyttah…"

"Do you not remember, lord? Both are dead," said Rhagnell. "Your quest has been successful. Prydn is safe."

Ardhu tried to smile; it came out a grimace. "Aye, I do remember. Ah...the pain..." He clutched his leg.

An'kelet knelt beside him, gave him a draught of strong beer from a handled beaker. "T'orc gored you with his tusk," he said. "It is a nasty wound. But I have seen worse. You are young. You will heal."

"Yes...yes." Ardhu lay back, his sweat-soaked hair a midnight stain across his white forehead. "I must get better. Morigau cannot be allowed to win."

At that moment, Hlwch Windyhand the Archer made a hissing sound from between his clenched teeth. He whirled around, snatching his bow from his shoulder and setting an arrow to the string,

"What is it?" asked An'kelet, rising and reaching for his spear.

"I can feel thunder in the ground beneath my feet," said the archer. "One comes, seeking us, following the trail our horses have left."

"Who would seek us?" asked Ba-lin and Bal-ahn almost in unison, those two identical youths who, men said, had but one soul between them.

"It could be Morigau," muttered An'kelet. "Maybe she has been watching our battles from afar. Or maybe it is more men loyal to Rhyttah. Prepare yourselves, men of the Warband!"

The warriors grabbed their weapon and stood, grim and silent, poised for attack. There was great crackling of branches and twigs, and a youthful figure on a lathered, staggering horse burst into the clearing. He stared at the circle of armed men, his eyes big and round with terror.

"Drem!" Anwas the Winged, who was lying on the ground, being treated for his own tusk-wound by Ka'hai, lifted a shaking hand to his kinsman. "Leave your weapons, men, it is Drem, my sister's son! What brings you here?"

Drem slid from his horse's back; he tried to walk toward Anwas, but his knees gave way and he fell heavily. "I have been riding for days with scarce a stop," he gasped. "I have been in strange lands under strange skies, menaced by boar and bear and wolf and cannibal-men! I come to bring word of a great evil, a terrible thing that has happened at Kham-El-Ard."

Ardhu staggered to his feet, grey-faced with pain and exhaustion, his eyes like shattered flints. "What evil? Speak, boy!"

Drem began to sob; great noisy ragged sobs. "The Queen...Lady Fynavir....she has been abducted."

A horrified murmur went through the warriors.

"By whom?" Ardhu demanded.

"By...by Melwas, King of the Summer Country."

Ardhu grabbed the lad's shoulder. "Do you know this for certain?"

Drem nodded. "I was with the Lady Fynavir when the evil bastards attacked. She told me to flee and raise the alarm, and so I did, but at one point I heard men near me so I hid in the bole of an old dead oak. While hiding, I heard them speak the name of Melwas."

"This is grave news indeed," groaned Ardhu, and he limped towards Lamrai, who was tethered to a tree. "Men, to your horses...we must ride for the Summer Country in all haste."

"Art...you cannot!" cried Ka'hai. "You will kill yourself!"

Ignoring his foster-brother, Ardhu tried to vault up onto Lamrai's back. The mare snorted and danced about, unnerved by the scent of blood and the boar on his clothes. Ardhu's strength failed, his arms giving way, and he sank back to earth, landing heavily on his wounded leg. His lips went white and he slumped on the ground in a half-faint, still clutching Lamrai's reins.

"Attend to the king, attend to the Pendraec!" Hwalchmai shouted, running forward. "Cousin, you mustn't be a fool! You cannot throw away your life, even for Fynavir! Women are sometimes stolen like cattle, that is how it has always been! What say you, An'kelet? Tell the fool to wait till he is well!"

An'kelet did not reply. He stood with night in his eyes, a great copper figure with the Balugaisa in his hand and his long Ar-moran daggers gleaming at his belt. He was, as Ardhu had first seen him, the man of bronze, inscrutable, god-like. A muscle flickered in his jaw, and then he was running, moving swift as lightning, hurling himself atop his horse, which was tethered beside Lamrai. Snatching up the reins, he gave a great cry and drove his heels into the beast's flanks.

It reared, not used to such violent handling, and with a harsh whinny, it bolted through the forest, An'kelet bent low over its flowing mane.

Like a man possessed the Prince of Ar-morah rode out across the bleak moors and sheltering dells, the bald hills and the black hills, heading south at great speed toward the Land of the Summer Stars.

CHAPTER TWENTY-ONE

Another day passed and night had fallen once more when the warriors of Melwas reached the Summer Country with their captive. Lying bound in the wagon, Fynavir could smell the scent of burning logs, animals, cooking. The skies above her blurred, the stars obscured by a haze of wood-smoke.

"Out you come." Melwas reached into the cart and dragged her out, cutting the bonds on ankles and wrists with his dagger. "Time to meet your new People."

Hand clamped on her shoulder, he pushed her toward a circle of mean-looking thatched huts. "People of the Summerlands, look what I have brought you!" He propelled her into a guttered street, a ring of flickering torchlight. "My new woman! Your new Queen!"

The folk of Melwas gathered around, staring at Fynavir—a dour, unsmiling crowd wearing tattoos of fabulous birds and beasts on their flesh and little else. Their woven skirts and trews looked crude, the cloth coarse, and their only jewellery was made of old cast-off bones—there was no gold or jet or other wealth. Their eyes hardened with suspicion as they gazed at the newcomer.

Watching those grimy, brooding faces, Fynavir remembered hearing that denizens of the Summer Country were a strange breed, ignoring the matters of the Five Cantrevs for nigh on a thousand years as they eked out a meagre existence in the shadow of the Great Tor. Perhaps, if they had no love of outsiders, she could play upon their fears and persuade them to ask Melwas to release her.

Taking a deep breath, she cried out, "People of the Summer Country, listen to me. Your lord, Melwas, has carried me here against my will. I am the wife of Ardhu the Terrible Head, anointed of Khor Ghor. I ask you to beg your lord to return me to my rightful home—death and destruction will befall you all if I am not brought to Ardhu's side!"

One solitary villager laughed. The others' faces remained like masks, fierce, mud-smeared. Melwas stiffened at Fynavir's side, and suddenly his fist shot out, striking her to the ground.

As she lay stunned, head reeling from the blow, he grabbed her by the hair and yanked her to her feet. "You will never try that trick again, woman!" he snarled, spittle from his cut mouth striking her cheek. "My people listen to me and no one else—do you understand?"

An old crone hobbled forward, pointing at Fynavir with a finger bent with arthritis. "Master, why this one, of all the fine women you could have had from the Summer Lands. She is as white as dead bone…it is unnatural!"

An unhealthy gleam entered Melwas's eyes. "Her whiteness is a sign of holiness, hag. Her mother is the Peaked Red One of Ibherna. She is the White Phantom, the White Lady, protectress of Albu. Any man who takes her as his own has right to rule as King as long as she is by his side."

"But you are already King here in the Summerlands," someone in the back of the throng shouted.

Melwas grimaced. "Aye, but what have our people become these long years? Hermits, hiding from a changing world. Friends to no one, not even each other! Yet once, long ago, we were Chosen People! My mother-ancestor, Evaen, was bathing in the lake when a great crane wrapped its wings around her in lover's embrace. Nine Moons later she bore a son, Trigaran, founder of our people, who wrought a magic bag made of Crane-skin from which our luck flowed…till it was lost by unwise fathers before me! Now, by taking this white woman, this spirit-touched one, I will restore the glory that was ours, before we were pushed into this marsh-bound land. She is Sovereignty and I will be the Sovereign through her—we will leave this place and take the lands and glory that is due us!"

"These tales sound fine to naive and youthful ears," the crone shrilled, waving her raddled arms, "but what of Ardhu Pendraec? Surely he will come for her and bring ruin on us all just as the White One said!"

"He is a mere boy!" Melwas shouted. "Aided by the trickeries of the sorcerer, Merlin! He will not prevail against us. He cannot even put a brat into his wife's belly!"

There was a burst of raucous mirth from the crowd. Standing beside Melwas, Fynavir shuddered with embarrassment. Melwas caught her chin in his hand, and pulled her towards him. "I will put an end to your barrenness," he grunted, flashing a lascivious grin that made the torn flap of his lips gape like a horrible second mouth. "I will ride you like my prize bull rides my cows, giving them new calves every spring!"

Fynavir shrank away, revolted and angry. "How dare you compare me to a cow?"

He caught her round the waist. "I dare, because that is what you are to me—a creature that brings me wealth and power, and will breed me heirs... You must understand this, white woman: you will be treated with honour if you obey my wishes, but if you seek to deny me what is rightfully mine, you will suffer. We are a harsh people in the marshes of the Summer Country; we do not throw flowers before the feet of our women and bow to their every whim like your southern tribes do. I expect obedience and compliance in all things." His hands wandered up from her waist, groping, seeking.

"Don't touch me!" she gasped. "Ardhu will kill you, you ill-visaged pig!"

"You need a lesson in humility, woman," he sneered, and with a vicious movement he suddenly ripped her dress from neck to hem. Bone toggles showered. She tried to cover herself with her veil-like hair, but he grabbed her arms and roughly pinioned them behind her back. As she started to sob in shame and fear, he smirkingly dragged her around the encampment like a prize beast. His men laughed, leered and made crude gestures, begging Melwas to throw her to them. After what seemed eternity, the marsh-king lost interest in the sport and pushed her down onto her knees in the churned mud in the centre of village. The mob sneered and hooted as she cowered; the women looked contemptuous and the men were still hot-eyed and foul-tongued with lust.

"This will be your Queen!" Melwas shouted again, prodding her roughly in the back of the leg with the toe of his leather shoe. "See how fair she is, how perfect, as befits a goddess? But she is also a woman, born of earth—she does not float in the sky with Sun and Moon..." He laughed lustfully, hauling Fynavir to her feet and yanking back her hair to expose her breasts. "Her paps are not made of gold, as you can see, and the Sun does not shine from her thighs! She is still a woman like any other woman, and will obey the lord who won her by right of capture!"

Hatred in her eyes, Fynavir stared up into his pitiless face. She knew her fate was sealed, that she could neither soften this warlord's will nor appeal to his followers for help. She had seen many men try to abduct Mevva and force themselves upon her, but her mother was a warrior as well as queen, and she had beaten every one of them in single combat and painted her flesh with their blood. Fynavir had no such strength of arms; all she had left to her was her defiance. "Right of capture!" she spat. "You fought no battle with my husband for me! You crept through the woods like a thief in the night, choosing a time when you knew Ardhu would be away! Not one blade was drawn, nor any arrow fired! You are a coward, a brute...and you will die for your dishonour of me!"

"Your tongue is too free, woman," he snarled back. "Put it to better use." He grabbed her shoulders and bent her backwards, forcing his broken mouth over hers, his hands rough and proprietary on her naked flesh.

"If you touch me again," she spat, when she was able to tear her mouth away, "I will curse you so that you are unmanned, and can never lay with a woman again! As the daughter of a goddess, you should fear my curses!"

Melwas made a sign of protection with his hand and spat. "You have said enough," he growled, his tone threatening. "More talk of curses and I will cut out your tongue!"

Roughly, he bundled her toward the largest hut in the village and shoved her unceremoniously through the door, while the villagers laughed nervously, ill at ease with the stranger-woman's talk of curses. Inside the hut was a low hearth filled with sputtering embers, an array of weaponry, drinking vessels, and a bed-place topped by many skins. Melwas tossed Fynavir on to the pallet and flung himself on top of her, filled with both anger and lust, trying to jam his knee between her legs and push them apart. She screamed and bit him; she did not care what punishment he gave, she would not let him defile her without a fight, poor as her effort might be. He slapped her face once, then yet again, and grabbed her flailing arms and pinned them at her sides. "The more you fight me, the more I want you," he snarled, panting, his eyes fixated on her naked flesh as she writhed beneath him, trying to shove him away.

Suddenly the door of the hut banged open. An old man entered; he wore a floor-length robe and his hair was cut bluntly at brow and mid-back, making him appear to wear a shining helmet of silver. He had a narrow, imperious face, the face of a man who was used to respect. Three serpents were tattooed on one cheek, and a grid pattern on the other. Fynavir guessed that he must be the tribe's shaman.

Scowling, Melwas swung round. "Why do you bother me, old one? Can't you see what I am doing?"

The old man looked sourly at him. "If you truly wish to marry this woman, certain procedures must be followed. You have stolen the White Phantom from the bed of another man, and if you take her to your own bed so soon, and she then grows great with child, there will be rumours that the child is Pendraec's, not yours. This could cause division amongst our people. It is my counsel that you do not lie with her for one passage of the Moon, until we know that she has no child in her."

"And if she does? I will not wait for her for nine months, Kanhastyr!" shouted Melwas.

"It will be dealt with," said the shaman Kanhastyr. "There are many ways to expel an unwanted child."

Melwas snatched a ragged skin from the floor and flung it at Fynavir who wrapped it around her nakedness. "So…you have a reprieve, then, bitch. One turn of the Moon. But I shall be watching you; you'll still be here with me every moment."

Grabbing her arms, he bound the wrists together with hemp rope and dragged her from the bed. He flung the end of the rope over one of the roof's supporting beams and, pulling down on the rope, hauled Fynavir almost onto the tips of her toes, her arms painfully extended above her head. He then secured the twine to an opposing beam. "I won't make it comfortable for you, I can assure you," he snarled in her ear. "You may regret you did not choose to willingly lie in my bed. And you'll end up there anyway."

He turned to Kanhastyr and beckoned him to go out of the hut. "If I must cool my head and my loins, Kanhastyr, then give me one of your potions to quell my ardour!"

The men exited the hut, leaving Fynavir to weep bitter tears of despair and pull upon the ropes that bound her until blood ran freely from her wrists.

An'kelet rode across the wilds of Albu like a man possessed. His horse stumbled with weariness, sweat lathered on its neck; he cursed it and shouted in frustrated temper, then cursed himself for his own impatience and begged the animal for its forgiveness. After all, if the mare had not bent its neck to him and allowed him to ride upon her back, his journey would be much longer.

Too long.

He tried to focus on facing Melwas and not to think of Fynavir in the hands of the dour chieftain who lived in the Summerlands. He did not know the man or what his intentions might be; Melwas might kill Fynavir to spite Ardhu and draw him into conflict; or sacrifice her for luck to the strange water-gods that lived in the bogs of his homeland. He might keep her as slave or concubine, or give her to his men as a diversion if she displeased him.

Terrible images flashed through his mind of her white, broken body sinking into the mud of the marshlands, her eyes staring blankly at the fading sky, her spirit lost forever to men. He fought to banish the images, to force them away, for he knew that such hideous fancies would weaken him, tying his belly into knots of anguish and making his spear-hand shake with rage and fear.

No. He had to collect himself, empty his mind of fearsome thoughts. He must be more than warrior now.

He must be a killer, with no thoughts of honour.

A killer, and a hunter.

A hunter whose quarry was the King of the Summer Country.

He reached the marshlands surrounding the Tor of Hwynn son of Nud shortly after Sunset. Clouds turned to flame in the West; weird night birds trilled and called. Marsh-mist coiled from the saturated ground and fey lights flitted over the bog—the spirits of lost men trapped between the Underworld and Otherworld. An'kelet turned his gaze from their tricksy light; they were dangerous, for they could maze a man and lead him to his death in deep water.

The marsh was not a safe place to wander after nightfall, so An'kelet halted his weary horse and set up camp, resting in the shelter of an upended willow that lay half-splayed in the green-dark bog-water, roots spiralling down into the murk. He tried to keep wakeful, but as the stars and Moon westered, and the chirping and croaking of bog-dwelling beasts dwindled into silence, he slipped into a deep, restless sleep.

He woke in the morning with the pallid winter Sun beating into his face. He groaned and quickly sat upright, ashamed that he had allowed his bodily exhaustion to overcome him.

Alarm promptly replaced his shame. He could hear voices nearby, coming closer. Cursing, he snatched the haft of his spear and crouched down behind the trunk of the willow, hoping he would not be spotted

"A rare find, Gam-el. I wonder where it came from." He could now tell that one of the speakers was a woman.

"From some fool who dared to walk uninvited in Melwas's lands!" the woman's companion replied. This voice was deep, a male's "He must have drowned in the bog. A bit of good luck for us—but not such good luck for him!"

The couple laughed raucously, and An'kelet suddenly realised the 'find' they were talking about was his horse. He had tethered the animal to a bush last night, but the mare must have broken free while he slept and wandered away.

Carefully, An'kelet shifted his position so that he could view the newcomers. They were standing a few feet away, an older man with a balding head and red beard and a woman whose face had a soft, sucked-in look from a lack of teeth. Both wore crude outfits of tanned hides, old and stained, and smelled very foul indeed. The man held An'kelet's horse by the rein.

"What should we do with the beast?" the woman eyed the black mare.

"Eat it?"

"Well, it's big and fat—tempting, I admit. But she ain't ours; she's on Melwas's land, so she belongs to the chief."

The woman sniffed and stared downheartedly at her grubby bare feet. "Not fair."

"It might be all right, O-on! Our chief is getting married in one moon, remember? He'll no doubt have the beast cooked up and we'll all get a bite anyway! Grand, it'll be! He might even look on us with favour because we found the animal!"

The woman rubbed her thin arms. "Maybe. But I don't like that idea of this marriage. It'll bring bad luck; I feel it in my bones. Why is Melwas so set on that strange whey-faced one? The woman is too white…it ain't natural."

"She has fine tits and a royal mother!" retorted the man. "That's good enough for him. It's not for us to question!"

The woman screeched and hit out at the man. "You weren't supposed to be lookin' at her…" They stumbled away, dragging An'kelet's mount behind them, the man laughing as the woman batted at him in mock anger.

An'kelet felt his pulse quicken. What was nearly a disaster might prove advantageous in the end. Despite his immediate urge to confront the couple and force them to take him to Melwas, he kept silent and let them go unmolested. Once the sound of their cackles and shrieks had vanished in the distance, he emerged from behind the fallen willow and followed the trail they had made through the reeds across the foetid marsh.

After several miles, An'kelet noticed the ground beneath his feet growing more solid. Up ahead, he could see a tract of dry grassland bordering a clear blue lake. Round houses clustered on the shore, while rows of tethered coracles bobbed in the shallows—the main occupation of the villagers was fishing, since neither farming nor animal husbandry fared well in such watery environs. A protective wall of sharpened stakes surrounded the houses, but there were no other signs of defence; bog and lake made impassable walls against incursions from the outside world.

An'kelet shouldered his spear and hurried toward Melwas's domain. The retaining wall, left unguarded, shielded him against any spying eyes. Bent almost double, he inched his way along its length down to the lakeshore.

By now the light was failing; the Sun still in winter's grip, the days still brutally short. Nightjars screamed as they dipped and dived over the water, and the Moon's ghost appeared, half full. The Western horizon spouted blood as the Sun fell away towards the lands of the Dead.

No one was about, so An'kelet silently slipped thigh-deep into the freezing water and thrust his spear through the bottoms of all the coracles except the largest and most sturdy one. The other craft sank soundlessly, trailing bubbles.

He then turned his attention to the settlement. Only a few hundred yards away women swished by in their long skin skirts, bringing in their weaving looms and drying racks for the night, while husbandmen penned the few scraggly cattle they owned and called in their roving dogs. Warriors staggered toward their hearths, already deep in their cups, unbuckling their dagger-belts and stone wrist-guards in preparation for drunken slumber. "Selgi! Selgi! Where is that brat of mine?" he heard a woman cry, her voice mixed with annoyance and worry.

The night drew colder and teardrops of ice appeared on the grass where An'kelet crouched. He watched the Moon sail overhead and the stars dance in their nightly procession.

Soon…soon…

A night-guard emerged from one of the huts and squatted beside a guttering fire between the dwellings. He carried an axe but after toying with it for a while, dropped it in exchange for the delights of his drinking beaker. Sighing, he stretched out his stubby legs toward the fading warmth of the fire-pit.

It was the last warmth he ever felt.

Swift as a striking snake, An'kelet leapt from his hiding place and flung himself at the man's back. Arondyt tore into the sentry's ribcage and pierced his heart, and he died with not so much as a cry.

An'kelet rose from beside the corpse, his hands and blade bloody. Battle-madness washed over him in dark waves, different from anything he had ever before experienced. His prowess in warfare had come from skill and his measured, thoughtful nature, not from the crazed rage that possessed many others. Yet now he was changing, his body tingling with adrenaline, his very features warped and twisted by the power of his wrath and his desire for the blood of his enemies. He had entered the state the priests called the hero's warp-spasm; half in the world of men, he was also half in the domain of the gods, his strength greater than ten, his aspect terrible and inhuman—a Sun with blazing eyes and pitiless death-rictus grin, and wild burning hair that blew out in the strengthening breeze.

Throwing back his head, he howled like some feral beast at the ascending Moon.

His cry brought Melwas's warriors running from their huts. Laughing like a madman, An'kelet charged towards them, slashing with Arondyt, severing arms and piercing legs and unguarded torsos. Screams rang out in the gloom as bodies toppled to the earth and blood fountained. One man leapt on An'kelet's back, and tried to drive a dagger into his throat; with a cry of amusement, An'kelet grabbed his assailant's arms and tossed him straight over his head into the fire-pit. The man's fur cloak touched the glowing embers and he ignited like a torch, and ran shrieking in agony throughout the village, a hideous fireball that eventually collapsed in a heap beside the lake.

"What do you want, bloody-handed stranger?" one of the men cried, trying to set arrow to his bow with trembling fingers. "We do not know you…we have no quarrel with you!"

"Oh, but you do!" shouted An'kelet. "Call Melwas to me and maybe some of you shall see the dawn!"

"I come!" a voice snarled behind An'kelet. Whirling, he saw the door of a large hut bang open, and a naked warrior step forward with a lethal-looking rapier in his hand. His hair coiled snake-like around his face, and his cheeks and mouth was marred by raised scars the colour of raw liver. Yellow wolf-eyes blazed from under scowling brows.

"Are you Melwas, King of the Summer Country?" asked An'kelet brusquely. He shoved his daggers into his belt, and reached to touch the haft of the Balugaisa where it hung in its sling across his back. It seemed to call to him, his favourite weapon, tempered in the poisoned blood of the monster Kon-Khenn.

"I am," replied Melwas. "Who are you, who attacks my people and disturbs my sleep?"

"Where is the woman…where is Queen Fynavir, wife of the Pendraec?"

Melwas flung his head back and laughed. "So that's what this is about, is it? The white bitch! But you, with your bright Sun-hair and foreign voice, are not her husband, Ardhu the so-called high king!"

"No, I am not. I am his right-hand man, An'kelet son of Bhan and the Lake Priestess Ailin, greatest warrior of the Western world, wielder of the long spear, Arondyt, sword of Light, and Fragarak the Answerer. Now tell, me, I will not ask again—where is Queen Fynavir?"

"Where do you think the slut is?" snarled Melwas. "In my hut, where else?"

The implications of Melwas's words, in addition to his nakedness, made An'kelet's growing madness spiral to even greater heights. A red haze clouded his vision; his lips drew back in a dangerous, animalistic grin. He said no more to his adversary, who stood, hands on hips, waiting for some type of formal challenge, a request for hand to hand combat for the possession of the woman.

Instead, in a vicious, purposeful motion, he yanked out the Balugaisa, took three long strides toward Melwas and thrust the spear straight into his belly with all his might. The king of the Summer Country uttered a strangled sound and clutched vainly at the spear. An'kelet continued to push forward, driving the barbs through flesh and bone, till the deadly head tore out of Melwas's back. An'kelet was almost breast to breast with his adversary, his eyes blazing with the changeling light of the warp-spasm, burning into his enemy's dying gaze.

"When you touched the Lady Fynavir, most perfect of women," he said, "your life from that moment was forfeit to me. For the evil and dishonour that you have done her, may your spirit be trapped forever in these bogs and never go to the house of your Fathers!"

Melwas tried to speak, but his mouth was gushing blood. An'kelet yanked back the spearhead with its fearsome barbs, and Melwas collapsed, his innards torn to ribbons by the brutal passage of the spear. An'kelet grabbed his opponent's hair and hauled up the body, slashing the face with Arondyt, before stabbing the blade repeatedly into the dead man's groin.

"There!" he cried, tossing the mutilated corpse at the feet of Melwas's oncoming men, who stopped abruptly in their tracks, fearful of this man of bronze with his mad eyes and death-wielding arm. "Melwas has no face and he is no longer a man… his spirit will not go into the Otherworld but will stay here unto eternity to pay for the sins of his days! Attend to him and do not raise your hand to me, lest you meet the same doom as your accursed master!"

The villagers started to shriek and wail, even the warriors hesitating to come forward against this wild-visaged foe with his terrible weapons. An'kelet lifted the bleeding corpse of Melwas and as one last indignity to the slain chief hurled the body at his followers. It crashed into them heavily, sending them reeling back, while An'kelet resheathed the Balugaisa and shoved his way into Melwas's hut. He paused, his throat tightening, as he saw Fynavir dangling from the crossbeam of the roof, her wrists black with caked blood, her only clothing a scrap of skin. Dark bruises marred her skin…cruel finger marks. Her head hung down, hair tangling over a face too thin, too pale, with huge circles underscoring the closed eyes. As he approached, she stirred, her head slowly lifting and her eyes flickering open.

"An'kelet…" her voice was a rasp in her throat. "Where is Ardhu?"

"Not here…" An'kelet could say no more, emotion rising in him.

"But you…you have come for me…" She tried to smile, her dry lips tremulous.

"I would never leave you to such as Melwas." He strode to her side and slashed through the ropes that bound her wrists.

Her arms fell to her sides and she stumbled forward, weak and fainting. He caught her as she fell, lifting her off the ground in his arms. .

"Melwas…he is dead, isn't he?" she whispered

"Yes."

"Good!" she said, with uncharacteristic viciousness. "But his men…they will kill you…us. I cannot flee with you as I am. You must leave me and save yourself."

"If I were to live and let you die, my own life would be worth nothing!" he said fiercely, brushing her knotted hair away from her bloodless face. "Either we both die here together…or we both live, to whatever end!"

Heading to the back wall of the hut, An'kelet gently set Fynavir down on the ground, where she rubbed her wrists and legs, trying to restore some circulation. While she did this, he cut a large gap in the wall with Arondyt and kicked out the wattle with several sharp blows. "Come, Fynavir," he said. "Throw your arms around my neck and climb onto my back. Hold on as tight as you can. That way, my arms will be free to fight off Melwas's men if need be."

Fynavir staggered up, clasping her shaking arms around him and folding her legs around his middle. With his two Ar-moran daggers in hand, Arondyt in the right and Fragarak in his left, he pushed through the gap in the hut wall and raced out into the night.

The village was a scene of tumult and panic. Women were screaming and keening over the bodies of the dead, while dogs raced around, maddened by the blood-scent and the commotion. Warriors loomed up out of the smoke and the reek, faces grim, leading ordinary farming folk armed with sickles and clubs studded with deadly flint spikes.

"There he is!" one screamed, and An'kelet felt the air ripple as an arrow whirred past his head. "The bastard who killed chief Melwas! He has taken the stranger woman, the white one of ill-luck!"

"Get them!" another voice howled, full of bloodlust and rage. "Sacrifice them both in the lake!"

An'kelet started to run. Fynavir was no great weight, but he was terrified an arrow or other missile might strike her exposed back. He had an awful vision of both of them impaled by a flying spear, bound together like lovers, flesh joined to flesh in the eternity of death. Please, great Ancestors, let her live. Goddess, if she is really a scion of your flesh, protect her now, I beg you...I beg you!

As they reached the edge of the village, a roaring tribesman suddenly jumped out from behind a hut, brandishing one of the lethal clubs An'kelet had spotted earlier. He swung it wildly at the Ar-moran prince, and one of its spines ripped into the muscle of An'kelet's left arm, drawing a gush of bright blood that drenched his sleeve. An'kelet leaped back, narrowly avoiding another blow from the club, and flung Fragarak at his adversary using his left hand, a move his enemy did not expect, for his gaze was fixed on the longer and more noticeable Arondyt. The blade somersaulted through the air, a spinning wheel of bronze fire, and struck the man firmly in the gut. He shrieked in shocked pain and crumpled to his knees, and An'kelet snatched the man's own weapon and hastily sent him to whatever gods or spirits he was vowed to.

Retrieving Fragarak, An'kelet began to run with all speed towards the lake. On his back, Fynavir glanced over her shoulder; through the shadows, she could see gesticulating figures silhouetted against new-kindled fires and the glint of flame on unsheathed metal. "They are coming! They will not give up until we are dead!"

"They may have no choice," said An'kelet, panting as he forced his legs to move even more quickly. He was now mere feet from the lakeshore, his keen eyes searching for the single coracle he had left afloat. And there it was, in the reeds, bumping gently against the half-submerged ruins of the coracles he had sabotaged.

An'kelet gestured to Fynavir and she released her hold of his neck. He lifted her into the coracle, and climbed in after her; it was a small craft, intended for only one sailor and their bodies were pressed together, his larger frame covering hers protectively. Pulling the Balugaisa from its sling, he put it to new use and pushed the craft away from the shore with a great thrust, shoving it out toward the centre of the night-shrouded lake.

"Look, they are getting away!" Torch-bearing figures were converging on the shore, running up and down as war-drums began to beat and horns blared in the shadows. Several more arrows whined in the air like angry bees and skittered across the surface of the water. "After them, in the boats... Melwas must be avenged!"

The angry villagers plunged knee-deep into the water, seeking the boats that they used everyday for fishing, the craft they knew they could manage like no others in all Albu. Their hands flapped about, groping and grasping in the cold waters...and then they found the sunken coracles, some upended, others sinking into the mud, all damaged beyond repair.

Angry cries went up, rising in intensity until all voices blended into one single voice that trembled and ululated, then fell in a series of wails and shrieks that sounded barely human. It was a dreadful sound and Fynavir covered her ears with her hands, even though she recognised that it was a cry of despair.

A cry of defeat.

The coracle sailed out into the lake, skimming across the wide waters under the Moon An'kelet and Fynavir had escaped. The gods, it seemed, had smiled on them.

CHAPTER TWENTY-TWO

Once An'kelet and Fynavir reached the far side of the lake, they beached the coracle and began to hastily make their way toward the South, using the conical bulk of Hwynn's Tor, black against the star-speckled mantle of the sky, as a way-marker. Fynavir was weak; her legs threatening to give way with every step, so An'kelet carried her at intervals. His own wounded arm was painful and still bleeding, a slow, dark trickle that soaked his tunic. It was not a serious wound, but he knew it needed to be washed and bound to avoid an infection that could prove lethal.

But there was no time to attend to such matters; they had to keep moving. The lands around were still hostile territory, and the news of Melwas's death would spread swiftly as fire, as such news always did. They had to reach the lands of the Dwri to be assured of safe passage to Kham-El-Ard.

"Do you know where we are?" asked Fynavir against his shoulder, her numb, bruised feet dangling over his arm. "How long do you think it will take us to reach home?"

"Two days or slightly more if we were both fit youths blessed with fleetness of foot." An'kelet smiled grimly. "But neither of us are fit, lady."

"I know…" She touched his wet sleeve, noting how he flinched. Her fingertips came away stained dark "We need to stop…there must be a safe place where we can make camp for the night."

"I believe we are travelling near the banks of the River Brui," said An'kelet. "Another few miles and we should be out of the Summer Lands, and into friendlier places. We must not become too over-confident and let our guard down, however. Enemies and desperate men are everywhere."

"An'kelet…" She had not asked it yet, but now, glancing down, he saw her eyes troubled, tearful. "Where is my husband? Why did he not come?"

"Ardhu is wounded—he couldn't ride, Fynavir. He took a deep injury to the leg while fighting T'orc. But do not fear, his wound should heal in time."

Fynavir was silent for a while, contemplative. "He couldn't come for me…but you did."

An'kelet glanced down at her. "I could no more leave you with that bastard Melwas, than cut out my own heart with my dagger. I swore an oath to protect you…and all that is in Ardhu's kingdom."

"So that is why you rescued me? Because you swore to guard Ardhu's chattels?" Her voice was slightly bitter, disappointed.

"No, not exactly." He gave her a crooked smile nearly as bitter as the tone of her voice.

She stared up into his face and suddenly the darkness and sorrow in her eyes lifted, as night lifts before the day.

They soon found the banks of swift-flowing Brui and followed it southwards. Eventually, they reached a spot where the river curved out and was fringed by a stand of weeping willows. Within this clump of tangled foliage, they found an old midden, heaped with shells, and the charcoal from a long-dead fire. An'kelet examined the burnt remains and deduced that they were old, their makers long gone from that place.

"We will stop here for the rest of the night," he said, setting Fynavir down on the dewy grass. "I will make fire." He went to the site of the old burning, and used his strike-a-light to ignite a small heap of dried moss, leaves and bits of wood. The ignited flame was feeble, but cast some slight warmth in that wintry world.

"Let me tend to your wound," Fynavir said, when he was done. "It cannot be allowed to fester. You could lose the arm—or worse."

They walked to the edge of the water and An'kelet knelt while Fynavir peeled away the shreds of his torn and bloodied sleeve, and laved the gouge in his upper arm with river-water until it was clean. An'kelet endured her ministrations in silence; not because of pain from the injury, which was slight, because he dared not speak, dared not move. Her close proximity, the touch of her hands on his skin, the glimpses of her body as she bent in the flimsy strip of skin she wore …he could scarcely endure it.

"I am no healer," she said. "But that will do until we can get you to see the Merlin. Now I must wash myself, the stink of Melwas's hut is still upon me and the stain of his hands…"

An'kelet caught her fingers, cold and white. "Fynavir, did he…hurt you?"

"If you are asking if he used me…no. But he was not…kind."

Turning her back to him, she let the filthy skin fall and waded out into the swell of the river. He could see bruises and wheals dappling her back and buttocks, and his heart twisted with anguish and rage. How could Melwas have done such a thing!

"Fynavir, be wary, the tow of the river may be too strong!" An'kelet shouted, as she swam out too far for safety, too far from his grasp. Even battered and bruised, she was beautiful and he would not be surprised if some river-spirit leapt from the depths to try steal her away.

She returned immediately, swimming into the shallows. "What's wrong? Your face, you are white as a bone!"

Words fell from his lips, unwise words, and unguarded, but exhaustion and emotion drove him. "I could not bear to lose you again. When word came that Melwas had abducted you, it was as if I had been pierced by a thousand spears."

"And you came for me. Alone, risking all, you came for me. I owe you so much. If there is a way to repay you…"

Heat jolted through him from face to groin, despite the chill of the winter's night. "I ask for nothing, but I also would refuse nothing that you willingly gave me."

She stood up in the river, water pouring in runnels off her bare flesh, and waded towards him. He sat on the bank, transfixed, unable to tear his gaze away from the sway of her full breasts, and from her rounded hips, the soft gold at their join filled with promise and desire.

His own desire rose up in him, and he reached to her, pulling her into his arms, his mouth hungrily seeking hers. Together they fell into the shallows, water surging about them. She tugged at his tunic, yanking it over his head, and at the lacings of his deerskin trousers. Her lips and fingers ran over his taut muscles, the Sun-bronzed flesh of chest and shoulders, teasing him, maddening him, making him ache with need.

Vaguely, through a haze of desire, he was aware he was making the most momentous and terrible decision of his life. He was about to betray the vows he made to his priestess-mother, that had made him the best and most noble warrior in the world.

Worse still, he was about to betray his friend.

His king.

But he could no more stop himself now than he could stop the turning of the seasons, the rising of the Sun. It was as if both he and Fynavir had been caught in some primordial spell that bound them together and dismissed all other loyalties, giving no heed to the fate that would befall them should their tryst ever be discovered.

The icy water splashing over their flesh did not quell their ardour; but instead heightened the sensations as they lay with the weeds twined around them, caressing their skin just as they caressed each other. It was as if the Brui cleansed them, washing away the past, moulding them anew, making them, for the first time in their lives, truly whole in their union with each other.

An'kelet gazed down at Fynavir, her head thrown back, eyes closed and her lips parted. Water swelled between her breasts, glittering. "Fynavir, Fynavir…" he chanted her name like a prayer, though he knew of no gods or spirits that would bless this union.

The union of traitors. A union that could bring down a kingdom.

She opened her eyes. He saw his own image mirrored in them, his spirit trapped in their depths in all willingness.

Nothing then mattered, not Ardhu, not his mother the Priestess, not his prowess as a warrior. The only thing that mattered was this night, and the heat of his heart, and the desire of the flesh.

***

Dawn came too swiftly, bringing reality with its blood red light. An'kelet woke, shivering, and glanced down. Fynavir lay asleep, half under him, wrapped in his cloak. The little fire was cold embers near her head. He shook his head, fearful and wondering and glad all at once, captivated by her beauty, her fragility, yet terrified at what he had done.

His need of her had changed him; he could not deny the unsavoury truth. The pure, almost holy quality that his mother Ailin had conferred upon him was gone, dead, charred like the ashes of the fire. It had died in Fynavir's arms. He was forsworn to both Ardhu and the Priestess Ailin of the Lake of Maidens. He would never be the same again.

Thinking of the night's passion, he shook his head in dismay. They had rutted like beasts out in the open, where any passer-by might have spotted them. And in the river, no less…the icy river! At the last, he had realised how cold he was, how Fynavir trembled against him like a leaf and seemed near to falling into a faint, and he knew that their actions put them both in danger of freezing to death. By the spirits, it was only just past Y'melc, too early for frolicking naked under the stars! He had carried Fynavir to shore and stoked up the fire he had kindled earlier, then bundled her under his cloak and warmed her limbs with mouth and hands. Eventually, they had both slept, growing warm by the crackling flames.

As he lay there, propping himself upright on one elbow, grief and consternation mingled on his face, Fynavir began to stir. She rolled over and gazed up into his eyes. She too looked troubled. Reaching up, she touched his arm. "An'kelet, what have we done? What are we to do now?"

He stared at the ground, unable to meet her anxious gaze. "Maybe…maybe we should head for the coast and take a boat to Ar-morah. My kin might give us shelter."

Fynavir shook her head. "No, no, that won't work. Ardhu would hunt us—he would have no choice, even if he had no stomach for it. The chiefs of Albu would demand that he take revenge, or else they would depose him as weak and unmanly. No, he would have to hunt us until one of us was dead. And if he were to bring his warband to Ar-morah, Albu would be open to sea-pirates, evil men and schemers like Morigau. They would pounce like a wildcat upon its prey, and the Isle of Prydn would burn."

"What would you have me do, then, lady?" His voice was strained. He knew what she was to say next…knew, because it was the only option.

"We must go back to Kham-El-Ard." Fynavir's voice wavered as she strove not to weep. "It is the only way. The only honourable way. We must pretend as if nothing has happened between us, that your loyalty to me is only through the friendship between you and my husband."

An'kelet pressed his hands to his forehead in frustration. "Ah, you cannot ask me to do this; it is beyond my endurance to see you at his side, in his bed, while I cannot even touch you…."

She took his hand, kissed the long, strong, golden fingers. "I will find a way. I will ask to go riding with you as my guard, and we can find some private place, some hollow… A stolen moment is better than no time at all…Ardhu would never suspect! He loves you as his brother!"

An'kelet groaned at her last words, self-loathing washing over him in a black tide. "That he does is the worst of it, Fynavir. For I am traitor to him, and unworthy to stand as a warrior of the Circle of Khor Ghor."

She pulled away, staring at the ground, embarrassed by his obvious distress. She had never seen him so distraught, so unsure—he who was so bright and strong and certain, the rising Sun at Midsummer. "It is the only way, An'kelet. I can think of no other, unless you leave me forever from this day onwards and make your own way to your people across the sea, or to Ibherna, or even to the dark forests of the middle-lands, where men are fierce and would welcome your warrior-skills. I could tell Ardhu a tale to cover your tracks—I could say you took a wound while fighting Melwas and died from fever, and that friendly locals made your pyre and I scattered your ashes into the river at dawn."

"Hush! All this talk of death!" He placed his fingers to her mouth, and then replaced them with his lips, in a kiss so deep, so powerful she felt as if he were trying to possess her spirit, to draw it from her body and bring it into him to join with his own spirit. When he finally released her, he pulled her tight against his chest and said, "I won't leave Prydn, my fair one; I will never leave you. For all the trials I may face, none could be worse than never seeing your face again. I will return to Kham-El-Ard with you, and play my part."

"It will be all right…you will see," she cried, heart leaping at the thought that he would be near her at Kham-El-Ard, and that she could somehow steal away with him. Ardhu would never find out; she would be careful and clever.

An'kelet looked at her sadly; his smile was thin and weak. "My love…it will never be 'all right'. Never again."

Fynavir and An'kelet stood at the gates of Kham-El-Ard, gazing out across the fields toward the ancient track called the Harrow or Temple Way, which came from the West to join the centre of all things at Khor Ghor. The Merlin stood beside them, brooding and silent; his raven-sharp eyes darting first to An'kelet then to Fynavir, searching, weighing each one up. They both stood straight as spears, neither looking at the other.

"My lord Ardhu is coming," said Fynavir. "My lord, the victor over the Chief Boar, will soon be home."

Messengers had come the day before; Ba-lin and Bal-ahn and the faithful young Drem. Fynavir had rewarded them with golden mead poured by her own hand, and with ingots of bronze, and amber amulets from the cold dark sea in the north where her long-dead sire had hailed from.

And now the great aurochs-horns were blowing, their voices deep on the wind, and the men of the warband and their banners were visible on the horizon, marching steadfastly for home. At their head was Lamrai, her grey mane tossing on the morning breeze, with Ardhu seated on her back, and the wan Sun glinted off his breastplate of gold and golden belt buckle and the polished surface of the Face of Evening. The people of Kham-El-Ard cheered as he rode toward them, their young king, the victor over many foes.

But Ardhu had no eyes for any of his people, as he spurred Lamrai into a sudden gallop, and charged up the crooked hill on which his fortress stood. His eyes were only for Fynavir, standing in her gold-beaded cape, with a headdress of swan's feathers upon her hair.

"My lady, it is good to see you unharmed!" He swung from his horse's back and tossed the reins to Ka'hai. "When news of Melwas's treachery came to me, I did not think there would be a happy outcome. Praise to the spirits that you are whole and well."

He walked towards her, and she could see that he had a slight limp, and winced slightly when too much pressure was placed on his left leg. She took his hands in hers, gently, and kissed his cheeks in greeting, and the people of Kham-El-Ard cheered even louder. Drums began to beat and a reed pipe wailed out; there would be much celebrating in Ardhu's great hall for the next three days till the new Moon.

Ardhu turned to An'kelet, who stood in silence, his arms folded and his head bowed. The young chieftain's eyes were full of gratitude. He clapped the taller man on the shoulder. "My friend, how can I ever repay you? I am eternally in your debt for returning Fynavir safely to me."

"It was my duty," An'kelet murmured. "I could do naught else."

"And you killed Melwas single-handedly, saving me the trouble!"

"He is dead indeed, and cursed beyond the grave."

"Then we shall all feast tonight, in my high hall, and the men-of-words shall tell tales not only of how Ardhu the Bear felled the Chief Giant and the Chief Boar, but how the brave An'kelet, Man-of-Many-Arts, saved Fynavir White Phantom, queen of her people, from the grasp of Melwas, king of the Summer Lands!"

The crowd roared their approval, and pressed forward eagerly, sweeping all into a vast celebration that lasted from dusk to dawn every day until the Moon was new.

It was the Time of the Bhel-fires, one of the most joyous festivals in all the year for the people of Prydn. A time to worship both Father Sun and Old Earth Woman, and invoke the Ancestors that they might confer continued fecundity on man and beast.

In the circle of Khor Ghor Ardhu stood with An'kelet on his right side and Fynavir on his left, and the Merlin before all three in his robe of many teeth and claws. Above them towered the immense Door into Winter, Portal of Ghosts; while from the other massive trilithons fell shadows that slunk and stretched and veered with the movement of the Sun. The gold dagger and inlaid axes on the Gate of Kings had been unveiled and glittered warmly in the rich, dying light; symbols of Ardhu's continuing power, the greatest reign of any in Prydn since the time of Samothos, who came to Prydn nigh on five hundred years ago, following the Westward paths of the sea.

Ardhu lifted his arms toward the scarlet West, his eyes dark with emotion. "Bhel-Sunface, to whom the pyres burn this eve, I offer you my thanks for the great blessings you have conferred upon me—the defeat of T'orc, and the fall of Melwas and return of Fynavir, my wife.... My wife, who is now with child and will give my kingdom an heir to take on my mantle when I am gone!"

The Merlin gestured to a priest-acolyte and a calf was led forward on a rope. Ardhu drew Carnwennan, and with a swift, brutal motion cut the animal's throat. It collapsed in a heap before the Altar Stone, blood pumping from the severed neck-vein and feeding the thirsty earth at the foot of the stone. Ardhu, without flinching, promptly slashed the palm of his own hand, letting red droplets fall to mingle with the calf's blood, signifying his own bond with the earth, with the stones of which he was earthly lord. Turning from the sacrifice, he took more blood from his hand and painted his face, and daubed it onto Fynavir's brow in the prescribed patterns of life and death and binding. Finishing, he turned to the silent An'kelet and used the last of the blood to draw similar marks on his cheeks and forehead.

"For you are as my family," Ardhu told his friend, his first warrior, acclaimed above all others in Kham-El-Ard. "So you shall share in this blessing. If not for your valour in the slaying of Melwas, this occasion would be one of sorrow and not joy."

An'kelet could find no words to say, but clasped Ardhu's hand in a tight grip.

The young chief did not see the shame and sadness in his eyes.

Instead, he turned back towards the Great Trilithon, its gigantic stones blood-hued in the Sunset, and spoke to the Merlin, a sombre figure reading omens from the death-throes of the calf that Ardhu had slain. "And what does the mighty Merlin, lord of seers, have to say upon this day? What words of advice have the spirits of this holy place whispered in your ear?"

Merlin sighed; he was getting old, and felt the pains of age more strongly every passing day. He wondered if Morigau had cursed him in some way. The thought made him cantankerous, and more afraid than ever that soon he would not be able to guide and watch over Ardhu and the Five Cantrevs of the West.

"They say only that when the enemies outside the fold are vanquished, the wise ruler will look for greater enemies within," he said sourly.

Ardhu shook his head, his eyes burning with the force of his belief. "I do not have that fear, Merlin. My warriors shall forever form a stalwart circle around me, even as the Stones of Khor Ghor stand in their unbroken circle for eternity."

He turned to Fynavir, smiled. "Are you ready?"

"I am, lord." She bowed her head, the blood on her face blazing like the sky.

"And An'kelet, my friend, my brother?"

The Man of Bronze raised his spear Balugaisa in salute to the stones, to the spirits, to his King…and to his Queen. "I am ready, lord!"

"Then let us go forth and feast, and jump the Bhel-fires on Kham-El-Ard!"

With the White Phantom and his chief warrior close behind him, the Stone Lord of Prydn passed under the colossal arch of Winter's Door and strode across the Great Plain towards the setting Sun.

BOOK TWO: MOON LORD

THE FALL OF ARTHUR, THE RUIN OF STONEHENGE

PROLOGUE—THE VISION

The last storm of winter shrieked across the Great Plain, blowing clouds of snow on its boreal breath and painting the stones of the ancestral temple of Khor Ghor with glittering patterns. Icy flakes crept into worn carvings and under lintels and made a frosty beard on the great Stone of Summer with its bowed head and glowering mouth.

In the heart of the circle, the old man stood alone, listening to the roar and shriek of the storm. His face was leathery, brown from the elements, hawk-like in profile; his free-falling hair, once as black as the birds beneath the capstones of the circle, was now a dull slate-grey, sullen and harsh as the stones themselves. He wore a calfskin tunic, fringed with bones and tusks, and a hat of beaver skin protected his head from the blast of the wind. In his hands he carried his seeing stone, a lump of rounded quartz bequeathed to him in youth by his long-dead mentor, Buan-ann, the Old Woman of the tribe in distant Faraon, where the holy mountain God of Bronze rose to heaven, the dark spikes of its summit visible all the way to the Isle of Ibherna. He raised the quartz to his eyes and breathed heavily upon it, his breath fogging the age-polished surface.

He was the Merlin, high priest of Khor Ghor, the Dance-of-Ancestors...and an old man with fear in his heart.

"What can you tell me, spirits?" he murmured to the seeing-stone, to the sky, to the thin dark bluestones rising round him like a ring of watchers, frozen tribesmen from some ancient time. "What do you see? Why have I felt fear in my heart from Solstice onwards?"

The wind howled louder, rising and ululating, filled with malice and the voices of the long dead who did not sleep easy in their barrows. With shaking fingers, Merlin slipped a handful of chosen berries beneath his tongue in order to commune with the spirit-world. Within minutes his vision blurred, dimmed, streaking away into nothingness. Dizziness overwhelmed him and he thudded to his knees in the snow, back resting against the Stone of Adoration, the focal stone of Khor Ghor, standing alone before the colossal arch of the Door into Winter, with its enormous capstone, attached by sturdy mortise and tenon joints, thrust up almost into the lowering snow-cloud.

In his age-spotted hands the seeing stone grew hot and Merlin fancied could see figures stirring in its heart, playing out some secret, sacred dance...No, not figures, not of men, at least... The image was of the Sun, a wheel of blood, dying over the altar of Khor Ghor as He did every Midwinter on the Shortest Day.

But this time, in Merlin's vision, Bhel Sunface did not rise again, as He had risen since the world was forged.

Instead His light became dim, obscured, a weak thing on the verge of extinction. The Sun in Merlin's seeing-stone was eclipsed by a Moon as black as jet.

CHAPTER ONE—YNYS YRCH

The King was dead

Loth of Ynys Yrch lay upon a bier of woven branches in the cult-house, his body puffed with putrefaction, rancid and purple after a week of death. Seashells covered his eyes, hiding their hideous fixed stare, while his jaw was bound shut with a strip of sinew to keep his mouth from opening in the endless rictus scream of the dead

Well might Loth have screamed, his tormented voice echoing in spirit realms above and below, for he had died not only horribly but ignobly, not on the field of battle or leading his men in the hunt but when he was lounging around his roundhouse with his warriors, drunk and stinking, a captive woman from a coastal tribe upon his knee. One moment he had been dandling the slattern with one hand and slurping from his big, ceremonial beaker with the other; the next he had clutched his throat and toppled to the ground, foaming and retching, the mead spewing from his mouth in a bile-filled fountain. The slave–woman ran off screeching while Loth continued to writhe in the rushes, face livid and his tongue thrusting from his mouth.

His men gathered round trying to rouse him, but he was past the aid of men; his throat rattled and he passed into the shadowy arms of She-Who-Guards, the protectress of the Dead and ancestral bones.

It was not just the Death-Spirit who roamed that night. Sinister as the Watcher herself, Loth's wife, Morigau of Belerion, had stolen in to his hut and claimed his corpse, carrying it with the aid of her sons and attendants to the great cult-house that sat in decaying splendour between the two ancient stones circles, Ring of Moon and Wheel of Sun, that stood on a long peninsula between two lochs, one saltwater, the other fresh. Morigau was priestess there, appointed after the mysterious deaths of her rivals, and it was her right to claim the body as Loth's wife, but men made the sign of evil as they saw her pass in her cloak of raven crow-feathers, with her followers carrying Loth's corpse high on their shoulders and the terns and sea-eagles wheeling hungrily above.

In the cult house with its red-painted walls and four jagged stones standing sentinel at the door, Morigau set about performing rites over Loth's body but she did not speak the words to assist the dead man's spirit upon its journey into the West. Instead, she cursed Loth, uttering dreadful chants to bind his spirit between the Lands of the Living and the realm of the Everliving Ones for eternity. A terrible punishment, the worst one could wish upon the newly dead.

She had hated her husband.

"Yes, Loth..." She trailed her index finger over the putrescent cheek of the dead man. The long nail would have drawn blood had there been any left to bleed. "I have my revenge at last. You beat me and humiliated me once too often—I, who am a priestess and of royal house, not some drab to warm your bed! Even worse, you maltreated my beloved boy, my beautiful one, who shall be king after you... and who knows what else he might be one day."

The sound of footsteps in the long, tomb-like passage leading to the inner sanctum of the cult house drew her from the reeking bier of her dead husband. Lips curved in a snarl, she groped for the honed flint dagger she always carried concealed in her robes... She knew that unrest grew in the tribe, and that with Loth's demise she and her four sons were in danger. She was not loved on Ynys Yrch and rumours had quickly spread that henbane-root had poisoned Loth's last beaker of mead; these harsh whispers were followed by hostile questions about the parentage of Morigau's boys, Agravaen, Gharith, Ga'haris, and, especially her eldest son, Mordraed who was potentially Loth's heir.

Morigau's lip curled contemptuously, giving her small, heart-shaped face an ugly, petulant look. Agravaen was obviously Loth's get, a surly boy, with not much of Morigau's blood in him: pimply, heavy-featured and a dullard, but strong of limb and single minded. Arrow fodder, maybe, but one who would do as he was told without thinking. Gharith and Ga'haris? Well, most men of the tribes had brown hair and eyes, as did both boys; and who could say for absolute certain who a child's father was, unless men came to locking their women away from all other male contacts?

She did not care overmuch what happened to those three anyway, legitimate or not. None of them could compare to Mordraed, her firstborn, her best…the one who deserved the world, and she would give him that if she could.

She breathed a sigh of relief as she recognised his familiar shadow in the corridor and re-sheathed her secret dagger. Moments later Mordraed strode under the arched door-lintel with its painted red diamonds and lozenges. Her other sons followed on his heels, a pack of eager puppies. Mordraed always led them, caring for his younger brothers in a way that Morigau, their mother, could not bring herself to. She had not wanted such a gaggle of children, only the one who would bring her desires to fruition, but they had come and she had whelped them like a bitch, and farmed them out to whatever village woman would suckle and tend them. Had her will been her own she would have exposed them, giving them to the spirits in return for greater gifts of power for herself but they were princes after all and Loth would have none of it.

"Mother, it is bad news, I fear." Mordraed crossed the room without glancing at his mother, making the required bow at the sacred shrine at the far end—a dresser similar to that seen in the local homes but larger and more finely crafted, filled with holy objects both on its shelves and under its stone slabs—strange little figurines of blobbed stone with crude eyes pecked on them and fine polished axe heads too good to be of use to any but denizens of the spirit-world.

"Tell me…"

Mordraed turned on his heel, folding his arms. He taut as a bowstring, every muscle quivering with rage. "The Boneman and Cludd rally the people against us. They cast blame on you not only for father's death but for the poor catch of fish and failed harvest of the past few years."

Morigau stood in silence, staring at her eldest son with her feral dark eyes. Despite the urgency of his words, the terrible truth he was imparting, she could not help but feel a surge of pride and of a fierce, almost unnatural love at the sight of him. I wrought this…. she thought. Me…

Her son. Surely a man-god blessed by the spirits, born of a coupling of sister and brother, in an act taboo and yet sacred, marking his special-ness.

In the dim light of the burning tallow cups that ringed Loth's bier he stood proudly alert, holding a short, composite bow with an arrow on the string. Dark and beautiful, he was like a hero from an old legend—hair the colour of jet fell in loose waves down his back, framing a high-planed face with a nose as straight as a blade and a mouth shapely if stern. Yet none could mistake his male beauty for effeminacy. Although not overly tall, his body was hard and lean, the muscles beneath his jet-studded leather jerkin perfectly developed from years spent mastering the art of the bow.

He was a deadly archer who seldom missed his mark.

And if any still believed him weak, fooled by the deceptive beauty of his face, his eyes would have told the truth. Deep as the sea, fathomless, they were a rare dark blue, so dark they appeared almost black, fringed by long lashes that he lowered to conceal his true emotions.

They were ice-cold eyes, which could at a moment's notice become blank and pitiless, wholly without compassion.

Death eyes.

Morigau, daughter of Y'gerna and half-sister to Ardhu Pendraec, Stone Lord of Prydn, loved Mordraed's eyes most of all.

"Mother!" Mordraed's voice rose, sharp and irritable. When she stared at him with such devouring intensity, it made him uncomfortable. "Have you not heard a word I said? Ack-olon thinks it too dangerous for us to stay on Ynys Yrch; he counsels that we flee for the mainland…."

Morigau hissed like a serpent, eyes igniting with anger. "How dare he suggest such a thing without consulting me first? What of your birthright? You should rule after Loth!"

Mordraed's lip curled. "It would seem many do not believe Loth was my father…Cludd, his sister's son, in particular. He has petitioned the Boneman to be instated by Mother-right and men rally to his cause."

"The traitors, the traitors…" Morigau cried, and she spat at Loth's fat, decaying body. The tallow-filled lamps that lit the chamber swirled, and suddenly the sinew supporting the dead king's chin snapped and his jaw sprang open as if to utter a horrible mocking laugh from whatever underworld trapped his spirit.

The two youngest boys screamed, flinging their arms round Mordraed, whose lightning hands brought his bow to the draw in an instant. He would kill Loth again, by the Moon he would, if the hateful old bastard were to return from the dead. Like Morigau, he had despised Loth, and the feeling had been mutual; Loth had suspected the boys parentage from the day he was born and Mordraed had heard the rumours too—snide comments from other boys, whispers behind the hands of gossiping women. He had cared little, for Loth had been harsh and cruel, taunting him and aiming blows whenever he passed by. He wanted no blood-claim on the foul old man…just chieftaincy over these storm-tossed isles as Morigau had promised since he was a tiny child, when she had given him a little bronze dagger and told him whenever he was angry to stick it into an effigy made of bones and straw that looked a little like Loth.

The tallow cups fluttered again and a swirl of salty sea-wind rushed down the passage. Someone else was coming, brought into the cult-house on the storm…

Torches flared and suddenly the whole chamber was brightly illuminated, shadows fleeing backwards in a mad umbrous rush toward Loth's bier. Cludd, the son of Loth's sister Clotagh, marched sternly into the chamber surrounded by upwards of a dozen men, some carrying fire-brands, other bearing unsheathed daggers and menacing clubs lined with spines of flint. The shaman known as the Boneman strode at Cludd's side, a scrawny elder with a cloud-grey beard to his waist and a necklace of men's finger bones jangling against his bony chest. He was the guardian of the crematory hearth in the Temple of the Moon, and acclaimed oldest man in the tribe, having lived nearly three Moon-Years…over fifty Sun-Turnings. He had staunchly opposed Morigau becoming a priestess from the moment she arrived on Ynys Yrch, a new bride with her belly already swelling—and was the only one of her rivals to live to confront her, for he would not treat with her in any wise.

Morigau's face was thunder-hued, her eyes sparking. "You have no right to come here! The spirits will curse you!"

"It is not the true men of Ynys Yrch who will be cursed," said the Boneman. "You are the one who is blighted. Your taint has scared the fish from our shores and caused the crops to wither. And so you must go, renouncing all ties to this island."

"And if I refuse?" She glared at him, gaze black with fury.

"You die, and your brood of bastards with you."

Cludd, a heavyset man who resembled his uncle Loth, circled round Mordraed, looking him up and down. The youth's fingers were still on his bowstring, his eyes murderous.

"You..." Cludd walked in front of him, arms folded over his broad chest, which bore two round sun-discs of sheet-gold—an assertion of power and authority, objects that proclaimed his wealth and lineage. "Put down that bow and you may live. I am not a harsh man; I have no real quarrel with you, Mordraed, despite the fact you are the scion of that she-bitch, Morigau. But you are to go from this place and never return, along with those surly whelps." He gestured to the cowering younger boys and scowling Agravaen. "Gods only know who their fathers might be but I have no doubt they are not spawned of my uncle, Loth. No more than you are."

"You dishonour me!" Mordraed snarled.

"No, that bitch has dishonoured you" Cludd jabbed a finger in Morigau's direction. "Now go, and take her with you…or you will all be burnt in the Bonefire by the next dawn."

Mordraed looked mutinous and would have drawn his dagger, but Morigau, standing nearby, began to waver. If someone, anyone had come to her defence she would have fought her ground. But she would not risk Mordraed in some hopeless battle, he was too important, even if he would not be King of Ynys Yrch after Loth. "We will go," she cried, thrusting herself between Mordraed and the stocky figure of Cludd. "But this will not be forgotten, Cludd, mark my words."

Morigau exited the cult-house, face almost demonic with despair and rage. The young boys scampered after her, wailing in terror as fat Agravaen pinched and swatted at them, taking out his own frustrations at losing his princely position in the tribe. Mordraed saw him jab his fingernails into Gharith's arm, drawing blood, and the older youth slapped his chunky hand away, then twisted the fingers back until he yowled like a wildcat. "Stop your foolishness," he warned Agravaen, "or you'll never wield dagger or bow again, I promise you, brother."

Agravaen scowled at him and pulled himself free, cradling his wounded hand, but he did as bade and ceased to torment Gharith and Ga'haris—he knew his older brother made no idle threats.

Huddled close together the outcast family hurried down the old path that led to the seashore. Crofters in huts stared out of their doorways, calling curses and spitting—Morigau had been hated indeed, well known for her evil dealings and bloody rites, and now that she had been toppled from power they were not afraid to show their dislike.

Half way to the shingle spit that faced the nearest point of the mainland they saw two men waving at them, beckoning them on from atop a dune of sand. Morigau's two loyal companions La'morak and Ack-olon. Not only her protectors, but also her lovers of many long years.

"Where have you been?" shrieked Morigau angrily as the little band neared the waiting men. She struck out with her fists, pummelling one and then the other. "You should have been at the temple, guarding us! Guarding my sons! No, you were off hiding, while that oaf Cludd threw us out like shite into the midden!"

A muscle twitched in Ack-olon's cheek but he managed to keep his composure. He was too afraid of Morigau, of her poisons and sharp knives, to answer her wrath with anger of his own. "We were helping, Lady; we had not abandoned you. We could do nothing at the temple in your defence—except die needlessly. So we stole away when tempers flared high and prepared a boat to take us to safety on the mainland. The boys will have to help paddle—they can do that, can they not?"

He gave Mordraed a mean, piggy-eyed look; Ack-olon had been Morigau's lover since they were little more than children and it irked him the way she fussed about the boy, treating him like he was already a little king, better than his brothers, better than him and La'morak, who were of high status clans themselves. Ack-olon was also privy to the truth—that

Mordraed was the child of a broken taboo, cursed, for he had been there that night when Morigau, masked as the raven, had seduced her own drink-addled half-brother.

Mordraed noticed the look and stiffened, his eyes turning black with fury. He hated the two men who were always sniffing about his mother, hated the sly jokes they shared, their wandering hands when they thought he could not see. How he wished Cludd had finished the two warriors, but he was certain that they had been, as Morigau had accused them, in hiding…or at best, preparing the boat to save their own skins should the worst happen.

"Of course I will help." He cast a frosty smile in Ack-olon's direction. "It would be rude of me not to help an old man."

Ack-olon's teeth gritted; a vein throbbed on his temple but he forced himself to turn away. At his side La'morak choked back a laugh.

"Old men…" Mordraed added.

La'morak's smile curdled like milk.

Mordraed carried on to the seashore, grinning, enjoying their almost palpable dislike.

A boat lay on the shingle, carved from a great log, long and slippery as a sea serpent. The wind was blowing fiercely, as it often did on those bleak treeless isles, and the waters beyond were choppy and wild. Clouds of spume blew past the faces of the refugees.

La'morak looked worried. "The tide is not good. The wind is up. It is a fierce crossing even for experienced sailors."

"We have done it before, we shall do it again," Morigau stated flatly.

"Maybe wait till dawn and see if the wind dies."

Morigau stared over her shoulder, head on one side, listening. A little bead of sweat appeared on her brow, to be licked away by the wind. "Are you deaf? Can you not hear? They proclaim Cludd as new king in the Circles of Sun and Moon. They are deep in their beakers and their anger rises. They will come looking for us, and if we are not gone they will tear us all limb from limb!"

"The boat it is then." Mordraed shoved Gharith and Ga'haris into the log-boat, and beckoned impatiently for Agravaen to join them. The loutish boy thudded clumsily into the craft, almost tipping it over before the party had even set off. Mordraed squashed himself in just across from him and grabbed a paddle made of driftwood, while Morigau sat with her back pressed against her favourite child and the youngest two crushed between her knees. Her two servants pushed the log-boat out to sea and began to paddle with all their strength against the fierce riptides. Mordraed joined them with his own paddle, amused to see how swiftly they tired, their brows lathered and dripping, while he was still fresh and keen, not even breaking into a sweat.

The wind blew and the craft skirled, swaying dangerously to one side. The youngest boys screamed and were violently sick, spewing over the side. Agravaen moaned horribly and slumped to one side, vomiting, his shifting weight threatening to spill them all into the cold, deadly embrace of the sea, where Mahn-ann waited with his scaly green face and hair full of fishes.

"Agravaen, control yourself!" Mordraed slapped the younger lad with an open hand, making him leap back howling from the side of the log-boat. "You had your man-rites a Moon ago—act like it, or I will smack your arse like a baby's!"

The boy glared mutinously at his brother and pressed his fingers to his red, stinging face but he obeyed, moving not an inch. Not one, for he knew Mordraed made no idle threats.

Finally, beyond all hope, the exiles spied land, grey and hazy in the approaching dawn. Seabirds were just waking, wheeling over the waves and the misted green shores. The boat ground onto a pebbly spit and its occupants tumbled out, the older men exhausted from constant paddling, the little boys worn out by fear, Agravaen still holding his churning belly and slapped cheek. Morigau and Mordraed, however, seemed untouched by the perilous crossing, eager to go on.

"We cannot linger here," said Morigau. "These lands are ruled by Loth's kinsmen, sons of his brother Urienz, who was killed by my kinsman Ardhu. They have no love of my blood or me. News spreads fast, and I fear we won't be safe long here either."

La'morak clambered up, unsteady, his face grey and stubbled in the murky dawn-light. "What is your plan, lady? Where is safe for the likes of us?"

She smiled; a smile that did not reach her green-brown eyes "We will be safe with my brother, the Foe-hammer, the Stone Lord. My dear brother in the south. How would you like that, my boys?" She turned to the youngest of her children, gesturing them close. "We will travel to the great temple of Khor Ghor and meet with Ardhu Pendraec!"

"My uncle!" Mordraed yelped in surprise. "Have you gone mad? From the time I was a babe you told tales of how much you hate him! Why would you go to him for help?"

She sighed and, unexpectedly, threw her arms around Mordraed's waist, making him flush with embarrassment. Agravaen made a disgusted noise, eager to score against the brother who had shamed him on the sea-crossing. "I do it for you, my beautiful son. For you."

"For me?" He shook her too familiar hands from him. "How exactly? I would be gladder if you raised a war-band to take back Ynys Yrch…my birthright."

"There is better for you than that harsh place of pigs and the wind!" Ignoring his obvious reluctance, she coiled a hand in his hair, ran lips like dried leaves along his cheekbone. "Mordraed, soon I will tell you…tell you all. But not now, not before your brothers. Not until we are away and safe from the savage kin of Loth."

Mordraed brooded for the next few days as they travelled through wild, wide lands fringed by mountains with heads cloaked in grey cloud and criss-crossed by thundering streams, swollen from winter rains and melting snow. Frigid rain pelted the refugees, sometimes turning to snow when they crested the highest hilltops—great flat flakes that slapped into their eyes and melted on their lashes. The wind was sharp as a blade, but fortunately, their sealskin capes and boots helped protect against both water and wind. The younger boys, less afraid now that Ynys Yrch was far behind them, started to laugh and play childish games, casting snowballs at each other and their brothers and catching snowflakes on their tongues.

Eventually the fierce mountains diminished and the great glens that gaped between their adamant feet fell away, and the lands around them became tamer, less stony and remote. Standing stones lined rills and ridges—territorial markers of the various northern tribes who lived in these regions: Painted Folk and Khaledoni mostly, both known as head-hunters and not the type of folk who would give the former queen of Ynys Yrch succour.

By a dark little wood of pine the travellers found the remains of an abandoned round house, roof shorn away by time and wind, an open pit gaping before its door where some Ancestor's long interred skull had been wrest from its long sleep when the hut's owner had decided, for whatever reason, to take all his own and flee.

Ack-olon and La'morak set about making a fire in the long-cold hearth and putting down skins for their mistress and her sons to sit on. Morigau ate a piece of dried fish from her pack, giving nothing to the boys who watched her hungrily, and when she had finished gestured for Mordraed to come to her.

She stroked his face, still smooth, a pretty youth's face but with a hardness beneath the glamour. "Your eyes are haunted. Can you not trust me?"

"No," he said, pursing his lips. "I cannot. You told me from the time I could walk that I would be king after Loth…and now you act as if I should smile at the loss of a kingdom. Smile…and go to the house of an uncle who is an enemy of my house, and beg him for scraps!"

"It is time for us to talk," said Morigau, and her lips curved into a crooked, almost sinister smile that made Mordraed feel vaguely uneasy. He knew his mother dealt in dark things; he had seen the blood on her hands, smelt the scent of death on her robes. But she was a priestess, she served the Blue-Faced One most of all, and the Dark Moon, and it was not for him to question.

"Then let us talk," he said gruffly. "Be out with it."

"Not here." Morigau took the sleeve of his jerkin and drew him from the hut toward the trees that surrounded it. "What I must tell you is not for the ears of your brothers. In fact, they must never know."

Intrigued though vaguely apprehensive also, Mordraed let Morigau lead him in the direction of the grove. Ack-olon and La'morak were huddled together in the hut's door, staring after them and nudging each other, faces smug with some private knowledge. He did not like that at all, and longed to slash away those smug grins with his dagger…

Morigau picked her way between the trees, which swayed and creaked in the rising wind. Dead branches lay denuded on the forest floor, peeling bark bleached silver-white like old bones. Fleshy mushrooms clustered in the damp, spores puffing up in a yellowish cloud as Morigau's feet passed, filling the night with vapours and strange earthy scents.

Where the grove ended, a worn path wound out into grassland long stripped of trees in some ancient clearance. Morigau strode out into the sea of grass, her long black hair streaming like a banner in the breeze. She walked so confidently Mordraed wondered if she had been here before; on her travels throughout the isle of Prydn before she finally settled down as priestess and wife to Loth of Ynys Yrch. Wondered if the empty hut and its rifled doorstep grave could have had anything to do with her previous visit…

Up ahead he could see the pinnacles of two stones, weather-pitted oolitic fangs that jutted from a cobbled surface still red from old burning. A huge recumbent stone weighing many tons rested between the knife-like flankers; it was streaked with quartz, but a thousand exposed and brutal winter's nights had cracked it, the cold splitting the great megalith so that its dark inner core lay open to the elements.

Morigau hastened to the recumbent stone and lithely vaulted onto it, sitting between the flanking stones as a queen would sit upon a throne. The Moon was behind her left shoulder, her face shadowed, her head a silhouette against the blazing stars.

Morigau revelled in drama and effect; Mordraed knew she was using her theatre on him now, to awe him, to make him fear. He made a soft snarling noise, hating such mummery. "Mother, it is too cold for these games. Say what you must and let us return to the fire!"

He moved another step closer. He was standing on the cobbles now, loose, jumbled, and filled with ash and charcoal. Objects crunched noisily beneath his ankle-high cowhide boots; glancing down, he started in surprise, for the things half-hidden in the gloom were white and rolling, fragile as eggs fallen from the nest of some giant bird. But suddenly, one tumbled toward him, pivoting as it struck against his foot, and he realised these frail objects were not eggs at all but the domed crania of neonates, newborn children.

He scowled and his spine prickled. "Why must death always go with you?" he spat at his mother, and he gave the nest of skulls a great kick. They disintegrated in a puff of white dust.

"Death is always with us." Her eyes gleamed, feral. "Look!" She reached forward and grabbed his arm, fingers digging like tiny knives into his flesh. "Is this not the bow-hardened arm that wields death?"

"Maybe…but you will not let me use it!" he spat at her. "Mother, you promised I was to be king… but you made us leave Ynys Yrch without a fight, stealing away like cowards in the night! I would have fought…fought to the death! For my honour...and yours."

"Throwing your life away would be stupid, Mordraed. Yes, I once saw you as a ruler on Ynys Yrch, a rival for my brother on his high hill of Kham-El-Ard. But I have seen…better things for you. My mind is never quiet, my son; it works night and day, devising, foreseeing. You will be a king, Mordraed, that is true…but you will be king of more than just a lonely, wind-scored isle. You will be master of all Prydn."

Mordraed's lip quirked. "Your brother would have something to say about that, I'm sure. Are your wits addled, woman? What are you thinking? That he will somehow see me as his heir? He has a son, does he not? He does not need a sister's son for inheritance; many tribes do not follow Mother-right any more."

Morigau licked her lips; they looked black, dry as dead worms in the shaky starlight. "I want him dead, Mordraed. Dead, so that all that I lost through him is restored to me—through you. The boy, of course, must die too. The woman, the White Queen, will become your woman, as she is Sovereignty and men will respect what she is, even if they have no love of you."

Mordraed's heart pounded. "This is madness! No one would follow me, a usurper!"

"No, Mordraed." She reached out and caressed his silky cheek, her fingers now oddly gentle. "They wouldn't. But you would not be a usurper. Mordraed, Ardhu Pendraec's young son is not his eldest. The eldest is…you. Know that you are Ardhu's son, so true heir to all he owns."

Mordraed jumped back as if she had struck him. The spot where her fingers had caressed him burned like fire. Cold waves of sickness and terror ran through him. "He cannot be…I knew my sire was not Loth…but Ardhu! He…he is your brother!"

"So he is, my son. The sacred blood of kingship flows doubly in you from our Ancestors in deepest Belerion."

Mordraed fought the waves of nausea that washed over him. His head spun. " You tell me I come from a union that was taboo! I am a creature born of great wrong!"

"Then turn that cursed birthing into a great right…" She reached down and caught his arms, drawing him towards her, pulling him near until he was almost lying across the great cracked block of the down-lying stone. She was stronger than a woman ought to be, strong as a war-goddess. "Look…look, Mordraed, see the Moon behind us, see her beautiful white skull? Near nineteen Sun turnings has the Moon's cycle, and you were conceived when the cycle was on its turn, so you shall come to your full power as it ends. Then shall great sacrifices be made, and Ardhu, my brother, will be amongst them. The Moon is your mother, my boy, not the Sun that rules Ardhu, and she will eclipse his Sun as in the days of old—and her shadows will not pass away. The very stones of Khor Ghor will tremble and fall before your hand, Mordraed, my one of Great Judgement, my son of the Dark Moon."

He knew not what to answer, but lay as one frozen, the horror of her words sweeping over him, the cold of the stone eating through his clothes, grasping at his beating heart as if to still it. Morigau reached under her cloak, drew out an obsidian blade set into a hilt of horn, and raised it, its edge winking dully. She kissed it and then with a sudden downward motion slashed Mordraed's left cheek. He screamed in shock and pain, and black in the moonlight, blood pattered onto the great block on which he lay.

Morigau skirled the flowing blood into patterns with her fingers. "It is done. You are sworn by the shedding of your royal blood to the dark Mother that rules the Moon. I am sorry about your beautiful face, Mordraed, but that is your sacrifice…to the one whose spirit will guide you…and to me. Come, I will make it better, so it will not look uncomely."

She drew him towards her; he whimpered like a child, hating himself, hating Morigau both at once. Morigau took her dagger again and refined the cut across his cheekbone, before taking blue powders from her belt pouch and rubbing them into the wound. "There..." she said happily, as if well satisfied. "You have nothing to worry about. A nice tattoo to mark you. You do swear to me, don't you, Mordraed? Swear to follow the Moon that helped make you...and your mother, your priestess, who only wishes the best for you...for both of us."

"Have I any other choice?" he said.

"No, you do not," she replied.

CHAPTER TWO—THE HALL OF THE STONE LORD

The youth ran along the crest of the chalk ridge, bent low to the ground, seeking animal spoor to follow. Frosty leaves crumbled beneath his feet, but his soft deerskin shoes made no noise upon them so light of foot was he. He was like a spirit, a pale ghost in the mist, fast moving and insubstantial in his tunic of white aurochs' hide and grey wolf-skin cloak, a tribute-gift to his father from a distant Northern king.

He was gifted and the spirits had touched him.

He was Amhar, son of Ardhu Pendraec and his White Queen, Fynavir.

Amhar had been born amid great fear. He had nearly killed his mother at the birthing, and Ardhu had ridden to Khor Ghor during her long travail and treated with the spirits to let them both live. The King had slashed his own flesh to give the Stones blood, to show them his suffering and willingness to sacrifice. And on a clear sunrise, after five bitter days, when the Ladies of the Lake crowded round the sacred pool moaning and chanting, the child finally slid forth into the waiting hands of Nin-Aeifa and Mhor-gan of the Korrig-han. "It is a man-child!" Nin-Aeifa had cried, lifting the red and purple infant up by his feet to drain the choking fluids from his lungs. The baby's mouth cleared and he started to scream, and Mhor-gan had taken her ceremonial dagger of finest flaked flint and slashed the cord that bound him to Fynavir, freeing him into the mortal world. He had then been swiftly carried to Khor Ghor in a red fox-skin and presented to the five trilithons, where the Ancestors watched with ancient eyes—the Portal-of-Ghosts, Throne of Kings, the Western Guardian, the House of the North Wind and the Arch of the Eastern Sky. The afterbirth had been burned before the Stone of Adoration as an offering and Merlin had anointed the child with animal fat, writing sacred, protective marks upon his skin while Nin-Aeifa sang strange women's songs in a high, trilling voice, driving off any evil spirits that might seek to snatch the young life away.

Amhar his father had called him, the child-name that would fool malign beings into passing him by, and then he was carried in his fox-skin back to Kham-El-Ard, his shrill cries tearing into the twilight. Face strained from the fear and elation of the day, Ardhu had called out to his sister, Mhor-gan, in the women's birthing house, "Does my wife yet live?' and when she told him yes, Fynavir would survive to raise her child, he and his chief man An'kelet, as drained and stark-faced as his lord, fell into each others arms and embraced with gladness, though Ardhu had no idea of the true reason for his friend's relief.

After his harsh entrance to the world, Amhar had thrived well enough, drank milking hungrily and obtaining a lusty wail, but he was a strange one, as was quickly noted by the folk of Kham-El-Ard. He resembled neither father nor mother. Although his eyes were green like Fynavir's and of similar shape, they were a darker shade than hers, a deep, rich, leaf green with hints of gold, like sunlight dappling a forest glade. Dark red hair streamed down his back; in shadow it almost took on a purplish hue, like wild foxgloves. He was prone ro strange fancies and dreams, and on rare occasions would grow very still and far away, as if entering another world; and he would fall to the ground and shake for a moment or two and sometimes utter a strange, unworldly cry as he fell. One of the healer-priests from Deroweth had examined him and suggested that they try to cut a roundel from Amhar's skull to let any evil spirits out, but Fynavir had screamed in horror and Ardhu had grabbed the priest and flung him out the door of the Great Hall at Kham-El-Ard.

"Get the Merlin before we even talk of such a matter, priest!" he shouted after him, and sure enough the Merlin soon came, stalking on his spindly legs up the crooked hill, his jaw-topped staff in hand and the bronze-bound skull of his totem-bird shining on his breast. He had gazed into Amhar's eyes, drawn his finger from nose to chin and told the boy to follow its path, and asked questions of the little lad that none could hear. And when he was done, he sat back and sighed. "He bears a mark, your son—a mark of the Otherworld. He would doubtless make a good priest were he not the Son of a King. When the spells come upon him, just leave him and watch he does not choke and he will return to you after he had travelled in other realms."

And so Amhar became known as one touched by the gods, and , fits aside, he also began to walk strange paths, daring to walk where others would not—out to the Spirit-Path that stretched across the fields alongside Khor Ghor, bounding the lands of the Living and the Dead, or to the barrow-downs of old Kings, white-capped and shining, where the wind was full of a thousand dead voices. Fynavir sobbed and railed at her son when she heard of his exploits, but he merely hugged her and knew no fear, and no harm came to him.

But his strangeness marked him, and because of this, even at sixteen summers he had not yet become a man. He had a child's dagger and a youth's slight bow, and still wore two braids in his hair, which would be cut off and burned in a bone-fire when he underwent the manhood rites. The Merlin said often that Amhar might make a better priest than heir to the chieftaincy of the West…but Fynavir had never quickened with child again, and Ardhu refused to think of his son as anything but a warrior who would follow him and continue the line of the kings of old. However, the uncertainty surrounding his life's path had delayed his time of passage beyond that of the youths born in the same year.

Amhar was not resentful, as other boys in his predicament might have been. Briefly he wondered why he must endure what most saw as shame…but soon decided the Ancestors must have some deep design for him. He had suspected the Old Ones' had favoured him since he was very small and had seen lights that no one else could see glowing amongst the barrows of the plain. Mother had hated those lights, and wept and cried and tried to cover his eyes. She was used to them now, though; she had come to realise her fey son would not change, nor would the Old Ones leave him be.

Amhar gazed ahead into the twilight as he walked through the valley of the Lakes, with the burial ground of kings on his right, hidden from view by a high crest of land, and the curves of the shining river Abona on his left, with the farms of men and the Hill of Ogg the Eloquent in the distance beyond. He could see the river was frozen, the spring coming late this year; white tendrils coiled from a layer of thick ice, and the trees overhanging it were rimed with hoar frost. He curled his toes, wondering if he could spare an hour or two to tie a pair of long, flat bones to his shoes and skate on the surface as he had done when he was younger. But no, the wind was picking up, tossing his hair and reddening his cheeks, and he knew he must not stay out much longer. His intention had been to catch a hare, to make its pelt into a hand-warmer for Fynavir, or even a deer that could bring much cheer to Ardhu the Stone Lord's table, but he had found no spoor from either beast in that wintry desolation.

He was just about to turn and head home, when he heard a noise, a vague murmur of voices, the words carried away on the shrieking breeze. Cautious even though the lands were at peace beneath his father's rule, he quickly dived into a bush and stared down toward the Deadlands where the great chiefs and kings lay sleeping in their earthen barrows, silent under a blanket of snow. Were they tossing and turning, trying to wake and speak with him?

His heart began to hammer, a dull thud against his ribs.

But no…the voices were not those of the Old Ones with their grinning fleshless mouths and dry sepulchral whispers that rasped from throats long vanished. A party of wanderers travelled along the downs, heads bowed as they pressed on into the wind.

Trying to capture a better look, he peered through gaps in the ice-rimed bush, pushing aside annoying fronds with cold fingers. What manner of men were these? Who dared to walk in those empty lands where spirits dwelt?

As the party drew nearer he could see there were seven in the group—an auspicious number. Two were men in their late prime, bearded and dark-eyed with fatigue, with huge fur cloaks, mangy from wear and weather dangling from their shoulders. They guarded a small dark-haired woman wrapped in the sleek hide of a beast unfamiliar to Amhar; she held herself with pride, like his mother, the Queen. A chunky beardless youth with shoulders like a bull marched at her heels, followed by two little boys staggering with exhaustion; Amhar guessed the woman must be their mother, but he was surprised by her lack of concern for them—she did not even glance aside when one tripped on a tree root, fell heavily and started to howl, his voice rising up into the twilight like the tremulous cry of a ghost.

Instead, it was the final member of the band, bringing up the rear, who strode over to pluck the child from his snowy bed, dust him off, and set him back on the path. A younger man, an adult by his weapons, but not much older than Amhar himself. He had long black hair, the front strands pulled away from his forehead and bound with a spray of feathers from some white seabird, and his cheekbones were sharp as knife-blades through obvious recent deprivation. Despite his thinness he moved with grace, like a wildcat; and he was clearly aware of all that took place around him; Amhar watched him scanning the horizons even as he righted the fallen lad.

Amhar leaned forward a bit further, trying to get a better view of the strangers as they passed beneath the ridge; and underneath him, a branch suddenly cracked. The young man below startled like a frightened horse, and with lightning speed fitted an arrow to the string of his bow. He gazed up to the top of the ridge, and Amhar, darting back into the safety of the foliage, saw the stranger's face clearly for the first time.

He nearly tumbled over with shock. The newcomer resembled his father, the King, and his aunt Mhor-gan—long-headed, with high cheekbones, narrow jaw, and even, defined features, though Amhar thought the cast of youth's face was far prettier than Ardhu's; indeed even prettier than Mhor-gan, who was a woman. But unlike his kinfolk the stranger's eyes were a deep blue, mirroring the fading sky as they swept the landscape, searching. Something in those fathomless, unreadable eyes made Amhar both fearful and elated at once.

Here, in the form of this dark stranger, was the beginning of his adventure, his quest—he knew it as surely as he knew the Spirits guided him. He wanted to shout out, to hail the youth with Ardhu Pendraec's face…but it was then his courage failed him, the fear overcoming the coil of excitement in his belly.

Before he dared speak to these newcomers, he must tell his father of their arrival and find out who they were and why they came to Kham-El-Ard, for he was sure that must be their destination. Shouldering his child's bow, he glanced once more to where the dark man stood with arrow to the string, and then burst from his hiding place and fled along the ridge into the gathering night.

"She has come." The Merlin stood behind Ardhu Pendraec, high king of Prydn, Stone Lord and master of the Great Trilithon. "As we knew she would. With the boy."

Ardhu sat on a fallen tree within the darkness of the wood behind Kham-El-Ard, down by the Sacred Pool, where, many Sun-Turnings ago, Nin-Aeifa, the Lady of the Lake, had gifted him the sword Caladvolc. Brown from years of riding in the sun, his face was grim, his youth fled, although in his green-dark eyes were vestiges of the young warrior he once was, full of fire, the conqueror of many and scourge to those who threatened Prydn's shores. A short beard that left his cheeks clean hid a small scar he had acquired from a sea-raider, and the first traces of grey glittered amidst his dark hair.

"Why, Merlin?" he questioned, sighing. "So many years have gone by and we heard nothing. Sometimes I almost fancied both she and her whelp were dead; life is harsh in the North."

"Morigau is harsher." Merlin's eyes were narrowed, his lips thin lines. "Her life there only strengthened her; tempered her will like strong metal. Hatred of you and all you stand for has kept her wrath ablaze when others' inner fires would have died to embers."

"What should I do?" The King grasped the hem of the High Priest's deerskin robe, shiny with the fats that he rubbed in to keep it supple and clattering with attached bones of animals and men. "Guide me, my mentor. All these years I have ruled well…and yet this woman and her brood bring me fear as no enemy from over the sea ever has! I do not want her at Kham-El-Ard." He struck his fists against the tree trunk, showering rotten shards of bark. "By Bhel Sunface, she already has come too near. Amhar spotted her party coming across the downs, and her brat drew his bow upon him. Gods, what if he had fired…"

"It is no use pondering what might have happened," Merlin interrupted. "That leads to madness. No harm came to Amhar." He began to pace, stroking his thin grey beard, fine as mist around his narrow, age-beaten face. "We must deal with the problem at hand…what to do with your sister and her children, if they have come to stay, which is what I expect. Her sons, if raised away from her influence, may yet grow to be doughty and loyal men who may serve your cause…Remember, the blood of U'thyr your father runs in their veins as much as Morigau's. It is better they grow to manhood under our tutelage than under hers."

Ardhu stared up at Merlin, eyes darkened by tree-shadows. "But what about…him…Mordraed? He…he is already a man; is it too late."

Merlin's breath hissed between his teeth; he glanced away as crows cawed, as though laughing, in the swaying canopy of branches above. "I do not know, my friend. Only the spirits know and often they mock at us men, and try to deceive. Now come, let us go and prepare for the arrivals and make what we can of this unexpected meeting."

Mordraed stared up at the Great Hall of Kham-El-Ard, high on its crooked hill. He felt over-awed, though he forced a look of cold indifference onto his features. Nowhere in his travels with his mother had he ever seen a building like the one that rose above him, stoutly made of carved and polished oaks. The hall shone in the sun like an earthly abode of the gods; he half- expected Bhel himself to burst through the lintelled doorway and burn all of Ardhu's enemies to ash.

But that was a foolish thought. He sneered inwardly at himself for his flight of childish fancy. Bhel did not walk amongst men. And the only one who would burst from those doors would be his mother's foe…his foe…his uncle Ardhu Pendraec. His uncle…and his father…

A knot of hatred mingled with revulsion curled below his breastbone. Why should Ardhu have such an abode, when he had committed such an unnatural crime with his sister? Even when Mordraed had been deemed Loth's heir, nothing on the Ynys Yrch could have matched the opulence of Kham-El-Ard; the monuments of the Northern Isles had been the greatest structures of their time, the very source of the religion of the Stones, but they had been decaying these last five hundred years till they were mere shells of their former glory. He felt suddenly very mean, poor, and insignificant, as if he were some unworldly rustic playing at being a prince. He glared at the people gathered on the hillside, the watchful warriors and gold-decked women who had come down from Ardhu's Great Hall to greet the strangers. Deep inside, he believed they were judging him, laughing behind their hands at his ragged clothes and uncouth ways.

Shoulders tense, he began to stride up the hill, following the wide, white path rutted in the chalk, ascending the heaped ramparts with their tall palisades and rows of stakes that could impale a man to the core. Ga'haris and Gharith trotted along behind him, big-eyed, craning their necks in both delight and fear, trying to take in all the sights and sounds of this new, alien place. Agravaen was like some lumbering halfwit, jaw agape, his breath railing noisily through his open mouth. Morigau was pinched-faced, sour, pushing forward between her two protectors, Ack-olon and La'morak, who looked as if they wished they were anywhere else but here.

Someone shifted in the crowd. "Bitch!" a woman yelled, and a rock sailed toward Morigau's head. The missile missed, thudding heavily on the ground near Gharith and Ga'haris; the two little boys clutched each other's hands and started to snivel.

Mordraed cursed and snatched at his bow, but Morigau shot him a warning look through narrowed eyes. "Hold your hand. Let us give them no more cause to hate us."

They entered the Great Hall, passing under the carved lintel where the bleached skull of a Sea-Pirate gazed down from where it had been fixed by a bolt of bronze—a warning to the enemies of Prydn. Inside a mixture of shadows and flickering light made the king's abode seem surreal, a place out of a dream. The floor was denuded chalk, scraped clean, then strewn with rushes that caught animal dung and the discarded bones from the warriors' feasts. Oak pillars held up the soaring pitch of the roof and were carved with knot-work, sun-wheels and crosses. On one loomed the Guardian of the Dead with her owl-eyes and on another a series of cup-marks that told the cycle of the Moon. Incense cups belched pungent herbal smoke, while clay containers full of lit tallow swung from cross-struts across the ceiling, sending a wavering light through the hall.

At the farthest end sat the man Mordraed knew must be the Pendraec—the Terrible Head.

His father.

The King of the Great Trilithon sat on a low seat draped in bearskin, its back and arms made from many-tined antlers and the scapula of an aurochs. He wore a helm of beaten bronze and Rhon-gom, the Lightning Mace that signified his lordship, lay across his lap, its polished fossil head gleaming in the fluttering light of the tallow cups. In a sheath of horn, the long sword Caladvolc hung at his side—the miraculous blade men said had come from the subterranean lair of a water-spirit.

As Mordraed had feared, the face beneath the elaborate helm was much like his own. Darker, somewhat rougher in its set, but the marks of close kinship were there. It was a kind face, or so it seemed…but Mordraed knew from his mother that the kindness was a sham. This man, this breaker of taboos, was unworthy to sit on the throne of Prydn. He was a usurper, a fraud, damaged and evil beneath the pretence.

He felt his anger rising and forced himself to look away, to study the others hovering behind the Stone Lord's seat of Power. Immediately he saw the White Woman, standing like a cold statue in rare, bleached white linen—the one Morigau had told Mordraed he must take because she was bound to the land, her body the kingdom he must claim. His stomach knotted. She had beauty, but she was old, lines creeping beneath her sea-green eyes, and she was so pale it was as if she were made of snow. Surely she would freeze the flesh of any man who dared to touch her…

His gaze was drawn sharply back to Ardhu as the Stone Lord moved. He had half-risen from his seat and was staring at Morigau, who stood before him, a leaf before the storm. There was no kindness in his face now; it was impassive as a standing stone. "What brings you to my hall, sister?" he asked frostily. "It has been many years since I heard of you, and had hoped to keep it that way. You are a serpent with fangs of honeyed venom."

Morigau hesitated a moment, then dramatically cast herself at his feet, flinging her arms around his ankles. "My brother, my kinsman, I beg you listen to me!" she wailed. "Great evil has befallen me and mine!"

"As well it might. The spirits will not smile on the likes of you."

"Loth, my husband, is dead. I am dishonoured…cast out from Ynys Yrch with my children."

"And this has what to do with me?" Ardhu kicked her away with a swift violent motion; she fell in a heap in the soiled rushes, her black hair hanging in disarray over her eyes.

Mordraed expected her to leap up in anger, casting curses at her brother, but she remained motionless, though two spots of angry colour gleamed on her cheeks. Slowly, she inched forward until she had prostrated herself before Ardhu's seat yet again. "I ask for your help…" she said in a faint voice, "not for me but for my boys, who have lost their inheritances…who have lost what was rightfully theirs due to lies and slander."

"Lies and slander? Knowing you, those 'lies' were likely to be true." Ardhu gave a cynical laugh and glanced knowingly at the two others who stood near the high seat—a tall, amber-headed man of great presence and a sharp-faced elder leaning on a staff who wore a bird-headed talisman about his neck. Mordraed guessed the first was the Ar-moran Prince, An'kelet of the Lake, Ardhu's most loyal companion, and that the greybeard was the Merlin, High Priest of the Stones of Khor Ghor, famed throughout Prydn for his power and his machinations that could raise kings to greatness…or destroy them.

Morigau cast her arms over her face and feigned a few harsh sobs. "My story of woe is not of my doing, and I say this to you, brother—kill me for my past misdeeds towards you if it be your will, but do not toy with me. And do not harm my sons, who are innocent of any wrong-doing."

Mordraed stared at his mother, writhing like a worm amid the dog-shit and chewed pork-bones, and cringed in utter shame. What game did she play? For her sons, indeed! When had she cared about any of them, save him alone, and she had never debased herself so utterly, even in his defence?

Ardhu sat back, playing with the Lightning Mace as if deciding whether to strike her skull with it and release her spirit to the gods. "Let me see these brats of yours," he said slowly. "I will decide whether I can train them to be of use to me and to Prydn—or whether they should be drowned like runtling puppies."

Morigau sprang from the floor and promptly grabbed the collars of Gharith and Ga'haris, thrusting them at their uncle. "My two youngest. Small but sturdy. They will be malleable to your will, lord-brother, I swear it. Whether as slaves or as soldiers, they will do you proud."

Ardhu Pendraec appraised the two boys, huddled together like small brown birds sheltering from the winter gales. His face softened almost imperceptibly. "You two…Do you know what it is to obey?" he asked, leaning forward until his gaze was level with theirs.

They nodded in unison. They certainly knew the consequences of disobeying Morigau.

"And do you know what punishments can follow disobedience?"

The boys' eyes slid to their mother, then back to Ardhu. They nodded again, silent and solemn.

"When you are grown would you swear to serve me and no other, joining the Men of the Tribe and maybe my warband if you have the skill?" Ardhu glanced from Gharith to Ga'haris. "That means I would be the one to give you orders, not Morigau. That means you will not see her or listen to her, only to me, your kinsman and king."

"Yes, lord!" piped up Ga'haris, the elder of the two by a year. His brother nodded furiously. Morigau was their dam, but both were old enough to realise they had no place in her world. "We would like that very much!"

"Then so be it." Ardhu clapped his hands. "Now, Ka'hai, come and take these lads and give them pork and bread. They are as skinny as skeletons; my kinswoman obviously never saw fit to feed them properly."

Ardhu's foster brother Ka'hai, comrade at arms and ruler of the stores of the Kham-El-Ard, stepped out from the press of the Stone-Lord's men and ushered the children from the Hall, casting a backwards glare at Morigau. He hated the woman, and his dislike grew even more intense when he saw the obvious neglect of her small sons. He had a pack of children of his own from his two wives and could not imagine such cruelty.

Ardhu turned back to his sister and her remaining sons. His eyes settled on Agravaen, bull-shouldered and bull-headed, full of adolescent gaucheness and half-bridled fury. Ardhu beckoned him forward curtly. "Why do you look at me with such rage, boy? What have I done to you?"

Agravaen was silent; he looked slightly confused, as if he had expected open anger from Ardhu to which he could respond with righteous anger of his own. "I…I don't…" he stammered.

"What is your goal in this short life, boy? Do you wish to be a warrior some day?"

"I am a Man of my Tribe—my rites were held two Moons ago. Of course I wish to be a warrior—that is every right-thinking man's desire, is it not?"

Ardhu smiled ruefully. "So many think, and indeed my own wealth has come from the use of dagger and axe. But never forget, boy, it is the man that tills the land and herds the beasts that puts food into your belly. It is the beekeeper that gets honey for your mead and the grain man who pounds barley into bread and who also brews the beer. A sword's edge has a much more bitter taste than sweet beer or mead. And often that draught is lethal—the cup of death."

Agravaen stared, trying to digest and understand his uncle's words. Farmers as important as warriors? What madness did his uncle speak! "All I know is that if you let me serve you and give me axe and blade, I will try to kill every enemy that comes against you!" he blustered impetuously. He was not quite sure why such an oath fell from his lips, when he had spent years hearing how his mother hated Pendraec, called him usurper and worse, but suddenly he just wanted to get away from Morigau—from her jibes about his lack of brain and her unflattering comparisons with Mordraed. He saw something different in the eyes of his uncle, something kinder and more accepting than what he was used to…and he gravitated towards it.

"Then, go, follow your younger brothers," said Ardhu, gesturing to the door "and remember that our eyes will be upon you at all times, watching how you behave."

Agravaen stomped out of the hall, flushed, embarrassed, and elated all at once. Ka'hai smirked behind his hand at his gauche manner, but managed to hide his laughter with a cough and took the lad out to the cooking hut where his younger siblings were already tearing at slabs of meat like hungry dogs.

Mordraed was left alone, before the high seat of the Stone Lord.

Suddenly the room went quiet and still. A dog whined; the fire-pit made a harsh crackling, spitting noise. Wind skittered over the roofline like the feet of malevolent spirits.

Ardhu's face was solemn; his hand gripped the haft of Rhon-gom until the knuckles were visibly white. "You, boy…" His voice was low, almost a growl. "Come to me. Kneel before your lord."

Mordraed took a step in his direction. His face was blank, a hard slate, his eyes shuttered. Arrogance and rage oozed from him, despite his chill demeanour; the truth was in his stance, in the tautness of his back and shoulders, the defiant tilt of his chin. He did not kneel, but continued to stand, staring down at this man who was both uncle and father.

Ardhu's breath hissed between his teeth; the rage of the Dragon, the Terrible Head. With a sudden rapid motion, he flung Rhon-gom to the ground, lunged forward, and grabbed Mordraed by the hair, twisting his head back before he had a chance to react. Ardhu's right hand moved like lightning, unsheathing his dagger Carnwennan, Little White Hilt, with its worn antler pommel on which he had carved a mark for every man he had slain in his eighteen years as Stone Lord of Khor Ghor. He pressed the honed blade to Mordraed's throat, drawing a bead of blood.

Everyone in the Great Hall of Kham-El-Ard gasped in horror, and Morigau cried out, her voice as harsh as a raven's caw and full of uncustomary fear.

"Why do you defy me?" Ardhu said, his tone even but with a hint of menace.

"My brothers did not have to kneel!" Mordraed gasped, starting to struggle but mindful of the sharpened bronze at his throat.

"They are children, or scarcely more so. You are not. You are of age to serve a master and serve him well or perish for your folly. Now…kneel."

Ardhu gave Mordraed's hair a vicious twist, forcing him down upon his knees in the rushes. Dog faeces oozed near his hand, along with a chewed bone, a pile of spittle. He writhed, burning with indignation, wishing he could reach his bow and make an end of this miscreant who tormented and shamed him in front of the people of Kham-El-Ard.

"Mordraed!" He heard Morigau's voice, desperate, strained, and he saw the hem of her tattered skirt flash before his face. "Do as your uncle says! Don't be stupid, boy!" She kicked him, the blow landing on his still unhealed cheek.

Pain and the surprise of Morigau's assault shocked him into stillness. Ardhu Pendraec slowly released his hair, allowing him to rise unsteadily to his knees before staggering to his feet. "You know where we stand then, boy," Ardhu said quietly. "You have the measure of me, and I of you. But it need not be this way. If you turn from your path of anger and serve me well…there is no telling how high you might rise within my warband. I would not reject you out of hand because of who your mother is."

Mordraed stared at him; hot anger dwindled to embers but a deep, bitter resentment remained in the pit of his belly, a hard indigestible knot. He did not speak but his mind churned. *Yet you have rejected me as your son…your eldest son… You would not dare acknowledge me for fear of your own life! You will pay for that cowardice, for the lust that made me what I am…by the gods and the spirits, you will pay, 'FATHER'…*

"I do not know what arts of war they have taught you on Ynys Yrch," Ardhu continued, "but in any case you will be under the tutelage of my best warrior, the Lord An'kelet, and he will teach you both the skill of sword and spear, but also the temperance with which you must use them."

At that moment, there was a movement from the shadows of the Hall and Mordraed saw a youth step past the pale-tressed figure of Queen Fynavir who, coming suddenly to life, tried to stay him with her outstretched hand. He gently disentangled her fingers from his cloak and stepped into the ring of firelight before Ardhu's seat of power, clearing his throat. "Harsh words have been spoken today, and maybe they needed to be," he said. "But in the haste of the moment, let us not forget that these newcomers are still kindred of the king, and words of kindness can often soothe the anger in one's soul better than those sharp as arrows. I, for one, will give greeting to my cousin Mordraed."

He walked swiftly towards Mordraed, long legs carrying him smoothly, confidently as any warrior, despite the fact he wore a short child's tunic of dark, plain wool. His long red hair burned upon his shoulders, the two child braids in the forelock that would be sacrificed to the Ancestors bound with twists of ancient gold. He wore a princely amber necklace, many strings of it wound over and over around his neck; some of the chunks were so large and clear, one could see bugs and beetles trapped within their hearts, preserved and imprisoned forever in those yellow tears of the Sun.

He halted before Mordraed, appraising him with thoughtful eyes of forest-green. "I saw you the other night," he said, "coming up through the barrow-fields. I nearly shot at you and you at me. Glad am I that it did not come to a war of arrows! Well met, Mordraed son of Loth, son of my aunt Morigau. I am Amhar, son of Ardhu, son of U'thyr…your cousin."

Mordraed stared at this slender youth, still wearing a child's garb but not a child in manner or bearing. Cousin…and brother. He felt a sudden shiver, he did not know why; as if somewhere, some barrow-ghost trod on the plot of land that would one day hold his own bones. Hatred was what he should feel…this boy-man was the one acclaimed as Ardhu's heir, the one who would rule the Five Cantrevs after Pendraec was gone, the one who held the positions that would have, should have been Mordraed's. And yet….he did not hate.

Amhar slipped a friendly arm over his kinsman's shoulder. "Come, you look tired. I am sure you are hungry. I will take you for food and then to lodgings. Tomorrow I will introduce you to my father's foremost warrior, the Lord An'kelet, who will teach you the warrior's craft. I will help you here, cousin; there need be no more battling between your folk and mine."

In silence, Mordraed moved toward the door of the Hall with the red-haired Princeling talking as if they had been the best of friends for all their lives. Mordraed briefly glanced over his shoulder and saw Morigau watching him depart, her face intense, twisted, almost demonic in the sullen red light of the guttering fire-pit.

She was smiling, her lips drawn back over her canines. It was the smile of a wolf.

CHAPTER THREE-COUSINS AND BROTHERS

Mordraed dropped into a crouch and circled his opponent, lip curled in a fierce snarl. In his hand he held a fine Ar-moran dagger, its blade a deadly rapier that could pierce a man's heart and kill him instantly before he even realised the blade had touched his flesh. His deerskin cloak was wrapped around his left arm—a makeshift shield. He was stripped to the waist, and his hair pierced by a thick pin carved from a human arm-bone; he had whittled it himself one day, when loitering out amid the barrows, hoping that by robbing it from the mound and setting his own seal on it, he would bind the Old One's spirit to him, fortifying him with the Ancestor's strength and prowess.

Across from him, also armed with a fine Ar-moran blade, was the Lord An'kelet, right-hand man of Ardhu the Terrible Head. Despite encroaching age—he was over forty—he still was near as lithe and supple as the youth he fought, and his looks were still striking, as if given him from the gods. He towered over most other men in the settlement, and muscle had not turned to fat as it did in many warriors who enjoyed much pork and mead. If the amber brightness of his hair was a little faded and laughter lines crept like fine-spun spiderwebs round eyes and mouth, none held it against him or spoke of the changes with disdain. He was, after all, the King's closest companion and the protector of the Queen Fynavir—he had saved her once, years ago, from the rival chief Melwas. If any whispered behind his back, it was only about the unusual fact that he had no wife, no woman at his hearth—his life was dedicated to serving the Stone Lord and to his Lady. Such dedication seemed strange, even unseemly, to some.

Mordraed was one of them. An'kelet had been appointed his tutor in war-arts, and he hated him nearly as much as he hated his uncle-father. Ardhu treated Mordraed well enough, a kind word of praise here and there but An'kelet…Mordraed fancied he looked down on him as if he were cow-dung stuck to the sole of his shoe. His did not contemplate for one moment that An'kelet hardly recognised him as anything at all; he was just a duty to be attended to on a daily basis.

"Come on, Mordraed…" An'kelet's lightly accented voice was sharp with irritation. "You can do better than this—I have seen you! You are lazy, that's what's wrong with you—too much time drinking and gazing at your pretty reflection in the river!"

Mordraed's usual simmering rage ignited and he lunged forward, dagger swinging in a shining arc. "You dare to criticise me, you who have no woman, but dote on the King's wife…"

The next moment he was down on his back with a hard thud, his head banging off the ground. An'kelet was kneeling over him, his blade Arondyt at his neck. "Beware of what comes out of your mouth, Mordraed, lest it bring you to ruin. And control that temper, boy, or you'll not live long enough to be a warrior of Ardhu's clan."

"Let me have my bow!" Mordraed panted, struggling to be free of An'kelet's hold. "Then you will see who is a warrior!"

"Enough of this folly!" An'kelet sheathed Arondyt, slamming the long Ar-moran dagger into its scabbard of horn. He sprang away from his floored opponent, brushing dirt off his long woven tunic with its amber buttons surmounted by golden sun-crosses. "I tire of this sparring…with word and otherwise. Go, and come back when you want to learn and not act like an angry bee!"

He stalked across the dun without a backward glance and Mordraed clambered to his feet, muddy and still angry. He was about to go after An'kelet, casting caution to the wind in his vain attempt to save face, when Amhar son of Ardhu, who had been watching the training within a crowd of half-grown lads, strode briskly to his side and placed a hand on his arm. "Kinsman, be still, fighting like this ill becomes warriors of Kham-El-Ard. We are all Ardhu's men; we must hold together and work out any quarrels between each other with cool heads and wise counsel."

"What do you know?" Mordraed said bitterly. "You are not even a Man of Ardhu's band yet… You are still deemed a boy, a child…"

He shut his mouth with a snap as Amhar gave him a reproachful look and bowed his head. No, he must use caution; it would not do well to insult this boy, his rival…his brother. Amhar was one of the few who did not treat him with suspicion in the high camp upon the Crooked Hill, and that could be useful in the end. Most useful.

"Forgive me," he murmured, though the words of apology came hard. He leaned over and picked up his discarded tunic and his bow. "I come from the North when men do not have gentle tongues. Let us go from this place for a while, I need to wash the dirt from me."

The two youths wandered down to a spot along the banks of Abona where the river widened just before it reached the great ford. Women were beating clothes on rocks in the current, and a cattleman drove a brace of cows across the water, scoring the unruly beasts with a switch as they rolled their eyes and lowed unhappily. Mordraed plunged into the deepest part of the swell, scrubbing at his bruised and dustied skin with a handful of river grit while the youngest washer-maidens giggled and eyed him with interest until their mothers slapped them and told them to look to their tasks and not to the newcomer.

Amhar sat on the bank, dangling his legs amidst the weeds. "Would you teach me some of your warrior-arts?" he asked at length. "The bow…I am good with a bow, but I know that you are even better, a true master despite your youth. Or…even the dagger…or war hammer."

Mordraed paused, pushing his wet black hair back from his high forehead. He stared at his young kinsman. Oh by the gods what disaster he could wreak on Ardhu's kingdom if he were to grant the young princeling's wishes! His mother would be dancing with glee if she heard Amhar speak to him so; the foolish boy was almost begging to be killed. And yet…and yet…

"It is really not my place," Mordraed said smoothly, gliding up to the bank, the water breaking into bright ripples about him. Caught in the sunlight, he looked like a young water-god risen from Abona's beds, the water-weeds snaggled in his locks, streaming down his golden skin. Across the ford the washer-maidens sighed, except for the few who found him strangely unsettling, as if he was one of the Everliving Ones from the Land of Youth— beautiful but cold and amoral. "You are still deemed a child, ridiculous as that seems, and I would not want to anger my uncle Ardhu the Terrible Head."

Amhar cast down his eyes and sighed. Ever since Mordraed and his brothers had arrived at Kham-El-Ard, he had felt restive and unsettled for the first time. He had begun to desire to be like others of his age, and take his place amongst the tribe, his father bestowing him with his first dagger and axe. He was a king's son, yet as a child he had fewer rights than the lowest of Ardhu's men. If he died on the morrow he would not even have his own barrow; he would be cremated beside Abona and his burnt bones placed into an urn, which would then be inserted into the side of one of the kingly mounds that dotted Moy Mor, Great Plain.

Mordraed forced a smile; his eyes were like hard darts, belying the smile, but the other youth did not notice. "Look, I see that you are sorrowful. I would not have that so, cousin." He leaned over, whispering in his ear: "If I promise to give you a lesson in arms, will you do something for me in return?"

Amhar nodded. "What do you wish? If it is within my power, I will give it to you."

"Take me to Khor Ghor, the great temple that lies so near to Kham-El-Ard and yet seems so far from us, like a place within a dream. Four months have I dwelt in the Lord Ardhu's camp, and never seen one of its famous stones! I have heard so much of its grandeur, I want to see it and worship my Ancestors, but I am deemed unworthy by uncle…"

"It is not that…" Amhar interrupted. He looked unhappy, troubled. "No one goes to Khor Ghor, unless the day is right. At the feast days the Merlin and the priests of Deroweth make offeringd there, and also when the Moon goes dark and when the Moon falls still. At high summer when the cuckoo calls and at midwinter when Bhel Sunface dies on the great Altar then not only do the priests go to the Stones, but ordinary men too—to marvel and to worship. But at all other times only the warrior-priests who guard the sanctuary and the ghosts of the Ancestors dwell within its mighty arches."

"But you have been there, have you not?" Mordraed pried. He had heard rumours of the boy's reputation for dwelling half within the realm of Otherness, of how he ran over the Great Plain without fear of the Unseelie, even to the great pale stripe of the Spirit-Path with its slumped chalk banks and crumbling barrow terminal marking the lands of Life and Death.

Amhar shuffled his feet uneasily. "Yes…but…"

"Then surely you can show me, cousin." Mordraed's strong hand fell on Amhar's arm. "We will be quick in what we do and not linger, and if any trouble comes of it, I promise that I, as a Man of the Tribe, shall take the blame, not you."

Mordraed stepped out of the river, shaking water from his hair, and wiped himself dry with a handful of leaves before donning his dark woollen tunic. He felt in his belt for his dagger as, with the young prince at his side, they followed the banks of the winding river toward the sacred stone circle on the Great Plain.

They came to Khor Ghor by the paths that crossed the great Barrowdown of the Kings, near the burial places of the earliest rulers of the Great Trilithon and the West, priest-kings and Tin-Lords of a bygone time when even the mossy and weather-lashed stones were fresh and new. On Feast-days and solstices the Sacred Avenue was used, running up from the Old Henge by Abona to the enormous mounds of the Seven Kings and away through the valley toward the monument, but Amhar had counselled against using such an obvious route, despite that its parallel banks offered protection from the malignant supernatural forces that wandered through those Deadlands. It would be too open to the eyes of the warrior-priests who prowled the area, bows in hand, watching for any who dared to break the sanctity of the monument.

Mordraed did not mind walking outside the protective banks. Other things he feared more than dead men, or so he thought—the dishonour of never regaining his promised birthright as a chief over men, and earning Morigau's displeasure, of having her behind him like a whip, striking him with her tongue and maybe even with weapons if he did not fulfil her desires. He grimaced as he thought of her. After Ardhu had first accepted him and his brothers into Kham-El-Ard, he had fully expected that Morigau would be sent into exile, with a death-ban on her. But Ardhu Pendraec was too clever to allow that. He wanted to keep her in his sights. However, he would not allow her to reside in Kham-El-Ard walls, so he had ordered her instead to live in the valley, near the House of the Ladies of the Lake, where his other sister, Mhor-gan of the Korrig-han, and the priestess Nin-Aeifa could watch her activities.

Mordraed had seen her sometimes on the hillside, dark-hooded, sometimes feathered like the scald-crow, watching him with her hot, deep eyes. He knew what she wanted, knew what she expected him to do. And he would do it; by the Ancestors, he would take what was his! And yet…he glanced at the red-haired youth beside him, guileless, his face innocent, almost like an idiot's, though Mordraed was well aware Amhar was no idiot. He was like Mordraed's youngest brothers, still deemed a child by the reckoning of the people. It was

210

dishonourable to slay a child, and warriors might not follow a ruler they thought dishonourable…

He made a frustrated noise and gripped the hilt of his dagger till its pommel bit into his palm. Amhar glanced over at him. "Are you all right, cousin Mordraed? We do not have to continue if you have changed your mind."

"I have not changed my mind." Mordraed stared away into the red-gold light of late afternoon, unable to look his kinsman in the face, fearful that Amhar might read the truth in his own eyes.

Mother will be proud of me…he thought, fingering his blade. Why he should care? He did not know but he did; and he cared for Mordraed, and the status of the bloodline he shared with many kings, as much as he cared for Morigau's wishes.

Up ahead he saw the great cluster of barrows on the South-Western side of the Stones strung out along the skyline. Mist was curling up from the cup of the valley as the Sun slipped down towards His rest and a chill crept into the air. The sky was streaked with fire and birds of prey soared shrieking overhead, seeking for mice and other prey amidst the clustered tumuli, their white chalk summits glowing golden as the long-buried grave-goods interred within.

Despite himself, his heart began to thud. He glanced sideways at Amhar, but the boy seemed totally devoid of fear; indeed, he seemed almost enraptured by the sight of the stones. He strode on ahead unaware of Mordraed's slowing footfall, his long slender legs parting the waving grasses. His gaze was firmly fixed ahead. "The priests, they go to meet the night guards up by the King barrows," he said. "We should have time…just a little time."

The two youths passed the last royal mound with its overgrown ditch and berm, and soon came upon the bank that ringed Khor Ghor, Tomb of Hopes, Throne of Kings…and Ardhu Pendraec's round circle where he gathered his men in the presence of the Ancestors to hold counsel for the good of Prydn. Across the white barricade of the ditch, not high enough to hold out beasts or men but instead holding in the powerful entities of air and sky and grave-mound, the grey Stones of Khor Ghor glimmered in the dusk, magic sentinels coloured with the dwindling light, first greenish, now rose-pink, now warm gold, the hues of the Sun, or nature, of Time itself. Crows chattered and squabbled, soaring in and out of the trilithons, those great mouths that yawned into the gloom like the mouths of long barrows, inhaling the cold mist of the Plain, exhaling ghosts into the growing dusk.

Mordraed paused, sudden waves of cold fear passing over him. What he had meant to do here suddenly seemed too great a thing. No matter what Morigau expected, no matter what he desired for himself…

"Come on, cousin!" Amhar was beckoning him forward. "If you are still up for it! We haven't much time!"

The slight challenge in the boy's voice hardened Mordraed's resolve. "I will see this place," he said tightly and he stepped across the ditch and ran toward the heart of the sanctuary, Amhar at his heels.

Inside the Stones, night was gathering. Mordraed stood in the centre of the circle, staring up, awed despite his efforts to feel nothing but contempt for this structure used by his father and his mentor, the Merlin, that axe-face old man whose voice was as harsh as the caws of the crows overhead. The five trilithons of the great crescent, each one representing a Cantrev of the West, huddled in on him, looming like unhappy giants; he felt suddenly smothered, realising for the first time how small and cramped it was inside Khor Ghor, despite the enormous size of the sarsen stones. The smaller bluestones crowded in even closer, eight times a man's set of ten fingers, looking like an army of people in the eerie twilight, frowning watchers, Ancestors of old sleeping in stone—for now.

"Can you feel them, cousin?" Amhar's voice was a respectful whisper. "The Old Ones? They are all around us. This circle is the beginning and ending of all things…"

Breath hissed through Mordraed's teeth. He wanted an ending here above all. His hand clutched his dagger hilt, slimy with cold sweat. He half pulled it from its deerskin sheath, careful to make no sound; but it was as if something, someone pulled on his arm, forcing his fingers to slide away… The Old Ones know what my mother wants me to do here! he thought wildly. They try to stop me!

Primal terror flooded him, despite his earlier confidence that no spirit would bring him fear. He fought the panic but it grew worse; shivers coursed down his body and his teeth chattered. The thought of the unseen and undead from the Not-World all around him, oozing up from the ground, from the pits in the bank, from the ditch, from the very Stones themselves chilled him, revolted him… How he hated this place, its stillness, its silence, the awful weight of years that seemed to deaden the very air within the inner sanctum. If ever he should become the king his mother dreamed of, he would slight this frowning, almost accusing monument…By the Moon Mother he would throw these Stones down and build anew, and drive these skulking, hated Ancestors away!

"Mordraed, are you all right?" Amhar shook him back to reality. The lad was standing at his side, his hair a dull dim red like the faded sunset. Hair the hue of old blood.

Mordraed shook his head to clear it, to sweep away images of dead faces, of eyeholes black with reproach. He had a duty; he must do what he knew to be right…for Morigau, and for his own future. "Cousin, this temple amazes me. Before we leave, come closer and show me the features that I must gaze upon and worship. I know little of what is here, being but a rude man of the North."

Amhar drew closer, trusting. He was mere inches away from Mordraed. He gestured up at the immense trilithons, naming each in turn. "That is Throne of Kings, where the true chief must swear to the Land upon the Sacred Sword-in-the-Stone. That is the Arch of the Eastern Sky, and that the House of the North Wind…and the one in the far West is dedicated to the Guardian, who protects our dead Ancestors. The tallest, Mordraed, is the Door into Winter, Portal-of-Ghosts, where Lord Bhel gives himself up above the Altar."

"What a noble sacrifice he makes each year…" Mordraed's voice was a low, dry hiss, vaguely tremulous. And so too will you…but only once… He put what he hoped was a brotherly arm around Amhar's shoulders, suddenly drawing him close against him. So close and tight he could not break free.

Amhar looked surprised and slightly confused.

Mordraed's knife, unseen in the gloom, slipped out of its sheath…

At that moment, the blaring of a horn was borne into the ancient circle, carried on the rising breeze. Its sound bounced around the megalithic rings, dull, ominous, and eerie. "That horn!" Amhar cried "Do you hear it?" He jerked free of Mordraed's slackening grip and ran to the edge of the Stones.

Mordraed stood panting in the centre of the place he hated, his plan in tatters and the enormity of what he had nearly done, what he had failed to do, washing over him like a dark, sucking tide.

A second later the fateful horn blared again, louder this time and clearer. Amhar turned to Mordraed, his face guileless; obviously, he did not realise how close to the Ancestors he had come. "Did you hear the horn, Mordraed? We must go with haste! That is a summons to all men of Kham-El-Ard. Something of great import has happened at my father's dun!"

Without another glance at his kinsman, he dashed out into the twilight, leaping over the ditch and away across the mist-bound rises and burial mounds. Mordraed stood alone for a moment inside the Stones, still shocked by the turn of events. The pillars of the ring seemed even darker now, almost angry; he imagined glowering faces, spiteful eyes, in their sides. This place meant him ill; he sensed it with every fibre of his being. Slamming his dagger home into its sheath, he ran like the wind after the cousin he had nearly killed, and the rising breeze snickered mockingly in the gaunt dark archways behind him.

CHAPTER FOUR—THE CART OF DEATH

The cart stood within the central enclosure at Kham-El-Ard, a hefty wooden wain with great round disc-wheels of solid oak. A dispirited pair of oxen was bound to it, their flanks grey and mud-splattered and ribs thrusting through shrivelled skin.

They looked half-dead, flies gathering round their slitted eyes, buzzing noisily as they feasted on oozing encrustations. But they did not look as foul as the man perched in the back, hunched and hooded, the gaunt shell of his body furled in a ragged skin that had patches gnawed out of it and sent out a reek of rotten flesh. Maggots fell from its folds, dripping down onto the burden borne by the strange cart...and that burden was most dreadful of all, worse than the staggering oxen or the emaciated carter.

The wain was filled with the dead, unbarrowed and unprepared for their journey into the Otherworld. Bundled together like piles of mouldering sticks, they sprawled on the bottom of the cart, legs tangled with arms, ribs mixed with finger-bones, skulls and pelvises rolling and rattling as the oxen stamped in their traces.

Around the cart the women of Kham-El-Ard began to keen, throwing their shawls over their faces to hide their eyes from such a hideous sight, which might blight their wombs to barrenness or mark the unborn with abnormalities. The warriors of Ardhu cried out in anger, and blades were raised and axes hefted; starting a war-chant, they circled the ominous carter with his burden of the dead, all the while blowing on the great bronze-bound horns that would summon all men to Kham-El-Ard in time of strife.

Leaving the comforts of his Hall at the first blasts of the horn, Ardhu Pendraec hurried toward the gate of the dun, where he could see people milling and hear the lamentations of the fearful women. An'kelet strode at his side, clutching his great barbed spear, the Balugaisa. The extended spines that could easily rip a man's guts from his body glinted wickedly in the light of the torches that had sprung into life all over the great fort on the crooked hill.

Ardhu felt uneasy. Years had passed without incident of note; he had fought off the odd sea-raider, trounced pugnacious chiefs who had challenged his authority, and had sat in judgement on disputes over stolen land, cattle and women, and meted out punishment for murder or blood-feud. Yet this one wraith-like man, in his unwholesome cart of death, filled him with more trepidation than a hundred bellowing, boasting warriors with sharpened axes, and he was not sure why.

Perhaps it was because he had dreamed so ill these many months, turning in restless sleep—dreamed of plague and famine, of Moons that ran red with blood and a Sun that failed. Of crops that stagnated in fields dry as dust, and rivers that shrank to leave foetid, muddy holes. He had even seen, in darkest nightmare, a circle like Khor Ghor, but not made of stones—it was wrought of human bones, a cage of ribs, a trap of death, with leg-bones for lintels, and skulls perched grinning above the entrance...

"Who are you and why do you come unbidden to Kham-El-Ard, bringing the naked dead with you?" he asked sternly, coming to a halt before the wretched cart. He had dressed in his old bearskin cloak, the preserved head moth-eaten and bare after many years of use, and he carried in his hand the sceptre Rhon-gom, so that this unwholesome stranger might know whom it was he dealt with.

The creature in the cart moved forward jerkily, motions resembling a spider dangling on a thread. "I am called Pelahan, and I hail from the East, O High King of Prydn," he rasped. "From the realm of the Maimed King, An-fortas, I come to beg for aid, for our land is dying—men call it the Wasteland and do not cross its borders. Crops fail, beasts die, and men starve. An-fortas himself was once a mighty and just chief and our realm a fair and fertile garden, but he has taken a wound that has crippled him so that he can be no true king and so the land fails and all in it."

Standing at Ardhu's shoulder, An'kelet shifted uneasily. "My friend, I beg you not listen to this ill-starred one. As tragic as his plight might be, what have we to do with those far lands and the sickness that assails it? What help could we give? We are warriors, not magic men."

Ardhu sighed and his fingers caressed the fossil head of Rhon-gom. "It is true…but men call me the King of all kings in Prydn. The protector. What would they call me if I refused to go? I have never baulked from settling disputes or putting down rebels when needed."

"But this is different," An'kelet insisted. "No one has ever come to Kham-El-Ard bearing such a grim burden, and looking half of the Otherworld yet begging for our aid."

The one called Pelahan cocked his head on one side and thrust back his voluminous hood, revealing a skull-like visage—his nose was gone, devoured by some flesh-eating disease, leaving only a jutting nub; and half his grey cheek had collapsed into his mouth, showing a row of bright white teeth through ragged flesh. The village women shied away, and their terrified wailing, which had dwindled when Ardhu appeared, started up in earnest. "If you do not come, the pestilence will spread," said Pelahan. "From one Cantrev to the other. Have you not noticed changes already, Chief Ardhu? A longer winter, darker nights, summers where the rains fall and the sun seldom shines? Have you not had rivers break their banks and wash villages away, and crops and children that have not thrived? Have your cows not calved dead things and the sows eaten their own sickly farrow? Tell me true that you have not seen these things!"

Ardhu's face paled beneath his tan. The last few years had seen poor crops and rain, endless grey skies that brooded like his dark nighttime dreams. On the last feast of Bhel there had been no glorious Sunset; the snow had fallen so heavily and the night had been so dismal that some believed Bhel was truly dead and would never rise again. And in the summer past, at Midsummer, the rain had fallen in sullen sheets until there were puddles circling the feet of all the stones in Khor Ghor, reflecting the worried faces of the Merlin and his priests. Word had come from the moors of the far West that the rain had been so severe many farms had been washed away, and the soil was ruined forever for the planting of crops. People began to abandon what had once been rich, fertile uplands, and headed for the valleys and coasts, leaving settlements, stone rows and temples to decay in the incessant rain.

Pelahan noticed Ardhu's expression and smirked, his teeth rigid as standing stones through curtains of livid flesh. "I knew it had come here too."

An'kelet tossed his head angrily. "Still, what has it to do with Ardhu? There have always been bad years; that is the way of things!"

"But the King is the land, and the land is the King," Pelahan whispered. "One fails, so does the other. This blight must be dealt with; otherwise, it will not be just the Maimed King's domain that is the Wasteland, but all of Prydn. And when the Land is weak, and under a cloud of shadow, then, too, will the enemies from the coasts come in their darting ships, like serpents of the seas."

"Ardhu, I do not like this wheedling, ill-visaged creature," said An'kelet. "Send him forth and let us burn the evil burden he drags with him!"

Ardhu Pendraec held up Rhon-gom and shook his head. "Peace, my brother. We cannot do that, as much as my heart tells me to. We must hold counsel with the Merlin at Khor Ghor; we must call the men to join in the Round and decide the best course of action. For all I shudder at the sight of this stranger, I fear there may be truth in his words. I have grown a better judge of men as my years have increased and do not feel that he means us harm, unsavoury though his aspect may be."

An'kelet sighed and clutched the Balugaisa tighter in his fist. "It will be as you say, lord. You are the Stone Lord, chief of chiefs of Prydn."

The men of Ardhu's warband gathered in the Stones the next day, his most loyal men through the long years. Foremost amongst them — Hwalchmai, still youthful and handsome; Ka'hai with his face creased in its usual concerned expression; Bohrs who was round as a barrel but strong as an ox; horse-maned Per-Adur whose haughty mien had long been tempered; Betu'or the ever-faithful, quiet and serious; the twins Ba-lin and Bal-ahn, still as one soul even marrying sisters so alike were they in temperament. Walking at the right-hand of his chief and friend Ardhu, An'kelet led them, an imposing figure wearing a gold headband and a long. dyed wool tunic with toggles of jet bound in copper wire.

Ardhu himself carried his shield Wyngurthachar, the Face of Evening, and wore his bronze helm that blazed like the Sun amidst the sombre stones. The breastplate of Heaven gleamed on his leather jerkin amidst its patterning of conical golden studs, and from his shoulders streamed a cloak wrought of a rare sky-blue cloth imported from far beyond the Isles, beyond even the Narrow Sea and the Middle Lands where Rhin and Rhon flowed, beckoning traders and adventurers—a gift of remembrance and thanks from Prince Palomides of the distant isle of Delos, who Ardhu had freed from slavery in his first battle by the Glein.

Merlin stood in the heart of the circle, staff in hand. He looked not only old but weary, as if he seldom slept, and many in the company noted that his staff was not solely for use in his magics, but needed for support. The hands clutching the worn ash-wood were gnarled and rimed with bumps—the painful, inflammatory bone-bend that afflicted most of the tribesfolk as they aged.

"My men, I call you, after many years, to accompany me on a quest." Ardhu took a deep breath. "If it is not considered too ill-starred by the mighty Merlin." He glanced towards his ancient mentor, silent in the shadow of the Stone of Adoration. "It is not, I deem, a quest of arms, but one of strangeness—evil magic might be afoot in lands beyond Kham-El-Ard. You have all seen the foul wain that has been driven to our gates, and its accursed master, who comes from a place in the East known as the Wasteland."

The men murmured; some were restless, especially the younger ones that were relatively new to the warband. They had heard of the deeds of years gone by—the Thirteen battles of Ardhu, beginning by the river Glein and ending under the bleak shadow of Mineth Beddun, the mountain of Graves, where he had shaved the beard of the evil giant Rhyttah and defeated T'orc, the otherworldly boar. They longed to do high deeds themselves but magic was something to be avoided. That realm was for the shaman, the priests and priestesses, the wisemen and women, even, to a lesser extent, the singers-of-songs. It was not for doughty men whose trust was in good bronze, well-shaped stone, and barbed arrows.

Merlin emerged from the long shadow of the greenish block that was the heart of Khor Ghor. His eyes were black beads rimmed with red; he had been consuming many herbs and mushrooms that would bring him into communion with the spirit world. In his shaking hand, he held up his seeing stone of quartz. "Yes, it is time for men to journey across Prydn and even beyond, finding that which all men seek to stave off the blight that comes to our lands."

"And what blight is that?" puffed Bohrs, folding huge arms covered in twisted tattoos. He had grown nearly as wide as he was tall in his older years, his beard hanging down to his waist and plaited into the woven girdle that encompassed his large belly. "Let me know who threatens the great peace brought by the Lord Ardhu and I will go forth and strike his head with my axe, the Foe-Smiter!" He fingered the large dolerite axe, its haft tied with bright strips of beaded wool, which hung at his side.

"It is not men…at least not yet." Merlin's eyes were hooded. "Though they will come in the end, sniffing at our doors like hungry wolves. It is time itself that brings us ill, as time always does…an end to all things both fair and foul. However, we can attempt to hold evil at bay for a while."

"How? We cannot turn back time," said An'kelet solemnly from his position beside his lord. "Every man grows old be he chief or farmer. The only ones who never age further are the blessed dead."

"To fall before the wrath of time is indeed the doom of men," continued Merlin. "But it must not happen before we can ensure the endurance of the peace that Ardhu has wrought. Many years of prosperity have we enjoyed, and if it is to remain so down the long ages, we must buy some more time, but change is coming, I know that, I have seen it…" He stumbled suddenly, eyes rolling, sweat glossing his brow. He leaned against a dark, spotted bluestone, hugging it like a brother. "The Dark Moon…comes…a time of betrayal, many betrayals. The cycle of Lady Moon reaches its end, but it is also the termination of a cycle of three, a holy number of fifty-six years mirrored in the shaft-pits around Khor Ghor where the most blessed and ancient Ancestors lie, looking to the Moon. Change is coming. Death is coming. The Wasteland will spread from east to west, but the Chalice of Gold will bring it back…for a while. The lamb will fall to the serpent's venom and men will sorrow, but his sacrifice will reap the weakness in our mightiest foes."

Merlin coughed and pitched forward, hand clutching his throat, the power of his prophecy sapping his strength. Saliva that was black from the herbs he had been chewing bubbled on his lips; his limbs shook as if with ague. Froth appeared at the corners of his mouth.

"Hwalchmai, Per-Adur!" Ardhu raced to the old man, catching him as he reeled and went to fall. "He is ill; this affliction assails him often these days…he is so old now, older than most men ever live… the strain of his knowledge is too much, the spirits seek to take him for theirs. You have healing arts, learned in these years of peace; use them now and then let us get him to Deroweth where priest-healers that are even more skilled will tend him. Once he is settled, we will heed his words and ride for the Wasteland and whatever fate awaits us."

Hwalchmai and Per-Adur, both of whom had learned healing skills at Merlin's own hearth, set about making the old man comfortable, turning him on his side and taking care he did not choke on his own tongue. A crude bier was made from twined skin cloaks, and the company of Ardhu Pendraec bore the ailing shaman to the sacred holding of Deroweth, with its timber cult houses, circular enclosure and metalled pathway that led to the flowing waters of the Holy River, Abona. The temple Woodenheart stood nigh to the side of the Great Henge, ringed by a shallow bank and ditch of its own, a forest of leafless trees guarded by several grey stones like warning fingers.

Ardhu was struck by the silence of the place as he entered the settlement bearing Merlin's limp form on its makeshift bier. Grass sprouted on top of the bank of the henge, marring its stark bone-whiteness, and thin beards of moss dangled from the lintels of Woodenheart, rustling as the chill wind blew. Some of the houses clustered around the site were falling into ruin, uninhabitable, their roofs patched with holes. Burial places had appeared on the periphery, ominous and oppressive, the dead encroaching on the living.

Ardhu shivered, and it was not just from the bite of the northeasterly wind. When had this decline begun? He could hardly remember. The festivals of his youth had seen so bright and vibrant…but now not so many came at Midwinter to feast on the young pigs and greet the re-born disc of Bhel Sunface. Men were busy in their own lands—settlements and farming had spread; fewer men herded, and fewer folk wanted to make the long journey on foot from across the Five Cantrevs and beyond.

Merlin was carried to his hut, the dwelling of the High Priest, which was situated on a slope that gave it prominence above the other houses. Two smaller thatched huts stood beside it, where food was cooked to feed the master of the central home. A semi-circular ditch open at the front ran around the dwelling, and a stout trilithon of wood reared up before the door, symbol of the power of its inhabitant.

Seeing Ardhu and the burden he carried brought the priests of Deroweth running from their cult-houses, pale with concern, chanting and burning incense in rounded cups to chase bad spirits away. The mightiest among them laid Merlin down within his hut, laving his face with water that had been poured over the holy ancestor-stones of Khor Ghor and then saved in dark pottery bowls that had been plugged by resins.

After what seemed a long while, the old man coughed and opened bleary eyes. He spat on the floor and struggled to sit up. "What are you all staring at?" he snapped, glaring at Ardhu who crouched beside his pallet, watching him. "What is this…a festival? Get you gone, Ardhu, and seek the Wasteland before its plague and famine comes to our door."

"So you will live then, Merlin." The corner of Ardhu's mouth twitching upwards, though his tone remained serious. "You will live to rebuke me one more day!"

"If I do not live to kick you into action, then my spirit will surely chase you down the long ages," rasped Merlin, eyes narrowing. "Now go!"

The wind whispered in the eves of Kham-El-Ard as Ardhu prepared to leave, ordering serving-men to pack food and skins and clean the edges of his weapons, Caladvolc and Carnwennan. Its sad soughing came hard to his ears, bringing memories of youthful days and happier times before the ravages of age and the wear of life had started taking toll on most of those he loved well. He felt his own back spasm, low in the lumbar spine, and bit back a rueful groan. Weakness had to be hidden even from his own loyal band. There was always someone who might, sensing weakness, turn upon him like a wolf…

"We do not all need to go to the Wasteland," he announced to his gathered warriors, who sat in a circle in the Hall, discussing all that had happened that day. "A few blades should be enough; I do not think this will be a battle of arms."

Bohrs harrumphed and folded his arms over his great girth. "No arms? Then what? Sorcery? That needs more swords, Ardhu, not fewer."

Ardhu shook his head emphatically. "No. It will not be that kind of fight. If it is a fight at all." His gaze raked over his men, taking in the glint of silver in hair and beards, the lines drawn on once youthful faces. There were new, younger men in the band of course, replacing those who died or were maimed in accident or conflict, but could they be wholly trusted, as he trusted his original band? He did not know; their loyalty hadnever been teated.

"Hwalchmai." He glanced at his cousin, who had defeated and taken the head of the fearsome Green Man of Lud's Hole. "Will you come?"

Hwalchmai rubbed his chin in thought, then nodded slowly. He had gone off adventuring on his own each spring and returned in the autumn for near on ten Sun-turnings, ever since his wife Rhagnell had died in childbirth. It was as if he could not abide to stay long at Kham-El-Ard with the bitter memories of Rhagnell, who was taken, along with her infant, near the Summer Solstice, although women loved his still-handsome face, and he had many lovers and children throughout the western villages.

"And you Bohrs?" Ardhu nodded toward the big man. "You may not have need to use your axe in this quest, my doughty friend, but I would gladly have it ready for service should the need arise."

"I am pleased at the thought of that, lord." A grin split Bohrs' face. "By the Everlasting Sky, I have been idle too long! I need to shift some of this…" He slapped his belly with his big thick hands, making his paunch shake and the younger members of the household laugh.

Hearing the laughter, Ardhu smiled ruefully. Twenty years ago no one would have dared laugh at Bohrs, a warrior as fierce as the wild boar of the woods. Now, to them, he was just fat, blustering Bohrs, a figure of fun to the upcoming warriors of the West who were not old enough to have known his reputation first-hand. Time was the doom of men; turning firm muscle to jelly and strong hands to quavering sticks, and making high deeds recede into the stuff of legend…

Turning from Bohrs, Ardhu nodded toward Per-Adur. "And you my friend…Over recent years your fame has grown not as a warrior, but as a healer. Where once your hand brought death, now it brings life. If this Maimed King needs one to attend to his wounded flesh, I deem that man should be you."

Per-Adur bowed. "I am grateful. I would like one last quest in foreign lands. I would heal this foreign king, but also, if need came, I would fight for you, as before."

"And what of me, Ardhu…lord?" An'kelet cleared his throat; his voice was strange, low and oddly reticent. "Do you require my presence on this journey?"

Ardhu gazed at his right-hand man, standing a head taller than most of the other warriors, still golden-bronze as in his youth but dimmed slightly, a hazy dusty bronze like the sun fading into the West at the end of a long, hot summer's day. An'kelet was staring at the ground, avoiding Ardhu's gaze. *He does not want to come with me!* Ardhu thought with a flash of surprised annoyance. He had imagined they would ride out together, as in the days of their youth.

"I would not force you," he said, somewhat coldly. "There are others who would be glad to join me."

An'kelet glanced up and Ardhu was surprised, again, to see that he looked relieved, almost glad. "Ardhu, friend, I give you my thanks. I have no stomach for riding out on such journeys. Not anymore. I will stay at Kham-El-Ard and guard your holdings…and your Queen." He glanced over his shoulder at the silent white figure of Fynavir, who went around the great hall with her women refilling the men's drinking beakers when they were empty. She looked up, as if suddenly aware of his attention, and blushed. Quickly she averted her face, bowing her head so that her thick braid of milk-pale hair swung in front of her visage and hid her flaming cheeks.

She was not swift enough. Ardhu, standing face to face with An'kelet, missed her expression; his friend's broad shoulder blocked his view. However, in the shadows, ignored as the newcomer not yet initiated as a member of the warband, Mordraed saw.

Saw and understood.

He had seen such furtive glances before, passed between Morigau and her many lovers while she still dwelt in the hut of her husband, Loth of Ynys Yrch.

The White Woman was cuckolding his father, the great and mighty Pendraec, the Stone Lord, king of the West. With his chief warrior, no less, the man he trusted above all.

Mordraed could have laughed out loud.

But he did not.

It was a secret he needed to keep…for a while.

Pushing a path through the assembled warriors, he raced out into the growing dusk. Dogs barked at him and women muttered darkly as he stormed through the busy heart of the dun, bowling over small children and sending squawking chickens flapping into the air. He did not care. Like a man possessed, he climbed onto the ramparts of Kham-El-Ard, where newly lit torches flickered in the dusk and danced along them. In the eastern sky the moon was rising, its sickly death-light bathing his face and hair, bleaching it of colour, making him a man white

219

as chalk, white as Death, born of the Old Woman in the Moon with her cruel sickle nose. "Soon, Mother!" he breathed to the rising crescent, holding up his arms to the pallid glow in the sky. "Soon the Sun shall lose its supremacy, and the Moon—and Mordraed son of Ardhu—shall rule over Prydn in its place."

.

CHAPTER: HAWK OF SUMMER

Ardhu awoke in the pre-dawn dark beneath the mound of furs in his cordoned-off bed-space at the rear of Kham-El-Ard's Great Hall. Gasping, he sat upright, trying to focus in the dark. The dream again...the cage of Bones. Death upon the land. A cup of gold. A cup of death...a cup of life. He shuddered; he would not sleep again tonight. The Otherworld was trying to intrude upon his life, through his dreams; he would not let malicious spirits gain any purchase.

Glancing over, he saw Fynavir lying curled in foetal position, like a corpse in a barrow, her breath a light rasp as she slept. She had shown little emotion when he had announced that he was leaving on a great Imram, a Journey, but he had expected no more. It had been long since things had been right between them, even before he defeated T'orc the Boar beneath the thundery peak of Mount Beddun when he was but a callow youth. For a while, when Amhar was born and there was much rejoicing in the tribe, a new warmth had grown between them, but over the intervening years it had faded again. She was quiet and dutiful, and men had not forgotten that she was the daughter of a Great Queen and, it was rumoured, a goddess of Sovereignty, so he would never do her any dishonour, for a great King must have a special Queen, for it was women who were bound with the earth that men walked upon...

But love...he smiled bitterly in the warm fuggy darkness...That was long gone, if it had ever existed in more than youthful fantasies. Gods, the hotheaded foolishness that had driven him to ask Chief Ludegran for her when he had known her all of one night! How green and impetuous he had been, a moonstruck boy! No wonder Merlin had been enraged! Beauty and status was not everything, nor was a dowry of gold and cattle...that was a lesson learned with age.

Leaning over, he took Fynavir's hand and raised it gently to his lips as he had not done for many Moons. He had to wake her, speak with her. An'kelet would not journey with him to An-fortas's domain, but another companion would take the long road to the Wastelands in the East. Fynavir would not be happy to hear his news, but it was her right to know before any other.

Fynavir rolled over and her eyes slowly flickered open; she blinked, confused, almost as if she expected another to be lying beside her, holding her hand. Abruptly she frowned, the corners of her mouth turning down. "What is it, husband? Why do you wake me before the Sun is up?"

"Shortly I leave Kham-El-Ard for the holdings of the Maimed King," he said, "and I have chosen men from my warband to ride out with me. But one place in my company is unfilled...the place that would have been An'kelet's had he desired to ride out with us."

Her face became shuttered, guarded; she yanked the fur about herself and stared off into the darkness. "What of it?"

"I have pondered who might take my chief warrior's place...and can think of but one. Fynavir, the time is come that Amhar is given a man's proper arms and place within the tribe. It is right that he puts aside the name of childhood and take on a new name and responsibilities. It is my will that he is given his manhood rites on the morrow, and then we will ride for the Wastelands of An-fortas."

"No!" Fynavir whirled to face him, eyes wild, a trapped beast's eyes, and she struck at him with balled fists. "You cannot! My son! What if anything should happen to him? He...he is all I have...! And he is your only heir..."

Suddenly, she dropped her hands and began to weep, rocking back and forth.

"Fynavir, his time has come," Ardhu said softly. He wanted to embrace her but feared she would strike out again. "All the boys born in the same year as Amhar are now accounted Men of the Tribe. Some even have wives! If you try to keep him as a boy forever, he will come to hate you. And although none speak ill of him now—none would dare—in years hence tongues might flap more freely."

"But…but what of his special gifts?" she whispered. "They do make him different, separate from the rest. The other lads do not speak to the Ancestors…and hear them speak back! They do not see the faces of long-dead warriors in the night!"

Ardhu had no more patience for debate. "No, and the other lads are not the sons of kings, wife. Amhar will not sit here weaving with women like some…some Fir-vhan, a man-woman! Nor will he be sent to Deroweth to don the robes of priesthood. He will become a Man of Kham-El-Ard and a true prince of his people."

"I curse you, Ardhu!" Fynavir rose, flinging a sheepskin around her shoulders, and she ripped aside the hangings that protected their cubicle from prying eyes. "You think to do right, but I know in my heart that your stubbornness, your desire to meddle in things that would be best left alone, will bring doom to us all! You may know about war and the ways of men, but I know about my child and what is best for him! Your decision will bring a day of wickedness to us all. I feel this in my heart!"

Sobs catching in her throat, she ran from the Hall, a pale creature seemingly of mist and ice; she raced into the darkened door of the women's house, where females of the tribe gathered when their monthly Moon-bleed was upon them and where it was forbidden for men to enter. Around Ardhu the men of the war-band stirred, woken by the sound of raised voices, and shifted aside their heaps of sleeping-furs and sheepskins.

Hwalchmai rolled onto his haunches and poked at the fire-pit with a stick, pushing back his sleep-tangled hair with his free hand. "Is anything wrong, cousin?"

"No." Ardhu shook his head. "Nothing is wrong, save a woman's foolish fancies. This will be a day of great rejoicing, not of sorrow. A day we have waited too long to see. Today my son Amhar will become a Man of the Tribe and join the warband of Ardhu Pendraec on his very first quest."

The Sacred Pool below Kham-El-Ard lay silent beneath the canopy of trees. Mist coiled from the surface, especially when the air was cool, for the water of the spring was temperate, heated by some hidden Underworld forge tended by a god or spirit so old even the Wise like Merlin had forgotten his name. On one side of the pool the warriors of Ardhu clustered together, faces painted with spirals and chevrons and zigzags and wearing ceremonial dress: headdresses of swan and jay and buzzard feathers and necklets of animal teeth—the beaver, the hare, the dog. Long cloaks, ochred familial plaques and shields proclaimed their lineages. The wealthiest wore their gold and bronze—all of it, no decoration spared—crescent collars imported from Ibherna, coiled arm twists and bangles, lip plugs and earlobe extenders, scintillating hair rings, and of course their collections of daggers and axes, some imported from the far shores beyond the Narrow Sea.

Ardhu stood amongst the company, holding Caladvolc unsheathed, its red-hot length glowing in the half-light. He wore the Breastplate of Heaven and a belt buckle made of gold to match, but little other adornment. It would be Amhar's day today, his investiture as true prince of Prydn, and Ardhu would not rob the youth of any glory. It was Amhar's time to shine; too long had he dwelt in the twilight.

On the opposite side of the pool Mhor-gan of the Korrig-han, Ardhu's full-blooded sister, waited for the new initiate to make his appearance. Ardhu had not asked her to come; indeed, he did not know how she, away in her thatched cult-house in the cradle of the valley, had learned of her nephew's manhood rites, unless it was true that she could speak with the birds of the trees, the worms and beetles of the earth and the capricious wind itself. She wore her customary green kirtle, the colour of both life and the dead, and over it a cloak made of badger skins, black-and-white striped, the light and the dark. Badgers' teeth, inordinately large and fierce-looking for a beast no bigger than a dog, clattered around her neck in a macabre necklace.

Ardhu gestured to Hwalchmai, resplendent in a diadem of hawk feathers that proclaimed his name—Hawk of the Plain and he lifted a cow-horn bound with bronze and blew upon it, a loud blast that sent birds shrieking from the tree-tops and rustled the leaves of the forest.

The greenery parted and in rode Amhar on a white mare. He wore a robe of the finest and palest linen, as white as the women could get it by bleaching it with urine. A golden band circled his neck but he had no other adornments. He had his boy's bow slung over his shoulder and a borrowed dagger in a plain leather sheath. His dark red hair was tied back, save for the two braids that would be shorn if he passed his rites.

Ardhu looked at him with a growing sense of pride. Yes, it was time indeed for Amhar to take his place within his people. He would have to prove himself, even though he was a King's son, but unlike Ardhu's own long gone initiation at the great henge of Marthodunu, there would be no chance of death or utter humiliation. Ardhu had outlawed such practices several years back, at least within his own demesne. What would it serve to have young men who need not be enemies fight to the death? Only the enemies of Prydn.

Hwalchmai blew his horn again and Amhar dismounted and knelt before his father on the bed of soft, rotting leaves that carpeted the forest floor.

"Today you come before me, my son and heir, to take your adult name and join us as a Man of the Tribe," said Ardhu. "But you must first prove that you are worthy. What skills have you gained in your years, Amhar son of Ardhu? Show us what you might bring to the People!"

Amhar rose and raised his bow. "I have learned the path of arrowflight, the magic of the hunt," he said, and he suddenly loosed an arrow from the string. It whirred away into the green gloom, a flash of white fletchings. A screech sounded from above and a bird suddenly tumbled from the sky, twirling as it plummeted down, to splash into the heart of the sacred pool. Thin streamers of blood fanned out along the ripples made by the falling body.

"Blood!" Mhor-gan's voice was a harsh whisper. "Blood of the sacrifice, given to the Ancestors this auspicious day!" She knelt on the bank, mud oozing round her ankles, and let her long fingers trail in the blood-tipped waves, her eyes reading destiny in the patterns.

Amhar turned from the pool and held up his bow. "Father, is that the shot of a boy or a Man of the Tribe? Can I lay this weapon down or must I return to my mother's hut for another year?" He spoke the ritual words clearly, without stumbling; he must have practiced long for this day, thought Ardhu with a flash of guilt.

"You may lay that weapon down," answered the Stone Lord.

Amhar took his boy's bow, turned it crossways, and with a violent motion snapped it over his knee. He cast the two pieces to the ground. "It is dead, as is he who was Amhar on this day."

"Show us what else the boy who wishes to join the men round the fires can offer us." Ardhu nodded toward Hwalchmai, who was drawing a bronze rapier from a cowhide sheath. He tossed the weapon to Amhar, who caught it deftly, and then drew a second long dagger from his belt, its hilt of amber pinned with gold studs—his blade the Piercer-of-Pain.

"Fight me, kinsman," he said to Amhar. "Do not hold back your strength. See me as the enemy who would keep you from your place amidst the People."

The seasoned warrior and the youth circled each other, moving in a crouch around the edges of the Sacred Pool. The watching men, excited at the thought of a fight, even if not one liable to cause serious injury, began to chant and stamp their feet. Axes were drawn and their hafts beaten rhythmically against the broad, bronze-bound faces of shields of oak and hide.

Hwalchmai made a sudden lunge forward, stabbing into the murky forest air. Amhar whirled away from him, and then circled round to engage, facing the Hawk of the Plain head on with neither fear nor reluctance. His borrowed weapon snaked out, striking, clattering against the slender, slightly grooved blade of Piercer-of-Pain.

Hwalchmai looked slightly surprised and drove forward, forcing the youth's arm up and exposing his side, a deadly move which could easily mean death to an enemy.

Amhar glanced down, realising his guard was off. Unexpectedly, he snatched back his blade from the deadlocked position, causing Hwalchmai to stumble forward in surprise, and at the same time grasped Hwalchmai's hair and drove his knee staunchly into his kinsman's stomach. The older man's knees buckled and he fell to the ground, winded, Piercer-of-Pain clattering from his fingers.

"You are quick and deal a fierce blow, young cousin," he said to Amhar, between gasps. "I deem you ready to join the King's warband. Or any other warband you choose!"

Amhar reached out a hand to help him up; Hwalchmai was clutching his tender belly, though grinning "Forgive me for your bruises, kinsman. I hope I have not caused you much pain. But I did as you asked and played the game as if we were indeed foes on the field."

Hwalchmai bowed, wincing a little. "You played it well."

Ardhu approached his son and clasped his wrist, raising his arm aloft. Amhar still held the long rapier given him by Hwalchmai; it shone like a needle of flame as sunlight filtered through the tangle of boughs above and struck the elongated blade. "So now the boy may fight alongside the Men of the Tribe, and leave his mother's hearth. He may eat with the Men and drink with the Men, and take to him a wife or wives of his choosing. Today he will give up the things of childhood and join ventures of the warriors of Ardhu Pendraec, lord of the Great Trilithon, Chief Serpent of Prydn—the Isle of the Mighty!"

The warriors started their chant, and blew upon horns to herald the acceptance of a new warrior into their ranks. Ardhu drew a razor from his belt-pouch and cut the two locks that symbolised childhood from the sides of Amhar's head, and Mhor-gan kindled a small fire on a heap of flints that crackled and turned white with the heat, and she burnt the hair and uttered words over it, offering its essence to the hungry spirits who clustered around that ancient site, the oldest of the old who had chased the great White Aurochs across a land of pine before any man herded cattle or used the plough, and who had raised three great totems on the Plain, facing the maximum rising of the Moon.

Then Amhar was taken and bathed in the holy Pool, clearing away the last vestiges of his old life, and then he was robed again and given a beaker of fermented milk mixed with blood, a ritual drink more potent even than the golden mead. He drank it in one and the ornate pot, already a hundred years old, was smashed to release its spirit, and its shards hurled into the springhead.

Mhor-gan came to him, the only woman present, the only female allowed to witness these rites, as priestess and seer, talker to the gods and spirits. She gestured him to kneel and painted signs of protection on his face with a stick of ochre, and she gazed upon him with both sorrow and tenderness.

"You are a special youth, this is beyond doubt," she said, taking his hands in her own. "But I can tell little more than that. The Ancestors cloud my vision with capricious mist, or perhaps Bhel Brighteye, who burns like the colour of your hair, had blinded me so that I may not look too deep into your Fate."

"I do not wish to know my Fate, aunt." Amhar looked into her eyes, earnest and serious. "It does not matter when or where or how, only that I do my best in the service of Ardhu Pendraec, Stone Lord of Prydn…my Father."

"May the Ancestors guide you, Amhar," Mhor-gan said, and she reached down into the Pool, still discoloured by the life's blood of the bird he had downed, and fumbled in the mud and leaves and accumulated sediments. When she withdrew her hand, she held up a strange stone of a type not local to the area, broken clean in half, with a deep indentation in one side. The stone was a deep red colour, almost the hue of fired clay, though slightly lighter towards the centre. She handed it to him, upended, almost as if she proffered a cup, a cup born of the natural world.

He glanced at her, wondering. "This is a talisman," she said, "left here in the pool by our most distant forbears; its magic is strong. As the days pass you will see it change; no longer red like blood, it will change to the colour of the evening sky before Bhel is gone but before Nud covers heaven with his cloak of stars. Drink from it, and it will surely protect you from all harm, imbuing you with the powers of the Ancestors."

"I thank you, aunt." He kissed her hand and hid the small stone cup inside his tunic.

Ardhu approached; in his hand he held a small wooden box bound with copper rivets. Opening it, he drew out first a fine flanged axe on a polished, hardwood shaft, and then a fine Ar-moran dagger with a gold pointillé hilt that matched his own older weapon. "These shall be your man's weapons from this day forward, Prince of Kham-El-Ard, Khor Ghor and the West. The axe is my gift; it is named Head-of-Thunder. The sword was made for you in distant Ar-morah, on the orders of the Lord An'kelet, and it has waited too long for your hand. Kos'garak, the Triumphant One, is its name."

Amhar took the axe and thrust it through his belt. The sword he raised before his face, examining its gold and bronze beauty. The pins adorning the hilt were no bigger than hairs, arranged in patterns by a master craftsman. "These are worthy weapons. I hope I will bring honour to you with them, Lord."

"And now I will give you one last thing!" Ardhu placed both hands squarely on the youth's shoulders and looked at him with wonder, so different in looks and temperament to either himself or Fynavir; this magical boy who had been born beyond all hope, and who now was a Man to ride out alongside him. "I will give you the name by which you shall be known forever more to the people of Prydn. Amhar the child is no more. From this day forth…you will be the Prince Gal'havad, the Hawk of Summer."

Leaving the Sacred Pool in the trees below Kham-El-Ard, Ardhu went to find the stranger Pelahan and his cart of stinking remains. Gal'havad followed his father, walking on his right as befitted the heir of the Lord of the West, and Bohrs, Hwalchmai and Per-Adur marched close behind.

When they reached Pelahan's wain of death, they saw the grim-featured man atop the cart, leaning over the dead and touching them, stroking their emaciated limbs as if willing them to live again. It was a tragic yet hideous sight, and Ardhu felt his stomach tighten in revulsion. The dead should be taken and disposed of decently, in an honourable way, lest their spirits be trapped on earth forever. "We are ready to go East with you, and see this desolate land of the Maimed King," he said to Pelahan, "but the cart will stay here, Master Pelahan, and the carrion you drag with you shall be burned and given to the river."

He approached the cart and yanked Pelahan away from his grim load. The strange easterner looked as though he might protest, then scowled and turned away. Per-Adur and Bohrs freed the scabrous oxen from their traces, and sent them away with smacks on the rump. Kindling torches, they hurled them amidst the dry stacks of bones, while Hwalchmai added dry tinder to keep the flames alight. Soon a roaring blaze took hold; skulls popped in the conflagration and the wood sides of the cart crumbled and disintegrated with a shower of sparks. Rancid smoke spiralled skyward, rising in a vast black plume over Kham-El-Ard.

When the blaze had died to embers, the women of Kham-El-Ard descended from the huts upon the heights and scooped up the ashes into bucket-shaped urns. They lugged them to the banks of Abona and tipped them into the swell, while chanting words to sooth any spirits angered by being cremated so far from their own ancestral land.

Fynavir came down from the long house to oversee the women's death-rites for the strangers. A thick fox pelt hung round her shoulders but she was shivering nonetheless; she looked suddenly aged and frail, her whiteness no longer of virgin snow but scored bone. Blue shadows underscored her eyes and her lips were pale, bitten. An'kelet accompanied her, steadying her with his hand as she navigated the uneven ground in her thin moccasins. The Armoran prince stared into the distance, his face like a slab of carved marble, still unable to meet Ardhu's eyes. Despite being the Gal'havad's trainer in arms, he had not been asked to attend the youth's manhood rites, and he knew Ardhu was angry with him for not joining the quest to the East. Angrier than he had ever been.

He knew too, that he deserved Ardhu's wrath…and more.

"Lady, greet your son, the Prince Gal'havad." Ardhu gestured to the youth at his shoulder. "He is now a Man of the Tribe."

Fynavir glanced up at her husband, her smile sickly. "And so he is, and now the son that was my joy is gone from me and wedded to the tribe. Just see that he is not gone forever, my husband! If he returns not to Kham-El-Ard unharmed from your hateful questing, I swear by the spirits I will curse you."

The gathered people gasped; they knew of Fynavir's heritage, of how her mother Red Mevva, was said to be a goddess, and her strange daughter the same, born of the white chalk, the bones of the earth. A curse from her lips would surely be of terrible potency.

Ardhu's eyes blackened with wrath, but it was Gal'havad who spoke, stepping between them, his arms outstretched: "Put this ill will to rest! I will not be fought over, and though I honour you both I will not be torn in two. If you cannot agree to have peace between you, I will hasten away, alone, to the Isle of Afallan or beyond. I shall not be punished for whatever anger lies between you, nor shall I be the cause of dissension in Kham-El-Ard."

Ardhu's face suddenly lightened and he hugged the slender youth. "Not only a Man this day, but a Wise man as well. My son, you are truly born of two worlds—the world of the warrior and the world of the priest. May this gift serve you well."

Fynavir flushed, she realised her outburst had gone too far. Tears filled her eyes. "His 'gift' may serve him well...or be his doom. May the gods protect him! I leave you now, to go upon your way, but I expect to see my boy returned, unharmed, within the next three months of the Moon."

She turned, her long white braid swinging, and marched back toward the hall of Kham-El-Ard, with An'kelet striding swiftly at her side, her protector, her rock against all storms.

Ardhu glanced at Gal'havad who was watching his mother's departure with a solemn, sad face. "Do not let her words disturb you. Affrighted are the hearts of some women, and never forget that your mother birthed you in much pain and that the spirits nearly took you and her to the Deadlands that day and she fought them and won both her life and yours."

"I will not forget her pain and sacrifice," said Gal'havad. "But I must speak truthfully—I am glad to be free upon the road and see the world beyond Kham-El-Ard with my esteemed father and his noble warriors. But before I go…may I say goodbye to my friend, cousin Mordraed? As he is not yet accepted into your warband, he was not permitted to attend my manhood trials, but I would wish him farewell before we travel East."

Ardhu frowned; a shiver of fear ran down his spine. He knew Gal'havad spent much time with Mordraed, and although keeping them apart would be problematic and bring difficult questions from both Gal'havad and others, he wished the two youths were not so close. Morigau was far away, living in a hovel in the lake valley under her younger sister

Mhor-gan's watchful eye, and he had barred her from entering Kham-El-Ard unbidden, but she was still the boy's mother and her stamp was impressed upon his personality. He did not dare trust him.

"No," he said firmly. "If he is not here now, you are not to run after him like some hound yapping at its master's heels. You are a prince and a boy no longer. He is of royal blood, too, but he is below you, as the earth is below the Everlasting Sky. His house is discredited and ruined. Do you understand, Gal'havad?"

The red-haired youth bowed his head. "I do, father," he whispered but there was a rebellious gleam in his eyes.

CHAPTER SIX—JOURNEY TO THE EAST

The company set off at daybreak, turning their horses' heads toward the great Ridgeway track that crossed Prydn, a route of traders and merchants and warriors for a thousand years or more. Pelahan had been given a spare pony; he sat hunched upon it like a black crow, an incongruous figure amidst the bright, decorous figures of the King's chosen men. Excited as a young puppy, Gal'havad kept spurring his mount on to faster pace and rushing on beyond the others, only to be called back to safety by Ardhu or Bohrs.

The band ascended the Ridgeway track near the Sanctuary, the thatched cult-house that guarded the main entrance to Suilven, Temple of the Eye, known by the tin-traders of old as The Crossroads of the World. Lines of standing stones snaked away from its lintelled doorway toward distant Suilven, where chalk banks towered over ditches that dropped down sixty feet toward the realm of the Underworld, creating a raised central platform that held three stone circles made of natural sarsen hauled from the nearby Downs. Gal'havad said wistfully that he would like to see these stone rings, so different from the familiar circle of Khor Ghor, and he stared with longing at a trickle of smoke coming from a fire in the heart of the Sanctuary, but Ardhu shook his head and frowned. "No, we have no time…you will go when there is peace in the land. All men will eventually see Suilven."

The Stone Lord turned his horse upon the Ridgeway and touched his heels to its flanks, driving the beast down the rutted chalk road, past tumuli swamped with trees and lonely pilgrims and merchants heading to and from the Great Temple, who stared and gawked to see a gold-clad lord before them, carrying his weapons of might and war. He knew Gal'havad would need to visit Suilven sometime, but he shuddered at the very thought of taking his son to that place with its dark woman-magic and for him, dark memories... It was there, on the Harvest Feast of Bron Trogran, that his half-sister, the bitter and venomous Morigau had seduced him—and he begot Mordraed upon her…

The Ridgeway wound East, toward the rising Sun and the accursed lands the travellers sought. It meandered through a flat, fertile valley, then rose gradually onto a high escarpment covered in deep yellow grass that tossed in the wind like a maiden's hair. They stopped to give the animals a rest, staring down at the smoky hills beyond, before faring on with speed, passing along the summit of a line of gentle hills that undulated like a snake, almost resembling a spirit-path, but made by the hands of gods rather than men.

As the day died the sky grew blood red, clouds burning in a great conflagration, and the travellers came to a flat plateau, with only a few bare dead trees upon it, limned against the crimson glow of the sky. A hundred yards to the right of the well-worn track, a long barrow crouched like a waiting beast, its portal stones up thrust like a row of teeth. "Here we shall stop for the night," said Ardhu. "The Ancestors will protect us."

They rode over to the mound, long fallen out of use, the entrance to the small cist-chamber blocked by rubble as if someone had striven either to keep the dead spirits inside or to keep grave robbers out— perhaps both. A façade of large flat-faced sarsens glowered into the gloom, the ones on either end of the façade taller and more pointed than the rest, giving it the appearances of fangs in an upended jaw. The body of the mound tailed back behind the heavy capstone of the penultimate chamber, its edges full of sharp, half-buried stones that had made their reappearance from the ground as the cairn shifted in partial collapse, heavy with the weight of untold years.

"What is this place called?" Gal'havad tethered his horse to a bush that grew alongside the slumping mound. He stared hard at the blocked entrance, as if willing the packing to fall away and the spirits of the place to rise and greet him.

"The Hill of the Old People is one of its names." Ardhu swung down from his horse. "It is one of the oldest of its kind, or so tales tell. The song-singers recite stories of how an earlier wooden house of the dead once stood below this stone house that lies before us. How chiefs battled over land and cattle at a camp nearby, and men, women and children were killed by arrow fire, with no mercy given. The survivors brought their bones here, when the birds on the high platforms had pecked their flesh and released their spirits, and a wooden death-hut, a new home to replace their ruined ones, was raised over them, and bowls and baskets placed beside them to be used in their next life. They lay here long, undisturbed. And then…" He wandered up to the sarsen façade, tracing the lichenous face with his fingers. "The Men of Metal came to Prydn after their long wanderings from the West, and a Smith, one of the first of his kind in all Prydn, set up his forge here, in the shadow of the great House of the Dead."

"Was he not afraid?" Gal'havad joined his father beneath the glowering stones. "Surely he would know that to build a smithy here was disrespectful to the Old One's spirits!"

"He may have been afraid…at first," replied Ardhu, "for they were not his Ancestors buried in the mound and they may not have been happy. They may have pinched him in his sleep, and brought cold winds to chill him and blow out his fires. But they brought him no real harm. Maybe they too were intrigued by his magic…the magic of smelting copper! And when men in local villages saw the fire-metal he wrought, bright as Bhel's eye, rings and axes and daggers—the villagers warmed to him and thought of him as a wizard as powerful as the village shaman. They brought him offerings here up at the Hill of the Old People, and said the gods had smiled on him, that he breathed Bhel's fiery breath into his works. Eventually they persuaded him to come down to their village and join them there as their own smith—they gave him a fine girl for a wife, a big hut, and many furs and weapons. But in order that he never leave them and take his magic elsewhere, they broke his left knee with a stone axe. They lamed him and he never wandered further."

Hwalchmai, who had joined his cousin and nephew, grinned and shook his head. "A fine story, kinsman. You would have made a fine Teller of Tales, Ardhu, had you not been destined to be King!"

Gal'havad glanced toward the dark passage between the flanking stones. He took a copper bangle from his wrist and placed it on the ground. "An offering to the Smith and to the Old Ones," he said, "for letting us stay unharmed in this place."

Ardhu patted the lad on the shoulder and began kindling a fire near the entrance of the tomb. The wind was rising, screeching through the spindly branches of the trees, making it difficult for the flame to catch. Shadows danced, flickering over the stony faces of the temple-tomb's façade. In the distance a fox yipped, its voice high and eerie. The moon was a pallid crescent soaring through the swaying tangle of boughs, casting a strange bluish light over the ancient structure.

At length the fire caught and held, warming the chilled group of travellers. Ardhu laid a joint of dried beef on the mound's capstone as an offering of his own and then gestured for Bohrs to share out food to the group. The companions ate in silence, except for Pelahan, who took his slab of meat and retreated to the farthest stone, where he gnawed on the joint like some kind of monstrous rat.

"Gods, he is an ill-favoured wight," murmured Hwalchmai, watching him out of the corner of his eye. "I wish he had not come on this quest with us. He is not a fit companion for kings…or any living man! He looks half a corpse!"

Ardhu grunted. "He is a guide…he may be of use yet. And if not, we will be rid of him soon enough. I have no desire to tarry on the road any longer than necessary."

Finishing his meal, Gal'havad got up and stretched his legs. He was intrigued by the strange man Pelahan, sitting with his back towards the others in his maggoty cloak. He approached him slowly, stopping a few feet away in case he was not welcome.

The hooded head swivelled round. "What do you stare at, King's son?"

"You are welcome at our fire," Gal'havad said bravely. "You need not sit outside."

Pelahan pushed back his hood; Gal'havad blinked at the site of his scarred face, the disease that ate at his very skull. "Do you not fear me, boy? Your companions do, I wager, even if they claim not to. Even your noble father, for in me he sees everything that he fears, the ruin of all he has achieved."

"I am not afraid," said Gal'havad. "You are a man, if a man afflicted. You are not dead...I have spoken to the real dead, out in the fields of Khor Ghor."

"You are a strange boy, different than the others." Pelahan's eyes were glittering specks against the livid mask of his face. "Maybe in you, a youth pure and innocent...and good...there is yet a chance. Even should your father fail, there may be one to take his place, one who can treat not only with men but with the spirits that surround us."

"My father will not fail!" said Gal'havad, his voice suddenly sharp. He turned from Pelahan, no longer wishing to speak with him.

Abruptly Pelahan leapt from his perch and grabbed the boy's arm. Gal'havad reached instinctively for a weapon, but Pelahan hissed like a striking serpent: "It is not me you need to fear, boy! Can you not hear the noise, feel the earth tremble? Horses are coming up the hill at speed!"

"Father!" Gal'havad raced back over to the fire as the warriors leaped up, daggers drawn, and stood back to back, facing the night and whatever hid in its depths.

"Horses? It cannot be horses!" snarled Per-Adur. "We are still the only tribe to ride the beasts for war...aren't we?"

"Apparently not," muttered Hwalchmai. "Look!"

Over the brow of the hill a party of riders appeared, waving brands as they galloped towards the barrow. They were dark-visaged, burly men, with long braids and long beards, and lattice tattooing over their eyes and on their muscled arms. The horses they rode were inferior to those of Ardhu's warband, short-legged and shaggy, with ugly raw-boned heads and crazed rolling eyes, but they moved at great speed, their heavy hooves churning up turf and mud and spraying it into the air.

Shouting and roaring, the men—ten of them—galloped up and over the far end of the barrow. The red light of the torches cast surreal flickering shadows over their features, making them look even more ferocious. One who seemed to be a leader flung back his shaggy head and howled like a wolf, as he drove his mount along the high ridge of the barrow. As he reined to a halt on the capstone he flung his torch down and drew a massive war-hammer with a haft dipped in pitch. Its head was crude, primitive, made of some rough crimson stone, and must have been nigh on a foot in length from end to end. He brandished it crazily, drunkenly, while his men whooped and cheered.

Ardhu raised Caladvolc; the guttering torchlight glimmered on the honed edge of its blade. "You! Lay down your arms. Know you not who you harry? I am Ardhu Pendraec, the Terrible Head, Lord of the Khor Ghor and the West, and with me are members of my warband, famed throughout Prydn and beyond!"

The big man with the hammer sneered. "I know who you are! We've been following you since you left Suilven!"

Ardhu's face whitened in rage. "And you dare to attack me, the overlord of these territories? You fool!"

"I never swore any oath to you, King of the West," the man sneered. "An old man, put in your high place years ago by the flummery of a wizard! Acclaimed king only because you stole a blade from an Ancestor's barrow! I, Khaw, challenge you for right of lordship…and for that pretty sword and gold lozenge you wear!"

Ardhu's eyes glistened, dark and deadly. "I brought peace to this land before you were spawned in whatever pit you come from. Do not break the Pendraec's peace or you will not live to see another dawn."

"Peace!" Khaw hawked upon the ground. "You have reduced us all to cowering women! Well, no more…it is the time for brave warriors to take what is able to be taken!"

He slammed his heels into his horse's flanks and the beast plunged forward, eyes wild. Ardhu raised Caladvolc and leapt towards his adversary, seeking to drive his blade into the horse's breast. Khaw, however, was too quick, and wrenched the beast's head away, forcing it to spin around in a circle. Caladvolc whistled harmlessly through the cold night air.

"You're not so quick any more, old man!" mocked Khaw. "Come, men, take down these braggarts from afar, these followers of womanish ways. It is no longer the time of the Farmer…it is a return to the age of the Warrior!"

Khaw's men surged towards the small party. Their eyes were alight with bloodlust and excitement. Bohrs loosed a bellow, loud as the call of a wild boar, and launched himself at the attackers, swinging his fine bronze axe. He struck the lead pony's knee, smashing it; screaming in pain, the animal went down on the mound, its legs thrashing and flailing, churning the ground to mud. Its weight struck against one of the stones supporting the capstone, and an awful groaning noise filled the air, stone shrieking against stone, grinding like the teeth of angry Ancestors. The support stone shifted, wrenched out of its bed, and suddenly part of the chamber collapsed with a roar. A gaping crater, a maw into the Un-world, opened in the side of the barrow and the pony and its rider tumbled in, both screaming in terror. The other riders yanked on their reins and tried to retreat as the top of the mound sagged, threatening to cave in completely. Khaw's face purpled with rage and he waved his war-hammer again. "To me, you fools!" he yelled. "Don't let this chance be ruined!"

Ardhu made a dash for the tethered horses, who were dancing in fright, pulling on their hemp leads. He grabbed Gal'havad by the arm, dragging the youth behind him. "Get on, boy!" he said, roughly shoving the youth onto his mare. "Ride, ride for the East with all speed!"

"But we…surely we must fight these traitors!" cried Gal'havad.

"If we must, but only if there is no choice—they outnumber us by many. We must not be stupid and arrogant. Now ride!"

"But you are the King…!"

"Just ride, Gal'havad!"

Ardhu struck the flank of Gal'havad's steed with the flat of his sword and the horse thundered away into the darkness. Seeing that the mare had reached the gleaming ribbon of the Ridgeway, he flung himself on his own steed and dashed after, with Hwalchmai and Per-Adur galloping madly at his back, shields raised to protect him from spear-casts or arrows. Bohrs lagged behind, having dragged Pelahan onto his steed; the overburdened animal whinnied and fought the bridle, while both men cursed and pummelled its flanks with their heels. Khaw was thundering towards them, his band closing rank around their treacherous lord, their eyes filling with bloodlust as they saw their quarry within reach.

Suddenly Pelahan whipped his hood back from his face and faced the mob. The moonlight illuminated his skull-like head, made black hollows of his eyes and an unholy cavern of his mouth and ruined cheek. He pointed accusingly at the warriors with skeletal hands and let out the most terrible ear-splitting cry, a high, thin ululation that rose and fell on the wind.

The superstitious men, not expecting to see such a tormented visage, yelled in fear and flung up their hands to make signs against evil. "It is a grave-wight!" one yelped, pulling his horse back with all his strength. "He has come from the barrow and is guarding the Pendraec and his men!"

"Don't be stupid…he is one of them!" snarled Khaw…but the moment's hesitation gave Bohrs and Pelahan the time they needed to escape. Bohrs got his beast under control and made a mad dash for the Ridgeway path. Pelahan bounced behind him on the straw-stuffed matt bound to the horse, clinging with bony talons to Bohrs' belt.

"By the gods, man," Bohrs yelled over his shoulder, "you did well tonight, unsavoury though you may seem. But…promise me one thing…promise you will never scream like that in my ear again! Nud's Clouds, I nearly shat myself!"

The companions thundered along the Ridgeway under the night sky with its cold unblinking stars, the eyes of dispassionate watching Ancestors. Ardhu called out to Gal'havad, and the youth drew on the reins of his steed and fell back alongside his father. "Do you think they will follow us?" the young man asked. His eyes were bright with both fear and excitement; Ardhu could see the stars mirrored on their surfaces, giving them an unworldly silver sheen, and he shuddered and touched the talismans he wore for safety, though not for himself but for the boy.

"They will follow," he said gruffly. "And look, down at the bottom of the valley. More of them."

Gal'havad stared down from the height of the ridge. In the darkness below, he could see a line of flickering torches. "These traitors deserve to die." His voice was gentle, almost a sigh, but there was a cold finality in it that made Ardhu shudder again.

"We will try not to engage them," Ardhu said, "but to outrun them. They are drunk; some will lose interest when the fire of the mead goes cold in their bellies. As for the rest…if we move swiftly we will come to Khiltarna, the Land Beyond the Hills, an area where chiefs are loyal to me. These brigands would not dare step beyond its border for fear of retribution."

The group galloped on, keeping a close eye on the torches swarming like angry bees at the lip of the hill. They heard some shouts from behind, but then nothing…no further taunts, no hoof beats.

Bohrs laughed. "Fools! All show and no guts!" He hawked over the side of the path toward the flickering torches massed below.

Ardhu looked wary. "Keep your wits about you…and your daggers to hand. Too much confidence is not wise."

He had no sooner spoken than Per-Adur uttered an oath and pointed to the slope on the right. The warriors' gazes were drawn upwards along the top of the ridge, where the stars were dancing over the swell of the ancient land. Six dark shapes loomed there, hard against the stars—mounted men. One moved, ever so slightly—a blade shone out like a tiny sun and then was hidden within a cloak.

"They have gone up and around us," whispered Per-Adur. "They know this land better than we do."

Ardhu took up his reins and pulled Caladvolc from its scabbard. "Ride!" he cried harshly. "Ride for your lives!"

The band shouted out to their horses and they resumed a mad gallop along the track. Their enemies atop the crest of the hill screamed war cries and hammered their heels into their own mounts' flanks. They flew down the hillside at a frightening, breakneck speed, skidding on the dew-drenched grass. Their horse's eyes were manic, their mouths foaming, their coats lathered as they sought purchase on the unstable ground.

"They are madmen!" shouted Hwalchmai. "They will be on us in a few seconds!"

On the left hand side, over the edge of the Ridgeway, Ardhu caught sight of a great flat-topped hill that rose unexpectedly out of the valley floor. It resembled an enormous barrow, though whether it was the tomb of a once-living man, a monument raised to a mighty Spirit like the Hill of Zhel, or a feature carved purely by the hands of gods when the earth was new, he did not know. Their other assailants were at its foot, milling and waving torches, shouting up to encourage their fellows.

Ardhu glanced at the enemy riders. They screamed and howled like wolves, gnashing their teeth and foaming like creatures gone mad. Their eyes started from their sockets, as wild as their steeds'; he suspected they were either lost in battle-frenzy or had taken potions to make them mad.

He looked back to the bald hill. Through the murk, he could just pick out a small narrow causeway joining its summit to the hillside. If his warriors could make their way across the causeway, they could try and make a stand, barring the hilltop against the men galloping from above and keeping the ones massed below where they were.

It was the only way to avoid a battle against berserkers in the dark.

"Men, follow!" he yelled, driving his stallion forward. "Quick, before they suspect!"

He pulled his steed's head around and scrambled up and over the side of the track. Hwalchmai and Bohrs yelled out in alarm at first, for it looked to the unknowing eye as if he was riding off the edge of the valley, casting himself and his mount out into the night sky. But then they spied the flat hill and Ardhu crouched low over his horse's neck, picking his way swiftly but carefully down the sharp slope towards it, and they followed without hesitation.

They heard startled yells on the slope behind them; obviously, their assailants had imagined, as they had done with Ardhu, that the men of Kham-El-Ard had made a suicide leap over the trail's edge to their doom on the valley floor far below.

The move down the slope gave them the time they needed. By the time the berserkers had reached the lip of the track themselves, Ardhu's men had reached the grassy causeway and were galloping like mad men onto the summit of the barrow-like mound.

Once on top of the hill, they flung themselves from their straw-padded saddles and sprang to defend the causeway. Axes and knives would not aid them here, not unless their enemies forced their way across; this was the territory of the archer, and like all men of both high and low status in Prydn, they had all learned archery from the time they were small boys. They kneeled on the damp soil, drawing back the strings on their short, composite bows, their deadly flint arrows with their long, tearing barbs aimed at the berserkers as they came thundering down the hillside towards the start of the causeway.

Hwalchmai's arrow flew true, striking the foremost in the shoulder. The man screamed and tumbled from his horse, rolling over and over on the ground. He tried to rise and pluck the arrow from his flesh, but he overbalanced and fell backwards on the sheer slope that overlooked the valley. Screaming, he began to slide on the wet, slippery grass, gathering speed as he rolled toward oblivion, toward the massed torches in the cup of the vale. A moment later he was gone, and the lights below swirled as the assembled warriors parted to avoid being crushed by his descending body.

"Well shot," Ardhu murmured to Hwalchmai out of the corner of his mouth.

"I wish Mordraed was with us." Gal'havad held his bow in hands that shook ever so slightly despite his best efforts. "He is the best archer at Kham-El-Ard."

Ardhu glanced at his son, then turned his attention back to the causeway, his face hard as granite. Yes, Gal'havad, he is that… but could I trust him not to put an arrow through my heart?

The remaining enemy horsemen were nearly at the tongue of land that joined the hillside to the mound. Hwalchmai loosed another arrow, followed in quick succession by Ardhu and Gal'havad. The darkness surrounding the warriors made aiming difficult, and this time no rider went down. Per-Adur cursed and fired four arrows in succession; they missed, but struck the earth before the hooves of the assailants' horses, frightening the animals, which neighed and reared and crashed into each other, threatening to unseat their masters.

"Come closer and next time those four arrows will be buried in your flesh!" yelled Per-Adur. He had become a healer in his later years, but had spent his youth in war-like pursuits, which he had never forgotten.

"Per-Adur, Bohrs…look!" Ardhu had crawled to the edge of the platform atop the broad mound. Below, the sea of torches was swaying, surging upward in a fiery tide. "The bastards are trying to climb the hill!"

Bohrs gave an angry roar. Spotting a large stone partly thrust up from the ground, he tore it from its bed. Raising it over his head, he cast it with all his strength into the massed enemy. Several torches dimmed and the sea of flames parted.

"Keep throwing!" Ardhu barked. "They might be put off. They may not know how few of us there are!"

Bohrs, Pelahan and Per-Adur rushed around the hilltop, ripping out stones and small shrubs and hurling them down into the valley. They yelled and bellowed, stomping around the barrow-top like wild men, hoping the noise and constant stream of missiles would fool and confuse their foes.

Ardhu, Hwalchmai, and Gal'havad continued to fire arrows toward the causeway—not wildly now, though, for the riders had drawn rein just out of bowshot, and it would not do well to waste their arrows if they could not reach their target. Ardhu and Gal'havad, being of highest rank, had fifteen arrows each in their quivers, while the other men had only ten.

"So now I have you, Pendraec." Khaw loomed out of the shadows, grinning. "Caught like a rat in a trap. I could wait here for days and starve you out, or call for my own archers to pick you off one by one…but the mob will be here soon enough and they will give you no quarter."

"You are a coward as well as a traitor!" Bohrs roared at Khaw. "If you weren't you'd settle this by armed combat, one on one. A man's battle! Not sitting on your horse, watching a few battle many, and with a boy and a sick man in our company!"

"Aye!" Hwalchmai cried. "You're craven! You need your band of drunken oafs to do your bloody deeds! Whatever the outcome of this day, you will live in infamy, and the spirits will curse you as will all true men of Prydn!"

"Be silent!" roared Khaw. "I am no coward! I wrestled a boar when I was younger than the lad you have with you! I have slain a bear! On one night alone I killed ten men who insulted me!"

"Then come forth and do battle with me!" shouted Ardhu. "Your grievance is with me, after all. Swear that you will let my men pass on unmolested and I will fight you in single combat!"

Khaw fell silent. His eyes rested on the unsheathed blade of Caladvolc. He had heard of its powers, of how the Lady of the Lake had guided the Pendraec to it in the Sacred Pool at Kham-El-Ard. He did not want to face its charmed blade.

Suddenly Gal'havad stepped forward, planting himself near the end of the causeway, his legs apart, his hair a bright banner in the wind on the height. "If you will not fight my father, fight me!" he cried. "You think the Stone Lord an old man—more fool you, Man of Contempt!—but if that is true, you would have no honour in fighting him. Fight me instead!"

An unwholesome grin split Khaw's bushy black beard. "From an old one to a boy. But at least your head would look pretty above the door of my hut!"

Ardhu grabbed at Gal'havad's sleeve, trying to draw him back. "No, you little fool, you cannot face him! This man is not a noble warrior; he is a brigand and a murderer. You have not fought to the death…you have not fought at all! I must be the one…"

Gal'havad glanced at his sire, and Ardhu saw his eyes shining silver again, unearthly in his white, intense face. He almost seemed a stranger, suddenly grown up, his youthful naivety fled…and there was something strangely of An'kelet about him too—his composure, his single-mindedness. "It is in the hands of the spirits, father. I feel it is right that I avenge the honour of our house, and cleanse the stains of Khaw's treachery with the shedding of his blood on this holy hill…which shall be known as the Pendraec's hill from now until the end of time."

Khaw had dismounted his horse and was slowly picking his way across the causeway. His men started to follow but Khaw waved them back with his huge stone war-hammer. "No, I do not want you. This glory is all my own," he sneered. "I will return before long, victorious, I am sure."

Reaching the summit of the mound, the rebel tribesman stood in front of the silent Gal'havad, hands on hips, raking him up and down with a mocking gaze. He flexed his brawny arms and tapped the head of his axe against his palm. "Do you fear me yet, boy?" he snarled. "Are you regretting your idle boastfulness?"

"I have no regrets." Gal'havad's voice was measured, almost without emotion. "The spirits have told me what I must do."

His hands moved; a white blur in the shadows. The dagger Kos'garak that he had been given only the day before flashed out and stabbed into Khaw's knee. The bigger man stumbled forward, roaring in agony, blood black in the moonlight. He had not expected such an attack; he had expected formality, the bragging and boasting of two warriors set to face each other in combat in the old-fashioned manner.

"You bastard!" he gasped, clutching at his leg. "You've maimed me. Dishonourable brat, that was not a man's move!"

"Dishonourable? You know all about that!" said Gal'havad. "I fight you as you deserve. You are devious and disloyal…a traitor to the West, and you shall die a traitor's death!"

Gal'havad was calm; he pulled his axe from his belt and strode towards Khaw. The hard edge, newly honed, shone blue, the redness of the bronze leached out by the starlight.

The older man cursed and attempted to hobble away, but his wounded leg buckled under him and he stumbled, lurching heavily to one side. Growling like a maddened beast, he swung out with his massive stone hammer, but its weight unbalanced him and he dropped to a half-crouch on the grass, fumbling with the weapon, trying to aim a good strong blow. Gal'havad took three long strides toward him and slashed down with his axe, striking his opponent's arm and shattering it at the elbow. Khaw's great war-hammer thudded uselessly to the ground, as its owner screamed in pain and sudden, overwhelming fear.

"To the spirits I give this evil man!" cried Gal'havad, raising his weapon. "Upon this dark day, my first blooding, a tribute to you Gods and to the Ancestors in the mounds!" He turned, whirling like a leaf on the wind, wielding his axe Head-of-Thunder two-handed for greater impact. The axe-head smashed between Khaw's eyes, shattering his skull and instantly sending his spirit into Otherness. It drank deep of the traitor's blood and brain, passing his strength into the bronze blade of the axe and into the youth who wielded it.

Gal'havad stood with arms and head thrown back, face so calm, so collected, it almost frightened Ardhu. Blood from the shattered skull had spattered his tunic and streaked his handsome face like war paint. Ardhu remember the first man he had killed, a Sea-Pirate on the river Glein, and how he had felt sick at the time, hating the blood, the stench, despite that the man was an enemy. Gal'havad looked almost…rapturous.

"Come, we must away now!" he said harshly, nodding towards Khaw's remaining men, who suddenly broke rank and fled from the edge of the causeway, galloping back down the

Ridgeway as if demons were pursuing them. "We don't know if they will return with reinforcements...or what the men below might do."

"No matter what they try, it is a steep climb up—it will take a while," said Bohrs. "Nonetheless, let us depart at once!"

The companions climbed upon their horses, Pelahan once again riding pillion behind Bohrs. Gal'havad's mount snorted and shifted, fearful of the blood-smell upon her rider; he stroked her neck with his gore-streaked hand and comforted her with soft words that belied the fact he had just brained a man.

Ardhu eyed his son as they galloped along the Ridgeway, leaving the crowds of enemies roaring in anger at the foot of the hill that would forever bear the name of Pendraec. "Are you all right, Amhar...Gal'havad?" he asked.

The youth looked over at him and smiled, teeth white between the streaks of red that criss-crossed his face. "I have never felt better, father. Like you, my role in life is to protect Prydn, and with my axe and dagger I will be as a spirit of vengeance upon the foes of my chief and my land."

As the Sun ascended the rim of the world, a burning disc that shot hot fire into the waiting heavens, the men of Ardhu crossed the border into the expanse of Khiltarna, the Land Beyond the Hills. Deep green rises, still purple with night-shadows, rolled away toward the horizon like waves. Streams ran between the rills and ruts, shining like strips of molten metal, and mist and low cloud hung white and languorous in the natural hollows of the land.

"We should be safe here," said Pelahan. "I know these lands well, having travelled here many times in my youth. The chieftains here are good men who do not seek to rob or harry travellers...as you said yourself, Lord Ardhu. I would counsel, though, that we abandon the Ridgeway, in case any of Khaw's followers decide to cross the border seeking revenge. We can follow the rivers, of which there are many here: Mymrim, Ghad, Khess and Ver, and in the North the tributaries of Great O-os, Ou'zel, Flyt and Hyz. Our arrival in the Wastelands will be delayed, but at least we will not have another evil encounter! When I deem that all is safe and quiet, I can easily pick up another path near Efyn Phen—the Ychenholt, the Oldest Road, which men say was used thousands of years ago by wanderers coming in from the Drowned Lands of the Dagarlad."

"It sounds a wise plan...so let us go." Ardhu flicked his reins against his horse's neck and urged her forward with the pressure of his knees.

The group left the track and headed down the valley. Finding one river, they crossed at the ford, and then hastened East along its bank, green with reeds and decked with white, waving water-lilies. They stopped to rest at noon, sleeping on their cloaks in the warm sun, and then continued with renewed vigour.

Dusk was falling when they spied a huge treeless hill looming on the horizon. The ruins of a round barrow crowned its summit. The long scar of a trackway marred its flank and curved up and over its bald head. Pelahan nodded in its direction. "Efyn Phen. From there we can pick up the Ychenholt that will lead us to the Wastelands."

They rode on and joined the path that stretched over the hill and wound into the East. By the time the night was half-through, there was a cloudburst and all were drenched and weary; so they left the track again and bedded down in a coppice, stretching a deerskin that Hwalchmai carried rolled in his pack on a wobbly frame made of tree-limbs. They managed to light a little fire, sputtering and without cheer, and drank some thin beer from a clay flask.

Ardhu glanced at Gal'havad. The youth was rocking on his heels, humming to himself as if he was mad. The rain had rinsed away some of the blood on his face but gore still clotted the edges of his hair and left large blots on his tunic. His teeth were chattering and his eyes bright and unfocussed.

"I knew he was not right!" murmured Ardhu, shaking his head. "No one kills a first time and acts as he did!" He went over to the lad, kneeling at his side, passing his hand before the blank-looking eyes. As he did so, Gal'havad unexpectedly let out one of his eerie cries, the sound that heralded his brief journeys to the Un-world, and he fell upon the ground, twitching and convulsing, mud mingling with the blood on his body and garments.

Ardhu fell to his knees and gathered him up, holding him close until the seizure had passed. The rest of the men glanced away; faintly embarrassed; they had heard of the young prince's affliction but it was not something spoken of at Kham-El-Ard, and it was infrequent enough to hide. It had not stopped the boy becoming adept with arms, after all—he had proved that when he slew Khaw as if he had been slaying enemies all his life.

Soon Gal'havad opened his eyes and seemed to come to himself. He did not remember falling, and recalled little of anything that had taken place since the attack at the Hill of the Old People. Reaching into his tunic, he pulled out the small cup-like stone his aunt Mhor-gan of the Korrig-han had given him, a gift from the unfathomable waters of the Sacred Pool. He stroked its rough surface and smiled; as Mhor-gan had predicted, its colour had changed from bold orange-red to a dusky purple. It was a cup of the evening, and he was the Prince of Ardhu's twilight.

"Father, pour me some drink into this cup of healing," he begged. "Then I may return to you all and continue the journey."

"Cup of healing…" Ardhu had not seen his sister's gift to the boy; he was dubious. Years of watching men die despite their amulets, despite their prayers, had robbed his faith in either charms or gods. Yes, he said the right words and made the required offerings, but if there was one thing he knew was true, it was that the Ancestors and Gods were capricious and often had no love of humankind.

"Yes." Gal'havad held it up, "My talisman. It will protect me."

Ardhu made a dismissive noise. "Your dagger-hand will aid you more," he said, but he poured some beer into the cup and helped Gal'havad, who still trembled slightly in the aftermath of his fit, to lift it to his lips. "But you won't believe me, will you? You have always been half of the Not-world, like my sister and the Merlin."

Pelahan came up at that moment; in the ruined leprous mask of his face, his eyes were strangely kind. More so than men of the axe like Bohrs, who had turned swiftly from the scene, embarrassed by Gal'havad's perceived weakness. "Are you hale, little lord?" Pelahan said quietly. "I do not forget that you spoke kindly to me in my affliction, and so I support you in yours."

Gal'havad nodded. "I am fine. Such turns are not new to me; I have always been this way. I am not ashamed. It is how the spirits set the fire within my head."

Pelahan gazed at the broken stone that Gal'havad clutched. "The broken cup…the colour of even's sky, a sign of the Otherworld, the mystic's sign. That is you, boy, the mystic-child, but not just a tool to whom the spirits speak but also a warrior with a blade in your hand." His sunken eyes suddenly glazed, and Ardhu, listening to this exchange, felt hairs rise on the back of his neck—was the ill-favoured man, wracked by illness, a seer himself? "Keep your cup at hand…but maybe you will also seek a greater cup of gold that will give healing to all."

"What do you mean?" Gal'havad frowned. "What is this golden cup of which you speak?"

"You may soon learn. But it is not time to speak of it yet. Not until we have seen the Maimed King." Pelahan suddenly shook his head as if to clear it and stalked towards the horses. "Now it is time we move on again. Come on, men of the West, we now ride down

Ychenholt toward the great Estuary of Met-Aras, where four rivers meet and the Kingdom of the Wasteland stands."

The warriors of Ardhu clambered up, soggy from the rain, hair hanging in sodden coils on their shoulders and their fur cloaks dripping water. Hwalchmai stamped out the sullen embers of their fire and they mounted and turned their steeds' heads toward the broad track. Soon, as the sky lightened, they began to chatter and joke with each other, even Pelahan. Gal'havad seemed to have completely recovered as if he had never been ill.

Only Ardhu remained quiet and dour, riding at his son's side. He had dreamed of a cup of gold, he who was born of good solid earth and dreamed only of hounds and hall, and who understood not the path of shamans and seers like the Merlin.

A cup locked in a cage of bone. A cup entwined with all their destinies.

CHAPTER SEVEN—THE TREACHERY OF MORDRAED

Mordraed lounged in the shadow of the Tor-Stone, a burial marker that pointed toward the line of undulating hills that led to Magic Hill in the East. Casually, he knapped a flint arrowhead, making its barbs as long and sharp as he could, deadly prongs that would rip the innards of any living creature it pierced. He was far from Kham-El-Ard, and was shirking his duties for the day, including his weapons training with An'kelet. He hated to admit it, but he was bored without Amhar…though how it would be between them now that the other youth had become a Man and taken his adult name, he did not know. If Amhar…Gal'havad now, he thought with a slight sneer…got above himself he would soon have to find a way to bring him down to earth again.

Suddenly he heard a sound behind him, a whisper in the grasses—light feet, almost as soft as hare-feet, but not so quiet that his keen ears could not discern the noise. Grabbing his bow, he leapt to his feet with an arrow on his string. "Who goes there? Show yourself."

A small dark head bobbed up from the tangle of grass and shrubs that grew in the field behind the Tor-Stone. A frightened child's face appeared through a haze of blowing green strands.

"Ga'haris!" Mordraed cast down his bow and ran forward, grabbing his younger brother by the scruff of the neck and swinging him round. "You little fool, creeping up like that. I might have shot you…and then I would have had to finish you off and bury you beneath the Tor-Stone!" He gestured to the menhir behind him, its shadow a long black finger stretching toward the two brothers.

Ga'haris looked terrified, almost as if he thought his brother might just intend to do away with him for disturbing his afternoon sojourn by the stone. Mordraed shook him lightly, frowning. "Little fool, I spoke in jest! I'm not mother…I would not give you to the stone! But I am wondering why you have come so far to seek me out! You and Gharith hardly pay me mind at all, now that you are wards of Ka'hai the Cook." He spoke the last with sarcasm.

Ga'haris grabbed his sleeve and clung. "I…I come because of Mother."

Mordraed's jaw tightened. "What of her?"

"I was playing late, down by the river. I heard a rustle in the bush, and then there she was, watching me. I was scared that someone would shoot her or spear her, 'cos she is not supposed to come so close to Uncle's fort…but she wasn't scared at all. She stepped right out and grabbed me, just as you did! But it wasn't me she wanted to see anyway; it was you. She's given me a message for you, Mordraed."

Mordraed felt his heart begin to pound. "What message was that, Ga'haris?"

"She says that now Ardhu is safely away, she wants to see you. Just for one night. Tonight. She'll meet you on the Prophet's barrow down near the house of the Ladies of the Lake. She says she has a gift for you."

Mordraed's eyes narrowed. Gifts from Morigau were often a two-edged sword. "I will go to her. "But you must tell no one, Ga'haris. Not Gharith, nor any other of your playmates. If you do, Mother would have no hesitation in giving you to the Stone…or the Earth…or the River."

"I promise, Mordraed. I won't tell anyone!" cried Ga'haris, his eyes full of pure terror, and he turned and bounded away like a terrified young deer.

Mordraed slowly followed him, wandering back over the stubbly fields, over a hill crested with the tall barrows of local chiefs and then down toward the Abona, sparkling in the late afternoon sun. He wondered what Morigau could want. He doubted very much it was just a mother missing her favourite son.

Night descended over the fort of Kham-El-Ard. Wood-smoke coiled from holes in thatched roofs, and shrill bone pipes skirled into the gloom, merry and inviting. Warriors strode in and out of the Great Hall of Ardhu, where the Queen sat with Ardhu's chair empty beside her. Despite her earlier anguish at the leave-taking of her son, Gal'havad, Fynavir now smiled and laughed. She wore a wreath of flowers in her hair, had reddened her cheeks with berry juice, and fressed herself in a fine shift of pale linen, thin and revealing, the firelight passing through its folds to catch on the rounded limbs within. A heavy shower of amber beads sewn in appropriate areas spared her modesty yet drew attention to her full breasts and thighs. Even at her age, she was the most striking woman in all Kham-El-Ard.

Mordraed sat in the shadows of the hall, a beaker balanced on his knee, his narrowed eyes fixed on the Queen. His earlier suspicions were still there, and had increased with every passing day. Since Ardhu had journeyed East, Fynavir and An'kelet had grown more relaxed in each other's presence…and then less careful. Others did not see, or else put evil thoughts from their minds, but Mordraed, searching for the signs, saw everything: the easy looks, the glances, a touch upon an arm, a smile. He had hardly ever seen the frosty bitch smile until she had been left alone with An'kelet—and to think he would have to mate with her when he became King!

Rising, he downed the rest of his mead in one go and made a move towards the open door. An'kelet, Prince of Ar-morah, arriving for the nightly feasting and story telling, blocked his path. He was a good hand's breadth taller than Mordraed, and the younger man felt a surge of irrational anger, as if the older man were looking down on him not just through his greater height but with arrogance and superiority. He noted that the foreigner was dressed up like some bright bird of prey, just like his whore, Fynavir—white feathers were braided in his amber hair and his tunic of painted leather was fastened with shiny jet buttons decorated with gold sun-crosses. A belt of fibres twined with bronze threads hung from his waist, fastened by a ring of polished shale, and his two famous daggers, Fragarak and Arondyt dangled conspicuously from it in sheathes of finest horn. "You leave the hall early tonight, Lord Mordraed?" he said, falsely polite. "Are you unwell? I note you did not come for your arms practice today."

Some of the nearby men sniggered and glanced up, hoping to see a confrontation.

"I did not want to tax you, my lord," said Mordraed, veiling his eyes with his lashes to hide the anger in them. His voice was measured, calm. "I have thought since the Stone Lord left that you have looked a bit…tired. As if something has kept you up at night."

An'kelet stared at him, stunned into speechlessness, his face blanching beneath his tan.

Mordraed tossed back his hair and suddenly cast him a razor-sharp grin. "And if you must know my business, I am faring out to meet a woman, Lord An'kelet. A woman! I know you might not approve, since you are so bound with honouring one woman only, being of great purity and holiness…our Great Lady, Fynavir of Ibherna!" He bowed exaggeratedly low in the direction of the Queen, the ends of his hair sweeping the rush-strewn floor.

An'kelet's fists clenched impotently, and Fynavir made a small gasping noise, which she covered with her hand. The warriors lounging about the hearth, already deep in their beakers, laughed, though not unkindly. This was not news. They knew An'kelet was the Queen's chosen champion and that he looked at no other woman. He had made much of oaths he had sworn to his own mother, a priestess of Ar-morah, which bound him to a chaste priest-like life. They did not see what Mordraed was implying.

Mordraed smiled again, a mocking, knowing smile, enjoying the discomfiture of his father's wife and her lover. Then, with another bow in their direction, he swept from the hall into the new-fallen dusk.

Reaching the main gate of the fort he was challenged by a red-faced, tawny-haired dolt of a guard; Mordraed could tell he was stupid just by the look of him. "Oh, 'tis you, Lord Mordraed," the guard stammered, when he stepped into ring of light cast by the man's torch. "You're king's clan so I can't stop you from faring abroad tonight if that's your will. But I'll be shutting the gates after Moonrise, and no one comes in again till dawn…not even relatives of Lord Ardhu."

"That's fine by me, man," said Mordraed. "I'm going to meet a lady, a fine lady. I won't be back ere dawn…if then."

The guard grinned and winked, making him look even more of a simpleton. "A good night to you then, Lord Mordraed."

A good night indeed…that was to be seen. Lithely Mordraed ran down the slope, passing the outer defences with their fierce, man-killing spikes, and entering the field beyond where the Avenue's banks glowed like two white bones in the thin Moonlight. He was glad to be away from the confinement of Kham-El-Ard, where there was always a smelly pork-chewing warrior to your left or right, and people prying into your business, watching you…even when you were of noble lineage. Freedom had been his when he lived on Ynys Yrch—freedom to run over the lonely isles and steal sea-birds' eggs from nests of the cliff and shoot at strange sea creatures that raised their blunt snouts from the swell. Strangers he shot at as well, those who dared to beach their coracles near Loth's settlement; and sometimes his arrows found their mark. He had taken a life before he was even accounted a man, which had pleased Morigau greatly.

He scowled. Although Kham-El-Ard was a great achievement, its buildings and organisation unmatched in Prydn, he did not enjoy its warm, muggy chambers and close quarters where spying eyes were rife and there was little freedom from those you despised. If…when…he was lord of Prydn he would ritually burn it down at the feast of the Bhel-fires, a conflagration that would surely please the spirits. And if he had his way, a few of the swaggering young warriors who had shown him disrespect would go into the fire as well—extra offerings to the Ancestors.

Striding across the field, he reached the Old Henge on the banks of Abona, its dark ditch sprouting thorny bushes, the vague reek of charnel coming from its central area, where ashes lay scattered amidst the pits left by missing stones. He could hear the river murmuring, its voice almost a chant; River-Mother was restless again, spring waking her from sleep after growing fat and slow with ice and excess water. Soon she would mate with her consort Borvoh, the Boiler, and run merrily on her way again, the Holy Cleanser who swept away the old and gave life to the peoples who dwelt near her.

Circling the henge, not wishing to disturb any ancient beings that might lie trapped behind its bank, he hurried down to the edge of the river itself. Rings widened on the water where fishes jumped, silver flashes in the dark, and the stars were like a thousand tallow-candles mirrored on the surface.

He peered at his own reflection too, the stars above him in a crown of light. Beautiful as one of the Everliving Ones who dwelt across the Plain of Honey. But cold, hard as a sarsen slab and death-eyed, with eyes blue, the colour of mourning.

Suddenly an owl shot out of the shadows, flower-faced and with eyes like golden lamps, and swooped above his head. Mordraed's heart sprang into his mouth and he fitted an arrow to his bowstring in an eye's blink, but he held fire and the bird flapped lazily Westwards, wings passing in silhouette over the circle of the Moon. An owl, the sign of She Who Guards, the Lady of the Barrow and the lunar mysteries—She was his mother as much as Morigau and would not harm him. Or so he hoped.

He followed the flight of the bird down the reedy riverbank, out into the valley where the river widened, becoming flat pools of slow-moving brackish water with lily pads floating languidly on the surface. He could see little of the local landmarks but knew that the hill of Ogg lay across the river, with its enclosure for cattle and outlying settlements of mean huts, and that above the steep north-eastern lip of the valley, lay the Hallows of the Kings and Queens—the great cemeteries of Khor Ghor, where long barrows, their wooden mortuary huts crumbled and their owners' bones in disarray, jostled against later round barrows, the graves of mighty individuals who bore gold and shale and jet and warrior's weapons for their journey across the Great Plain. Next to them stood the women's tumuli, their small central tumps holding skeletons of high-status females whose bony claws clutched items for use in the After-Life: amber and faience beads, incense cups and awls, pendants shaped like the halberds of their men.

Mordraed did not want to go too near these mounds, nor catch sight of Khor Ghor in the far distance, its stones floating like ghostly heads in the night. He had no wish to linger with the dead like his mother and Amhar… Gal'havad. He mouthed the youth's new name with petty mockery, still hating that the boy at last had man's status in the tribe.

Up ahead he saw the river flare even wider, almost becoming a small, glassy lake, and in the most still, sluggish part of its swell, a thatched hut that teetered on long stilts that raised it above the water level. The cult-house of the Ladies of the Lake—his aunt Mhor-gan, the one they called Khorreg, the elf-woman, and her mistress, the one-eyed hag called Nin-Aeifa, who was said to have guided his accursed father to the sword Caladvolc. He would not be knocking on their door at this late hour!

Retreating from the riverbank and the spindly-legged house, Mordraed hurried in an uphill direction, following an indistinct track through berry bushes and gorse. Oaks and hazel trees towered over him, branches rustling in the wind, and holly hedges bled red berries. Thorns tore at his clothes and hair. He started peering right and left; he knew that there was a barrow-hill of great age and veneration nearby, where a great prophet of the times of King Bolgos rested, separate in death from others as he has been separate in life due to his great wisdom.

He spied the hill first—solitary and grass grown, its deep ditch full of offerings deposited by the local people of the valley. And then… she was there, crouched on the tomb's summit like a marker-stone—Morigau, sister of Ardhu, her hair down, flowing free in black waves to her waist, her cloak of feathers billowing around her, its tattiness hidden by the darkness of the night.

"Mother." He stepped towards her. He did not really know if he felt happy or not to see her.

"My boy!" She sprang down from that hill of the ancient dead and flung her arms around his narrow waist, kissing his face and mouth in a way he thought unseemly. Uncomfortable, he pushed her back an arm's length and frowned.

"Are you not glad to see me?" she said. "It has been such a long time. You have been remiss. I thought you would have sought me out at least once since entering my brother's hall."

"I would not have my head on a spike or be watched more closely than I already am in Kham-El-Ard."

"Does my brother mistreat you?"

"No, he does not. Yet I am well aware of my position in his domain. If I stepped out of line, I would be crushed like an earthworm under Ardhu Pendraec's heel."

"And what of your brothers? I have seen Ga'haris, but not the other two."

"They are fine, happy and well fed." Mordraed spoke with slight maliciousness. "Much more so than on Ynys Yrch. Agravaen loves the Pendraec, despite all the tales you told of his evils; he follows him like a loyal hound and is sure he will be an esteemed warrior in his warband some day. He never speaks of you."

Morigau's black eyes sparkled. "He is a useless boy, worse than Loth ever was...arrow fodder as I said before. But he may prove useful to us yet, as he is so stupid, so gullible."

"Ardhu's son is friend to me." Mordraed decided he would tell Morigau about Gal'havad, but he would keep silent about his failure to slay the young prince within the stones. "That may also prove useful."

Morigau nodded. "I had heard this rumour, and saw the way he greeted you in Kham-El-Ard. Pah, a weak, effeminate-looking boy not fit to rule the West. Fit only to feed the dark earth. Not like you, my Mordraed, my Dark Moon."

"There is more," continued Mordraed. "A discovery much more important to our cause. But I would not speak of it here; it is cold and the night is deepening, and gods know who or what might be lurking in the brush...maybe even those two raddled hags from the Lake."

"You are right." She ran down the barrow's slope, lissom as a girl, and beckoned him to follow her. "We need to talk where unfriendly ears cannot hear nor eyes see... I also have a gift waiting for you, my son...an important gift to aid you on your road to greatness. I chose it with you alone in mind—Ga'haris should have spoken of it, but pah...the boy is probably as addled as Agravaen! I risked Ardhu's wrath and eluded the mean eyes of my sister Mhor-gan to fare beyond and get it for you. Come and see...but do not be ashamed for me, though I live in a hovel and not the stately abode I am due. Curse my brother and his meanness for keeping me in such a state!"

They walked together down the night-furled valley, Morigau clinging to her son's arm as if he were a lover. She could not stop touching him, his arm, his shoulder; he held his head high and ignored her. Soon a ramshackle hut, small and poorly constructed, came into view, its walls painted with magic symbols to frighten off both spirits and passing men. A pig snorted in a pen, and came snuffling up to the fence as Morigau approached. The animal was a big fat sow, horrid and slug-like, its skin bone-white and dotted with sores. "She is an oracular pig," Morigau explained, poking at the creature with a stick until it squealed and bit at the wood. "I use her in hopes that she will soon tell me of the fall of my brother."

Mordraed entered the hut, bending under the low doorframe. The inside of the hovel smelt foul; rot, sweat and ordure mingled to form a heady stew. La'morak and Ack-olon, Morigau's guards and lovers, were squatting in the corner, so grimy and dishevelled they looked as if they had been rolling in the pen with the oracular pig. A cheerless fire of green wood that spat and hissed burned on a central hearth, and a small, faceless stone idol that Morigau must have brought from Ynys Yrch crouched on a plinth before it. Some wild beast had been killed and blood and tangled innards lay reeking at the foot of the plinth.

Morigau kicked Ack-olon aside and threw down a skin for Mordraed to sit on. She then poured him a drink of honey-mead in a crudely fired beaker. "I stole the honey from Mhor-gan's own beehives. She never knew," she said with satisfaction.

Mordraed tipped back the mead—thank the spirits; at least it was not foul. He was disgusted by the squalor around him, and, despite himself, wished he was back at Kham-El-Ard where the women frequently brushed out the hall with branches and threw dry reeds on the ground. The sullen glowers of Ack-olon and La'morak annoyed him too; it was plain to see they hated him being there. The thoughts of his mother coupling in that sty with the two of them, dirt-caked and grunting, made the gorge rise in his throat.

He fingered the beaker Morigau had given him, fingernail tracing the impressions of wheat around the rim. "Do you want to know what I have found while dwelling with my fa...Ardhu?" he asked.

"Of course," said Morigau. "Tell me any news that might help our cause!"

"My eyes are very keen," he said at length, "and, while in Ardhu's hall, I have seen something no one else has noticed. Or if they have, they have put the thought from their minds and pretended it was other than it was."

"Oh?" Morigau poured a beaker of mead for herself—it was a man's drink, but she was a priestess and normal rules did not apply to her. "And what might that be? I am intrigued, my son."

Mordraed grinned the nastiest grin possible, no light at all in his dark, deep-sea eyes. "You know the Ar-moran, An'kelet of the Great Spear? Ardhu's most loyal friend?"

"Aye." She leaned forward, mouth shining with the thick, sweet mead. Lips too full, too lush, parted over her straight white teeth. "What of him? I have heard that despite his status he takes no woman, that he is loyal only to Ardhu's household only." She laughed. "Are you going to tell me he shares my brother's bed as well…ah, my dear, it would not be the first time a king's shield-brother was something more to him besides!"

Mordraed shook his head fiercely. "No! It is nothing like that! The bronze man…he beds the Queen, the White Woman! And Ardhu Pendraec is too convinced of An'kelet's friendship and the honour of his pasty whore to even notice what is going on within his own dun!"

Morigau's mouth dropped open in surprise and then she started to laugh. Clutching the edge of her cloak in her hands, she strutted around the flickering fire in a victory dance. Ackolon and La'morak glanced at each other before bursting into laughter themselves.

Morigau ceased her dance and knelt back down beside her son. "What welcome news! If there is one thing that can destroy a man, this is it. His woman a wanton slut…and bedding his closest companion, no less. And Ardhu a king, who's household should be above reproach! How all men in Prydn will laugh at his shame! So tell me, Mordraed, what have you seen, what proof of this treachery have you to show Ardhu?"

Mordraed shifted uncomfortably, unnerved by her hot eyes, her hot breath burning against his neck. "None as yet. I know I have read the signs clearly, though…I am no fool. But as you might imagine, if I were to leap up and denounce them both before the warriors, hatred and anger would be directed at me before them and doubts cast upon my word…because I am your son."

Morigau slapped her hands against the dirty, threadbare dress straining over her thin thighs. "Aye…aye, you are right. I would not have you put at risk by denouncing them openly… but, let me think…what about your brother Agravaen? You say he has grown loyal to my brother. Others must see his devotion. If you were to…guide him…let him discover the lovers…Well, we all know what he is like, he cannot keep his big mouth shut, and he would doubtless roar the place down in dismay if he is as loyal as you imply."

Mordraed rubbed his chin. "I could probably arrange such a thing. Agravaen is none too clever and would never wonder if I were suddenly to befriend him."

"It is set then," said Morigau. "Oh, how I wish I could be in Kham-El-Ard to see Ardhu's kingdom crumble, his family in ruins…just as my inheritance, my family was ruined by his father, the usurper U'thyr Pendraec!"

She rocked on her heels, face scowling and ugly as she remembered her past—being tossed from her mother's hut when her new man moved in, the beatings when she, a difficult child who heard black barrow-voices in her head, screamed and howled and bit both her foster-dam and her own mother.

Mordraed shivered; she looked like some kind of fell spirit, a death-wailer or the river-watcher who beat men's bloody death-shrouds on rocks in streams, as she teetered back and forth on her grimy, heels. Suddenly she shook her head, and the fierce glare of total hatred vanished from her eyes. "Your news brings another question to my mind," she said in a heavy, triumphant voice. "If the Ar-moran has been bedding the Queen for a long time, who is to say if the boy men call Prince is in fact Ardhu's get? He does not look like our family. If that doubt could be sown, and the troublesome bastard removed one way or another, a space would open for the rightful heir. You, my son, Mordraed."

Mordraed grunted. He had not even thought of such a thing, which surprised him, for his mind often moved in such directions, even as Morigau's. Secretly he thought his mother was wrong, red hair popped up unexpectedly in many families, but putting the seeds of doubt in men's minds would do no harm.

Morigau continued, "Be that as it may, I had another reason to call you here—not just to see your mother who wishes you only the greatest fame and honour, who worships you as she could no other man." She sidled up to him. "The gift…the gift I spoke of. I am sure you will be pleased. I chose it just for you and risked much to get it…Come with me."

She guided him round the back of the hut, next to the pig's reeking sty, where a small lean-to of woven branches drooped against the hut's outer wall. Mordraed frowned; what on earth could she be about to show him?

Morigau bent over, staring into the shadowed lean-to. "There you go, Mordraed, your gift… Khyloq, my present to you…your bride!"

"What?" Mordraed pushed Morigau roughly aside. Under the branches, huddled in the corner and shivering uncontrollably, was a girl. Long auburn hair a shade darker than Amhar's fell in sodden, dirty tangles over her torn and sodden tunic. Her ankles and wrists were bound, and the twine on her ankles tied to the supporting posts of the lean-to, which would have come crashing down on her if she struggled for freedom.

"Who is she?" he hissed, and when Morigau just laughed, he grabbed his mother's shoulder and shook her violently, until her head snapped back. "Speak, woman! What is this about?"

"She is Khyloq neq Khunedda, daughter of a powerful chief of the middle-lands. A good lineage, my mother's mother's sister was married into the clan, and for the most part the men descended from the old Tin-Lords. I stole her."

"Stole her?" Mordraed stared at Morigau, incredulous.

She waved her hand as if he was silly and childish for being so shocked. "Stole. Abducted…no matter. Her father would not countenance a match since we lost Ynys Yrch, so La'morak, Ack-olon and I took her by night, in the old way. She will make a good wife to you I am sure. She was not much trouble, not too wilful on the road here. Only bit Ack-olon once."

Mordraed exploded. "How dare you do this evil thing? A match and I am the last to know! Have I no say?"

Her black eyes glittered and suddenly she was not just Morigau, but the death-crone, the queen of the Dark Moon, ruling over him, who was only the Moon's servant. "No, you do not. Never forget, my son, that without me to guide you, you will be just another discarded chief's bastard, doomed to watch the less worthy claim things that should be yours."

Mordraed was almost incandescent with rage but managed to control himself. "And what of the White Woman? Did you not say that I must have her as my own, that she is Sovereignty and will confer rulership of the Land onto me? And if you insist on lumbering me with this girl—I cannot take her back to Kham-El-Ard; I am not even in the King's warband as yet and have no wealth to keep a woman!"

"Khyloq will remain with me," replied Morigau. "She will stay a secret until you are well settled on Kham-El-Ard with Ardhu's golden breastplate on your tunic and the Lightning Mace in your hand. You will marry Fynavir…but once the marriage is consummated Khyloq can be brought forward, as second wife. No one will object; a king can have all the wives he pleases. Only Ardhu's foolishness keeps him from taking another besides his white bitch. You will need an heir and quickly; you need to establish yourself before other chiefs decide they have right to the domains of the West. Fynavir will not give you sons; I have heard that the birth of her brat tore her womb and that is why she has been barren ever since. Once you have lain with her and all know that you have ploughed that sacred earth, you can do what you like…" She grinned unpleasantly, rubbing her chin. "If you truly despise her…Well, that can be dealt with in time…It would be most unfortunate if Fynavir died soon after you assumed the position of Stone Lord, but she is growing old, after all…The problem may even be dealt with for you; once Ardhu knows that she lies on her back for An'kelet of Ar-morah he may get the guts of a proper man and put her to death!"

"But then I could not claim her…and right of rule through her."

"No." she agreed. "But his actions would make him accursed, although in the right. Either way, you win, my Mordraed."

"You are a creature of much spite," Mordraed muttered, "But I do not doubt you have my interests at heart…"

"I do. And since I am the one of all our clan who has both intellect and courage," she said coldly," I will be coming to Kham-El-Ard as your advisor when my brother is deposed. And replacing that old fool, the Merlin as priest. I will rip his stringy guts out and divine from them in the very heart of Khor Ghor! Now, no more talk… look at the girl; what do you think? Does she stir you?"

She grabbed the girl's arm and yanked her forward so that Mordraed could see her more clearly. Khyloq whimpered and Morigau struck her, and then ripped her tattered, sodden robe away. She shoved her forward, pulling back her hair and exposing her white body. "Do you like her?" she asked. "So pretty at that age, before the sagging that comes from bearing too many brats."

"Mother, stop that!" Mordraed snarled and pushed Morigau out of the way. Taking off his cloak he tossed it to the soaked, shivering girl, whose tears were now mingling with the rain. "If you are determined this thing must be done, then she will be considered one of our clan and it would be dishonourable to abuse her! In fact, if she is to be mine, then I say to you…leave her be. She can contribute to the chores of the household—by the Ancestors, someone needs to clean this shite-hole up—but she will not be beaten or abused, not by you and not by those two miserable miscreants squatting inside your hut. If I hear otherwise, you will answer to me."

Morigau suddenly bowed her head. "I hear you, son. My boy is grown—he speaks like a man and a king now."

"I will take the girl inside," Mordraed continued, his voice still sharp. "What were you thinking of, tying her up outside like a goat or a dog? She might have died of cold, and a charge of murder would be raised against you, not just abduction!"

He guided Khyloq into the hut and sat her down beside the fire. Looking at her in the flicker of the flames, he found her quite comely—a heart-shaped face, light green-amber eyes, and a lithe wiry body with long legs. Reaching out, he touched her breast. She gave a little gasp and tried to draw away. He drew her closer "No." He shook his head. "You are mine. You heard my mother Morigau. That is why you were taken. For me. We are of noble house; do not be fooled by this vile shack. One day you may not live in such squalor but in a chieftain's hut with gold and amber at your throat. I do not take you to dishonour you and then discard you."

Behind him, he could hear Morigau chanting, speaking words of the marriage rite that would bring fertility to the union and bind them together before the Ancestors. She shuffled round the pair, hopping on one foot in the traditional spell-caster's position hurling fragrant herbs into the embers then dousing youth and maiden with sprinklings of oils and powders. She had stripped off her deerskin tunic and wore only a necklace made of spiky bones carved into phallic shapes. Red ochre signs were drawn around her breasts and above the join of her thighs. She danced and writhed, waving a rattle—the noise of which would frighten off any malign spirits who might seek to steal the bride's fertility or the groom's potency.

Kneeling beside the couple, she took a lump of ochre and chalked signs on Khyloq's torso to match her own. Khyloq protested, but feebly; Morigau was wiry and strong. Watching her straddle the girl, Mordraed began to feel the first surges of real desire, the need to touch and explore that white flesh, to quench the fire of his loins in the cave between her legs. He ripped at the ties on his deerskin trousers as Morigau shoved Khyloq's thighs apart with her knee. Khyloq cried out, but now Mordraed stifled her cry with his mouth, pressing his tongue in between her teeth.

Morigau backed away from Khyloq and took her son's hand, guiding it between the girl's legs. "She will welcome you. The gate will be open. Let your union be fruitful and blessed."

Mordraed straddled Khyloq, pressing her down into the fur on the floor. She struggled, pushing up against him but the touch of her skin made him even more excited. Suddenly he noticed his mother's men staring, their faces looming over the mean fire-pit, distorted with lust and eagerness. He pulled his cloak over his back, hiding himself and the lying girl below him. "At least have the decency to turn your ugly faces away!" he ordered "And if you ever look at my wife with lust again, I will blind you with my dagger and feed your eyeballs to the crows!"

Morigau laughed. "I will attend to the needs of my men. They will soon forget pretty new flesh." She wrapped a strand of La'morak's lank hair around her hand and yanked him towards her.

Mordraed turned back to Khyloq, propping himself up on his arms to look down at her. She had ceased to resist and stared back at him with an expression that blended defiance, resignation, and something else, too, something he'd seen in other women's faces when they looked at him. Captive or no, she was not blind to his charms. "I won't hurt you," he said, "as long as you do not bite me or scratch me…much."

"I won't then," she whispered. "Unless you ask me to."

He laughed and dived on her, throwing her deep into the fur, and in the next hour forgot about pleasing his mother, or his hatred of Ardhu, or the treachery of An'kelet and Fynavir. Khyloq, perhaps wisely realising she had no chance of escape and glad at least that he was not a smelly old brute who took pleasure from beatings or humiliation, was less reticent than he had feared. When he was done he collapsed across her, and slept almost immediately, snoring lightly with his face buried in the long red coils of her hair.

And dreamed of red hair, but not that of the chieftain's daughter Khyloq, his captive bride.

The foxglove hair of the friend who was yet his foe—Amhar who was now Gal'havad.

CHAPTER EIGHT: THE MAIMED KING

In their nighttime camp beneath a lone pine under strange, unfamiliar eastern skies, Ardhu was woken from sleep by a sound he had not heard for a very long time. He rolled over and stared at the sky, saw wings white against the golden-red orb of the rising sun. Beside him, Gal'havad stirred. "What is that sound?" he said sleepily. "It is like the wail of a lost soul seeking its barrow-mound."

Pelahan, cooking a hare on a makeshift spit in a little hollow near the camp, glanced up. "It is a seagull, little lord. We are almost at the Wastelands now. The great waters of the Northern Sea will be spread out before you once we pass the next hill."

The companions rose and broke their fast, then mounted their steeds once more. They fared into the burgeoning light, passing stunted shrubs beaten low by the wind and spare, tall trees of a type unseen in their western home. More gulls appeared, screeching and flapping overhead, squabbling over titbits found amidst the grasses, which were long and tough, yellow under the strengthening sun.

"There's a strange smell in the air" Gal'havad raised his head and took a deep breath in through his nose. He licked his lips. "I can taste something in my mouth also."

"That is salt from the sea, Prince," said Pelahan. "The whole sea is awash with it."

"It tastes like tears," murmured Gal'havad, wiping his mouth on the back of his hand.

Pelahan nodded. "Aye. Some say the saltiness is the tears of the Maedh'an na Marah, the Maidens of the Wave, who have the lower bodies of fish but wish for two legs, so that they can come on shore and couple with their mortal lovers. Instead they must take their men Underwave where they drown."

The trail wound up a shallow slope, cresting a dune made of sand and earth, and once on top Pelahan signalled for a moment's halt. He turned his cadaverous face into the wind and let out a long, painful sigh. Ardhu was sure he saw tears standing in his weary, faded eyes. "The Wastelands lie before you," he said.

The companions looked. Ahead they saw an endless stretch of coastline, sand mingling with rough flinty shore. Sea grasses blew, hissing in the wind, and water streaked in amongst them, making small freestanding islets where birds nested—terns, gulls, plovers. The water beyond was choppy and dark, and the sky above it a flat iron-grey. A northern sea, colder and less kindly than the turquoise waters off the coasts of Belerion in the farthest west, and even more fierce than the Ibhernian Sea, which formed a barrier between Prydn and its sister isle.

"It will not be long now before we reach the Maimed King," said Pelahan. "I pray he still lives. I have been gone long and all his men have abandoned him. He is alone, in his agony and despair."

"Before we meet this King, tell me more of what has happened here," said Ardhu, as the party descended the dune and cantered along the bleak seashore under the threatening sky, with frightened nesting birds bursting up before their horse's hooves.

"King An-fortas ruled the East, the land of Y-khen, for many years; he held this coast as you held the west, keeping back raiders who came across from the Flatlands in their boats seeking land and occasional plunder. But he grew old and he refused to see that he could no longer war as a young man; he fought a Northern Man from the Ice Mountains, huge as a giant with hair the colour of the sun, and though he killed the invader, he took a dagger-wound in the thigh which crippled him. Now you know the law, Terrible Head…a king yourself. A king who is blemished bodily cannot reign. The King and the Land are united in the eyes of the Spirits, and if one is damaged and failing, so will the other be. But the people loved An-fortas and none wished death to him, so he ruled on and did not hand his kingship to his son. His health worsened, no healer could cure his wound… then a sickness came, and whole villages perished from the delta right down the coast. At one time, the sea-strand was alive with fishermen, but look now, it is empty, a place where the gulls play with dead men's bones. Aye, those plague-touched men did not even get a pyre for their last journey, but lay where they fell, food for birds and crabs."

They travelled on a short way, clambering over dunes, forcing their way through tangled bushes stiff with salt. Suddenly Hwalchmai gave a shout. Rising in his saddle, he peered into the distance, eyes shaded by his hand. "I can see a structure built upon the beach. Birds gather over it, like those that hover over biers where the dead are laid that their spirits may be set free."

"I fear we may be too late," said Pelahan grimly. "Let us ride with haste."

The companions cantered down the beach, splashing through the tidal pools, and soon reached a circular structure wrought of stout timbers like Woodenheart, where the rites of the newly dead were spoken. However, there the similarity ended–unlike Woodenheart, its carefully shaped posts were crammed closely together, forming a tight barricade against both the inward-creeping tides and the intrusion of the outside world. The wood it was carved from was dark, smoothed by the abrading salt and spray, and it held a sombre, almost menacing air. A small v-shaped entrance was the only passage into the interior, the gap so small it was impossible to get a clear view of what lay inside.

The companions dismounted and Pelahan fell to his knees in the sand as if overcome, holding his head and rocking back and forth, gibbering in the strange eastern dialect which held words unknown in the rest of Prydn due to migration from the Lowlands and the far North.

Ardhu approached the timber circle with caution. Bowing before it, he cast down some bluestone chips he had brought from Khor Ghor as an offering to its guardians, whoever they were. Then he squeezed himself through the v-shaped entrance; no mean feat, despite that he was still a slender and wiry-built man.

Inside Ardhu beheld an unsettling sight. A giant tree trunk stood upended, its head buried deep in the sands, burrowing down toward the Underworld. Twisted roots snaked toward the hazy sun, and the marks of axes could be seen preserved upon them where the tree had been hacked from the ground. Upended cinerary urns circled it and clustered around the walls of the enclosure.

On this makeshift altar lay the body of a man, spread-eagled, staring open-eyed at the heavens. He was old but still tall and muscled, with white hair and beard that streamed down the protruding roots of the stump. Fine clothes he wore, a tunic of woven nettle-fibres, a belt held in place with polished bone hooks and a necklace of hundreds of perforated shells that clattered in the sea breeze. His legs were bare, spread apart. In his right thigh was a great gash, open like a mouth, its lips stained black with putrefaction.

Ardhu went to his side and held his golden armlet in front of the open mouth. The metal fogged; the man still lived.

"Per-Adur!" he shouted. "Come at once. The Maimed King is in here…we must get him out and tend to him. There may not be much time!"

Per-Adur climbed through the narrow gap, puffing and panting as he did so, and rushed to his lord's side. Disgust darkened his face as he smelt the odour of rancid flesh. "I will do what I can," he said, "but this is not a good place, in this house of death. Do you not mark what this circle, lord? The Maimed King has come here to give himself to his gods."

"Well, pray they will not take him yet," said Ardhu, "at least not until I know what ails this land and how it may affect the rest of Prydn."

Between them the two men lifted the supine body of the King. He was heavier than he looked, and his head flopped forward as if he were indeed dead. Carefully they squeezed him through the gap in the timber posts and laid him out on the sandy ground. Hwalchmai, Bohrs and Gal'havad stared, dumb-founded.

Pelahan rose from the ground, wiping his haggard, deathly face, and beckoned to Ardhu's men to follow him. "This way, with the King. We will take him to the old village where the people of the East once lived in joy. An-fortas's hall still stands, though ruinous."

Crossing the salt-marsh with the Maimed King lying over the neck of Per-Adur's horse, the company reached dryer land and a deep stand of tall pines. Inside, amidst the green of the trees, was a shallow ditch with a dilapidated wattle fence spanning it. Passing this ramshackle palisade, the companions entered the remnants of a village. Huts lay tumbled in the pine needles, roofs ripped away by the winds, amidst a sea of animal bones, not from any merry feast but from beasts that seem to have died where they stood and then were left to decay.

The central hut, large and thick-walled, still retained its wattle roof, and it was here Ardhu's men carried An-fortas the Maimed King. They placed him on a bier made of their fur cloaks and saddle blankets and Per-Adur knelt to minister to him, while the others stoked up a fire to warm the dreary place.

"It is bad," said the healer, as he prodded inside An-fortas's wound with a pair of fine bone tweezers. "I have never seen worse. I am surprised he has survived this long. There is only one chance…and that is if I can burn the wound with fire and purify it. However, to do such a thing to one so ill might be worse than letting him go to peaceful rest amongst the Ancestors."

"Peaceful rest?" Pelahan's voice was hoarse. "Feel how he burns already!" He placed his mottled hand on the sick man's brow. "Surely your craft could bring him no more pain that what he suffers now."

"You were told," said Bohrs, a bit gruffly, "that we are warriors, not magic men. Maybe you should have asked the Merlin to come here instead."

"If he dies," said Pelahan, "it is the beginning of the end of all Kings of this Age of Men. For you, too, Ardhu Pendraec." He rocked back onto his heels, suddenly staring at his ruined hands as if they were alien to him. "I have not told you the whole story, men of the West," he murmured breathlessly. "I am not just the servant and messenger of An-fortas. I am his son. The people who pass this accursed place on the long trade-roads into the West, call me the Fisher King, for that is all I can do now, with illness consuming my flesh…fish these coasts to provide some small sustenance for me and my failing sire. Once we were masters over these lands and all in them…this settlement was called Kar-Bonek, and was a mighty centre of trade, where chiefs from the Middle and Low-lands exchanged metals and riches with us…but now my father lies fallen, with a wound that will not heal, and I…am the lord of naught but fish! I should have listened to the shamans and done what needed to be done when his illness unmanned him, but I would not move my hand and take up the flint knife. I loved him too much, and that was my weakness…and so the Spirits struck me down as well. Then fatal illness ravaged our tribe, and the Ghort, the hunger, the famine, followed pestilence. The Spirits are angry, and the Land withers and is not reborn in spring."

Gal'havad approached An-fortas's bier and gazed into the face of the mortally sick man. Grey and soft it looked, as if already mouldering. "The look of the Otherworld is about him," he said softly. "His spirit seeks to leave the flesh that trammels it."

"I fear you are right," Per-Adur murmured in a low voice. "But let us get water into him; he probably has not had drink or nourishment for many days."

"Here…you may use my holy cup." Gal'havad took out the twilight-hued stone cup that came from the Sacred Pool and proffered it. "This is the cup bestowed upon me by the Lady Mhor-gan. She is a great magic-woman, a priestess, and the water it came from is blessed above all others, the birth-pool of Abona. Maybe its qualities can revive the Maimed King."

Per-Adur's expression was dubious but he bowed his head in agreement… after all, what harm could it do? Taking the small stone cup from the youth, he filled it with water from his pig's bladder flask and handed it back to Gal'havad. "The cup is yours to use, my Prince."

Gal'havad leaned over the Maimed King, thinking how mighty he must have been in his youth, a golden warrior who could cast spear and shoot bow and fight enemies with his axe. Now he was just a broken shell, his kingship robbed by the wound in his leg. Quietly he mouthed a prayer to Nud Cloudmaker, who, besides being lord of the Milky Way and Snarer of Souls, was a healer-god with a pack of red-eared dogs that licked the wounds of the afflicted until their poisons dissolved. Gal'havad wished such magic dogs would appear now; though even hounds of the Underworld might be hard pressed to heal such an evil wound as that in the thigh of An-fortas.

The water from the little cup trickled onto the parched lips of the King. Gal'havad gently pulled the cracked lower lip down to allow more of the fluid to get into the injured man's mouth. An-fortas made an unexpected gasping noise and began to writhe on the furs, fighting his fever, perhaps fighting his imminent death.

His eyelids flickered, and suddenly he gazed up straight into the face of Gal'havad. "Who is this I see?" he croaked, voice rasping out of his parched throat. "Are you one of the Everliving Ones, come to guide me across the Great Plain to Moy Mell beyond? Are you, with your bright hair like flame, the Peaked Red One?" He spoke an ancient eastern name for Bhel in his Year-End aspect, when he carried his burning light down into the depths of Winter, leading a spiral-trail of spirits behind him.

Gal'havad touched his red hair, pushing it back from his face so that An-fortas could see him clearly. "No, lord. I am just a mortal man. I am Gal'havad of Khor Ghor, son of Ardhu Pendraec the Stone Lord of Prydn, and I am here, with my father and the best of his men, to aid you and your son, the Fisher King."

"Gal'havad." The old man grasped his sleeve with shaking fingers. "Hawk of Summer…a saviour come from the Summerlands, despite your protests that you are just a man… I can see purity and goodness in you, with my failing eyes; maybe you of all men could bear the cup of gold that can restore the world, the cup that was taken away."

"What cup is this, Lord An-fortas?" asked Ardhu uneasily, remembering his dreams, remembering the muttered words of Merlin as he fell deep in trance in Khor Ghor.

An-fortas paused, chest heaving as he struggled to take a normal breath. "In better times I had a golden mug wrought for me from the finest gold in Ibherna. Many Moons their smiths laboured to make it true and fair—a rimmed beaker, with a handle fastened to it by gold rivets. It was not a cup for a chieftain to hold in his hand to show off to his underlings—it was a sacred holy thing, whereby men could commune with the gods by drinking mead flavoured with henbane, which would open the door of the Un-world to them. It was for communion with the sky, with Bhel himself, and also for libation to the Earth, to the Lady whose womb we all return to. It could never be set down, for its bottom was fashioned in a curve."

"What happened to it?" asked Ardhu. "Is it still here?"

An-fortas shook his head weakly. "When I first was wounded I tried to do magic on myself, even bathing the gash with water mixed with special potions in the cup itself. Nothing worked, and one day in anger, I hurled the cup across my hut and dented both handle and base. I know not how tales of my rash anger spread beyond the East, but a Moon-turn later nine maidens, a sacred number, came riding hence on ponies, beautiful girls…no, priestesses, from the isle of Ibherna. They looked on me with pity but also anger, when they took the cup and saw its damage. It was the metalworkers of that green isle who had wrought it, at my behest, and they told me it had been bathed in the sacred basin that was the Cauldron of Rebirth of their chief-god, Dag. Now, they told me, it must go back to be repaired and re-consecrated…and that with my unhealed wound I was no longer a king and no longer worthy to hold it." Tears of despair leaked from the corners of his dimming eyes. "I fear they were right. Once they had left, my kingdom was laid waste utterly, the plagues coming and the sand rising in great storms to cover all, and I have become the ruined creature that you see."

Bohrs was scratching his beard. "This holy cup…" he said. "If we were to fetch it back for you, fixed and made holy again, could that help? Is that what you think?"

An-fortas sighed. "I do not now think there is any help for me in this world. But there is more to this world than me."

He glanced at Ardhu. "You have been a good lord of men," he said. "All know the name of Ardhu Pendraec. But goodness is not enough. Dark times are coming to us all. The Wasteland is like a growth; it is a blight on Prydn, but beyond that it is also a death of hope…and that in turn makes man's mind a Wasteland as surely as a field that gives forth no corn."

"I do not understand," said Ardhu. "I am not a shaman like the Merlin. What I know is what is bought by sword or by trade."

"Know this," said An-fortas, "the King is the Land, the Land is the King. When the land is empty of seed, it must be filled anew in order for living things to grow—the corn, the barley, and the little apples on the trees. If the old King cannot plant the seed and make it come to fruition, he must feed the soil with the very essence of his life."

A silence fell over the men in the chieftain's hut. "He is raving," murmured Hwalchmai, shaking his head. "His long illness has addled his mind."

"Find the cup." An-fortas's voice sank to a whisper. "Maybe it is the one thing that will save Prydn from the Wasteland. Maybe the glory of the Quest will save a king from the perils of encroaching age…" He took another heaving breath, his lungs rattling. "Do not try to heal me further. I must fight my fate no more. Carry me back to the Holy Circle on the strand and let me go to my Gods with dignity. Would that I had heard them calling me home years ago when first I was wounded, and heeded that call."

"No…" Pelahan the Fisher King's voice was a low groan of misery. "Father…do not ask this, not yet. I have brought them hence to save you…"

"It is his wish," said Ardhu darkly. "And if he speaks truth, then it should have been done long ago. But by the Eye Goddess, I wish the Merlin or some other shaman was here to oversee this act."

The warriors of Ardhu carried the Maimed King back down towards the sea. Behind them the pines rustled, their needles smelling fresh and alive. All around the salt marshes gleamed under the light of a huge Moon that cast a light-trail across the swell of the sea. The Moon's face was tinted oddly red, darker than a harvest moon. Their passing feet crunched on pebbles and then brushed through shifting sands.

Soon they saw the funereal timber circle, the Milky Way of Nud Cloudmaker a misty, boiling streak overhead—his enchanted cloak in which he snared the spirits of men to pass on to his son, Hwynn the White, lord of the Underworld, for judgement before they were sent West.

Ardhu and Hwalchmai gently manoeuvred An-fortas through the entrance to the shrine and laid him back on the natural platform formed by the upside-down tree. Its huge coiled roots thrust up into the night, embracing the limp and failing body of the old man. He stared up at the sky, eyes losing their focus, glazing as they looked into otherness and eternity.

Ardhu's breath emerged a ragged fog before his lips and he loosed his dagger Carnwennan from its sheath. "If I must, I will do this thing as King of Prydn." He rubbed at his thigh, suddenly aching as it often did on chill nights such as this—his thigh, wounded long ago by the tusks of the Boar T'orc, the ravager of Prydn sent to plague him by his sister Morigau. But he was healed, well healed…and not so old or so frail…not yet…

Unexpectedly, Gal'havad came up beside him; his pale face awash with a faint sheen of sweat, his forest-green eyes burning with strange passion. "Father, I will do it, if that would please you more."

Ardhu shook his head violently. "You are too young for such dealings, which are the territory of priest and shaman! I must stand in, as called for, for I am King."

"I will be King after you," argued Gal'havad, "and I am touched by the spirits—the Merlin himself said so and you have noted it yourself. A few days ago I sent a traitor to his death and the torments that will await him in the Un-world; now, showing great mercy, I will send this good chief to the Plain of Honey, as he wishes and as the Great Ones wish."

Ardhu stared at his son—the shining face, the dark red hair like a burnished shield in the dimness, the white cowl of Nud's starry mantle above his slender shoulders. "Do as you will, my son. You are accounted a Man of the Tribe, and you have your own special wisdom; more, in some things than I, or so it would seem."

Gal'havad drew Kos'garak from his belt. Starlight glinted on the three golden rivets holding the hilt in place. Three times he circled the failing Maimed King, the fallen giant lying on the upturned stump in the centre of the funerary wooden ring. Beyond the shrine the waves went thump, thump, thump, beating watery fists against the shore, a solemn drumbeat in the night.

Then he bent over the Maimed King and solemnly cut one wrist with his knife. A thread of redness slid from the gaping cut and trickled into the damp soil at the foot of the trunk. He then proceeded to the other arm and opened the second vein, allowing more blood to feed the earth, the hungry earth that was withering and dying without a whole and hale king to reign over it. The Maimed King did not move, seeming not to feel the cuts, the beginning of his life slipping away.

Gal'havad moved the dagger upwards, letting it rest for a moment beneath the white bearded chin. He hesitated a moment, face taut with the enormity of what he had chosen to do, and then with a sharp and brutal motion, he drew it across the Maimed King's throat, instantly severing the great vein of life. The air went red with spray, and the old man gave one great gasp as his spirit fled upward into the sky, vanishing into the star-spangled cloak of Nud.

Gal'havad sheathed his dagger and knelt down in the sandy soils, heaving with sobs, suddenly overcome by the enormity of the sacrifice. Ardhu went to his side and tried to raise him, but he felt heavy, limp, and the pain that sometimes needled Ardhu's leg shot through him, making him unable to lift him further.

Pelahan appeared at the entrance of the wooden ring; no tears for his father marred his ruined face, but his eyes were without light, black and hopeless. He was the one to wrench Gal'havad to his feet, gaze into his face and shake him lightly to bring him to himself. "Look at me, boy. You did what I could not; you did what had to be done, what should have been done long ago, and I thank you."

Gal'havad turned and brought out his small stone chalice, glittering faintly in the gloom. Gently he filled it with the blood of the fallen king, the holy blood that fed the Land. "By the power within this font of life, I swear I will find the golden cup of King An-fortas," he said quietly," though I may fare to the end of the world and die in the attempt."

"Make no vows of such a nature" Ardhu said sharply, eyes narrowing. "Do not forget who you are…"

But Gal'havad's green eyes were stubborn. He said nothing, but stood with the blood running over his fingers.

"We will bury him, now, in a place no one shall ever find him, giving him back to the earth that it might grow strong again with his sacrifice," said Pelahan. "Will you help me one more time in this, King of the West?"

Ardhu nodded, his face grey and weary. "This one more thing…yes. Then I must be away for Kham-El-Ard, to talk with Merlin and Mhor-gan and see what counsel they can give about the blight on Prydn and on this cup of gold that An-fortas spoke of."

Pelahan stood aside and Per-Adur and Hwalchmai climbed into the ring, making gestures against evil when they saw the dead king lying on the tree stump, the blank surfaces of his eyes reflecting the stars and his blood, now a dark viscous stream, puddling on the ground beneath him.

"It is time to bury my father," said Pelahan. "He will not lie here, though our Ancestors and elders did. His is a different death, his flesh not given to the birds and beings of the air, but to the earth and the marsh, the dark wet places that breed new life."

Ardhu's men lifted the body of An-fortas for the last time and carried it forth on its final journey. His corpse was heavy, stone-like, on their shoulders. They bore him far inland, into a land of marshy pools where terns nested and green tongues of heatless flame flittered over the bog, the malevolent souls of Ancestral ghosts.

A jetty of woven withies thrust out into the marsh at its deepest point, the remnants of an old track like that found crossing the fens of Afallan in the West. A rotted stump of an old idol sat at the end of the jetty, its head split so that one could not tell if it was meant to be a male or female deity…and the body gave no indication, for it was a hermaphrodite, with pendulous wooden breasts and a detachable phallus.

Pelahan walked slowly to the end of the withy pier and beckoned the others forward. He took the body of the Maimed King from them and shut his eyes with gentle fingers. Removing his own deerskin cloak he wrapped An-fortas in it, hiding face and hands and feet, and pinned it fast with his own crutch-headed cloak-pin. He murmured words none could hear, nor wanted to for they were words of new king to the old, of a contrite son to a father had he failed. He then raised the body to a kneeling position on the edge of the jetty and let it fall.

With a thick, slurping splash it hit the murky water. Nesting birds whirred up, affrighted, squawking their anger and terror into the gloom. The wrapped bundle bobbed for a moment on the swell, then spiralled down into Otherness, bubbles bursting as it passed into forever.

Overhead the first glow of dawn touched the sky, red as the blood of An-fortas's final wound.

Red as the blood that still marred Gal'havad's garments and skin, patterning his face like morbid tattooing.

Ardhu glanced wearily toward the morning star, Light-of-Day, just rising in the Eastern sky, a pure white flame. It was the only pure thing he had seen for days. All else seemed rotten, putrescent.

"Come," he said, his voice hoarse, ragged. "Let us collect our horses and set out upon the long road home. And may we never return here to the place, unless its fate is changed and its eternal winter turns to spring."

CHAPTER NINE: THE RITUAL SHAFT

Mist swirled around the Stones of Khor Ghor, exhaled from the ground by spirits of the ancient dead. Above, a reddish, mottled moon was shining amidst a circle of feeble stars. Slowly the Merlin hobbled toward the great ancestral monument, his weary feet dragging as he limped up the Avenue. He leaned heavily on his staff, stopping every now and then and scowling. How he hated the growing frailty of his body! His acolytes had tended him well in Deroweth but they told him he needed to rest, that in his last trance, when he had fallen amid the Stones, a malicious spirit had elf-shot him in the temple, causing his left side to freeze. Whether he would ever recover completely was unknown; many men died from such venomous shot, and those that survived were often left blighted, their faces and limbs forever frozen, words slurring in their throats.

But he was not like other men. He was the Merlin, shaman and High Priest of Khor Ghor! He would not lie abed and be spoon-fed slop by women! He would resume his position until the gods of the Everlasting Sky saw fit to smite him down forever. No, he could not die yet and go to the long house of his Ancestors, not while he felt there was wrong afoot in the lands of his people. Not when he sensed the realm he had struggled to build, with Ardhu as his chosen instrument of power, was shaking, shuddering at its foundation. Destruction and desolation dwelt in the East, where Ardhu was now, but day by day more reports came from West and South and North… crops failures, feuds over land, disease that caused abandonment of settlements. Some messengers came seeking the advice of the Merlin or the war-lords of Ardhu's court, but more often these days the displaced, the starving came to Kham-El-Ard, walking on blistered bare feet, clad in naught but the rude skins of beasts as if they were men from a thousand years ago or more. Their sunken cheeks were as sharp as those of skulls, and hollow eyes looked accusingly at the frail, bent figure of the Merlin, as if saying, "You promised more. We had more. But it could not last…the dream has died."

"The dream will not die!" Merlin cried out, to himself, to the ghosts and otherworldly beings that floated in the field between the Dance-of-Ancestors and the great Spirit-Path that divided the Lands of the Living from the Domain of the Dead.

He was nearly at the Stone of Summer, circled by its ring-ditch; beyond its vast bulk, the henge bank was a chalky blur in the moonlight. The Three Watchers, Guardians of the Door, rose like twisted fingers to beckon him into the heart of the Great Sanctuary, cave of the Sun, Womb of Time, and entrance to the worlds of the Unseen.

Out of the corner of his eye he saw something move, flitting amid the Stones. Breath hissing between his teeth, he drew the honed flint dagger he always carried at his waist. And then laughed…for between the Stones hopped a large grey-brown hare, one of the sacred beasts of She-Who-Guards, whose faceless plaque towered on the Western Trilithon. It loped away into the coiling mists, vanishing over the hump of the bank.

He followed the animal's passage with his eyes and suddenly his laughter curdled in his throat. He caught movement again near the northernmost of the Four Stations. This time, it was no animal.

He was certain it was not a guard sent from Deroweth; he had seen the warrior-priests traversing the Great Plain as he had crossed from the Spirit-Path to the Sacred Avenue. It also looked too slight to be a grown male…maybe a boy…or a woman.

His eyes narrowed and his thin fingers gripped his dagger hilt. There was one woman he hated—and feared—above all, the woman who was Ardhu's sister, mother of the bastard Mordraed. She of all women would not fear to come here by night, treating with her dark spirits of chaos and death, her hands skimming through spoil on the bank, seeking bone fragments and tiny ear-bones for her spells and brews. How he wished he could have found a way to dispose of her, without starting a blood-war with her kin. He had whispered fell words to the wind, cast evil curses in the direction of her hovel in the river valley, but like old roots grown tough she did not sicken and die but became harder, tougher. True, her behaviour had been exemplary since Ardhu took in her sons, but Merlin knew she was not the kind to bury her hatreds or give up fighting for what she believed was rightfully hers…

He stalked toward the short, squat station stone, his dagger glinting in the pallid light, ready. He had little strength, but by the gods, he would do his best to stop the she-bitch if indeed it was her.

The figure turned and a hood was thrown back. For a moment, seeing wild black hair and dark eyes, Merlin thought it was indeed Morigau, but he quickly recognised the gentler cast of the features of Mhor-gan, Ardhu's younger sister, one of the Ladies of the Lake.

"By Great Bhel, Mhor-gan, I nearly struck you with my sacred dagger," he said harshly. "I thought you were Morigau."

Her black brows rose. "And what made you think of my wayward sister?"

"Because I know too well that she is not sitting in her hut weaving and making pots like normal women! I cannot read her mind, but I know her thoughts are dark. She did not come to Kham-El-Ard just for the protection of her sons, for whom she cares little."

"She cares for one," said Mhor-gan carefully.

Merlin sighed. "Yes, Mordraed…the child of Ardhu's folly. 'Man of Judgement' is what his name means…I can only guess why Morigau named him so."

"They say he is very skilled at arms," said Mhor-gan, "and that, if the other men concur, Ardhu will allow him into his warband by the Winter Solstice, if not before. He is also…friends…with Gal'havad."

Merlin's face twisted, his eyes pained. "Yes, I have seen how Mordraed has availed himself of young Amhar's good nature. What can I say to make them part? What, even as high priest, can I do? Ardhu once spoke of killing all brats born in the month of Bhel-fires when he knew Morigau was carrying his seed, but it was I who cautioned him against such a rash act. Now I do not know if I was wrong."

"The boy has done no evil…yet," said Mhor-gan. "And may not; it would be unfair to judge him for the shadows that lay upon his birth."

"As you say…but I am still troubled. And I deem you are too, for why else would you wander here alone after Moonrise?"

Mhor-gan pulled her cloak tightly about her and stared at the sky. Her breath was a fog around her pale lips. "Yes, you are correct, Merlin. I am troubled. I have hardly slept in weeks; my dreams are evil and unsettling. So I came to pray for guidance at the Stones…and now that you are here, I shall also seek counsel with wise Merlin. I knew in my heart you would be at Khor Ghor tonight…and that you have felt my unease too."

She looked at him, her countenance suddenly grown very white. "Merlin…my bees have gone."

He looked quizzically at her, not understanding. "Gone?"

"Fled away. Flown in a great cloud to the south. I do not know why. And the plants I grow with Nin-Aeifa, she of Great Esteem, they have not sprouted, or if they have, they turn to slime when we harvest them. The Great Lady herself has dreamed and spoken in her dream-state; she told of a far-off mountain that breathes flame straight from a pit where malignant fire-spirits dwell…and with the coming of the flame and smoke there will be a year of no summer, a year when night and day are much the same. A time when Bhel will weaken when he should wax strong."

Merlin tried to laugh. The sound fell dead amidst the pillars of Khor Ghor. "Bad years come…it has happened before in my long life. They pass. As for this dream of Nin-Aiefa's…surely it is but an unsettling dream, or betokens other than it seems."

Mhor-gan glanced at the sky; ragged clouds were covering the Moon, wrapping the stars, making them wink out, one by one. "The worst has not come yet, Merlin. But it is coming, I am sure of it. Have you not noticed? On some nights Bhel's visage is bloody...as it is in Winter. The Sky looks streaked by blood. Even the Moon's face is sometimes tinged with red. It is the beginning...of what could be the end of time."

Merlin hunched over, suddenly looking as old as the Stones themselves, a creature old as the time that Mhor-gan thought might end. "We must fight against this threat if we can."

"But can we?" said Mhor-gan. "It is not a battle for blades and arrows...though they may have their part." She tossed back her head, scenting the air. "I can almost smell ash upon the wind, the scent of crops rotting in the fields. The Land is losing its power, Merlin...can you not feel it in the earth below, the air above?"

Merlin's voice emerged a harsh croak; he despised himself for the feebleness of it. "I can feel it, Lady Mhor-gan. And if it is my counsel you seek, I can tell you nothing...only that I am afraid. There... I have said it. The great Merlin, high priest of Khor Ghor, is full of fear."

"And where is Ardhu, my brother, in this time of peril..." Mhor-gan said softly. "The King who is the Land itself, bound body and blood to earth and stone, who lies with the White Phantom daughter of Intoxicator?"

"You know where he is, lady. He seeks the Maimed King in the East, to put right what has gone wrong in that domain."

"Do you think he will succeed?"

Merlin stared at the ground; he spat the next word out like venom. It hung between them on the cold night air. "No."

Mhor-gan moved forward, touching the old man's shoulder. "Merlin, we must speak more of this matter...in the presence of Nin-Aeifa. Come with me to our House of the Spirits in the land of the Lakes. It is not good for you to be out here in these cold mists so long; you are not well...I can see the frailty in you."

Merlin pursed his lips, shaking his head. He tried to avoid Nin-Aeifa, the only woman he had ever loved, long ago beneath the apple-blossoms of the Isle of Afallan where the fey King Afalak harvested the sacred fruit for his brother, Hwynn the White Fire, to succour the dead passing West into immortality. They had come together like the clash of swords, the snarl of summer lightning, but had parted at destiny's whim, their individual paths mapped out by the powers that moved the earth and sky. He feared her now, old and strange, with her one blind eye that gazed into Otherness...She was at the Beginning of him, and perhaps she too would have a part in his Ending...

Mhor-gan took Merlin's arm like a solicitous daughter. He could smell the scent of her—Abona's water and wildflowers. "Come," she said, her voice kindly, warm.

He peered into her face, so like her malevolent sister's, yet like Ardhu's too. Dark and light, foul and fair. Shadows coiled in her eyes; he could not read her thoughts there.

A shiver of fear rippled through him; in the Stones, the black-plumaged birds that nested under the lintels let out a harsh cawing and flapped up into the heavens, disturbed by something unseen, perhaps a passing fox that ran between the uprights.

What would be, would be.

Huddling into his cloak, he let himself be led like a sacrificial beast on the long path over the barrow-downs to the House of the Ladies of the Lake.

The house within the Lake was lit with tallow cups when Merlin and Mhor-gan arrived. Nin-Aeifa sat cross-legged on a cowskin, eyes closed, deep in meditation, the yellowish light flickering over the sharp planes of her face. Her hair had turned stone-grey over the years, but she had caked it with chalk paste and twisted it into braids that had solidified and fanned out from her head like pale, frozen snakes. A necklace made of faience baubles and hundreds of tiny pink shells from the distant shore swung around her neck, and from her belt, cinched tight at the waist with a clasp of polished antler, dangled perforated lumps of shale, amber and quartz, their surfaces pecked with designs.

"Merlin…it has been long since we have met," she murmured, without even opening her eyes. Her voice was deep, rich as wood smoke…unchanged from what he remembered from his youth.

"Nin-Aeifa…" he breathed her name, could say no more. He felt suddenly dizzy and weak. The herbs she burned in a hearth behind her set up a stink that made his eyes water and his head spin.

Mhor-gan guided him to a small wooden stool near her mistress and helped him to sit comfortably, then brought out a red, handled beaker filled with rich, thick mead. "The last for a while, I fear," she said sorrowfully. "Now that my bees have gone."

Merlin took a draught of the mead; the potent liquor steadied him. Nin-Aeifa opened her eyes and fluidly rose to her feet; in silence, she glided towards him. He could have almost sworn her bare feet did not touch the clay floor.

"Merlin," she said. "You see the world of beyond even as I do."

"It has been my gift and my curse. As it is yours."

"You have seen then the darkness and the cold that is to come, the withering of the land?"

"Seen it? Lady Nin-Aeifa, already there are a trickle of people arriving at the gates of Kham-El-Ard, homeless and starving. I have done more than merely 'seen' it in a dream. It is here, though as yet the trickle has not become a flood."

"Then you will not be angered by what I have to say to you."

He spread out his thin, knotted hands on his skin-clad knees. "I will make no promises on that, Nin-Aeifa. Speak."

She took a deep breath, clutching her quartzes and ambers and stroking them like talismans. "The King is the Land and the Land is the King… Merlin, my brother, my lover—the reign of Ardhu Pendraec is nearly at an end. The hand that was strong begins to grow weak. The Sun that was bright is eclipsed by a dark Moon. The skies grow dim with ash and winter grows long. The White Queen who was the earth that mated with the son of the Sun turns her face away…her favours granted elsewhere. What will save the Land? I do not know if anything will. But, time out of mind such bleak events lead to one thing…the Great Sacrifice. The Greatest Sacrifice of all."

Merlin coughed, mead spewing from his damaged mouth and running into his long grey beard. His eyes were wild. "No! You speak madly, woman, seeress or not! Kham-El-Ard and Khor Ghor are still beacons to men, a hope for peace and for alliances. Ardhu may no longer be young, but he is hale…gods, no! He…" the words slurred between his wet and shaking lips, 'he is like a son to me, the son I was denied when I chose my calling. At first, yes, he was only a pawn, a boy born of a union I devised; I was great in ambition then. But as time passed by, he became more to me…no, do not speak to me of the Great Rite and of Ardhu! It will never happen by my hand."

"If you will not, then you must at least step aside and let the Wheel of Fate turn as it will, making no interference. Fate may well play its own hand before these days are over…" Nin-Aiefa's voice was a rasping whisper like the wind in fallen autumn leaves. A haunting sound. Merlin remembered suddenly their first meeting in Afallan, near the Holy Tor of Hwynn son of Nud, where she had held a rapier to his throat. Fair and perilous she had been, and though her beauty had now faded into Winter, she was still perilous…the Lady of the Lake and its dark secrets and woman-magic.

He struggled to his feet despite his weakened left side, ignoring the cries of Mhor-gan, who tried to comfort him, to pull him back down onto the stool. "I will listen no longer to this madness! And if I hear you plot against the lord of Kham-El-Ard, I will send the Stone-Lord's warband to burn this hovel to the ground!"

"You accuse me of speaking madness?" cried Nin-Aeifa. "You refuse to listen, although the signs are there for all with eyes to see! You threaten those whose serve the Immortal King Afalak, and Hwynn son of Nud? You have passed from wisdom, old man...the dictates of your heart have addled your brain!"

"I wish I had never laid eyes on you," he snarled, shaking with rage. "You hard, unnatural bitch. And, you, Mhor-gan of the Korrig-han, you wish me to tear the heart from your own brother...but maybe I should not be surprised... all the spawn of Y'gerna are the same except for Ardhu, who was tempered by my hand."

He stumbled toward the door, desperate to be away. Suddenly, his head lolled forward, and there was a sensation of something dropping away within his skull. Lights scintillated in the corners of his eyes. He had been drugged.

"No!" he howled, falling to his knees, thrashing the air around him with his arms. His staff fell with a clatter, the jawbone on the end snapping and rolling away across the floor.

Mhor-gan hurried to his side. "Merlin, you must heed our words. Do not fight us. We have no wish to harm you, who are a priest of high esteem, one of the greatest of your order."

"You have betrayed me, and betrayed Ardhu and Albu the White..." he gasped, striking out at her with a bunched fist that had no more clout than a falling leaf.

Nin-Aeifa glided over to him and stared down; her visage pinched, twisted with a bitter sorrow. "Mhor-gan, take him to the holy place as planned. All has been made ready for him."

Mhor-gan pulled Merlin to his feet, trying to be gentle. He fought her but she was the stronger, and he found himself being propelled out into the dawn. In the East the Eye of Bhel was just rising, a red ball over the edge of the Great Plain. Bloody light flooded the fields and the swells of the river Abona became a stream of gore.

Merlin was taken up a rise, past many a death-house grown with grass. Skylarks soared overhead and other birds darted and skimmed in the waving grasses; the souls of the dead taking flight on this morning of ill-omen.

Up ahead by a stand of trees he could see a shallow barrow, a cup-like depression that surrounded a hole that gaped like an ebony mouth in the verdant earth. A small wooden shrine shaped like a miniature trilithon marked the crater and protected whatever lay below from the worst excesses of the weather. The place exuded a certain menace, and Merlin's heart banged against his ribcage in sudden frenzy.

He should have known what this place might be, but in his old age he seldom came past the Down of Kings, leaving the land between the barrow-hills and the shores of Abona to the ministrations of the Ladies of the Lake and those from the Deepwood Valley who followed them. He wondered what had been happening here, out of sight and out of mind, and thought again of the feel of Nin-Aeifa's cold blade against his youthful throat.

Mhor-gan was pressing him on toward the mounded ring that circled the black pit, and he could see that her face was drawn and uneasy, as if she hated what she was about to do. "Mhor-gan..." he said, using no formalities of title, speaking to her as an equal and Ardhu's sister. "Think, woman, of what you do! Think of your brother...surely you do not wish to see him die!"

"All men must die, Merlin," she responded, her voice a mere whisper, and she dragged him on until they stood together on the edge of the shadowy crater, staring into the heart of the earth.

Merlin writhed, trying to free himself one more time. Gazing down the shaft, he could see that it descended deep into the bowels of Prydn, reaching toward the Underworld and, perhaps, the realms of the restless dead—those who were the shades of evil men, who sucked marrow from bones and were in constant need of supplication lest they cause havoc amongst the living. The tunnel was at least a hundred feet deep, cut straight into the chalk with picks of antler, and a hemp rope ladder dangled down the side and vanished into its depths. A charnel smell wafted up from the hidden depths, tainting the fresh morning air with the hint of old death.

"Merlin, you must go down," said Mhor-gan. "I beg you not to fight me. I have no wish to bring you harm."

"Are you to kill me too…make of me a sacrifice?" A sudden hopeful light gleamed in his tired old eyes. "Could you do this—and spare Ardhu?"

She looked him up and down in sorrow, the scrawny legs and arms, the mouth that now hung at a crooked angle from being elf-shot. "No, your blood would not suffice. Though you are wisest of the wise, you can not stand in for him, his tanist. Maybe once, many years ago, but not now."

She gave him a gentle push from behind and, hands shaking, he began to climb down the rope ladder. Turgid darkness embraced him and the chalk walls rising on either side sweated water and other noxious substances. After what seemed an eternity of dangling in the darkness, his feet touched a solid surface. He released the rope ladder and it was hastily snatched up by Mhor-gan, out of reach. He found himself standing on a packed chalk floor beside a stout post the height of a man; he leaned upon it to steady himself then grimaced as he saw the brown, congealed mess that smeared the wood and the white animal bones strewn at its foot. On the ground beside the post were sleeping furs, baskets of food, jugs of water and mead.

The trap had been waiting for him for some time, it seemed, and he had fallen straight into it.

"I will come back each day to check that you are hale and to bring you food and drink." Hearing Mhor-gan's voice from above, he glanced up and saw her head silhouetted against a tiny circle of brightening sky. "I pray soon this time of evil will pass and a new day dawn, and then you will be freed again to live your last years with the honour you deserve."

He spat at her and hurled a curse, which she deflected with a movement of her hand. Then he crouched amidst the congealed flesh and bones and howled in bleak despair.

CHAPTER TEN—BETRAYAL OF LOVE

Mordraed lounged in the corner of the grounds of Kham-El-Ard, his back against the wattle wall and his legs stretched out before him. Battle-training was nearly over for the day and he was surrounded by a dozen other youths, laughing amongst themselves, showing off bruises they had obtained from mock-fights with the likes of the Lord An'kelet and the twin warriors Ba-lin and Bal-ahn. Agravaen was out on the training ground now, Ba-lin facing him as his opponent—he looked big, red and sweaty, like a trussed pig, thought Mordraed uncharitably, his eyes narrowing as his half-brother shuffled and puffed around the marked-off ring, thudding clumsily from side to side on his graceless feet. Agravaen would have looked almost comical, a buffoon to jeer at, except for the obvious power in his bull-neck and muscled shoulders, and the determined expression in his eyes.

He wanted to be a warrior. He wanted to be firmly placed at the Stone Lord's side.

His desire was perfect for Mordraed's plans, for it would cloud Agravaen's already dim thoughts...

Smiling, Mordraed turned his attention to his fellows. His keen gaze drifted past those who were the sons of Ardhu's favourites and sought out those who were...different. A rag-tag of boys who had come from across the Plain in hopes of being one of the chosen men; youths who were clearly unsuitable and would never be picked by Ardhu for his warband—those quick to violence, who loved to kill or torture; those unable to take orders, always angry and restive, their own wants placed before others'; and those who were simple, easily swayed and easily impressed, not knowing their own minds yet...if they ever would. These youths had warmed to Mordraed over the past weeks, clustering around him like moths drawn to flame, impressed by his prowess with weapons, his slick tongue and dark wit, and the kinship he shared with the Stone Lord of Khor Ghor.

Little did they realise how Mordraed despised them, hating their fawning, their crudeness, their stupidity...

But they could be useful.

"How do you find the training?" he asked breezily of one dullard sporting a black eye and with teeth already bashed in during some earlier brawl.

The youth, Wyzelo, wiped his sweaty, flushed face on his arm and sidled over to Mordraed. "Good enough. But I'm tired of all this playing at being a warrior. Why can't we join the Stone Lord's band and fight our enemies for real, bashing in their skulls and winning glory?"

"Why indeed?" Mordraed shrugged gracefully. "Haven't you guessed, my friend?"

The thick-head glanced at Mordraed, big pale eyes stupidly bovine in the red platter of his face. "No..."

Mordraed flashed him another smile, full of false ruefulness. "Well, the sons of his first faithful are always going to take precedence over other contenders, are they not? They even rank above me, though I am the King's...nephew. As you know, I have not been inducted into the Stone-Lord's warband as yet. Who knows?—if it pleases my uncle I may never well be. The same goes for you."

"That is not fair!" Wyzelo cried. "I'm as good as any of them, if not better..."

Mordraed raised his hand. "Peace, friend. It would not do well to have the Lord An'kelet or Ba-lin and Bal-ahn overhear your words. You'd be cast out for certain. And I, for one, know your value, and would not see you sent away." He sighed, staring at the sky. "One day I may reclaim all the lands that should be mine. I would need a warband like Ardhu's then. If that should happen, would you be my man, Wyzelo? My main warrior, ready with axe and arrow to defend what is mine by right?"

"I would!" Wyzelo answered enthusiastically. "You seem like a wise and noble master to follow! You are young, whereas the Stone Lord grows o..." He shut his mouth with a resounding snap and reddened, realising he had spoken rashly, and in front of the King's own kinsman.

Mordraed put a hand on his shoulder. "Don't worry, Wyzelo," he said smoothly, "I promise your words shall remain a secret. A slip of the tongue, that is all...Say, since you seem so wise and knowledgeable yourself, maybe you could assist me...Who else in Kham-El-Ard is like you, neglected despite your worth? Who else might seek a place within a fighting band?"

Eager to draw the attention away from the folly of his loose tongue, Wyzelo promptly gestured to several other youths standing on the sidelines while Agravaen blundered around the training ground, swinging his axe at the fleet-footed Ba-lin. "Over there...my companion from the same village, Mor Bethuinn...Kehul, Fial and Belenion. You can see they are well grown and full of courage, but the masters here keep saying we are not ready to join the warband."

"A shame...they look like they have the makings of doughty warriors. Meet with me on the morrow, Wyzelo. In the fields by the Old Henge, where it is more private. Bring your friends. We will talk more then."

"I will, great Mordraed of the Stone Lord's clan," said Wyzelo with enthusiasm, and he hurried away toward his fellows.

Mordraed smirked to himself, watching the rough country youth disappear amid the gaggle of boys. It couldn't have been easier. He had always had a nose for sniffing out dissatisfaction, perhaps because he often felt so dissatisfied himself.

Turning from Wyzelo and the other youths, he set his attention back towards his brother Agravaen. He was hand to hand with Ba-lin now, daggers locked, striving for supremacy. Agravaen's lumpen face was bordering on purple, his eyes slitted and watering, his lips curled back over his strong white teeth. Suddenly Ba-lin's knee shot out, catching him in the groin. Agravaen fell like a stone, clutching his crotch. His mouth worked soundlessly for a moment in his agony, and then he got his breath back and loosed the most awful roar of pain and rage...while the youths packing the training yard fell about howling with mirth.

Ba-lin nudged the curled-up boy with his knee. "In a battle you play to win, young Agravaen. Was my move fair? No. But remember...your opponents wish to keep their lives, so they will do anything to shorten yours..."

"Get up." Mordraed walked over to his brother and dragged him to his feet. "You are making yourself a laughing stock... again."

Agravaen's face was puce, twisted in pain. "It's his fault! He tricked me when I came close to bettering him...A few more blows and I could have killed him!"

"You are training; you are not meant to kill anyone. Especially one of the Stone Lord's prime warriors." Mordraed's tone was derisive. "But come, I must talk to you where the others are not listening."

They walked around the side of the hall of Kham-El-Ard and sat in its shadow, out of the way of dogs and carts and men herding beasts, and women coming up from Mother Abona with pots upon their heads. "I have seen our mother," said Mordraed, noncommittally, his tone level.

Agravaen's eyes narrowed. "Mordraed, let me speak plainly here...I do not care. In fact I hope never to see the bitch again. You...you... she loves but the rest of us were as shite on her shoe, to be wiped off and thrown away as far as possible. She...she is a liar, brother. She told us tales of the wickedness of Ardhu, but look...he has taken us in, housed and fed us, almost as if we were his own sons!"

One of us is... The corner of Mordraed's mouth quirked up; a bitter smile, a cold smile that matched his deep-sea eyes.

"So your loyalty is to Ardhu now," said Mordraed, his voice low. "You want nothing more than to serve him."

"Aye," breathed Agravaen, "that is why I try so hard to become a great warrior. I want nothing more than to ride beside him in his warband. But it seems all I do goes amiss…" He scowled and picking up a lump of dried dung from the ground, hurled it angrily across the fort. It bounced off a wooden post on the ramparts and a dog ran out and began to worry it. "I am like that dog, Mordraed. I only get the shite."

"It doesn't have to be so." Mordraed's voice descended to a bare whisper. "There is much afoot in Kham-El-Ard that our uncle had no idea about. Things that could bring his kingdom crashing down…"

Agravaen made a gasping noise. "Treachery?"

Mordraed turned his head, catching the younger boy's gaze in a long, level, intent stare. "Of the worst kind, Agravaen. The Lord An'kelet…and the White Woman…they are more to each other than they should be. They are lovers, I know it."

Agravaen shook his head. "You must be wrong. An'kelet is his friend, close as a brother! He honours the Lady Fynavir, worships her as a goddess. He would not do such a vile thing."

"Because he is the perfect warrior?" Mordraed sneered. "Grow up, little brother. No man is that perfect! Did you really think he has dwelt all these years without a woman?"

Agravaen leapt to his feet, fists clenched. "If what you say is true, why have you not spoken to Ardhu?"

Mordraed spat on the ground. "What…and end up with my head on a pole outside the gates? You know how it is, brother. He tolerates me, but he trusts me less than you and our brothers because I am older and he thinks I am under Morigau's sway. An'kelet and I have no love for each other and he is a favourite; I would never be believed. However…" He sprang up, leaning in toward the stockier youth. "This might be an ideal opportunity for you. If you were the one to reveal the trysts of An'kelet and Fynavir, then surely our uncle would mark your loyalty and reward you by allowing you into his warband."

Agravaen scratched his chin, covered with scraggy, downy black traces of a beard. "Maybe you are right…maybe that would work. But…I have never seen the Queen with An'kelet. How would I manage to catch them? You do understand that I must see their treachery myself and not rely on rumour."

Mordraed draped his arm about his brother's broad, muscular shoulders. "I will help you. My eyes and ears are keener than yours. It is my joy to help you improve your lot; after all, we are kin." His smile was wide, friendly but his eyes diamond-hard.

Agravaen smiled back, the smile as naïve and trusting as a child's.

The messenger came from the East, from where he had been keeping watch over the borders of Ardhu's lands. Smeared with dust and sweat from the long ride, he entered the Hall of Kham-El-Ard and stood before the seat of the Queen. "I bring news, blessed Lady."

Fynavir sat before him, palely shimmering like some spectre, her hands outspread on her lap, fingers splayed like icicles on the woad-stained blue fabric of her dress. Her face looked even whiter than usual; she bit her lip in consternation. "Speak!" she nodded. "Keep nothing back. If you bring ill news of my husband or my son, say it now and do not hide it with gentling words."

The messenger cleared his throat. "The King of the Wasteland has passed into the Land of his Ancestors, despite the best efforts of Ardhu Pendraec and Lord Per-Adur. Even now, the Lord of the West travels home with the Prince Gal'havad at his side. Within three downings of the Sun, he will be back at Kham-El-Ard."

Fynavir released a shuddering sigh. "My son…he is unhurt, praise Bhel. My thanks for your tidings, messenger. Go to the fire-pits and you will be fed and given drink and money of copper rings. I must myself move in haste to prepare for Lord Ardhu and Gal'havad's homecoming."

She left the hall, hurrying out amongst the round huts that belonged to the warriors. The wind lifted her hair, tearing it free of its long plait, and men stared, but she ignored them. Finding the largest hut, surrounded by a wooden palisade and a ditch, she passed the threshold and went inside.

Inside An'kelet, Prince of Ar-morah, lay abed under a pile of skins, still sleeping, for the hour was early. Hearing the noise of an intruder, he sat up at once and reached for his blade, Arondyt. When he saw Fynavir silhouetted in the doorway, he cast the blade down and grinned. He threw off the skins and stepped forth naked, his tall frame still lean and muscled and golden despite his age. He pulled her into the circle of his arms and she leaned heavily against him, pulling his head down to hers, her mouth seeking his with almost desperate urgency.

"Fynavir, why do you come here like this?" Suddenly he drew away from her and reached for his tunic and trews. "It is not safe. The Sun is too high in the sky, all must have seen you. We must not become careless, even though Ardhu is not here. Other eyes than his may be watching. Not all are friends to us and men's tongues often wag when they are idle."

"I have reason." She reached for him again, arms locking around his neck, her white hair falling like a shower of snow over his chest and arms. "A messenger came this morning. Ardhu is on his way back from the Wasteland. In three days he will be home." A sob tore from her throat. "I have missed Gal'havad, but I cannot lie… in the depths of my being I almost hoped this time would never end. For the first time in all these long years, we could be together as we wished, every day…and almost…" her lips trembled, "every night."

He took her by the shoulders, shaking her lightly, gently. "Fynavir, remember what we do is a grave wrong! Ardhu would have every right to kill us both if ever he found out."

She pressed herself against him, shivering. "Why have the gods cursed us so, making the love between us a thing of darkness and treachery?"

"Why, indeed…" he said with sadness, stroking her hair.

"Let us ride out…" she said. "One more time…let us lie together. Just one more time before he comes back, and I must do my duty by him…and you yours."

"Fynavir, I do not think it is safe…We must go about our daily lives, as we always have."

"Please…One hour with you, that is all I ask… that I may think on it during all the lonely nights."

He groaned and pressed her close. "I am a fool…but when could I deny you anything, Fynavir, my love…my doom."

Down by the river Mordraed perched on the grassy bank, dangling his legs in the swell. Agravaen was stomping out into the swell, holding up a long bone harpoon, his face crinkled in concentration as he tried to spear a fish for that night's supper. Other youths milled around the trees that grew along the Abona, drinking from water-skins and chewing strips of dried meat as they blathered about non-existent battles and their prowess in them. Mordraed lazily eyed this young unruly pack …Wyzelo and his friends, the malcontents, the disobedient, the thick-in-the-head. A slavering band of dogs, all of them, scrabbling to get to the top, but dogs could be trained to be loyal with a few thrown scraps…then these dogs would bark for him.

Rising, he casually sauntered towards them. "How is it with my brothers?"

"Not good!" yelled one he knew was called Belenion…the Henbane. Mordraed wondered if the scrawny, hooked-nosed lad was as venomous as his name. "Not enough mead…no women…nor any war! I came here to be a great warrior and I am sent running about like a little boy with a wooden blade every day while the 'great chiefs' look on and laugh. Tired of it, I am! I want to decorate my hut with the jawbones of my enemies!"

"Your hut?" said Wyzelo. "You don't even have a house of your own yet. We sleep together in one hut like children or beasts."

"It is not as it should be." Mordraed sighed deeply, theatrically. "I do not know how my uncle cannot see the wrong that is being done to you. I would not treat you so, mighty warriors that you are. I fear the men around Ardhu have poisoned his mind. I mean, what is An'kelet but a foreign prince? Loyal he might have seemed over the years, but who is to say treachery does not dwell in his heart and that he does not covet all Ardhu owns? Maybe he has just been biding his time."

"Bloody foreign pig," grunted a skinny gap-toothed boy named Ic'ho. "You should be in Ardhu's circle, Mordraed, and treated with just as much respect as An'kelet. You are of the blood of kings. His blood. Why does he ignore you in preference to outsiders?"

Mordraed licked his lips. Now was the moment. He could feel the tension in the air, the dissatisfaction growing into anger and disdain. The moment might pass, he might find he had been presumptuous and incur anger or puzzlement from this fractious band of youths, but he had to speak now or forever hold his tongue. "If I asked it and…if my uncle does not acknowledge your worth…would you be my men, my followers instead? Although I have no land as yet, who knows what the future may hold? After all…" His eyes were shining, his breaths short and shallow, "Prince Gal'havad is Ardhu's only heir; his union with the White Woman has not been blessed. And Gal'havad…he is not hale, he has fits and sees the spirit-world. He is more suited to be a priest than a king! Who knows, his affliction may even shorten his days. If he were to die young and have no heirs of his body…who knows what I might be then?"

"King Mordraed!" shouted out Ic'ho, laughing, obviously drunk. "With us at his side as his chief warriors!"

The rowdy youths hooted and whooped, circling Mordraed. Laughing, they lifted him to their shoulders and raised their axes to him in honour.

Agravaen sloshed his way out of the river, scowling at their antics, and tossed his harpoon on the ground in frustrated anger. "What foolish mummery is this? Mordraed, if any from Kham-El-Ard should hear you, it might not go well for any of us!"

Mordraed laughed scornfully at him. "It is only a harmless game," he mocked. "Why so serious, brother?"

Agravaen's face purpled. "And why so reckless, Mordraed? It was never like you…and I do not like it."

At that moment, the sound of hooves interrupted the brothers' verbal sparring. "Someone rides out from Kham-El-Ard!" cried Wyzelo, pointing east with the haft of his axe. "I see An'kelet of Ar-morah upon his stallion…but he does not ride alone. Another is with him."

Mordraed shaded his eyes with a hand and stared towards Kham-El-Ard. He could see An'kelet's amber hair shining in the sun, and his checked cloak, woven with the lozenge pattern of his high-born clan, streaming out behind him in the wind of his speed. Beside him on a smaller horse rode a figure wrapped in a rust-coloured fur, a voluminous skin hood pulled up to hide the face. He immediately knew there was only one person it could be.

The White Woman, the treacherous Queen.

He knew at once his hour was here and he must seize the chance. Whirling on his heel, he gestured to the band of drunken youths, to red-faced Agravaen with his angry expression. "Follow me!" he cried. "Let us go into the wilds after them."

"But why?" asked Belenion, staggering drunkenly on the river's edge. "I don't care where An'kelet of Ar-morah goes!"

"Do not question!" Mordraed's hand caught the front of the other's woven tunic, almost causing the youth to trip and fall into the river. "That is an important lesson you must learn…if you wish to be accounted in any chief's war-band! Listen, all of you, if you want to rise in esteem, come with me now and bring your weapons. This may be a day for great feats of arms, I promise you all. A day that will go down in the memories of men!"

The youths grabbed their axes and untied the peace-strings that bound their copper daggers into their sheaths. The drink was hot in them, stirring them to act. Agravaen stormed up to Mordraed, huffing and heaving; Mordraed noticed for the first time how tall he had suddenly grown…they were now nearly the same height, almost eye to eye. "What are you planning, brother?" he snapped.

"To root out treachery, if there is any to be found," said Mordraed. "Is that not what you want too—to keep our uncle's domains safe? I told you I would let you have the honour of bringing any evil to his attention."

Agravaen grunted, unable to deny his elder sibling's words. "I would bet on this being a fool's chase. But let us go and see, and if you are wrong, I want you to bring me the best bit of beef at the fire tonight and refill my beaker before your own."

"It will be as you wish," said Mordraed excitedly. "Now let us hasten, in case we lose their trail. But do not let them see you…that is most important." He glanced sternly around the gathered group of young men. "Keep to the bushes, keep to the reeds—use every trick of woodcraft you have ever been taught in order to be silent…and safe. Remember, it is An'kelet of Ar-morah who is our quarry today, and he is the greatest fighter amongst men—or so they say. Luckily, he does not seem to have his spear, the Balugaisa, with him—which must mean the Spirits are smiling upon us."

The youths raced down the river bank, single file, sobering up now that the chase was on. Mordraed grasped Agravaen's arm, and pushed him after the rest. "Hurry up, brother. We are the sons of kings—we must lead these cattle and prod them to do what they must."

The group continued along the Abona, nearly to the dwellings of the Ladies of the Lake, but suddenly, as the river spread out into multiple channels, the trail went dead, the clear passage of the horses veiled by the wetness of the ground. The youths groaned and started complaining bitterly that an afternoon's good drinking had been spoiled by a fool's errand.

"Shut up!" Mordraed cast them a dark glare that made them all fall silent. Flinging himself onto his knees, he scanned the water-logged ground, the patchy grass, searching for signs of hoof prints. At length he found a depression in the soil, recent, an earthworm coiling on the disturbed surface. "Further down the valley, to the north… I think they are heading toward the Great Enclosure."

"The Great Enclosure!" Agravaen's face paled. "That's where they used to take the dead. It's an evil place…why should they go there?"

"That is obvious," said Mordraed, face glowing with self-pride at his deduction. "They think no living man would dare set foot among the place of the dead so it would be ideal for their immoral tryst. Come, let us hurry and catch them."

Bow in hand, he raced toward the North, with his pack of youths running like faithful but ill-trained hounds behind him.

An'kelet and Fynavir rode up to the banks of the Great Enclosure, where up till a Moon's Year ago the dead priests of Khor Ghor had lain on wooden platforms, awaiting the cleansing of the flesh and the freeing of their spirits. The rite had since fallen out of use as burial customs changed and the dead now went straight to their barrows still clad in flesh.

An'kelet swung down from his horse and let its reins dangle; the animal immediately started to crop the tufted grass. Striding over to Fynavir's mount he lifted up his arms for her to come to him. She put her hands on his shoulders and let him lift him down onto the ground. She stared around—the low encircling bank, the empty pits where wooden excarnation platforms had stood. As she moved her foot, teeth fallen from the rotting bodies of long ago tinkled in the grass.

"I hate this place," she breathed. "I can almost smell the scent of decaying flesh...though they are long gone..."

"It is not a nice place," said An'kelet. "But it is a safe place. No one comes here anymore, and the bank protects from prying eyes."

"The spirits look on." She glanced around the site, bleak and unwelcoming, raked by a chill wind that stirred her hair and her fur cloak. "They will know what we have done."

"But they will not disturb us. Nor will those who have no mortal tongues speak of our joining to others."

He took off his cloak, spread it on the ground. The teeth were shining, pearlescent, in the grass, precious tokens of death and ending. They were not as bright, though, as the warm amber of An'kelet's hair, the rings bound in it shining in the muted sunlight. Fynavir sank to her knees, and pressed her hands to her face. "I begged to be alone with you, I cannot deny it," she said. "But now I feel a great fear in my heart, such as I have not felt before."

"I will chase that fear away." He knelt beside her, freeing her hair, his mouth on her neck against the warm pulse of life. She reached up to touch his face, the mane of amber hair. The pale, cloud-swathed blob of Bhel above suddenly picked out strands of silver; she had not noticed them before.

"Seventeen years we have met in secret," she whispered. "Seventeen years we have betrayed Ardhu. We are growing old, my love. How can we continue as we have in the years to come?"

"That is in the hands of the gods," he murmured. "Do not think of it now." He drew her on to his lap, moving her woven skirts aside, his hand questing up her thigh. She stifled a moan as his fingers touched her and she wrapped her legs around his back, pulling herself in against him. She was shivering, both from the cold of the wind and from excitement...and from fear too; no matter his comforting words, a sense of doom and despair and melancholy lay on her like a shroud.

He reached out and unfastened the jet toggles on the front of her kirtle, and pushed her back onto his cloak. His hands were ice-cold as he caressed her. It was always like this, when they could escape from Kham-El-Ard alone...a union in haste, brief rutting like beasts on the ground, then quickly up and back to the fort on the Crooked Hill, with leaves and grass brushed from clothes and smiles of falseness on their lips. That was the price they had to pay for their forbidden love, being forever false and forever fearful...

An'kelet knelt above her and pressed her legs apart, and she felt him slide inside her. Her fear vanished in a shower of pleasure and she writhed against him, drawing him closer. She gazed up into his face, her pupils dilated with her desire...and suddenly she let out a terrible scream.

"An'kelet, someone is here...behind you, on the bank!"

He pulled away from her, cursing, and snatched up Fragarak from where he had tossed it aside on the fur. To his dismay he could see a familiar figure on the bank of the Great Enclosure, staring at him with a shocked, snarling, angry face.

Agravaen son of Morigau.

Their eyes met and held for a moment. Then, Agravaen pulled his war hammer from his belt and rushed towards him uttering a blood-curdling howl, "Traitor! Traitor!"

An'kelet was not afraid—he'd trained this clumsy, over-eager boy, knew Agravaen's only advantage in any battle was his brute strength. But he was also concerned as to what he should do. Killing the lad was his first instinct. But Agravaen was Ardhu's nephew and had been taken under his protection; the Stone Lord's wrath would be terrible…but the boy could not be allowed to tell anyone in the tribe what he had seen.

Dagger in hand, An'kelet stalked Agravaen, who eyed him with both rage and terror. The youth swung his axe from side to side, seeking an opportunity to strike an arm or a leg, shattering the bone and making a cripple of his older, more skilled opponent. An'kelet circled him at a distance, attempting to find a place from where he could dart like a serpent and strike with his honed Ar-moran blade, the hot bronze cutting into kidney, heart or lung, or biting through the great vein in the neck. He would try to make the death quick, because his quarry was Ardhu's nephew and he would not have his friend's kinsman suffer overlong.

Suddenly he heard Fynavir cry out behind him. He whirled on his heel just in time to see Mordraed leap over the embankment and circle her throat with his arm, pressing on her windpipe and felling her immediately. The northern Prince dragged her along the ground, his dagger pressed to her neck, his eyes glittering like hard stars. His beautiful face took on an almost demonic look as he grinned at An'kelet, his expression victorious...

"Let her go!" An'kelet felt the first surge of the battle-fury, the Warp-Spasm, come upon him. His head swam, his voice thickened and deepened. He had never trusted this dark, quick-tongued youth from Ynys Yrch, not for one moment since he had arrived. He should have been sent from Kham-El-Ard with his accursed dam—if not sent to the spirit-world. Mordraed was touched by evil like his mother; he was the snake that bit a man's ankle in the grass; he was the disloyal dog that savaged its master's hand. He was the Darkness to oppose Ardhu's Light…

"Let her go?" Mordraed's fingers reached up to stroke Fynavir's face; even as she struggled to breathe, she recoiled from his touch as if stung. "A traitor to the Stone Lord? No, An'kelet of Ar-morah, you and she shall both answer to Ardhu Pendraec and to the spirits you have offended with your lust and your deceit."

An'kelet gave a cry and rushed forward, dagger upraised. He would kill this arrogant youth and then he would take Fynavir, whether she willed it or not, and flee with her to Ar-morah. Many of his kinsmen still dwelt on the long tongue of land that jutted into the Narrow Sea and they would shelter him and show him loyalty. Even in recent years he had traded with them, bringing in daggers with gold pointillé hilts, fancy, prestigious pots with handles and rounded brass helms in continental style. He would have the priestesses of his mother Ailin's order break Fynavir's marriage bonds and he would wed her himself as he should have done years ago, before he brought Ardhu to the Dun of Ludegran, her foster-father.

An'kelet's mad headlong rush brought him within feet of Mordraed. The younger man roughly thrust Fynavir from him and struck out with the flat of his bow, catching An'kelet across the upper face with a whip-like motion. It was a dishonourable battle-move but highly effective, momentarily blinding him, making him see only stars and swirling blots of light. Tears of pain streaming down his cheeks, An'kelet staggered back from his opponent, hands instinctively reaching to his stinging eyes.

Mordraed laughed and struck out again, the top section of the bow cracking down on An'kelet's exposed right wrist; the Ar-moran was not wearing his archer's wristguard for he had only brought his daggers with him... This blow, however, was not as accurately aimed as Mordraed's first and failed to make An'kelet drop Fragarak. Vision slowly recovering, An'kelet lunged at his youthful enemy, sure that once he had his footing he could bring him down rapidly and finish this fight.

He was surprised when a dagger of bronze rose to meet his blade, not as long as the near-rapier he carried, but broad, with a deadly gleaming tip. Thrust into flesh and turned, it would wreak terrible damage. The hilt was of dappled horn and had several deep spirals grooved upon it, looking in some aspects like a spirit-face, the eyes of the Watcher. It slammed against Fragarak, and the bronze blades sparked as they sawed on each other. The hand behind the weapon was rock-hard, steady, immoveable…

An'kelet smiled grimly. Had he really expected any less? He had been training Mordraed himself these past months. But when had the youth become so strong of limb and fast? When had he, once the greatest warrior in the known world, begun to weaken and grow slow?

Still, he was not done yet. Suddenly pulling back from his opponent, he drew his other dagger, Arondyt, and made a sharp thrust at Mordraed's midriff. Fast as the serpent Mordraed recoiled, and then, as the blow went wide, he swung round in a semi-circle, kicking the weapon from An'kelet's hand with a blow so hard An'kelet felt the muscles tear from his forearm to the shoulder. He staggered and dropped Arondyt, his arm hanging numb and useless at his side.

Mordraed tossed back his raven-hued hair, laughing. He preened himself like the black bird of prey he resembled. "Surely you are not finished already? I am enjoying our little sparring match, Lord An'kelet! Our first real fight."

"You mock me but by the end of this day you will beg me for mercy…" gasped An'kelet, but even as he spoke the words a terrible sensation of doom and fear came over him, such as he had never experienced before. His words felt hollow, untrue. Pain lanced down his arm; his slashed eyes were still throbbing and blurring. He realised he did not have the heart for these battles any longer, nor the strength of a man less than twenty Sun-turnings.

He was done.

"An'kelet!" he heard Fynavir cry out. Having recovered from Mordraed's stranglehold, she rushed across the grass toward him, her unbound hair flying out in a white cloud. He grabbed her to him, uncaring now that any man should see them together.

And at the moment many did see…for the banks of the enclosure were full of young men, whooping and shouting, brandishing bronze and copper and stone axes, their faces flushed with misplaced pride and too much mead. He recognised them all, had given training to most, and with despair he realised that they were the displaced and dissatisfied, the youths he had told Ardhu would never be men of the warband—those who liked blood too much, or mistreated women and weaker men; those who imagined themselves stronger and greater than they were.

"You have done this, haven't you?" he gasped at Mordraed. "These creatures are your curs, eating the scraps of lies you throw them."

"Curs they may be," said Mordraed. "But I can assure you, Lord An'kelet, they have the bite of wolves."

He made a gesture with his hand to the young men on the enclosure bank, and with a frenzied roar they rushed in at their quarry, dragging along an axe-brandishing Agravaen in their mad headlong charge. Thrusting Fynavir behind him, An'kelet shouted a war cry of his own and hurled himself at the first line of youths, his unexpected burst of strength driving the first enemies back and bowling several of them over. He leapt upon the fallen, stabbing one man through the eye with Fragarak, and breaking the other's spine with a downward hard stamp of his foot. Screams rose to the heavens and blood fed the hungry grass.

Fynavir was screaming, hysterical, frozen to the spot by the horror and unreality of what was happening. Mordraed swung round and struck her across the face to silence her, his blow throwing her to the ground where she lay dazed, redness leaking from her cut lip.

An'kelet shouted in rage to see her struck in such a manner, and vented the full force of his fury on those before him, grabbing two of his assailants and smashing their faces together, hitting them repeatedly as blood spurted and teeth cracked and fell from their red mouths to join the lost teeth of the long-dead in the grass. Casting their limp bodies to one side as a child would hurl a corn-dolly; he once more fought his way towards Mordraed at the edge of the earthwork. "I…will…have you…" he gasped. "You…are the rot in Kham-El-Ard…"

Mordraed cast him a pitying look, deliberately meant to infuriate. The look one might give a fool or simpleton. His eyes flicked across the circle.

In his rage and panic and eagerness to get to Mordraed, An'kelet had failed to notice that he was being stalked…

Agravaen son of Loth was thundering up behind him, wild and hostile, his archaic stone war-hammer upraised.

"Don't kill him, Agravaen!" Mordraed called out. "I want to see him confess to his crimes before Ardhu and be suitably punished!"

An'kelet whirled around, grappling for the haft of Agravaen's hammer…but he could not get a grip on the sweat-streaked wood with his damaged hand. If he dropped Fragarak, he might be able to over-power the stockier but less skilled man…but it would be a great risk to attack without any weapon save his own strength. Realising his opponent's disadvantage, Agravaen bore down on him like some rushing monster, a beast half-man, half-bull, and the youth's war-hammer smashed into his temple.

Lights exploded in An'kelet's head and he staggered and fell to his knees, blood running into his eyes. Seeing him fallen, his enemies howled and yelled and piled in on top of him, punching and kicking, tearing away his weapons and pinioning his arms behind his back.

Watching, Mordraed felt a sense of elation so great he thought his heart might burst. He threw back his head and screamed this first victory to the ever-changing skies.

CHAPTER ELEVEN—THE TRIAL OF FYNAVIR

The small party of horsemen cantered down the Harrow Way, the ancient track which crossed the summit of Harrow Hill, wound past the temple of Khor Ghor, and then fared on into the farthest West. Behind their shoulders the sky was the colour of an old bruise, filled with impending storm; a low rumble of thunder filled the charged air, and sullen flashes of lightning crowned the Eastern line of hills—Harrow, Beacon, and Magic Hill, where Bhel's face first rose at the beginning of the World of Men.

"Nearly home," said Gal'havad, leaning over his mount's neck and urging it to greater speed with the pressure of his heels. Despite the company's failure to heal the Maimed King, the young man's mood was lightening at the prospects of a homecoming—he wanted to see his mother again, to put things right with her after their last fraught parting, and to see his friend Mordraed, whom he had parted from without even a farewell, and tell him of his adventures as a Man of the Tribe.

Riding ahead of the others, Gal'havad soon reached the foot of Kham-El-Ard, raised like the prow of a sea-going ship that sailed into the Sunrise. He was surprised to see no workers in the surrounding field systems, and no one coming and going about their business on the hill. It was almost as if Kham-El-Ard had been abandoned. He bit his lip fearfully, and let his gaze travel up the earthen ramparts to the timber palisades rising above, but there was no sign of a battle or any destruction; all was as it should be, save for its eerie quietness. One thin streak of smoke came from one hut inside the Dun, to be dispersed in the storm-laden air.

Heart pounding, he slammed his heels into his mount's flank and drove it up the hill at great speed. Coming to the great gates, many times his height, he was stunned to see no guards on duty, as if they had all been called away elsewhere. He saw a few women in the distance, but they were scuttling between their huts like small beetles, faces downcast, moving rapidly as if terrified.

What was going on?

He glanced toward the Great Hall. He could hear voices now, a low ominous rumble just like the thunder in the distance. It was a different sound from what he remembered—no laughter, no song-singers, and no women chattering. It was a dark sound, an angry sound like disturbed bees buzzing in a hive.

"Ka'hai!" The name was torn from his mouth in almost a scream as he saw Ardhu's foster-brother suddenly appear in the door of the hall and glance out.

The older man's heavy brow furrowed and he strode forward, waving his arms, waving Gal'havad away. "No! Amhar…Prince Gal'havad…you mustn't come in here, you must not look! Where is your father? Where is Ardhu?"

Gal'havad flung himself from his steed and rushed toward Ka'hai and the gaping doorway behind him. "What is wrong, Ka'hai? Where are the people? Why do you bar me from my own home?"

Ka'hai caught the youth's shoulders, swinging him in a semi-circle, trying to turn him aside. "Gal'havad, a terrible thing has happened in your father's absence. You will be told all…but we must wait for the Stone Lord to arrive before more is said of this evil matter!"

"Tell me, Ka'hai!" Gal'havad wrenched himself free. His face was the colour of the chalk. "I am the Prince of Kham-El-Ard!"

Ka'hai began to weep, great unmanly sobs that made his broad shoulders heave and shake. It was like watching an oak tree fall, felled by an axe. "I cannot speak of it, Gal'havad. I cannot!"

Gal'havad raced past him, leaving Ka'hai bent with his grief. Running into the hall, he pushed through a sea of bodies toward the Eastern end where his father's high seat stood. As he drew near to the antlered chair, he could see his cousin Mordraed standing separate from the rest of the crowd. He was dressed in his finest warrior's garb, his hair braided with gold, and in his hand he held a black basalt stone axe of ancient type—a symbol of authority. Two white streaks were painted on each cheekbone—warrior's face-paint, worn in time of action— and he had darkened round the edges of his eyes with charcoal, making their blue colour stand out even more vividly. Behind him his lumpish brother Agravaen, also carrying a stone hammer and wearing his finest clothes and trinkets, stood like some shaggy and pugnacious hill-troll. Other youths that Gal'havad barely knew were clustered in the rear; they strutted about in unruly fashion, weapons clearly on display, full of pride and overconfidence.

"Mordraed!" Gal'havad thrust the crowds aside, struggling through the press of bodies towards his kinsman. "Tell me, I beg you…what has happened in my absence? Where is my mother, Fynavir?"

Mordraed jumped a little at the sight of the other youth but immediately regained his composure. "I am sorry to speak words that will grieve you," he said…loudly, so that all assembled could hear. "But the Lady Fynavir is being held a prisoner. And so is the Lord An'kelet!"

"A prisoner!" Gal'havad stopped in his tracks and stared at Mordraed as if he had gone insane. "But she is the Queen of Kham-El-Ard! And An'kelet is my father's closest friend! Mordraed, what madness do you speak?"

The insincere smile vanished from Mordraed's lips. "Your dam is a traitor and the Lord An'kelet, the foreigner, with her. There is no easy way to say it, my friend…but as you are now a Man of the Tribe I will speak to you as a Man and not a child. Fynavir of Ibherna has played the whore for An'kelet of Ar-morah for many years and now she has been caught…"

Gal'havad stood as if he had been struck, blood draining from his face. Unable to speak, he mutely shook his head in denial.

At that moment, the crowds behind him parted. The angry buzz of voices within the hall fell still. Ardhu stood in the doorway, hard-faced as a sarsen stone, with Caladvolc a brand of fire in his hand. Hwalchmai and Per-Adur flanked him with weapons ready as he entered the Great Hall and strode purposefully toward Mordraed on the raised area near his seat of power. His gaze burned into the dark youth, taking in his stance and attire. Anger flared within him, and old mistrust.

"You!" he shouted. "Why do you stand there, as if you were lord of Kham-El-Ard? Where is my queen and my chief-warrior? What have you done with them, bastard?"

He raised his sword but at that moment Mordraed did something Ardhu had not expected. Casting down his weapons, the son of Morigau flung himself to the floor at his feet, falling face down in the rushes in a position of utter subjugation and humility, his back and neck exposed to potential blows from above. "Great Stone Lord," he said, "I beg that you do not bring the force of your wrath down on me, who only has the honour of your house foremost in my mind. I have done nothing to shame or betray you, you who are my close kinsman…unlike others who are dear to your heart."

Distrust still burned within Ardhu, and reaching down he grabbed Mordraed's tunic and hauled him roughly to his feet. "Do not seek to flatter me with words, son of a woman with a snake's tongue," he spat. "Speak now and speak clearly…and tell me what has happened here!"

Mordraed nodded toward Agravaen. "It is my brother who you must ask, lord. He is the one who first saw that a great wrong was being committed on you under your very roof."

Ardhu frowned, perplexed. Agravaen! He had watched the thick, rough boy blossom these past months, becoming dedicated to war-craft and eager to please him. Stupid he might be, but Ardhu had seen no malice or duplicity in him. He wanted to serve. He wanted to be in the war-band, away from the malign influence of the mother who thought of him as less than nothing, a child she would have exposed on a cliffside if she had had the choice.

"Agravaen..." Ardhu ordered, "Speak!"

The boy lumbered forward, licking his lips nervously. His eyes darted from Mordraed to Ardhu to the rush-strewn floor. "Terrible Head, please do not be wrathful, for I am loyal to you" he said, his voice cracking. "But I have ill news for you. When I was out...hunting...with my companions I saw An'kelet of Ar-morah and Lady Fynavir ride out into the Valley, their manner passing strange. Unbeknownst to them, I followed the trail of their horses to a hidden place and there I saw a sight that will burn in my mind forever—they lay together rutting like beasts upon the grass. My Lord..." his voice rose and his eyes rolled almost hysterically—he was obviously terrified, fearing that Ardhu's wrath at this evil news might be directed at him, "they must be put to death, given to the Stones! All will be made right then."

Ardhu went rigid. "Be silent!" His fist shot out, striking Agravaen full in the mouth. He fell backwards, lips swelling and bleeding.

Spinning around on his heel, Ardhu approached Mordraed, yanking him roughly towards him by the front of his tunic so that they were mere inches apart. "Take your brother and get out!" he shouted. "Remove yourself from my sight. If you have harmed them, my wife and chief warrior, I will have your innards ripped from your body as you watch..."

"They are both unharmed." Mordraed's voice was flat, cold. "My men have them bound in the cave below Kham-El-Ard, waiting for the Stone Lord's justice."

Ardhu stopped and suddenly stared straight into Mordraed's face, incredulous. "Your men? Mordraed son of Morigau...in this place nothing's yours!"

His arm shot out, striking the young man just as he had struck his younger brother. Mordraed staggered back but did not fall beneath the blow; he stood wiping blood from his lip where one of Ardhu's twisted bronze armlets had cut it, his deep blue eyes blackening with hatred.

Abruptly those fathomless eyes became shuttered, the face expressionless, revealing nothing more. He bowed curtly to Ardhu. "I will go as you decree, my uncle." Grabbing the arm of the still-reeling Agravaen, he propelled the younger man out of the hall and away amidst the huts clustered on the hilltop.

Ardhu turned, his visage grey, strained. "Ka'hai!" he called for his foster-brother, who knelt, still wracked with grief, by the doorway of the Hall. "You have been with me from the time I was a babe; brother of my heart, if not my blood. Come with me, and support me as you did when I was a child. I need you now as much as I need the arms of men like Bohrs and Hwalchmai."

Led by Ka'hai, Ardhu left Kham-El-Ard and took the long spiralling pathway down to the waters of the Sacred Pool that lay below the vast bulk of the Crooked Hill. There were signs of great trampling and tumult in the undergrowth, clods of earth torn up and smears of blood on foliage and ground.

"They are imprisoned in the cave, Ardhu," said Ka'hai tearfully. "Ba-lin and Bal-ahn are on guard, along with many others. An'kelet, as you might imagine, was not easy to subdue. He killed two of the yearling boys from the local settlements when Agravaen discovered his...treachery, and injured many more. He was only taken because Agravaen smote him unconscious with his hammer; but even that was only a small respite...once he woke the battle fury came on him and he slew again and again. Blood was spilled in Kham-El-Ard where blood has never been spilt before, and you can see by the gore around us that he was still fighting when we managed to drag him here."

Ardhu nodded stiffly. "Where are the dead?"

Ka'hai gestured to several biers lying beside the pond, covered with painted deerskins. Flies buzzed about them in clouds. "We have done no rites for them, Ardhu, to send them over the Great Plain to the Land of the Ancestors."

"And why has this not been done? Where is the Merlin?"

Ka'hai shrugged his shoulders. "That is the other evil news I must tell…we do not know what has happened to wise Merlin. He has not been seen for days, at Deroweth, Kham-El-Ard or Khor Ghor."

Ardhu ran his hand over his brown hair in an agitated motion. "Evil news indeed, Brother Ka'hai. All goes amiss for me in these dark times." He strode over to the biers and dragged back the deerskins one by one. Beneath the hides lay tangles of putrefying flesh, splintered femurs and ribs poking up from blackened stumps that seemed scarcely human, especially since beasts had been gnawing on them in the night. "Have them taken to the Old Henge and burn them on pyres," he ordered. "Have all the priests come from Deroweth to chant and sing and send their spirits on their long journey…then have them taken to Khor Ghor and interred with honour."

"But many of them were a bad lot," exclaimed Ka'hai. "Defiant and rebellious… they would have soon been sent home to their families."

"No matter," said Ardhu. "In rooting out the poison in the midst of Kham-El-Ard, they did me a great service and hence they shall have fitting burial in the Tomb of All Hope."

Leaving the reeking biers, he walked on toward the cave in the broad chalky hillside where An'kelet and Fynavir were imprisoned. As he neared it, he could see two dozen of his men surrounding its mouth; they had set up a great blockade in the entrance, an infill made of a stout tree trunk. They were clearly ill at ease, with drawn bows, daggers and clubs at the ready.

Ardhu approached Bal-ahn who stood nearest to the entrance, his bronze axe in his hand. "Unblock it," he said, nodding toward the makeshift barricade. "I will speak to them."

"Lord, no," said Bal-ahn uneasily. "An'kelet's strength in his anger is that of ten men…we could barely control him as it was. I would counsel you, as your companion of many years, to build a great fire here in the cave mouth, using the tree at kindling, and finish this vile matter in the only way it can end."

Ardhu's eyes glinted dangerously. "I do not ask for your counsel. Drag the tree away so that I may go inside. An'kelet of Ar-morah will not harm me."

Bal-ahn inclined his head and gestured to the other warriors to start removing the barrier. They chopped at the tree with their axes, hacking out a space where their chief could pass. "I will come with you, Ardhu," said Bal-ahn when the last cut was made.

Ardhu put his hand on his shoulder, more weary now than angry. "My thanks…but it is for me alone to do."

Taking a deep breath, Ardhu slid through the gap and entered the cave. The thin sunlight entered with him and lit up the mossy, stone-filled floor and the two figures crouched at the back amidst the rubble. He could see Fynavir's pale hair, unbound and tangled, and her tear-streaked face, marred by bruises, floating like a sad moon in the shadows.

Beside her An'kelet stirred. Abruptly he stood up, and Ardhu noticed that his tunic was stiff with gore. Blood also matted his hair and stained his arms and face. A wound on his temple leaked slowly, but most of the blood upon him was not his.

Slowly, he approached Ardhu. His eyes were wary.

Ardhu unbuckled his belt, with Caladvolc hanging from it, and cast it to one side. "I am not here to kill you," he said, his voice flat. "Not yet at any rate. I have come to hear, from your own mouth, what has happened. An'kelet of Ar-morah, my chief warrior, my friend… I want truth from you for once and for all. Have you lain with my woman?"

An'kelet took a deep, shuddering breath and suddenly fell to his knees before Ardhu. "Pick up your blade and smite me to the death!" he cried. "For I have betrayed you. I have lied to you long enough and would have an end. But do not harm Fynavir; I seduced her when she was lonely and weak."

"No, An'kelet, no!" Fynavir ran forward and threw her arms around her lover, almost as if Ardhu was not there at all. "If you die, then I will go with you to that Otherland!"

Ardhu stood unmoved, his cheeks grey. "She is as guilty as you. Her face tells me the truth about what has passed between you more than any words. You both deserve to die."

"Have mercy, Ardhu," An'kelet whispered hoarsely. "Not on me, for I know what I deserve. But on her. She is only a weak woman…"

Ardhu glared at Fynavir. "I did not say I would kill her, only that she deserves to die. No, she will stay here. She is the Land, or so the people think, and though she is barren soil, failing of even her beauty…" he spoke harshly, words deliberately cruel, "she is still considered the daughter of a Goddess on Earth. So she shall stay, by my side and in my bed, and she shall be punished besides in any way that I see as fitting."

"If she lives, I can ask for no more. Now take Caladvolc and drive it into my heart. We are undone, I have broken all my vows, and I cannot bear the shame."

Ardhu picked up the sword and drew it from its sheath. The blade gleamed red as blood as the faint beams of sunlight trailing into the cave struck it. Fynavir began to whimper, "No, no, no."

Ardhu approached An'kelet and placed the sharpened tip of the blade against his chest. Caladvolc shook in his hand. Tears streaked his cheeks as his arm muscles tensed, ready to thrust the sword into the heart of his long-time friend. An'kelet bowed his head, closing his eyes, lips moving in silent prayers to the gods of the Underworld, to Hwynn the White and his father Nud, asking that they might forgive him his crimes and still welcome him onto the Plain of Honey.

Suddenly Ardhu's arm dropped. He gave an awful, strangled cry of mingled grief, anger and despair and thrust Caladvolc, not into An'kelet's heart, but into his side above the hip.

An'kelet gasped and twisted in agony, grabbing at the blade that pierced him. The edges sheared into his fingers, drawing more blood.

Teeth gritted, Ardhu took a step back and yanked the blade from the wound. More blood flowed, pooling on the cave floor. Fynavir curled into a ball, sobbing. The redness from her lover's wound soaked into her hair, turning it bright crimson.

Ardhu slammed Caladvolc into its sheath, uncleaned, still dripping. "I will not take your life, in gratitude for the years you have served me. But now, wounded by my hand, I will send you forth to live or to die as the spirits see fit, but to receive no aid or succour from any man, woman or child in Kham-El-Ard, Deroweth, or the Place-of-Light. The Crossroads of the World and the entire West is barred to you also, and if you set foot in my territory, by Bhel's face and the Everlasting Sky, I will hunt you down and kill you like a wild beast."

He backed up to the barricade in the cave mouth and shouted for Bal-ahn and the others to come and widen the gap. The men of the war-band poured into the cavern, setting hands upon An'kelet and dragging him out into the open air. Curses they flung at him, for what he had done, and they spat at him and made signs against evil. Holding his injured side, blood welling through his bone-white fingers, he looked from face to face—the men he had fought beside and the lads he had trained as warriors. They had been his friends, his companions, his students…now they gazed at him with hatred, his sworn enemies unto death.

"What shall we do with him?" shouted one. "Let us take him to the river and drown him, and let her waters cleanse away his sin!"

"No!" Ardhu shoved the man out of the way. "Lay no hand upon him. He is a disease, a blight amongst us. Let him go and crawl into some hole and bleed to death, his blood feeding the land of our forebears, the land he has sullied!"

He turned to An'kelet himself, his eyes tormented. "Get you gone, before I change my mind!"

Gasping, hands pressed to his leaking wound, An'kelet limped down the steep, wooden slopes toward the riverbank, a red ragged figure of death and despair. "No, no, do not let him go to die in dishonour…" Fynavir ran from the cave and collapsed at her husband's feet, clinging in supplication to the fringe of his tunic.

Ardhu dragged her up roughly and grabbed her face in his hands, twisting her head so that she was forced to watch her lover stagger away into the trees. "Look upon him well, woman," he said, voice heavy with weariness and grief. "It is the last you will ever see of him."

That night at Kham-El-Ard there was a great storm. Thunder crashed overhead and shook the great posts holding up the hall to their very foundations. Men sat about silent and grim, holding their heads in their hands, while women squatted in the rain, wailing as if there had been a death.

Eyes red-rimmed, Gal'havad paced before his father's high seat, restive and anxious, angry and sorrowful in turn. Ardhu slumped on the chair of antlers, leaning his head on his hand, his visage ashen and his gaze unfocussed. "My father, listen to me," Gal'havad begged. "You must let me speak to my mother, to find out the real truth of what has happened!"

Ardhu's lip curled. "There is no need. All was confessed."

"You will not kill her." It was a statement, not a question, and edged slightly with danger.

Ardhu glanced up at his son; the youth's face wore a determined hardness he had not seen before…and yet it shone with almost an inner light, a pure flame that made him bow his head in shame and glance away again. "No, I will not have her put to death. She is the daughter of the Goddess on Earth. She is the Land. Whatever man takes the White Woman will be King."

Gal'havad sighed in relief, his shoulders slumping. He suddenly looked very young again, young and frail.

"But she will have to be punished."

Gal'havad raised his head, eyes starting to smoulder anew. "Punished? What punishment do you propose? Tell me!"

Ardhu raised his hand; his jaw was set. "It is not for you to question me. I am Stone Lord of Prydn, the Terrible Head, master of the Portal of Ghosts. Go from my sight until you are called for. I dismiss you from my Hall, Prince Gal'havad."

"Father, you cannot…!" Gal'havad's voice rose sharply and he took a long stride toward Ardhu's seat.

Bohrs blocked him, shaking his wild head. Gal'havad glanced down and saw that the burly warrior had his dagger drawn, gleaming in his clenched fist. "You have drawn blade on me," he said, incredulous.

"I wouldn't gladly use it, lad," the heavy-set warrior mumbled. "But you have to go as Ardhu commands. Just do as he says. He will come round…with time."

Gal'havad's mouth trembled. "Pray to the spirits it is so…and that this madness that is on him soon leaves!" Turning from Bohrs, he fled from the great Hall and out into the storm.

Ardhu stared after him, eyes dull and without emotion.

Gal'havad staggered through the lashing rain, soaked to the skin, his hair plastered to his skull. He wandered aimlessly amidst the huts, not knowing where to go. His usual place was in a cordoned-off area at the back of the Hall, near the quarters of his parents, hidden behind a hedge of skins stretched over wooden frames to create a private space. He shivered, his teeth starting to chatter as water trickled down the back of his neck.

Suddenly he spotted a familiar figure limned against dull firelight in the low-hanging doorway of the hut where young warriors were quartered while they did their training in arms. "Mordraed!" he shouted, springing forward.

Mordraed stiffened as Gal'havad burst into the hut like some creature borne of the raging storm, his hair a slick stream the colour of old blood against his white forehead, frigid water showering from his short, ox-skin cloak. Gal'havad came to him and cast his arms around him in a deep embrace, seemingly unaware of the rigidity of the other youth's shoulders, the unfriendly set of his mouth.

"Mordraed, cousin, glad am I to see you." Gal'havad's voice was thick with emotion, bordering on tearfulness. "My world has grown dark and crazed, and I need to see one who is not part of that madness."

Mordraed forced a smile upon his face as Gal'havad glanced up; it would not do to let the boy see that he was annoyed by this unexpected intrusion. He put what he hoped seemed a comforting arm around his cousin's shoulders and drew him in toward the tiny fire that burned in the centre of the hut. The other lads who had fallen under Mordraed's sway stared at the newcomer, some with near-open hostility despite his rank. Gal'havad appeared not to notice their stares and scowls.

"Now, what is bothering you?" Mordraed poured a weak beer into a crude black pot and handed it to Gal'havad. "Has Ardhu chased you from the Hall too?"

Gal'havad nodded dismally. "He is maddened with grief. Somehow I must convince him that he must not hurt my mother. He intends to punish her, but will not say in what way. I fear he will harm her in his anger."

Mordraed rolled his eyes. "Gal'havad, consider it fortunate that she has not been put to death. She is, after all, a whore and a traitor."

"Do not speak of her so!" Gal'havad shot back. "It is not your place to judge!" His hand instinctively went to his dagger-hilt.

Mordraed's lips curled. So the boy had got some fire in his belly since going on his little quest into the East!

"Forgive me for my hard words, cousin. If it comforts you, my own mother is no better! Here, sit by our fire…we are all outcasts here, all those who do not quite fit into your father's plans. He blames me and Agravaen for his sorrow too, you know; for although it was through us the traitor An'kelet was apprehended, we still have been banished from the Great Hall." He sighed. "I just hope it is not a permanent ban. Otherwise, I will have to leave for distant lands to seek my fortune."

"No…you cannot do that, Mordraed!" cried Gal'havad. "You…you are my only friend here. I have no others my age, and now that my mother is in disgrace and my father cold as ice to me and unwilling to listen, I would be greatly sore of heart if you left. You…you are like a brother to me."

Mordraed almost laughed at the irony of Gal'havad's words. "If you truly feel that I am your brother, then you must speak for me and for Agravaen…when the Stone Lord is calmer, that is."

"I will," said Gal'havad staunchly, "for all the good it will do."

They fell silent and Gal'havad squatted by the fire, drying himself, and downing the rancid beer Mordraed had given him. Eventually the flames in the fire-pit died to embers and youths began to sprawl out under their fur cloaks and sheepskins, coiling together on the rushes like a pack of weary hounds. Gal'havad glanced around unhappily, unused to sleeping in such cramped conditions; but eventually he lay down facing away from the others, turning his face into the darkness. Soon the sound of soft, rhythmic sleep-breathing reached Mordraed where he sat a few feet away, finishing the last of the sour drink in his beaker.

Mordraed put the mug aside and slowly eased himself down into the rushes, lying flat on his belly. If he stretched out, he could almost touch Gal'havad's back. One hand slid down to his hip, his finger hooking round the hilt of his dagger, drawing it an inch from its sheath. He had polished and sharpened it just the other day. One quick stab in the dark, and it would be all over…he would have done what he had intended to do in the Stones, had the malevolent Old Ones not prevented him. Eyes burning with a feral light, he reached out, his fingertips brushing his half-brother's shoulder blade. Here, right here…one swift deep thrust and the knife would pierce the heart from behind…

But no…what was he thinking! Suddenly he snatched his hand back as it had been burned. It would be foolish to act now. Yes, foolish. He would be the first suspect if the boy was found dead, he knew that. Already Ardhu had grave doubts about his loyalty. Possibly he might be able to pass the blame onto Agravaen—maybe claim that his younger brother had been jealous of his friendship with Ardhu's heir—but he doubted such a story would deceive the Stone Lord for long.

Vengeance must wait. But it would come.

Slowly his eyelids drifted shut over his death-blue eyes, and he sprawled next to the youth he had sworn to kill, throwing his arm over the sleeping youth's shoulders, seeing no incongruity in using his intended victim's body-heat to warm himself in the draughty hut. He slept deeply, his hand still curled round the hilt of his dagger—and did not dream.

The priests came from Deroweth, highest priests and the Elders in flowing robes of bleached linen, with blue kirtles for the priestesses, green for the seers and speakers with the dead, and rust for the temple guardians and acolytes. They gathered in Kham-El-Ard before the doors of the Great Hall, and a huge beaker filled with mead flavoured by meadowsweet was passed between priests and the highest ranked warriors of Ardhu's band. The pot was an enormous, ancient example, impressed with wheat grains and fingernail patterns; it was broken after the draught was drained and its shards buried in a pit near the threshold, alongside the offering of a newborn lamb. Then the priestesses poured fermented milk into coarse, rounded black pots and passed these to the women of the tribe, the ladies who accompanied the great warriors of Ardhu Pendraec, before depositing them at the fortress's entryway, symbolic of the fertility of man and beast and a tasty offering to passing ghosts borne on the bitter wind.

On his high seat, Ardhu sat decked out in his full regalia—the lozenge and belt buckle of gold, the shield that was the face of Evening, Little White hilt and Caladvolc the Hard-Cleft, sword from the Sacred Pool. Rhon-gom the Lightning Mace was in his right hand, wreathed in bright strips of rolled cloth decked with talismans. These adornments had been newly added to the mace, and men wondered to see them for they were tokens of coming change. Ardhu's gaze was still haunted, but the deadness of the weeks before had lifted from his eyes and a new purpose gleamed in them.

He gestured to the foremost of the priests to come before him. "Gluinval, is there still no word on the whereabouts of the Merlin?"

Gluinval shuffled forward in his pale and frothing robes, a spray of dog's teeth round his neck and a crow's skull plaited into his long sandy beard. "No word has come, Stone Lord of Khor Ghor. It is not unknown that wise ones of our order foresee their own deaths and go into the wilds to meet in their chosen way the shadow that stands at every man's shoulder. I fear this may be true with the Merlin, blessed be his name among us! None may ever know where the bones of wise Merlin lie."

Ardhu gripped the haft of Rhon-gom and a spasm of sorrow crossed his features. "I knew this day would come," he murmured, half to himself. "But why now? He is still needed…more than ever the good counsel of my friend Merlin is needed!"

Shaking his head to clear it, he focussed his attention back toward the priest Gluinval. "So, if Merlin does not return, who will take the place of High Priest of Khor Ghor?"

"It will be decided in a testing of wise men, as it has been done for centuries. But we must wait till at least three Moons have passed, and we are sure the Blessed Merlin has gone to the Realm of Ancestors."

"And for now? Who leads the priests; who guards the Doors between the worlds of the Living and the Dead?"

"The Merlin taught me, from my youth. I am senior among the wise of Deroweth."

Ardhu leaned forward, his eyes suddenly darkened, growing wolfish in his thin, sun-darkened face. "Then tell me, as a wise man of Deroweth, what do you deem the fitting punishment for a faithless wife? But not any faithless wife, who might easily be put away or given to a bog to appease gods and men. A wife who is also Queen, not just by virtue of marrying a man of status, but by her own lineage, which is bound to the spirits that rule the very soil we walk on."

Gluinval licked his lips, knowing full well that Ardhu spoke of Fynavir and her betrayal. "Lord, according to the legends of our People, passed down by many tongues since the days of Samothos and Bolgos, a capricious woman of great beauty called Tlatga once lived in Belerion. They said her father was Lord Bhel himself, that he came as lover to her dam while she made offerings inside a chamber of the Old Ones on Midsummer morn. Her hair was fire from Bhel, her body white as the chalk of our blessed Plain, but her heart was frivolous and her actions unwise. She played two brave chieftains false and set them snapping like dogs at each other's throats, driving their warriors to great battles not for cattle-wealth, lands or weapons…but to posses this faithless woman's body. The crops withered and failed, neglected in their fields, and common men starved, while noble warriors, cruelly slain, rotted in their barrows. When the foolish chiefs realised what they had destroyed for the desire of Tlatga the Fair, they put their enmity aside and turned on the one who had scorned them both. They decreed that Tlatga would atone by ploughing anew the earth ravaged by her folly. Alone, she would pull the plough through the ruined fields in the manner of oxen; a shameful task for the daughter of Bhel—but after the thing was done, the Land was at peace and returned to its health. Tlatga was given to both chiefs, one through the dark months and the other the light months, for the rest of her days."

Ardhu looked thoughtful for a moment, then he bowed his head. "To draw a plough like some humble beast, to grovel in the mud before the folk of Kham-El-Ard…I deem this a fit punishment for infidelity. No blood is spilt, no death will come, yet the affront to me and to the Land itself is made good. It will be done."

He rose from his seat and beckoned to Hwalchmai, standing on his right in the place that had been An'kelet's. "Cousin, with the departure of the traitor An'kelet of Ar-morah, I bestow on you the honour of being my right-hand warrior. Would that my eyes had not been blinded in the past and I had set you in that position from the start. Now I ask you to bring Fynavir of Ibherna to me, that her punishment is meted out without further delay."

Hwalchmai bowed. "It will be done, Stone Lord. I will fetch her myself."

He strode from the hall and returned shortly leading Fynavir, whose hands were bound with twine behind her back. She came without resistance, looking thin and frail, her uncombed hair matted over lifeless eyes circled with darkness. The same kirtle she had worn in the cave, streaked with An'kelet's blood, hung rank and stinking on her gaunt frame. She no longer looked beautiful, but as if she was half in the spirit-world and longing for death.

She stood before Ardhu's seat, unable to meet his eyes. "Kill me," she said dully, her voice a dry rasp. "It is what I deserve. It is what I want. It is what the Gods will ask of me as atonement."

"They would not desire the blood of one so faithless!" Ardhu's voice was the lash of a whip. "And so you shall not die as is your wish. But you will atone for what you have done; you have cursed the Land by your actions and brought it to barrenness…and so you will plough it by your own hands, white as the chalk, and perhaps make it whole again. And then you will lie in my bed and be as you should have been had you not shamed yourself with An'kelet…my right-hand man…my friend of long years! Maybe then the spirits will take away your barrenness and give us more sons, that my Lands may be guarded by strong hands and Gal'havad have many kinsmen to stand at his back when the time comes for him to assume my mantle."

Fynavir made a strangled sound in her throat and looked as if she might collapse at Ardhu's feet. Ardhu rose from his seat and steadied her, taking her arm with surprising gentleness, as if he was a doting husband and not a man betrayed, wrestling with his own anger and need for revenge, fearing also the darkness and desolation he had seen in the East, the creeping cold and the steady flood of the rain.

She did not resist him. Her eyes held nothing, no fear, not hatred. Nothing.

They left the Hall and processed down the hill, surrounded by Ardhu's chief warriors. The priests of Deroweth followed, chanting and making gestures against malevolent beings from the unseen world. Drums were beaten, and people from both the dun and Place-of-Light came running up from the river and the fields to see what was happening at Kham-El-Ard.

In the marshy lands near the Old Henge Ardhu stopped the procession. "Kneel, woman." He gestured to Fynavir and then to the ground. She slumped to her knees in the grass, obedient, her head hanging. Ardhu grasped her thick hair in one hand and lifted it, yanking her head up and back, while drawing Caladvolc with the other. The watching people gasped, imagining for a terrible instant that he intended to behead her on the spot. Instead he swung the sword is a sideways motion and the blade sheared through her snow-pale locks, leaving only a few inches curling around her head. "This is the first offering, the first penance of the faithless wife," he announced, holding up the hank of hair so that the gathered throng could witness its cutting. "Let the priests take it and give it to the Great Ones."

Acting as high priest in the Merlin's absence, Gluinval took the hank of shorn hair and, followed by his entourage of priests and seers, carried it through the entrance of the Old Henge. In the centre of the earthen ring, they built a cairn of small stones to which they added a magic brew—the bones of a frog, the skull of a bird, an eel and a dog's tooth, all mixed up with hazelnuts, yew-berries and toadstools. Fynavir's hair was spread over the top like a protective covering, and Gluinval used a flint strike-a-light to set the whole cairn on fire then danced wildly around it with his fellow priests, as the acrid smoke from the burning hair and magic stew coiled into the air.

When the pyre was reduced to ashes, the priests gathered up the remains and brought them in an urn to where Ardhu stood with Fynavir kneeling silently at his feet. The people from the local villages gathered round, wailing and crying out at this terrible sight they had never thought to see—their Queen shamed and their King seeking retribution for the wrong done to him. Fear gripped them, and horror; rumour had spread quickly of the Queen's infidelity, and all knew what that could mean for their continued existence. They knew the gods would be angry, and the Old Woman of Gloominess would walk long amongst them, bringing a long Winter. Already they had seen too many grey skies, too many tears from the sky that washed their livelihood away.

Ardhu gestured for Fynavir to get to her feet; she seemed unable to control her shaking limbs, so Hwalchmai lifted her up from the ground, his face grim, hating every moment, and forced her to face her husband. Ardhu stared at her, eyes unreadable, his mouth a tight, thin line, and then he raised Caladvolc to her neck and this time cut off her filthy rags, leaving her naked to the eyes of the assembly. Gluinval reached into the urn he carried and brought out a handful of still-warm ashes, blackening her face with them—a mark of shame—before tracing symbols on the rest of her body that told of her shame, her dishonour of her lord's bed. She recoiled as the priest touched her breasts and wept silently as two priestesses strode over, dragging a crude plough, and fastened the straps of its harness around her.

The crowd's hysteria was rising; people screamed out unintelligibly and fell writhing on the muddy ground as if possessed by spirits out of darkness. The throng pushed forward, toward Ardhu, toward Fynavir bound to the plough—to what purpose none knew, perhaps no real purpose, only to move and cry out and wave their fists in both protest and agreement at the punishment of the woman who had been their queen for so long. Ardhu's war band shouted at them and drew their axes, menacing the villagers as they drew too close, forcing them to take several paces backwards.

Ardhu turned angrily from them and grasped the handles of the plough, his knuckles bright white as he gripped the splintering wood. "Go, faithless bitch!" he snarled at Fynavir. "Let us finish this for once and for all!"

Fynavir lurched forward, struggling in the traces. Mud splashed up her ankles and she almost fell. The plough bit into the ground and partly sank, as the soil was so saturated from the unseasonable rains. "Go on, use some strength, woman!" Ardhu raged, all his anger and hurt and loss bursting forth in a frenzied tide. None in Kham-El-Ard had ever seen him so angry, he who was known for being measured and calm, who raised his hand in wrath only at utmost provocation. "You are the daughter of a goddess, aren't you? Special? An'kelet certainly thought you were special! He knew well the power in your thighs! Show me, your husband, what you are truly made of!"

Fynavir made a strangled sound and flung herself forward once more. Rain began to sluice down from the empurpled sky, making her shorn head frizz and curl like a lamb's fleece, streaking the ashes on her skin until she looked like some strange striped beast, a creature of light and shadow.

Someone laughed in the crowd of villagers and suddenly the mood became even uglier. A sod flew, striking the back of Fynavir's calf. "I curse you, White Phantom!" a woman shrilled, her voice so taut and high–pitched it sounded barely human. "Your lust has doomed us! My bairn has died, I have no milk…and the rains still come. This is your fault! You have cursed the Land. You are barren after one child due to your sin! You have brought evil on us!"

The crowd's wailing ceased and a dark murmur came from them, a sound like thunder over distant hills, a murmur low and ominous. Several people rushed forward, arms swinging wildly, to be forced back by the men of Ardhu's warband.

Ardhu ignored them, wrapped in his own private misery, intent on taking his own vengeance for the wrong that had been done him. "Pull harder, faster, woman!" he gasped to Fynavir, wiping the rain from his face with his arm. "Or do I have to smite you like a stubborn ox."

Fynavir yanked on the traces with all her remaining strength. Her eyes were screwed shut against the rain, against the sight of her vengeful, grief-maddened husband, and the people who, having been won to her cause over the long years, now cursed her name and called for her death. The priests and priestesses clustered together near the Old Henge, colourful damp blobs in the rainstorm, chanting and singing, swaying in a sickly rhythm that made her head spin and her stomach churn.

"I wish my heart would burst and this torment be over forever!" she suddenly screamed, and she threw herself forward, the hemp ropes of the simple harness biting into her bare flesh, burning like brands, cutting red channels. The world spun and she fell into the half-ploughed furrow, rain showering over her, churning the mud and the blood where the ropes had torn her flesh.

The crowd let out a terrible noise, a frenzied inhuman shriek, and they tried to surge forward once again. This time their intentions were clear; glassy-eyed, maddened by fear and superstition, they would tear her to pieces in the furrow and scatter parts of her body far and wide across the Great Plain in an attempt to restore the failing fertility of the soil of Prydn.

Hearing that awful, crazed cry, Ardhu suddenly seemed to come to himself, as if from a dream. He glanced at the roiling horde and a needle of fear pierced his heart. Not only Fynavir was in danger… they gazed on him with mad, accusing eyes too…the old king, the king whose power was waning, whose arm was growing weak. He abruptly dropped the handles of the plough and sprinted to Fynavir, drawing Carnwennan and slashing the ties that bound her.

The crowd broke free at the moment, one man rushing forward swinging a great club over his head. He shoved past Bal-ahn, who struck out at him with his axe, only to find his aim ruined as hysterical tribeswomen leapt up at him, biting and clawing, trying to pull him down, to rend him as they sought to rend Ardhu and Fynavir.

"Keep back…it is your King you threaten!" Ardhu warned in a great voice, reaching for Caladvolc's gold-pinned hilt.

The huge, wild-haired man staggered crazily on, showering mud, his eyes rolling and his club making whistling noises as it smote the storm-laden air. Per-Adur sprang into his path, thrusting at the man's throat with his dagger, seeking the great life-vein that stood out like a twisted pulsing rope. The attacker roared like a wild beast, and his club smashed into Per-Adur's arm and drove him backwards, his feet sliding in the churned-up mud. He tried to gain his footing, to reach his enemy's vital parts with his knife, but the wild man whirled the club again and with a crack it smashed into the side of his head. Silently he pitched face forward on the ground, his yellow hair reddened with blood, the left side of his face crumpled and ruined, the cheekbone and jaw shattered.

Ardhu reached for Fynavir, who lay floundering in the mud at his feet. Freezing brown ooze sucked at her smeared flesh, drawing her into its sombre heart, towards the Land of the Dead. Gasping, breath rattling, she lifted a pitiful, shaking hand to her husband. He hesitated for one moment, staring at her in her misery, then suddenly grasped her hand and pulled her free of the mud. Dragging her under his bearskin cloak, he held her tight against his left side so that his right arm was free to defend both her life and his own.

The berserker charged towards them, waving the club that was smeared with Per-Adur's blood. "Die…!" he cried. "I will loose your blood so that the Land will flourish once more and we will all live…"

"If you want blood to feed the earth, Man of the Tribe, let it be your own!"

A new voice rang out across the churned up field, making Ardhu whirl around in alarm. Squinting through the lash of the rain, he saw his son, Gal'havad, riding from the gates of Kham-El-Ard like the storm-wind, striking his steed with his heels to drive it on to greater speeds. He had the same strange, almost fearsome light in his face that Ardhu had seen in the East; the face of a man truly touched by the Ancestors, not quite in the world of mortal-kind. His red hair flamed upon the breeze; his eyes were the colour of the Otherworld and the grass that grows on dead men's barrows. Upon him he wore the true regalia of the princes of the West: golden tresses in his hair, beads of amber at his neck, sun-crosses on the buttons of his madder-red tunic. His Ar-moran dagger, Kos'garak, gift at his manhood ceremony, shone in his hand, hot and deadly, its blade thinner, longer and more piercingly sharp that those wrought in the Five Cantrevs.

Without a moment's hesitation he bore down on the berserker. The man raised his great club again, brandishing it in defiance, but Gal'havad behaved as though the weapon were a child's toy, a stick wielded by a petulant boy. Knocking the weapon aside, he forced his plunging mare straight at the man, his gaze riveted on the coarse red face, the mouth open like a dripping cavern. His arm shot out, his dagger shining, his blow straight and true, quicker than the lightning flashes that came over the distant hills. Kos'garak bit the throat of his enemy and passed through flesh, sinew and bone in a crimson shower. The crazed man gurgled once and tumbled like a fallen stone into the furrow, lying amidst the mud, the worms and his own warm blood.

Gal'havad wheeled his horse around and faced his father. His breath came in ragged gasps, as if he was drawing in his slain foe's life force with every inhalation, and his dagger slewed off a shower of deep life's blood that struck Ardhu's lathered tunic.

"There has been enough bloodshed and unwholesome deeds for today," Gal'havad said chillily, and his voice held a certain authority that astonished and even frightened Ardhu. He knew he should have been angry—Gal'havad had been banished from the Hall after his first outbursts about Fynavir, and it was his intention that the boy not witness her ordeal, but he could not deny that Gal'havad's unexpected arrival may have saved both his life and hers.

The crowd was dispersing now, their wails and shouts becoming sobbing and low keening. Gal'havad edged his mount closer to his father and held out his arms. "Give her to me," he said.

It was not a request.

To his own surprise, Ardhu the Stone Lord complied, lifting the crumpled figure of Fynavir in his arms, mud and blood and streaking ash, and laid her over the front of Gal'havad's steed, across the young warrior's knees. Gal'havad steadied her limp body against his shoulder and covered her nakedness with his cloak, and then, without another glance at his father, he galloped back towards the black cone of Kham-El-Ard, the fortress of the Crooked Hill.

Gal'havad came to his father's seat later than night. The warband had been sent from the Hall; outside, above the rumble of the storm, they could be heard drinking and carousing in the huts, while pipes skirled and drummers beat a strong tattoo that mingled with the thunder.

The Hall was dark, the fire nearly out. Ardhu sat in his chair, leaning back, feeling the ache in the leg that had been wounded so long ago, in the shadow of Mineth Beddun, the mountain of Graves. It was always so now, when the weather turned foul.

He peered through the smoky shadows at Gal'havad, still wearing his princely attire, although he had cleaned the blood from his arms and hands, even scrubbing his nails of any gore.

"You had been told to stay away until you were summoned," Ardhu said accusingly. "I swore I would not hurt her. You disobeyed me."

"I saved you," said Gal'havad softly, inclining his head.

Ardhu gave a deep sigh. "Aye, I cannot deny that. For that I am grateful." He stood, stepping up to the youth. "Sometimes I think you see things that I do not, Gal'havad, with your eyes that gaze into the spirit-world like a priest's. Even if you were disobedient I owe you for your actions this day…name what you desire of me, and it shall be given."

Gal'havad licked his lips and shifted uncomfortably. "My father, I ask that you admit my cousins Mordraed and Agravaen back into the Hall. They sought to help you when the Lord An'kelet's duplicity was exposed, and you have repaid their loyalty ill by driving them away. They should be rewarded, not punished! Both should be admitted to the warband as befits faithfulness and their rank as the sons of kings!"

Ardhu let out a long drawn breath. "Agravaen, he is stupid…but yes, I can see he would be loyal to me, and his arm is strong. But the other one, Mordraed….you do not understand, Gal'havad."

"Do I not?" Gal'havad's fine brows rose. "Then maybe you should tell me, and not keep me in the dark! I know there is bad blood between you and his mother Morigau; maybe that should be put to rest at last."

Ardhu groaned and shook his head. "It can never be so."

Gal'havad folded his arms across his chest "You said you would grant me what I wish. That is what I wish—for Mordraed and Agravaen to join the war-band and have the rank in Kham-El-Ard that they deserve. If you do not trust Mordraed, you can trust me; I will keep watch over him and guide him if he goes astray. He will listen to me, I am sure of it…and I am sure he will serve you well; he is the best archer I have ever seen…" His voice rose and his eyes danced with delight; he sounded like a young child now, all enthusiasm for an older sibling or friend that he admired out of all proportion. "Together as kinsmen, I am sure we could accomplish so much, father! If we do quest to find the Maimed King's cup of gold, I am sure Mordraed will be a much-needed help on the long road."

Ardhu shook his head again, feeling suddenly old and drained. "You love this cousin from the North, don't you?"

"The spirits did not see fit to give me a brother to stand at my shoulder. They gave me Mordraed instead."

Ardhu went cold; he was glad the hall was dark so that Gal'havad could not see the sudden pallor of his cheeks. He longed to shout the truth, the terrible truth…but his tongue felt thick and heavy, and trembled like that of an old man shaken with palsy. There was nothing he could do or say that would not reveal the shamefulness of his past and condemn him. He should have been the one to pull the plough and heal the Land, not just Fynavir; he was as guilty as she.

"I will grant your wish," he said heavily. "Mordraed and Agravaen will be admitted back into the Hall and accepted into the warband. But if I get any scent of dissension or strife, they will both be cast out, not just from the Hall but from Kham-El-Ard itself."

Gal'havad bowed low; he was smiling, a happy youthful innocent smile that tore at Ardhu's very core. "Father, I swear you will have no cause to regret this day."

Gal'havad retreated from the Great Hall, feeling cheerful and light of heart. Almost immediately Mordraed appeared through the spray of the wind-driven rain and swooped on him like some dark bird of prey, drawing him into the lee of one of the round huts clustered around the dun. "What did he say?" he asked sharply, clutching Gal'havad's arm

"It is good news, cousin. His anger has abated. You—and Agravaen—are permitted to enter the Hall again…and he has said he will have you both amidst his chosen warriors. A time of great questing may be coming, you know, if the Stone Lord and the priests will it; what adventures we will have together, Mordraed!"

"What adventures indeed," Mordraed said dryly, his teeth a flash of white in the murk.

"And now we should go to our beds…it has been a hard and wearying day for all in Kham-El-Ard."

The red-haired youth looked suddenly drawn and he staggered slightly and leaned against the side of the hut; Mordraed wondered if he was about to have one of his fits and commune with the Otherworld. He hoped not; to witness such a vile event would be shameful and embarrassing. But luckily Gal'havad shook his head as if to clear it, then pulled himself upright and began to limp away. He paused after a few steps and glanced over his shoulder. "Are you not coming, Mordraed? Are you going to stand out in the rain all night?"

Mordraed drew up the hood of his sealskin cloak, which he had brought from Ynys Yrch and was sound protection from inclement weather. "I have an errand to run, dear cousin. Do not wait for me tonight, but look for me on the morrow."

He turned on his heel and stalked towards the gates. They were ready to be closed for the evening but the same simpleton he had spoken to weeks before was on guard, and he passed unchallenged. Like a shadow, he descended the ramparts and crossed the flooded field. Finding the riverbank, he followed the course of the Abona into the deep valley beyond, seeking out the hut of his mother Morigau.

CHAPTER TWELVE—THE LILY-MAID

An'kelet sprawled on his back amidst the growing greenery on the banks of Abona, staring with rapidly dimming eyes at the faded sky. The ground beneath him was soaked with river water and with his own blood. Around him river-reeds and lilies dipped and swayed in the breeze, as if bowing in honour of the passing of he who was once known as the greatest warrior in the West.

After Ardhu Pendraec had wounded him with Caladvolc, he had managed to stumble a few miles upstream from Kham-El-Ard and then bind his own wound, packing it with mosses and sap as he had been taught by his mother, the Priestess of the Lake in distant Ar-morah, Land of the Sea. However, as he tried to follow the river's course to safer lands where he could escape the Stone Lord's wrath, the wound started to go bad. Having lost his two famed daggers, Arondyt and Fragarak, when he had been taken prisoner by Mordraed and Agravaen, he had to quickly knap a blade of flint…with which he re-opened the wound to expel a stream of vile, reeking pus. Cleaning it till blood ran afresh, biting on a whittled tree branch against the excruciating pain, he began walking again, though fever burned in him, and the bleeding started once more, though at least the blood and the wound smelt clean.

Eventually, despite his great strength, blood loss and pain overcame him and he collapsed, expecting never to rise again. Gasping for breath, his lungs aching, he had turned his gaze on Bright Bhel, his face an umber ball trailing towards his rest below the Western horizon, and prayed for a quick death before the wolves and other scavenging animals smelt the scent of his blood and tore him to pieces.

But Bhel hid his bright Face behind a cloud, and An'kelet of Ar-morah did not die. He lay, staring up at the heavens as they changed from blue to gold to purple, his mind running over and over the folly of his life, the events that had led to this ignominious death on the riverbank. Fynavir…the White Phantom…he had known better than to touch her, to break oaths to both the spirits and to his King. A small bitter gasping laugh came from his peeling lips. But how could he have denied his own heart and not died anyway, just as bitter, just as destroyed in mind and body?

"Come, Hwynn, White One!" he groaned. "Take me away and be done with it! I wish no more to suffer the hurts of the world of mortal men!"

As he spoke he caught the sound of movement in the growing twilight, amidst the thick trees that grew along the riverbank. He tried to prop himself up on his elbow to see who was watching him. Maybe it was Hwynn himself, mounted on his horse of bones, his hair and his face and the blade he carried tongues of white heatless fire. If it was, he would welcome him in a strong embrace and draw in his cold breath that would still the heart forever…

Again, he heard a noise, the crack of a branch. Hwynn? No. Maybe a badger…maybe a brigand who was out to see if any rich pickings could be found on the fallen warrior in the forest. An'kelet flexed his fingers. Well, if any miscreant tried to rob him, he had just enough strength left to wring the bastard's neck and send his spirit shrieking into Ahn-un—the Not-World. Ahead of him the bushes parted, showing dewdrops and sending up a flutter of moths. A figure stood in the shadows, bent forward, on tiptoes, almost like a frightened deer poised for flight. But it was no beast of the forest, nor was it skull-faced Hwynn.

It was a young girl.

She took another tentative step towards An'kelet and he could see her clearly now. She was tall for a woman and slim built, with long, straight, shining hair mixed between dark gold and leaf-brown. She wore a soft deerskin tunic belted with cord that was looped through a shale ring. The hem reached only just above the knee, leaving her long legs bare.

Slowly she approached and leaned over him, her hair falling forward like a stream of poured honey. Her face was a pure, sweet oval, her wide eyes a deep blue touched with violet…much like the twilight that even now cloaked the riverbank and all around it. She said nothing, and he wondered for a moment if he but dreamed; or if she was some sprite of the woodland or water, come to claim his life-essence for her own.

But then she spoke: "You are sore hurt! Can you hear me?"

He moved his mouth; suddenly his tongue felt tingly and he struggled to talk.

"Hush!" She knelt beside him. "You must not expend your strength. I will help you…if I can."

She reached to a bulging pouch fastened at her belt and opened it, revealing an array of herbs and seeds. "My mother was the village healer ere she died. She taught me her craft well…or so I am told."

An'kelet reached toward her, his shaking fingers, cold and numb, touching her arm, bronze from lots of sun and outdoor living. So different from Fynavir's snow-white flesh, the only other woman he had ever touched…Warm and alive…and he felt so cold, like the soil of the burial mound.

"Who…are…you?" he slurred.

"My name is Elian," she said. "I come here to pick the lilies every spring. The folk in the village where my father is chief call me the Lily Maid."

Elian dragged An'kelet up river to a little grove of alder trees, where she had rigged a tent of hides for use as a shelter while she gathered her lilies and herbs from the forest. She had wanted to take him back to the small settlement where her father was chief, but he had begged her not to. He could not of course tell her why, but she had not questioned, just stoically grasped hold of his arms and pulled him along through the damp grasses. She was surprisingly strong for a woman, and he guessed she did much outdoors work and the tending of beasts, despite her father being a minor chief.

In the tent, she pulled away his sodden tunic, breath hissing through her teeth as she saw his wound.

"Is it bad?" he said.

"Bad enough, I will not lie. But I think, if the spirits will it, then you will live. I will clean the gash properly…but then I will have to sew it shut. Have you heard of that method of healing before?"

He nodded. "Yes, but I have never seen it done, and I have never taken such a deep wound before now. It sounds painful."

"It will be," she said with honesty. "But it is your best chance if you wish to recover."

He closed his eyes and lay back, face very drained and pale. "I am not certain that I do, lady."

"That is a wicked thought," she said, wiping at his wound with a large flat leaf. It brought immediate cooling to the tortured flesh. "You are not an old man yet. The gods would be angry if you willed yourself to an early death."

"You do not know what has befallen me, girl," he breathed, closing his eyes as she probed deeper into the gash and daubed unguents on the raw, torn flesh. "If you knew what an evil bastard I am, you would not lay your hand upon me."

Elian's lips pursed. "I do not know what has befallen you, but I can guess. I had a brother once, now dead. He fought with a local chieftain over some petty matter and died for his pigheadedness. If you are like other men, I imagine you too fought over some triviality."

An'kelet let out a bitter laugh, despite his pain. "It was hardly trivial, lady. But it was foolish, and the folly was mine. I betrayed my friend in the foulest manner…and left a helpless woman on her own, to face punishment and maybe worse."

Elian's eyes were fixed on An'kelet's injury. For some reason she did not want to hear of the stranger's 'folly'…or this woman he had left behind. "It is in the past now. The spirits have seen fit to let you live despite the ills you did. Now…I will give you something for the pain that you must face." Reaching to her bag, she drew out some willow bark. "Chew it," she ordered. "Suck the moisture from the bark. Old Saille the willow goddess sends a gift to soothe pain in her woody flesh."

An'kelet placed the shreds of bark into his mouth, then lay back as Elian took a long fine bone needle from her pack and threaded it with a thin strand of gut, the end of which she bit off with her teeth. "You must not move," she said. "You must stay completely still as I work."

"I will do my best." An'kelet closed his eyes.

Elian leaned over him and the needle entered his flesh. He bit his lips until they were ragged but made no outcry, no unnecessary movement as she darned his flesh, drawing the torn edges of his wound together. "You will have a scar," she said as she finished, "But I would not worry too much. You have a handsome enough face and every warrior has scars."

He was half-fainting with pain, but managed to utter a small, weak laugh. "I promise I will not worry about the scar, Elian."

She took her needle, cleaned it and wrapped it, then turned back to her patient. "I must go now. My father will be worried otherwise and I do not want him to come searching for me. He is very protective since my brother died. You do not want to be found, either…and…" her mouth quirked, "maybe I do not want them to find you. You are my secret, a gift brought to me by the Lady River. But tell me, what should I call you? There must be a name I can call you by, even if it is not your true one!"

He could barely think through the haze of pain and the weakness of his body. "Some have called me Longhand in the past. It was when I was a Spearman. But now..." He stared down at his hands, shaking faintly in the dimness. "You may as well call me Nohand, for I have not any weapons, not even one of my daggers."

"It will not always be so," Elian said firmly. "You shall be healed, Longhand, and you will eventually take up arms again and win back your honour."

He shook his head, his smile grim. She could not see it in the gloom. "No, my honour can never be regained. At least not in this land. But thank you for all your aid, Elian the Fair."

He heard the hiss of her breath between her teeth. "I will be back tomorrow, Longhand."

Over the next few days An'kelet's condition worsened. Fever burned in him, and he knew not himself but raved and tossed on the ground. Elian knelt at his side in the little skin shelter, heating rocks on the fire to make the tent warmer. If he could sweat out the evil humours, there might be a chance for him. The girl scowled, shaking her head in despair. She did not understand why he sickened so. She had cleaned the wound well and treated it with the freshest plants; and even now, it did not stink of putrefaction, nor were its edges discoloured. It was as if bad spirits were at him, tormenting him, trying to drag him into the realm of Not-being. Well, by Bhel and the Everlasting Sky, those foul creatures would have a fight on their hands—if Elian daughter of Phelas of the tribe of Astolaht had anything to do with it!

Singing softly to herself to distract from the gravity of the situation, she went to the river and drew water into a big clay bowl. Taking it back into the shelter, she used a wad of dried moss to sponge down the feverish man, wiping beads of sweat from brow and body. It was frightening…not only was he hot, but his strength seemed to dwindle and his flesh with it, as if it was burning off in a fire that raged inside.

"You will not die, you will not die," Elian repeated over and over, as she held the moss sponge to his lips, squeezing it so that water dripped into his mouth. "But maybe…" She looked into his closed, pale face, the sweat standing out like jewels on his brow, "maybe the problem is that you do not wish to live. Well, if you stand on the dark edge, I will draw you back! Whatever you have done and to whom, one so fair of visage does not deserve an end such as this, surely!"

For several more days she tended him, staying awake all night least he should have need of her care. She had lied and told her father she would be gone for a few days to the distant home of the Ladies of the Lake, to worship at their women's hut and to learn more of herb craft and the like. It was her ambition to be the Holy Woman and healer of Astolaht, so Phelas thought nothing of her hasty departure—women's business was not for men to question—though he insisted she take a bow and quiver of arrows for protection. He had made certain that she knew how to protect herself since her eldest brother, Ro'chad, had died defending their livestock from cattle-raiders.

Elian had sworn not to sleep as long as she felt Longhand's life might be in danger. But on the fourth day weariness overcame her and she slumped on the floor next to the mound of skins where her patient lay, and she slept, curled into a tight ball beside him.

She awoke to the sound of the dawn chorus and, peering through the tent flap, saw the Moon was setting, a thin ghost sailing West through the trees. She cursed herself for her weakness; she should have stayed awake! Panicking, her eyes flicked to her patient, fearing the worst…she had been sound asleep for hours.

He was very still, very quiet. She could not hear the troubled breathing that had plagued him these past nights. Oh no, what have I done! she thought, reaching for his slack wrist… She found the beat of his life-force almost right away. His skin was cool, no more sweat washed over him; gazing at his face, she saw that, though pallid, he looked more relaxed. His breathing was slow, rhythmic.

A great joy welled up in her.

The stranger from the river would live.

An'kelet recovered slowly. At first his legs would not hold him at all, and when he tried to rise he fell down again, almost taking the shelter of skins with him. Elian propped him up and helped him back onto the nest of skins she had made. "Too soon, friend Longhand," she said. "Recovery may take some time. I will bring you food and drink to cheer you and make you hale."

"I am shamed," he said, a shadow on his handsome though drained face. "You, a maid who is not my wife, must tend to my needs like a newborn babe. I cannot even piss by myself. That is shameful."

"It cannot be helped," she said. "And do not fear, Longhand, I live in a house with no women, just my father and remaining brother, and I am not ignorant of what a man looks like."

He blushed furiously. Elian had to bite back a laugh; he was so much older than her, old enough to be her father, and yet he flushed like a young innocent lad at her joking words! She wondered where he had come from to have such strange manners and bearing; her father's age he might be but Phelas

was nothing like Longhand—he was a stout, balding man with wispy grey hair and a worried-looking face scored by years of wind and weather.

"I am sorry, Longhand," she said kindly. "I speak and do things plainly, which is how it has always been with women in my family. It is probably not the custom of your people for women to speak so freely of such things."

An'kelet dragged himself into a sitting position. "I feel filthy, having lain here for so long. Can you get me to the river?"

"Not yet…I fear its swell would be too strong and you would be dragged down to the bed of old River Mother! I would not let her have you after all my efforts to keep you in Tirr nambeo, the Land of the Living! A few more days…maybe a week… and hopefully you should be well enough to brave the cold waters. I will wash you as best I can in the meanwhile, if you do not mind."

He nodded, and she took out some soft wads of moss from her leather bag. Going outside she dipped them in the river then returned and began to slowly lave his skin, pushing aside the blood-stained and crusted tatters of his tunic. The palm of her hand came to rest on his chest, and she suddenly realised, as if for the first time, how strongly muscled he was despite the wasting of his illness. A warrior's physique…so different from the farmers and herdsmen of her small holding, short men who grew bow- legged and round-hipped from squatting round their fires. She also appreciated that, before his wounding, he had been well-fed…and she now suspected, of high status. She plucked a button from his ruined tunic and examined it in the dim light—although damaged and broken in two, it was a piece of jet with a rim of imported gold.. She had never seen the like; her mother had owned one bead covered in thin gold foil, but that was all. She stopped washing her patient, her hand still resting on his chest, and suddenly a shudder, half fear, half pleasure, shot through her and her face reddened to match his earlier. He noticed her hesitation and looked at her quizzically. She noted, as if for the first time, his eyes were almost an amber colour, warm and deep.

"I must do something about new clothing for you," She drew away. "This garb has grown rank and needs to be cast away—it will attract unwholesome spirits by its blood-smell. I will see what I can take from my village. I will need to be careful, though, lest I am questioned."

"Yes. No one must know. If you care for my life, my existence must remain secret."

"I do care for your life, Longhand." She gazed at him and suddenly her eyes were shadowed. She turned away abruptly, reaching for the flap of the tent. "I will return tomorrow. Rest well."

She came back the next day, carrying a large spotted skin wrapped round her shoulders. She had taken it from Astolaht only after much harassment from her brother, who had stared suspiciously at her from over the rim of his beaker and asked why she was flitting back and forth from Astolaht like some piece of wind-blown marsh-gas. He wanted to know if she had a man, and was taking the skin so that she might lie with him on it. She had reddened to the roots of her hair, both angry and embarrassed, and smacked him in the face with her balled hand, making him bellow with anger, and then they had both railed at each other and tumbled in the grass outside their father's hut. It was only Phelas threatening to beat them both that made them spring apart and stand, breathing heavily, giving each other poisonous glares.

"And what are you doing with that skin, daughter?" Phelas had glowered at the dishevelled girl, her kirtle torn and hanging from one shoulder. "You have not been home much of late; you have been flying back and forth with scarce a word for your kin…"

"As I said!" snapped Tirre, his eyes flashing. "A lover!"

Chief Phelas swung his fist and struck Tirre, shocking him into silence.

"I told you," said Elian. "I have made a pilgrimage to the Ladies of the Lake. They have instructed me how to become one with the air we breathe, the earth we stand upon, the water of Mother Abona. And in order to accomplish that, I must have space to find peace, to enter the spirit world…and not be bothered by oafs such as Tirre!"

Phelas sighed, looking at his daughter with her gleaming oval face, honey hair and sun-bronzed skin. She was too old to be unwed, he knew that…but she was all he had left of her mother, whose marriage to him had been a love-match, and he did not want to part with her as yet. "I do not know if I believe you or not," he grumbled. "But whatever it is you do, daughter, take care. You are more precious to me than the sun-metal gold."

"You need have no fear," she had said, but she found her eyes darting away from his face, full of guilt. Throwing the deerskin over her shoulder, she had run into the dappled forest and not looked back.

But now she was here, back in her little shelter with Longhand, and was using her needles and gut strings to sew him a simple long tunic out of the deerhide. Carefully she scratched the hair away with her flint scraper, wanting to show him that she had some skill. She could have done better, making him both close-fitting trousers and a shorter, fitted shirt, but she did not dare be so familiar as to measure his frame with her hands. She hoped he would not mind her poor efforts.

He watched as she sewed, silent as he lay on his bed of furs. She noted his colour had all but returned and there was new life in his eyes and a renewed lustre to his hair. It fell in loose waves over his shoulders, rich amber to match his eyes. She had not shaved him while he was ill, even though it had obviously been his custom, for she had feared she might cut him as he tossed in his sickness, and now there was red-gold upon his chin and round his lips. A lord of bronze and gold, born of the river and the sun.

Elian bit her lower lip and glanced down at the skin in her lap, sewing furiously. Why was she thinking such things? He was a stranger, she did not even know his true name, and he was old...for all that he still held the power of youth in his arms. He would get well, and then he would go...

Elian the Lily-Maid realised with sudden awful knowledge that she did not want the stranger to leave. She wanted him to stay, and be with her. She was not as the other girls in her village, already dandling babes round their fires; and he was not like the men of her clan. Whatever evil he claimed he had done mattered not one bit to Elian of Astolaht.

Longhand sat up, stretching out his legs in his old, cracking trews, stiff with dirt. "I thank you for your efforts, Elian. Do you think it possible that I might enter the river today and wash the dirt from me, now that you have made new clothes? I feel stronger by the day. I do not think the river can take me."

"Yes...yes, I think so..." Her voice was scarcely more than a whisper. "But I must come with you, in case you fall."

They went down to the river and Elian sat upon the bank amidst the tufted grass. The wind was blowing and the lilies she loved to gather nodded their heads. Bits of blossom off the trees blew in white showers and curled on the river's swell.

Unselfconsciously, but with his back to her, An'kelet slipped into the cold Abona, releasing a little gasp as its coldness bit into him. Gingerly, he removed the torn and blood-smeared shirt and then the scored trousers, letting them drift away as an offering to the spirits who ruled the watery places, to Mother Abona, the Great Cleanser, and her consort, Borvoh the Boiler, churning and twisting in the weirs. He was reminded of his initiation at the temple of Khor Ghor so long ago, where the Merlin had dunked him in Abona's swell, purifying him before he took his oaths in the Throne of Kings before the Stone of Adoration and Ardhu Pendraec, the Stone Lord of Prydn. Oaths he had broken... His mind cast back to another river, dark under a midnight sky hard with stars like the inside of a broken bluestone pillar, where he had first betrayed his king and lay with the White Woman, Fynavir of Ibherna, Ardhu's chosen Queen.

The pain of the loss of both Fynavir and Ardhu, his friend since youth, was like a sharp twisting knife inside him, and he stumbled on stones in the riverbed. Buffeted by the waves, his knees gave way, threatening to throw him down to be swept to oblivion, to eternal forgetfulness. Elian gave a little cry and ran out into the water to steady him, and suddenly she found her arms around him, tall and golden bronze and naked, like some god of the Sun come to earth…even if that god was growing weary and faded, passing towards winter.

He stared down at her, her honey hair in damp coils against his chest, her tunic, wet from the river, clinging to her lithe young body. Suddenly he felt something he had not expected to ever feel again—the stirrings of desire. Until now, such sensations had been reserved for Fynavir, and guilt had accompanied them…guilt for the breaking of his oaths to both his priestess mother in Ar-morah and to Ardhu. Now those oaths were long gone, no longer binding him before man and spirits…he owed no loyalty to Priestess Ailin, on her Lake Isle where men died every nineteen turnings of the Sun, nor did he owe allegiance to the Stone Lord, who had cast him from Kham-El-Ard to die. He was going to live instead, though, by the art of this fair-faced girl who clung to him as if they were already lovers. She could heal him in more ways than she knew, freeing him from the ties that had bound him for so long… In the back of his mind he knew that this sudden rush of lust was not right, not in his state of mind and not as an outlawed man who must soon, now that his wound was healing, flee these lands before he was tracked down by Ardhu's men. To take her and then leave was against the honour he had always lived by, instilled in him by the virgin Lake Maidens in his mother's domain…but by the spirits, he wanted nothing more than to cast her on her back and quench the memories of all he had lost in soft yielding flesh.

Elian glanced up at him expectantly, her eyes wide and the pupils dilated, her mouth parted and breathing ragged, and he knew then that she felt what he felt too. She had not come there that day to nurse him; she wanted his body as much as he desired hers. Grabbing her shoulders he pushed her back towards the shore, ungentle in his urgency, rougher than he would normally have been with Fynavir. Reaching dry land, he swung her up into his arms and entered the shelter where she had tended him.

He dropped her onto the furs on the ground, hardly noticing how heavily she fell, and that her eyes had darkened, not with desire, but a hint of fear. Kneeling over her, he yanked the ties on her wet tunic, peeling it away from her body. He caressed and fondled her, none too gently, making Elian utter a small cry, though he did not know whether with pleasure or pain.

"Longhand," she managed to gasp, grasping at his bare shoulders, almost holding him off. "Please… I have not been with any man before."

He scarcely heard her but ran his hand up the inside of her soft thigh. She flinched. He could not wait, did not want to. Pushing her thighs farther apart, he lifted her slim hips and flung himself on top of her. She flinched again, more strongly and bit her lip, and suddenly he saw a tear of pain run down her cheek. A pang of guilt struck him and he wiped the tear with his hand, but then the need of his body overcame him, and he took his pleasure with little thought of hers. She cried out now, and he knew it was not with pleasure, and he pressed his hand over her lips so he would not hear. She writhed under him, suddenly frightened, as if fearing he would suffocate her.

Suddenly, it was all over, and with that rush of release, terrible shame flooded over him. "O gods, what have I done!" He dropped his hand from her mouth.

Hastily he rolled away from her. She lay on the furs like a frightened animal, breath coming in huge gasps, skin smeared with dirt and his sweat. Her knees were hugged to her chest, her eyes wide and fearful, and the whites too big.

"I told you I was tainted!" he shouted, loathing in his voice. "You should have kept well away and left me to die! I was meant to die…it was decreed so by Ardhu Pendraec!"

She struggled up, covering herself with her arms. "The Stone Lord? Why…what was he to you?"

"He is the one I betrayed! I took his woman to my bed, even as I took you. The Queen…the White Phantom. The one woman I should never have touched."

A look of horror crossed her smudged and tear-streaked face. Rumour had come down the Great River of the wrath of Ardhu at finding his wife unfaithful, and how he had punished her by sending her into the fields to pull the plough like a beast. "Who are you? What is your name?" She had half-guessed his identity already, but needed to hear the truth from his own lips.

He stood up, dirt-smeared, his hair a tangle of copper and leaves. "I am An'kelet, prince of Ar-morah, son of the priestess Ailin and King Bhan…once wielder of the spear called Balugaisa, once esteemed companion of the circle of Khor Ghor. Now I am an outlaw, bereft of all honour, a liar, a thief and a defiler of women."

She dragged one of the skins around her and rose to stand beside him. She was shaking, her teeth chattering. "This can be made well, just as your body was made well. You can come to my father's village with me…I will hide you. My father will be angered when he finds out we have been together, but when he knows it is my choice, he will come round and help you."

He glanced sideways at her and shook his head. "No. It cannot be. I will not hide away in any village till I am hunted down like a beast…and bring Ardhu's wrath down on your people. I will go this very day…back to Ar-morah, across the Narrow Sea." He strode from the tent, picking up the tunic she had made for him and yanking it on, before pulling on his worn calfskin boots with their felt inserts. "I thank you for the kind gift of this garment…and…" he stared down, fiddling with the belt, adjusting it to fit his dwindled waistline, "and for all else you have given me."

Elian scrambled from the tent, dropping the fur in her haste. "No…no!" her voice was a moan of torment. "Do not leave…not like this…not now, I beg you. I…I cannot face returning home full of shame. Oh, I have been such a fool…a fool! I beg you not to abandon me…I …Over the days I tended you, I have come to love you, An'kelet of Ar-morah!"

"You will survive your wound of the heart, as I have survived wounds of both heart and flesh, lady," he said softly. Reaching forward he gently embraced her and kissed her bruised mouth—as a lover this time, rather than a ravisher. "You are fair to behold; any man would be glad to share your hut. But it cannot be me. I must go from Albu the White or spend all my life a fugitive."

"Then take me with you," she whispered.

"I cannot. I will not lie to you…my heart will always be with Fynavir, wife of Ardhu. That is the doom the Spirits have laid on me. You deserve more than to be second best."

He released her and began to stride purposefully down the riverbank, into the trees. "Don't leave me!" she shrieked at his back, falling to her knees. "I cannot bear it! I will not live with the shame you have brought to me! You have used me and now you abandon me…you may as well have put a dagger through my heart! You have killed me, An'kelet of Ar-morah!"

An'kelet broke into a run. He did not glance back. He vanished into the woodland as the rain began to fall, a thin, drizzly, drenching mist.

Elian the Lily-Maid of Astolaht tumbled to the ground like a sapling struck by lightning and lay unmoving, white and cold on the banks of Abona, with the rain washing her flesh as if seeking to rinse away the sorrow and the bitter truth.

CHAPTER THIRTEEN–OATH TAKING

Rain poured down out of a leaden sky, a solid sheet of water that slapped the stout timbers of Kham-El-Ard. Solstice was nearly upon the people of the Plain and the Place-of-Light but it was hard to believe it was summer. A chill hung in the air and the crops were dying where they grew, black rot speckling their roots. The fields were swamps, though the hills and hollows looked greener and more fecund than ever, but man could not live upon grass like a beast.

Ardhu Pendraec stood on the walls of his hilltop dun, staring at the winding, widened curve of the river, with the trees beyond sinking into mist-caps and the distant rises cloaked with helms of grey cloud. Despite the punishment of Fynavir and his own offerings to the spirits at Khor Ghor, nothing had improved in Prydn, neither with the weather nor with the actions of men. For the first time in many years a rumour came of a raiding party down on the south coast; dark-bearded men in sky-blue cloaks, seeking tin and copper and bronze, but with sword-blades rather than through legitimate trade. In the East, rumour had it, men raided cattle and women as they did in the days of their forebears, and rough brigands overthrew lawful chiefs and set themselves up as petty kings. And from the Middle-lands up as high as Peakland where the henge of Ar-bar stood on a limestone plateau, there were reports of a plague that killed men, women and children within a day. Pyres burned day and night on the Peaks and the air was black with the greasy smoke of the crematorium.

Ardhu frowned, his fingers twitching round the cold hilt of Caladvolc. Despite having broken An'kelet's influence and casting him forth to die, despite the atonements he had made to the spirits—sacrifices, prayers, fasts and dances, Fynavir had not quickened again. She was quiet in his presence and did not deny any demand he made upon her, and her shorn hair had grown swiftly and now lay on her shoulders like a boy's, but she had grown thin, the flesh burned from her with sorrow, and she did not ever laugh or smile, not even when Gal'havad came to visit her, holding her hands and speaking gently to her.

Ardhu knew there was only one thing left to do…follow what the Maimed King had suggested ere he gave himself up for the ruined Land. The Quest. The Quest for the Chalice of Gold, the beaker of Plenty, that had been taken by its makers and protectors back over the sea to the isle of Ibherna. He had lived long enough and seen enough to question in his heart whether the gods cared enough about men to place great powers in a thing wrought by mortal hands…but he knew others believed in its power, and, perhaps, that gave it the greatest magic of all. Its finding would be a token that he, as King, could still bring prosperity to Prydn, that age had not weakened his hand or his skill, and that the Cup of Gold could be the Cup of Plenty and the wheat sway in sun-burnished fields the next year.

And if it did not work, and the rains still came…he shivered and his blood felt as ice in his veins.

No, it must work, and he would announce the departure of the warband on an Imram, a Great Journey, as soon as possible. He would send messengers ahead to the ship wrights of Ynys Mhon, who would be well paid—with gold—to make two long, seaworthy boats in the style of continental craft that would hold twenty warriors and their weapons. From those rocky shores, dotted with the tombs of the Ancestors, his warband would fare to Ibherna where the Cup lay hidden in the Hollow Hills of the people who dwelt there.

But first the warband must be readied and new warriors sworn in at Khor Ghor. Replacements for An'kelet and for Per-Adur, whose head-wound caused him dizziness and ringing in the ears, and for Ka'hai who these days preferred to order the stores of Ardhu's household to fighting. Gal'havad would have his official Coming of Age ceremony before the

Stone of Adoration, as befitted the Prince of the West…and also, as Ardhu had promised, Agravaen and Mordraed would take oaths as loyal warriors of the warband.

The Stone Lord's eyes narrowed slightly. Since the unhappy homecoming from the East and the banishment of An'kelet, Agravaen and Mordraed had worked hard to keep a place of respect in Kham-El-Ard. No ill word had come from any quarter regarding either of them…and yet Ardhu still felt uneasy. Not of Agravaen, guileless and eager to please, dreaming of glory. But Mordraed, always Mordraed, with his beautiful but closed face, and that slightly sardonic manner that none could fault yet none could trust. Yet he had done no wrong and Gal'havad was by his side most days, just like any adoring younger brother.

Of course, that is what he is, Ardhu thought, with a sudden stab of guilt. Does Mordraed know? Has Morigau told him the truth?

He prayed to Bhel and all the spirits of Earth and Sky that Gal'havad would never learn his father's darkest, most shameful secret.

The Rites of the New Warriors began shortly before dusk on the Night of the New Moon. The rain had eased a bit, and clouds scudded across the vault of heaven, flickers of flame as the dying sun caught their underbellies. Up the Avenue came a stream of celebrants carrying burning brands, the men on the right side of the bank and the women dancing down the left. They lined up near Heulstone, the Stone of Summer, before turning to gaze down into the valley bottom, where the initiates were being brought up from the river Abona by the priests of Deroweth.

The three youths were guided past the Stone of Summer. They walked sun-wise around its grey bulk while the priests chanted and bowed and laid down offerings of dried wheat, little sheaves that tore apart on the rain-sweet wind.

They were then led into the heart of the circle past the Old Man and the Mother Stone, the two foremost bluestones, and the priests gave them beakers of mead to smash at the Stones' feet and burnt oat cakes to leave so that the spirits could sup as they pleased.

Upon reaching the Stone of Adoration, its greenish flanks glittering dully in the cooling light, the priest Gluinval, who performed the necessary rites for all religious matters in the Merlin's stead, squeezed through the narrow gap of the Great Trilithon, Portal of Ghosts, wearing a headdress with the bleached antlers and skull of a deer dead for nearly a millennium, and a robe painted with solar and lunar symbols of the Everlasting Sky. He raised a red-painted rattle and shook it, making a thunderous noise that bounced around the five inner Trilithons.

One of his acolytes lifted a perforated cow's horn and blew upon it, making a mournful noise that echoed alongside the din of the rattle. At that moment, Ardhu Pendraec stepped out from behind the mighty southern trilithon the Throne of Kings, with its inlaid carvings of daggers and axes. He wore a long woollen robe dyed with great art to match the colour of the sky, the colour of the holy ancestral bluestones, and on his breast gleamed the golden lozenge that proclaimed his kingship. He wore no helmet, for this was not a place of battle, but a thin band of bronze held the greying dark wings of hair away from his forehead. Blue beads dropped from the ends of his shoulder-length hair. In his hand he held the unsheathed Caladvolc, sword of bitter edge, undefeated in battle.

He gestured with his free hand for Agravaen to approach. The youth, his hair twisted into a knot on the side of his broad skull and blue paint running in zigzags across his eyes, lumbered toward his uncle, sweat beading on his brow in nervousness. "Agravaen son of Loth of Ynys Yrch, do you come here before the Ancestors to serve the Stone Lord of Prydn?" Ardhu asked, his voice sounding almost not his own in that sacred, enclosed space.

"I do, Stone Lord." Agravaen knelt on the packed chalk, and leaned forward to kiss the damp ground, the bones of the earth, as was customary. His flat, unappealing face came up white. "I will serve until my axe breaks and my dagger shatters and the breath goes forth from my body and my spirit flies over the Great Plain…" he mumbled the ritual words.

Mordraed watched him, lips compressed into thin lines. He knew his younger brother meant every word. It was embarrassing to watch him grovel and look up at Ardhu Pendraec with the eyes of a soft seal pup…but what else could one expect of a dolt such as Agravaen?

By the Throne of Kings, Ardhu touched the blade of Caladvolc to Agravaen's brow and then his heavily muscled shoulder. "You oath is accepted before your chief and your Gods. You, Agravaen son of Loth, shall join the warband of Ardhu Pendraec in this Round, this Dance of Great Ones."

Agravaen clumsily clambered to his feet and was escorted by priests to the Stones known as the Three Watchers, where he was given a ritual libation of fermented milk.

Ardhu and Mordraed stood looking at each other across the circle, silent, unsmiling. Gluinval made a hissing noise behind his antlered mask and suddenly downed his rattle. The air seemed to crackle between older man and youth; their gazes sparred, though neither spoke a word, and both wore expressions that were deceptively bland and calm. Ardhu was resplendent in his royal robes, the last beams of sunlight tracing the geometric patterns on the breastplate of Heaven…but Mordraed, standing before him, surely seemed his equal in that moment, almost a dark twin…but younger, the upcoming challenger, the future whether good or ill. Of similar height to Ardhu, his bare arms, wrapped in golden coils, were strong with the power of youth and his black hair fell in shining waves down his back, twined with feathers white and dark. His face was that of one of the Everliving Ones, too still, too perfect…almost pretty but with an edge hard as a sword blade.

"Come here, Mordraed." Ardhu's voice was a harsh rasp. He did not speak the usual formal words, but it made no difference.

Mordraed walked forward, gait stiff. He bowed before Ardhu and then, as Agravaen had done, knelt and kissed the earth. He made sure, though that his face remained clean; he would not root on the ground like a pig, as his brother had done. He spoke the ritual words, clearly; his voice as pleasing as his face and form.

Ardhu approached him with Caladvolc; the older man's hand shook slightly. Mordraed noticed it instantly and suppressed a mocking smile.

Ardhu touched the point to Mordraed's brow and then to his shoulder, as was customary…but suddenly he whipped it aside and pressed the blade's lethal tip against the base of Mordraed's throat. "You will be in my warband, and you will fight at the side of my son, Gal'havad." He emphasised the 'my son,' "And if you betray me—or—him…by the Ancestors I will take this blade and give you to the Stones. Do not suppose that…because we share blood…I would not do it."

Mordraed's eyes blazed; people outside the circle and the priests were craning their heads, wondering why he had not been released from the Circle to join Agravaen at the Three Watchers. "I know exactly what you would do, lord," he said, rather impudently. "It is what any king would do if faced by betrayal." As I would do to you, the biggest traitor of all—to the laws of our people and to your sister and your eldest-born son!

"So, once again, we understand each other."

"I have always understood, my uncle."

"Good. Now stand beside me and await the coming of Gal'havad, your kinsman and my heir. I want you to swear not only to me this day, but to him."

Mordraed's expression became one of confusion; he had not anticipated being asked to perform such an act. "This is highly unorthodox," he spat, his eyes seeking Gluinval, as if hoping for intervention from the priest.

"Maybe it is," said Ardhu firmly, "but it is what I wish."

Gluinval began to move again, as if released of some spell. The rattle whirred, and Gal'havad came forward from his waiting place behind the outer ring of bluestones. On the journey up the Avenue from Kham-El-Ard he had worn a dark fur cloak and cloth hood in stark contrast to the high status warrior's garb of the other two youths, but now he had shed them and stood forth clad as the Son of the Terrible Head, the Prince of Evening, Gal'havad the Hawk of Summer. He wore a long woven robe made by his aunt Mhor-gan of the Korrighan; it was fringed with strands of glowing bronze and an inlaid chevron pattern ran around the hem. The colour of the robe was like nothing Mordraed or indeed Ardhu had ever seen on textiles before; a rich purple, the colour of the dying day, similar to the hue of the sacred cup Gal'havad carried as a talisman. Indeed, the dye used to get the colour had come from scraping the sides of similar stones within the Holy Pool below Kham-El-Ard—all carefully harvested by Mhor-gan and her mistress, Nin-Aeifa, Lady of the Lake. Besides the robe, he wore an archer's wristguard of greenstone studded with golden pins, and a vast crescentic necklace of amber beads. He also bore a new ornament, a gift from Ardhu upon this special day—a black jet lozenge, identical in design to the Breastplate of Heaven, a token of the symbols of kingship he would one day inherit.

He strode up to the Stone of Adoration and suddenly a shaft of light, the last of the day, streaked through the arch of the western trilithon, the Gate of the Guardian, and pierced the sanctity of the great circle. Stones turned green-gold then golden-pink; Gal'havad's auburn hair ignited, a stream of fire upon his shoulders; while his high pale forehead, struck by that glorious ray as it speared the gathered clouds of dusk, seemed to burn with an unearthly flame.

Ardhu stared in wonder, and Mordraed felt his belly give a queasy jolt. Gal'havad seemed more than just a youth of noble lineage come to take his vows within Khor Ghor. He looked like a priest-king, one who would mediate between the gods and men but who also had the authority to rule. Mordraed frowned, a twisting serpent of jealousy rising in him; he wondered if he, even with his years of practice, could keep the expression of hatred and envy from his face. But it was not just envy…a frisson of fear shot through him at the same time. What if Gal'havad prevailed against him, loved as he was by the spirits of this grim circle? He stared around at the Sun-touched Stones towering overhead …by the Moon, he wanted to see those huge sarsens fall, shattered on the ground…

A moment later the clouds bunched and the light-beam failed. The Stones descended into darkness, turning slatey then a sullen blue. Cold shadows fell over Gal'havad, extinguishing the light in his face and the fire of his hair. Mordraed smiled to himself, coldly; yes, that is how it should be and would be…the light of this touched and tainted youth diminished, cut off. Forever, when Mordraed found the right moment to remove his rival and claim the inheritance that was rightfully his.

Ardhu gestured to Gal'havad and his son went to him, walking three times around the Stone of Adoration and then laying his hand upon the inlaid golden dagger on Throne of Kings. The Terrible Head spoke to the youth of the Land and of duty, and the sacred responsibilities that came with being the Stone Lord of Prydn. Watching, Mordraed stifled a yawn; these pretty speeches seemed nothing but meaningless babble to him. A waste of time. For Gal'havad would never rule after Ardhu. Never.

Suddenly he felt Ardhu's sharp hazel eyes upon him. He jerked back into total alertness, schooling his face to look serious and sincere. Ardhu held out a hand toward him. "Remember what we spoke of, Mordraed Sister's Son," he said softly. "It is time for you to swear to the Prince Gal'havad, that he may have a faithful and loyal protector and servant."

Gal'havad's expression was one of surprise, but also of warm gladness. Mordraed came before him and knelt in a way he hoped would seem humble, and took his hands in his own. "I swear," he said, his voice barely above a whisper, "to serve you and be at your side, as if you were my brother…" His lips curled slightly, hidden by the raven-wing fall of his hair.

"Swear…" Ardhu loomed over Mordraed, vaguely threatening, his fingers playing with the hilt of Carnwennan, his dagger. "Swear that you will bring him no harm. Swear by the Everlasting Sky."

Mordraed writhed in irritation. "I swear…" he suddenly raised his voice, glad to see the black birds that nested in the Stones fly in fright at the unexpected sound, "that I will never raise blade in anger against my kinsman and my prince, the Lord Gal'havad of Kham-El-Ard. And if I should in madness and folly commit such a base act, may the Everlasting Sky fall upon my head and my bones remain unbarrowed for eternity." *I may speak the words you crave, father, but how can such an oath be binding when you have forced it upon me? And my mind is quicker than yours…There are many other ways to rid oneself of troublesome kin besides daggers and axes…*

Ardhu grunted and gestured that he might rise. Mordraed got up, and Gal'havad embraced him, giving him the kiss of peace on either cheek. "I am so glad you have sworn your loyalty to me, Mordraed, my dearest cousin. You will be as high in my esteem as An'kelet was to my father…before…before…" He abruptly bit his lips and glanced down, realising that he had spoken rashly.

Ardhu appeared not to have noticed. "Let us go forth and let the people of Kham-El-Ard and the Place-of-Light see their Prince. Then we must make ready for a great Imram, a great journey…to find the Golden Cup that lies across the sea in Ibherna."

CHAPTER FOURTEEN—TRIPLE DEATH

Ardhu sent messengers to the far west the next day. Boats would be built, sturdy enough to carry his war-party to Ibherna's shores. Gold he sent with the horsemen, as payment to the shipwrights, who lived on the headland on the tip of Mhon, and also to the priests of the Shrine of the Dark Grove, for their prayers in seeing Ardhu's men across the treacherous waters that separated the sister isles.

Then he called his men to his Hall and chose those who would be his companions—chief amongst them being Bohrs, Hwalchmai, Betu'or, Ba-lin, Bal-ahn, Mordraed and Gal'havad. "Go to your women and your families and make your farewells," he said sternly. "We will not linger long, but will leave at first light tomorrow. We will go for blessings at the Crossroads of the World, then hasten to the shores of Mhon, where we may depart Prydn if the seas are calm enough. If they are not, we will wait and sacrifice a horse to the waves. Bring your talismans, and bring your sharpest blades, your most doughty axes. We dwell in dark times, when even the Sun is not so mighty as he used to be...Let us show the people of this land, this holy isle of Prydn, that still their King fights for them, that he is still strong and one with the Land itself and will bring its flourishment once more!"

He finished his speech to great cheers, and men began to beat drums and dance, while others ran about packing provisions and attending to the horses of the warband.

Mordraed walked with Gal'havad through the heaving throng. "Are you excited, cousin?" asked Gal'havad. Little children were clustered around him, trying to touch his purple robe for luck. "To go out into the world and see the great and magical things that lie beyond?"

"Very excited," said Mordraed dryly, not meeting his eyes.

"I must say farewell to my mother." Gal'havad sighed. "She seldom smiles or even weeps these days...but I know, beneath her ice, the pain is raw, and that she would not have me leave."

"I have a woman to see as well," said Mordraed. "Do not expect me back in Kham-El-Ard before our leave-taking at dawn."

Gal'havad glanced at him, brows lifting in surprise. "What is this, Mordraed? You have not told me of any woman!"

"I do not tell you everything, little cousin," said Mordraed mockingly. "And do not ask me...I will not share her with you!"

He turned and left before Gal'havad could ask any more questions, striding through the open gates, and down the hillside towards the shining band of Abona without a backwards glance. Pressing forward without delay, he soon reached Morigau's hovel, its roof even more unkempt than he remembered and its door-frame leaning at an awkward angle. The oracular pig in its pen lifted its ugly porcine head and grunted at the sight of him.

Hearing the snorts and squeals of the pig, Morigau stuck her head out of the doorway. When she saw the arrival was her son, she ran forward with a glad cry. "Again...it has been too long, Mordraed. How fares my boy?"

"Well enough," he answered. "Tomorrow Ardhu's warband, of which I am now a sworn member, sets out for Ibherna, on some fool's chase to find a Golden Cup."

"A cup?"

"Yes. Ardhu believes it will bring hope and goodness back to the Land. The fool."

Morigau's thin but strong arms wrapped round Mordraed, drawing him against her lean, wiry body. He tried not to flinch in revulsion as she stroked his back with her long-nailed hands. "There is only one way to restore the failing of Prydn," she whispered her breath hot against his ear. "A new king, young and virile and beautiful. You, my Mordraed."

"I will be ready for it when that time comes," he said.

"It will be soon." Her deep eyes misted, seeing into Otherness. "There is change…in the air about us, in the water that flows, in the earth in which we barrow our dead. An old king will die, another one will come to replace him."

"I will need your help," he said. "I have sworn an oath to raise no hand against Ardhu's heir, Gal'havad. And yet I must. I know it is weak of me to even question what I must do, but an oath is powerful…"

"Any oath sworn to Ardhu is not valid…he who is no rightful king, who broke the greatest of taboos…"

Mordraed glanced at her, amused since she also had committed the sin of which she accused her brother…and he was the fruit of that folly. She appeared not to notice.

"But if it troubles you, there are other ways. I can make poisons that could fell a hundred strong men! Use such a draught to kill the boy and you would not be forsworn; you would have raised no hand against Ardhu's heir."

Mordraed rubbed his chin thoughtfully. "It could work. No marks and no trace. What brew can you give me that will do the deed but with little outward sign?"

"Come with me, Mordraed."

She took him into her hut. It was a little less rank than he remembered but still close and smelly; Ack-olon was cleaning a skin by the sputtering hearth while La'morak chewed on a piece of meat in the corner. Khyloq was stirring a pot full of some revolting gruel, her face smeared with ash and grease and her expression one of bored annoyance. As she saw him, her green eyes flickered in the thin oval of her face. After the initial awkwardness of their forced marriage, she had swiftly warmed to him, perhaps seeing him as her protector from the excesses of Morigau and her two warriors. Any shyness gone after the first clumsy night, she was eager to please him every time he visited, dragging him out behind the hut and down to a secluded spot down by the river, where she would lift her ragged skirts for him.

"Mordraed, you have come…" She dropped her ladle and stroked his arm with her grubby work-worn fingers.

He shook her off. "A moment, woman," he ordered, his gaze fixed on Morigau. "I must attend to more important things than you."

Morigau was prying amidst clay vials and pots lined against the wall. She sniffed at some and eventually brought up a little urn stoppered with blue clay. "This one," she said with satisfaction. "Mixed in a drink it will not smell and will have little taste. It is fast and it is deadly."

Mordraed took the urn and carefully tucked it into his belt pouch. "That is what I need. May it work as well as you claim."

"I am mistress of the art of creating poisons," she said. "What do think happened to Loth of Ynys Yrch? Do not doubt me…I, who, through my gods-given craft, shall be mother and priestess to the new King of Prydn before this year is gone!"

"I do not doubt you—I would be afraid to, mother! Now, I will say you farewell—until this quest of Ardhu's is over. Listen to word brought down the great Ridgeways, that you will know when to expect me home."

She clutched him to her, kissing his mouth in a way that was not altogether seemly, as Ack-olon and La'morak sneered in frustration. Pulling away from her, he grasped Khyloq's grimy wrist and led her from the hovel and away down the hillside to their usual spot. She undid the ties on her scruffy brown kirtle but he seemed distracted and did not look at her. "Go take a bath, girl," he said. "You smell of the pig."

She quickly ran down to the river, then returned dripping wet and wrapped herself around him, shivering in the cold. He still seemed barely interested; he kept reaching to the pouch at his waist, fingering the small urn tucked inside that carried death. "Mordraed, won't you touch me?" she breathed in his ear. "I have missed you, though I know you have many things to think of. Killing people...becoming King...doing what your mother says..." She spoke the last words with a hint of jealousy and spite.

Mordraed swung round on her, grabbing her long water-darkened red hair. "Do not speak of Morigau like that! Who do you think you are?"

She tried to tear herself away but he dragged her closer. Rather than looking fearful, however, she looked rebellious. He liked this expression far better than when she appeared meek and cowed. He felt the stirring of desire.

"I know who I am," she panted, standing with her hands on his shoulders, almost as if pushing him away—except that she was in fact leaning towards him, her white skin dappled with shadows, smelling of river water and the woodlands. "I am Khyloq, daughter of a noble chieftain and of good blood...and I am wife to Mordraed son of Ardhu son of U'thyr Pendraec the Terrible Head. When he is King of Kham-El-Ard and all of Prydn, I shall sit beside him as his best woman, for even if he must wed the White Woman as Morigau claims, I will be the one to bear him sons. Sons that will rule Prydn after him"

She suddenly snatched his hand and pressed it to her bare stomach. "Stupid man! Do you not notice that my belly has grown? Already you have put a bairn inside me. The Ancestors have smiled on our union"

His jaw dropped. "Why did you not say something sooner?"

She flicked back her fiery mane. "I would not tell of it before a few moons had gone by, lest evil spirits snatch the baby from the womb. Stupid man; why do you look so surprised by my news? A baby is what comes when you plough the furrow. Surely Morigau taught you that!"

"You are a sharp-tongued little shrew, aren't you?" he said, half-laughing, drawing her close against him and running his hand over the slight swell of her stomach, wondering at the strange, old magic that had seen fit to make his seed quicken to life.

"I am," she said. "And one day I will be lady of Kham-El-Ard, and my son and yours will be prince of all Prydn!"

Shortly after sunrise the next morning Ardhu's war party set off toward Suilven, the Crossroads of the World, as he had decreed. It rained and the wind blew, howling across the sky as though winter still held sway in Prydn, although it was actually nigh on the Summer Solstice. Several men had whispered that it was ill-luck to leave at such a time, before Bhel Sunface had sent his shaft of light into the holy circle in the red sunrise of the longest day, but Ardhu paid these whispers no heed. He knew it would be deemed equally unlucky if he stayed to lead the ceremony, and no Sun and no warmth came. Instead, he gave the honour of his place to the newly appointed high priest, Gluinval, and to Fynavir, an unusual move, for such acts were not often the province of women, but he was eager to show the people that he had accepted her back ...though he knew the truth of her silence, and to even look on her half-grown hair and wan face felt like a dagger thrust in his gut.

A few paces behind Ardhu and his chief warriors, Bohrs and Hwalchmai, Gal'havad rode beside Mordraed, happily surveying the rain-washed countryside. "I look forward to seeing Suilven," he said. "I have heard it is much different from Khor Ghor...much bigger...and there is a mighty hill where some say Bhel sleeps and is reborn, and a tomb of the Old Ones where the spirits fly after dusk..."

"Aye, and it's such a magic place, all the priestesses have three tits and an extra eye in their forehead," said Mordraed dryly.

"Do they?" gawped Agravaen, who was riding just to the rear of his older brother.

"Of course not, you dolt," laughed Mordraed, and Gal'havad laughed too, while Agravaen flushed red and murmured, "I knew that!"

Other than Mordraed occasionally tormenting Agravaen, the ride across the Plain and beyond, following the great Ridgeway track, was uneventful. Mud sloshed underfoot and hail beat into the company's faces as they crested Red Horn hill, but it did not slow their progress, and soon the wooden posts of the Sanctuary became visible on the horizon, dim under a soggy cloud cap. The door was barred and no fires burned.

As they drew near, Ardhu reined in his stallion and paused for a moment, remembering a time he had been here as a young man no older than Gal'havad, and how his actions could have ruined all he had worked to obtain. But it had all turned out for the best. None save Merlin knew of his dark secret…unless Mordraed himself knew.

Ardhu glanced furtively over his shoulder at the dark-haired youth riding behind him, the wind blowing his black mane straight back from his high forehead. He still didn't trust him, but looking at the boy, relaxed and even smiling as he talked with Gal'havad and Agravaen, he found himself wishing the path of fate had been different. Maybe he should have killed Morigau and taken the child, raising him as his own…well, he was his own. Then, perhaps, there would be no fear of what darkness might be lurking in Mordraed's head. Certainly he was a warrior one could be proud of, bold, fearless, a lethal archer…with a face and form that spoke of the ancient lineages of the West. It was cruel fate that Mordraed resembled Ardhu's family so much, when Gal'havad resembled no one…

He scowled, not allowing his thoughts to travel any further on that road, and slammed his heels into his steed's flanks, driving the beast away from the shuttered Sanctuary towards the twin lines of menhirs, diamonds and longstones, which wound down from the Ridgeway toward the heart of Crossroads of the World. The rest of the warband followed him, unaware of the doubts and fears that roiled within their leader's mind.

They did not enter the great circles of Suilven, protected by their monumental chalk-cut ditches, but instead turned toward the Hill of King Zhel, rising like a snowy cone with a pool of wind-rippled water hugging its feet. Passing by, with an offering of gold and bluestone chips given to the waters, they came at last to the tall rows of wooden buildings that formed the Palisades. There they were greeted by the folk of Suilven, who took their steeds to pens and fed and watered them, and brought forth champions' portions of meat and huge ceremonial beakers slopping thick, honey-rich mead.

Once this greeting was over, Ardhu travelled on foot back into the Great Circles to meet with the priestess who presided over Suilven. In his youth, the Holy One had been a great, fat old woman called Odharna, but she was long barrowed, her spirit now dwelling among the Ancestors, and her place had been taken by the Esteemed High Lady Mako'sa, She-who-Dispenses-Food.

Mako'sa was unusually tall, with a thin brown face and grey-black hair threaded with blue faïence and wrapped into coils on either side of her head; an added pad of horsehair gave her tresses towering height. Madder dye had given her robes a blood-red hue, and her cloak was wrought from the skins of hares—her totem animal. The hares' heads had been left on and were bound with fine bronze thread.

"Welcome, Stone Lord," she said, as she sat cross-legged outside of her cult-house within the great earth-ring of Suilven. "It has been long since you came to visit us at the Crossroads of the World."

He nodded. "My business has always been at Khor Ghor. I do not think the great priestesses of this place need the help of any mortal man to run their temple."

"No, that we do not," said Mako'sa. "But we are surprised to see you now, unbidden and carrying your axes and daggers of war. "

"The world is changing, priestess. You will have seen how Bhel fails and the rain comes." He held up his hand to the sky; it was raining again now, a thin drizzle. Water beaded on his greenstone wrist guard.

"Yes, we have seen it." Mako'sa's eyes turned grey as the soggy sky. "There is little that the Eye of Suilven does not see, Ardhu Pendraec. So a quest it is, for you and for your men. A quest to save the Land? Or to save your life?"

He went ashen. "What have you seen, Lady?"

Rain trickled between her dark brows, furrowed from age and weather. She must have been over fifty, a great age for a woman; though such advanced age was not infrequent among the priestesses of Suilven. "I have seen the fate of kings, Pendraec. As it always must be."

"We all die and go to the Ancestors, that is true," he said gruffly. "But I have no intention of going anytime soon, and it is my Land that worries me more than the fate of my body. Crops are failing, Lady Mako'sa; children with bellies swollen from hunger die in ditches."

"And so you will fare over the Sea to seek the Cup of Gold, the Cup of Plenty, that stands within Spiralfort, where the lamps of Uffern burn. Hoping its powers will restore what has been lost."

"Yes…the tale of the Cup was told to me by the Maimed King of the Wasteland ere he died."

"Perhaps hope in the quest is the thing…rather than the finding," Mako'sa said quietly.

He ignored her; perhaps not understanding her words or choosing not to understand them. "I have brought my men here not just for rest and food but for your blessing."

"And they shall have it, for what it is worth," said Mako'sa, bowing her head. "Bring them to me."

The warriors of Ardhu's band came one by one to the cult-house of the Esteemed Lady Mako'sa, each one bowing before her door with its carven poles that showed the faces of many beings both foul and fair, their eyes made out of pebbles polished from years of supplicants touching them for luck. Whatever she said or did with each man of the tribe within the stout walls of the house was never spoken of, either by the priestess or the warrior, who, his brow marked with a sign made of animal fat, marched back to the encampment at the Palisades. It was secret and made sacred before the spirits.

Gal'havad, looking a bit pale and queasy, went into the cult house before Mordraed, who waited impatiently outside the skin-hung door, striding back and forth with a petulant expression. Gal'havad was not long and came out bone-white and quite unsteady on his feet. Mordraed saw him stagger and lean against one of the totem poles, hand pressed to his midriff as if he was about to be sick.

"What is wrong with you?" Mordraed caught him, as his knees buckled.

"It is nothing. Go and have your blessing from the Great Lady."

Mordraed cast a distasteful glance toward the hut door. Scents of burning herbs, unwholesome and possibly hallucinogenic, drifted out towards him. "I think not, cousin. My fate was already mapped out by the spirits at the hour of my birth…that is my belief; I do not think a blessing, even from a powerful priestess, can change what is destiny."

He helped Gal'havad from the henge and out into the now-darkened fields. The Moon came out above, slicing through the sky; the stars were hard eyes, watchful and unfriendly. Mordraed breathed a little sigh; he was well aware that out here, beyond men's comforting fires, there was no one around. No one but him and Gal'havad, cousin, half-brother… and rival. It seemed the perfect place to finish his unsuspecting kinsman. Yet somehow he could not bring himself to find his dagger hilt. Not here. Not yet. Striking down a man who looked as weak as a babe was not honourable. And of course there was the forced oath, sworn before the Stone of Adoration, that he would raise no hand to Gal'havad.

Inside, he felt something he had not expected.

Pity.

It was as if he gazed at one of his two youngest brothers when he saw the ailing Gal'havad. He shook his head, wondering at his own feelings, despising himself for this unbidden weakness. He cursed silently and dropped his arm from his companion's shoulder, and at that moment Gal'havad toppled over into the growing corn and was noisily sick. His limbs jerked and Mordraed realised he was having one of his fits where he entered the Otherworld.

The sight of Gal'havad helpless and unmanned, lying twitching in the corn, filled him with revulsion, but again… that sense of pity rose up in him, snaring him, twisting his gut. Gal'havad could not stop his spells, could not control the forces that tormented him…Mordraed would hate to be so out of control, used by spirits for reasons unknown…

"Gal'havad." He crouched down beside his half-brother. Mercifully, he had ceased shaking and lay crouched on his side like a corpse in a barrow, pale-faced and with closed eyes, his breathing rapid and shallow. "Gal'havad, can you hear me?"

Slowly Gal'havad's eyelids flickered. His expression was one of disorientation. "I am sorry, Mordraed," he whispered, "that you have seen me so."

"I know of your strange spells," said Mordraed bluntly.

"Will you help me back to the encampment, cousin?"

Mordraed put his arm around Gal'havad's narrow waist and assisted him to his feet. He staggered slightly and put a hand to his face. "They are getting worse, Mordraed," he whispered. "The fits. There is great pain in my head too, and a blinding light. In the morn I ofttimes void my stomach; the other youths think it is because of too much mead but it is not."

"You bear a burden, Gal'havad." *And so you should have been a priest and not a king's heir…and then I would not have to kill you!* "Come; let us get you back to the Palisades."

Reaching the encampment, they entered the hut that had been set aside for the younger members of Ardhu's warband. As Ardhu's heir, Gal'havad had a section separate from the others, with fur-draped screens separating his bed-space from that of the others. Mordraed shoved the hangings aside and ushered Gal'havad through, and the red-haired youth collapsed in a weary heap on the bare chalk floor, still looking wan, weak and drained. "Mordraed, will you stay with me?" he asked, almost plaintively, as if he were still a little boy, and not a warrior who had already proven himself at Pendraec's Mount and who had ritually taken the life of the Maimed King.

Mordraed shifted uneasily; he did not wish this, but what could he say? "Yes, if that is your will."

He sat down uncomfortably on the ground near to his half-brother, stretching out his legs before him. Gal'havad shifted and laid his head on Mordraed's knee. He turned his head to gaze up at Mordraed, "I am afraid," he said quietly.

A cold sensation passed through Mordraed. *Do not look at me…Do not look at me…* He tried to ignore the intense, unwavering stare of his young half-brother. "There is no need to fear." His voice sounded harsh, the caw of the gorecrow.

"I dream of the barrow, Mordraed…Sometimes I cannot see myself upon my father's high seat or …growing old."

"All who live dream of the barrow now and then," Mordraed said shortly. "Do not think of it more; it can make a man mad. Rest or you will not be able to continue with the Pendraec's quest. I will watch over you; if you sicken again I will call the priestesses."

"My thanks, Mordraed." Gal'havad closed his eyes. "You are good to me. I often feel bad that you have no inheritance like the one I do, that your lands were lost when your father Loth died. I swear that one day I will see that you have lands aplenty and many head of cattle."

Mordraed was taken aback. "You...you would? You would give me those things, which would make me nigh as powerful a chief as yourself?"

"Of course I would. I swear it by our shared blood."

His voice was growing faint, heavy with need for slumber. Cushioning his face with his hand Gal'havad was soon asleep, head resting on Mordraed's knee. The older youth sat as if frozen, horrified by the intimacy of Gal'havad's touch, his face nearly as white as his half-brother's. Oath or no, he should end this now, snap this sickly boy's neck like a wounded animal's, free the wretched spirit-touched youth from his blighted life...He could claim he had another fit, that he fell at an awkward angle and his neck snapped...

But he could not bring himself to touch him...Anger and emotions he could put no name to welled up, a coil of conflict. Moving Gal'havad's head onto the ground with a gentleness incongruous with his inner turmoil, he covered his half-brother with his own cloak, then raced from the hut out into the darkness.

Merlin paced around the bottom of the sacred shaft, a caged beast trammelled by walls of chalk. He touched the place on the wall where he had tried to mark off the days and nights of his imprisonment...how many had it been? He was losing track of time now, as he grew weaker and more despondent.

"I must get away!" he muttered to himself, staring up at the tiny circle far above that allowed a glimpse of the darkling sky. He knew, felt it in his bones, that there was much amiss in the outside world. Ardhu...he must go to Ardhu, warn him, help him before it was too late.

He sighed and sagged against the chilly chalk wall. Yes, he was wrong to try and stave off what the Ladies of the Lake termed as 'Fate'...but how could he not? He had made Ardhu, engineering even the union that brought about his birth...how could he abandon him to wanton destiny now?

Suddenly he heard a noise from above, the sound of feet skimming grass. He stared up, rheumy eyes straining in the gloom. Moments later, Mhor-gan's face appeared at the lip of the shaft, gazing down. "Merlin?" she asked. "Are you hale? I have brought more food and a warmer garment."

Merlin made no answer. It was doubtful Mhor-gan would fall for his wiles, but he must try. She would be the one to appeal to if all else failed; Nin-Aeifa's heart was long ice towards him, and Mhor-gan had always been the softer of the two priestesses, her heart fair and true, like her brother's.

He crouched down, curling into a ball and putting his arms over his head. Opening his mouth, he let out what he hoped sounded like a pain-wracked moan.

High above him, Mhor-gan looked alarmed. "Merlin, what ails you?"

"The elf-stroke..." He touched his cheek. "It has happened again. You must help me lest I die here like a trapped animal."

"I will come down at once." She dropped the rope ladder down the side of the pit and began to descend.

Reaching the bottom, she knelt beside Merlin as he crouched on the floor. His heart was pounding and he resisted the urge to lunge at her and battle with her for the ladder and freedom. Instead he held out what appeared to be a weak, quavering hand. "Help me, Mhor-gan," he implored. "I wish to smell the pure night air one more time if I am to die."

"You will not die," she said fiercely. "Here, put your arms around my neck and I will bear you to the surface. I will take you to Nin-Aeifa's abode for warmth and healing."

305

Merlin staggered to his feet and climbed upon her back. He trembled as he wrapped his bony arms around her neck. She did not know the trembling was from excitement, from anticipation of freedom.

"How is your grip, Merlin?" she asked, concerned. "Can you hang on?"

"My fingers will hold…I think…" he said in the weakest whisper he could muster.

Mhor-gan began to climb the ladder, clinging to the ropes till her fingertips turned white. Like her brother she was not overly tall, with Merlin being slightly the taller, and he could tell that it was a strain on her to carry him in such a manner, tiring her, sapping her of strength.

He smiled, there in the dark, out of sight.

After what seemed an eternity, they reached the top of the ritual shaft. Gasping, Mhor-gan crawled on all fours upon the grass, Merlin still with his arms looped around her neck, dragging on her like a dead weight.

"Are you well, Merlin?" she panted.

"I am…" he said, and suddenly his voice was deeper, stronger…and the quivering hands that flapped so feebly at her throat were now tightening on it with intent.

She tried to cry out, but Merlin pressed her face down into the grass. "I will not harm you, for you are a priestess and the spirits would not be pleased," he said, drawing off his belt and binding her arms together. Then, still pushing her into the ground, he tore strips from the hem of his robes and threaded them through the belt, tying her arms to her ankles so that she could not rise and pursue him.

"Merlin…" Gasping, Mhor-gan rolled onto her side, red marks from his fingertips glowing on her neck. "I meant you no harm; you know that; we only wanted to keep you from rash actions …"

"Rash actions—what? Saving Ardhu? Killing myself? No matter what you think is the right course for Prydn, woman, I will tell you one truth—you and your sisterhood will have no say in the fate of Merlin."

Leaving her struggling against her makeshift bonds, he began to run jerkily uphill. Adrenaline pumped through him, giving him a strength of body he had thought long gone. He knew he teetered on a dagger's edge, pushing himself beyond the limits of his failing flesh, but he no longer cared. This would be the last quest of the Merlin, and he would gladly look good to those Ancestors who awaited him in the spirit-world upon the Plain of Honey.

Following the top of the ridge he set his course toward the East and the hill of Kham-El-Ard. His heart leapt in his bony chest as he saw its dark hump rising like a land-locked ship against the star-strewn sky. He could see torches flickering on the ramparts; smell the comforting scent of fires and animals, of human life.

Ardhu, Ardhu, my son…I pray you are still there, and that you are safe…

He puffed up the hill, staggering over to the gate guards who stood on duty all night. They gawped at him like simpletons but opened the stout oak gates at once to allow his passage. Hair wild, robe flapping around his knees, he stumbled across the inner yard and burst into Ardhu's Great Hall…

And found it almost empty. Neither the Stone Lord nor his prime warriors were to be seen—no Ardhu, no An'kelet, no Hwalchmai, no Bohrs. A few idle-looking louts lounged around the fire-pit, frowning in Merlin's direction as the freezing night air washed in over them.

The old shaman felt fear grip beneath his breastbone. "Where is Ardhu Pendraec?" he rasped. "Where are Prince Gal'havad and Lord An'kelet?"

One of the youths sitting at the fire snickered. "An'kelet? You are out of touch, old man! He is gone from here, by Ardhu's will. By now, he is probably dead in the forest and being eaten by beasts. Where in Prydn have you been? He was fucking the bloody Queen!"

306

Merlin's face went bone-white and dizziness washed over him. "And Ardhu?"

"Gone to find the Cup of Plenty over in Ibherna." The youth, Mordraed's friend Wyzelo the Weasel, belched and flicked a greasy pig-bone into the fire. "Waste of time, if you ask me. We should be fighting the tribes who have become unruly, not chasing such womanish dreams!"

"And Gal'havad is with him?"

"Yes, pretty boy has gone."

Merlin felt his dismay turn to sudden anger. Striding to Wyzelo's bench, he caught the youth's throat in a clawed hand, almost knocking him from his perch. Wyzelo's beaker went flying and rolled in the dirt. "Who are you to speak so of the prince who will one day rule you? And who do you think it is that you speak to now, boy?"

Wyzelo made a squeaking noise, so high-pitched and effeminate that his half-sotted companions fell about the place laughing.

"I am the Merlin," snarled the old man, his eyes burning into Wyzelo's. "Have I been gone so long you do not recognise me? Or has this place gone to ruin so swiftly that men no longer honour those whose hard work brought them here?"

"Merlin!" He released Wyzelo as he heard a familiar voice behind him. Turning, he saw Ka'hai striding towards him from the outside ward, pinch-faced and worried. "Glad am I to see you…but so surprised that I shake like a leaf in the wind! It was rumoured you were dead!"

"It seems reports of my death were highly exaggerated," said Merlin dryly. "Do I look like a dead man to you? Now tell me, for you I know I can trust…has Ardhu indeed gone to Ibherna for this Cup of Gold?"

Ka'hai nodded. "Yes, he left a few days ago, travelling first to Suilven for blessings on his quest, and then intending to ride for Mhon, where he has paid for ships to be built on the strand. He has taken twenty of his best men, including Gal'havad. Mordraed his sister's son also rides with the company."

Merlin's face whitened. "Mordraed! I can hear by your voice, friend Ka'hai, that you feel about this news as I do. Why should he take on the whelp of the bitch who tried to bite him?"

Ka'hai sighed. "Gal'havad wishes it…he seems besotted with the man, as if he has been bewitched! Mordraed also exposed the treachery of An'kelet and Fynavir—maybe Ardhu feels he owes him something for that deed."

"He owes that one nothing! This is evil news indeed." Merlin shook his head, chewing his chapped lips as he thought about what he should do. "Ka'hai, I cannot linger here…I must ride and catch up with Ardhu if I can. Have a horse brought for me. Quick, man…all we hold dear may depend on it! Ardhu is as your brother, and if you love him, you will do as I say!"

Ka'hai opened his mouth as if to protest, but Merlin's eyes glowed like brands, feral and bright, and the warrior dashed off into the gloom, returning shortly with a fine, grey-maned horse. "This is Per-Adur's steed. He is injured and will not ride again for a long time, maybe never again. Take it, with his blessings, and may the spirits smile on you and on my chief—and foster-brother—Ardhu Pendraec."

Merlin clumsily pulled himself up onto the horse's back; he was never much of a rider, less so with his weak elf-shotten side. But he would do what he had to. "Watch these dogs well," he said, pointing with a sideways motion of his chin toward Wyzelo and his loutish fellows as they lounged about inside the Hall. "I think they have been fed scraps that tempt them, and would soon gladly bite the hand that feeds."

Clapping heels to the grey mare's flanks, he shot out of the wooden gates of Kham-El-Ard and into the night, heading toward the circles, avenues and ditches of Suilven, and the great Hill of the Eye in its pool of moon-silvered water.

The second night at Suilven rolled round. Ardhu himself had gone for purification and blessing at the springhead near the Hill of Zhel, and none were allowed to witness this ritual cleansing of a King save Priestess Mako'sa and her acolytes. Even the lesser holy men and women were forced to wear blindfolds and masks to hide their eyes from what it was forbidden to see.

Sitting alone on the towering bank of the henge, watching the sharp sickle of the moonrise in the east, Mordraed felt uneasy and restive, eager to be off. Too many women here, intelligent fierce women whose sharp gazes could scry a man's soul. Too much like his mother, only worse, for they did not hold him dear. He feared to look them in the eye, lest the truth of his heart be read and they should fall upon him, rending him limb from limb in fury and feeding his blood to the earth.

His blood instead of Ardhu's; he—Mordraed—the tanist sent to try and appease the Spirits so that the old king could live to fight another day…

He shook his head angrily. Such an end would be unnatural and wrong…the young should not die before the old; the weak should not hope that the young offer themselves up to the gods in their place.

Suddenly he heard a noise, the faint thud of hooves on chalk. Turning, he peered into the gloom, his keen eyes catching sight of a figure at the end of the avenue of stones that ran from the portals of Suilven to the Sanctuary on its plateau overlooking the shallow vale.

A man on a horse, riding at great speed toward the sacred Circles. Riding as if he fled from, or to, the world's ending.

A sense of alarm filled him, though he did not know why, and slinging his bow across his shoulders, he leapt from the bank and jogged down the Avenue, keeping close to the flanks of the giant pillars that marched away into the gloom, an army of stalwart stone.

The thundering hooves drew closer, and he could hear the heavy laboured breathing of a horse pushed almost beyond its endurance. Hastily he slunk into the lee of an enormous diamond-shaped menhir, leaning against its craggy face, willing himself to appear invisible, to become part of the stone itself. He could feel its cold surface burning into his back through his thin summer tunic, and see the rough lichens that made patterns like gurning faces on its broad spine.

Out of the gloom the rider came flying…grey-white steed, grey-white man with long hair and beard a ghost-like misty trail on the wind. He caught a brief glimpse of an intense hawk-like face, withered as an old apple, but with eyes burning like fire, like fallen suns.

A face he knew and had hoped never to see again.

The face of Ardhu's counsellor, the shaman Merlin.

Merlin, who had used his unclean magics so that U'thyr could bed Y'gerna of Belerion and beget Ardhu, throwing Mordraed's mother aside as if she were an unclean rag, taking her inheritance and birthright from her. His mother, who was a powerful magic-woman in her own right, who could have been as great as the Merlin himself if given a chance. Or so she had always told him…

Like most of the others in Kham-El-Ard and Deroweth, Mordraed had thought Merlin was dead when he vanished without a word…or that he had become crazed and run amok in the woods as his kind were wont to do, struck moon-mad by their constant communication with the spirit-world and by the potions they consumed all their adult lives.

"You may wish you were dead, old man," he muttered between clenched teeth, sliding out from behind the great stone, a darker shadow blending with other shadows. "And then you may well find yourself in the spirit-world in truth!"

Bow in hand, he began to track the trail of the Merlin across the circles of Suilven. His face became very still and white, intense, between the midnight wings of his hair. All his senses felt heightened; he knew he was on the edge of something great, something terrible, something that would change the course of his life forever.

Tonight Mordraed was what his mother had taught him to be.

Tonight he was the Hunter and the Merlin was his prey.

Merlin rode his lathered horse over the fields and into the sacred hollow near the springhead of Suilven. Ardhu's ceremony was over and the King was gone, returned with his retinue to the Palisades, but Mako'sa remained at the spring, reading things from past and future in the deep, clean water that flowed from the body of the Earth in that hallowed space. The masks of her followers, removed once Ardhu's cleansing was over, had been thrown into the bubbling waters where they hovered and eddied a few inches below the surface, like the images of strange otherworldly creatures, unravelling and unbinding as the gentle current buffeted them to and fro. Torches set along the banks sent fiery ripples across the swell and made strange shadows dance.

Mako'sa watched, visage solemn, painted with white chalk so that her long thin face almost appeared a skull. A time of unravelling and unbinding…a time for new beginnings. Kneeling on the flat sarsen stones that spanned the spring, she drank of the holy water, hoping to receive blessing and wisdom.

And saw, to her surprise, a reflection appear in the water behind her left shoulder, grey and ghostly, as if an Ancestor had wandered from the old chambered barrow on the hill and come to gaze upon her rites. She sat up immediately and turned, the decorative bronze wires and faience beads on her elaborate hairpiece clattering and clacking with the speed of her motion. Her hand went to the little flint dagger, sharp as a razor, that hung at her belt, its blade painted with protective symbols. It was the life-seeker for taking sacrifice, but it could also command the dead should they rise from their sleep as fractious ghosts.

But it was no ghost that stood before her, silvered in the starshine, hair and beard wildly tangled and his robes drenched with sweat. She knew that face, lean as her own, a bird's face within a man's. It was the Merlin, chief priest of Khor Ghor.

Merlin, who Ardhu had told her was reckoned amongst the dead. But who was clearly not, his breath steaming hot with life before his cracked lips.

"High one," she said, "why do you come to me like this, weary and wind blown? Where have you been for so long, O wise one, making the song-singers and the priests and priestesses mourn you as one who has gone over the Plain in the Snare of Nud the Catcher?"

"A prisoner have I been," he answered, "held by ones who I never thought would mean me ill." He was at the top of the little dell that encircled the spring, still mounted on his froth-mouthed steed. Carefully he slid from its back, letting the reins dangle, and walked stiffly towards Mako'sa. "But no more. I seek Ardhu Pendraec, to advise him as I have always done. To keep him safe."

Her brows rose slightly. "He is not some youth to keep safe anymore, Merlin. He will be what he will be. He has proposed a quest of great holiness and he has had blessing from the Eye of Suilven, and bathed in the blood of the Great One who birthed the Sun Himself, whose body is represented in the Holy Hill. He will fare forth to Ibherna with his band of chosen men to find the Cup of Plenty, which lies in the valley of the River of the Great White Cow—locked within Spiralfort, fortress of the Flaming Door, where the lamps of Uffern burn both night and day."

Merlin seemed to sag, his shoulders slumping. "I can see no good in this quest. Only death. A symbol of Hope he seeks and maybe he will find it…but I feel it will be bought at a terrible price."

"What would you have me say, Merlin?" said Mako'sa quietly. "Should I have denied my blessing? He would have gone anyway, without even asking the spirits to strengthen his hand."

Merlin knelt by the water, staring at his own ragged reflection. The ends of his beard and his snarled hair fanned out on the swell. "Does the Land need blood so much?" he said hoarsely.

"The Land fails…the Moon is red, Bhel himself bleeds and turns his Eye from us. Ash of the pyre has fallen in the North."

"Could I not stand for him? It was done so in older times, Mako'sa."

She pulled her cloak around her, as if suddenly chilled by the wind. "No. I think you know that you have grown too old to take his place."

"So others have said…but I am still the Merlin!"

"And may you be long among us, with your wisdom. But making of yourself a sacrifice will not avert Ardhu's doom. I certainly will not be the one to lay hand upon you, nor would any of the wise."

Merlin's shoulders slumped. "I would speak to him at least."

She touched his arm lightly, an expression of pity on her face. "There will be no harm in that. You were as a father to him as well as mentor."

Suddenly the Merlin raised his head. His eyes narrowed, became secretive, and his nostrils flared as if he was scenting the breeze like a beast. A strange expression crossed his thin features and he licked his lips in nervous agitation. He was gazing intently over Mako'sa's shoulder and the priestess felt a shudder of fear ripple up her spine.

She wondered if her initial thought had been correct; that an old spirit was indeed wandering about out of its bone-chamber, creeping closer to the place of power where the water flowed from the womb of the earth, feeding the Khen and the great pool at the foot of Zhel's hill. "What do you see, O Merlin?" she asked.

He shook his head. "N…nothing…just an old man's fancy." He knelt on the sarsen stepping-stone bridge again. "Lady, would it be possible for me to stay here awhile on my own? To pray to all the Mighty Ones that these troubles will pass?"

Mako'sa hesitated then nodded. "To any other I would give only refusal. But you are the Merlin, and the events of these grim times are bound to you, heart and soul and body. Stay here awhile, as you wish. I will not stop you. I will go to the Palisades where the feasting has begun."

She bowed to him and then, drawing her cape around her, walked away beyond the ring of flickering torchlight and out across the fields of blowing grass. She did not gaze back…perhaps was afraid to, fearful of what she might witness.

Merlin wiped a hand across his sweat-stained face and clumsily rose to his feet, stepping off the bridge and raking the nearby shrubbery and trees with a burning gaze. His stance was not one of a man about to pray to his gods but one who expected to face an enemy "Come out, son of pestilence," he snapped. "I know you are out there. Let us not play these games but put an end to this foolery for once and for all."

The bushes rustled, and it was not the wind.

Out of a haze of green boughs stepped Mordraed, the Moon shining behind his dark head, the light of the guttering torches around the spring giving a bloody hue to his features. He looked so like Ardhu at the same age that a terrible pang of sadness ripped through the Merlin—sorrow for what was gone, for what was fading from Prydn, for all the bright summers of the past years that were now blurred into a rosy memory. He even sorrowed for

Mordraed, beautiful but twisted, child of a broken taboo, pawn of a malevolent mother who had groomed him to the darkness for so long he could never see the light.

"What do you stare at, old man?" Mordraed's voice was cool, silken, deadly.

"A traitor. A would be kin-slayer." Merlin spoke softly.

"You presume."

"I know."

"And why are you here, after going missing for many months? Your own loyalty is in question, vanishing when Ardhu Pendraec needed your counsel most!"

"I do not tell serpents such as you my business. Step aside, Mordraed. I will go now to Ardhu's side and speak to him." He took a long, determined stride in Mordraed's direction.

The young man blocked him, sneering down into his face. "What lies will you whisper to him, old man? He doesn't need to hear the prattling of one nearly in his dotage!"

"I'll tell him the truth and he will believe me. The truth that you seek his chieftaincy, to cast him down. You have already cut him like a dagger when you disgraced his queen…"

"The whore disgraced herself…" retorted Mordraed.

"And caused him to drive away his strongest warrior…"

"A traitor of the greatest kind…I would have killed An'kelet for his actions had it been up to me!" Mordraed tossed back his hair, his eyes on fire. "Besides, you can say what you will; he has heard all these things about me and more and still has allowed me into his band. You tell him nothing new."

"But there is more, and this will interest him—your trips to the hut of your mother, Morigau, who was forbidden to meet with you. What does she tell you, what has she given you for your journey to the West? Come, Mordraed, we both know she is a master poisoner! And the red-haired girl that you rut with down by the river; who is she? Not a local woman, that is for sure. My watchers have said you call her wife and that her belly is full. And even if your sly secret doings do not move Ardhu to anger, I will lie to him of more dark deeds…not because untruths fall easy from my tongue, but because I know what you are and what you will do. He will believe any tale I tell him of you, for he trusts me…and not you."

Mordraed blanched. He had not thought the old man might have been having him watched. Nor that a holy priest of Khor Ghor would admit to telling blatant falsehoods to get what he wanted.

Merlin reached out, shoving Mordraed backwards with a sharp motion of his hand. A strange expression was in his eyes; desperate and feverish. Sweat sprang out on his forehead. "So out of my way, Mordraed son of Morigau."

"You will tell my father nothing!" Mordraed flung down his bow onto the grass and caught the old man by the shoulders, whipping him around.

"You will have to kill me then." Merlin's eyes, struck by the moonlight, were two eerie silvered pools.

"I should have done so long before now!" cried Mordraed, and he lunged at Merlin catching him around the throat and hurling him down on the sarsen stone bridge that spanned the bubbling waters of the sacred spring.

Merlin's head hit the ground with a crack and he lay there gasping. Mordraed was kneeling over him, hands clawing at his neck, seeking a stranglehold. Merlin choked and spluttered, writhing, but he managed to tear the clutching fingers away from his windpipe and throw the youth back, half into the water. "Come on…" the old man sneered, between gasps for breath, livid marks already glowing on his throat. "I am but a dry stalk, and you young and fresh; is that the best you can do? I had imagined your dam raised you as a killer…"

Mordraed flung himself forward, grabbing a handful of Merlin's robes, pulling him off the bridge into the water. They stood together in the swell, facing each other, the old man all grey and white, a spectre seeming half of the spirit-world, and the youth all darkness and fire, with eyes like the night sky, sucking in the torchlight.

Mordraed lunged, throwing his adversary backwards in a violent motion. Merlin stumbled and his head struck the bridge with a crack. Blood suddenly poured into the swirling waters, curls of it flooding outwards to stain both opponents with red. Merlin raised a hand to the stream, his palm coming back crimson. Lights fragmented in his brain. "And so the first blow is struck…" his voice was tremulous and yet full of rapture at the same time.

Mordraed stared at him; he could almost fancy the old fool was laughing through his pain, while staring at the blood coming from his head as if it was a marvellous, wonderful thing. The most wonderful thing he had ever seen.

Mordraed snarled in perplexed frustration and laid hold of his adversary again, hurling him bodily into the shallows. He collapsed, face down, in mud and water and blood, his arms flung out, his fingers digging into the streambed. Panting, eager to end this madness for once and for all, Mordraed flung himself on the aged shaman and thrust his head under the water. Merlin jerked and writhed and blood-tinged bubbles rose to the surface, bursting horribly like boils on the swell.

Merlin went limp and Mordraed backed away, panting, but then he heard a tormented groan… he was still not dead, and there was a disturbing hint of mocking laughter even amidst his agony. He lifted his head and craned around, his bloody, muddied face staring up like some horror from the Un-world realms. "I thank you, Mordraed," he croaked. "You have killed me by the sacred way, as no other dared to do—the threefold death of strangling, wounding, and drowning. My sacrifice may not save Ardhu, but maybe if the Ancestors are pleased it will give him more time, more strength. Strength to defeat the likes of you. And as a dying man, and high priest of the Door into Winter, I will speak one last prophecy meant just for you—you will never be king in Ardhu's stead. By the Everlasting Sky, if I have to fight Hwynn and Nud themselves, I will return from the Otherworld to stop you!"

"Be silent!" Mordraed grabbed a heavy chunk of sarsen from the streambed and slammed it into his victim's head.

Merlin ceased to move. Shaking, Mordraed pulled him into the centre of the spring and weighted his body down with stones. He yanked off Merlin's talismanic pendant, the bronze-wrapped skull of his totem hawk, and tossed it far out into the water, in case the shaman's spirit-beast might rise and attack him. Swiftly Merlin sank, bubbles rising and breaking around his body. The blood trails slowed to trickles and dispersed on the swell.

Mordraed crawled onto the bank, shivering, staring at the spot where the corpse had vanished. The unfurling masks from the earlier rites bobbed around it like sinister guardians. Hot and cold shudders ran through him. He had done what he intended, what he knew he had to do. The old man would have destroyed him otherwise; he had always been an enemy. But his last words… a curse and a powerful one, born in blood.

"But it will not come true!" Mordraed made the symbol to avert evil with his hand, though he knew it was too late for the words had been spoken. "By Bhel and the Everlasting Sky, I will be King!"

CHAPTER FIFTEEN— THE SPOILS OF AHN-UN

Ardhu's warband left the Crossroads of the World at the rising of the Sun. Horns blew mournfully and drums were beaten, dull rumblings bouncing from the enclosures of the Palisades to Zhel's hill and back. The Sun, to everyone's surprise, showed its face after days of gloom, the rain-clouds rolling back from the East like great moving bruises staining the arch of the sky.

It was a good omen. Ardhu sat astride his horse staring up at the brightness, letting the meagre warmth caress his face. The Sun-rays caught on the Breastplate of Heaven and Caladvolc's gold decorated hilt and turned them to flame. He raised the Lightning Mace in salute to the glowing Face of Bhel and the company began to move, leaving the Palisades and heading uphill in a westerly direction.

Mordraed stared over his shoulder as the warband moved off. He was white-visaged and twitchy, expecting at any moment to hear screams from the direction of the sacred spring. Perhaps he had not pinned the body down well enough or deep enough…maybe there was bloody residue along the waterline that the priestesses would notice.

But no sound of discovery came, only the shrill shrieking of the wind as it whipped over the crest of the hill, past the hump of the chambered long barrow on its summit. Mordraed forced himself to look ahead and suddenly smiled grimly, realising the significance of this place. The tomb of the Ancestors…where Ardhu had broken the great taboo and mated with his own sister. Mordraed raised his hand to his forehead and saluted the Old Ones who had gathered around the illicit lovers that night and breathed upon them, ensuring that a spirit would enter Morigau's womb to be reborn in flesh. Ensuring that he would be—a new powerful life come out of the Un-world of the ancient Dead.

The huge blocking stone of the mound flashed by, stern and forbidding, and then the company was beyond the boundaries of Suilven and out into fields full of blowing grass and fleeting cloud-shadow. Mordraed clapped his heels into his horse's flanks and galloped on ahead of the others, even outstripping Ardhu, although it was insulting and inappropriate for him to outride his chief.

Ardhu frowned as he saw Mordraed race past, a blur of darkness, but decided to hold his peace. Why make trouble, just for the sake of reeling in one invigorated by the high spirits of youth? He had more on his mind that making unfriends with his wayward and trying bastard.

He had the Imram to think of, his Quest. The journey to the West that would either save his kingdom …or destroy it.

The two ships glided across a smooth and silvered sea, under a pale sun enfolded in thin cloud like wisps of a sky-goddess's hair. Ardhu knelt in the prow of the foremost, that he had named Pridwen, pleased that the weather had been fair and the crossing easy—the sea between Ibherna and Prydn was often treacherous and cruel, swallowing the craft of even the most experienced sailors. He glanced over his shoulder, noting the seasick greenness of Gal'havad's face and the almost rapt, excited expression on Mordraed's. He felt uneasy and turned back into the spray.

The lead ship ground ashore in a narrow estuary, its banks lined with drifts of wind-carved pale sand. Ardhu and his men leapt ashore and dragged the boat up onto dry land, then stood knee deep in the tide to take hold of the second boat and haul it in beside the first. When both boats were secured, the companions scanned their surroundings. They were at the mouth of an estuary filled with islets and sandy banks; a river as wide and bright as Abona coiled away into a smoky green distance. There were no signs of any habitation, just a few stark cairns on the nearby hills, their ruined portals gaping at the sky. Seabirds wheeled overhead, wings flashing in the pallid sunlight, their cries mournful as those of barrow-ghosts.

Ardhu put his hand on the shoulder of Betu'or, one of his oldest companions, whose life he had spared in his manhood rites at Marthodunu. "Will you stay with the boats, my old friend?" and when he saw the warrior look downcast "someone must, Betu'or. We cannot risk that they are stolen or destroyed; if anything should happen to them, it is likely that we will never escape this island."

"I will stay," said Betu'or, "although I would rather be at your side. I want to do more for your cause, Lord Ardhu, than sit on a beach with my feet in the sand."

"You will one day, Betu'or, the Knower of Graves," said Ardhu softly, clasping the warrior's arm fondly. "Your day will come when you can do more for me."

Leaving Betu'or to make camp on the strand, Ardhu led his small warband away from the water and into the hilly lands beyond. Hwalchmai trudged next to his kinsman, loosening the peace- bindings on his axe in case he should need to use it. "Do you have knowledge of where we must go? Although Ibherna is small compared to Prydn, yet I think we should be weary treading all of it!"

Ardhu nodded. "I spoke for many days with the wise of Deroweth about this very matter. If our calculations are correct, we have come aground at In'var Kolptha, named for a great warrior who drowned here in the tides at the dawn of time. If we proceed inland, following the River of the White Cow past the Stones of Balytra, we should come to the place we seek, that our people name Spiralfort and the God's Peak, and the men of Ibherna the House of the Good God and Young Sun. What reception we will have there, I cannot say, so we must be careful in all we do and say. The men of Ibherna, it is rumoured, are even fiercer than our own warriors and follow ancient ways that we now shun."

"Well, if they start aught with no good reason, they will have a taste of my axe," grumbled Bohrs, stomping up beside Ardhu and smacking his unsheathed weapon against the palm of his hand.

"I would have no fighting, unless it is absolutely necessary," said Ardhu. "We do not come to fight."

Bohrs looked disappointed. "Just a few heads to crack, Ardhu…just to show them who is mightiest."

"No! Not unless there is no other choice!"

"Well…" Bohrs scratched his beard," I cannot see them giving up this Cup of Plenty or whatever it is, just like that. So I am sure there will be head-cracking to be done. And lots of fighting."

Walking at Ardhu's side, Hwalchmai shaded his eyes with a hand. "Maybe you will get your chance soon, Bohrs. I see armed men on the rise up ahead."

The warband moved on, grouping together to create the impression of solidarity. On higher ground in the distance stood three standing stones, weirdly whittled by the wind, the tallest aligned with a rocky island out at sea which faced the rising Solstice Sun in Winter. Between these gnarled pillars, dwarfed by their lofty height, stood a group of warriors, not as many as Ardhu's band, but fierce of visage and strange and magnificent in manner of dress.

Ardhu was the richest chief in all Prydn, but these men dripped gold as if it were no more precious than clay beads. Huge crescent collars gleamed like Moons around their necks, and twisted, spiralling armbands shone on tattooed arms. Cloak fasteners with terminals the size of a man's fist glowed in the sunlight. Gold coils hung from earlobes, and dark and fire-hued tresses were bound with scores of golden rings. It was no surprise that they were wealthy though, even those who were not chiefs—Ibherna's mines exported massive amounts of copper to the mainland coasts all the way to sun-soaked Ibher, and gold was traded as far away as the Middle-lands between the Rivers Rhin and Rhon, and even to the farthest North near the Bheltis Sea.

Ardhu approached the warriors cautiously, holding out his empty hands to show that he brought no threat. He knew a little of the tongue of Ibherna, from Fynavir who was daughter of the red Queen Mevva, who still lived, although now a very great age, in vast holdings further North. Not that the language was difficult to comprehend if spoken slowly; the Tin-men had colonised Ibherna as well as Prydn and brought with them what became the language of trade. Once established, this tongue swiftly became the common speech, with older tongues falling aside and vanishing in its wake.

One of the men stepped forward; obviously a leader or shaman. He had a face much beaten by the sun, with rheumy blue eyes bright against the leather of his wrinkled skin. A huge red eye was drawn in ochre on his forehead, and on the end of his staff perched a skull that was also daubed with the same eye. He wore a bell-shaped tunic, with zigzag patterns threaded with fine hairs of bronze crossing it many times.

"I am Kichol, priest of Bal'ahr, he who is the Eye of the Dying Winter Sun," he announced. "Who are you who come unbidden to Ibherna, bearing weapons of war?"

"We carry our weapons because we are men and warriors," replied Ardhu. "Not because we choose to offer battle to the brave and noble folk of our kindred-isle. We come to visit the sacred sanctuary on the River of the White Cow, where it is said the God sleeps in his mound with white swans circling."

"The road to that place lies hither." The shaman of the Red Eye of Bal'ahr pointed with his staff toward the river. "Not just to the Home of the Good God, House of the Sun, but also to Dubad, The Hill of Darkness and Cnobga, mound of Bui the Hag. But there is a toll for foreigners who use the old way to the Palaces of the Ancestors."

"And what is this toll?" said Ardhu uneasily. He mistrusted this man, with his silent comrades who had neither smiled nor spoken, but stood still as the stones behind them, glittering in their masses of gold.

"You must leave one of your companions to be given to Bal'ahr with the turning of the tide," Kichol replied, almost hungrily. "When the sun rises he will be bled into the waters. It will be an honourable death."

Ardhu's face darkened with anger. "What you ask can never be, old man. I do not give up my sworn warriors lightly, and never to strange gods!"

"Then you shall not pass my lands!" Kichol struck the butt of his staff against the ground and the warriors beside him drew copper blades from their belts. At the same time, a dozen other men sprang up from behind rises and bushes. Men with bows, men with blowpipes, men with spears and gleaming daggers.

"I knew they would prove false! They wanted this from the beginning, I could see it in their eyes!" roared Bohrs and he flung himself toward the Shaman of the Red Eye with all the fury of a charging boar, his axe swinging in his hand.

Kichol's warriors loosed blood curdling war-cries and circled around Ardhu's band, spitting and cursing at them, making magical signs against them as if they were demons. But it was these servants of Bal'ahr who resembled demons; these warriors with the lurid red eye of their fierce and ancient solar god daubed upon their foreheads and the skulls of small birds and animals plaited into lime-caked hair—crows, eagles, voles and mice—all making a macabre tinkling as they moved.

One leapt directly in front of the warband, defiant, hungry for engagement, a red whorl of paint bleeding on his bare chest, a dagger in one upraised hand and a blow-pipe in the other.

"Take him down!" yelled Ardhu as the man put the reed pipe to his lips and glanced about him seeking a victim. Bohrs was standing on the warrior's right; the man shifted in his direction and filled his lungs with air.

Hwalchmai shouted out and hurled himself at the warrior with the blowpipe, stabbing his flank with his rapier and ripping upwards toward the ribcage. The man staggered and dropped his own knife under the onslaught, but kept a tight grip on his blowpipe. Shoving Hwalchmai away from him, he blew hard upon the carved tube, showering the men of Ardhu's warband with deadly spikes like so many thorns...

Mordraed spat a curse and dived into a nearby bush, dragging Gal'havad with him; he had used the blowpipe to hunt birds for sport as a boy and guessed the tips were poisoned. Ardhu flung up Wyngurthachar and the spikes struck harmlessly against the bronze surface of Face of Evening.

Not all were so lucky. Agravaen was struck, a dart protruding from his cheek. He roared in fear and anger, swatting at his face. Staggering, he thudded toward his assailant and smote his head with a dozen frenzied blows of his war-hammer, spilling the man's brains on the ground before collapsing, hands pressed over his swelling flesh.

Several other members of the warband likewise fell, rolling in spasms on the ground, froth bubbling on their lips as poison seeped into their blood. Next to Ardhu, Glu Mightygrasp went down with a thud, gurgling as his throat constricted, and a flying spear went into him, pinning him to the earth and finishing him. Arrows whined, killing Anwas and Ellidur outright, going right through their shields of oak and leather, and giving Bal-ahn a scraping wound to the shoulder. Mordraed and Gal'havad returned the arrow-fire from their position in the bushes. Their lower angle helped them as they fired upwards with lightning speed, their hands a sweaty blur, their white fletched arrows arcing toward the enemy on the rise. Screams rent the air and several of Kichol's warriors tumbled down the rise—eyes and throats and hearts pierced by the deadly barbs of the arrows of Ardhu's two sons.

More warriors arrived, though, running pell-mell from the tangle of birch, elm and alder that grew along the waterway, and they charged toward the Stone Lord's warband with almost crazed abandon. Ardhu had Caladvolc out and slashed around him, fighting his way toward the Shaman of the Red Eye, who was screaming, dancing, and chanting in frenzy, inciting his men to slaughter, calling down the wrath of spirits and gods on the strangers who had set foot upon the blessed island without leave. A warrior leapt out at Ardhu, wielding two long knives of Ibher bronze; Ardhu flung up Wyngurthachar on his left arm and smashed it into the man's jaw, shattering it until it hung at a strange disjointed angle before cleaving his skull with Caladvolc and kicking the body away.

"I will kill them all!" Ardhu shouted at Kichol, holding up his dripping blade as proof. "Call them off or they all die this day and your bloody god will have his red tribute!"

Kichol halted for a moment, and Ardhu, drawing ever nearer, could now see his eyes, blood shot and wild. There was fear in them. Adrenaline shot through Ardhu, the excitement of the hunt, the kill, the anger of being attacked so needlessly. Casting aside Wyngurthachar with reckless abandon so that he could use weapons in both hands, he raced towards his opponent. The shaman's remaining men saw the shield fall, and rushed in toward Ardhu's unprotected left side, but Mordraed rose to his knees, all darkness and serpent-grace, and fired a stream of arrows that felled many. Sprawled in the grass at his side, Gal'havad had run out of arrows but grabbed a miscast spear and flung it with all his strength at the bare legs of the opposing warriors, impaling one and tripping others, who went down shrieking like demons from the deepest pits of Ahn-un.

Ardhu had almost reached Kichol. He still held Caladvolc in his right hand, but now in his left he held the Lightning Mace, symbol of his authority as Lord of the Great Trilithon. With a cry he brought the mace down on his opponent's skull staff, splitting the pate of the death's head in twain in one motion, breaking the other man's symbol of power with his own.

Kichol fell back, recoiling in terror, but Ardhu launched into him, battering him with many blows from the huge polished fossil head of the mace. One blow struck the man's brow where the bloody Eye of Bal'ahr was painted and blood spurted out, streaking Ardhu's tunic and face like war-paint. The priest of the God of the Winter Sun crashed to his knees, and as his head lolled forward, Ardhu brought down Caladvolc with as great a force as he could muster, shearing the head of his enemy from his shoulders. The body fell back, headless, against one of the three tall pillars crowning the slope. Rooks and ravens began to wheel overhead, cawing and cackling as they awaited their meal.

In the distance, there came the yammer of hounds, eerie howls that grew in intensity. Someone else was coming.

Ardhu whirled away from Kichol's corpse and snatched Wyngurthachar from the ground. "Run!" he shouted to his men. "More of our foes are on the way…and they have brought beasts to track us. Leave the dead; we can do no more for them!"

"And the wounded?" Ba-lin shouted, staunching the bleeding flesh-wound that scored his twin brother's shoulder.

"If they can run with us, bring them…if not, drag them if you have the strength. But if their injuries are too great…" Ardhu closed his mouth with a snap, his eyes grown hard and steely. All knew what he meant.

Bohrs's big, rough face creased up and he began to weep—he who was as hard as the sarsens of Khor Ghor. "I will do the deed, Stone Lord."

"No, I will," said Ardhu grimly, drawing Carnwennan, his white-hilted dagger, from its sheath against his lower leg. "Turn away, all of you."

Mordraed and Gal'havad scrambled over to Agravaen who lay thrashing on the bloodied ground. A purple stain smeared his cheek; his eyes were glazed, unseeing. With a grunt of exertion, Mordraed yanked him up and slung him over his shoulders. He staggered under the dead weight; Agravaen was a good hand taller than him and heavily built.

"I will help you!" cried Gal'havad, rushing to his side.

Mordraed scowled at him. "Help me? Why should you help me! Don't get in my way, boy!"

"I want to help! He is my kinsman too!" Gal'havad grasped Agravaen's dangling legs, taking some of his weight. "Let's run. I can hear the dogs getting closer."

The two youths staggered down to the riverside, plunging through the marshy pools that rimed the overgrown banks. The remaining warriors of the warband raced at their heels, followed in the distance by Ardhu, ashen-faced, his hands crimson from his last, lethal gift to those who had served him.

On the distant horizon another warband appeared, wearing the same mark of Bal'ahr the Winter Sun on their foreheads. Before them loped great grey-coated hounds the likes of which the men of Prydn had never seen, shaggy and near as tall as a man. They raced before their masters like dogs of the Un-world, howling and baying, their tongues lolling horribly.

Catching up with the main body of the survivors, Ardhu gestured ahead to a curve in the river, where a thick patch of elm, ash and alder grew on the far bank. "Get into the water at that spot!" he shouted. "Cross to the trees. Maybe the dogs will lose the scent." He sounded doubtful. Desperate.

The band plunged into the river, splashing and going under as the muddy river bottom gave way beneath their feet. Mordraed slipped and was momentarily pulled under by the slow, strong current; he resurfaced cursing and blinking water from his eyes; not only briefly blinded, but with a wet bowstring that would render his weapon unusable. And Agravaen…where was he? He had lost hold of him…He glanced about wildly. He had no great feeling for his younger brother but he could not let him drown or fall to a bunch of savages.

A few feet away he saw Gal'havad struggling in the swell, bracing the supine body of Agravaen against his shoulder and fighting to keep his head above the water. "Over here, Mordraed!" he gasped. "Hurry, I cannot hold him much longer."

Mordraed struck out swimming and managed to get hold of Agravaen again. Between him and Gal'havad they hauled his limp form to the shore and then into the relative safety of the trees. Once hidden in the tangle of foliage they halted, staring back at the progress of the other men. Most were nearly across the river, showering mud and water as they slogged through the shallows. Only Ardhu and Bal-ahn hung back, standing on the far bank amid the swaying reeds. Bal-ahn with his shoulder streaming dark blood and a face as deathly as that of Hwynn, god of the Mortuary.

"With this wound bleeding freely, the hounds will sniff me out for sure." Brought on the wind, Bal-ahn's words were carried across the holy river of the Great White Cow. "And I am too weakened to swim such a current. I will stay and hold them off as best I can. It may give you more time, Lord."

"Bal-ahn...you cannot." Ardhu's voice was weary, heavy. "You know what that will mean. You know there can only be one ending if you remain here."

Bal-ahn drew his dagger, an imported blade from Ar-morah, long and deadly. "I do."

"I cannot ask you to do this."

"You have not asked me, Lord. I choose to do it."

Standing ankle-deep in the mud on the opposite bank, Ba-lin listened to his brother's words and his cheeks drained of colour. Splashing back across the river, he reached Bal-ahn's side and grabbed his uninjured arm. "We were born of one womb; it is said we share one soul between us," he said fiercely, though his voice trembled. "If you make a stand here, my brother...you will not stand alone!" He drew his own dagger and stood at Bal-ahn's side, ready to share his twin's death as he had shared his birth.

"Go, Stone Lord." Bal-ahn glanced desperately at Ardhu. "I can hear the enemy drawing close; they have not given up the chase!"

Ardhu embraced each of the brothers quickly. He was as white as they, his eyes dark hollows, his hands trembling with emotion. "Farewell, my greatest friends of these many years. May we meet one day in the banquet halls of the Ancestors on the Plain of Honey!" Whirling on his heel, he dived headlong into the river and swam with the agility of a salmon to the far shore. He had just reached the bank and scrambled into the shadows of the trees when the first of the great hounds padded into view, a great creature near as tall as a pony, with a dun coat and swinging tail like a club. Its lips peeled over its fangs as it saw the twins waiting with drawn daggers on the riverside.

And then, with a blood-curdling howl, it bounded towards them.

In the little wood, Ardhu gathered his band together. Nine...that was all that were left. Nine, including an injured Agravaen. All had come to ruin. Why had the Ancestors turned against him in such a manner?

"We must keep going," he barked gruffly. "Ba-lin and Bal-ahn will hold them as long as they can but they are far outnumbered, and our foes know this area while we do not."

"Which way?" gasped Hwalchmai, slapping his sodden hair out of his eyes.

"Down the river. Keep following the water but do not go too close to the edge lest you are spotted by enemies on the other shore."

Mordraed fumbled in the calfskin pouch hanging at his belt. He felt the vial of poison there; undamaged, its stopper still sealing its contents, praise the spirits. "My bowstring is wet; I cannot shoot at our foes. But I also have a slingshot. I will take any down with that, if I can."

They began to run again, Mordraed and Gal'havad pulling Agravaen's supine form along the ground, one arm each; he was proving too weighty to carry between them. Woodcraft was forgotten as they crashed through vines and growing shrubs, desperate to put as much space between them and their pursuers as possible. In the distance they could hear the great dogs barking and howling in canine fury; then men were screaming, shouting, their voices eerie and hideous and distorted on the rising wind.

They forced their way through the greenery for what seemed an eternity. Eventually Ardhu held up a hand for a halt. "I hear nothing now. We will find a place where we may rest and tend the wounded. Leave the river and head for that rising ground…" he pointed through the tangle of trees to a grey outcrop of stone furred with mountain-ash and ferns. "There's an open spot above the treeline where we can watch for the approach of any enemy."

The companions veered away from the River Boann and began to climb the escarpment. A few hundred yards below the top, in a bald space denuded of greenery, stood the retaining circle of a ruined roundhouse. The band climbed into the safety of its sheltering walls and then collapsed, some leaning against the tumbled stones, panting, others falling full out on the ground, their strength almost completely sapped.

Mordraed and Gal'havad placed Agravaen on Mordraed's skin cloak and Mordraed tried to give him some water. He could not swallow. "Let me try," said Gal'havad and he took his little violet-coloured cup from the safety of his tunic, filled it with a bit of weak ale from his flask, and pressed it to Agravaen's dry and peeling lips.

Mordraed scowled, sitting back on his haunches. Gal'havad was like a child, playing with his silly talisman, a stone scraped out of the bottom of a pool. And yet…he saw Agravaen's eyelids flicker. The big lad glanced around dazedly. "I…I have done well this day, haven't I?" he asked. His voice was strange, lost; his eyes glazed and unfocussed.

"You killed your enemy, so yes," replied Mordraed.

"I have done well for the Stone Lord, then?" Agravaen asked, letting his head fall back on the earth with a thud. His mouth trembled slightly; a purplish stain deepened his lips.

"Aye." Mordraed's voice was sharp. "What a good warrior should do for his chieftain."

Agravaen's hand shot out, catching Mordraed's wrist and drawing him down until their heads were close together. His fingers were icy. "I know…what is in your heart…brother…" he whispered, and suddenly there was bloody foam leaking from his mouth. "Don't do it. Our mother is not right. Turn from your path, Mordraed, or you will die…"

Mordraed listened in horror. What if Gal'havad or any of the others heard? Leaning down, he pressed his hand over Agravaen's mouth, trying not to recoil at the feel of his hot spittle against his palm. "Be silent…the poison makes you rave. Be still, we will do what we can for you, perhaps the dart did not go too deep."

Agravaen stared up at his older brother, unable to speak due to the pressure of his hand. His eyes suddenly darkened with a look akin to hatred, and then he made a gasping, wheezing noise and began to jerk and spasm.

Gal'havad heard the sound of his heels drumming the loose stones. "Mordraed, what is happening?"

"Get back!" Mordraed swung out at him with his arm, gesturing him away. "This is not for you to see, Prince of Kham-El-Ard!" Bitterness and rage dripped from his words and Gal'havad stood as one stunned, too fearful to move.

Agravaen lay still. His eyes were wide open, sightless, and a trickle of yellow foam ran from his mouth. Mordraed wiped his hand on the grass, face contorted. "He is gone to the Ancestors…Leave me, Gal'havad. I will make a burial pyre for him."

Having heard the commotion, Ardhu strode over and looked at the inert body. "I feel grief that Agravaen has gone to the long-house of his fathers," he said formally, "but there can be no pyre. The smoke would be a clear sign to our foes."

Mordraed's eyes crackled. "So you think it acceptable that a man of your own royal house, your sister's son, lays unbarrowed as food for wild dogs and wolves…"

"I do not," said Ardhu wearily. "But we are in danger and the needs of the living must outweigh those of the dead. Remember, Mordraed, in the days of our forebears, the bodies of the dead were laid open to the sky for many Moons before they were burned or placed within their mounds."

"I will build him a small cairn at least," snarled Mordraed. "High on the hill above, where the Sun will touch. No thanks to you, Stone Lord, and no honour to your kin."

Ardhu turned his back to his bastard son. No use in argument that would solve nothing, especially with Mordraed who seemed to crave confrontation at every turn. He was sorry to see Agravaen dead, he had been loyal despite his upbringing in Morigau's household, but he could not make exception for him.

Mordraed angrily grabbed Agravaen's body beneath the arms and started to drag him out of the hut circle and further up the slope, while the other members of the warband stared, motionless. They knew him little, as he was one of the younger members, and had rarely mingled outside of his group of fractious youths who had few prospects.

Gal'havad, who had watched the exchange between his father and friend, suddenly leapt forward as if released from a spell. "I will help him!" he cried, and raced after Mordraed.

He soon caught up with the dark-haired youth and in silence grasped hold of Agravaen's legs. Mordraed stared at him, surprised, then nodded curtly in acceptance of his help. Between them they wrestled the young warrior's body to the crest of the hill, where they found the shattered cairn of an earlier people, its inner stones, covered with Suns and spirals, now open to the frowning sky. They placed him in the unroofed entrance passage and tucked his knees up to his chest, laying his head to the North so that his unseeing eyes faced East toward Bhel's glory. Mordraed began to hunt out rocks from the fallen dome of the mound and placed them over him, one by one, heaping them up into a pointed cairn. Unspeaking, Gal'havad worked steadily beside him, until, by the time the sky had darkened to purple and the light of a big Moon turned the hilltop to white-silver, the body of the dead youth was completely covered, safe from the predators that roamed the wild places beyond the firelight.

Upon finishing, Mordraed fell back against the retaining circle, breathing heavily, rubbing his blood and earth-stained hands over his hot, sweating face. He felt wearier than he had ever felt; he who was graced by the spirits with good health and strong limbs…and his mind was in turmoil. Agravaen dead…his ally, even if only to use as a shield against the hostility of others. And if that was not bad enough…there, across the river when they were attacked, he had lost yet another chance to claim his birthright. He could have finished it off then, quickly and easily. Two arrows gone astray in the heat of battle…Ardhu Pendraec and his son Gal'havad dead in one tragic accident. None would have dared blamed him, and he would have made the suitable show of grief.

He moved his knuckles across sore, burning eyes. What was wrong with him? Why had his arm turned soft? No…no, nothing was wrong! It had just not been the right time to make such a decisive move, that was all…if he had killed them, the remaining warriors of Prydn might have lost heart and been overwhelmed by their enemies, and he would have swiftly met the same fate he had dealt out.

"Mordraed, are you all right?" he heard Gal'havad's voice through what seemed a heavy mist. He managed to force his eyes open and glare blearily at his half-brother, who knelt on the lichenous stones, hand on his shoulder.

Mordraed shrugged him off. "Why?" His voice was dry, cracked. "Why did you come up here to bury Agravaen with me?"

"It was right. Agravaen deserves to lie in honour. My father was wrong not to help you himself." Gal'havad hung his head. "I would aid you in whatever you asked, Mordraed. You are my brother."

A cold chill swept through Mordraed, piercing him to the heart. It was as if a barrow ghost had prodded him with an icy skeletal finger. The heavy mist of exhaustion fell from him, and his dark eyes narrowed. "Brother…what do you mean?" Could the boy know? Had he known all along?

Gal'havad's face was open and guileless. "I know we are really but cousins, yet I have no brother of my blood and I have always looked to you as I might a brother."

"You are a fool, then…" Mordraed scrambled up.

Gal'havad stared at him. "You are not yourself…but I understand."

Mordraed stormed down the hill, slipping on the shale, eyes burning, tearing with an emotion he could not fathom. *Oh my little brother…it is you who does not understand. I AM myself. Completely myself. And that shall be your undoing…*

Ardhu led his remaining men down the river in the dark. Fish flopped in the swell, the wind sobbed in reeds and withies. Animal eyes, luminous as floating moons, shone out of bushes, then vanished into the tangle of foliage on the banks.

"I can smell a tang in the air," hissed Hwalchmai. "Can you smell it too, Ardhu? Wood smoke."

Ardhu lifted his head, scenting the air like an animal. "Yes, I smell it too. But not just wood smoke. Flesh cooking. Let us hope…" his smile was grim, a shadow deepening his eye sockets till his visage looked a skull, "it is animal flesh. Although men say the folk who dwell at Spiralfort are wise and peaceful. If what I have deduced by the stars is correct, we should be drawing near the bend of the River of the White Cow, and will soon see the great sanctuary of God's Peak."

"Let us pray to the Ancestors that you are right about the peacefulness of the folk who dwell there," murmured Hwalchmai.

"They wrought the Cup of Gold for the Maimed King," said Ardhu.

"Aye…but they took it away again," said Hwalchmai darkly. "A capricious folk, whose motives we do not know."

Ardhu glanced over his shoulder at his dwindled warband. Their faces glowed pale in the starshine. Mordraed and Gal'havad were at the rear of the party, walking side by side… Mordraed's visage was dark, shuttered, his lips drawn into thin lines, his hair whipping his cheeks like the wings of the flesh-hungry raven. Ardhu felt a sudden, irrational surge of fear; the like of which he had never felt before, even in his first battle by the Glein, when he was scarcely more than a boy. He gripped the hilt of Caladvolc, tempted to draw it, although he knew he would appear mad to his men.

Trying to get hold of his emotions, he turned in his saddle and gestured to the two youths. "Come to me, both of you. Gal'havad, you must stand with me as Prince of the West. Mordraed, I take it you have restrung your bow? We may have need of it."

"It is done," said Mordraed flatly. "My weapons are always close to hand, Lord Ardhu."

I would wager that they are indeed, my serpent son born in shame and shadow! But oh gods, I must trust you now because I have no choice and almost no men left…

The course of the River Boann turned abruptly, and in an instant, the trees vanished, leaving a wide open vista. The companions stopped and stared, for before them, on the northern side of the Holy River of the White Cow, was a marvellous complex, with features both familiar and alien to them.

On the top of a slight slope stood a huge mound, not as large or as conical as the Hill of Zhel, but wide and drum-shaped, a sun-disc with a mighty white quartz revetment and decorated kerbstones that gleamed blue in the moonlight. A circle of about thirty massive stone blocks surrounded it, shutting out the profane world and holding the powers-that-be in. Two timber structures stood close at its side—a smaller, linear one in the West, facing the Land of the Ancestors, and an enormous circular one in the Southeast, filled with many rows of pits and posts and fronted by a pair of gigantic stones similar in function and appearance to the Three Watchers of Khor Ghor. Torches and fires flickered by stones and wooden posts, making shadows dance, and the smell of roasting flesh permeated the night air. By the entrance passage of the great mound a pair of stone lanterns could be seen burning—the famed eternal night-lamps of Uffern, the Very Deep.

"So this is it!" Bohrs stood staring, arms folded over his barrel chest. "The place they call Spiralfort, the God's Peak."

"And also Kar Pebir, the Flaming Door, and Fortress in the Middle-of-the-Earth," said Hwalchmai. "or so the song-singers tell, when they fare across Severna's sea."

Gal'havad looked across the rippling waters of the river at the mound and its satellite structures. A strange sensation gripped him; fear and yet elation, a sense that here destinies converged...it was just as he had felt when he first set eyes upon his cousin Mordraed walking through the snow across the barrow-grounds of the kings.

"Father..." he swivelled round in his saddle to face Ardhu. "Let us cross the river and come to this place. I can sense the Cup we seek is here, waiting for us to claim it."

"We will not be hasty," said Ardhu. "We must be cautious, though I have heard the folk of the God's Peak are hospitable, enemies of those who attacked us on this bitter day. The headman is said to be a wise man called Maheloas."

The companions walked a little further, crossing the Boann at a place where there was a natural ford with signs of passage. White cattle sacred to the spirit of the river moved through the waters with them, passing back and forth under the vast haze of the Milky Way, the cloak of Nud and skyward path of the Dead.

An unbroken line of men and women confronted them, trudging across the grass towards the great mound on the height. Torches flared and they gazed at rows of faces, young and old, some masked, others bare. The strangers were impassive, neither friendly nor fierce, and it seemed their eyes, glimmering in the red torchlight, scryed the truth of their souls.

Ardhu stepped forward, hands held apart, far from the hilt of Caladvolc. "We come in peace. Is there one here who goes by the name of Maheloas?"

An old man left the throng and walked in stately manner towards Ardhu. He reminded him of the Merlin, a lean wiry figure with sweeping grey-black hair and a long beard plaited with beads wrapped in golden foil. Beneath bushy brows that rose like wings, his eyes were a pale, striking blue, the colour of thick winter's ice upon the tarn. He wore a shaman's robe with a great wheel painted upon it in ochre; the wheel was crisscrossed with lines that showed the movements of the Moon. "I am Maheloas," he said. "High Priest of the Houses of the Holy—of the Cave of the Sun, and of Cnobga the Hill of the Hag Bui, and Dubad the Hill of Darkness where the Winter Sun is swallowed. And you I know, though we have never met. You are Ardhu Pendraec, King of Prydn, and husband to Fynavir, daughter of Mevva the Intoxicator."

Ardhu's eyes widened in surprised. "How do you know who I am?"

Maheloas smiled, his face creasing into a thousand lines. "Wanderers come bringing tales of strife and sadness in Prydn. They say the King, the greatest lord since the days of Samothos the Tin-Lord, seeks to find the Cup of Plenty that will bring new life to a barren old world."

"That is what I would do." Ardhu inclined his head.

Maheloas scanned Ardhu's face with his ice-cool eyes. "And yet...I do not feel belief coming from you, Lord of Prydn. You do not believe any Cup of enchantment can save your land."

Ardhu glanced up again, suddenly fierce, his gaze green-dark fire. "What I believe or do not believe is of importance to no one but me. I do what I must and have the blessings of Deroweth and Suilven for this quest."

"You will be welcome here." Maheloas smiled benevolently and held out his hand. "But if you do not believe, the Cup will never go with you. And if you try to take it by force, not one of your men will leave this place alive. I do not threaten this in anger, King of Prydn, I tell you only what must be. We took the Cup back from the Maimed King long ago, when he fell into folly and ruin; it is precious to our people because the gold from which it is beaten was bathed in the blood of our Good God Dag who, with his consort Ahn-u makes all the land fruitful."

Ardhu bowed, and then ran his hand across his tired eyes. "I speak from weariness…half my men are dead, including kin and friends of many years, and we have been running from foes for hours. I beg you, Maheloas, to let us rest awhile and then we may talk of the Cup."

Maheloas nodded. "I will agree to that, Stone Lord of Prydn. Follow me."

The priest led the band to the Eastern enclosure beside the great Mound of Spiralfort. An outer ring of mighty totem poles surrounded an inner ring of cremation pits lined with clay, where animal carcasses burned, tended by veiled women in strange broad hats of woven river rushes. The ground was thick with ash; the air greasy and rank with smoke. Beyond the crematory hearths were three inner rows of pits in which the charred remains were strewn—burnt, blackened ribs and cow's heads with horns, parts of goats and sheep and deer, even a wild horse. A large clay mound, pale and tumescent, stood at the end of the vast enclosure, reminding the warriors of Prydn of their own sacred space at Marthodunu, lying in its valley midway between Suilven and Khor Ghor.

"This is Wheel-of-Offering," said Maheloas. "Where we give to the spirits the bounty of our land both night and day."

"You do not feast here yourselves?"

"At the times of darkness and light—yes. Now and for the next few months only the spirits will sup. We have enough for ourselves in our settlement on the hither side of blessed Boann. That we have so much to spare should show you, who has ceased to believe, how we are blessed by the Ancestors and Great Ones."

"But have you not noticed the change in the weather, the gods turning their faces away? Surely it has come to you too."

Maheloas did not meet Ardhu's probing gaze, but continued to walk amidst the smouldering and bone-filled pits. "If the rains come, we pray harder and make more and greater sacrifices… The Old ones will listen."

More sacrifices…Ardhu's stomach lurched; he had had enough of sacrifice. The loss of Ba-lin and Bal-ahn burnt his memory like the fires around him, while the smell of hundreds of lumps of burning meat made hot acid leap into his throat.

Maheloas took the men of Ardhu from the great Eastern circle to a more intimate structure in the West, where twin rows of massive parallel posts stood like sentinels, the early morning mist swirling around their bases. One of the standing stones of the circle surrounding the passage tomb was trapped within this artificial forest, a lumpen grey ghost glimmering in the torch light. A low roof made of plaited river-reeds lay over the top of the posts, casting deep shadows that hid whatever lay in the sacred space at the back of the structure.

Out from the entranceway of this mysterious cult-house stepped a girl who greeted Maheloas in a soft, musical voice. Next to Mordraed, Gal'havad made a small noise in his throat. Mordraed was about to cast him a scathing glance…but then he saw the torchlight illuminate the maiden who walked gracefully towards them.

She was slight and her hair was as black as his, curling to her waist, twined with blue beads and roundels of carved bone. Crescent earrings imported from the realm of Ibher hung from her lobes, and an intricate gorget ribbed with golden beads clasped her neck. In contrast to the darkness of her hair, her skin was white as if she seldom walked under sun, flawless and unmarked—this proclaimed her status, that she need not work tending the crops or herding the cattle. In the small, perfect oval of her face, her eyes were a clear, deep blue, the colour of Mordraed's own eyes, but lacking their coldness—instead they were filled with a calm clarity. In one hand she held a bowl bound with bronze, in the other a sceptre similar to Ardhu's Lightning Mace, its shaft cut with deep spiralling grooves and its polished stone head pinned on by golden studs.

"I am Ivormyth daughter of Maheloas," she said simply. "I am the Maiden of the Holy Cup, its servant and its Guardian. Be welcome here, to the House of the West."

She gestured with her hand and the companions entered the cult-house, bowing to the great standing stone confined within its walls. Inside were two other young women, near as beautiful as Ivormyth, who brought out bowls of ancient design, wreathed in spirals and brimming with pork, and tall fine beakers impressed with wheat and nail-marks like little crescent Moons.

"This is the House of Vedu," said Ivormyth, placing the symbols of her rank on a dresser of stout withies at the back of the hut. "House of Intoxication." She handed Ardhu the largest of the beakers, a huge drinking vessel as red as fire. Honey-mead swirled in it, with tiny flowers added for sweet flavour dancing on the swell.

Ardhu clasped the beaker and raised it above his head as expected, then drank it to the dregs in one. Ivormyth took the empty pot from him and smashed it against the single standing stone, the pieces spinning out across the room. "The spirits welcome you," she said. "Sit and rest and my sisters will tend your wounds."

The warband sat down on the floor, humble and quiet in the presence of these sacred maidens. Ivormyth and her two companions went amongst them, bringing food and drink and bowls of clean water and moss to tend their scrapes and gouges.

Mordraed was unable to keep his eyes from Ivormyth as she bent and knelt beside the warriors, graceful as a willow wand. Khyloq and the child in her belly were forgotten; they fled from his mind like mist. House of Intoxication indeed! He had not expected this; suddenly he felt a little less angry and confused. If he could take this girl back to Prydn it would please him; there was no law that said a man could not have many wives, it all depended on wealth…and stamina. He grinned. Once Ardhu was out of the way and Mordraed claimed his rightful place, he was sure he would soon be richer than Samothos and Bolgos in their golden barrows!

And then Ivormyth was there, standing demurely in front of Mordraed, offering him a beaker. He leaned forward, taking the drinking cup slowly, letting his long, slim fingers slide against hers. He smiled, tossing back his hair, confident that she would look upon him with favour; he had long known how the women of the tribes desired him. Why should she be any different? They were alike; both beautiful, both high status; it would be an excellent match.

To his surprise, she did not return his smile. Her lips were pale straight lines and her eyes cool. Without a word or gesture, she turned away and faced Gal'havad, who sat beside him. "You are the son of Ardhu Pendraec?" she said. Her voice was lilting music; it infuriated Mordraed to hear it wasted on his younger brother.

"I am. I am called Gal'havad, the Hawk of Summer, Prince of Evening. My mother, Queen Fynavir, is from your fair country." Gal'havad got to his feet and made a small, courteous bow. "The Ancestors bless the day of our meeting, Lady Ivormyth of Spiralfort."

Mordraed's eyes widened in fury. The little bastard was trying his wiles with the girl! Gal'havad, the pure one, the different one who was more apt to speak with ghosts on the Plains than women!

New hatred coiled in Mordraed's heart; how did Gal'havad dare, when Mordraed had made it obvious where his interests lay! He let his thumb touch the hilt of his dagger. He should have finished it before; well, the time was coming. None would gainsay Mordraed son of Morigau and the Pendraec.

Ivormyth gave a hand-signal to the other maidens and together they left the cult-house. Dawn was coming; light seeped through cracks in the roof and the torches were guttering, but the companions were all weary, and lying down they slept like dogs round the hearth, sated with meat and drink.

Gal'havad and Mordraed alone remained awake. Mordraed would not look at his brother, but stared moodily into space. Gal'havad seemed not to notice. "Cousin, I am filled with a great joy," he said impetuously. "This is a great and holy place; I can feel the spirits of the Old Ones all around me. And the Lady Ivormyth…it is as if she holds my destiny in her hands, I can feel it."

"I would imagine that is not all you would like to feel," said Mordraed with heavy sarcasm.

Gal'havad frowned, his brows drawing together. "Mordraed, what do you mean?" And then, as the words registered, "Mordraed, that is an unjust thing to say. I would not dishonour a lady of such high rank and beauty. Or any other, for that matter."

"Oh noble Gal'havad," mocked Mordraed. "Spare me your words of honour and let me sleep."

He flung himself on the ground, back to Gal'havad. The red-haired youth stared at him for a while, noting the tenseness of his back and shoulders. His eyes were closed but Gal'havad knew he did not sleep. For the first time a little cold finger of doubt touched Gal'havad. Mordraed had always been quick to anger and sharp-tongued…but in the last few days there had been strangeness in him. Reaching into his tunic, he pulled out the violet cup from the sacred pool at Kham-El-Ard, given him by his aunt Mhor-gan. He held it to his face, feeling the stone, washed smooth by five thousand years of gentle waves, against his cheek, reminding him of home, of the forests and the Plain, of the Stones of Khor Ghor in the morning mist, and the great hump of the Spirit-Path streaking toward the rising Sun.

He wished he was home now, and that this quest was over.

But that was not to be. He was in the Land of the Setting Sun, at the Temple of Spiralfort, for good or for ill. Stretching out on the ground, he fell into an exhausted sleep alongside the rest of the companions, the little violet cup clasped like an offering between his fingers.

Gal'havad woke later in the day. He could hear people moving around him, and the sounds of dogs, animals and people outside the cult-house. He sat up, scrambling to his feet, and suddenly he realised something was wrong. Something terrible.

His talisman was gone.

Cursing, he searched through the rushes on the floor, searched through the calfskin bag at his waist and in the folds of his clothes.

It was gone. The violet cup of twilight, his talisman of protection, his gift from Mhor-gan.

Angry and desperate, he whirled around to see who else was in the hut. His father was standing by the doorway, with Bohrs, and Hwalchmai…all trustworthy, kin or as close as kin. The other men too, he trusted; they had not even been lying near him. Mordraed had slept at his back, of course; he was still nearby, sitting cross-legged in the rushes, honing his dagger blade and seemingly unaware of Gal'havad's distress.

"Mordraed!" he called out. "Have you seen my cup?"

Mordraed craned his head around, continuing to work his blade with the flint sharpening-stone. "No. Should I have?"

"It is missing. I had it in my hands last night!"

"And you went to sleep with it on show?" Mordraed rolled his eyes. "Not wise, little cousin. No doubt one of these foreign savages has made away with it. Do not worry yourself…it was just a trinket. I am sure Mhor-gan will dig up another one for you when we return home."

Gal'havad's shoulders slumped. Maybe Mordraed was right; he attached too much importance to his aunt's gift. No matter the truth, he could do no more to find the talisman; he could not accuse Maheloas and his people of theft for fear of causing an affront that might lead to all their deaths…

Sighing, he gathered his cloak up and walked toward Ardhu, trying not to think of his missing gift. Mordraed rose and followed him, hiding a slight smile behind the fall of his hair. The little fool wasn't looking so sure of himself today…

Ardhu peered out of the cult-house into the bright sky. "Maheloas is coming for us. I believe we are to have a testing of sorts."

"I would test my axe on some heads," murmured Bohrs.

"Again…" Ardhu cast him a warning look, "no fighting unless we have no choice."

A shadow fell over the threshold, stretching inward over the great stone that was the heart of the house. Maheloas was there, a fox skull bound in the upper section of his hair and its bright pelt falling across his shoulders. Skulls of cranes and swans dangled from his cloak, making an ominous clack and clatter. In his hand he carried a great, antiquated crook made of stone, its front wreathed in jagged patterns. "Come, my guests." He gestured with his thin, knotted hand. "You will eat with us and we will speak of the quest you have come upon and what you desire."

He led Ardhu and his warriors across the green vista outside the great Ancestor tomb. Even in broad daylight it was a magical place, all its features now clearly revealed. The grassland swept away toward the river, dropping in stepped terraces toward the foaming, frothing cauldron that was the heart of Boann, River of the White Cow. Birch trees tossed their branches on the far riverbank, silver dancers amidst solemn alder and magic hazel, so beloved of shamans for their wands. Deer flitted amidst the trees, passing like shadows as they migrated towards the distant peak of Redmountain, the source of many streams and tributaries that merged their strength with the holy river.

The group passed East toward the rising Sun, back toward the crematorial pit circle with its still-burning offerings. The vast entrance of the passage tomb came into view, clear now in the light of day, a place of power, of the spirits, of life and death. White quartz fronted the mound here, a wall that had buckled and slumped, fallen after uncounted nights of rain and wind and erosion. A huge stone blocked the way to the passage, an enormous prone block carved with art—huge swirling spirals locked together, looking to some like the orbs of the Watcher who protected the souls of Men, to others like a great bull ready to charge, to yet others a vast sea with waves curlingoverlooked by the bright stars that were the Ancestors.

Behind the portal-stone, above the dark womb-passage, was a stone box; the place where the beams of the Midwinter Sun would pierce the mound, lighting the holy of holies, drawing the spirits from the cremated ashes that lay in huge carved bowls in niches inside. Ardhu recognized the significance, even as he observed the box, for its purpose was similar to that of the Great Trilithon, which on the same day also framed the Sun, drawing its rays into the circle and bringing life to the spirits.

Leaving the entrance of Spiralfort behind, the company circled the mound alongside its vast decorated kerbstones, partly hidden by the collapse of the heavy cairn material, which was already over a thousand years old. In the East loomed the pit-circle with its many rings of posts, and by its entrance, guarded by the two flanking stones like grey needles, a small domed hut that they had not noticed last night amidst the flickering fires and the smoke of the cremated offerings.

Maheloas guided them to the hut door. Inside, the beehive hut was dark and dank, the clay walls oozing moisture. Incense cups burned, the fragrance of herbs mixed with the pervasive aroma of charred meat. Ivormyth knelt on the floor, her two attendants beside her. Her bowl stood before her knees, while the sceptre lay near her right hand. She had assumed a new robe, thin as mist, her flesh, painted with ochre, gleaming tantalisingly through the folds.

Maheloas gestured for Ardhu and his band to be seated and they settled themselves on the floor. Ivormyth's women rose and, as before, brought mead, bread, and meat, which were consumed in silence. When the remnants of the meal were cleared away, Maheloas rose to his feet and gazed first at Ardhu then at each of his men in turn.

"You have come many miles from Prydn to Ibherna to see the Golden Cup of Plenty, Blessed by the Good God, old master of all," he said. "The Maimed King held it once but it passed from him when he became unclean and doomed. You wish to take it again, to bring hope and maybe more, for it is said all things of goodness flow from its depths. But not all may touch the Cup, and already once have hands not worthy enough held it, diminishing its power. Ardhu Pendraec, Stone Lord, you have already admitted the belief is not in you—you will not touch or bear the Cup of Gold. But of those who travel with you, your loyal companions, I cannot say."

The old man gestured to the warband. "Look upon what you see here before you…the Cauldron that is always Full, the Sceptre that a king bears, the Maiden that is the Land. Choose between them, warriors, and choose wisely. One may be He Who Sees Beyond to the true Nature of the Cup."

Bohrs pushed forward, ever eager, and grasped the bowl in his thick hands, lifting it above his head. "A full bowl of food and the full bellies of the people is always a good thing! Without food, where would we be? Dead!"

The companions laughed, though Ardhu with unease. What if this game was played to deceive and the prize would be snatched away, with no real chance of winning it?

Hwalchmai stepped forth next, reverently lifting the sceptre with its flashing pins of gold. "A peaceful land with a strong lord to rule over it is good land. When chiefs fall to warring, the land and its bounty is diminished."

Hwalchmai placed the sceptre back into its place and was about to sit back down at Ardhu's side, when Mordraed shoved him aside, almost making him drop the holy relic in his hands. Mordraed's eyes were hot as brands as he stared at Ivormyth, who sat head bowed, her hair pooling around her like black water. "It's the girl, isn't it?" he cried. "The other objects merely fool the greedy and the power-starved…the food bowl for Bohrs who dreams of naught but haunches of roast pig and beakers of beer, and the sceptre for Hwalchmai, a landless kinsman eternally basking in the glory of his betters! The girl is the key…She is Sovereignty, the Cup is her, and I will claim her here and now!"

Reaching down, he grasped Ivormyth's slender wrist and yanked her to her feet, his expression one of triumph.

Ivormyth glanced up, eyes flashing, and slapped him with full force across the face.

"Bitch!" He dropped her arm and drew his dagger as Maheloas leapt up to pull Ivormyth away. Ardhu and Hwalchmai swung into action, grabbing Mordraed's arms and pinioning them behind his back, while Bohrs ripped the knife from his hand and flung it upon the ground.

"You dishonour me!" Mordraed screamed, incandescent with rage. "It was the true answer, the meaning of the Cup…but you have no intent of giving us the treasure, do you, Maheloas? Your savages probably want to cut out our hearts and give them to your god, Bloody Crescent!"

"Enough!" Ardhu's fist shot out, striking Mordraed in the mouth and drawing blood. The blow was strong enough to drive Mordraed to his knees, head reeling. "You will not insult our hosts. If you do not hold your tongue, I will give you to the spirits myself!"

Maheloas walked across the hut and stared down at Mordraed. "You were wrong, boy. Wrong. As were the others. The Cup is bound with all you have seen, and yet none. Its true meaning remains locked from you, and none here is noble or pure enough to witness its brightness, the Sun bound in a Cup of Gold. I would ask you now to leave the Mansion of the Good God and his Son. Follow the river back to the shore, take ship and do not look back. We will not harm you if you agree to this, but if you do not go in peace, I cannot guarantee your safety."

"Wait!" It was Gal'havad who spoke now. Clambering to his feet, he faced the shaman. The light shining through the door at his back turned his hair into a halo of fiercest flame. His face was translucent pale, the face of one of the Everliving Ones who guarded the islands of the West. "I have not spoken yet. I beg you listen to me. I know the secret of the Cup of Gold."

Maheloas's brows rose; his shrew gaze scanned the young, ardent face before him, lit by an inner light that was almost not of the world. "Speak."

"The mystery of the Cup is not in plenty, power or sovereignty. The secret is in here." He laid his hand on his chest. "Its power is what is means to the man who holds it, who believes in its worth. It is nothing and everything."

Maheloas's lips drew to narrow lines. "Who are you, boy, who speaks words of a priest but wears a warrior's garb?"

"I am Gal'havad, Hawk of Summer, prince of the Twilight."

A sigh slipped from Maheloas's lips. Unexpectedly, he sank down on one knee and clasped Gal'havad's hand in his own. "You are the one. Dark and light, youth and death, warrior and mystic. You have won the right to the Cup of Gold for your people."

Ardhu and his men stared, overjoyed at this sudden change in fortune, victory snatched from the jaws of defeat. Mordraed half-scrambled to his feet, snarling, and was slapped down to the ground again by Ardhu, who planted his heel upon his son's wrist, pinning him to the spot.

Ivormyth, with great dignity, collected the bowl and the sceptre. Gravely she bowed to Gal'havad and placed them into his hands. "These will you have, lord of the Golden Cup: the Bowl of Plenty, the Sceptre of Power…and I will also be yours if that is your wish."

"I wish it, lady," he replied, blushing.

Maheloas came between them and took their hands and clasped them together. "An alliance between our people. This is good. On the night of the third day the Moon is reborn and then will the Lord Gal'havad claim the Cup and all the other treasures he has won."

The warriors of Ardhu Pendraec rejoiced, and so did the people of God's Peak, the Spiralfort of the Good Dag and his Son. People danced around the stone circle throughout the day and night, and beakers were filled, and drunk and smashed. Offerings were given in the pit circle and to the maiden of the Holy Chalice and her chosen one, Gal'havad, winner of the Cup of Gold. The folk of Ibherna came from all around, climbing up the terraced hillside from the river to gift them with fruit and wheat sheaves and to give Ivormyth ancestral gifts to take to her new home in Prydn, the Isle of the Mighty—barrel-shaped beads and schist plaques of jadeite, a miniature axehead pendant and two polished balls for fertility.

Ardhu relaxed for the first time in many days. He drank from the same beaker as Maheloas, as they would soon be kin with the joining of his son and Maheloas's daughter. He vaguely wondered how Fynavir would react when Gal'havad returned from his travels with a bride as well as the holy vessel; shocked no doubt, but perhaps since Ivormyth was of her own folk she would come to be glad.

As Ardhu drank to the health of the couple and the renewing of Prydn, Mordraed sulked, sitting in the blue shadows of the mighty God's Peak, his back against a slab of intricately carved stone. He had been made a fool by the riddles and games of Maheloas and his haughty daughter, and by his own father, who should have stood up for him and not treated him like some miscreant. As for Gal'havad…envy gnawed at Mordraed. He could scarcely believe it. A mere few months ago, his half-brother had been just a boy, not even accepted as a Man of the Tribe, and now he was some kind of hero and about to wed the woman Mordraed desired for himself…

Cold snakes of fear writhed in his belly and suddenly he felt deathly ill. Gal'havad was becoming too powerful, too popular, despite his physical frailties, his shaking illness. It was time to act, time to make an end as he had sworn to do. He had been weak, and too merciful, sparing his half-brother too many times. It was time to do the will of Morigau, and to take the destiny he was owed.

He rose, heart hammering, gazing toward the cult-house where Gal'havad was ensconced with the girl, receiving gifts from the tribesmen of Ibherna. This deed had to be done; it was what he had been trained for, what he was sworn to do. So why did he feel so sick and shaken and sad…somehow so appalled and yet so intent on Gal'havad's death?

"Am I falling ill?" He brushed his arm across his forehead. He did feel slightly hot. A fine sheen of sweat glistened on his brow. He did not understand this; he was never sick. But it would make no difference.

The deed had to be done.

When the Moon was reborn, Gal'havad would claim the Cup of Gold as Maheloas had decreed.

When the Moon was reborn, Mordraed would be waiting.

For he was the Dark Moon, eclipsing the light, son of a broken taboo. Fingers trembling, he touched the scar on his face where Morigau had marred him, marking him as the chosen one of her malevolent lunar spirits.

In the time of the Dark Moon, death walked.

Ivormyth moved like mist across the trampled earth before the portal stone of God's Peak. Twilight had fallen and a purple haze hung over the land, giving it a surreal glamour, where trees and rocks and river seemed strange and distorted, half in the world of reality and half fading into an Otherness. Reverently she knelt in a dip in the ground before the tomb's entrance and left an offering, a rounded ball of quartz, amidst a pile of older gifts peeping through the soil—pebbles from distant seashores, a stone phallus, tools that had been used to prepare the dead before they were cremated and their ashes placed inside the passage-grave. Then, rising, she stoked the eternal flames–the Fires of Uffern—that burned in stone lanterns on either side of the portal of God's Peak. Imported oil spat and flames curled into the dusk, spitting and sizzling. The vast carved stone of the many spirals lit up, its tangle of lines seeming to curl and coil as shadows raced over its surface. The white quartz revetment behind gleamed with a spectral bone-light as the Moon, reborn, rose in the East and soared toward that ancient place of Ancestors.

Ivormyth bowed to the entrance-stone and then sprang lightly up and over it, vanishing into the blackness of the great cairn.

As she vanished from sight, Mordraed slid out from behind one of the boulders of the surrounding stone circle. He was not quite sure what he intended to do—only that something this night would change…change forever.

Carefully, quietly, he slithered on his belly over the spiral stone, and crawled on hands and knees into the passage, keeping low in the darkness to avoid detection. Gravel and bits of charred matter ground into his palms but he made no outcry. Glancing up, he could see spurs of stone jutting into the long, narrow tunnel; this ancient grave was almost barricaded across its width, as if to dissuade all but the most determined from entering.

Continuing on, he eventually spied Ivormyth in the furthest chamber. Having lit another stone lantern, she was on her knees making obeisance to whatever spirits her tribe worshipped. Her back was to him, and she faced a niche carved with a triple spiral; it was here the Winter sun fell at dawn, the shaft of the sun piercing the dark womb of the holy hill. Other recesses also became visible, dark mouths in the tentative light; in them stood vast stone basins, decorated, filled with a jumble of cremated human bones. An astounding cantilevered dome covered the final chamber—the true turret of Spiralfort, the God's Peak.

Mordraed gazed on this holy of holies with awe and for a moment his resolve wavered. The spirits here were strange to him; they almost seemed to sap his power, making his hand tremble and his heart heavy. But despite his sudden unease, he crawled over the shallow sill-stone into one of the niches and wedged himself in behind one of the cinerary basins.

He was quiet, using all the arts of moving silently that he had learned from the hunt…but Ivormyth heard something nonetheless, a shuffle, a breath in the shadows, and she turned her head swiftly and for a second he thought he was undone.

But she made no move, perhaps thinking it was a friendly spirit, some old mother from times past, or even just a small animal rummaging in the tomb, or leaves blown in on the wind. Turning back to the holy of holies, she reached into the fire-lit niche and drew out a beautiful cup.

Mordraed had never seen its like before. Fashioned like a drinking beaker, it was wrought from a single lump of pure gold, with descending rows of corrugated rills whose edges caught the flickering light. Unusually it had a grooved handle, also of gold, riveted on by tiny lozenges that resembled Ardhu's breastplate. Reverently she lifted the Cup, touching the cold metal to her lips.

"Blessed Cup of Plenty, one of the Hallows of these isles," she breathed. "Wrought by the bright lords from Murias, across the sundering sea, fashioned in the breath of Dag the Good God whose Cauldron is never empty. Now to pass to the Prince of Evening, to restore the fortunes of his land and augment those of mine."

So saying, she reached to a woven basket she had brought with her and removed a wooden keg and poured a draught from it into the Cup. She tasted it herself; allowed to touch this man's drink because of her priestly status. Satisfied the drink was properly brewed, she set the Cup carefully on a jutting ledge of stone, where it gleamed like a fallen sun. The drink within it, whatever it was brewed from, shone the colour of dark, arterial blood.

Rising, Ivormyth bowed to the Cup, to the Ancestors that surely swirled, bone-dust and ether, in such a holy, ancient space. "I will return, O Mighty Ones," she murmured, "with he who will become one with me, who will drink the Breath of Life from this Cup of Plenty and unite our isles forever."

Turning, she swept down the passage, her robes trailing behind her like mist.

Mordraed's heart almost leaped from his chest it beat so hard. This was the moment…the moment of his destiny, his triumph. Surely it was meant to be, all his mother had worked for. The spirits had guided the arrogant bitch Ivormyth away, and left the Cup unguarded. The Cup that Gal'havad would drink from.

The Cup he would poison.

Laughing under his breath, he reached inside his jerkin and drew out the tiny clay vial Morigau had given him. At the same time he drew forth Gal'havad's tawdry purple cup, which he had stolen in the night. Hurling it to the floor, he smashed it in two and ground the bits into the dust. If it did protect from poison—and of that he was doubtful—its power was truly shattered now.

Slinking forward, he approached the shimmering Cup of Plenty. It beckoned to him, almost daring him to take it for his own, but he resisted. It would be more useful as it was...the Cup of Life...but by his design an instrument of death. Unstopping Morigau's flask, he poured its contents into the Cup. Acrid fumes rose then dispersed throughout the chamber.

The sound of approaching voices at the passage of God's Peak made him whirl around in alarm. Ivormyth and Gal'havad were entering the tomb. Quickly he shoved the empty poison vial in his tunic and scuttled away to hide behind the huge funerary basin in its niche. Hot-eyed, he watched as his half-brother and the girl Ivormyth came into the terminal chamber of Spiralfort.

Ivormyth gestured for Gal'havad to kneel and he did so at once, bowing his bright head. With her thumb, she traced patterns in ochre on his brow and cheeks. "Tonight you take the Holy Cup as your own; you are chosen, you will unite two lands. A new Sun will come; dawn will be bright. I will leave you here a while to ask the spirits about your path; what they will desire of you when you are a king of men. Drink freely of the elixir whose secret was passed down to us, time out of mind, from Ancestors long dust upon the Fields of Gold. It will help you see the Otherworld and know the Truth and your ultimate Destiny."

"Will you stay with me?" he asked.

She shook her head but reached out and squeezed his hand. "No, it is for you alone as the one who is pure and holy enough to claim the Cup of Dag. But when it is over, my father Maheloas will join us and we will lie together this night and every night until forever."

He grabbed her then, rough in his haste, and kissed her lips, her cheeks, her hair, and Mordraed, in the niche with the old bones scattered around him, grimaced in revulsion and envy. But then he stifled a laugh upon his sleeve. Envy? No need. Ivormyth would have a cold bedmate before the light of dawn...

Ivormyth pulled gently away from Gal'havad and, casting him one last smile, retreated down the corridor. Gal'havad knelt on the floor, hands spread out as though in supplication, staring at the Cup on the ledge before him. It seemed a long time before he moved; Mordraed chafed impatiently in his cramped hiding spot, willing him to drink.

Finally he climbed to his feet and took hold of the Cup. Light from its pure gold surface cast a warm glow on the cold grey stones of the burial chamber. "Spirits, I know not what your plan is for me. Whatever it is, know that I have always served you well. Maybe, within the draught from this blessed Cup, all the mysteries of the heavens and earth shall be revealed to me."

Mordraed shuddered as the younger man spoke; it was almost as if he knew, suspected. And yet...he raised the Cup, first holding it above his head as if to show the Spirits that he was ready to accept what Fate they brought him, then bringing its shining rim to his lips.

He drank deep, finishing the Cup in a single draught.

He stood for a few minutes, eyes closed, arms outstretched, almost god-like in the flickering of the stone lamp. Then, he began to choke. His eyes shot open and he fell to his knees, hand clutching at his throat.

Mordraed did not know why, but he could not watch in secret any longer. He burst from his hiding place and skidded across the cairn floor to tumble down a few feet from Gal'havad.

His heart was racing, its furious beat making him nauseous, and sweat sprang on his brow, but it was cold as ice-water. What have I done? What have I done? his mind screeched, unbidden.

"Mordraed…" Gal'havad's voice was a croak; he dragged himself towards his half-brother with an effort, his arms trembling like leaves in a high wind. "The gods, the Eternal Ones on the Plain of Honey…they have called to me… I must go to them…For me, the Cup has come with a great price, but I am sure this is indeed a gift and not punishment by the Great Ones… I will never again shake with the illness-inside-my-head when I am gone across the Plain…"

His face was white and earnest, his eyes unfocussed and dazed. "Mordraed," he suddenly said, his voice small, like a child's. "Take my hand. It is growing dark…so dark…"

Mordraed hesitated, waves of sickness rushing over him. To take the hand of the man he had slain… Slowly, reluctantly, he took the other's hand, not quite knowing why he did so, when it would be so easy now to turn away. This ending was not as he expected; in his mind's eye, he had seen himself standing over Gal'havad's inert form, the proud conqueror, shouting his triumph to the world. Instead, he felt sick, as if heart and guts were wrung from within, and all he had striven for and desired so much seemed bleak and pointless as an old worm-eaten skull. Gal'havad had stood in his way, but he had helped him too, had sworn to give him lands and riches had he lived to be king. And surely he would have kept his word, for Gal'havad was a man of honour…unlike Mordraed, son of the serpent-woman, with her cold blood running in his veins.

Unexpectedly Mordraed began to cry. It burst from him like a wave from the sea, unwanted and unstoppable.

"Don't grieve for me," Gal'havad whispered, squeezing his fingers with rapidly dwindling strength. "It is the will of the Ancestors. That must be why my own cup went missing, it was taken from me by the spirits so that I could enter the doors of their domain."

Mordraed wept even harder, guilt and remorse and anger and other feelings long suppressed rose in him like a furious storm. The remains of Gal'havad's talisman lay a mere foot or two away, crushed by his feet. His! Not the spirits'… Even in dying, Gal'havad was deluded; there was none whom the Gods loved, only those whom base men hated. Men like Mordraed, lusting for power at any price…

Was the price too high to pay?

Gal'havad slumped back onto the cold flagstones, the Cup lying fallen beside him, his hair a radiant sun wheel around his drained face. "Farewell, my friend," he muttered. "I can see the steeds of the sea with white warriors riding on them wielding long spears of light. They come for me, to bear me to the lands where falls not the rain, nor snow, nor any tears, where Sun and Moon are never dim, and there is no sorrow. I…I…" His voice was barely above a whisper; a haze of bloody mucus marred his pale mouth. "I…will miss you…you were like my brother…"

"I…I am your brother." Mordraed leaned over him, his tears falling freely onto his pallid face, and kissed him on the mouth, as if hoping his pain and the poison that destroyed his innards would pass to him too.

Gal'havad gazed up at him and smiled through his pain. Then suddenly he took one great gasping breath and no more.

A dark madness grasped hold of Mordraed, a monster lurking in his head that sank claws and teeth into his brain, into his very spirit. He flung himself down across the inert body of Gal'havad and screamed his rage and fear and grief and confusion into the echoing chambers of God's Peak.

Ardhu's men heard the first cry, a haunting howl so agonised it sounded scarcely human. Standing beside her father Maheloas, Ivormyth gave a terrified gasp and dropped the beaker she had been holding for a celebratory draught when Gal'havad emerged from Spiralfort. It smashed on the cobbles, dark contents staining white quartz like blood.

Ardhu sprang forward, throwing himself with abandon into the mouth of the tomb, Hwalchmai and Bohrs hot on his heels, and the other three men behind them with drawn axes. They skidded and slid in the darkness, shouting in anger and pain as they crashed into the jagged juts of stone that thrust out into the narrow passage.

At last Ardhu stumbled out into the awful, flickering light in the terminal chamber. He saw the corbelled dome, stained with soot; he saw the side transepts with their beautiful yet sinister basins filled with pale ash and clinkers of welded human fat and hair.

He saw Mordraed crouched down on the floor, a crouched shadow on the dusty flagstones. He saw the Golden Cup, the prize he had sought for his Land, fallen, dented, rolling in the wind that blew up the central passage.

And he saw Gal'havad lying as if asleep, his hair the setting sun around him, his face as white as the chalk of the Great Plain, or the Mother Moon, or the bones of the dead. His lips curved in a faint, unfathomable smile, as if he knew some eldritch secret, some special mystery reserved for him alone…but they were blue, with no breath passing between them. The Prince of Twilight had passed into the twilight of Ahn-un…and his passing brought darkness and night to the heart of Ardhu Pendraec.

"What have you done?" Ardhu screamed at Mordraed. Grabbing his shoulder, he wrenched him up and flung him away from the body of Gal'havad.

Mordraed hit the wall and slumped back to the ground, throwing his arms up over his head. "I did not touch him!" he gasped. "I swear it. The spirits have taken him; he was always close to their world!"

Ardhu drew Caladvolc, its long blade a tongue of blood in the fluttering lantern-light. His eyes were stony, maddened. Hwalchmai clutched his chief's sword arm, trying to wrest the weapon from him. "No, Ardhu…do not do this, you cannot shed blood here…You have no proof, it may not be a lie…the boy is clearly grieved!"

They strove together for a moment or two, then suddenly Ardhu let go of the sword hilt. Caladvolc clattered to the ground. Ardhu stared at his fallen weapon, and then at Gal'havad's body. Mordraed was forgotten. Ardhu's visage drained, becoming nearly as pale as that of the dead youth, and he crashed down on his knees.

At the entrance of Spiralfort, the warriors of Ardhu could hear Maheloas and others moving, calling out and asking what was wrong. The men drew their axes and daggers, ready to defend their mourning chief and the body of his son, though there were only four of them. Mordraed, slouched against the wall, choking with the madness of his unforeseen grief and guilt, was forgotten.

"Do you think they have murdered him?" Bohrs glanced at Hwalchmai. "Was this their plan, to poison Gal'havad? But why? They seemed peaceable and kindly hosts!"

"I do not know." said Hwalchmai shook his head grimly. "But in my heart I do not think they are to blame. Maybe the gods did but act…Gal'havad, may his spirit travel light to the Uttermost West, was purer of mind and body than the rest of us…but he was unwell and becoming more so. Whatever the truth, Maheloas's folk must not come in here and see Ardhu in his grief…We will come out when we are ready. Block the entrance if you must, till Ardhu is himself again."

Bohrs thrust his corpulent frame into the narrow passageway. "Hold, friends!" he shouted down the shadowy corridor. "A great evil has fallen upon us. Let us deal with this as best we can, in the way of our people, and when we are ready we will come out to you."

333

Hwalchmai went to Ardhu and laid a steadying hand on his shoulder. "Kinsman," he said gently. "We need to take him from here. The people of Maheloas are wondering what has happened. This is their tomb of Ancestors; we cannot keep them from it for long."

Ardhu lifted his head; Hwalchmai gaped for it was as if the hand of time had struck his cousin a resounding blow. He looked as deathly as Gal'havad, waxen, suddenly aged. Slowly, like a very old man, he clambered to his feet. "Lift him," he murmured his voice grating in his throat. "Bear him from this place as one would a returning warrior."

Hwalchmai and Bohrs went to Gal'havad and gently lifted him, wrapping him in his cloak. They supported his head, while the other men lifted his legs, and they raised him to their shoulders. Ardhu picked up Caladvolc from where it had fallen, and holding it aloft like a brand began a slow march from the heart of God's Peak, leading the makeshift funeral cortege. Mordraed scrambled up and staggered behind the others, ignored as if he did not exist.

The warband exited the tomb with grave dignity, watching the faces of the tribesmen gathered in the forecourt. The horrified expressions of Maheloas and Ivormyth immediately told them that their hosts had not played them false; that they had nothing to do with the death of Gal'havad.

Ivormyth began to wail and keen, tearing her hair; Maheloas tried to draw her to him but she pulled away and ran toward Ardhu and his men. "What evil had befallen? What evil?" she cried. "Oh, let me see him, who was the Prince of Twilight, who was to be my husband!"

In silence, Ardhu gestured to his men and they laid their burden on the earth before the spiral stone that was the Watcher's eyes, a Bull, a Wave of the Sea. Ivormyth knelt beside Gal'havad, leaning over his body and rocking with grief. Briefly she kissed his pale lips, and her face twisted. "There is death in his mouth! I can taste it. Such bitterness was not in the draught I gave to him!"

Immediately Bohrs's gaze swivelled to Mordraed, crouching by a kerbstone like some crushed spider, his hair a tangled web over his white, red-eyed face. "You! What were you doing in there? You had no right to be within the sacred space!"

Mordraed raised his head; he looked haunted…and hunted; he knew his position was a precarious one. "You cannot blame me!" he gasped. "He was my…cousin, I loved him, we fought side by side! I went in there to…to protect him! I suspected from the start that all was not as it should be. The girl…she attached to him as a burr sticks to a horse's mane! She hardly knew him, it was not natural! I hid to make sure he would not be harmed…but I failed him; he drank that cup of poison before I could make myself known and strike it from his hands."

Hwalchmai frowned. "Inside God's Peak you said that you thought the spirits had taken him. You mentioned naught of poison."

Mordraed licked his lips; he pointed a shaking hand of Ivormyth. "She mentioned the poison; she damned herself out of her own mouth."

Ivormyth cried out, angry and grief-stricken at once. "I noted the taste of it upon his lips; I would hardly have done the act then announced it to you and my folk!"

The tribesmen behind Maheloas began to murmur, angered by Mordraed's accusations. The flames of the eternal lamps of Uffern gleamed on newly drawn daggers.

Maheloas held up his arms, shaking his head is dismay. "Enough, all of you! Put up your blades! Evil has marred this night already. Ardhu Pendraec…" he took a stride toward Ardhu and clasped his arms at the elbow; Ardhu barely moved, hardly reacted; his face was near as lifeless as that of Gal'havad, "I swear by the Almighty Sun, by the Good God, by Ahn-an whose breasts are the Mountains, and by Crooked Krom who carries the Grain-of-the-World upon his back, that my people and I are blameless of any wrong doing in this matter. I can only guess what happened to your son. Maybe the spirits did reach out to take him; it is not for me to say. Or maybe you can think of other possibilities…" His pale blue gaze, glistening, slid toward Mordraed. "But be that as it may, do not bring your anger and your bloodshed to this place. I would counsel that you go back to Prydn as soon as your grief is no longer raw. You may take the Cup with you; for it was won by the Prince of Twilight."

Ardhu jerked into life, shaking his head as if to clear it from evil dreams; perhaps he hoped he truly did but dream and he would awake and the world would be in its normal balance once more, and Gal'havad would rise from the ground, with laughter on his lips and the sunset trapped in his locks. "There is no point in taking it, this Cup of Life that brought his death! If the world was barren and failing before; it is truly the Wasteland now, at least for me. And so it shall ever be."

Stooped like some hoary elder, he turned to his warband…what remained of them. Only five still lived, including Mordraed. All in all, including himself and Betu'or, if his loyal friend had survived the wait upon the sea-strand, only seven of his once mighty warband would return to Prydn from Spiralfort. He had failed utterly; once he had been as the rising Sun, growing brighter and more powerful in strength…now it was as if his Sun had tumbled from the sky, leaving a bleak world of Winter and despair in its wake.

Hwalchmai made a coughing noise. "Ardhu, I know this is a time of great sorrow but we must decide and decide quickly…what are we to do with Gal'havad's body?"

Startled, Ardhu glared at him. "We take him home, to the sacred cemeteries of Khor Ghor."

Bohrs nervously shifted from one foot to the other. "Ardhu…my friend, my lord of these long years, it is not possible. You know that. We cannot carry a body with us while travelling many days, nor can we afford to tarry here while he lays open to the sky. We must bury him in Ibherna, wherever we are permitted…"

"No!" A muscle jumped in Ardhu's jaw. "He will not stay in the land where he died! I forbid it!"

Maheloas stepped forward, his hands clasped, his fingers knotted together, working nervously. "He died while in our territory; we will help you," he said gravely. "Our great Ancestor-tomb has been made unclean by the evil that has happened today. We must sanctify and purify…with fire."

"You would cremate him. Burn him on the pyre."

Maheloas bowed his head. "If it is your will."

Ardhu passed his hand over his brow, lines of strain clear on his face. "So be it…I can see no other way. Once the deed is done, I can take his bones back to Prydn to be buried in earth-houses of his own Ancestors."

Maheloas gestured towards his waiting people, the grim-featured warriors, the weeping women. "We must make ready a pyre for the Prince of Twilight, the holy one, the Cup-winner…he whom the gods loved so much they have taken him to the Plain of Honey this very day. Go to the House of the West and prepare it to receive Gal'havad, son of Ardhu Pendraec."

T he pyre was ready by Sunrise. Gal'havad had been laid on an oak plank in the centre of the timber cult-house, knees curled up as if asleep, his face turned toward the East as was the custom of his people. Burnished copper, his long hair lay spread out over his shoulders and around his face, and his woven cloak, coloured violet with the dye from the magic stones in the Sacred Pool behind Kham-El-Ard, covered him from mid-chest to feet. His amber necklace hung about his neck, glowing, its strange insects frozen in time; and he too, given false semblance of life by the dawn, seemed to be caught in time, a vision to be remembered for eternity by all who gathered there.

The men of Spiralfort gathered around him, placing brush and dried reeds around his bier to help fuel the fire. Heaps of skins lay round as offerings, and women brought meadowsweet and wild flowers in great bunches and beakers of drink so that he would not thirst upon his Great Journey. Maheloas danced and invoked the Sky, the Ancestors, the Earth itself, and with Ivormyth laid protective lumps of quartz, the stone of the Moon, the stone of the Sun, around Gal'havad, placing one clear fine rock before his face so that his spirit, if still travelling to the West, could clearly see the way within its depth.

Ardhu took up Gal'havad's dagger, the gift from An'kelet for his manhood rites. He broke the tip, drawing blood from his own hands as he killed the spirit of the weapon, sending it to the Deadlands alongside his son. Likewise he took Gal'havad's bow and with a great cry snapped it in two across his knee before placing the fragments across Gal'havad's legs and tipping the contents of his quiver of arrows after it.

Lastly Ivormyth brought the Cup of Gold, the fatal Cup that had brought death and not the renewed life Ardhu had hoped. Hands trembling, she set it down on the bier close to Gal'havad's hand. It had been a relic, sacred to the God Dag, but her people wanted nothing to do with it now; its magic had turned bad, feast falling to famine.

This last act done, Ardhu and his men and the folk of Spiralfort departed the House of the West, Maheloas cutting the throat of a black-faced lamb against the blocky standing stone in the doorway to sanctify and seal the funeral chamber with blood. Once outside, he gestured to his followers and they set many brands alight with their flint strike-a-lights. Solemnly, he handed one to Ardhu. "It is your right, Ardhu Pendraec, to start the flames that will light his way to the land of the Ancestors."

Ardhu walked toward the cult-house, grey as a winter's night, no life in his eyes, like a dead man who yet walked. He paused for an instant, gazing into the gloom of the chamber, taking in one last glimpse of Gal'havad that must last him to the end of his days…and then, with a violent motion, he thrust the burning torch into the reed thatching.

A whooshing noise filled the air and the thatch caught alight. Flames raced up the roof and over it in a searing sheet. Ardhu's warband and the people of Spiralfort hurled their torches after it, adding to the conflagration. A wind, blowing from the East, fuelled the fire and it sprang ever higher, roaring and crackling. The chamber was consumed, as twisted orange flames spiralled into the air and oily smoke belched above the quartz-faced mound of God's Peak.

Maheloas began to chant before the burning house, and his men followed suit, rubbing ash and dirt on their cheeks to emulate the dead man within the tomb of fire. The women hewed off hanks of their own hair and flung it into the inferno as an offering to any passing spirits; it sizzled and sparked, sending up a horrible, acrid scent that mingled with that of the pyre.

Then Ivormyth walked toward the pyre, slowly, stately, a strange twisted expression on her face—suffering mixed with determination. She dropped her spotted cowskin cloak to the ground and the watchers gasped as they saw that she was arrayed with gold from head to toe— a gorget with flower-faced terminals, buttons like rayed suns with jet surrounds, a belt of woven strands closed with a massive polished buckle. She drifted towards the burning hut, her hair streaming out behind her like a tendril of escaped smoke.

She halted near the entrance, blinking as smoke and glowing embers billowed around her. Nothing could be seen of Gal'havad amidst the smoke and fire. The stone in the mouth of the hut seemed to glow with a sullen reddish light as flames licked greedily around it.

Ivormyth looked from her sire, Maheloas, to Ardhu and then to Mordraed, who stood behind the rest of Ardhu's warband, pushed to the back, forgotten in their grief for their lost prince. White as bone, his countenance was wracked by sorrow…and guilt. He held his arms protectively across his body, as if expecting blows from some otherworldly agent.

"I was named as the killer of Gal'havad son of Ardhu by one of this company," Ivormyth said in a clear, ringing voice, her gaze still locked on Mordraed. "That was the cruellest lie ever spoken by man's lips on this Isle of the Blessed. I have harmed none in my short life; I served my father and the Ancestors well. I was to wed the Prince of the Twilight, and was glad to do so. I was happy to lie at his side in life…and to prove that I am no murderer, I will show all how true I am to him and to his blessed memory. Today I will join the Prince of Twilight as his bride in the realm of the Not-world."

Maheloas gave a terrible scream and lunged for his daughter, suddenly realising her intent, but Ivormyth was too swift for her elderly father. Swift as a deer, she hoisted her robes round her calves and sprang forward, hurling herself into the flames of Gal'havad's funeral pyre. She began to scream as the hungry flames roared up to meet her, but as if by the hand of a merciful god, the roof-beam of the house cracked and collapsed inwards with a resounding roar, bringing the walls down with it, and scattering red-hot embers everywhere. Ash and hot sparks fountained up then showered over the horrified onlookers. The standing stone inside the hut seemed to wobble in its pit, and suddenly it cracked at the base and shattered, spewing steaming fragments all over the scorched ground.

Maheloas was on his knees, rocking with agony. His hair smouldered; his mouth hung open in a soundless scream. He ripped off the ceremonial mask he wore and hurled it into the fire. "Get your son's bones and go from here," he said to Ardhu Pendraec, when words would come. "It was a black day for both of us when you set foot upon this isle!"

CHAPTER SIXTEEN-THE LADY IN THE RIVER

The remnants of Ardhu's warband trudged back to the sea-strand where they had first set foot ashore. For the first time since they had entered Ibherna luck was with them, and they were neither attacked by the tribe of Bal'ahr nor any other man or beast upon the road. Ardhu walked ahead of the others, face sarsen-hard and unnaturally aged, holding in his arms a coarse cinerary urn that contained the charred bones of Gal'havad. Bohrs and Hwalchmai flanked him, axes upheld in a symbol of respect to the remains of the young lord of Kham-El-Ard—while Mordraed, shunned by the others, staggered in the rear of the party, haggard as a wraith, a figure almost to be pitied in his abject misery.

Betu'or was sitting down by the boats, still faithfully on guard, a spear across his knees. He leapt up, kicking sand over his small fire, when he saw familiar figures crest the rise…then stopped in horror as he counted the men before him and realised what his chieftain bore in his arms.

"No, it cannot be so!" he cried, falling to one knee as the sand eddied around him, as golden as the Cup they had sought…and left behind, charred in the ruins of the cult-house at God's Peak.

"Sadly, it is indeed so. Gal'havad son of Ardhu has gone to the Ancestors." Hwalchmai came down beside Betu'or and raised him with a hand. Ardhu said nothing; he merely clutched the urn and stared out, stone-eyed, to sea. "And only seven of us will return to Kham-El-Ard…and that is if the tides are with us and we do not founder." Hwalchmai followed Ardhu's gaze out to the choppy grey water; bunched clouds loomed like giant's heads on the horizon and the wind was singing.

"The wind is not right." Betu'or held up a string of lank seaweed, watching the direction in which it swung. "The Moon had a sick hue last night, and the dawn was the colour of blood…both ill omens for sailing."

"I will stay no longer, not even if Ga'o the Wind Spirit blows his fiercest blasts and Mahn-ann brings down the roiling mists of Symmerdim." Ardhu's face was impassive, like granite. "The very soil of this place screams out against us, and if we linger too long I am certain not one of us shall return to Kham-El-Ard. Betu'or, we will only need Pridwen for the journey home, for there are but seven of us left; destroy the other boat, so that none can follow us. We have met many here who have no love for the men of Prydn."

Betu'or drew his axe and started to hack at the lesser of their two sturdy boats. Wood cracked and splinters flew. Hwalchmai and Bohrs joined him, smashing the carefully wrought timbers with great force until the craft lay in shattered pieces upon the strand.

Then the warriors gathered together and pushed Pridwen out into the swell, with Ardhu seated in the prow, facing his homeland, the urn and its precious contents held fast between his knees. Once Pridwen was afloat in waist-high water, they hauled themselves over the side and took up their flat paddles—all except Mordraed, who crouched at the far end away from his fellows. He looked ghastly and began to heave over the side, his hair hanging in the salty water. The others ignored him, disgusted.

The crossing was bad, with a high wind taking them farther down the coast, but not as bad as it could have been; at least no storm-god had swept in to try and capsize them, and no Maidens of the Waves tried to draw them onto hidden rocks. Before long, the shores of Prydn became visible under a helm of grey drizzle. Pridwen had been driven off course by the capricious winds, but it had turned out to be no bad thing—the cliffs on the horizons were familiar to the warriors; the red and pale cliffs and sea stacks were the bastions of the Land of the Dwri, the People of the Water, one of Ardhu's own holdings through his father, U'thyr Pendraec.

Sailing into a sheltered cove with a huge, storm-carved arch that opened to the wild seas, Hwalchmai, Bohrs and Betu'or leapt into the shallows, dragging Pridwen up across the loose shingle on the beach until its prow came to rest against a vast weedy rock. As the company disembarked, climbing stiffly out onto solid land, the towering cliffs above became filled with spear-carrying men who waved their weapons with menace.

Ardhu set down the precious urn that contained Gal'havad's remains, took Rhon-gom from his belt, and held it aloft so that all could see the symbol of his sovereignty. Immediately the tribesmen on the heights cast down their spears and began running down paths on the cliffside to greet the King of the West upon the cold seastrand.

Their leader was a man known to Ardhu; a youth of twenty summers called Ithel who had been at Winter Solstice celebrations at Deroweth for the last two years. He was distant kin, a grandson of one of U'thyr's sisters.

As Ithel jogged down the beach, shouting out a greeting to his kinsman, Ardhu held up his hand for him to halt. "Ithel, we come to the lands of the Dwri with no tales of glorious questing and its rewards. We went over the waves with death at our shoulders, and death is all we have brought back to Prydn." He nodded grimly towards the rough black urn at his feet.

Ithel stared at the coarse pot, not understanding its significance.

Ardhu bowed his head. "That urn contains the bones of Gal'havad, prince of Kham-El-Ard, my only son and heir. He died upon the Imram, the…gods…" he swallowed, fighting for control, '…took him at the moment of our victory…for he was too good to walk longer amidst mortal men."

Ithel looked thunderstruck, his cheeks draining at the gravity of this news; he made the sign against evil with his hand. "My …my lord…these are unwelcome tidings indeed! Sorrow is in my heart and will be in the hearts of all true men of Prydn, Great Stone Lord. May the spirits give you ease."

"I will have no ease for the rest of my days, be they long or short," said Ardhu bitterly. "And the spirits? They have turned their faces from me. But if you would aid me, there is something I would have you do…to honour Gal'havad. Send your most reliable men across Prydn, to every camp and settlement you know. Let them spread the news of the death of my son, the Hawk of Summer, who has now passed from us as summer passes to winter. Let all of Albu the White and even beyond weep for the Prince of the Twilight."

Ithel bowed. "It will be done, Ardhu Terrible Head. I will see that all men know and honour the memory of Gal'havad. Fires will burn to light his bones home to the houses of his forebears." He turned, shoulders slouched with the heaviness of his assignment, and scrambled back up the cliff, gesturing to his men to follow. Once they reached the cliff-top there was scuffling and commotion on the height, and then, against the faded, dismal sky, a tongue of flame blossomed. It spiralled upwards, smoke trails billowing above its burning heart like the hands of departing spirits. It was joined within a short while by a blaze upon the summit of the opposing sea-cliff, matching the first in ferocity and intensity.

Ardhu picked up the heavy urn, cradling it in his arms, and began to climb the steep slope from the cove, his steps slow and lacklustre, the steps of a mourner.

And so the bones of Gal'havad the Son of Ardhu, the Prince of Twilight, began their long journey back to Kham-El-Ard.

The Land was in mourning. Ithel's messengers had spread the unhappy news, carrying it through all of Dwranon and as far afield as Khor Ghor and Suilven, while other men continued to pass the tale of woe on through all the villages of the West right down through Duvnon with its twisted tors to the craggy tip of Belerion where the land meets the sea. Mounted on a steed borrowed from Ithel's holdings, Ardhu rode slowly through Dwranon with the cinerary urn in its place of honour before him on the horse, and his men gathered around him like a guard, marching sombrely on the long road home. Mordraed, though still pale and wretched, had regained some of his equilibrium and even marched at their side, though the others still ignored him. They could accuse him of nothing, and his grief seemed real enough, but his behaviour in Ibherna and its consequences had estranged them even more from him. But he was Gal'havad's kinsman, and had been his friend, so they had no right to bar him from the funeral procession.

They passed the great Mai Dun Fort of the Plain, where a causewayed camp had crowned the hilltop in the days of the Ancestors, a place where feasts had taken place and marriages were contracted and the silent dead had watched over all from platforms raised to the Everlasting Sky. A great long barrow, so large it seemed more a bank than a mound, stretched along the brow of the hill like a dark, undulating worm. As the warband passed on the track that skirted the foot of the hill, small figures scurried along the barrow's length and suddenly its humped back burst into flame—beacons lit to honour the dead youth whose charred bones were carried ever onwards towards Kham-El-Ard.

It was the same at the Great Dragon Path of Dwr, white-banked and massive under a stark crescent Moon, trailing away into the distance as far as the eye could see. As Ardhu and his companions processed along its length, the night air was suddenly filled by smoke and ash, and flames from hastily ignited brushwood pyres lighted the Spirit-Path and all its satellite barrows. And the people of the Dwr came from hut and farm and settlement, some travelling many miles, whitening their faces with chalk and smearing their bodies with charcoal, and they wailed and keened and cried, dancing and drinking themselves into a frenzy in honour of their lost prince.

Within a few more days, Ardhu's warband reached the Harrow track, the Way of the Temple, and came at dusk within sight of Khor Ghor. Stark, eternal, it gleamed hazily in the purple of the twilight, the trilithons a faded red, like old blood, surrounded by the ever-circling black birds that made their homes beneath the lintels.

Ardhu drew rein, watching as night drew down its cloak, furling the Seven Kings on their high ridge and the Spirit-Path with its attendant barrows. All was silent, still, save for the distant yipping of a fox…

And then the lights began, twinkling in the gloom, myriad tongues of flame that leaped down the Avenue's parallel banks, over the rounded heads of the Seven Kings, and along the top of the Great Spirit-Path itself. A drum rolled, its sound awful and solemn, reverberating within the massive Stones that made up the holy circle, and the shrine itself came to life with fire. The darkened stones turned red once more, flickering torches moving between the archways, and suddenly the tops of the lintels were ablaze, as flames shot high into the air before dissipating in an instant, some magic wrought by the priests of Deroweth in tribute to Gal'havad and his passing from the world of men.

Dismounting his steed and passing the reins to Hwalchmai, Ardhu started down the Avenue, the urn heavy as stone in his arms, and the fires burning around him, blinding his eyes.

And so he came to Kham-El-Ard and found its people waiting for him, lining the path that led up the hill with torches burning in their hands, and on the top of the ramparts were fires so great it almost looked as if the entire wooden fort was alight. He could hear the flames roaring, and huge clouds of smoke and ash puffed into the night air, obscuring the stars.

As he ascended the path, men and women knelt before him, weeping and crying out, rending the earth with their hands. He passed them, stony-faced, and then, just within the great oaken gates, halted and placed Gal'havad's urn upon the ground.

Across the yard from him stood Fynavir, face daubed with chalk, as was customary in times of mourning, her unearthly whiteness and the thinness that had come upon her since the banishment of An'kelet making her look like a skeleton that walked. Upon her shoulders gleamed the golden shoulder-cape that she had worn to their marriage-feast, still as bright as the day it was made...though the linen that drooped from its eyelets hung in tattered grey shreds, a shroud that tangled around her gaunt limbs.

Ardhu went to her; he clasped her hands. She stared blankly at him, her fingers not enclosing his. He sank to one knee before her and suddenly he wept, for the first time since Gal'havad had died. "Forgive me," he said. "I have not brought him back to you."

"I know..." she said. "The whole land has mourned for him."

"The gods willed that he go to the Undying Realm..." Ardhu said feebly, brokenly.

"I know that too. But everything to me is lost, grey ash on the wind. If the spirits would take me away to be with him, I would gladly die this very instant."

She knelt in the dusty soil beside him, great sobs tearing from her chest, and he held her and wept with her, and it was as if, for a moment, the tears washed away some of the dark stain that blighted their marriage, joining them in purpose if only for a brief time. When their grief was at last spent, they both rose and walked, hands clasped, to Gal'havad's urn.

"Where shall we bury him?" asked Ardhu. "I leave it for you to choose, my Queen. We can build a new barrow on the Plain or inter him in the edge of one of the great mounds of the Tin-Lords that cluster in the fields."

"I do not want him far from me," She wiped her red-rimmed eyes. "I want to gaze out and see where he is, and think upon him until the end of my days. Can we not build him a fitting grave near us here at Kham-El-Ard?"

Ardhu inclined his head. "It will be done, Fynavir, my Queen,' and so the order was made—and a barrow raised below the ramparts of Kham-El-Ard the Crooked High Hill, a fine round tumulus overlooking the curves of bright Abona, which flowed between the stands of ash, and elm, and stout oak that grew behind the hill. Fires were kindled along the banks of the river from the fort all the way to Deroweth and drums were beaten and cattle slaughtered and eaten in a vast funeral celebration. Men and women danced with mad abandon, and leapt through the clouds of flame and smoke...and beside them Mordraed danced harder and longer than the rest, almost till exhaustion took him.

Then Gal'havad's urn was lowered into a central grave-pit and a vessel full of meat placed beside it, along with bronze pins and amber beads and worked flint. Earth and chalk was shovelled over the pit with a cow's scapula, and great wailing went up from Fynavir and the women of the tribe, who cast themselves into the barrow's newly-dug ditch, tearing at their hair and faces, their beauty turned to ugliness as death itself turned all that was fair to ash.

Mordraed sidled over to one of the slaughtered bulls and bathed his hands in the blood welling from its slashed neck; he rubbed it through his hair, painted it on his chest and arms and cheeks. His fair face took on a demonic scarlet hue, his dark blue eyes vivid against the crimson gore. He scarcely seemed human, more like a spirit of war, of death.

He was the Dark Moon.

He was Death.

The grief that had almost felled him in Ibherna had dissipated and a renewed anger had replaced it. Anger toward Ardhu Pendraec. It was his fault Gal'havad had to die. If Ardhu had acknowledged Mordraed and given him his rightful due, Gal'havad could have been allowed to live. Mordraed was wise. Mordraed could be merciful if he chose. He would have sent Gal'havad off to the priests at Deroweth; he would have been happy there, talking to spirits, with holy men to tend him in his illness...

Mordraed shot Ardhu a venomous glare through the haze of the burning. The Stone Lord, dancing with his warriors in a circle around Gal'havad's barrow, did not notice him. A cold, hard emptiness rose up in him, filling his belly like poison, mingling with the hatred of his heart.

Soon…let it be…Let there be an end!

Let him come into his birthright and take Ardhu's head in battle and give it to the Great Circle…before he destroyed the loathsome place forever, breaking its malign power with the breaking of its Stones.

Mordraed left the funeral celebrations after Sunset, when most of the mourners were drunk and ill, glutted with the mead and meat they had wantonly consumed. Keeping to the bushes, he dashed along the riverbank, the wind ruffling his gore-clotted hair. Light was failing, but the twilight would be his friend, hiding him from any curious eyes, from the men of the Stone Lord, his enemies, who did not trust him.

He was doing his duty.

He was visiting his mother, Morigau, to tell of his victories.

She was waiting for him on Prophet's barrow, as if she knew he would come, her unbound tresses a dark foaming cloud like the smoke of Gal'havad's pyre. She sprang down the hill, lithe as girl, and hurled her wiry arms about him, kissing his cheeks and mouth. His lips stung with her assault and he yanked his head away, noticing his mouth was bleeding at the corner. "So you have done it…at last," she breathed, "You've killed the precious prince, Ardhu's boy. I wonder how my brother feels to lose what he holds most dear. A just punishment for him. Tell me, my darling Mordraed, was the death long, did he suffer as I have suffered…"

A wave of nausea crashed over Mordraed. Suddenly he felt pure, blinding hate toward Morigau…the same kind of hatred he felt towards Ardhu. "Shut up, your unnatural bitch!" he spat. "It is ill to gloat over the dead! He did not deserve to die, mother, and although he needed to be removed, I will regret killing him until the day that I too fare across the Great Plain. One day the Spirits will sit in judgement on me for giving him that poison draught…"

Morigau's eyes narrowed angrily; but her voice dripped with sarcasm. "What is wrong with you, boy? I did not bring you up to have such weak, womanish thoughts. What is the matter, why do you care so much for his fate; were you his lover?"

Mordraed whirled around and struck her so hard that she fell to the ground. "Never speak of such things to me again, women!" he snarled. "Or you may find yourself as dead as Gal'havad!"

Morigau laughed; a high crazy sound. She pressed her hand to her face, already swelling from his blow. "I am glad you have not completely lost your spirit. Don't forget, that although you may not approve of the things I make you do…it is for you, for all of your close kin. You will thank me one day when you are the most powerful chief in all Prydn!"

Mordraed grunted and turned from her. He could see Khyloq in the field, pressing on towards him through the long summer grasses. Although he knew he had only been away a few weeks, the swell of her belly seemed much bigger now, more obvious to his eyes. He thought of the child inside her dragged screaming into the world by Morigau when the time came—to be taken and used by her just as she had used him, to be moulded into her creature, her pet, maybe even the one who held the poison chalice for him if he displeased her. Fear ate at him, and hatred, deep hatred that expanded in his heart and consumed like fire…

Khyloq reached him and stood arms folded, red hair tumbling in burnished coils around her. Her face was dirty, her feet bare. "You've been a long time coming to us," she said curtly. "You've been back in Kham-El-Ard for days!"

"Gal'havad had to be buried with proper rites," he said shortly. "I could not leave without remark. And it was only right I honour him." He cast a fierce glance at Morigau as if daring her to disagree.

Khyloq pressed herself against him; she stunk of the pigsty and he guessed she had been mucking it out while Morigau waited for him. "I am glad you are back; I heard most of Ardhu's men were killed. Are you glad to see me? Do I look fair to your eyes after so long away?"

Mordraed's lip curled. "You look fat. And filthy. But I will be glad enough of your company when you are washed."

"Yes, go lie with her." Morigau stepped up to him, still rubbing her swelling cheek, though in an almost reverential way, as if his blow had been as soft and desirable as a kiss, perhaps even more desirable. "Maybe it will put you in a sweeter mood."

"I am not here for dalliance," Mordraed said dismissively. Khyloq looked furious, flushing as red as her hair. "I want to know what is to be done now. Gal'havad is gone, but Ardhu remains strong, with many loyal men around him. Now that his only heir is dead, he may well take another woman since the White One seems barren. He could beget more sons yet. I must move and move swiftly, but how can I, when he still has his warband, depleted though it is through his foolish Imram?"

"He must leave Kham-El-Ard." Morigau smiled. "He must fare abroad with his men, and leave you behind with those who are loyal to you. Then you will be free to make your move, with few to withstand you…and I will be free to leave this hovel of my exile, and help raise you to the position for which you were born."

"Leave Kham-El-Ard? Why would he? He is deep in grief, and has no reason to leave his home to go questing once more."

"The madness of his grief may be his undoing," she grinned. "I can turn the dagger of pain that is already in his heart. Believe me; I have not been idle in your absence, my son. I have travelled far and found out many things. My hands have not been idle. Wait and see. Watch the River, my son. Abona will bring you a gift."

Night lay over Kham-El-Ard, uneasy, dreaming night. Torches on the stout earthworks twinkled like fallen stars, while the true stars, shining through tufts of fast-moving stratus, glimmered on the moving swell of Abona. Mist coiled from the temperate surface of the Sacred Pool and crept through the trees like a living thing.

Inside the fort, in his sleeping quarters at the back of the Great Hall, Ardhu tossed restlessly, as he had done every night since Gal'havad died. Coiled at his side but not touching him, Fynavir wept quietly in her sleep. He averted his face, unable to bear the sight of her tears.

In the hut assigned to youths in training, Mordraed too lay sleepless in the dark. Now that Gal'havad was dead, he had been excluded from the warband, thrust back into the quarters of the inferior young men who would never make warriors. He sprawled under a patchy old skin, listening to the chorus of snores around him, the rattle of mice in the rushes. He was not one of Ardhu's chosen men any longer, so this would be his band instead, a band where he was no follower, obeying orders, but where he was the unquestioned leader. His warband would have no old men like the king, no fools with high ideals and their endless prattle of honour. Killers, berserkers, the foolhardy and the vainglorious would serve Mordraed well.

He grinned, fingering his dagger blade in the dark. The new would sweep out the old; the fierce would put down those that had become tame as old dogs.

Suddenly his ears caught a sound, brought on the night-breeze—an alarmed shout from one of the night watchmen on the ramparts. Mordraed sat up, head on one side, listening intently. Another shout came, louder than the first. Footsteps sounded across the dun and he heard the creaking of the gates of the fort as they were dragged open.

Something was happening, something abnormal.

Mordraed sprang up and kicked the shoulder of Wyzelo, who sprawled near him in the rushes, mouth hanging and snores emerging. "Quickly, up, up, Wyzelo…all of you!" he cried, glancing at the other supine shapes scattered across the floor. "The watchers have left their posts. Some ill is afoot."

The youths clambered up, bleary-eyed and yawning, and with much grumbling followed Mordraed from their hut like a flock of bad-tempered sheep. A stream of curious people hurried past them, heading toward the open gateway. Ardhu and Fynavir, dressed hastily in tunics and cloaks, strode through the middle of the crowd, surrounded protectively by the remaining members of the warband. Everyone looked disorientated and confused.

They proceeded to the riverbank, far below, led by the gate-guards with drawn bows. The Sun was just peeping above the eastern horizon, a streak of blood-red between the boles of the trees. Its rays stroked the flowing waters; caressing the hair of old River-Woman…and illuminating a strange craft that floated along Abona's swell.

A deep dug-out canoe was drifting aimlessly along the current. An old man sat in it, shoulders bowed, face chalked to reflect death and grief. Before him, in the prow of the boat lay a girl as fair as the sunrise, stretched out on her back, her hands holding pebbles of magic white quartz. Flowers were heaped around her, lilies and flags, foxgloves, red campion. Two pots stood by her head, one filled with milk, one with grain, and an awl and two scrapers had been placed at her side.

As beautiful as she looked, her features made rosy by the warm dawn-light, there was a livid hue marring the cheeks, the full mouth.

She was dead.

Ardhu pushed through the crowd of tribesfolk and warriors and reached the river bank first. His face looked haggard and strained and angry. "What do you here, bringing this strange burden to Kham-El-Ard?" he asked. "She should be taken to her people and buried in their rites."

The old man glanced up; tears had made snail's tracks through the white chalk paint on his cheeks. "I come here because I want vengeance, reparations…although nothing can bring my daughter back to me."

"What has this to do with the folk of Kham-El-Ard?" snapped Ardhu, irritation obvious in his voice.

"Everything!" The man poled the craft to the shore and clambered onto the bank. He marched up to Ardhu and stared into his face without flinching. "It was one of your warriors that brought this doom upon my daughter…my beautiful daughter who was more precious than the Sun and Moon to me."

Ardhu frowned. "I do not understand. How did she die? There is no mark upon her. What has happened here? Speak clearly, old one!"

"I am Phelas of Astolaht," said the man. "And my poor dead child…" he gestured to the body in the boat, "is Elian, known as the Maid of Lilies. I will tell you her tale and you will know why I have come here in my grief…Several Moons ago Elian found a wounded warrior from Kham-El-Ard on the edges of our territory; she saved his life with her healing arts and nursed him back to health…and he repaid her by forcing himself upon her, then casting her aside like a broken beaker. Her heart may have healed from that wicked deed, but there was more…he left a child in her belly. The shame was too much for her to bear. She wished to rid herself of her burden but her simple remedies did not the job. So she went to another wise-woman in the valley and gave herself into her care but the woman's arts failed and she died in my arms, in agony…" He stopped, his face crumpling.

Mordraed felt his heartbeat quicken at Phelas's words and he craned his head to see the dead Elian and her father. A 'wise woman'…Could it have been his mother and her poisons? Morigau had told him to 'watch the river.'

Ardhu's lips tightened as he stared down at Elian's still countenance, the cheeks slightly speckled with livid stains.. "Who is the warrior of my band who has done this grave deed?"

Phelas's breath was a sob. "An'kelet Prince of Ar-morah."

Ardhu's breath whistled between his teeth; a muscle jumped in his jaw. "He is long gone from here…he may even be dead. I wounded him with Caladvolc…"

"He is not dead." Phelas shook his head. "Elian healed him. When he abandoned her to her fate, he told her he was heading back to his domain in Ar-morah, over the Narrow Sea."

Ardhu stood in silence. Indeed, it seemed the whole of the world had grown silent, save for the soughing of the breeze and the continual gurgle of the holy river.

Suddenly Fynavir, pale and sharp as a winter icicle at her husband's side, fell to her knees beside the riverbank and began to sob.

Ardhu whirled, an awful rage in his face. Even his oldest friends recoiled—none had seen such a terrible expression of anger, grief, and despair. "Cease your noise!" He grabbed Fynavir's arm, hauling her roughly to her feet. "Look! Look what he has done to this innocent girl! Look what evil he has wrought. What kind of a creature did you lie with, Fynavir of Ibherna?"

Fynavir struggled free of Ardhu's grip. Tears spattered from her eyes, but there was fire in her stare for the first time in months. "One who loved me…as you did not. One who valued me not because my mother was god-touched, because I am the White Phantom, but because I am Fynavir. Think on that, Stone Lord."

Tears still falling, she gazed down at Elian…this girl who An'kelet had taken in her stead, taken cruelly and thrown aside if the story was true. Taken and then killed as sure as if he had stabbed her with his Ar-moran dagger. It was beyond bearing…even the memory of their love was now tainted, mould upon the blossom. Choking back sobs, she picked her way back toward Kham-El-Ard in the chill dawn, while the crowd murmured and stared at her retreating back.

"What do you intend to do?" asked Phelas, facing Ardhu again with an air of defiance, as if daring him to do nothing. "This foul deed must not go unpunished. When you took power, ruling the Great Trilithon and assuming the mantle of that king of old, Samothos, you swore to defend Prydn from all evil. Instead, by taking the foreigner from Ar-morah into the fold, you brought it to us. My daughter has paid the price for your folly, Stone Lord."

Listening to his words, Mordraed jabbed Wyzelo in the back with a finger. "You…I need you to speak for me," he whispered in his ear. "Now. Shout out that Ardhu should take his warband and ride for Ar-morah to take vengeance on An'kelet for his crimes."

"Why me?" Wyzelo was still half-asleep, his hair sticking up in tufts around his bovine face. "Why not you? You're kin!"

"He won't listen to me; he no longer trusts me. But seeking An'kelet is the right thing to do; you know that, don't you, Wyzelo? Deceitful killers and adulterers cannot be allowed to live. He has murdered this girl with his lust and he has made a fool of the King. Ardhu must go forth across the seas and slay him…" His eyes narrowed. "And if he goes, that leaves our lot in charge at Kham-El-Ard, Wyzelo. His band is so depleted, he will need to take them all, leaving just us. Think of it. Something of merit to do, rather than waiting for scraps to be flung to us."

Wyzelo nodded, expression brightening at the thought of a Kham-El-Ard where he could have his say. "I did not think of the benefits to us. I will put in a word, Mordraed."

The warband had gathered in a circle around Ardhu and Phelas. "I counsel a cool head," Hwalchmai was saying. "A vile thing has happened, and I would not have expected it of An'kelet, but what can we do? He is far from here, hidden in his ancestral lands. It would be foolhardy to follow him."

Ardhu drew Caladvolc, holding it out before him. "But when men hear that he has escaped my justice, what will they think? That the sword of the Terrible Head is weak, that he allows treacherous men to go free."

"Who cares what others think?" said Hwalchmai, testily. "We know the truth…"

Ardhu slammed Caladvolc back into its sheath. "I care. For once rumours spread that I am not in control of this Land and all that is in it, then a darkness will spread, like a night that has no day following. Evil men will come as they did of old—raiders will burn the coasts and chieftains who dwell within our very midst will turn to bloodshed and plunder."

"You should go, lord!" Seeing his opportunity, Wyzelo shouted out, his voice booming amongst the trees. "Bring the miscreant to his knees! Take his head for your hut! Restore the glory of Kham-El-Ard!"

"Shut up, boy!" Bohrs looked Wyzelo up and down contemptuously. "Why do you speak, when you are not even a man of the warband but a useless ox who fails in his training?"

Wyzelo reddened and his teeth clenched but Ardhu held up his hand. "No, even such as he should speak, for he will have to fight should our borders ever fall. I have made a decision; when I saw the body of the Maid of Lilies, I knew it to be right. We will cross the Narrow Sea to Ar-morah. Every able man of the old company will come with me, even you, my brother." He patted the shoulder of Ka'hai, who stood with a worried frown at his shoulder. "It will be one final last flowering of our might, to make this Land safe forever."

CHAPTER SEVENTEEN—THE TIME OF BURNING

The journey across the Narrow Sea was surprisingly smooth, the winds favourable and the seas calm, though Ardhu was glad they had to go no farther South, for just beyond lay the Little Sea, Mar-Byhan with its many green islands, and then the vast curving expanse of the Great Bay, where the tides were always capricious, sending unwary Tin-men to watery graves for the last five hundred years.

The company sailed round the jagged tip of Ar-morah, so similar in appearance to the coast of Belerion, and set ashore below a headland crowned by a massive cairn made of many steps. It dominated the landscape, grey and brown, its pebbled layers rising towards the horizon and its summit surrounded by wheeling, screeching seabirds.

Climbing to the top of the cairn, Ardhu gazed out across a land of verdant fields and grey rock that shimmered under the watery sun. He sighed, wishing he had been able to bring the horses with him on this journey…but it would have been far too dangerous to take such animals in their relatively flimsy craft. Cattle and sheep, yes, if kept with careful handlers and tied well—horses, no.

Hwalchmai came up next to him, the daggers and axe in his belt jingling as he walked. "Where now, Ardhu? How do we find An'kelet in this great space?"

Ardhu waved his arm in an Easterly direction. "I suspect he has gone to ground in the forest of Bro-khelian, which lies in the territory of Ar-goad, the Land next the Wood, somewhere in the middle of Ar-morah. Within its depth he was born to Ailin, the Priestess of the Lake Maidens and King Bhan, and he claimed his kin still had holdings there amidst the trees."

Hwalchmai frowned, squinting into the distance. "We will be far from our ships…I do not like it, Ardhu."

"Nor do I, cousin." Ardhu placed a hand on the other's shoulder, leaning on him for a moment as if for support. Then he pulled away and drew himself up to his full height. "But my choice is made and whatever the spirits have destined for me, I will accept."

The warband trudged on amidst a landscape of golden gorse and speckled boulders, of fallen tombs and standing stones that seemed to point the way across Ar-morah, as well as to the Moon, Sun, and stars. As they settled down to camp for the night in the lee of a bald hill, they heard the drum of hooves and saw a solitary rider on a stocky pony galloping over the terrain towards them. Immediately the archers raised their bows, and Hwalchmai and Bohrs readied their axes in case of attack.

But Ardhu, leaving Caladvolc sheathed, walked forward alone to meet the rider. It was a youth of about fourteen Sun-turnings, with honey-bronze hair and long limbs tanned golden from the sun. He reminded Ardhu of a younger An'kelet. "Who are you, boy?" he called out. "What is your business with us?"

"Are you Ardhu Pendraec, king of Prydn?" the boy shouted, leaning over his pony's neck.

"I am. Who asks?"

"I am Brandegor, kinsman to An'kelet of Ar-morah, who dwells in his ancestral holdings in Bro-khelian. He has given words to me that I may speak them to you."

"Speak, then, Brandegor kinsman of An'kelet. You have nothing to fear from me."

"An'kelet says that if you come in peace you may meet with him within the woods of Bro-khelian. But if you bring war to his door, you will never go home alive…the forest will have your bones, the moss will consume you, and you will pass from this earth as if you have never been."

Bohrs made a growling noise. "He presumes…We should cut the trees with our axes and then burn his blasted forest."

"Be silent Bohrs," frowned Ardhu. "Such talk does no good. Let me think…" He passed his hand across his brow. "Brandegor, bring An'kelet this message from me—I do not come in friendship, because there is much in Prydn that he must still be taken to task for. But I will not bring my warband into the forest. Instead I will come alone. We will meet one on one, as princes and warriors, and make a final end to what is bad between us."

Bohrs made a derisive noise. "Are you mad, Ardhu? He knows the forest!"

"And I know him," said Ardhu. "It is the only way." He nodded toward Brandegor. "Go now, with all haste, to announce me to your chief. I will follow as quickly as I may."

The youth bowed his bright head. "I will tell the Lord An'kelet of your decision." He struck heels to the pony's flanks and galloped toward the tree-furred hills on the horizon.

Bohrs stared moodily at Ardhu. "I pray you have done the right thing, Stone Lord," he murmured. "An'kelet is not the man who was once your friend, and how can you ever trust him?"

Ardhu shrugged. "I do not trust him. But I will face him, and let the Ancestors decide between us."

In Kham-El-Ard Mordraed crouched on the ramparts, watching the river and the fields below and occasionally glancing over his shoulder at the inner bailey of the fort. Under a weak blue sky, pale and vapid after yet another summer rainstorm, people went about their daily business—herding beasts, weaving, making reed baskets, cutting wood, cooking. Dogs yapped and barked and children ran screaming amidst the huts. Lazily Mordraed counted the men folk, sizing them up—most were either very old, lame in some way, or very young, with the exception of his band of perennial ne'er do wells, who stalked about swilling beer from their beakers and brawling with each other.

It was as he had hoped. The only important member of Ardhu's warband left in the dun was Per-Adur, whose head-wound had never really healed and now suffered shaking fits similar to those of Gal'havad…Mordraed shuddered, lips curling into a snarl. He would not think of Gal'havad, would not let his foolish grief cloud the days leading up to his great glory.

Staring back out into the fields, he spotted a band of strangers coming from the direction of the ford. Straining his eyes into the bright midday light, he saw Wyzelo marching at their front, his expression one of self-satisfaction. He smiled to himself. The great oaf had done one thing right, at least—he had gone and collected all his kin and fellow malcontents from their villages on the edges of the Plain. They had dwelt too long in the shadow of Kham-El-Ard and now they wanted more.

As he did.

Wyzelo led the newcomers up the crooked hill to the wooden gates of the fortress. They came slowly, seemingly no threat to anyone, a crowd of stout lads with poorly knapped axes and flint knives, little copper amongst them. In Kham-El-Ard the tribesfolk stopped their weaving, potting, and scraping skins and turned to stare at the newcomers. Women, sensing something amiss, called their children to them and bustled them inside their houses. The men came up from the fields and from the river, frowning, wishing they had their daggers, but they had not taken such weapons to their daily toil.

Only Mordraed's chosen, the unfit and the uncouth, seemed pleased to see the newcomers. Still slurping from their beakers, they grinned and nudged each other, obviously enjoying the discomfiture of the rest of the tribefolk.

At the gate, one youth with a spear stepped forward and barred their way. "I know you, Wyzelo," he said, "but these others have no right to be here, and you have no right to bring them in the Stone Lord's absence."

Wyzelo looked the youth up and down mockingly. "I think you'll find you are wrong," he drawled. "I think you'll find things are changing here, and that I can do as I bloody like."

"You've gone mad!" hissed the youth with the spear. "You've had too much sun!"

Mordraed stood up. He climbed gracefully down from the ramparts, and padded cat-like toward the stand-off at the gate. Smiling a dangerous smile that did not reach his eyes, he put his hand on the young guard's spear, pushing its sharp tip towards the ground. "Step aside, my friend, I would advise it."

The youth erupted in anger, though dawning fear was clear in his face. "Who are you to tell me what to do? Ardhu's nephew but a man disgraced, cast out of the war-band…"

Mordraed's hand shot out, catching him round the throat in a vicious grip. In an instant he was on the ground, helpless and gasping. Mordraed pulled his bow from his shoulder and fitted an arrow to the string, pointed toward the youth's chest. Women screamed inside the dun and old men flurried, too fearful to get involved but craning to see. Mordraed's fellows began to strut up and down in front of the tribefolk, smirking and swinging their axes, daring the people of Kham-El-Ard to come forward.

Mordraed lifted his head, his glance raking over the assembled villagers. "I will tell you and this…" he kicked the fallen guard, "who I really am and why I it is my right to command all within these walls. Listen well, you sheep, you worthless cattle! Ardhu Pendraec is no fit master for you; he is fit only for the grave. Not only have the land and crops failed, showing he is no longer rightful king…he is the breaker of taboos, a dealer in the forbidden. He has lied to you for years, pretending he had favour with the Spirits—but they had no love of him! The White Phantom was barren save for one sickly son, who the Ancestors have now taken. The Spirits cursed Ardhu and rightfully so!"

"How can you speak such treachery?" one elder cried, his voice tremulous. "Your tongue is that of an adder!"

"Is it, old man?" Mordraed's eyes crackled. "Look at me, all of you. What do you see? Am I not in the image of the Stone Lord himself and all his Ancestors before him in Belerion and Dwranon? Do I not look, more than nephew, but more as son? That is because, you fools, I am Ardhu Pendraec's son, born of his own sister, the Lady Morigau. He begot me in forbidden union and deceived you all, while robbing me of honour and birthright!"

A hush fell over the crowd, a horrified silence.

Mordraed's lips tightened to lines. "He has gone on his fool's quest to Ar-morah, leaving his lands yet again. He is no fit leader—may the sky fall on his head and the sea eat his bones! I will take his place here, as is my right by the strength of my arm, ruling over you in high Kham-El-Ard from this day forward."

"You cannot do this unjust deed!" a voice roared. Across the dun hobbled Per-Adur, leaning on a stick for support. Despite the injury that made his gait unstable and his limbs shake, he still managed to clutch a bronze axe in his free hand. "No one will follow you, son of a serpent-woman and witch! If what you say is true, you are cursed by your birth and by your actions."

Mordraed stared at the shambling figure of what had once been a proud warrior. He felt nothing but contempt. Per-Adur would be better off with the Ancestors. His eyes turned hard as diamonds, cold as winter. "Kill him!" he said to Wyzelo, and then, sweeping his gaze over the whole of the inner bailey. "In fact…kill them all. Only keep the White Woman…for me."

Wyzelo and several of his companions lunged forward toward Per-Adur as people shrieked and howled and ran about madly in panic. Drunkenly, Mordraed's followers drew their weapons and chased the villagers, baying for blood like mad dogs. The youth at

Mordraed's feet recovered from the compression on his throat and tried to get a firm grip on his fallen spear. Seeing his arm reach out, Mordraed spat disdainfully on him and shot him through the heart with an arrow.

Wyzelo and his cronies now had hold of Per-Adur. He swung at them with his axe, knee-capping one and sending him rolling in the dirt in agony. Wyzelo kicked his staff from under him, and the injured warrior staggered forward, unbalanced. Mordraed ran over to him, striking him with many blows from his fists, before snatching the older man's streaming hair, worn, as customary, in an upswept style like a horse's mane. It was perfect to grab hold of.

Mordraed forced Per-Adur to his knees, dragging him around so that his face was toward the village…and the terrified people who ran screaming through the huts, falling to dagger, rapier, axe blow and arrow's flight. "Look your last on Kham-El-Ard!" he snarled. "Look your last on the Sun." He dragged Per-Adur's head back, forcing him to stare into the sky at the glowing disc of Bhel Sunface. "Now look at me…your lord, your death." He twisted Per-Adur's head again, until their eyes locked. "I am Mordraed, son of Morigau, son of Ardhu. I am the Dark Moon, and I am vengeful! Fear me and despair."

"I fear neither death nor you," Per-Adur croaked. "You are a deluded fool. By the gods, you will pay dearly for this act." And he spat at Mordraed, the spittle hitting the Moon-scar on his cheek.

Mordraed's dagger flashed in the sunlight. Per-Adur crumpled to the ground in a spreading pool of blood. The yellow mane of his hair turned red.

Mordraed took his dagger and licked it, bringing the essence of the dead man's power into himself, and then wiped the other side of the blade across his cheeks, painting himself with this symbol of victory. So it had begun…what he had been born to do…

Glancing around he saw bodies strewn, men, women, children, dogs, even a pony. His band was running wild throughout the dun, screeching like wild animals and destroying anything in their path, their distorted faces barely human and their arms red to the shoulder with gore. One took a brand from a fire and shoved it into the thatch of a hut; it exploded into flame as the youth shrieked with crazed laughter.

Mordraed cursed. He raised his own dagger and shouted a halt. Reluctantly his band ceased to chase the remaining villagers and came slowly towards him, grinning like the fools they were. "Enough!" Mordraed shouted, fixing them with a hard stare. "Put out that fire, you idiots! We don't want to destroy Kham-El-Ard; it is to be ours, the finest and most powerful settlement in all Prydn."

Wyzelo, Ic'ho and a few others hastened to beat out the flames. The fire died away as the hut collapsed inwards, walls and roof disintegrating. Mordraed gestured to the cowering survivors of the raid, a handful of terrified, ashen-faced women and girls, a dozen wailing young children. "I am merciful; these creatures have survived thus far, so I shall spare them. We need women to cook and mend our garments. You can have them for slaves or bedmates, if you desire any of them."

The youths of the band rushed towards the women, who screamed. Mordraed called his men back again, his voice taut with annoyance. "Later, you dogs. We have work to do! Where is Fynavir…has anyone found the wife of my father, the faithless whore they call White Phantom?"

"Here, Mordraed!" Two youths came forward, dragging Fynavir between them. She showed signs of having fought them and her gown hung in tatters, but she hardly resisted them now; in her thin face her eyes were dead, hopeless. Her cheeks as white as her hair, which hung down knotted and in disarray. She resembled one Moon-mad.

Mordraed stared at her and felt sick; he was to bed that…old, cold as snow, dead as a piece of bone? She…who was Gal'havad's mother? At the thought of the half-brother he had murdered, his sensation of sickness deepened; a cold ripple travelled up his spine, as if somewhere a man had stepped on the ground where his barrow would one day be raised. No, he would not think on it…Gal'havad was meant to die; his death was due to Ardhu's actions; Mordraed was only the agent, the one who struck the blow. The spirits surely had meant for it to end that way or they would have intervened.

Fynavir pulled away from her captors and stepped right up to him so that they were face to face. She was a tall woman, not much smaller than he. He could see her eyes beneath their pale gold lashes, green like Gal'havad's had been, and the lines that showed her age and suffering, marring what once had been a face of great beauty. She showed no fear, no hate, just a dull resignation.

"Why have you done this terrible deed, Mordraed? Why? When Ardhu was so good to you, giving you a place in Kham-El-Ard, letting you befriend his only son? Gods, I wish he had never been so trusting…yes, I know what the warriors whisper about my son's death…and it is only because Ardhu is fair and would not accuse you without proof that you yourself do not lie dead!"

Mordraed's lips quirked up; more of a grimace than a smile. "Lady, I see no one has ever told you the truth…neither the Merlin nor Ardhu Pendraec himself. You say Ardhu is good to me? He has me here on sufferance! Humiliates me! He withholds deserved rank and respect!"

"Why do you think you deserve anything, as son of the woman who hated her brother and continually strove against him?"

"Because I am Ardhu's son!" Mordraed grabbed her roughly by the shoulders and shook her. Fynavir looked genuinely shocked; her hand flew to her mouth and her knees buckled and she fell to the ground.

"Yes, know the truth, woman. Know what you married." Mordraed clutched her wrists and yanked her roughly back onto her feet. "Know also that I will take you in his stead, make you my own woman. You are the White Woman, the Sovereignty of Prydn bound within you, and now you are mine…and the lordship of Prydn with you."

"You are mad! I would sooner slit my own throat that let you lay a hand on me!"

"That I cannot permit." He gestured to two of his men, who stood nearby, grinning. "Take her away and guard her well. Make sure no sharp objects come near her hands." Reaching out, he ran one thumb down the side of Fynavir's long pale neck, trying not to shudder…she felt as cold as the snow she resembled. Cold as a dead body. God, how he hated the thought of bedding her! "You will have a small reprieve to get used to the idea of being my woman…I have other things I must attend to before you, Lady of Kham-El-Ard."

Whirling on his heel, eager to put her from his sight, he motioned to Wyzelo and the rest of his warband. "Take any horses than remain in Ardhu's stables. Bring your weapons. We ride to Deroweth."

Fynavir, caught in the strong arms of her captors, stared at him with dawning horror.

"What are you planning, Mordraed?" she screamed.

White teeth flashed against his dark, handsome face. "I go to get a blessing from the priests, lady. For our marriage."

Mordraed's warriors began to laugh and make obscene jokes. Fynavir was dragged away, struggling furiously, screaming and begging Mordraed not to go to Deroweth.

He shut his ears to the noise and turned to Wyzelo and the others. "We must destroy all the priests, or they will turn their magics on us and kill us all. So show no mercy. You need feel no guilt, no fear of wrathful spirits—the priests have supported my corrupt sire for years, so they too are corrupt and deserve to die like dogs. Burn them out. Cleanse their evil with fire!"

The horses were brought and torches lit and passed out to every man. Mordraed swung up on the back of a black mare, one of Lamrai's foals and a favourite of Ardhu, and took up a brand in his left hand. Rising high in the saddle, like some vengeful young god, he thrust the flame toward the fading sky. "With fire," he cried, "we shall destroy our enemies. Fire…to burn away the darkness, to burn the sins of the world to ash!"

The young acolyte Dru Bluecloak strolled between the stout, rectangular houses of Deroweth, carrying a beaker of mead for his master, the high-priest Gluinval. Behind him trundled two serving woman, hauling a huge cauldron-like pot of boiled meat. The Sun had just set, and a purple cloak of twilight lay over the sacred space and the Plain beyond, furling the stunted head of the Khu Stone, stone of Dogs, that pointed the way to Khor Ghor. Woodenheart was a black blot, its posts rising up like a forest of bare trees, and the causeway to the river shone pale dull silver. Night-loving insects made strange chirping and chuntering noises in the growing dark, while a fox yipped somewhere in a clump of bushes, a noise that sounded eerily human.

Dru Bluecloak cast a jaded glance at the two women struggling along behind him with the great cooking pot. They were spilling broth and scalding each other, and scolding each other too, in some sort of ludicrous rivalry of incompetence. "Come along," he said testily. "The High One will not wait much longer to take his meat and drink!"

Suddenly one of the women gave a cry. She dropped her end of the cooking pot, making her companion stagger forward and almost fall face first into the cauldron. "Oh, look, look both of you! Down by the Abona! The stars…the stars are falling to earth!

"What?" her companion shrieked, still trying to gain her equilibrium. "Where?"

Brow furrowed in annoyance, Dru Bluecloak turned sharply around, ready to lash both women with the sharpness of his tongue for their foolish imaginations. Instead, his tongue cleaved to the roof of his mouth, and his heart began to pound like a solstice drum. He stood transfixed for a moment, unable to move or speak, then released a great and terrible cry. The beaker tumbled from his hands, smashing on the ground.

"Those are not stars! They are torches! Torches born by men on horses! There is no reason why such men should come to Deroweth except for evil…Run, run!"

The first horse came into view, bursting through the night vapours sailing from the river. A warrior with a grinning, painted face sat astride it, torch in one hand, battle-axe clutched in the other. He paused for a moment, surveying the settlement, then hammered his heels into the horse's flanks, driving it forward into the enclosure. Waving his axe, he screamed a war cry, and thrust the torch into the thatching of one of the many huts that clustered around the chalk banks. Flames leaped into the growing shadows.

The acolyte and the two women fled, screaming, the females bounding like hares across the field and into the shadows that furled the Khu Stone. Dru Bluecloak hoisted his robes around his knees and ran toward the High Priest's hut, with the timber trilithon standing proud and tall before its doorway, marking it as a place of high status. Gluinval emerged even as he reached the door, staring in wonder at the younger man's stricken face and breathlessness, his feebly waving arms.

"What is amiss?" he asked urgently. "Why do I hear screams and smell smoke? Have you set the cook-hut on fire?"

Dru Bluecloak's mouth opened and shut; no words would emerge. He shook his head weakly and pointed with a shaking hand into the gloom.

Gluinval let his gaze follow the trembling hand of the acolyte. Brightness was appearing all over Deroweth, the brightness of flames—flames that blossomed in the dark like hot orange flowers. Flames that ate and gnawed at huts with vicious incandescent teeth, twirling up and consuming walls, devouring thatched roofs with a terrifying hunger. In the direction of Woodenheart there was a groan and a crash so loud it sounded as if one of the mighty oak posts had been tipped from its pit. Screaming and shouting followed the sound, and course, drunken laughter.

Grasping his staff, the High Priest strode forward to defend his enclave. Acolytes and other priests could be seen fleeing through the smoke and fire, chased by men on horseback who swung at their skulls with honed axes of bronze. Some priests had robes aflame and screamed like terrible demons of darkness as they burned to death even while in flight.

"Who commits this act of sacrilege?" Gluinval thundered, glancing right and left. He wielded his staff like a weapon, held rigid across his body as a protection. "A curse be upon your head—you shall have no happiness from this hour forth, you shall not prosper in aught that you do. Whatever you touch will wither and die. Your blood will feed the earth in penance for your crimes, no barrow will hold your bones, and your name will be spat upon unto eternity…"

"Save your curses, greybeard." Mordraed rode out of the smoke on his stolen steed, ash on his cheeks and falling from the flowing darkness of his hair. In his lean face his eyes were blue cold stars. "I am cursed already by the circumstances of my birth. I care not for your curses."

The high-priest glanced up, recognising the young man instantly. "You! You are the Stone Lord's nephew!"

"No, priest," sneered Mordraed. "Not his nephew, his son. And soon I will be his bane!"

Mordraed forced his mount forward; it whickered and fought his control, frightened of the growing flames, the screams of the dying all across the settlement. Gluinval swung out with his staff but Mordraed struck out with a huge black basalt war-hammer and shattered it in the middle. Laughing, he herded the priest back towards his hut, through the arch of the wooden trilithon, and into the narrow doorway. Behind him his men rushed in, eager for sport, and he gestured to them to barricade the door from without.

"We have a rat in the trap," he said. "Put it to the torch."

Wyzelo thundered up to the hut and hurled his brand into the thatch; others joined him. Smoke spiralled, and there was a flicker as the thatching caught…and then the roof exploded, showering sparks into the night air. Watching the destruction, the young men roared in approval and dismounting their steeds, they began a war-dance, a victory dance fierce and terrible to behold with the firelight shining on polished weapons, and on glistening, sweating torsos and on the glassy surfaces of drink and blood-crazed eyes.

Behind the hut, hiding in the mud at the bottom of an animal pen, Dru Bluecloak wept in sorrow and terror. "My master, my master," he sobbed, but as he heard the roof cave in, he knew there was no hope of the High Priest's survival. "I will go to Ardhu Pendraec…I will bring him back to take his vengeance and right this wrong!"

Hauling himself over the fence of the pen, he ran for his life out past the Khu Stone and across the Plain, into the Deadlands where he prayed his enemies would not follow.

Mordraed saw a flash of blue heading West, but paid little heed. One lowly servant was of no interest to him. He turned his attention to the wooden trilithon before the High Priest's burning hut, lit luridly by the dancing flames.

"Wyzelo… come help me. We must bring this thing down."

Wyzelo and his fellows crowded around. They hacked at the huge oak posts with their axes, hammering at them in frenzy as if they were hated enemies. Other warriors joined in, scraping at the bases with picks and other implements they had found around the site, trying to undermine the structure. Yet others gathered kindling and stacked it around the bottom of the posts.

When the structure seemed sufficiently weakened, the two posts full of notches and rocking in their beds, Mordraed kindled two torches and thrust them into the pyres that had been built around their feet. The dry tinder caught instantly and flames darted up the sides of

353

the trilithon, fanned by the nightwind blowing from the East. Higher and higher they roared, twisting around the posts in an all-consuming embrace, illuminating the underside of the wooden lintel. The old wood, already dry from untold years of exposure, crackled and began to glow as the flames burnt through the surface towards the core.

Up and up the conflagration rose, eating, consuming. Ashes started to fall through the showering sparks, and for a brief instant the entire shape of the trilithon was lit up, a stunning red-hot beacon against the starry sky. Then, with an unearthly groan, one leg of the structure slumped forward. The whole structure wavered back and forth, back and forth in unearthly motion.

"Get back!" shouted Mordraed, gesturing wildly to his celebrating warriors. "It's coming down."

The youths scattered in all directions, as the burning wooden trilithon seemed to dance in its pit. Wood crackled and snapped, and in a blazing flash of flame the whole structure collapsed, one post completely fallen, the other tilting at a disjointed angle. The blazing lintel was cast into the darkness, where it continued to burn.

Mordraed raised his axe to the sky in victory. "The priesthood of Deroweth is cast down! Next we will bring our vengeance to Khor Ghor. A Moon will rise there to replace the failing Sun. But not tonight!" He motioned for his men to take to their horses once more. "It is still an unsafe place in the dark, and I have more pressing matters. We ride to collect my mother, the esteemed Queen Morigau of Ynys Yrch, and take her in triumph to Kham-El-Ard."

Morigau and Khyloq squatted amid the rushes in Ardhu's Great Hall gleefully rummaging through Fynavir's personal possessions. Morigau had appropriated her golden shoulder-cape, ripping away the aged fabric and replacing it with weavings in her own colours. Khyloq was fingering a huge crescent-shaped jet necklace with shale spacer beads, holding it up to her throat and admiring her reflection in the blade of a ceremonial dagger.

Several feet away Mordraed sprawled across Ardhu's throne of antler tines, a beaker of mead clutched in his hand. He had washed the ash and blood from his face and was dressed simply in a close-fitting deerskin tunic and leggings, but on his head he wore a circlet given him by Morigau, wrought of two strands of gold from the rivers of her birthplace, Belerion, beaten into fine sheets and fastened by rivets. She had hidden it amongst her possessions for years, waiting for this day.

"Tonight you will bed the White Woman," Morigau said cheerfully, trying on coiled armlets and bronze finger rings, "so you will be wedded to the Land in the eyes of the people. You have sent men to Place-of-Light to tell them that you have taken Ardhu's throne?"

"Yes." Mordraed's voice was curt. "I have sent guards to make sure none of the villagers there try to take up arms or send messengers to Ardhu while he is in Ar-morah. The more time he is gone, the more resistance I can devise against him."

Morigau rose and went to her son. She kissed him on the cheek, twining her fingers in the long black silk of his hair. "Don't look so sullen, my beautiful child. We are attaining all that we have ever desired."

He gave her an inscrutable look. "Did you ever ask what it was I desired?"

She seemed surprised. "Surely this is it…"

He waved her away as the doors opened and one of the men came in leading two young boys—Gharith and Ga'haris. Although they were being brought to greet their own mother and brother, they looked terrified and clutched each other's hands as they were herded down the hall.

Morigau frowned to see them; she had almost forgotten they were in Kham-El-Ard. "The brats," she hissed under her breath.

The children were brought before Mordraed's seat. He leaned forward, placing his hands upon their shoulders with surprising gentleness. "Don't be afraid," he said, "I won't hurt you. Indeed, now that I am master of Kham-El-Ard, it will go better for you. I will make sure you rise in position, and have many heads of cattle and as many lands as I can spare. I only ask that when you are grown you do not raise hand against me, but serve me well. Will you, my small brothers?"

Looking from one to the other, the boys both nodded gravely. They did not understand what was going on…but they trusted Mordraed. Their older brother had always watched out for them, even while Morigau ignored them.

"Then go and sleep well, and do not fear. Any that wish you harm, will have me to contend with."

The children bowed and were led back out of the Hall. Morigau glanced at Mordraed with a raised eyebrow. "They were terrified," he said testily. "I wanted them to know their lives and futures are safe with me."

Morigau's lip curled. "Mordraed, you must learn to be harder. If I were you I would have them drowned in the Sacred Pool like unwanted puppies! They have seen your actions today, what you have taken solely with the strength of your arm…What makes you think in a few years they will not do to you what you did to Ardhu? I counsel you to have them put to death"

His eyes were ice, and furious. "You unnatural bitch. You are their mother. Do not ever speak of such a thing to me again." He leaned forward, a vicious smile twisting his lips. "I have followed your orders long enough anyway. Now I have something I want from you…"

She frowned, twisting a coil of her hair with sudden nervousness. "And what is that?"

He nodded toward the end of the hall where Morigau's long-time companions, La'morak and Ack-olon, stood in the light of the flickering tallow-lamps, haggard-faced and out-of-place amidst the raucous youths of Mordraed's warband, who played games with coloured pebbles, drank copious amounts of beer and wrestled with each other in the rushes. "Those two….your 'attendants.'"

"What of them?"

"I have always hated them. I want them dead."

Morigau straightened abruptly, high colour flaring into her cheeks. "They have served me since before you were born!"

Mordraed cast her a sharp glance. "I know how they have 'served' you! Listen, I have done your bidding in all things so far, even when I did not agree. I am not yours to move as you will, like the game-pieces my men play with. I am now your lord, mother, even if you are priestess here. Do what I command you!"

She looked furious, as if she would explode. But there was also resignation in her face; she knew Mordraed would not be moved. "Do what you will," she spat. "I can find other younger servants who interest me more anyway. Just do not expect me to watch the execution! Now I will go prepare for your union with the White Woman—I am sure you are looking forward to that."

Lips curved into a rigid sneer, she stormed from the Great Hall, striding straight past Ack-olon and La'morak without giving them even a glance. The two men moved to follow their mistress but Mordraed leapt up from his high seat, casting his beaker to the ground and drawing his dagger. "Halt, you!" he shouted down the hall. "Do not move!"

Ack-olon and La'morak stared at him and then at each other in growing fear and confusion. The young men of the warband ceased their gambling and brawling and set down their beakers. All eyes turned expectantly on to Mordraed. Tension grew in the room; the air crackled with it.

Smiling cruelly he glided down the hall, hair of shadow, eyes blue death, gold fire on his brow. His lips smiled but it was not a smile one wanted to see. He nodded to the warriors nearest to the two older men, who were already loosening the daggers at their belts.

"Kill them," he said softly.

Mordraed stalked toward the hut where Fynavir was imprisoned, guarded by several warriors in case she attempted to escape. As he neared the entrance he saw that it had been decked out for the marriage-rite, the high doorframe twined with flowers and greenery. Bowls of milk to please passing spirits and encourage fertility were laid out before the door. Not much chance of that, he thought sourly, his stomach suddenly churning. She is a barren stalk…

Morigau appeared, as if from nowhere, wearing a wreath of hawthorn and cloak dyed red with madder. In silence, she laid down chalk balls and phalli before the threshold while Mordraed watched. He noted that her eyes were red-rimmed …had she wept for Ack-olon and La'morak, whose heads now adorned the gates of Kham-El-Ard? He hoped so with all his being; it was time she felt some of the suffering that he had felt at Gal'havad's death.

Coming over to him, she took his hands and daubed them with life-affirming ochre, whispering spells to make him potent and Fynavir fertile…although she was nowhere to be seen, the unwilling bride held captive inside the hut. Mordraed resisted the urged to heave as Morigau finished her ministrations. He had never felt less like lying with a woman; in fact, it was as if someone had tossed freezing river water over his loins.

"Mother," he whispered thickly. "I do not want to go through with this."

She cast him an evil look. "You must…even if only once. To make the marriage with the Land."

He gritted his teeth. "I do not think I can."

A mocking laugh left her lips. "Oh, so that is the problem. Fear not… I can brew you a potion that will make you like a bull with a herd of cows."

"No! I have had enough of your potions."

"Then let your anger fuel your lust, my son." She leaned against him, hand to his face, her nails caressing the scar she had placed on his cheek. "Think of all the injustices Ardhu has done to you and your people. Think of how this will be the ultimate vengeance against him! Think of this, and take his White Woman; fill her with your fury and make her scream for your mercy!"

Mordraed tore away from his mother in disgust and pushed his way into the hut. Inside were the guards and a gaggle of women who had been preparing the marriage-chamber for his arrival. Fynavir lay naked and motionless on a pallet of furs; she had been washed and painted with the customary designs. She almost looked dead; there was no resistance in her, her eyes closed and her legs drawn up in foetal position.

Mordraed gestured to the grinning men and the frightened, pale-cheeked women. "Get out."

They hurried from the hut, leaving him alone with his father's wife. He flung off his cloak, pulled off his leather tunic and trousers, and knelt on the pallet, staring down at her, his breathing slow and heavy. So beautiful once, he knew…but ruined now. He let his hands slide across her ribcage and hollow belly, feeling her shudder with revulsion at his touch. He tried to conjure up the anger that would bring the lust Morigau had spoken of, but he felt nothing except a vague sense of sickness. And guilt. This was Gal'havad's mother, and he had killed her son. Now he planned to destroy her further by dishonouring her.

He suddenly felt exhausted, his head heavy as a stone. He just wanted to lie in the dark, alone.

He must have made a small noise, a soft groan, for suddenly Fynavir opened her eyes and glanced up at him. Again, he was shocked by her eyes; green like Gal'havad's, bringing with them bitter memory...He recoiled, staggering back and falling onto the floor near the fire-pit.

"Are you ill?" her voice was heavy, dull. "I thought you had come to rape me, you, the strong conqueror who takes all!"

Anger rose in him and he leapt back onto the pallet, throwing his body over hers and pressing her down into the furs. "How dare you speak so to me?"

"If I displease you, kill me." She sounded as weary as he felt. "I would prefer it."

"I don't want to kill you. And, truth be known, I don't want to bed you either."

She stared up at him. "I...I don't understand..."

He shook his head. "I do not want you to understand. I just want..." He picked up his discarded cloak and flung it at her. "I want you to leave. To go from Kham-El-Ard. Now. This night. The men are getting drunk; they will not notice, not if you go to the back route, the escape route that leads down from the rear of the fort to the Abona. Behind the goat pens. Can you manage it in the dark?"

"I...I, yes...I can."

"Then go."

She wriggled out from under him, dressing quickly in her discarded robes and wrapping the cloak he had given her around her shoulders. Going to the doorway, she glanced back at him, sitting on the furs, his shoulders slumped, a figure of gold and shadow in the fluttering, failing light of the tallow lamps.

"Why have you decided to free me?" she asked once more, softly.

He raised his head and his eyes met hers. Cold, dark blue eyes beneath lashes long and black that a girl would have been proud of. But there was something new in that sharp, uncompromising gaze, something she had not seen in Mordraed before tonight. It horrified her, because she guessed its meaning.

She gasped and staggered, clutching the doorframe for support. "You are freeing me because you feel guilty! It is in your eyes, your face! So it is true what men whisper...you killed my son! You are suffering torment for his death!"

The solemn mask of Mordraed's face shattered, twisting as if she had drawn a blade and stabbed him. "Just go, get out!" he rasped. "Before I change my mind!"

She fled, and Mordraed curled up on the floor, his arms flung over his head, crying out in rage at the gods who had afflicted him with this madness.

CHAPTER EIGHTEEN—THE FOREST OF BRO-KHELIAN

The Forest of Bro-khelian gleamed golden in the late afternoon sun. A magical place it seemed, the leaves of the deciduous trees light-spangled, the scent of greenery and running water permeating the air. Ardhu walked silently along its mossy paths, past dolmen capstones long fallen and hidden by foliage, through tangled briar-thickets where blossoms masked sharp thorns, and over streamlets where mists coiled like shy water-spirits, touching his legs as he passed. His men waited at the forest's edge as promised and to leave them made him uneasy, but so far he had seen nothing of danger in the confines of the wood.

By the time the light had just started to fade, he reached a spring, which bubbled up out of the ground and filled a basin half-natural and half-wrought by human hands, its bottom lined with water-rolled quartz pebbles. Kneeling, he laved his face and took a deep refreshing draught. The day had been hot—the climate in Ar-morah was warmer than that of Prydn—and he was growing weary of the long walk.

As he knelt on the lip of the basin, the cool spray descending on skin and hair, he suddenly caught sight of a reflection in the crystalline water behind his left shoulder. A wavering image of a face...a face he knew, a face he had once loved... Leaping up, his hand went to the hilt of Carnwennan and he dropped into a crouch.

An'kelet of the Lake, prince of Ar-morah and son of a priestess and a sacrificed king, stood on the edge of the clearing where the spring flowed, watching his former friend with sombre eyes.

Ardhu felt a slight stab of envy, just as he had when he first met An'kelet in Prydn when they were both young, himself little more than a boy. Despite the hardships of the years and the wound Ardhu had given him on their last meeting, An'kelet looked hale and hearty, his youth and vigour restored now that he was back in the land of his birth. Indeed, caught in the rose-glow of the dying sun, he almost seemed a god, his amber hair flowing from beneath a pin of polished bone; jadeite pendants around his neck; gold upon his arms and at his belt and upon his brow. He wore leather calfskin breeches and a fringed jerkin that was open to the waist; Ardhu suspected this choice was deliberate, for it showed the jagged white line of the scar from the injury he had dealt him with Caladvolc.

"Ardhu..." An'kelet stepped forward, unarmed, although Ardhu could see gold-hilted Ar-moran daggers at his waist. "So you have come chasing me. I suppose I should have expected it. Eventually it had to become known that you did not kill me."

"It became known, that is true," snarled Ardhu. "Along with the evil that you wrought upon the one that helped you escape my justice."

An'kelet's expression changed to puzzlement. "I know not of what you speak."

"Have you forgotten so soon? Ah well, your ignorance proves your baseness. I am here to finish what should have been done in Prydn...by the Ancestors I will feed your blood to the earth for all that you have done." Drawing Carnwennan, he flung himself with wild abandon at An'kelet. His sudden burst of rage clouded his aim, and An'kelet carefully sidestepped his headlong rush, and he went crashing into the foliage.

"Must it come to this, our troubles brought even to the green glades of Bro-khelian?" said An'kelet sadly.

"Yes, it must! Have you forgotten what has gone before? You escaped justice and wreaked more evil before your departure..." Ardhu crawled from the greenery, ripping vines and fronds away from his face. "Don't you remember?" he flung at his former friend with venom. "You begged me to kill you. I was the fool and did not smite off your head with Caladvolc. Now I will claim it, as I should have done back in Prydn."

An'kelet raised his hands; he still had not drawn blade. "I was ready to die for my sins at Kham-El-Ard...but the spirits spared me. None have survived the blade of Caladvolc save I. Does that not tell you, Ardhu, my old friend, that the Ancestors have some plan for me? I do not think we have come to the end of our tale as yet."

"You have come to the end of yours!" Ardhu spat, and he charged madly at his former friend once again. He halted, skidding on moss, as An'kelet folded his arms. "Draw blade, damn you. Do not make me kill you with dishonour."

"I will not draw weapon on you; you are still my lord. And despite all that has gone awry, I still think of you as my friend, my brother in heart if not in blood."

Ardhu stood spitting with rage, his face suffused with colour. "Curse you...curse you! If you will not draw weapons, fight me without! Fight me!"

An'kelet undid his belt and flung it aside with his golden-hilted daggers attached. "This I will do, though with a heavy heart."

The two chieftains lunged at each other, grappling. An'kelet was taller and in youth had been the stronger, but his belly-wound, though well-healed, was still tender and blood-loss had sapped his former strength. Ardhu, on the other hand, was fuelled by his anger, his grief, his loss, and his strength flourished until he was an even match to the man who once had been known as the most powerful warrior of the western world.

Grunting, they fell and rolled on the moss, rose again, struck out with fists and feet. Ardhu managed to hurl An'kelet against a tree, and An'kelet, recovering almost instantly, retaliated and flung Ardhu straight over his head, sending him crashing into the waters of the fountain.

Soaked to the skin, an oath on his lips, Ardhu sprang back up and attacked An'kelet with renewed fury, seeking to fling himself on his back and get his hands round his throat, to twist his head backwards and break the spinal column. But An'kelet guessed his intention and tucked his chin low, and grabbing Ardhu's legs by the calves he heaved him up high, throwing him into a nearby bramble bush.

And so it went on for many an hour, with neither man gaining the advantage. The glade and the waters near the fountain were trampled to mud, the bushes were rent and branches of the trees snapped. The daylight died in the West and the forest turned the hue of blood. An'kelet and Ardhu drew apart, seeking a moment's respite to regain their strength, and stood staring at each other across the waters of the spring. Both were muddy from head to toe, bruises blooming like dark flowers on their flesh, blood on cut mouths and on their battered hands.

"Do we go on?" said An'kelet softly. "Does this not show that we are equal before the spirits? Would it not be better if we put our strengths together and fought as one instead of fighting each other?"

"Have you forgotten? You dishonoured my marriage bed! You had my woman!"

"I know, Ardhu...it is the shame of my life... But, listen...I tell you, I did not take Fynavir to dishonour you or without thought or guilt for my action. Nor did she betray you lightly. It was as if—do not be angry at my words—we were fated to come together. It was as if the spirits and gods had decreed it so, and we could no more deny it than we could stop the rising of Bhel."

Ardhu hunkered down, suddenly weary. He did not want to hear these words yet somehow knew he needed to. And to accept them. That was what tormented him the most; that Fynavir had wed him and he had been too blind to see that her heart was with another. Secretly, it had made him doubt his own kingship; the people thought the White Woman was the Land, the spirit of the chalk personified...and the man she bedded the rightful master over all. An'kelet had been her true choice of mate...Ardhu had been endured and no more, and had been too deluded and sure of his own claims to see it. Was he just a tool of the Merlin as many of his enemies had claimed? Maybe An'kelet should have sat in Kham-El-Ard, the greatest warrior of all with his great barbed spear, the Balugaisa, and the White Phantom at his side...

Across the glade, An'kelet was washing his bloody, swollen hands in the spring. The dying light turned his curling hair red, red as Gal'havad's. Ardhu felt his throat tighten. No...he could not allow himself doubt or grief at this moment, when he must steel himself against all weakness and summon his last vestiges of strength, and end this rivalry for once and for all. Hopefully, if the Ancestors willed, with his one-time friend dead at his feet.

"I was greatly grieved to hear of Gal'havad," An'kelet said suddenly. "News of his death reached me here; all the traders on the coasts were abuzz with it. I went to the great stepped-cairn on the headland and stared across the sea that sunders us and wept for him. I imagined—it may have only been in dream—that I could see the beacons burning on Prydn's far shore all through the night."

"Fires burned on every hill." Ardhu's voice cracked. "The banks of Abona blazed with great pyres; the waters themselves looked to be aflame. No man has been so mourned in Prydn as Gal'havad, the Prince of Twilight. And now I am lost, my strength failing...and I have no heir."

Both men fell silent, staring at each other over the darkening water.

"I would throw in my lot with you again, Ardhu," said An'kelet softly. "If you can forgive me my sins against you. I cannot replace him...but I can fill one space at your side and firm your hand if it wavers."

"And the girl? What of the girl?"

"Girl?" An'kelet frowned in perplexity. "You speak in riddles, Ardhu! I know of no girl."

"Elian...the Lily-Maid. She died through your dishonouring of her, and her father begs for retribution. He brought her body to Kham-El-Ard and many of my men cried for your death when they heard she came to grief by your hand. And so I came here, to finish it...and you."

An'kelet passed his mud-splotched hand across his brow. "Elian! This is evil news you bring! She was a sweet and trusting girl. I behaved shamefully with her, that is true; my mind was not right, so ill and grieved was I, but I never wished her ill. I cannot bring her back, for no mortal can tread beyond the Great Plain and return a living man...but I will send restitution to her father, as poor a thing as that might be."

Ardhu was silent. The anger and the pain inside him was a tight knot. And yet, he wanted to trust in An'kelet's words, wanted things to be between them as they were of old. But, with Gal'havad dead, and Fynavir a creature in perennial mourning, a withered white flower that knew no spring, surely that could never be again.

Or perhaps there was a way...a sacrifice of pride, an acceptance of what was once unacceptable.

"An'kelet..." his words came in ragged pants. He did not know where they came from or how he managed to speak them. "I want you to ride with me again. I have never lied and will not lie now. If you return with me to Prydn and stand by me in all things and help me restore the Land to what it should be, I will not only forgive your sins against me but reward you above all men. Above anyone. I will take you and Fynavir before the priests at Deroweth and I will give her to you. If she is spirit-of-Earth, it was you she chose, not me, no matter how I wished otherwise...who am I to force her to remain at my side? I should praise her for her sense of duty! And you...if the White Woman has chosen you, and remained loyal throughout all these long years, then why should you not, as the greatest warrior in the Western World, be king of Prydn after me? In older times a King could choose his own successor; it need not be the heir of his body."

An'kelet stared at Ardhu in shock. "You would do that…even though many men would speak ill of you for it and even laugh behind their hands?"

"I care nothing for the laughter of fools," Ardhu said angrily. "For the first time in months it seems darkness is lifting from my eyes, and I see clearly what must be done. An'kelet, will you return with me? Will you be the heir to Kham-El-Ard should I fall to my enemy's daggers or to evil magic?"

An'kelet strode forward, through the spring and he grabbed Ardhu's hands in his own and went down on his knees in the mud and water. "Oh my friend," he said, and his cheeks were wet. "I had only hoped you would accept me at your side again. Yes, I will return to Prydn with you. And yes, I will be your heir if that is your wish…although you will live many years yet!"

Ardhu laid his hand upon the mane of waving amber hair. He felt strangely at peace. "I have missed your company, An'kelet," he said. "Can we not now go from this place of fruitless battle, and eat and feast as we did in the days of our youth?"

An'kelet leapt up, eyes warm honey-amber. "We can and we shall. I will take you to the settlement of my kin, and have your warband sent for, and we will dine on suckling pigs and fish of the sea. I look forward to seeing old familiar faces again…Hwalchmai, Bohrs, Betu'or, and hearing the tales they have to tell."

CHAPTER NINETEEN-DESECRATION

The Sun bled between the bruise-dark clouds tiered over the edges of Moy Mor, the Great Plain. Heat mingled with the promise of thunder and later rain. Heat waves shimmered above the soil; the first real heat in the long damp summer that had spoiled crops all across Prydn.

In the heart of Khor Ghor Mordraed stood staring at the sky. The Sun was coming out...surely that was a good omen for his reign? And yet, the sky behind was dark as if Tar-ahn the Thunderer was angry, and Bhel's Eye was a burning red slit, an evil eye watching him with scorn...

Shuddering he turned from the stormy sky to the activities taking place within the great circle. Morigau was there, dressed in the robes of a priestess, her face painted with Moons. Child crania clacked round her neck on a thong and her belt was full of fingerbones reddened with ochre. She had taken magic draughts and her eyes were wild and crazed; she swayed from side to side, staff in hand, mumbling gibberish then suddenly becoming lucid, shouting out to proclaim her son as rightful lord of all Prydn—Mordraed, the Dark Moon, who had wrest power from the waning son of Bhel and who would bring back the Old Ways of the Land, before the Tin-men came. The days when Moon with her skull-face was Mother of all, and even the mighty Sun was in her cold shadow.

She raised her arms, her tattered raven-feather cloak, patched many times, streaming out around her. "Hark now!" she howled like a mad woman. "Mordraed of Ynys Yrch has won the right of kingship in the Five Cantrevs. He will restore us to the glory we once knew. We will bring down the Stones of this tainted place, this haven for fools, this place where the true powers were forgotten and false ones venerated!"

Behind Morigau, Mordraed's men worked steadily, raising a great wooden cage around one stone of the Great Trilithon, the southern one nearest to the Throne of Kings with its axe and dagger carvings. Others were digging with antlers picks at the base, sweating profusely in the heat and white with chalk dust. Yet others were dragging bundles of kindling and pitch-lined buckets full of river water. They worked steadily, occasionally glancing up to listen to Morigau's proclamations, but many looked uneasy as if they hated and feared what they had been commanded to do.

Mordraed stalked back and forth between the bluestones. The red sun, glancing off his golden circlet, made the metal hot and his head pound like a drum. "Mother, the men look unhappy," he whispered testily in Morigau's ear. "It is not their wish to slight this place. What can I do? If they turn from me now, I have failed."

"Promise them the world." Her dark eyes gleamed. "They are stupid oafs, without the high ideals so beloved of my brother. You will not even have to keep your word, just throw them a few scraps and kill any who complain." She gave him a mocking glance. "You will have to work a bit harder to keep them, my son. I cannot believe you let the White Phantom slip away so easily when she was such a important symbol to the people."

Mordraed bridled; averting his head so she could not see the truth within his eyes. "She spent the hour in my bed; that was time enough for the deed to be done. Why endure her whey face beyond that? I would have to watch my back at every turn!"

Turning from Morigau, he stepped toward the working men, inspecting the woodwork circling the massive southern stone of the Door into Winter. "This is good," he said loudly. "You will all be blessed by Mother Moon and the Ancestors. Tonight we will all feast—you may bring all your families, and you will have the best of the pigs—Champions' Portions, for that is what you are: champions of Prydn, cleansing the old, evil ways to make way for the new. Gold I will give you, and amber for your women, and you may divide amongst you the weapons, cattle, sheep and women left by the men of the unclean and unworthy Ardhu Pendraec, whom the gods once favoured, but now is fallen in glory. The unnatural man who has left you in time of need to go to Ar-morah on a fool's quest!"

Leaning over, he inspected the crater that widened at the foot of the stone. The upright rose many feet above his head, casting a black shadow over him, its stone foot held in place only by the remains of ancient packing and the wooden supports constructed to stabilise it while the underminers worked.

It was time.

Backing away from the stone, its grey face a stern warning, he gestured to Wyzelo, who was directing the men in the slighting. "Let us begin," he said. "Light the fires."

Flushed with excitement, Wyzelo flung the dry kindling into the pit and lit it. Flames crackled and licked around the edge of the pit and the half-buried base of the stone. More kindling was dumped on and the flames sprang higher, blackening the face of the monolith. Earth began to give way, and the huge sarsen swayed dangerously, the wooden cage around it groaning as over forty tons of rock strained against it.

Morigau began to shriek and wail, dancing in circles and chanting, her eyes rolled back in her head as if she had gone mad. Spittle shone on her mouth, trailed down her chin. She writhed sinuously around the bluestones, a serpent-woman spitting out words of hatred and venom. "The Dark Moon is risen, beloved of old Moon Mother who was here before the Sun himself!" she cried, pointing with a clawed hand to the ghost of a Moon between the brooding tiers of cumulous. "The old ways will return with the rule of my son, Mordraed the Dark Moon! My brother has made you not-men, giving gifts only to his favourites. You will all live as men were meant to—making war, gaining cattle, earning glory. And Mordraed shall be your ruler, cruel and yet benevolent to those who follow his path."

The youths roared, calling out Mordraed's name in proclamation. They started to dance, weaving in and out of the Stones, striking them with hands, with axes, driving themselves into frenzy, all their frustrations and hatreds blazing out in this act of ultimate desecration. Mordraed stood near the base of the unstable stone, watching his men, sweat pouring down his forehead as the fire flared. He ripped off his smouldering jerkin and stood naked to the waist in the blistering heat, ash smearing face and body, his hair lifting and crackling in the updraft. "Today the first stone of Khor Ghor falls!" he cried. "Today the Dark Moon rises over Kham-El-Ard and my sire's evil reign is ended forever!"

He glanced up at the encased stone of the Great Trilithon. The wooden struts were beginning to ignite; flames licked the lowest rungs with harsh red tongues. "Get behind it!" he shouted to his men, waving his arms, his motions almost as frenzied as Morigau's. Fear and excitement shot through him like a spear. "Push it…push it into the pit!"

The youths ceased their victory-dance and rushed up to the great standing stone, some eager to bring it down, others more reticent. Not all in Mordraed's band believed the desecration of the temple was wise; they thought of eyeless skulls deep underground and fleshless mouths of Ancestors in rictus-screams of rage. Others, more practical than superstitious, thought on what might happen if the stone fell awkwardly, crushing or trapping them beneath its bulk. No man could survive being struck by such a weight.

Mordraed gestured again, a downwards motion with his arm. The young men pushed, trying to tip the mighty stone that had stood framing the south-western sky for over five hundred years. At first little happened. The flames licked higher, shooting up the front of the menhir, burning the wooden scaffolding away utterly and sending clouds of rank smoke and burning ash billowing high into the air.

With the wooden support completely engulfed in flame, the stone began to slowly lurch forward, straining towards the huge pit that had been dug at its foot. The intense fire that burned in the crater roared up to meet it, funnelling round it as the wind blew, and sending the men behind running for safety. One or two howled, burnt by the searing updraft, and ran out of the Circle onto the Great Plain where they fell into the long grasses, writhing in agony.

And then the earth began to buckle. A strange shriek filled the air, as if the stone itself was crying out, the spirits locked within its heart wailing in rage and despair, and with deadly speed it plunged forward into the fire-pit blazing at its foot. The huge stone bulb at its base pulled up from the ground as it descended, showering chalk and packing material, and sending men flying across the Circle as if they were no heavier than feathers.

Mordraed leapt back as the megalith came down, roaring like a giant creature that had taken on a life of its own. It struck the Stone of Adoration, ripping it from its socket and beating it into the earth with its enormous weight, then cracked through the middle as it rocked back and forth over the sandstone block that had been the heart of Khor Ghor. Instantaneously the giant lintel that spanned the top of the trilithon was thrown violently through the smoke-filled air and landed near the Guardian's Gate with a noise like a thunder-clap, leaving the remaining half of the Door into Winter standing alone with its naked tenon thrust like a dagger at the storm-laden sky.

"It is done!" screamed Morigau. She was half-white with chalk dust, half-black with ash. Her eyes were wild, ecstatic. "The Moon has smiled on us and felled the Sun!"

Mordraed approached the fallen stone. Fire was still licking it from the pit below, but the flames were beginning to go out, smothered by its fallen bulk. He should have been pleased; he had always hated this place of Stone Ancestors, of memories. But he felt strangely empty and afraid...the remaining Stones seemed to cluster about, the bluestones huddled like conspirators, a wall to hold him in. To pinion him, while punishment was meted out to him for all his evil deeds...

Overhead the ominous sky grumbled.

A storm was coming!

Moments later, the sky roared again, shouting the agony of the desecrated Stones, the angry Ancestors. Huge forks of lightning pierced the ebony clouds, spearing down amidst the barrows of the Seven Kings on their rise. Sulphurous smells filled the air; hair stood on end with static charge. Another boom sounded, the drum of a waking god, followed by the piercing crack of a thunderbolt. The sky turned a sickly yellow and suddenly the circle was filled with eerie ball-lightning, spinning and bouncing from stone to stone like a living entity, lighting up frowning faces and carvings from the days of old.

Mordraed's men screamed at the sight of the unnatural balls of light and they fled the ruined inner sanctum and cowered within the ditch. Even Morigau, her sanity returning, yelped in fear and ran from the circle dragging Mordraed behind her as torrential rain began to lash down.

"What have we done?" Mordraed gasped, huddled in the ditch beside his mother, rainwater streaming down his face, his bare chest. He shivered wildly although even with the storm it was not cold. "This is a sign! It is not good, not good at all." He held his head in his hands, his heavy, aching head that seemed to pound every waking hour and sometimes even woke him from sleep.

Morigau recovered her composure and sneered at him. "Don't be a fool. The storm-god Tar-ahn smites the Stones even as you did! He joins you in their destruction. Men will come to see this as a sign of his approval, even if they are frightened now. Men, especially the mindless dolts of your warband, are fearful of change, fearful of anything beyond their customary rutting and fighting. But they will adapt. Now, come...we must hasten to Kham-El-Ard and shower them all with food and riches! You must get out before the tribes and show yourself to be the most generous lord that ever walked beneath the Everlasting Sky!"

Drums boomed within the high ramparts of Kham-El-Ard. Men danced and drank, chased the unwilling women who were the wives and daughters of those who had gone to Ar-morah with Ardhu. Gold was distributed, animals slaughtered and eaten, clothing divvied up, and weaponry and jewellery fought over. Drink-fuelled youths grew angry and tussled with their fellows; split eyebrows and bloody noses abounded and threats and curses rang out.

Mordraed watched for a while, face pinched with distaste. How he hated these quarrelsome and greedy fools! He could never trust them; one foot wrong and they would tear him to pieces…

He shuddered and walked away to the Great Hall, Khyloq trailing behind him like some lost sheep. She was wearing so much pilfered amber and jet jewellery he though her neck might bend and snap. It sickened him.

Without a word, he took off his dagger belt and cloak, flung himself onto his pallet and yanked a skin over him. Khyloq crawled under the fur, trying to rub seductively against her husband. He felt her growing belly press against the small of his back and to his horror, felt the thing inside her stir, just a little...

Cold terror ran through him; icy sweat broke out on his forehead despite the warmth of the night. This was a magic he did not understand—woman's magic. What if it, this unborn brat, was planning evil even when in the womb, eager to come forth so that it could steal all he had striven for…just as he had taken all that his father Ardhu Pendraec had attained?

Jerkily he tore himself out of Khyloq's embrace and stood up. He hoped she could not see in the smoky darkness that he trembled from head to foot.

"What is wrong?" she asked. "Come lie with me…you have paid me little attention of late."

"Nor shall I, if you continue to whine," he snapped. "Go to sleep. I need time…alone. I will return to you later."

He picked up his discarded belt, fastening it tight about his waist and strode back out of the Hall, feeling stupid and angry at the same time. Outside in the dun the fire-pits were starting to gutter, and inebriated men sprawled about, their drinking-vessels strewn around them. From the clustered huts came continual waves of irritating and disturbing noise; harsh laughter, a barking dog, a woman's screams.

Mordraed glanced towards the gate. A single guard stood there, leaning against a huge post, but he was obviously drunk, his head lolling onto his chest.

Anger flared inside Mordraed…at himself as much as anyone. What was he thinking to let these fools go mad like this? Ardhu was in Ar-morah…but he would be coming back, unless An'kelet killed him in battle. He would be back! And even with his smaller forces, Ardhu would swiftly overwhelm these undisciplined idiots unless Mordraed established some kind of order…and swiftly. He had to find Wyzelo, the most receptive of that unruly bunch, and get him to try to drag his fellows from their mead and women and ready them for the conflict that was almost certain to come.

Approaching the fine, large roundhouse he had bestowed on Wyzelo, he heard a lot of groaning and panting coming through the open doorway. He's got some slut in there…Mordraed thought with a grimace, as he stepped over the threshold.

On the sleeping pallet he could see two figures writhing on a nest of skins, clawing at each other's flesh like beasts. The white moons of Wyzelo's fat, moving buttocks were an unwelcome sight to Mordraed's eyes.

And then it all got worse. As Mordraed took another step into the hut he could clearly see the female entangled with his prime warrior, her hair spread out across the skins like coiling snakes and her head arched back, her lean brown body slippery with sweat, her mouth drawn back in a taut grin that was almost deathly.

It was Morigau.

She had not seen Mordraed. She pulled Wyzelo down on top of her, curling her legs around his back. He groaned and rolled heavily onto her, while she laughed as if she had won some huge prize by taking him to her bed.

Mordraed stood and stared in shocked silence, unbelieving. He knew she had many lovers over the years, but other than Ack-olon and La'morak she had never mentioned names and he did not ask. But now, she was here, playing the slut with his warrior, his most trusted man, who was young enough to be her son, manipulating him and binding him to her will, just as she had done with Mordraed from childhood onwards…

He must have made a sound because Morigau's expression rapidly changed. She glanced over and saw him standing in the doorway, eyes feral, too bright in the taut white mask of his face, his breathing suddenly erratic, strangled. "Mordraed, why are you looking so stricken?" she taunted. "You killed my companions of many years…Did you think I would live alone forever more like some dried-up crone? I found new flesh…as I warned you I would." She ran her nails down Wyzelo's broad back, laughing. Wyzelo jerked uncomfortably, all desire gone with a wave of embarrassment; still locked in her embrace, he looked both afraid and confused.

Mordraed felt his hands knot into fists. Strange rushes of hot and cold flashed through his head, his heart; he wondered if the spirits, the angry spirits from desecrated Khor Ghor, were coming to punish him. "You are a foul, wanton creature," he snarled, his voice thick; it felt as if his tongue would not move correctly to form words. "I think it is true what men say; your mind is possessed by evil spirits."

"You sound like your father, your oh so righteous father, Ardhu Pendraec. And who are you to judge me? It is obvious to any with eyes that you loved that dead half-man, Gal'havad…a man and your own half-brother! If I am foul, you have wallowed in the filth with me." Morigau's eyes were blazing, mad, with too much white showing; her lips were drawn back almost in an animalistic snarl showing pointed white teeth.

Looking at the twisted countenance of his mother, something snapped in Mordraed's skull. The pounding in his head that had assailed him for days suddenly became a violent hammering. He said not a word but lunged towards the pallet where Wyzelo and Morigau lay, still entwined.

Wyzelo reacted first, trying to disentangle himself from both furs and Morigau. "Mordraed…my lord…no, no!" he squealed, sounding like a pig brought to the slaughter. He half-turned, trying to rise, one arm flung up defensively to shield himself. "It was nothing…I was drunk…"

It was too late. Mordraed's hands were lightning and his long Ar-moran rapier was in his hand. In deadly silence he thrust downward with the long, fire-red blade, piercing straight through Wyzelo's heart and driving the long, spiked tip into Morigau beneath him. Wyzelo had no chance to scream, but blood rushed from his mouth in a great burst and his body collapsed over Morigau's, twitching in death throes. Morigau started to scream; the blade had entered her chest, but not deep enough to kill. She heaved at the heavy body of Wyzelo but could not move him.

"Mordraed, Mordraed!" she cried. "Why have you done this to me? I gave you the world…the world!"

He knelt beside her and viciously gripped her hair in his hand. His face was inches from hers. His blue eyes, death eyes, burned into hers. "You gave me ashes, mother…ashes and dust."

"Oh, let me go, take out the blade…help me!" She writhed in pain, her blood mingling with Wyzelo's on the pallet. "I won't speak more of Gal'havad; I swear to you…I won't try to tell you what to do…"

"Too late…" he said coldly, but he withdrew the Ar-moran danger from Wyzelo's corpse and from Morigau's chest.

She sighed and gasped with relief and pain, tried to stem the bleeding with her hands. "I knew you'd see sense. You are angry…that is good. It shows you are a man and not some tame creature. Call the healer now; I am losing much blood…"

"I told you, mother…too late."

The dagger suddenly flashed down again, plunging into her ribs. The blade struck the floor on the other side of her body and snapped, leaving Mordraed with a useless horn hilt and fragment of bronze in his grip.

Morigau made a gurgling, gasping noise and clawed at the broken blade. "You…you have slain me. I…I am your mother."

"I know," he said, bending over her so that his lips almost touched her greying cheek. His breath blew hot against her ear. "I am indeed your son—you made me what I am and now you pay the price."

Mordraed walked out of the hut, the bloody broken rapier in his hand. A crowd had gathered; rough young men suddenly sobered by the screams and noises. Mordraed gazed around him and then flung the gory dagger-hilt to the ground before them. "Morigau is dead," he said defiantly, "and so too her leman, Wyzelo. She was a sorceress, a witch who had dread spirits in her head. She would bring only ill to the people of Kham-El-Ard. And to me, your chief."

The people in the dun were silent. Mordraed heard a faint whimpering and saw his two small brothers hiding behind taller members of the crowd. They clung to each other, as ever, two little dark birds huddled against the storm.

Going over to them, he sank to one knee and took them in his blood-stained arms. They shivered, as cold as winter ice, afraid to touch him in return. "Forgive me," he said. "It had to be done. For all of us."

"But…but she was our…" began Ga'haris in a tiny, tremulous voice.

"I know…But there is much you do not understand. She would have killed you one day, I swear it. With me, you will be safe as long as you are true to me."

He turned from the boys and gestured to his silent men. "The time of feasting is over. You have your gold, your bronze …now you must work to keep it. Put down your beakers and lift your axes. A guard must be put on Kham-El-Ard and Place-of-Light at all times. No strangers must go in; no one must fare out, unless I give him leave. I want men in the woods, men on the Ridgeways and the Harrow track. I want others to fare to the coast and watch the movements of any ships across the Narrow Sea. For, unless the Ancestors smile on us, Ardhu Pendraec will be returning to Prydn. And he will want his fortress…and his revenge."

CHAPTER TWENTY—THE DARK MOON

Ardhu Pendraec sat with An'kelet of Ar-morah in the wood of Bro-khelian, two chieftains side by side, united in friendship once again after their bitter separation. Ardhu's warband was gathered around a fire, laughing and merry-making, as in old times. Joints of roast pork lay spread out before them, brought on wooden trenchers by members of An'kelet's fair-faced clan, and there were also shining silver fish from the nearby Little Sea, cooked in nests of sweet yet salty weeds gathered from the water's edge. Big, multi-handled beakers different in design from those in Prydn were passed through the group, brimming with thin, grape-based alcohol unlike anything the men of Albu had tasted before. Branches spread above the company like an enchanted, green canopy; and in the boughs the birds were singing without care. A golden haze hung over the whole of the haunted forest, enfolding it, embracing it, almost making Ardhu feel he was in a protected Otherworld where harm could never come, where grief could not find him.

But in his heart, he knew that could never be.

Evil and sorrow would always find a path.

And so it was, while they feasted and the Sun faded and the stars came out, that Dru Bluecloak, one-time acolyte at Deroweth, arrived after a long and perilous journey at the forest's edge, seeking Ardhu Pendraec. He was met by the men of An'kelet's tribe who patrolled the edge of the woods with their man-high yew bows, and taken into the heart of the forest where An'kelet had his holdings away from the prying eyes of outsiders.

"My Chief, one is come from Prydn bearing news," said the leader of the patrol, bowing before An'kelet, who sat cross-legged on a sheepskin, holding a pork joint in his hand. "He wears the robes of a priest in training."

Ardhu and An'kelet both frowned and glanced at each other in consternation. "Bring him forward," ordered An'kelet, setting his food aside.

Dru Bluecloak stepped from behind the warriors of An'kelet's clan. He was maybe five and twenty Sun-turnings but looked ten years older, his hair knotted and his beard wild and dark lines underscoring haunted eyes. The blue cloak of his order was stained and torn, and his shoes were ragged flaps bound to bloodied and blistered feet with leather ties. "I...I come from Deroweth," he said, his voice high and wheezy, as if he struggled for breath. "I bear grave tidings."

Ardhu's visage became stone. He sat up straight, fingers on Caladvolc's hilt in an instinctive gesture. "Speak these tidings, holy man."

Dru's mouth worked; he licked his salt-cracked lips. "It...it...is Mordraed, Stone Lord, your kinsman of Ynys Yrch."

A chill rippled up Ardhu's spine, despite the balminess of the evening. "What of him? Speak!"

Dru bowed his head; tears stood in his eyes. He blinked them away. "He has...raised men against you and burned Deroweth to the ground. I saw him burn the High Priest alive; I survived only by fleeing like a coward. I made for the coast and heard more news while hiding there; the land is ablaze with it. Mordraed has desecrated the stones of Khor Ghor, toppling the Door into Winter...and he has also taken the dun of Kham-El-Ard as his own. When I heard those tidings, I knew I had to fare across the Narrow Sea to find you."

"And Fynavir...the Queen?" An'kelet leaned forward, a dangerous light in his eyes. "What news of her?"

Dru choked and coughed, staring at his feet. "Men say Mordraed swore to have her as his own Queen, because she is the White Woman. But it did not come to pass. She is gone."

"Gone?" There was a dangerous note in An'kelet's voice.

Dru shrugged. "That is what is whispered. None know where. Pray to the spirits she is safe in hiding."

Ardhu glanced at An'kelet, his look agonised. "I have been such a fool," he said hoarsely. "I came to Ar-morah seeking your death…and in my stupid need for vengeance, I left my realm open for evil to take hold. And now the worst has happened. Mordraed! I should have guessed!"

An'kelet was white as bone beneath his golden tan but he managed a tight-lipped smile. "Maybe it was meant to be, Ardhu. Maybe if you had stayed in Prydn he would have come at you at night, stabbed you while you slept. Maybe the Ancestors guided you here not for war that would solve nothing but for us to reconcile so that we can stand together against Mordraed." Reaching out he clasped Ardhu's hand in a tight, firm grip. "We will stand as brothers again, fighting side by side…and we will surely win."

"But your weapons…I took them from you, destroyed them. The Balugaisa…"

An'kelet shook his head. "Do not fret over their loss. More have been made for me by my people. Now…" He leapt to his feet, tall and imposing as a god under the swaying trees. "I must summon the tribes of Ar-morah to join me if they will. Your band is sadly depleted, but I will fill the ranks of your host from the Land of the Sea." Brow furrowed in concentration, he began to pace. "We have some ships, in which we sail the coasts of the West from here to Ibero, trading tin…and you have a few boats too—but not enough for our purposes. I will sacrifice some of the trees of Bro-khelian to build more, and will have the best wood-carvers employed upon this task. But preparations will take time, even if it is done in all haste and orders given today. Then we must look for the right auguries, divined in the entrails of a bull slain upon the strand, and for the turning of the tide."

Ardhu bowed his head, resigned, through frustration shone in his eyes. "Although time is doubtless against us, there is no choice in the matter unless we learn how to fly across the Narrow Sea like the gulls. I praise the Ancestors that you are here to help, An'kelet of Ar-morah, my brother in all things, lost to me through our mutual folly and blindness but now returned to me and to my cause."

Ardhu's warband began to shout and cheer, beating the hafts of their axes against the earth. "Ardhu! Pendraec!" they chanted over and over and then "An'kelet!" until the magic forest of Bro-khelian rang with the sound, echoing from crystalline spring to mossy dolmen, from solitary standing stone to spreading trees with their leaves aflutter in the night-wind.

Ardhu stood amongst his men with Caladvolc unsheathed, holding it up to the black vault of the sky, and An'kelet joined him with a new spear whose head burned like fire, raising the weapon until its tip joined with the blade of Hard-Cleft, and both knew in that moment that this was the hour that men must stand together or all they worked for would be lost, and that nothing must ever come between them again lest the Prydn they had striven for fell forever into darkness.

The Feast of the Rage of Trogran had just ended and the earth of Prydn baked in the hot sun. The constant drenching rains that had afflicted the country for so long had ceased, but this was not the normal heat of summer. It was humid warmth, thick and sticky; the wind hot and burning to the eyes and throat of man and beast. The skies were not clear summer-blue but massed with storm clouds that unleashed their fury every evening, then rolled back to brood on the edges of the horizon like strange, megalithic formations of the heavens. The Sun was a dim blob amid the frowning, twisting trilithons of the clouds, a bleeding and baleful eye that cast lurid light over the Great Plain with both rising and setting.

Mordraed shifted uneasily under the gaze of that dwindling red eye as he stood upon the ramparts of Kham-El-Ard. Crackles of lightning began over Magic and Harrow Hill and a low wind moaned in the trees down by the great river. Mordraed shivered, despite the stormy heat; he felt troubled and alone. Bron Trogran was a celebration of fertility, when crops were gathered in and thanks given to the Ancestors for the bounty of the earth, but the time it took place was also the month of death, when, in the days of Samothos the first Tin-Lord, the Corn-King would die with the last cut sheaf, a gift to the Corn-Woman whose body incubated the wheat. He did not know why this old rite, now reduced to a play of men and women in masks, wielding sickles that cut only sheaves and not flesh, bothered him so, for it was always the Old King who would fall, be taken back into the earth, his blood and bones feeding the crops for seven Sun-Turnings, while a young newcomer took his place to restore the Land.

The young Challenger never failed, never died…

Nor would Mordraed fail…

Another shudder gripped him and, despite the heat of the day, he felt cold to the bone. At the start of Bron Trogran, Nin-Aeifa the Priestess of the Lake, had left her watery dwellings and made the journey to Kham-El-Ard. Men had stopped and stared and prostrated themselves on the ground, for despite her great age, she was still very fearsome, painted blue and white, her kirtle shining like fish scales, her hair matted with lime and decorated with shells. She had walked into the dun, bold as a she-wolf, and stood before Mordraed's seat, unafraid, although a naked axe-blade lay across his knee.

"I have a message for you from the High Priestess of Suilven and the Nine Ladies of the Lake," she had intoned, fixing him with her terrible single blind eye, milky and blue, that saw into the Otherworld as well as the hearts of men. "News has reached Suilven and Glasduin of the murder of the priests of Deroweth and the slighting of Khor Ghor. These deaths, these desecrations, are abhorrent to us and to the Spirits. Neither you nor any of your people may attend—or celebrate—the Feast of Bron Trogran, lest your sins blight the earth and the crops and anger the Ancestors. This Ban, spoken at the Full Moon, in the Great Cove of Suilven, will be for your lifetime and three men's lifetimes beyond. So it shall be." She then spat at his feet, and slammed her wizened hawthorn staff on the ground three times to seal the ban.

"I care not," he had snapped back, half minded to kill the loathsome woman and throw her body into the pigpens where the perennially hungry swine would devour her stringy frame to the bone.

But he had held back from touching her, as her horrid, damaged eye fixed on him again, unblinking like the eye of a corpse. "Where lie the bones of wise Merlin?" she breathed, so quietly that only he could hear, and he realised that she, half in trance-state, exhaled damning words torn from some unknown realm. "He who had the triple Death that was forbidden to him. Maybe nowhere, maybe everywhere—in the air that surrounds you, the earth below your feet, in the flame that burns, in the water where he was drowned…"

Mordraed had leapt from his seat in alarm at these last words. She knew! Nin-Aeifa and the priestesses of Suilven knew he had killed the Merlin! "Men!" he had shouted, in frenzy "Get this creature from my sight before I kill her with my own hands and feed her to the pigs!"

But Nin-Aeifa had cast him a contemptuous glare and turned and walked proudly away of her own accord, and none, even Mordraed, had been brave enough to touch her as she descended the hill of Kham-El-Ard and headed for the Old Henge and the river. "Remember, Mordraed of Ynys Yrch," she had called back over her shoulder. "Three lifetimes beyond your own…though I daresay your own life will be a short one. I do not foresee your days being long and fruitful, for darkness is within you."

Mordraed rubbed his arms at the memory and scowled into the thunderous late afternoon. She had cursed him…or maybe it was just empty words meant to frighten, to take the resolve from his sword-arm. He did not believe in curses, at least when the fires were bright and weapons close to hand. What was wrong with these fools, why were they so against him? Yes, perhaps he had been harsh in his punishment of the priests of Khor Ghor, but they were corrupt, pawns of Ardhu—surely the Priestesses, who were deemed to be wise, could see that the Priests had lost their way? Surely they were aware that the realm was falling into ruin because Ardhu was old, weak, unfit...no true king.

He began to pace, high on the rampart, walking with the ill-controlled tension of a caged beast. He had hardly slept...since she had died, impaled on his dagger. Hardly slept as he waited for news to come from the South. News of Ardhu...Was he dead in Ar-morah, fighting An'kelet for lost honour, or was he on his way back to Prydn with anger and vengeance in his heart?

Down by the Abona he caught a slight movement in the trees and saw several of his men running to ascertain the cause of the disturbance. His heart began to hammer against his ribs as he saw a dishevelled rider loom out of the murk, half-falling from his horse in exhaustion. He could see the man gesticulating wildly as the warriors surrounded him and he heard raised voices, though he could not make out the words.

A second later one of the men broke away from the horseman, and ran haphazardly toward the gate. As he approached, legs pumping, Mordraed could see the scaly pallor of his face, the terror in his eyes.

He knew what news he would bring.

Ardhu, his father and his bitter enemy, was on his way back to Kham-El-Ard.

Mordraed gathered his bow and strapped on his quiver of arrows. He lifted his new dagger, which the smith had forged for him after he broke his rapier in Morigau's body, examining it for balance and sharpness. It was good...he had asked that it be made longer and broader than was the fashion; now it looked almost a twin of Ardhu's Caladvolc the Hard-Cleft.

He called it King-killer, in hope.

All around him the people of Kham-El-Ard milled; the air was crackling with fear, with tension. Women wept outside their huts; even though they were Ardhu's people they feared they would be caught between the two opposing forces and killed by either blade or fire. Even Mordraed's own sworn men looked fearful, their bravado leaving them as they realised they would truly have to face the wrath of the Stone Lord, wielder of Caladvolc, and his sworn companions, who had years of battle experience and an innate discipline and purpose that they lacked.

Khyloq came running, her flame-hued mane a tangle, and flung her arms around Mordraed's waist. "I hear the cursed one comes! Kill him, my dark Lord. Let me be set up as a true queen of Prydn, with none left to question my right!"

"Get off me!" Mordraed grabbed her wrists and pushed her away from him. "I do not have time to think of you and your wants..." Yet as he looked at her, with her swelling belly and her eyes full of both desire and fear, he suddenly thought, *She must go from here...If the day goes wrong, anything could happen. Ardhu would not kill a woman, but I do not trust the motives of my own men...And my brothers, would any spare them?*

"Look..." His voice was kinder and his hands slid to her shoulders, squeezing gently. "I am going to send you from here, and I want you to take Ga'haris and Gharith with you. It is not safe in Kham-El-Ard for a woman...particularly my woman. Go down the Abona, into the valley, and seek the Priestesses of the Lake. They are my enemies, but they would not harm or turn away another woman, I think, and I pray they will not turn away innocent children either."

"I do not like this idea!" Khyloq gasped, clutching his leather jerkin. "It is as if you prepare for your death!"

"I do not prepare for my death," he said, a dangerous edge in his voice, "but I leave nothing to chance…I am not a fool. Now get my brothers and go, and do not tarry upon the path!"

She left him, tears running down her cheeks, and soon he saw her, wrapped in a woven shawl that covered her bright head, picking her way down the hillside toward the Abona, clutching the hands of his young kinsmen tightly in her own.

Turning from the sight, he cast his gaze over his own men—the stupid, the violent, the malcontent, the idle who only spoke of great deeds and did none. They seemed completely dwindled in his vision, hardly a warband, just a rag-tag bunch of brawling and boastful boys; even if their numbers surpassed his father's, they would never be able to withstand an onslaught from Ardhu's experienced warriors for long. If hatred and blood-lust spurred them on at first, their ardour would soon diminish and they would break and scatter, to be hunted down and slaughtered.

Something within him bent, twisted. There had been so much death already. Why needless slaughter, even of such cattle as these? He raised his hand, gesturing for their attention. "Listen, listen, I have made a decision! I will fare to Khor Ghor…on my own. You must all stay here, holding the dun. When Ardhu Pendraec arrives, tell him to stay his hand and swear that you will do the same. Then tell him that I am on the Great Plain, at the Stones, and that I await him there. He must come alone, bringing none of his followers. We will do battle, one on one, as men and chiefs, and the Spirits will decide between us. If I should fall…" he took a deep breath, "I would council you surrender to him, and pray to the Ancestors he gives you mercy. If I win…then you may strike at his men with all your fury, for their spirit will be broken."

The youths of the warband reacted with horror and an angry murmur went up. They had long wished to engage in battle with their sworn enemy, and had filled the fort with round stones to cast down at their opponents. Their blades were freshly sharpened and their arrows tipped with venom. The idea of hiding behind stout oak walls and waiting for an outcome held no appeal.

Mordraed glared at them, staring them down with eyes of bitter ice. "I do this to save your skins, you brainless fools!" he snarled. "Do you understand nothing? I have given you gold, amber, axes and status as men of the tribe. Now grant me this one bit of loyalty in return, damn you all to Ahn-un!"

They recoiled from him, fearful of his wrath, their anger hidden if not truly quelled. Mordraed turned scornfully from them, almost hating the sight of their hard, stupid faces… "Remember what I have told you," he said icily, and he strode forward into the storm-laden afternoon seeking the Sacred Avenue that would lead him to his destiny.

Ardhu, An'kelet and their men reached Kham-El-Ard late the next day. The woods and fields were quiet, brooding under the hot sky; it was strange to see no harvesters, no washerwomen, no children playing in the river. The landscape seemed almost empty, part of the Deadlands…except for the fort of Kham-El-Ard on the crooked hill, its gates shut and barred, its ditches full of newly honed wooden stakes, and trails of wood smoke seeping from its many hearths to darken the skies above it.

Ardhu stared at the barricaded dun, his lips thin lines and his jaw tight. Deep anger flooded him, and he longed to charge up the hill and set a great tree trunk against those gates, his gates, but he knew such an action would be counterproductive. Those holed up within his dun would heave rocks upon his head, or boiling water, or animal dung, and with the height and the protection of the stout oak walls, the defenders had the clear advantage.

Seeing his friend's expression, An'kelet laid a steadying hand on his shoulder. "It would not be wise to act in haste. "I will go up to the gate and speak with them."

Ardhu nodded. "Take care, An'kelet. They may shoot at you before you speak. These are not true warriors; they are rabble corrupted by Mordraed."

An'kelet raised his round shield of leather and wood. "I will take no risks." He trudged towards the fort, his spear carried on his back in its sling rather than in his hand. Raising a clenched fist, he pounded on the great wooden gates. He could hear voices muttering behind. "Open the gates!" he shouted. "I am An'kelet, prince of Ar-morah, companion of the Stone Lord. How dare you bar entrance to the King of the West, the lord and builder of this dun?"

A coarse red face popped over the breastwork. "Kham-El-Ard is Ardhu Pendraec's no longer. Now it is held by Mordraed, lord of the Dark Moon."

"If that is so, tell Mordraed to come forth and speak to us—if he dares!"

"He is not here," replied the man.

"Well, where is he?"

"Gone to the Stones," the warrior shot back. "He has asked that we pass a message on to his adversary, Ardhu Pendraec."

Hearing these words from his position at the bottom of the hill, Ardhu quickly rode up beside An'kelet. "What message is this? Speak!"

"He says he will fight you man to man in the Stones. Whoever wins will be king of Prydn…the other will be in his barrow. He says that if it is settled in such a manner, we can avoid bloodshed; he has ordered us not to attack you unless you do not agree to these terms. "

An'kelet glanced uneasily at Ardhu. "I do not like this overmuch."

Ardhu took a deep breath. "I would not have the people inside Kham-El-Ard harmed, nor do I even greatly desire the heads of the dolts who bar our way. I will do as Mordraed asks; maybe it is the best way to settle this forever..."

"I do not trust Mordraed; he is a snake." An'kelet shook his head darkly. "I will come with you to Khor Ghor."

Overhead, the gateman leaned further from the parapet, shaking his head. "You must go alone, Pendraec. That is the order of Lord Mordraed. If you try to take men with you, we will ride down from the hill and join battle. Then we will fire this place and burn it to the ground."

Ardhu took a deep breath, thinking of all the men and women he knew who were captive in the dun. Ka'hai's wife and children, close as kin; he knew the big ugly man was fretting at the bottom of the hill, thinking of what their fate might be. "I will go alone. I am not afraid."

An'kelet paced uneasily. "If it is your wish. But let me have my say, since we are friends again and you have named me heir. It is late in the day and although the nights are light, still it will not be overlong before the Sun sets; it is not good to fight in the dark."

Ardhu laughed darkly and unsheathed Caladvolc. "I do not intend to fight at night. Before the Sun is down, it will be finished."

"If you are not back here by Moonrise, grant me permission to send men to find you," said An'kelet grimly. "Grant me that much, at least."

The Pendraec inclined his head. "It is granted."

He swung down from his steed and handed the reins to An'kelet. The taller man raised a quizzical eyebrow.

"I will go on foot," said Ardhu, "following the Sacred Avenue from the River. Khor Ghor has already suffered at Mordraed's hands; I would not disrespect it further by riding a beast beyond its banks, even on this day…this day of reckoning."

He turned from the fortress gate, the late afternoon sun flashing on his breastplate and buckle of gold and on the surface of the Face of Evening, his shield. He raised Caladvolc and he raised his copper axe, saluting bright-faced Bhel as He soared through the skyway on his journey to the West. He embraced An'kelet, kissing him on either cheek, and then his kinsman Hwalchmai, and also Betu'or, Ka'hai and Bohrs, who stood with his jaw agape, for the Stone Lord had never behaved thus before when battle was imminent. It was almost like a farewell…

Then, his leave taken, Ardhu strode down the hill toward the chalk banks of the Avenue. He did not look back.

Mordraed sat inside the circle of Khor Ghor on the fallen lintel of the Door into Winter. Moodily he stared out across the Great Plain, where the long grasses rippled in the late Sun like waves on a strange green sea. Every now and then he took a sip of water from a small clay flask or chewed on a strip of dried beef. He would not eat more, for he wanted his belly to be empty when the time for battle came; he did not want his body to be sluggish from consuming excess food or drink.

After a while he got up and started to pace. Ash from the destruction of the trilithon eddied around him, small black whirlwinds against the wrenched chalk. The bluestones frowned, close as conspirators, while beyond them the arches of the outer circle grinned, as if mocking him. Maybe Ardhu would not come. Maybe he was too afraid, or had some other plan…

He grimaced. He had to come; an ending had to be made. Overhead the westering Sun beat heavily on his head, increasing the throbbing in his temples that had gripped him for days…no, weeks. He hated it, both the pain in his skull and the relentless heat of Bhel; but not to worry, soon the Sun would fall from heaven and the Moon would rise, and it would be his time, the time of the Dark Moon…

A sudden noise, scarcely more noticeable than a breath of wind in leaves, made his spine prickle.

He was not alone.

Limbs tense, adrenaline rushing, he pivoted around, bow in his hands and an arrow to the string.

Ardhu Pendraec, father and uncle, chief and rival, stood in the gap that led to the Southern causeway, the reddish light of late afternoon flaming on his regalia, turning the unsheathed blade of Caladvolc to bronze flame.

Mordraed fired two arrows in quick succession. Ardhu flung up Wyngurthachar and the swan-feathered shafts bounced harmlessly aside, skittering in the dirt. He then sprang at his opponent, faster than one who was not in full bloom of youth had a right to be, and crashed his full weight into Mordraed before he could release another arrow, striking him in the belly with his shield and throwing him back onto the shattered block of the Great Trilithon.

Mordraed landed heavily, his bow tearing from his fingers, breath forced from his lungs with the force of impact. Almost immediately, he recovered, thrusting himself up on his elbows and flinging himself forward against Ardhu's shield and trying to wrest it from his father's arm.

Grappling together, they staggered across the circle, bashing into bluestones and tripping over chunks of wreckage from the broken trilithon. Mordraed gave one vicious wrench and twisted Ardhu's wrist, near breaking the bones, and Wyngurthachar tore loose and clattered to the ground. Grinning, Mordraed snatched it up and flung it outside of the circle. Now Ardhu's left hand side was open to attack, vulnerable.

Ardhu stared at the man before him…this thing he had made in one night of folly so long ago it seemed like a terrible, twisted dream. So alike in face and form, but Mordraed with a prettiness about him that contrasted with the ice in his eyes, the cruel and uncompromising set of his mouth. The downing Sun shone on the black river of his unbound hair and warmed his cold features. His skin was unadorned, with no sacred marks upon him for protection, nor were any talismans bound to his deerskin jerkin or belt; it was obvious he believed he needed no help from the Spirits to win this fight.

"I should have killed you as a child," Ardhu said harshly.

Mordraed smiled and drew his new long sword from his belt, the blade fashioned just for his hand. King-killer. "But you did not and now I shall kill you."

They engaged in the centre of the circle before the fallen half of the Great Trilithon and the crushed, half-buried Stone of Adoration. Bronze smote against bronze with metallic clangour and sparks flew into the air. In the West, through the towering arch of the Gate of the Guardian, the Sun was rapidly descending, spraying out spokes of incarnadine light like gore from a fatal wound. Above the Stones, the vault of the Everlasting Sky resembled a blood-stained shield. Sullen clouds towering on the horizon turned crimson and broke apart, burning like a thousand heavenly funeral pyres, a thousand fallen monuments. Nearing the edge of the horizon, the lurid, watchful red eye of Bhel looked distorted and huge, black cloud-streamers darting over its surface as it began its final descent into the Land of the Dead. Trapped in its last bloody rays, the stones of Khor Ghor burned out against the failing twilight sky—red, gold, green, beacons lit in a final blaze of glory before night fell forever.

Ardhu and Mordraed did not speak, nor meet each other's eyes as they slashed and parried and hacked at each other with their keen bronze blades, seeking to wound and then bring down. Mordraed fought like a wild animal, hoping his youthful strength and unbridled rage would carry the day; but Ardhu was more experienced and patient, his blows less frenetic and more accurate, and he countered every move the younger man made with consummate skill, stepping aside and around when Mordraed lunged in his direction, hoping to bring blade to flesh.. He was aware that his shield arm was unguarded and his left flank open to attack, but as Mordraed bore no shield himself, Ardhu did not greatly worry about it. They were equal, like the Days when Light and Shadow balanced in the great Circle…

Mordraed's face was pallid, sweat streaming into his eyes as he struggled to get in under Ardhu's guard. He had not expected the old fool to be so sprightly still, to have such an arm of stone. He had underestimated his father sorely. But if he could not best him by swift blows and sheer force, other forces could and would come into play…

Stabbing and parrying with his long sword, he gradually managed to work Ardhu around in a semi-circle until the last hot piercing beams of Sunlight flared on the older man's helmet and breastplate…and shot into his face, making him squint against the harsh burning glow in the farthest West.

"Fool!" shouted Mordraed as he saw Ardhu try to shade his tearing eyes with his left hand, an instinctive gesture. He gave a great leap forward, throwing himself onto Ardhu, trying to smash his knee into his groin or belly and render him helpless. Ardhu staggered back under his son's weight, Caladvolc lowered to waist-level in defence of his lower body, and Mordraed's blow went wide, his kneecap meeting with force against Ardhu's hip bone. It was not what Mordraed had hoped for but a violent impact nonetheless, which made Ardhu's leg crumple beneath him, pins and needles rippling down his thigh.

Mordraed saw the agony in his father's face and rushed him again. Off-balance, Ardhu was hurled backwards, slamming into one of the mighty grey pillars of Throne of Kings on the Southern side of the circle. Anger flared in his eyes, and he swung Caladvolc in a shining arc towards Mordraed's head, eager now to end this in the only way it could end…in blood and death.

Grinning now, sensing that the tide might be turning in his direction, Mordraed threw his blade up to meet that of his father. The Hard-Cleft was like a tongue of burning flame in the dusk and, gleaming, King-killer leapt forth to answer its challenge. The two swords smote against each other with force, sparking and sawing. Aware that Ardhu had nowhere to go with the massive trilithon at his back, Mordraed relentlessly pushed his advantage, drawing in closer and closer till they were almost touching, hip to hip, shoulder to shoulder. Upwards he forced Ardhu's hand, a move he had learned from An'kelet whilst in training at Kham-El-Ard. He saw Ardhu grimace, and try to twist Caladvolc for a sharp downward thrust.

Mordraed used his last reserve of strength to slam his own sword heavily against Caladvolc, a blow violent as a thunderclap. Ardhu's hand snapped back and the blade of Hard-Cleft struck the face of the trilithon behind him, smote the stern grey sarsen that was one of the hardest stones on earth.

And shattered…

Glittering in the embers of Sunset, shards of the sword from the Sacred Pool, gift of Nin-Aeifa of the Lake, spun across the circle and came to land amidst the ashes left by Mordraed's destruction. Stunned, Ardhu stared at the hilt and jagged fragment in his right hand. The useless stump…his broken kingship.

At that moment Mordraed struck. Lowering his sword-arm, he grasped Ardhu's shoulder and yanked him close, almost as if he would embrace him. But it was no tender moment of forgiveness. Lips curved in a triumphant leer, he thrust King-killer into Ardhu's unprotected left side and twisted the blade.

Ardhu's face whitened with shock. Mordraed began to laugh, driving the blade deeper. "I knew I would prevail," he gasped. "The Old King always dies at the hand of the new in the month of Death!"

Behind Mordraed's shoulder, the uppermost rim of the Sun was finally sinking under the horizon. The sky and the Circle were the colour of old blood. Real, fresh blood poured from Ardhu's side and reddened his pale and draining lips as his knees gave out from under him and he slumped to the ground at the foot of Throne of Kings, the inlaid daggers and axes shining out above his dark head.

Mordraed withdrew King-killer and raised it in triumph, red rivulets from the gutter of the blade streaking down his arms, his face, his chest.

And then…there it was. A soft sound, a faint movement in the deepening twilight near the Gate of the Guardian, no more substantial that the beating wings of a moth…

Afraid of new attackers, Mordraed whirled on his heel, weapon at the ready. The remaining fragments of brightness in the West briefly dazzled his eyes...and then, as he struggled to adjust his vision, he spied a figure gazing through the arch of the trilithon. Red blood-ruby hair, long robes wrought of twilight and eventide mist, a sad, solemn face he knew so well—object of love and hatred. Eyes green as the grass on a barrow-hill and deep as death caught his and held him in a reproachful stare.

"No!" he screamed, the word wrenched from his constricting throat.

Unwillingly he staggered in the direction of the vision, the apparition.

It changed.

The Merlin stood before him, not the old feeble man crippled by elf-shot whom he had dispatched to the Otherworld, but a strong youthful shaman in a great ceremonial headdress of horns and bone. His visage was dark and saturnine, strong lines running from nose to mouth, lips curved in mockery and deep dislike. His robes frothed around his ankles, blending with darkness; on his breast his hawk talisman gleamed, its eyes shining like molten bronze and its open beak dripping the blood of the sacrifice…

No words came from his lips but Mordraed heard cold, familiar words echo inside his head, first spoken Moons ago, "You will never be king in Ardhu's stead…if I have to fight Hwynn and Nud themselves, I will return from the Otherworld to stop you!"

"You won't stop me!" he shrieked, waving his sword like a madman. "My reign is destined!"

His back was turned to the crouched, wounded form of his father. He did not see Ardhu move, crawling on his knees, one hand pressed to his bleeding side, the other stretching toward his lower leg.

Mordraed had forgotten, in his moment of triumph, his moment of terror…

He had forgotten Little White Hilt, the Sword from beneath the Stone, the dagger that had given Ardhu his right to rule the tribes of Prydn…

Until it bit deep within his lower belly, tearing into his entrails, a fatal blow from which no man could recover.

Mordraed dropped to the ground, the pain, the fear, making the shadows and spectres that assailed him flee from his mind. There was no Merlin, no Gal'havad within the circle of Khor Ghor. Only him, with the horn-hilted dagger protruding from his side, and Ardhu Pendraec, bleeding from a similar wound beside him, their blood co-mingling, pooling on the ash and chalk. "This…cannot…be…" Mordraed gasped, disbelieving. "I…was…destined…"

He was clutching Ardhu's shoulders, trying to keep from collapsing; it almost looked as if they embraced as kinsmen, not as bitter enemies struggling against each other till the last. Ardhu glanced up at him, and his pinched, grey face was twisted with sorrow. "You…my son…were deceived…"

As Ardhu spoke, a horn suddenly sounded outside Khor Ghor, its notes bouncing eerily from stone to stone. Hoof beats made the earth tremble.

Ardhu glanced with swimming vision to the East, where a round, pale Moon-ghost floated in the sky. The Moon had risen. His men were here.

Mordraed craned his head toward the noise of the horses. He could see the dim shapes of men entering the stones…saw daggers drawn and bows with barbed arrows on the string. Ardhu's warriors!

Releasing Ardhu, he started to crawl on all fours toward the entrance of Khor Ghor, toward the Watchers and the Stone of Summer…toward the ghost Moon, the blessed Mother Moon to which he was sworn, as it soared higher into the night-time sky.

Instinctively his hand went to the hilt of Carnwennan, pulling it free of his flesh; blood flowed with renewed intensity and he stared at it, streaking down his legs, covering his hands, shining in the bitter Moon-light.

His life, slipping away, feeding chalk, stones, and Ancestral bones buried deep beneath him.

Coldness seeped through his limbs, a strange tingling; he struggled to breathe. An iron taste hung in his mouth and he felt something wet on his lips that was not saliva.

Behind him he could hear shouts from Ardhu's warriors, knew that they were preparing to leap upon him, to rend him limb from limb with their axes and daggers. They would take his head, they would take his heart; his pieces would be scattered on the plain and his spirit would never rest. An ignominious death, devoid of honour. A traitor's death.

He heard Ardhu's voice rise, shaking, hoarse, as if from a great distance. "Men…finish him! But not with your blades. Give him to the Circle in the old way of our ancient forebears, to atone for his crimes against the Ancestors. Give him to the Circle that his spirit might be trapped here for eternity, guarding what he has tried to destroy."

Mordraed halted, mid-crawl. Behind him, he could hear footsteps, heavy breathing.

He knew what his fate would be now…both relief and a curse.

Drawing himself up onto his knees through his pain, he flung his arms open wide in token of his submission and looked up toward the ascending Moon, the bone-white eye of She-Who-Guards, the Protectress of the Dead. On the pitted surface he swore he could see the face of Morigau gazing down at him, filled with love and hate and pride and mockery…

Three arrows flew. Three arrows struck.

One hit Mordraed's breastbone and then glanced aside into his heart.

Mordraed fell face first on the ground, arms still outstretched, and the men of Ardhu's warband took his body by the arms and dragged it to the terminal of the henge-ditch near Heulstone, where they dug a hasty pit. They threw the corpse in with little care, taking his weapons as trophies but leaving his archer's wristguard because he was a man of high status. They placed shards of bluestone around him, to bind his spirit with the power of the sacred Stones, then covered the crouched body with chalk and spoil and debris.

Done, the warriors returned to the inner sanctum of Khor Ghor. Ardhu had propped himself up against the Stone of Adoration; his breathing was shallow and laboured, a cold sweat gleaming on his brow. His mouth shone dark red. Hwalchmai, Bohrs, Ka'hai and Betu'or flung themselves down at his side, trying to staunch the wound in his belly with torn shreds from their cloaks but the bleeding would not stop.

Hwalchmai leaned over and laved his cousin's forehead with water, while Ka'hai steadied him. Ardhu swallowed, and reached out to clasp the hands of both Hwalchmai and his foster-brother, who was weeping openly. "I am glad you are here with me…at the end," he whispered. "And Bohrs too." He glanced at Bohrs who had got up and stood miserably beside the Door into Winter, his shoulders shaking. He wept freely, though in silence.

"It is not the end, lord," said Betu'or brokenly.

"In this life, it is." Ardhu closed his eyes. "I can see the long house of my Fathers across the Plain of Honey. Its doors lie open for me, in a land where falls not the rain, nor the snow, nor any tears; where there is no sorrow and no life's ending. I can see Gal'havad there, on shores awash with crystals and dragonstones, with the wind in his hair and light in his eyes…and the Merlin is with him…They wait for me…"

"Betu'or…" his voice was fading; his fingers, cold, touched Betu'or's arm. "Long ago, I spared your life; now it is time you did something for me in return. The sword…the sword Lady Nin-Aeifa gave me…It must go back whence it came. Back into the Sacred Pool, into the holy waters. Will you take it there and return it to the spirits? I ask you because you are Betu'or, Knower of the Graves…Will you find the watery resting place for this thing of power?"

"I will, lord," said Betu'or, and he picked up the broken shards of Caladvolc, held them to his face and wept.

Ardhu gazed up at the sky; the clouds had suddenly rolled away and the heavens were bright with a thousand stars. The Cloak of Nud, the Milky Way, stretched above the Stones and into infinity. He smiled. He could hear the Hounds of Hwynn the Fire-White, god of the Mortuary, baying faintly and then louder, as they sallied forth from Hwynn's stronghold at the Tor and came towards him.

And then he was away with them, over the Great Plain and into the ultimate West.

CHAPTER TWENTY ONE—INTO ETERNITY

An'kelet camped before the gates of Kham-El-Ard with his men around him in hastily thrown-up tents and shelters. Every now and then, he glanced into the shadows by the banks of Abona. The Moon had long risen and Ardhu had not returned from Khor Ghor; he had sent Ardhu's most trusted warriors after him as agreed...but they had not returned either.

A knot of dread had settled in his belly, cold as the bone-white Moon floating in the sky.

Where could they be?

Suddenly, he heard the hammering of a horse's hooves. Grasping his spear, he raced in the direction of the noise. A pale grey horse was flying down the Avenue, heedless of any missiles fired from the ramparts of Kham-El-Ard, where Mordraed's warriors foamed and fretted like mad dogs bound on the lead.

The horse wheeled to a halt near An'kelet's encampment and the Ar-moran prince saw Hwalchmai, Hawk of the Plain, drop from the saddle-pad, his knees almost giving way as his feet struck the ground. He staggered toward An'kelet, footsteps so laboured and heavy that An'kelet thought he might be wounded.

"Hwalchmai, what has happened?" he shouted, hurrying towards the shambling figure.

Hwalchmai said no word. He glanced up at An'kelet, his eyes shining and wet, star-silvered. Reaching under his short fringed cloak, he drew out Ardhu's Lightning Mace, symbol of the Stone Lord's authority in Prydn. Its fossil head was smeared with blood.

Kneeling on the ground, he bowed his head and proffered the Mace to An'kelet.

And above him, the men waiting in the fort of Kham-El-Ard, seeing this as a token of Mordraed's victory, went wild.

Dawn broke, sullen and red. Blood and fire everywhere, in the sky, on the river, on the ground. The Sun was a hot ball of flame over the horizon, while beneath its rays Kham-El-Ard burned, the greatest fortress in that age of the world, gone forever. Great oak posts toppled and tumbled into the defensive ditches, while gouts of flame shot heavenward and black smoke curled, a shroud that blocked half the morning sky.

An'kelet leaned on his spear, breathing heavily, his heart a stone. He had tried to avert such a disaster but Mordraed's men, believing their master was victorious, had acted in berserker fury, flooding down the Crooked Hill like a hive of angry bees, breaking the truce between the two warbands in their madness. An'kelet's more experienced warriors had taken them on in one great wave, driving them back up to the gates, killing half of them with arrowfire alone. Upon sensing imminent and utter defeat, Mordraed's band had acted with rashness, firing the dun around them as they retreated into its interior. The dry posts and the thatched huts and Hall had ignited almost instantly.

Everything lay in ruins...and yet An'kelet had won.

"Look." At his side Hwalchmai pointed to the Sacred Avenue. "He comes. Ardhu comes home...one last time."

An'kelet shaded his gaze against the brightness in the heavens. On the Avenue he could see figures moving slowly, heads bowed in mourning. A supine figure lay across their shoulders, raised up toward the strengthening face of Bhel.

"We will go to the River," he said. "And wait. Then we will prepare him for his last journey and do what must be done."

Betu'or the Knower of the Graves stood beside the Sacred Pool at the foot of Kham-El-Ard, the place where the Old Hunters had gathered millennia past to hunt the great cats, the antlered deer, the mighty aurochs that could feed a whole tribe for a whole Moon. Coils of mist twisted from the waters; below the greenish surface, amidst moving weeds, bubbles streamed to the surface and burst.

Betu'or stood on the pool's edge, one foot in the holy spring, one on dry land—standing between the worlds of men and the watery Otherworld. In his hands he held the two shards of Caladvolc Hard-Cleft, shattered against the stony flank of Throne of Kings. He held up the pieces to catch the light, to let all those assembled in the woods behind see that they were truly broken, their spirits released forever and sent from the domains of mortal men.

A sigh went through the assembly, flowing out into the bright morning, and with that Betu'or flung the shards high into the air over the Sacred Pool. They spun in mid-air, shining like gold, like fire, like the tears of the Sun, and then, still whirling, they tumbled into the heart of the waters and were consumed, swallowed into the deep depths whence they came.

An'kelet, holding the Lightning Mace before him, led the mourning party from the Pool down to the fords of Abona. There, on a huge oak plank, lay Ardhu Pendraec in splendour, extended on his back, rather than in the usual crouched burial position of his people, signifying that he was more than mortal man, that he, alone of men, walked with the Great Spirits, the Gods and Ancestors. His face had been painted with ochre, giving him the semblance of life, his hair had been washed and combed down; he looked as if he merely slept, waiting for the right hour to rise. The Breastplate of Heaven gleamed on his chest, reflecting the moving clouds, and Wyngurthachar lay above his head, and all around him the folk of the Lake Valley and Kham-El-Ard placed armfuls of meadowsweet and campion, the red flower of champions.

Beside him, guarding the bier was his sister Mhor-gan in her priestess's robes of death-green. Her hair was unbound in mourning and her face drawn with grief. Nin-Aeifa stood next to her, a very old woman now, but still tall and straight, her grey braids clattering with quartz beads and shells. Seven women circled them, priestesses with moon-collars and necklets of faience beads shaped like tiny blue stars.

The Nine Ladies of the Lake, drawn together on this day to honour the Stone Lord, to bear his earthly remains away on his final journey.

As An'kelet, the warband and the villagers watched, the holy women took up the oak plank with Ardhu's body and placed it reverently on a wide wooden raft anchored within Abona's swell.

"Where will you take him?" An'kelet breathed, sinking to his knees at the water's edge. "Where can I go to place offerings to the spirit of my friend?"

Mhor-gan looked at him solemnly. "He will have no known grave, prince of Ar-morah. Dark times will come to Prydn with his death; and warfare…I think you, as his successor, know that. There can be no risk of his bones being disturbed. Let it be thought he is everywhere and nowhere, like the noble Merlin…his grave and ultimate fate unknown. Maybe he will lie in a deep cave, under the protection of the Great Spirits; or maybe he will merely lie atop a hill in a coffin carved into the form of a boat, sailing the seas of time toward the Tor of Hwynn and beyond. Maybe some men will even believe he is not truly dead but has been taken by the Nine Maidens for healing in the Garth of Afallan, ready to return when he is needed again by his people."

She turned from An'kelet and gestured to Nin-Aeifa to join her. They boarded the raft with the Maidens gathered around them, and knelt in a ring around Ardhu's body, singing and chanting and keening. Then the ropes mooring the raft were cut and they slipped slowly, mournfully, down the breast of Mother Abona, the Holy River, the Cleanser, away past the grieving people, past the Old Henge, away into the wilds of the lake valleys, away into eternity.

EPILOGUE—DAWN

For the next eighteen turns of the Moon, An'kelet of Ar-morah, heir to the legacy of Ardhu Pendraec, strove to build a new settlement to replace fair, doomed Kham-El-Ard; he chose a place on the hither side of the Plain, not far from the charred remains of Deroweth, but not so close that the angry ghosts of slain priests might disturb the slumber of the inhabitants. Between bushes and sylph-like trees, the ravaged stones of Khor Ghor frowned in the distance, shimmering in sunlight, standing bleak as skeleton bones in the morning mist.

Men seldom went there anymore. Some still visited, curious as much as worshipful, and carved axes on the stones, in imitation of those graven on the Throne of Kings but the days of the Great Feasts at Midsummer and Midwinter were over; the people now lit fires within their own home villages and jumped the flames among folk they knew. Once An'kelet had tried to rouse enthusiasm for a rebuilding of the shrine and he took the tribe's holy man and a force of ardent youths, and they dug pits all around the Stones, hoping, perhaps, to add more monoliths, to rebuild the structure anew.

His plan did not work. Men drifted away, putting up single stones near their hamlets and worshipping at cult-barrows; after what had happened at Khor Ghor, the death and the destruction, it had become little more than a haunt. Only the ever-present birds remained, nesting under the lintels, squabbling over long-dried bones in the ditch.

It was the way of time...felling and changing.

An'kelet sighed. He could not resurrect what the spirits had doomed to die. Khor Ghor was meant to go. So instead he turned his thoughts to other things pressed to the back of his mind through the long painful months after Ardhu's death.

Fynavir.

He had asked the folk of Place-of-Light, the Valley, and the Plain if they knew of her fate after the night of her forced marriage to Mordraed. They knew nothing, only that she was gone, but many hinted she must be dead, maybe even by her own hand, through shame and bitterness.

An'kelet could not bring himself to believe it.

And one bright day of sunshine and showers, he found himself walking down the river to the House of the Ladies of the Lake. If any would know Fynavir's fate, it would be those wise women who saw all, in both the realms of the living and the dead. He pondered why he had not sought them out earlier, and hung his head in shame—it had been too painful to see them, those women who had borne his friend on his final journey, carrying him to a resting place they would not even reveal to him.

He spied their hut ahead, standing on its long spindly legs in the river's swell; ancient Nin-Aeifa squatted outside the door, dandling a raven-haired infant on her knee and singing to it as it gurgled and wriggled, while two young, brown-haired boys splashed in the water nearby, trying to spear the fish that darted below the surface. An'kelet did not know whose the baby might be, but with a jolt he recognised the boys—Gharith and Ga'haris of Ynys Yrch. Ardhu's nephews...and half-brothers of Mordraed.

As he drew closer, the boys glanced up and fell silent, their harpoons clutched in their hands. The elder sprang from the river, dashed inside the house, and brought back Mhor-gan of the Korrig-han, leading her by the hand.

She walked toward An'kelet and gave him the kiss of peace on either cheek, and he felt his heart near break again for she looked so much like her dead brother; the same smile, set of cheekbone and jaw, the dark eyes mixed with forest green. "I knew you would come," she said softly. "I am only surprised it took you this long."

An'kelet nodded toward Ga'haris and Gharith, who had resumed their play in the water of Abona. "It seems you have made the House of the Lake something of a refuge."

Her white teeth flashed. "Indeed. Many have been under the care of the Ladies of the Lake; some shall stay with us as servants…others must find their own path in the world."

He was silent a moment, an awful thought filling his mind. "That infant…Surely it is not…"

"No. Not hers. His. Mordraed's. But do not look unkindly on it because of its parentage. Remember, it is still Ardhu's grand-child, no matter what evil its father did."

He leaned over her, a good head and shoulders taller and gently took her arm. "Where?"

Mhor-gan nodded toward the vale-side, overlooking the old barrowfields of the early Kings. "Beyond. She goes there often, to look and to remember."

"Should I seek?" His eyes were weary, tired. He pushed his amber hair from his brow. "Or is it too late? Is it tearing open an old wound, making it bleed again?"

Mhor-gan touched his face with her fingertips. "Go to her. There are some wounds that cannot be healed…but many that can."

He turned from the river and headed over the hillside toward Khor Ghor. He could see it in the distance, with the barrows of the old kings lying before it like supplicants, dappled by Sun and by cloud shadows. The skylarks were dipping and swirling in the grass, and a small, fierce hawk soared against the Sun, reminding him poignantly of the Merlin.

And then he saw a woman, kneeling in the long waving grass, simply dressed in a woven kirtle, with a large basket of plaited river-reeds at her side. He frowned at first for the hair that coiled on her shoulders was an earthy brown, not the white mist he had expected, but as she moved, hands seeking in the grasses, he recognised the curve of cheek, her sweet long neck, that he had kissed, that he had loved. She had used dyes to disguise herself, so none would suspect.

He began to run, unable to help himself…though he felt an eager fool, he who was now Ardhu's heir. Fynavir shifted in the grass and stood up, her face calm and her eyes shaded by her fair lashes, so incongruous with her dye-stained hair. "An'kelet. Or should I now speak of you as Stone Lord?"

He halted, hands dropping to his sides. "You know then that Ardhu passed the mantle on to me."

She nodded. "I was surprised to hear such news…but I am glad you were reconciled. And that you were with him at the end." She pressed her knuckles to her mouth, her voice faltering. "What was it all for, I ask you? I ask the spirits day and night. We ruined it, An'kelet; between us, we made the great thing he wrought fall to ashes."

He went to her then and held her, and she wept against him for a while, and he wept too against the darkness of hair that had been white as snow.

"He will never die," he then said quietly. "He is legend now, Fynavir. In a thousand years or more they will still tell his tale, though it will be changed by many tongues and many retellings."

"That is some small comfort."

"Sometimes…" he clasped her hand, twining his fingers with hers, "a small comfort is all we have."

Together they turned and faced the Stones, distant on the Plain, the remaining half of the Door into Winter a barren stick with its naked tenon stabbing the sky, and An'kelet took his axe from his belt and saluted the temple three times with blade upraised—for Sun, for Moon, for Ancestors. Then he gathered Fynavir beneath his cloak and led her from that place of loss and memory, from the realm of the Dead to the realm of the Living.

To start anew.

To live in the new age that must come.

THE STONEHENGE SAGA HISTORICAL NOTES

All the places in THE STONEHENGE SAGA are real but given new names. The rituals are of my devising based on findings and comparative anthropology. The reconstructions of clothing, jewellery and weaponry are based on actual finds in prehistoric barrows; many of the inspirations for my characters' personal effects are in Devizes or Salisbury museum, Wilrshire, U.K..

For further reading, books on British prehistory by Aubrey Burl, Mike Parker Pearson and Barry Cunliffe are recommended

I have also had requests for a list of character names. I have included the main ones and a complete list will be appearing on my blog in the next few months. below. As for pronunciation, most names sound roughly how they are spelt. C is always hard, never an 'S' sound and 'ch' is as in the Scottish 'loch' and never as in 'change.' A single F is pronounced V. Ardhu can be pronounced in two ways, however—Ar-dee (as in Welsh) or Ar-doo (as in Irish.) Take your pick!

By the way, I was once accused of using 'made up fantasy' names instead of nice 'Celtic' ones—in fact, none of the names are made up, at least not in the way implied; they are a combination of Indo European rootwords and deconstructed Brythonic and Goidhelic names for the most part. I see no problem with this, as the language of the day is not known; it may have indeed been an early form of a Celtic language, but it would not be identical to today' words, even as the Brythonic of the Roman period does not equate to Welsh today.

For further discussions of Stonehenge, King Arthur, folklore, myth, linguistics, archaeology and more, visit stone.lord.blogspot.com

If you have enjoyed this book, please have a look at the other historical and fantasy fiction by J.P. Reedman:
    RICHARD III:
    I, RICHARD PLANTAGENET-Tant Le Desiree Part 1.
    The young Duke of Gloucester at Barnet and Tewkesbury. His fights with

George and married to Anne Neville. The Scottish campaigns.

I, RICHARD PLANTAGENET- Loyaulte Me Lie Part 2.
Kingship. The mystery of the Princes. The betrayal of Buckingham and the Stanleys. The final charge at Bosworth.

Omnibus Edition of I, RICHARD PLANTAGENET CONTAINING BOTH PARTS now available in Kindle and Print. Over 230,000 words!

SACRED KING.
Historical fantasy novella set at the time of Bosworth…and beyond. The afterlife of the King in the twilight realm of faerie…which Richard sees as Purgatory. A tale of hope and redemption, and of the finding of the long-dead King in a Leicester car park. A chance find…or not? The Return of the King.

WHITE ROSES, GOLDEN SUNNES.
Compilation of short stories (156 pages) of stories about Richard III and his family, frequently dealing with Richard's childhood and youth. Includes the tragic tale of his brother Edmund of Rutland.

MEDIEVAL:
MISTRESS OF THE MAZE. The story of Fair Rosamund, the mistress of Henry II. Captive in a bower, Henry sought to keep her safe from the wrath of Eleanor of Aquitaine.

MY FAIR LADY - A Story of Eleanor of Provence, Henry III's Lost Queen. First person fiction on the life of this half-forgotten Queen, who was the wife of Henry III, mother to Edward Longshanks…and one time regent of England. Set at the time of the second Barons' Revolt. An Amazon Best Seller in Historical Biographical Fiction and Medieval Historical Romance.

THE HOOD GAME-RISE OF THE GREENWOOD KING. A pagan retelling of the Robin Hood legend. Robin of Sherwood fans will enjoy!

FANTASY:
ELVINGSTONE-Fantasy gothic romance. A young dancer is whiskered away to a crumbling mansion owned by Alaric Stannion. What lies within the mound in the old graveyard? Will Arabella ever be able to fathom the house's secrets and live safely with her love?

BETWEEN THE HORNS: Tales From The Middle Lands.
Collection of humorous fantasy stories for all ages, set in a mythical central European country where each of the towns tries to out perform the others in its celebration of the seasons. A land between the Horn Mountains where giant hares lay eggs, trollocs dwell and the Krampus whips unruly children, where witches control the weather and look for fat boys to eat, and the Erl King rides in bleak midwinter. In the vein of Tim Burton.

MY NAME IS NOT MIDNIGHT
Dystopian fantasy set in a post apocalyptic 70's Canada. A young girl sets out on a quest to fight the religious oppression of the Sestren. In the vein of Philip Pullman.

THE STONEHENGE SAGA

Names of main characters and places

Abona--The River Avon. One of the great sacred rivers of Britain and also its tutelary goddess.
Ack-olon-lover and servant of Morigau
Afallan- The Apple Garden. Avalon
Agravaen-son of Morigau, half brother to Mordraed
Ahn-ann—a shadowy mother goddess figure. Also known as Ahn-u
Ahn-is—priestess witch slain by Ardhu
Ahn-un-The Not World or Un-world. The Otherworld.
Ailin of the Lake of Maidens-Priestess and mother of An'kelet
Albu-The White. Name of the lower part of the British Isles encompassing the White Cliffs of Dover. Roughly England
Ambris-high priest of Stonehenge, mentor of Merlin, kinsman of U'thyr
Amhar- Child name of Gal'havad, son of Ardhu and Fynavir
An-fortas-The Maimed King, king of the Wasteland
An'kelet- Equivalent to Lancelot. From an older form of the name. In Stone Lord, the suffix or prefix 'An/ahn' refers to a goddess/god or supernatural place.
Ardhu-Dark Bear, Merlin's protégée who becomes the Stone Lord of Khor Ghor.
Ar-morah-Land of the Sea. Brittany in France, which was once known as Armorica. Homeland of An'kelet
Arondyt-one of An'kelet's daggers
Art'igen-The Bear-that-is-to-Be. Ardhu's childhood name
Astolaht-village of Elian the Lily Maid
Bal-in and Bal-ahn-twin warriors who are followers of Ardhu
Balugaisa—barbed spear of An'kelet. Spear-of-Mortal-Pain
Belerion-Cornwall
Betu'or-Knower of Graves. First a combatant then friend to Ardhu. Bedwyr in Arthurian legend
Bhel Sunface-'Shining' spirit of the Sun.
Boann—spirit of the River of the White Cow in Ibherna—the Boyne
Bohrs-One of Ardhu's prime men after an initial clash
Boneman, the—priest of the stones of Stenness
Breastplate of the Sky. Golden lozenge worn by Ardhu. Similar to that found in Bush barrow near Stonehenge
Bresalek-the name of the Green Man of Lud's Hole-the Green Knight
Brig-ahn-priestess of Brygyndo. Brig-high, royal
Bro-khelian-the forest of Broceliande in Brittany
Brygyndo. Fiery Arrow. High One. 3 faced goddess Equivalent to the goddess Brigit.
Buan-ann—the real name of the Old Woman of No name, Merlin's first mentor
Caladvolc the Hard-Cleft- Ardhu's blade, equivalent to Caliburn. The name seems to derive ultimately from Caladbolg, sword of an Irish mythological hero
Carnwennan- Little White Hilt. Ardhu's dagger,taken from a burial cist—the sword from beneath the stone
Crossroads-of-the-World-another name for Avebury, given by later traders
Dag-father god in Ibherna
Deadlands, The -the West where spirits went; also referred to liminal areas like the fields around the Cursus in Dorset and at Stonehenge

Deroweth-settlement at Durrington Walls

Din-Amnon—the stone circle where the young Merlin saw the red and white dragons

Dindagol-Gorlas's holding on the headland in North Cornwall. Birth place of Ardhu. Modern Tintagel

Dragon Path of Dwr-the Dorest Cursus

Drem-brave youth and messenger from Kham-el-Ard

Dru Bluecloak-acolyte at Deroweth

Duvnon-Devon. Land of Dark Valleys.

Dwr, Dwranon Dwri—Dorset and the folk who live in it. The People-from-across-the-Water

Eckhy-priest of Stonehenge; his ghost speaks to Merlin

Ech-tor- father of Ka'hai, foster father of Ardhu. First element of name means Horse

Elian—healer who finds An'kelet wounded. Her love for him ends in tragedy

The Feast of the Rage of Trogran—another name for the Feast of the Corn-Lord in August

Fhir-Vhan-the Man-Woman- Cross dressing figure at the Sanctuary, considered sacred. Curses Ardhu. A skeleton of mixed male/female parts was found buried at the Sanctuary

Fragarak the Answerer-dagger of An'kelet

Fynavir- The White Phantom. Daughter of Queen Mevva of Ibherna, becomes Ardhu's wife. Name is equivalent to Irish Findabhair, daughter of Queen Meadbh and of course Gwynhwyfar/Guinevere

Ga-haris- son of Morigau, half brother to Mordraed

Gal'havad-Son of Ardhu and Fynavir, Hawk of Summer, Prince of the Twilight. Mystic and warriors, attainer of the Golden Cup

Gharith-son of Morigau, half brother to Mordraed

Gleyn-river where Ardhu's first battle takes place page

Gluinval- priest who takes over from Merlin at Khor Ghor

God-of-bronze-the Holy Mountain in Wales. Carn Menyn in the Preselis

God's Peak—a name for the ritual complex at Newgrange

Gorlas-an obnoxious and war like petty chief of Cornwall. Husband to Y'gerna, mother of Ardhu

Great Barrowhill-mound that once stood inside Marden henge—the Hatfield barrow. Now destroyed

Great Trilithon, The—as it is today…the Great Trilithon. Also known as the Portal of Ghosts and the Door into Winter, and Door of the Setting Sun

Ha-bren- The Severn River and its tutelary goddess

Hill of Suil-Silbury Hill. Hill of the Wise Eye

Hwalchmai- Hawk of the Plain, Ardhu's kin and one of his chief companions. Defeater of the Green Man/Green Knight

Hwynn the White Fire—god of the Mortuary. Equivalent to Gwynn Ap Nudd, the Faerie king who lives in Glastonbury Tor

Ibherna-Ireland.Ireland was known as Hibernia by the Romans, perhaps NOT land of Winter but from land of the Iverni, who were a tribe. The bh here is pronounced as V

Ickenholt-The Icknield Way

Ivormyth-tragic daughter of Metheloas, briefly betrothed to Gal'havad

Ka'hai-Ardhu's foster brother and close friend

Kaladhon-a name for what is now Scotland

Kar Sarlog- hill encampment. Old Sarum

Keine. Mother of Merlin. Takes from the Saint Keyne, but interestingly means 'nothing' in German

Kham-el-Ard-Crooked High Place- Equivalent to Camelot. Vespasian's camp hillfort in West Amesbury

Khaw-a rebel chieftain

Khiltarna- The Land Beyond the Hills. The Chilterns

Khyloq—Mordraed's wife

Khen the Head River-the river Kennett near Avebury

Khelynnen-Fynavir's serving woman

Khor Ghor-Dance of Spirits of Great ones—Based on the recorded named Choir Gawr, the Giant's Dance. Choir hear is related to the word 'chorea' not 'choir.'

Khu Stone,the-- Stone of Hounds or dogs. The Cuckoo stone in the field by Woodhenge. A Romano British shrine with child burial/dog skull was unearthed here

Kichol of the Red Eye- priest of Ibherna who serves a bloodthirsty solar god

Kon-khenn-sea monster whose bones were said to be the spikes on An'kelet's spear

Krom the Bloody Crescent-dark god of the grain in Ireland. Received human sacrifice every seven years

Lamps of Uffern-two stone lamps outside of Gods Peak

Lailoq-'friend' Child name of Merlin.

La'morak-lover and servant of Morigau

Loth-King of Ynys Yrch, the Orkneys. Enemy to Ardhu

Lud's Hole-abode of the Green Knight. Lud's Chapel

Maedh'an na Marah-Maids of the Waves, mermaids

Maheloas-priest and tribal headman at Gods Peak

Mahn-ann- sea-spirit. Equivalent to the Irish Mannanan

Maigh Dhun-Fort of the Plain. Maiden castle in Dorset

Mako'sa- priestess of Silven, Odharna's successor

Marthodunu-enclosure of the Plain. The ceremonial site of Marden in Wiltshire

Melwas of the Summerlands-King who abducts Fynavir

Merlin. Also the Merlin- Adopted name of Lailoq taken from his totem animal

Mevva- Irish tribal Queen known for her fierceness and lust. Name refers to mead—hence 'the Intoxicator'. Mother of Fynavir

Mhon—Anglesey, still known as Mona. The Mother Isle

Mhor-gan of the Korrig-han-sister of Ardhu, friend to him, priestess

Mineth Beddun- mountain of the Graves. Scene of a battle

Mordraed—illegitimate son of Ardhu and his half-sister Morigau. Ardhu's greatest enemy and his bane. Name means 'judgement'; equivalent to Irish Midir and later Moderatus.

Morigau-half sister to Ardhu, his most bitter enemy, mother of his son Mordraed

Moy Mell, the Plain of Honey—Where dead warriors go after death

Moy Mor, The Great Plain-Salisbury Plain..and also the Plain the spirits of the dead travel over

Nin-Aeifa-Priestess of Afallan. Equivalent to Vivian/Niniane

Nud Cloudmaker- Hwynn's father. Also known as Snarer and Snatcher. Also God of the Milky Way. Equivalent to Nuada/ Nodens

Odharna-high priestess of Suilven—Avebury

Ogg-a god of eleoquence, hill name after him

Old Circle—the henge at the end of the Stonehenge Avenue, recently

Palomides-a slave of the Sea-pirates, freed by Ardhu. A Greek from Delos, long said to have ancient ties to Britain

Pelehan-the Fisher King, son of the Maimed King

Per-Adur-One of Arthur's chief warriors

Phelas-father of Elian

Rhagnell-wife of the Green Man/Knight; takes up with Hwalchmai

Rhyttah-gigantic warrior, slain by Ardhu.

Rhom-gom- Ardhu's ceremonial mace/sceptre. The Lightning Mace. Similar to that found in Bush Barrow

Sacred Dragon Mound-Dorset Cursus

Sacred Pool,The- spring and pool behind Vespasian's camp. Has been used for feasting and ritual deposition since Mesolithic times

Samothos—one of the first of the Tin-lords or kings. One of the beaker people and a metal prospector, now seen as semi-mythical

Sanctuary, The-timber and stone circle attached to the Avenue of Avebury. Called the Sanctuary in 'real life'

Seven Kings, The- Very large barrows on the ridge to the east of Stonehenge. They are called the Seven Kings in modern times as well as in STONE LORD and MOON LORD

She-Who-Guards-death goddess, watcher of the dead.

Sherdan-Palomides' name for the Sea-pirates

Sovahn-feast, equivalent to Samhain

Spiralfort—another name for Gods Peak-Newgrange

Suilven-Place of the Eye. Avebury Stone circles

Tarn Wethelen—the site of Mount Pleasant in Dorset. Both real and fictional places were burned in a great fire.

Tirre-brother to Elian

T'orc—a giant boar trained by Ardhu's evil sister Morigau

U'thyr Pendraec, a chief of the Dwri, father of Ardhu. Ardhu the Chief Dragon or the Terrible Head

Urienz-cousin to Loth, Ardhu's enemy

Vhortiern- Great Lord. Merlin's chief

Wastelands, The—eastern lands hit by plague and famine. Norfolk.

Woodenheart-Woodhenge

Wyngurthachar-Ardhu's shield. The Face of Evening. Carved with representation of the Watcher of the Dead

Wyzelo-the Weasel. Companion of Mordraed

Y'gerna—mother of Ardhu, Mor-ghan, Morigau

Ynys Yrch—Isle of Pigs, the Orkneys

Y'melc-feast of Lambing, Feb 1

Zhel—aspect of the Winter Sun, said to be buried in Silbury in a golden coffin